Chain of Iron

THE ELDEST CURSES
With Wesley Chu
The Red Scrolls of Magic
The Lost Book of the White

The Shadowhunter's Codex
With Joshua Lewis

The Bane Chronicles
With Sarah Rees Brennan
and Maureen Johnson

Tales from the Shadowhunter Academy
With Sarah Rees Brennan, Maureen Johnson,
and Robin Wasserman

Ghosts of the Shadow Market
With Sarah Rees Brennan, Maureen Johnson,
Kelly Link, and Robin Wasserman

THE LAST HOURS

BOOK TWO

Chain of Iron
CASSANDRA CLARE

WALKER
BOOKS

First published in Great Britain 2021 by Walker Books Ltd
87 Vauxhall Walk, London SE11 5HJ

2 4 6 8 10 9 7 5 3 1

Text © 2021 Cassandra Clare, LLC
Jacket photo-illustration © 2021 Cliff Nielsen
Interior illustrations by Kathleen Jennings © 2021 Cassandra Clare, LLC

This book has been typeset in Dolly and Pterra

Printed and bound by CPI Group (UK) Ltd, Croydon CR0 4YY

British Library Cataloguing in Publication Data:
a catalogue record for this book is
available from the British Library

ISBN 978-1-4063-5810-0
ISBN 978-1-4063-9847-2 (Export/Airside PB)
ISBN 978-1-5295-0093-6 (Illumicrate)
ISBN 978-1-5295-0092-9 (FairyLoot)

Cover artwork for Illumicrate and FairyLoot editions © 2021 Dan Funderburgh

www.walker.co.uk

MIX
Paper from
responsible sources
FSC
www.fsc.org   FSC® C020471

For Rick Riordan. Thanks for letting me use the noble name di Angelo.

PART ONE

– ❊ –

LITTLE GAMES

You will soon hear of me with my funny little games. I saved some of the proper red stuff in a ginger beer bottle over the last job to write with but it went thick like glue and I cant use it. Red ink is fit enough I hope.

—Jack the Ripper

LONDON:
EAST END

It was strange and novel to have a human body again. To feel the wind stirring his hair and the cold particles of snow stinging his face as he made his way along the cobblestones. To swing his arms and measure the new length of his stride.

It was just after dawn, and the streets were mostly deserted. Every now and again he caught sight of a costermonger pushing his cart through the snowy street, or a charwoman in her apron and shawl hurrying to the drudgery of her work.

As he skirted a heap of snow, he stumbled and frowned to himself. His body was so weak. He needed strength desperately. He could not go on without it.

A dark shadow passed in front of him. An old man in worker's coveralls, cap pulled down low over his head, slipping into an alley off the main thoroughfare. As he watched, the man settled himself on a crate, leaning back against the brick wall. Reaching into his threadbare jacket, the man drew forth a bottle of gin and unscrewed it.

He stepped soundlessly into the alley. The walls rose on both sides, cutting off the weak sunlight. The man looked up at him out of bleary eyes. "Wot d'ye want?"

The adamas knife flashed in the dim light. It plunged into the man's chest again and again. Blood rose, a fine spray of red particles dyeing the filthy snow scarlet.

The killer sat back on his heels, breathing in. The energy of the man's death, the only useful thing the mortal creature had to offer, flowed into him through the knife. He rose and smiled up at the milky white sky. Already he was feeling better. Stronger.

Soon he would be strong enough to take on his true enemies. As he turned to leave the alley, he whispered their names under his breath.

James Herondale.

Cordelia Carstairs.

1

THE BRIGHT WEB

And still she sits, young while the earth is old,
And, subtly of herself contemplative,
Draws men to watch the bright web she can weave,
Till heart and body and life are in its hold.
The rose and poppy are her flower; for where
Is he not found, O Lilith, whom shed scent
And soft-shed kisses and soft sleep shall snare?
—Dante Gabriel Rossetti, "Body's Beauty"

A smoky winter fog had settled atop the city of London, reaching its pale tendrils across the streets, wreathing the buildings in dull tinsel. It cast a gray pallor over ruined trees as Lucie Herondale drove her carriage up the long, neglected drive toward Chiswick House, its roof rising from the fog like the top of a Himalayan peak above clouds.

With a kiss on the nose and a blanket over his withers, she left her horse, Balios, at the foot of the front steps and set off through the remains of the terraced garden. She passed the cracked and ruined statues of Virgil and Sophocles, now overgrown by long tendrils of vines, their limbs broken off and lying among the weeds. Other statues were partially hidden by overhanging trees and unpruned hedges, as if they were being devoured by the dense foliage.

Picking her way over a toppled rose arbor, Lucie finally reached the old brick shed in the garden. Its roof was long since gone; Lucie felt a bit as if she'd come across an abandoned shepherd's hut on the moors. A thin finger of gray smoke was even rising from within. If this were *The Beautiful Cordelia*, a mad but handsome duke would come staggering across the heath, but nothing ever happened as it did in books.

All around the shed she could see small mounds of earth where, over the past four months, she and Grace had buried the unsuccessful results of their experimentation—the unfortunate bodies of fallen birds or cat-slain rats and mice that they had tried over and over to bring back to life.

Nothing had worked yet. And Grace didn't even know all of it. She remained unaware of Lucie's power to command the dead. She did not know that Lucie had tried *ordering* the small bodies to come back to life, had tried *reaching* within them to catch at something she could draw into the world of the living. But it had never worked. Whatever part of them Lucie might have been able to command had fled with their deaths.

She had mentioned none of that to Grace.

Lucie gave a philosophic shrug and went up to the massive wooden slab of a door—she did sometimes question what the point was of having a door on a building that didn't have any roof—and tapped a coded pattern: one two, one two.

Instantly she heard someone crossing the floor and turning the bolt, and the door swung open. Grace Blackthorn stood in the doorway, her face set and serious. Even in the foggy weather, her hair, loose around her shoulders, glinted silvery bright. "You've come," she said, sounding more surprised than pleased.

"I said I would." Lucie pushed past Grace. The shed had a single room inside with a floor of packed earth, now partly frozen.

A table had been pushed against the wall under the Blackthorn family sword, which hung from coarsely forged iron hooks. On the table a makeshift laboratory had been constructed: there were rows of alembics and glass bottles, a mortar and pestle, and dozens of test tubes. An assortment of packets and tins took up the rest of the table, some lying open, others emptied and collected in a pile.

Next to the table was a fire that had been laid directly on the ground, the source of the smoke escaping from the missing roof. The fire was unnaturally silent, emanating not from wood logs but from a mound of stones, its greenish flames licking greedily upward as though seeking to consume the iron cauldron suspended from a hook above it. The cauldron held a simmering black brew that smelled earthy and chemical at the same time.

Lucie approached a second, larger table slowly. On it rested a coffin. Through its glass lid she could see Jesse, exactly as he'd appeared when they were last together—white shirt, black hair lying soft against the nape of his neck. His eyelids were pale half-moons.

She had not confined herself to birds and bats and mice. She had tried commanding Jesse to come back to life too, though she had been able to do it only during the short periods when Grace had gone to fetch something and left her alone with Jesse's body. She had fared even worse with that than she had with the animals. Jesse was not empty, as the animals were—she could feel something inside him: a life, a force, a soul. But whatever it was, it was anchored in the space between life and death, and she could not shift it. Even trying made her feel ill and weak, as if she were doing something wrong.

"I wasn't sure if you were still coming," Grace said crossly. "I've been waiting forever. Did you get the thorn-apple?"

Lucie reached in her pocket for the tiny packet. "It was hard to get away. And I can't stay long. I'm meeting Cordelia tonight."

Grace took the packet and tore it open. "Because the wedding's tomorrow? But what's it got to do with you?"

Lucie looked at Grace hard, but the other girl seemed genuinely not to understand. Often Grace didn't seem to grasp why people did things if the answer was *because that's how friends behave* or *because that's what you do for someone you're fond of.* "I'm Cordelia's *suggenes*," she said. "I walk her down the aisle, but I also provide help and support before the ceremony. Tonight I'm going out with her to—"

Whoosh. Grace had upended the packet into the cauldron. A flash of flame licked toward the ceiling, then a puff of smoke. It smelled of vinegar. "You don't have to tell me. I'm sure Cordelia is not fond of me."

"I'm not going to discuss Cordelia with you," said Lucie, coughing a little.

"Well, I wouldn't like me, if I were her," said Grace. "But we don't have to discuss anything. I didn't ask you here for chitchat."

She gazed down at the cauldron. Fog and smoke collided together in the little room, surrounding Grace with a nebulous halo. Lucie rubbed her own gloved hands together, her heart beating quickly as Grace began to speak: *"Hic mortui vivunt. Igni ferroque, ex silentio, ex animo. Ex silentio, ex animo! Resurget!"*

As Grace chanted, the concoction began to boil more rapidly, the flames beginning to hiss, rising higher and higher, reaching the cauldron. A bit of the mixture bubbled over the side of the cauldron, splattering onto the ground. Lucie instinctively jumped back as green stalks burst out of the ground, growing stems and leaves and buds as they shot up almost as high as her knees.

"It's working!" she gasped. "It's really working!"

A quick spasm of delight passed over Grace's normally expressionless face. She started toward the coffin, and Jesse—

As quickly as they had sprung up, the blooms withered and dropped from the stems. It was like seeing time itself speed faster. Lucie watched helplessly as the leaves fell away, and the stalks dried and crackled and snapped under their own weight.

Grace stood frozen, staring down at the dead flowers lying in the dirt. She glanced at the coffin—but Jesse had not moved.

Of course he had not moved.

Grace's shoulders were stiff with disappointment.

"I'll ask Christopher for fresher samples next time," Lucie said. "Or more powerful reagents. There has to be something we're not getting right."

Grace went to stand over her brother's coffin. She placed the palm of her hand against the glass. Her lips moved, as if she were whispering something; Lucie could not tell what. "The problem isn't the quality of the ingredients," she said in a cold, small voice. "The problem is that we're relying too much on science. Activators, reagents—science is woefully limited when it comes to feats like the one we are attempting."

"How would you know?"

Grace looked at her coldly. "I know you think I'm stupid because I never had any tutoring," she said, "but I did manage to read a few books while I was in Idris. In fact, I made it through most of the library."

Lucie had to admit that Grace was at least partially right—she'd had no idea Grace was interested in reading, or in anything really besides torturing men and raising Jesse from the dead. "If we don't rely on science, what are you proposing?"

"The obvious. Magic." Grace spoke as if she were instructing a child. "Not this—this child's play, working spells we got from a book my mother didn't even bother to keep hidden." She practically spat the words with contempt. "We must draw power from the only place it can be found."

Lucie swallowed. "You mean necromancy. Taking power from death and using it to work magic on the dead."

"Some would consider that kind of magic evil. But I call it necessary."

"Well, I would call it evil," Lucie said, unable to keep her frustration from her voice. Grace seemed to have come to a decision without her, which was definitely not in the spirit of their partnership. "And I don't want to do evil things."

Grace shook her head dismissively, as though Lucie was making a fuss over nothing. "We must speak to a necromancer about this."

Lucie hugged her elbows. "A necromancer? Surely not. The Clave would forbid it even if we could find one."

"And there's a reason for that," Grace retorted sharply, gathering up her skirts. She seemed ready to stalk out of the shed. "What we have to do is not altogether good. Not . . . the way most people think of good, at any rate. But you already knew that, Lucie, so you can stop pretending to be so much better than me."

"Grace, no." Lucie moved to block the door. "I don't want that, and I don't think Jesse would want that either. Could we not speak to a warlock? Someone the Clave trusts?"

"The Clave may trust them, but I do not." Grace's eyes burned. "I decided we should work together because Jesse seemed to like you. But you have known my brother very little time, and never when he was alive. You are hardly an expert. I am his sister, and I will bring him back—whatever I need to do, and however I need to do it. Do you understand, Lucie?" Grace took a deep breath. "It is time to decide whether you care more about the precious sanctity of your own life than you care about giving my brother back his."

Cordelia Carstairs

*   *   *

Cordelia Carstairs winced as Risa fixed the tortoiseshell comb more tightly in place. It anchored a heavy coil of dark red hair, which the lady's maid had convinced her to put up in an elaborate style she promised was very popular.

"You needn't go to all this trouble tonight," Cordelia had protested. "It's just a sledding party. My hair's going to end up a mess no matter how many pins and combs you poke into it."

Risa's disapproving look had prevailed. Cordelia assumed she felt that her charge should be making an effort to look good for her fiancé. After all, Cordelia was marrying James Herondale, a catch by any standards of society, Shadowhunter or mundane—handsome, rich, well-connected, and kind.

There was no point in saying that it didn't matter how she looked. James wouldn't care if she showed up in an opera gown, or stark naked for that matter. But there was nothing to be gained in trying to explain that to Risa. In fact, it was much too risky to explain it to anyone.

"*Dokhtare zibaye man, tou ayeneh khodet ra negah kon,*" said Risa, holding up a silver hand mirror for Cordelia. *My beautiful daughter, look in the glass.*

"It looks lovely, Risa," Cordelia had to admit. The pearl combs were striking against her dark ruby hair. "But how will you ever top this tomorrow?"

Risa just winked. At least someone was looking forward to the next day, Cordelia thought. Every time she thought about her wedding, she wanted to jump out of the window.

Tomorrow she would sit for the last time in this room, while her mother and Risa wove silk flowers into her long, heavy hair. Tomorrow she would have to appear as happy a bride as she was an elaborately dressed one. Tomorrow, if Cordelia was very lucky, most of her wedding guests would be distracted by her clothes. One could always hope.

Risa smacked her lightly on the shoulder. Cordelia rose obediently, taking one last deep breath before Risa tightened the laces of her corset, pushing her breasts up and straightening her spine. The nature of the corset, Cordelia thought irritably, was to make a woman aware of every minute way that her shape differed from society's impossible ideal.

"Enough!" she protested as the whalebone stays cut into her skin. "I did hope to eat at the party, you know."

Risa rolled her eyes. She held up a green velvet dress and Cordelia stepped into it. Risa guided the long, fitted sleeves up her arms, adjusting the frothy white lace at the cuffs and neckline. Then came the process of fastening each of the tiny buttons that ran up the back of the dress. The fit was snug; without the corset Cordelia would never have managed it. The Herondale ring, the visible sign of her engagement, gleamed on her left hand as she lifted her arm so that Risa could arrange Cortana across her back.

"I should hurry down," Cordelia said as Risa handed her a small silk handbag and a muff to warm her hands. "James is hardly ever late."

Risa nodded briskly, which for her was the equivalent of a warm hug goodbye.

It was true, Cordelia thought, as she rustled down the stairway. James *was* hardly ever late. It was the duty of a fiancé to escort a lady to parties and dinners, fetch lemonade and fans, and generally dance attendance. James had played his part to perfection. All season long he had faithfully partnered her at all sorts of eye-wateringly boring Enclave events, but outside of those occasions, she barely saw him. Sometimes he would join her and the rest of his friends for excursions that were actually enjoyable—afternoons in the Devil Tavern, tea at Anna's—but even then he seemed distracted and preoccupied. There was little chance to talk about their future, and Cordelia wasn't sure precisely what she'd say if there was.

"Layla?"

Cordelia had reached the sword-and-stars-tiled entryway of the house, and at first saw no one there. She realized a moment later that her mother, Sona, stood by the front window, having drawn back one of the curtains with a narrow hand. Her other hand rested on her rounded belly.

"It *is* you," Sona said. Cordelia couldn't help noticing that the dark shadows under her mother's eyes seemed to have deepened. "Where are you off to, again?"

"The Pouncebys' sledding party on Parliament Hill," Cordelia said. "They're dreadful, really, but Alastair's going and I thought I might as well keep my mind off tomorrow."

Sona's lips curved into a smile. "It's quite normal to be nervous before a wedding, Layla *joon*. I was terrified the night before I married your father. I nearly escaped on a milk train to Constantinople."

Cordelia took a short, sharp breath, and her mother's smile faltered. *Oh, dear,* Cordelia thought. It had been a week since her father, Elias Carstairs, had been released from his confinement at the Basilias, the Shadowhunter hospital in Idris. He'd been there for months—much longer than they'd first expected—to cure him of his trouble with alcohol, a fact that all three other members of the Carstairs family knew but never mentioned.

They had expected him home five days ago. But there had been no word save a terse letter sent from France. No promise that he would return by the day of Cordelia's wedding. It was a wretched situation, made more wretched by the fact that neither Cordelia's mother nor her brother, Alastair, was willing to discuss it.

Cordelia took a deep breath. "*Mâmân.* I know you're still hoping Father might arrive in time for the wedding—"

"I do not hope; I know," Sona said. "No matter what has waylaid him, he will not miss his only daughter's wedding."

Cordelia almost shook her head in wonderment. How could her mother have such faith? Her father had missed so many birthdays, even Cordelia's first rune, because of his "sickness." It was a sickness that had gotten him arrested in the end and sent to the Basilias in Idris. He was meant to be cured now, but his absence so far was not promising.

Boots clattered down the stairs, and Alastair appeared in the entrance hall, dark hair flying. He looked handsome in a new tweed winter coat, though he was scowling.

"Alastair," Sona said. "Are you going to this sledding party as well?"

"I wasn't invited."

"That isn't true," Cordelia said. "Alastair, I was only going to go because you were!"

"I have decided that my invitation was sadly lost in the post," Alastair said, with a dismissive wave of his hand. "I can entertain myself, Mother. Some of us have things to do and cannot be out cavorting at all hours."

"Honestly, the two of you," Sona scolded, shaking her head. This seemed to Cordelia to be highly unfair. She had only corrected Alastair's untruth.

Sona placed her hands in the small of her back and sighed. "I ought to speak to Risa about tomorrow. There's still so much to be done."

"You should be *resting*," Alastair called, as his mother headed down the corridor toward the kitchen. The moment she was out of sight, he turned to Cordelia, his expression stormy. "Was she waiting for Father?" he demanded in a low whisper. "Still? Why must she torment herself?"

Cordelia shrugged helplessly. "She loves him."

Alastair made an inelegant sound. *"Chi! Khodah margam bedeh,"* he said, which Cordelia thought was very rude.

"Love doesn't always make sense," she said, and at that, Alastair looked quickly away. He had not mentioned Charles in Cordelia's presence for some months, and though he'd received letters in Charles's careful handwriting, Cordelia had found more than one tossed unopened into the dustbin. After a moment, she added, "Still, I wish he would send word that he's all right, at least—for Mother's sake."

"He'll come back in his own time. At the worst possible moment, if I know him."

Cordelia stroked the soft lambswool of her muff with one finger. "Do you not want him to come back, Alastair?"

Alastair's look was opaque. He had spent years protecting Cordelia from the truth, making excuses for their father's "bouts of illness" and frequent absences. Some months ago Cordelia had learned the emotional cost of Alastair's interventions, the invisible scars he worked so diligently to conceal.

He seemed about to reply when outside the window, the sound of a horse's hooves echoed, their tromping muffled by the still-falling snow. The dark shape of a carriage came to a stop by the lamppost in front of the house. Alastair twitched the curtain aside and frowned.

"That's the Fairchilds' carriage," he observed. "James couldn't be bothered to pick you up, so he sent his *parabatai* to do his job?"

"That is not fair," Cordelia said sharply. "And you know it."

Alastair hesitated. "I suppose. Herondale has been dutiful enough."

Cordelia watched as Matthew Fairchild leaped lightly down from the carriage outside. She couldn't stop a flash of fear—what if James had panicked and sent Matthew to break things off with her the night before the wedding?

Don't be ridiculous, she told herself firmly. Matthew was whistling as he came up the front steps. The ground was white with snow, tramped down here and there with boot prints. Flakes had already come to rest on the shoulders of Matthew's fur-collared greatcoat. Crystals glittered in his blond hair, and his high cheekbones were flushed with cold. He looked like an angel painted by Caravaggio and sugar-dusted with snow. Surely he wouldn't be whistling if he had bad news to deliver?

Cordelia opened the door and found Matthew on the front step, stamping snow from his balmoral boots. "Hello, my dear," he said to Cordelia. "I've come to bring you to a large hill, which we will both hurtle down on rickety, out-of-control bits of wood."

Cordelia smiled. "Sounds marvelous. What will we do after that?"

"Unaccountably," Matthew said, "we will climb back to the top of the hill in order to do it again. It is some kind of snow-related mania, they say."

"Where's James?" Alastair interrupted. "You know, the one of you that was supposed to be here."

Matthew regarded Alastair with dislike. Cordelia felt a familiar sinking of her heart. This was how it always went now, when Alastair interacted with any of the Merry Thieves. Suddenly, a few months ago, they had all become enormously angrier at Alastair, and she had no idea why. She couldn't bring herself to ask. "James was called away on important business."

"What business?" said Alastair.

"No business of yours," Matthew said, clearly pleased with himself. "Rather walked into that one, eh?"

Alastair's black eyes glittered. "You had best not lead my sister into trouble, Fairchild," he said. "I know the kind of company you keep."

"Alastair, stop it," Cordelia said. "Now, are you really skipping out on the Pouncebys' party or were you just needling Mother? And if the latter, do you wish to accompany Matthew and myself in the carriage?"

Alastair's gaze flicked to Matthew. "Why," he said, "are you not even wearing a hat?"

"And cover up this hair?" Matthew indicated his golden locks with a flourish. "Would you blot out the sun?"

Alastair wore the sort of expression that indicated that no amount of eye rolling would be enough. "I," he said, "am going for a walk."

He stalked out into the snowy night without another word, the effect of his exit dampened by the snow swallowing up the tread of his boots.

Cordelia sighed and started down the walk with Matthew. South Kensington was a fairy tale of white houses frosted in shimmering ice, the glow of the streetlamps shrouded in halos of snow-softened mist. "I feel I am ever apologizing for Alastair. Last week he made the milkman cry."

Matthew handed her up to the carriage seat. "Never apologize for Alastair to me. He provides me an adversary to sharpen my wits on."

He swung himself up next to her and closed the heavy door. The silk-lined interior of the carriage was made cozy by soft cushions and velvet curtains over the windows. Cordelia sat back against the bench, the sleeve of Matthew's greatcoat brushing her arm reassuringly.

"I feel as if I haven't seen you in an age, Matthew," she said, happy to change the subject. "I heard your mother was back from Idris? And Charles from Paris?" As Consul, Matthew's mother, Charlotte, was often away from London. Her son Charles, Matthew's brother, had taken a junior position at the Paris Institute, where he was training in politics: everyone knew Charles hoped to be the next Consul someday.

Matthew ran his fingers through his hair, dislodging ice crystals. "You know Mother—the minute she steps from her carriage she's off and running again. And of course Charles lost no time in coming home to see her. Reminding the Paris Institute of how close he is to the Consul, how much she depends on his advice. Pontificating to Father and Martin Wentworth. When I left, he had interrupted their chess match to try to drag them into a discussion of Downworlder politics in France. Wentworth was looking a bit desperate, actually—probably hoping Christopher would cause another explosion in the lab to give him an opportunity to escape."

"Another explosion?"

Matthew grinned. "Kit almost blew off Thomas's eyebrows with the latest experiment. He says he's close to making gunpowder ignite even in the presence of runes, but Thomas has no eyebrows left to give to the cause of science."

Cordelia tried to think of something to say about Thomas's eyebrows but couldn't. "All right," she said, hugging her arms around herself. "I give up. Where is James? Has he taken fright and legged it for France? Is the wedding off?"

Matthew pried a silver flask from his coat and took a nip before replying. Was he buying himself time? He did look a bit worried, Cordelia thought, though anxiety and Matthew were things that rarely went together. "That's my fault, I'm afraid," he admitted. "Well, me and the rest of the Merry Thieves, to be fair. At the last minute, we just couldn't let James tie the knot without throwing him a party, and it's my job to make sure that you know nothing of the scandalous proceedings."

Relief passed over Cordelia in a wave. James wasn't abandoning her. Of course not. He never would. He was James.

She squared her shoulders. "Since you just told me that the proceedings will be scandalous, doesn't that mean you've failed in your mission?"

"Not at all!" Matthew took another drink from the flask before replacing it in his pocket. "I've only told you that James is spending the eve of his wedding night with his friends. For all you know, they're having tea and studying the history of faeries in Bavaria. I'm meant to make sure you don't learn otherwise."

Cordelia couldn't help but smile. "And how do you intend to do that?"

"By escorting you to scandalous proceedings of your own, of course. You didn't think we were *really* going to the Pouncebys' party?"

Cordelia drew back the curtain of the carriage window and looked out into the night. Instead of the tree-lined streets of Kensington, shrouded in winter snow, they had arrived at the outer edge of the

West End. The streets were narrow and thick with fog, and crowds of people milled about, speaking in a dozen languages, warming their hands over fires in oil drums.

"Soho?" she said curiously. "What—the Hell Ruelle?"

Matthew cocked an eyebrow. "Where else?" The Hell Ruelle was a Downworlder nightclub and salon, operating a few nights of each week in an outwardly nondescript building on Berwick Street. Cordelia had ventured there twice before, months ago. Her visits had been memorable.

She let the curtain fall and turned back to Matthew, who was watching her closely. She pretended to stifle a yawn. "Really, the Ruelle again? I've been there so often it might as well be a ladies' bridge club. Surely you must know a more scandalous place?"

Matthew grinned. "Are you asking me to take you to the Inn of the Shaved Werewolf?"

Cordelia hit him with her muff. "That's not a real place. I refuse to believe it."

"Believe me when I say that there are few places more scandalous than the Ruelle, and none I could take you to and expect James to forgive me," said Matthew. "Corrupting one's *parabatai*'s bride is not considered sporting."

The laughter went out of Cordelia; she suddenly felt very tired. "Oh, Matthew, you know it's a fake wedding," she said. "It doesn't matter what I do. James won't care."

Matthew seemed to hesitate. Cordelia had broken with the masquerade, and he was clearly taken aback. He never remained speechless for long, though. "He does care," he said, as the carriage turned onto Berwick Street. "Not, perhaps, in the way everyone imagines. But I don't think it will be a hardship to be married to James, and it is only for a year, isn't it?"

Cordelia closed her eyes. That was the agreement she had made with James: one year of marriage, to save both their reputations. Then she would sue for divorce. They would part amicably and remain friends.

"Yes," she said. "Only a year."

The carriage drew to a stop, just beneath a streetlamp whose yellow light illuminated Matthew's face. Cordelia felt a small catch at her heart. Matthew knew as much of the truth as anyone else, even James, did, but there was something in his eyes—something that made her fear for a moment that he suspected the last piece of the puzzle, the bit she'd hidden from everyone but herself. She couldn't bear to be pitied. She couldn't bear it if anyone knew how desperately she loved James and wished the marriage were a real one.

Matthew pushed the door of the carriage open, revealing the pavement of Berwick Street, glossy with melted snow. He jumped out and, after a quick conversation with the driver, reached up to help Cordelia down from the carriage.

The Hell Ruelle was reached through the narrow alley of Tyler's Court. Matthew took Cordelia's arm and tucked it through his, and together they made their way through the shadows. "It occurs to me," he said, "that while we may know the truth, the rest of the Enclave doesn't. Remember what pests they were when you first came to London—and now, as far as that smug bunch is concerned, you're marrying one of the most eligible bachelors in the country. Look at Rosamund Wentworth. She's gone and gotten herself engaged to Thoby Baybrook just to prove you're not the only one getting married."

"Really?" Cordelia was highly entertained; it had never occurred to her she had anything to do with Rosamund's sudden announcement. "But I assume that marriage is a love match."

"The timing raises questions, is all I'm saying." Matthew waved a hand airily. "My only point is, you may as well rejoice in being the envy of all London. Everyone who was snide to you when you first arrived—everyone who shorted you because of your father, or muttered rumors—they'll be eating their hearts out with envy, wishing they were you. *Enjoy* it."

Cordelia chuckled. "You always do find the most decadent possible solution to any problem."

"I believe that decadence is a valuable perspective that should always be considered." They had reached the entrance of the Hell Ruelle and passed through a private door into a narrow hallway lined with heavy tapestries. The corridor was seemingly done up for Christmas (though the holiday itself was weeks away); the tapestries were adorned with green boughs wound with white roses and red poppies.

They found their way through a labyrinth of small salons to the octagonal main room of the Ruelle. It had been transformed; shimmering trees, their bare boughs and trunks painted white, stood at intervals, festooned with dark green wreaths and dangling red glass globes. A glimmering mural portrayed a forest scene: a glacier edged by a grove of snowcapped pines, owls peeking out from the shadows between the trees. A black-haired woman with the body of a serpent coiled around a lightning-struck tree; her scales gleamed with gold paint. At the front of the room, Malcolm Fade, the purple-eyed High Warlock of London, seemed to be leading a group of faeries in an intricate dance.

The floor was piled with heaps of what looked like snow, but on closer examination was delicately cut white paper, kicked up in drifts by dancing Downworlders. Not everyone was dancing, of course: many of the salon's guests were crowded at small circular tables, their hands wrapped around copper mugs of mulled wine. Nearby, a werewolf and a faerie sat together, arguing about Irish home rule. Cordelia had always marveled at the mix of Downworlders that attended the Hell Ruelle; enmities out in the world between vampires and werewolves, or between different faerie courts, seemed to be suspended for the sake of art and poetry. She could understand why Matthew liked it so much.

"Well, well, my favorite Shadowhunter," drawled a familiar voice. Turning, Cordelia recognized Claude Kellington, a young werewolf musician who oversaw the entertainment at the Ruelle. He was seated at a table with a faerie woman with long, blue-green hair; she stared curiously at Cordelia. "I see you brought Fairchild," Kellington added. "Convince him to be more entertaining, will you? He never dances."

"Claude, I am crucial to your entertainments," Matthew said. "I am that irreplaceable thing, the eager audience."

"Well, bring me more performers like this one," Kellington said, indicating Cordelia. "If you happen to meet any."

Cordelia couldn't help but recall the performance that had so impressed Kellington. She'd danced on the Ruelle's stage, so scandalously that she'd rather shocked herself. She tried not to blush now, but rather to appear a sophisticated sort of girl prepared to dance like Salome at the drop of a hat.

She nodded at the decorated boughs. "Is Christmas celebrated at the Hell Ruelle, then?"

"Not exactly." Cordelia turned to see Hypatia Vex, the patroness of the Hell Ruelle. Though Malcolm Fade owned the place, the guests were invited by Hypatia; anyone she disapproved of would never make it past the door. She wore a shimmering red gown, and a gilt-dipped peony was tucked into her cloud of dark hair. "The Ruelle does not celebrate Christmas. Its attendees may do what they like in their own homes, of course, but in December the Ruelle pays homage rather to its patron with the Festum Lamia."

"Its patron? You mean . . . you?" said Cordelia.

There was a hint of amusement in Hypatia's distinctive eyes with their star-shaped pupils. "Its cosmic patron. Our ancestor, called by some the mother of warlocks, by others the Mother of Demons."

"Ah," said Matthew. "Lilith. Now that you point it out, you do have rather a lot more owls in the decor than usual."

"The owl is one of her symbols," said Hypatia, gliding a hand along the back of Kellington's chair. "In the first days of the Earth, God made for Adam a wife. Her name was Lilith, and she would not be subservient to Adam's wishes, so she was cast from the Garden of Eden. She mated with the demon Sammael, and with him had many demon children, whose offspring were the first warlocks. This angered Heaven, and three vengeful angels—Sanvi, Sansanvi, and Semangelaf—were sent to punish Lilith. She was made barren by the angels, banished to the realm of Edom, a wasteland of night creatures and screech owls, where she resides still. But she stretches out her hand sometimes to assist warlocks who are faithful to her cause."

Most of the story was familiar to Cordelia, though in the legends of Shadowhunters, the three angels were heroes and protectors. Eight days after a Shadowhunter child was born, a ritual was performed: the names Sanvi, Sansanvi, and Semangelaf, chanted as spells, were placed upon the child by both the Silent Brothers and the Iron Sisters. It was a way of locking the soul of the child, Sona had explained to Cordelia once, making them a closed door to any kind of demonic possession or influence.

Probably best not to mention that now, she thought. "Matthew did promise me scandal," she said, "but I suspect the Clave frowns on Shadowhunters attending birthday parties for well-known demons."

"It isn't her birthday," said Hypatia. "Merely a day of celebration.

We believe it to be the time she left the Garden of Eden."

"The red baubles hanging from the trees," Cordelia said, realizing. "They're apples. Forbidden fruit."

"The Hell Ruelle delights," said Hypatia, smiling, "at the consumption of that which is forbidden. We believe it is more delicious for being taboo."

Matthew shrugged. "I can't see why the Clave would mind. I don't believe we need to celebrate Lilith, or anything like that. It's really just decorations."

Hypatia looked amused. "Of course. Nothing else. Which reminds me . . ."

She glanced meaningfully at Kellington's faerie companion, who rose and offered Hypatia her seat. Hypatia took it without a second glance, spreading her skirts out around her. The faerie melted back into the crowd as Hypatia went on, "My Pyxis has been missing since the last night you were here, Miss Carstairs. Matthew was here too, I remember. I'm wondering if I might have inadvertently made a gift of it to you?"

Oh no. Cordelia thought of the Pyxis they had stolen months ago: it had exploded during a battle with a Mandikhor demon. She looked at Matthew. He shrugged and nicked a mug of spiced wine from the tray of a passing faerie waiter. Cordelia cleared her throat. "I believe you did, actually. I believe you wished me the best of luck for my future."

"Not only was it a thoughtful gift," Matthew added, "it was very helpful in saving the city of London from destruction."

"Yes," Cordelia agreed. "Instrumental. An absolutely necessary aid in preventing complete disaster."

"Mr. Fairchild, you are a bad influence on Miss Carstairs. She is beginning to develop a worrying amount of cheek." Hypatia turned to Cordelia, her starry eyes unreadable. "I must say, I'm a bit surprised to see you tonight. I would have thought a Shadowhunter bride would want to spend the evening before her nuptials sharpening her weapons, or beheading stuffed dummies."

Cordelia began to wonder why Matthew had brought her to the Ruelle. No one wanted to spend the night before their wedding being scorned by haughty warlocks, however interestingly decorated the surroundings. "I am no ordinary Shadowhunter bride," she said shortly.

Hypatia only smiled. "As you say," she said. "I think there are a few guests here who've been expecting you."

Cordelia glanced across the room and saw, to her surprise, two familiar figures sitting at a table. Anna Lightwood, gorgeous as always in a fitted frock coat and blue spats, and Lucie Herondale, looking neat and pretty in an ivory dress with blue beading and waving energetically.

"Did you invite them?" she said to Matthew, who had turned up his flask again. He tipped it into his mouth, grimaced at finding it empty, and tucked it back into his pocket. His eyes were glitter-bright.

"I did," he said. "I can't stay—must make my way to James's party—but I wanted to make sure you were well accompanied. They have instructions to dance and drink the night away with you. Enjoy."

"Thank you." Cordelia leaned in to kiss Matthew on the cheek— he smelled of cloves and brandy—but he turned his face at the last moment, and her kiss brushed his lips. She drew away quickly and saw Kellington and Hypatia both watching her with sharp eyes.

"Before you go, Fairchild, I see your flask is empty," said Kellington. "Come with me to the bar; I'll have it refilled with anything you like."

He was looking at Matthew with a curious expression—a bit the way Cordelia recalled Kellington looking at her, after her dance. A hungry sort of look.

"I've never been one to turn down the offer of 'anything you like,'" said Matthew, allowing himself to be spirited away by Kellington. Cordelia considered calling out after him but decided against it—and anyway, Anna was gesturing at her to come join their table.

She took her leave of Hypatia and was halfway across the room when something caught her eye in the shadows: two male figures, close together. She realized with a jolt that they were Matthew and Kellington. Matthew was leaning against the wall, Kellington—the taller of the two—bending over him.

Kellington's hand rose to cup the back of Matthew's neck, his fingers in Matthew's soft hair.

Cordelia saw Matthew shake his head just as more dancers joined the throng on the floor, cutting off her view; when they passed, she saw that Matthew was gone and Kellington, looking stormy, was headed back across the room toward Hypatia. She wondered why she had been so shocked—it was hardly news to her that Matthew liked men as well as women, and Matthew was single: his decisions were his own. Still, Kellington's overall air discomfited her. She hoped Matthew would be careful—

Someone placed a hand on her arm.

She whirled to see a woman standing before her—the faerie who'd been seated with Kellington earlier. She wore a dress of emerald velvet, and around her throat was a necklace of gleaming blue stones.

"Forgive the intrusion," she said breathlessly, as though nervous. "Are you—are you the girl who danced for us all some months ago?"

"I am," said Cordelia warily.

"I thought I recognized you," the faerie said. She had a pale, intent face. "I quite admired your skill. And the sword, of course. Am I correct in thinking that the blade you bear is Cortana itself?" She whispered this last part, as though just invoking the name took courage.

"Oh, no," Cordelia said. "It's a fake. Just a nicely made replica."

The faerie stared at her for a moment, and then burst out laughing. "Oh, very good!" she said. "I forget sometimes that mortals joke— it is a sort of lie, isn't it, yet meant to be funny? But any true faerie would know the work of Wayland the Smith." She gazed at the sword in admiration. "If I may say so, Wayland is the greatest living metal-worker of the British Isles."

That brought Cordelia up short. *"Living?"* she echoed. "Are you say-ing that Wayland the Smith is still alive?"

"Why, of course!" said the faerie, clapping her hands, and Cordelia wondered whether she was about to reveal that Wayland the Smith was in fact the rather drunk goblin in the corner with the lampshade on his head. But she only said, "Nothing that he has made has passed into human hands in many centuries, but it is said he still operates his forge, under a barrow in the Berkshire Downs."

"Indeed," Cordelia said, trying to catch Anna's eye in hope of res-cue. "How very interesting."

"If you had any thought of meeting Cortana's maker, I could take you. Past the great white horse and under the hill. For only a coin and a promise of—"

"No," Cordelia said firmly. She might be as naive as the Ruelle's clientele assumed her to be, but even she knew the right response to a faerie trying to make a deal: walk away. "Enjoy the party," she added, "but I must go."

As she turned away, the woman said, in a low voice, "You need not marry a man who does not love you, you know."

Cordelia froze. She glanced back over her shoulder; the faerie was looking at her with all the dreaminess gone from her expression. It was pinched, sharp and watchful now.

"There are other paths," the woman said. "I could help."

Cordelia schooled her face to blankness. "My friends are waiting for me," she said, and walked away, her heart hammering. She sank into a chair opposite Anna and Lucie. They greeted her with cheers, but her mind was miles away.

A man who does not love you. How could that faerie know?

"Daisy!" Anna said. "Do pay attention. We're fussing over you." She was drinking from a tapered flute of pale champagne, and with a wave of her fingers a second one appeared, which she handed to Cordelia.

"Hurrah!" Lucie cried in delight, before returning to ignoring her cider and her friends completely, alternating instead between scribbling furiously in a notebook and staring into the middle distance.

"Did the light of inspiration hit you, pet?" Cordelia asked. Her heart was beginning to slow down. The faerie had been full of nonsense, she told herself firmly. She must have heard Hypatia talking to Cordelia about her wedding and decided to play upon the insecurities of any bride. Who didn't worry that the man they were going to marry might not love them? In Cordelia's case it might be true, but anyone would fear it, and faeries preyed upon the fears of mortals. It meant nothing—just an effort to get from Cordelia what she had asked for before: a coin and a promise.

Lucie waved an ink-stained hand to get her attention. "There is so *much* material here," she said. "Did you see Malcolm Fade over there? I adore his coat. Oh, I've decided that rather than being a dashing naval officer, Lord Kincaid should be an artist whose work was banned in London, so he fled to Paris, where he makes the beautiful Cordelia his muse and is welcomed into all the best salons—"

"What happened to the Duke of Blankshire?" said Cordelia. "I thought fictional Cordelia was about to become a duchess."

"He died," said Lucie, licking some ink off her finger. Around her neck, a gilded chain gleamed. She had been wearing the same plain gold locket for several months now; when Cordelia had asked her about it, Lucie had said it was an old family heirloom meant to be good luck. Cordelia could still remember its presence, a gold flash in the darkness, the night James had nearly died from demon poison in Highgate Cemetary. She did not recall having seen Lucie wear the necklace before that time. She could have pressed Lucie on it, she supposed, but she knew she kept her own secrets from her future *parabatai*—she could hardly demand to know all of Lucie's, especially about a matter as small as a locket.

"This sounds like quite a tragic novel," said Anna, admiring the way her champagne reflected the light.

"Oh, it's not," said Lucie. "I didn't want fictional Cordelia to be tied to only one man. I wanted her to have adventures."

"Not quite the sentiment one might hope for on the eve of a wedding," said Anna, "but I applaud it nonetheless. Though one hopes that you will continue having adventures even after being married, Daisy." Her blue eyes sparkled as she lifted her glass in a toast.

Lucie hoisted her mug. "To the end of freedom! To the beginning of a joyous captivity!"

"Nonsense," Anna said. "A woman's wedding is the beginning of her liberation, Lucie."

"And how is that?" asked Cordelia.

"An unmarried lady," said Anna, "is perceived by society as being in a temporary state of not being married, and in hopes of becoming married at any moment. A married woman, on the other hand, can flirt with whomever she wants, without damaging her reputation. She can travel freely. To and from my flat, for instance."

Lucie's eyes widened. "Are you saying that some of your love affairs have been with ladies who are already married?"

"I am saying it is the case more often than not," Anna said. "It is simply the case that a married woman is in a freer position to do as she pleases. A single young lady can hardly leave the house unaccompanied.

A married lady can shop, go to lectures, meet friends—she has a dozen excuses for being away from home while wearing a flattering hat."

Cordelia giggled. Anna and Lucie were always able to cheer her up. "And you do like a lady in a flattering hat."

Anna raised a thoughtful finger. "A lady who can choose a hat that truly suits her is very likely to have paid attention to every layer of her ensemble."

"What a wise observation," said Lucie. "Do you mind if I put it in my novel? It's just the sort of thing Lord Kincaid would say."

"Do as you like, magpie," said Anna, "you've stolen half my best lines already." Her gaze flicked about the room. "Did you see Matthew with Kellington? I hope that doesn't start up again."

"What happened with Kellington?" Lucie inquired.

"He rather broke Matthew's heart, a year or so back," said Anna. "Matthew has a habit of getting his heart broken. He seems to prefer a hopeless love."

"Does he?" Lucie was scribbling in her book again. "Oh, dear."

"Greetings, lovely ladies," said a tall young man with dead-white skin and curling brown hair, appearing at their table as if by magic. "Which of you dazzling beauties yearns to dance with me first?"

Lucie leaped up. "I shall dance with you," she said. "You're a vampire, aren't you?"

"Er—yes?"

"Capital. We shall dance, and you will tell me all about vampirism. Do you stalk beautiful ladies through the streets of the city in the hopes of snatching a sip of their genteel blood? Do you weep because your soul is damned?"

The young man's dark eyes darted around worriedly. "I really only wanted to waltz," he said, but Lucie had already seized him and dragged him out onto the floor. Music rose up in a surge, and Cordelia clinked glasses with Anna, both of them laughing.

"Poor Edwin," Anna said, looking out at the dancers. "He has a nervous disposition at the best of times. Now, Cordelia, pray tell me every detail of the wedding plans, and I will get us some fresh champagne."

2

ALL THAT TURNS

If sometimes, on the steps of a palace, on the green grass of a gully, in the mournful solitude of your bed chamber, you wake up, the intoxication diminished or dispelled, ask the wind, a wave, a star, a bird, a clock, all that flees, all that moans, all that turns, all that sings, all that speaks, ask what time it is; and the wind, the wave, the star, the bird, the clock will answer you: "It is time to become intoxicated! To not be the martyred slave of Time, be intoxicated; be unceasingly intoxicated! With wine, with poetry, with virtue, as you wish.
—Charles Baudelaire, "Enivrez-vous"

"Look out behind you!" Christopher barked in alarm. James ducked hastily out of the way. Two werewolves flew past them, locked in drunken combat, and crashed to the floor. Thomas held his glass above his head to keep it safe from the jostling crowd.

James had not been sure that the Devil Tavern was the right place for this party, given that he was there several days a week anyway, but Matthew had been insistent, intimating that he'd arranged something special.

James glanced about at the chaos and sighed a quiet inner sigh. "I rather imagined a more sedate evening."

Things had not been so riotous when they first arrived. The Devil was doing its usual lively, friendly evening business, and James would have been happy to slip upstairs to their private rooms, as he had so many times before, and simply relax with his oldest friends.

Matthew, however, had immediately climbed onto a chair, demanded the entire pub's attention by clanging his stele against the metal chandelier, and cried out, "Friends! This evening my *parabatai*, James Jeremiah Jehoshaphat Herondale, celebrates his last night as a single man!"

The whole pub had whooped and cheered.

James had waved a hand to thank and dismiss his well-wishers, but it seemed they weren't done. Downworlders of all kinds approached to shake his hand and pound his back and wish him happy. To his surprise, James realized that he knew most everyone present—that he'd known many of them, in fact, since he was a boy, and they had watched him grow up.

There was Nisha, the "oldest vampire from the oldest part of this old city," as she always said. There were Sid and Sid, the two werewolves who were always arguing over which of them could be "Sid" and which must be "Sidney." The odd cluster of hobgoblins who chattered among each other, never spoke to anyone else, but periodically sent free drinks to other customers, seemingly at random. They surrounded James and demanded he finish the whiskey in his hand so that he might drink the whiskey they'd brought to replace it.

James was genuinely touched by the outpouring of sentiment, but it only made him feel even more uneasy about the nature of his marriage. *It will all be over in a year,* he thought. *If you knew that, you would not be celebrating.*

Matthew had disappeared up the stairs soon after his speech and left the rest of them to be surrounded by the rowdy revelers getting drunker and drunker in James's honor, until, of course, the inevitable moment when Sid threw a punch at Sid and a roar of equal parts approval and mockery rose from the crowd.

Thomas, a scowl on his face, used his broad frame and considerable muscles to maneuver the three of them into a less crowded corner of the room.

"Cheers, Thomas," Christopher said. His brown hair was ruffled, his spectacles pushed halfway up his head. "Matthew's special entertainment should be starting . . ." He looked hopefully toward the stairs. "Any minute now."

"When Matthew plans a special something, it's usually either terribly delightful or delightfully terrible," said James. "Do any of us want to take bets on which this will be?"

Christopher smiled a bit. "A thing of surpassing beauty, according to Matthew."

"That could be anything," said James, watching Polly the barmaid march into the middle of the fray to pull the Sids apart as Pickles the kelpie took bets on who would be the winner.

Thomas uncrossed his arms and said, "It's a mermaid."

"It's a what?" said James.

"A mermaid," Thomas repeated. "Enacting some kind of . . . sultry mermaid performance."

"Some friend of his from the demimonde, you know," put in Christopher, who seemed pleased to know the word "demimonde." Admittedly, Matthew's frequent assignations with poets and courtesans were a far cry from Christopher's tinctures and test tubes, or Thomas's extensive library and intensive training regimen. Nevertheless, they both seemed relieved to have spilled the secret.

"What's she going to do?" said James. "And . . . where is she going to do it?"

"In a large tank of water, one hopes," said Christopher.

"As for what she will do," said Thomas, "something bohemian with bells and castanets and veils. I imagine."

Christopher seemed concerned. "Won't the veils get wet?"

"It will be an experience never to be forgotten," Thomas went on. "So says Matthew. Surpassing beauty, and so on."

Without thinking, James found himself reaching for the silver bracelet on his wrist, running his fingers absentmindedly across its surface. He barely noticed its presence after all this time—Grace Blackthorn had entrusted him with it when he was only fourteen. But James had been trying hard not to think of Grace as his wedding approached.

One year, James thought. He must put Grace out of his mind, for one more year. That was the promise they had made to each other.

And he had promised Cordelia, as well, that he would not see Grace alone or behind her back: if anyone found out, she would be humiliated. The world must think their marriage was a marriage in truth.

The thought of going through with his wedding to Cordelia while still wearing the bracelet made him ill at ease. He reminded himself to take it off, when he was back at home. Removing it might be a slight to Grace, but leaving it on felt like a slight to Cordelia. He had decided when it had all happened that he would not betray his wedding vows by word or deed. He might not be able to control his heart or his thoughts, but he could remove the bracelet. That much lay within his power.

At the other side of the room, Polly was ordering around a small team of brownies. They had set up a stage at the far end of the room, on which sat, indeed, a large glass tank of water. A pair of brownies moved candelabras around to provide theatrical lighting, and others scampered about, clearing the floor to make way for an audience.

The stairs rattled; Matthew was hurrying down, his bright hair the color of candlelight in the haze of the bar. He had taken off his jacket and was in shirtsleeves and a green-and-blue-striped waistcoat. He flipped himself over the staircase banister and landed on the stage. Standing behind the tank, he held up his hands for quiet.

The din continued unabated, however, until the first Sid brought his massive fists together above his head and shouted, "Oi! Quiet or I'll crush your mangy skulls!"

"That's right!" agreed the other Sid; apparently they had put their differences behind them.

There was a fair bit of grumbling, and a nearby werewolf muttered, "Mangy! *Well!*" But eventually, the crowd quieted down.

"Steady on," James whispered. "How is a mermaid going to get down the stairs?"

There was a pause, and Christopher, who had taken off his spectacles to clean them, said, "How did the mermaid get up the stairs?"

Thomas shrugged.

"Good evening, my friends!" Matthew called, to a smattering of polite applause. "Tonight we have something truly exceptional to present to you in honor of an old friend of the Devil. You have been kind enough to tolerate the presence of us Merry Thieves for several years now—"

"We just thought you Shadowhunters were raiding the place," Polly spoke up with a smirk, "and taking your time about it."

"Tomorrow, one of us—the first of us—marches to his doom and joins the ranks of you poor married sods," Matthew continued. "But tonight, we send him off in style!"

Hoots and cheers accompanied shouted jests and pounding on tables. A satyr and a squat horned creature near the front stood up and pantomimed a lewd embrace, until someone threw a sausage at them. At the piano, one of the hobgoblins struck up a light comic tune. Music filled the room, and Matthew held up his witchlight. Glimmering, it illuminated a figure descending the stairs.

James wondered for a moment whether this was the first time someone had used a witchlight rune-stone as stage lighting before he realized what he was looking at and his mind went blank. Christopher made a small noise in the back of his throat, and Thomas stared wide-eyed.

The mermaid had human legs. They were long and really quite shapely, James had to admit, loosely draped in diaphanous skirts made of woven exotic seaweeds.

Unfortunately, from the waist up she was the front half of a gaping, staring fish. Her scales were shiny metallic silver and reflected the light in a way that almost, but not quite, distracted from her dinner-plate-size, unblinking yellow eyes.

The audience went mad, cheering and hooting twice as loudly as before. One of the werewolves howled, "CLARIBELLA!" in a mournful, yearning voice.

"May I present," Matthew cried with a grin, "Claribella the Mermaid!"

The crowd whistled and banged their approval. James, Christopher, and Thomas struggled to find words.

"The mermaid's backward," said James, having regained some of his vocabulary—though perhaps not all of it.

"Matthew hired a reverse mermaid," Thomas agreed. "But why?"

"I wonder what kind of fish she is," said Christopher. "Are mermaids a specific kind of fish? Sharks, or herring, or such?"

"I had kippers for breakfast this morning," Thomas said sadly.

The backward mermaid began to swing her hips side to side, with the ease of a practiced cabaret dancer. Her mouth bobbed open and closed in rhythm with the music. Her small fins, on either side of her body, flapped.

To Matthew's credit, the rest of the Devil Tavern crowd seemed to be unironic admirers of Claribella and her performance. When her dance was finished she retreated behind her tank, at least in part to protect herself from her most ardent devotees.

"She does have a certain way about her," Christopher said. He looked over at James hopefully. "Eh?"

"We should have gone to the Pouncebys' sledding party," said James.

"Perhaps a quiet evening upstairs?" said Thomas sympathetically. "I'll cut a path through the crowd."

As they followed Thomas through the surge of Downworlders, Matthew, who had been selling tickets for private sessions with Claribella, saw them and leaped down from the stage.

"Seeking the beautiful solace of solitude?" Matthew asked, taking James's arm. He smelled like Matthew always did—cologne and brandy, singed with a bit of smoke and sawdust.

"I'm going upstairs with the three of you," said James. "I wouldn't call that 'solitude.'"

"Quiet, then," said Matthew. "'Thou still unravish'd bride of quietness, Thou foster-child of silence and slow time—'"

As they reached the steps, Ernie the tavern owner jumped up on the stage and attempted to dance with Claribella—but with only a pair of stubby fins, she easily eluded him and leaped headfirst into the tub of gin inhabited by Pickles the kelpie. She emerged a second later, blowing a spout of gin as Pickles neighed in delight.

They made it to their private rooms upstairs, Thomas bolting the doors firmly behind them. It was cold, and a steady leak was dripping water from the ceiling onto the worn carpets, but James found it a welcoming sight anyway. This was the headquarters of the Merry Thieves, their bolt-hole, their place away from the world, and the only place James wanted to be right now. The snow had picked up and was coming down in whirling white gusts against the leaded glass windows.

As Thomas carried over an empty pot to catch the leak, Christopher knelt in front of the fireplace and examined the logs laid within it, damp with melted snow. He took an object from his pocket, a metal tube attached to a small glass flask—a delivery method for a chemical fire starter of his own invention that he had been working on in recent weeks. He threw a switch, and the flask filled up with a pinkish gas. There was a small pop and a brief flash of a flame shooting out the end of the tube, but it quickly extinguished itself and thick black smoke poured into the room.

"I didn't expect that," Christopher said, trying to stopper the tube with the end of his handkerchief. James exchanged an exasperated look with Matthew, and they ran to open the windows, coughing and gasping. Thomas grabbed a tattered book from the shelves and tried to fan the smoke toward the window. They opened the rest of the windows and doors and grabbed whatever was at hand to wave the acrid smoke around the room until it finally dissipated, leaving a bitter stench and a scattering of black soot on every surface.

They slammed the windows closed. Thomas went into the adjoining room and returned with dry wood: this time, when Christopher tried to light the fire—with ordinary vesta matches—it caught. The four of them crowded around the circular table in the middle of the room, all shivering; Matthew caught James's hands and chafed them between his own.

"Well, this is a fine way to spend the eve of your wedding," he said apologetically.

"Nowhere I'd rather be," James said, his teeth chattering. "You're the only ones who know the truth about this wedding, for one thing."

"Thus freeing us from the usual expectation that this penultimate evening must be enjoyable," Matthew said. He let go of James's hands and set out four cups. Picking up the brandy bottle, he poured a measure into each.

His tone was light, but there was an edge to his voice, and James wondered how much Matthew had had to drink before he'd even arrived at the tavern tonight.

"The regulars seemed to enjoy Claribella's performance," Thomas said.

"Did you know she was a reverse mermaid?" Christopher asked, his lilac eyes wide with innocent curiosity.

"Er," said Matthew, refilling his mug, "not as such, no. I mean, the booker said she was backward, but I just thought he meant she was poorly educated, and I didn't wish to be a snob."

Thomas snorted.

"You might have asked to see her before booking her," James said. He took a sip from his mug; the brandy began warming up his insides as the fire, now crackling, had started to warm his outside.

He'd meant it as a joke, but Matthew looked wounded. "I made an effort," he protested. To Thomas and Christopher he said, "I didn't hear any magnificent ideas from the rest of you for tonight."

"Only because you said you had it handled," Thomas said.

"The important thing," Christopher said, looking alarmed at the potential for conflict, "is that we're all together. And that we get James to the ceremony on time, of course."

"Of course, because the groom is champing at the bit to be married," Matthew drawled, and they all looked at each other, as alarmed as Christopher. The four of them argued or fought very rarely, and James and Matthew almost never.

Even Matthew seemed to realize his comment had cut too close, the skeleton of the truth gleaming like white bone through dirt. He pulled his flask from his coat and turned it upside down, but it was empty. He tossed it onto the nearby sofa and looked at James, his eyes bright.

"Jamie," he said. "My heart. My *parabatai*. You don't have to do this. You don't have to go through with it. You know that, don't you?"

Both Christopher and Thomas sat motionless.

"Cordelia—" James began.

"Cordelia might not want this either," said Matthew. "A sham marriage—not what a young girl dreams of, surely—"

James stood up from the table. His heart beat a strange tattoo inside his chest. "In order to save me from being imprisoned by the Clave for arson, destruction of property, and the Angel knows what else, Cordelia lied for me. She said we spent the night together." His tone was harsh, each word clear and precise. "You know what that means for a woman. She destroyed her own reputation for me."

"But it isn't destroyed," said Christopher. "You—"

"Offered to marry her," said James. "No, scratch that, I told her we were getting married. Because Cordelia would indeed be the first to turn away from such a union. She would never want me to do something I felt compelled to do, never want me to make myself unhappy for her sake."

"Are you?" Thomas's eyes were clear and steady. "Making yourself unhappy for her?"

"I would be more unhappy if she was ruined," said James, "and I had the blame for it. A year of marriage to Daisy is a small price to pay to save us both." He exhaled. "Remember? We all said it would be good fun? A lark?"

"I suppose the closer it gets to the day, the more serious it seems," said Christopher.

"It is not a light business," said Thomas. "The runes of marriage, the vows—"

"I know," said James, turning away toward the windows. Snow seemed to have swallowed all of London. They sat captured in a pinpoint of light and warmth, in the center of a world of ice.

"And Grace Blackthorn," said Matthew.

A short silence followed. None of them had spoken Grace's name in front of James since his and Cordelia's engagement party, four months ago.

"I don't know what Grace thinks, actually," said James. "She was very strange after the betrothal—"

Matthew's mouth twisted. "Even though she herself was already betrothed and had no business—"

"Matthew," Thomas said quietly.

"I haven't spoken with her for months," James said. "Not a word."

"You haven't forgotten that you burned down that house for her, have you?" Matthew said, refilling his cup.

"No," said James tightly. "But it doesn't matter. I made a promise to Daisy, and I will keep that promise. If you wanted to prevent me from doing the right thing, you should have started the campaign quite a bit earlier than the night before my wedding."

Everything was very quiet for a moment. The four of them were still, barely breathing. Snow dashed itself against the panes in soft explosions of white. James could see himself reflected in the glass: his own dark hair, his pale face.

At last Matthew said, "You are right, of course; it is only perhaps that we worry that you are too honest—too good, and goodness can be a blade sharp enough to cut, you know, just as much as evil intent."

"I am not as good as all that," said James, turning away from the window—

—and suddenly the room and his friends fell away, and he had the sensation of falling, twisting and turning through a long expanse of nothingness, though he was also standing still.

He had landed on a hard patch of earth.

No, not now, it can't be. But as James got to his feet, he found himself in a barren wasteland, under a sky covered in ash. It wasn't possible, he thought—he had seen this shadow realm fall apart, as Belial howled in rage.

The last time he was in this place, he had watched Cordelia drive her sword into Belial's chest. An image of her appeared unbidden in his mind, striking the blow, her sword out and her hair streaming, as if she were a goddess captured in a painting: Liberty or Victory leading the people.

And then the world itself had yawned open as the sky split and red-black light fell upon the crumbling earth. And James had watched Belial's face cave in and his body shatter into a thousand pieces.

Belial wasn't dead, but he had been so weakened by Cortana that Jem had said he would not be able to return for at least a hundred years. And certainly since that moment, all had been quiet. James had not seen his grandfather, nor a hint of his grandfather's shadow realm. But who else but Belial could have drawn James here now?

James spun around, narrowing his eyes. Something about this place, which he had seen so many times in dreams and visions, was different. Where were the piles of bleached bones, the dunes of sand, the twisted and gnarled trees? Far in the distance, across a desolate expanse of weed-choked scree, James saw the outline of a massive stone structure, a towering fortress rising above the plains.

Only human hands—or intelligent ones, at least—could have built such things. James had never seen a hint of such history in the desolation of Belial's realm.

He took a cautious step, only to feel the air slam into him like a wave. He was blinded, forced choking to his knees, and yanked into a depthless blackness. He hurtled again through nothing, twisting and flailing until he landed roughly on a hard wooden floor.

He forced himself up onto his elbows, inhaling the stink of burnt chemicals mixed with damp wool. He heard voices before his vision cleared, Matthew's rising above the other two: "James? Jamie!"

James coughed weakly. He tasted salt, and touched his mouth with his fingertips. They came away black and red. Hands caught his wrists; he was hauled up roughly, an arm around his back. Brandy and cologne.

"Matthew," he said, in a dry voice.

"Water," Christopher said. "Do we have any water?"

"Never touch the stuff," said Matthew, settling James onto the long sofa. He sat down next to him, staring so intently into James's face that, despite everything, James had to stifle a laugh.

"I'm fine, Matthew," said James. "Also, I don't know what you expect to discover by looking into my eyeball."

"I've got water," said Thomas, pushing past Christopher to offer James a mug: James's hands were shaking so badly that his first swallow went half down his windpipe, half down his shirtfront. Christopher pounded him on the back until he was able to gulp air and breathe, and drink properly.

He set the empty mug on the arm of the sofa. "Thanks, Thomas—"

He was caught, suddenly, in a fierce hug from Matthew. Matthew's hands were tight on the back of his shirt, Matthew's cold cheek against his. "You went shadowy," Matthew said, his voice low, "as if you were going to disappear, as if I'd wished you gone and you were vanishing—"

James drew back enough to smooth Matthew's hair away from his forehead. "Have you wished me gone?" he said teasingly.

"No. Only I wish myself gone, sometimes," Matthew said in a whisper, and it was that rarest of things where Matthew was concerned, an entirely true statement with no mockery or teasing or humor to be had.

"Never wish that," James said, and sat back enough to see the other two Merry Thieves, and their worried expressions. "I turned into a shadow?"

Thomas nodded. Matthew was leaning against the back of the sofa now, only his right hand wrapped around James's wrist, as if he were reassuring himself that James was still there.

"I did think that rubbish was over," James admitted.

"It's been months," said Christopher.

"I thought it couldn't happen to you anymore," Thomas said. "I thought Belial's realm was destroyed."

James looked at his friends, wanting to reassure them—*it doesn't mean anything, there could be any sort of reason for it to happen, I'm sure it isn't important*—but the words died on his lips. The bleakness of the place was still too close to him, the acid taste of the air, the distant fortress shrouded in smoke.

Someone had wanted him to see it, he thought. And it was unlikely to be someone who wished him well.

"I know," he said at last. "That's what I thought too."

The air outside was so cold it seemed to shimmer as Cordelia, tipsy and giggling, clambered down from the Institute carriage and waved a vigorous goodbye to Lucie. Behind her, Cornwall Gardens was dark and shuttered. "Thank you for the party surprise," she called, closing the carriage door. "I never expected to spend the night before my wedding playing tiddlywinks with werewolves."

"Did you think they were cheating? I thought they were cheating. But it was terribly amusing regardless." Lucie leaned out the open window and blew Cordelia a dramatic kiss. "Good night, my dear! Tomorrow I will be your *suggenes*! We will be sisters."

Cordelia looked momentarily anxious. "Only for a year."

"No," Lucie said firmly. "Whatever happens, we will always be sisters."

Cordelia smiled and turned to go into the house. The front door had opened, and Lucie could see Alastair in the doorway, holding an upraised lamp, like Diogenes looking for an honest man. He nodded at Lucie before pulling the door shut behind his sister; Lucie tapped the side of the carriage, and Balios started up again, the sound of his hooves like muffled rain against the snowy ground.

She sank back with a sigh against the blue silk seat, suddenly tired. It had been a long night. Anna had slipped away an hour or so after midnight with Lily, a vampire from Peking. Lucie had stood firm—she'd wanted to remain at the Ruelle as long as Cordelia was amused; she knew her friend was half dreading the next day. She couldn't blame her. Not that people didn't get married for all sorts of reasons of expediency rather than love, but even if it was temporary, it was very dramatic. Cordelia would have to put on quite a performance tomorrow, as would James.

"Penny for your thoughts," said a low voice. Lucie looked up, her mouth curling into a smile.

Jesse. Sitting opposite her, his face illuminated by the rosy glow of the carriage lamp that filtered through the window. She had trained herself not to jump when he suddenly appeared between one moment and another; in the four months since they had become reacquainted, she had seen him nearly every night.

He always looked the same. He never gained an inch in height, or his hair an inch in length. He was always reassuringly dressed in the same black trousers and white shirt. His eyes were always deep and green, like verdigris on a tarnished coin.

And his presence always made her feel as if delicate fingers were walking up her spine. Shivery and warm, all at the same time.

"A penny is very little," she said, keeping her voice light with an effort. "My thoughts are most interesting and should require a greater outlay of cash."

"Pity I'm stony broke," he said, indicating his empty pockets. "Did you have a good time at the Ruelle? Anna's outfits are truly spectacular; I do wish that she could advise me on waistcoats and spats, but, you know . . ." He raised his arms, gesturing at his never-changing attire.

Lucie smiled at him. "Were you lurking about? I didn't see you."

It was rare that she didn't see Jesse if he was present in a room. Four months ago, he had given his last breath—once imprisoned in the golden locket she now wore around her neck—to save James's life. Lucie had been worried afterward that the loss would mean Jesse might fade away or disappear; while he remained bothersomely insubstantial, he was still very visible, if only to her.

He leaned his dark head back against the blue-and-gold upholstery. "I may have popped by to make sure you got into the Ruelle safely. There are a lot of suspicious types around Berwick Street at night: thieves, cutpurses, rapscallions...."

"Rapscallions?" Lucie was delighted. "That sounds like something from *The Beautiful Cordelia*."

"Speaking of which." He pointed an accusing finger at her. "When are you going to let me read it?"

Lucie hesitated. She had allowed him to read some of her earlier novels, like *Secret Princess Lucie Is Rescued from Her Terrible Family*, which he had enjoyed very much, especially the character of Cruel Prince James. But *The Beautiful Cordelia* was different. "I'm polishing the book," she said. "It requires polishing. All novels must be polished, like diamonds."

"Or shoes," he said dryly. "I've been thinking of writing a novel myself. It is about a ghost who is very, very bored."

"Perhaps," Lucie suggested, "you should write a novel about a ghost who has a very devoted sister and a very devoted ... friend who spend a great deal of their time trying to figure out how to make him not a ghost anymore."

Jesse didn't reply. She'd meant to be amusing, but his eyes had gone dark and serious. How odd that even when one was a ghost, the eyes were the window to the soul. And she knew Jesse had a soul. And that it was as alive as anything else living, desperate to be free in the world once more, not sentenced to a half-existence of consciousness that came only at night.

Jesse glanced out the window. They were passing through Piccadilly Circus, nearly deserted at such a late hour. The statue of Eros in the center was lightly dusted with snow; a lone tramp slept upon the steps below it. "Don't have too much hope, Lucie. Sometimes hope is dangerous."

"Have you said that to Grace?"

"She won't listen. Not a word. I—I don't wish you to be disappointed."

Lucie reached out her hand, still in its blue kid glove. Jesse seemed to be watching her in the faint reflection traced against the inside of the window, though of course he could not also see himself. Perhaps he preferred it that way.

He turned his own hand over, palm up. Drawing off her glove, she rested her fingers lightly on his. *Oh.* The feel of him—his hand was cool but slightly insubstantial, like the memory of a touch. And yet it sent sparks through her veins—she could almost see them, like fireflies in the dark.

She cleared her throat. "Don't worry about me being disappointed," she said. "I am terribly busy with important things, and I have a wedding to arrange tomorrow."

He looked over at her then, smiling almost reluctantly. "You're the only one planning this wedding?"

She tossed her head, making the flowers on her hat tremble. "The only competent one."

"Oh, indeed. I recall the scene in *Secret Princess Lucie Is Rescued from Her Terrible Family* in which Princess Lucie bests Cruel Prince James at the art of flower arranging."

"James was very annoyed by that chapter," said Lucie, with some satisfaction. Light glowed into the carriage as they passed the streetlamps: outside, a lone policeman walked his solitary beat before the Corinthian portico of the Haymarket Theatre.

She could no longer feel Jesse's hand against hers. She glanced down and saw that she seemed to be resting her fingers against nothing—he seemed to have gone from slightly to entirely insubstantial. She frowned, but he had already withdrawn his hand, leaving her to wonder if she'd imagined things.

"I suppose you'll see Grace tomorrow," Jesse said. "She seems unbothered by the wedding and appears to wish your brother well."

Lucie couldn't help but wonder. Grace was a subject she and Jesse could only touch on lightly. She never saw them at the same time, since Jesse lay unconscious during the day, and Grace had difficulty getting away from the Bridgestocks and Charles during the night; Jesse often visited her, but she never spoke to Lucie about their conversations. For all that Grace and Lucie were working together to save Jesse, the topic of him as he was, now, was an awkward one.

Jesse did seem to understand that Grace had gotten engaged to Charles in order to be protected from Tatiana's influence, and that James and Cordelia were marrying to save Cordelia's reputation. He even seemed to think it was the right thing to do. But Jesse loved his sister with a great protective love, and Lucie had no desire to discuss with him the fact that she worried Grace had broken James's heart.

Especially not while she still needed Grace's help.

"Well, I'm glad to hear it," she said briskly. Turning out of Shoe Lane, they rolled through the iron gateway of the Institute and into the courtyard. The cathedral rose above them, dark and imposing against the sky. "When—when will I see you again?"

She immediately wished she hadn't asked. He always turned up, rarely missing more than a night between their meetings. She shouldn't press him.

Jesse smiled a little sadly. "Would that I could make an appearance during the wedding. It is a pity. I would have liked to see you in your *suggenes* dress. It looked like a butterfly's wings."

She had shown him the material—an iridescent peach-lavender shot silk—before; still, she was surprised he recalled it. Lights were coming on in the Institute; Lucie knew that her parents would soon be emerging to welcome her back. She drew away from Jesse, reaching to gather up her discarded glove, as the front door of the Institute opened, spilling warm yellow light across the flagstones.

"Perhaps tomorrow night—" she began, but Jesse was already gone.

GRACE:
1893–1896

Once upon a time, she had been someone else, she remembers
that much. A different girl, though she had the same skinny wrists and
white-blond hair. When she was still small, her parents sat her down
and explained that she and they and everyone they knew were not ordinary people, but the descendants of angels. Nephilim, sworn to protect
the world from the monsters that threatened it. The girl had a drawing
of an eye on the back of her hand, from before remembering. Her parents put it there, and it marked her as one of the Shadowhunters and
allowed her to see the monsters that were invisible to others.

By all rights, she should be able to remember the details of her parents' faces, the house they lived in. She had been seven years old—she
should be able to remember how she felt in the stone room in Alicante,
when a crowd of adults who were strangers to her came and told her
that her parents were dead.

Instead that moment was the end of feeling. The girl who had
existed before she went into the stone room—that girl was gone.

At first the girl thought she would be sent to live with other members of her family, though her parents had been distant from them and
they were strangers. Instead she was sent to live with an entirely different stranger. All at once she was a Blackthorn. A carriage of ebony as
black and shiny as a pianoforte came to fetch her; it brought her across

the summer fields of Idris, to the edge of Brocelind Forest, and through elaborately filigreed iron gates. To Blackthorn Manor, her new home.

It must have been a shock for the girl, going from a modest house in the lower part of Alicante to the ancestral house of one of the oldest Shadowhunter families. But that shock, and indeed most of her memories of the house in Alicante, were gone like so much else.

Her new mother was strange. At first she was kind, almost too kind. She would grasp the girl, suddenly, around the waist, and hold her tightly. "I never thought I would have a daughter," she would murmur, in a tone of wonder, as though she were telling someone in the room who the girl could not see. "And one that came with such a pretty name, too. Grace."

Grace.

There were other, more frightening ways that Tatiana Blackthorn was strange. She took no action to keep up the house in Idris or prevent it from falling into decay; her only servant was a sour-faced and silent maid who Grace rarely saw. Sometimes Tatiana was pleasant; other times she harshly ground out an unending litany of her grievances— against her brothers, against other Shadowhunter families, against Shadowhunters in general. They were responsible for the death of her husband, and the whole bunch of them, Grace came to understand, could go to the devil.

Grace was grateful for having been taken in, and she was glad to have a family and a place to belong. But it was a strange place, her mother never really knowable, always busying herself with odd magics in unlit back corners of the manor. It would have been a very lonely life, if not for Jesse.

He was seven years her elder, and pleased to have a sister. He was quiet, and kind, and he read to her and helped her make flower crowns in the garden. She noticed that his face was a blank when their mother went on about her enemies and the vengeance she craved against them.

If there was anything in the world that Tatiana Blackthorn loved, it was Jesse. With Grace she could be critical, and liberal with the slaps and pinches, but she would never lift a hand to Jesse. Was it because he was a boy, Grace wondered, or was it because he was Tatiana's child by blood, while Grace was only a ward she had taken in?

The answer mattered little. Grace didn't need her mother's adoration, as long as she had Jesse. He was a companion when she needed one most, and so much older that he seemed almost grown to her.

It was a good thing they had each other for companionship, since they rarely left the grounds of the manor, save when they went with their mother on her brief trips to Chiswick House, a vast stone estate in England that Tatiana had wrested from her brothers twenty-five years ago and now jealously guarded. Though Chiswick House was near London, and thus a valuable piece of property, Tatiana seemed determined to watch it rot away too.

Grace was always relieved to return to Idris. Being close to London did not quite remind her of her old life—that had turned to shadows and dreams—but it did recall to her that she had a past, a time before she had belonged to Jesse, to Tatiana, and to Blackthorn Manor. And what was the point of that?

One day Grace heard a queer thumping noise coming from the room above hers. She went to investigate, more curious than worried, and discovered that the source of the noise was, shockingly, Jesse, who had set up a makeshift knife-throwing gallery with some straw bales and a hessian sheet in one of the high-ceilinged, airy rooms on the manor's top floor. They must have been used as training rooms by the house's earlier inhabitants, but her mother only ever referred to them as "the ballrooms."

"What are you doing?" asked Grace, scandalized. "You know that we aren't meant to pretend to be Shadowhunters."

Jesse went to retrieve a thrown knife from a straw bale. Grace couldn't help but notice he'd very accurately hit his target. "It's not pretending, Grace. We are Shadowhunters."

"By birth, says Mama," she said cautiously. "But not by choice. Shadowhunters are brutes and killers, she says. And we're not allowed to train."

Her brother prepared to throw the knife again. "And yet we live in Idris, a secret nation built for and known only by Shadowhunters. You bear a Mark. I—ought to."

"Jesse," Grace said slowly. "Do you really care so much about being a Shadowhunter? About fighting demons with sticks, and all that?"

"It's what I was born to do," he said, his brow dark. "I have taught myself, since I was eight years old—the attic of this house is full of old weapons and training manuals. It's what you were born to as well." Grace hesitated, and a rare memory surfaced in her mind—her parents throwing knives into a board hung on the wall of their small house in Alicante. They had fought demons. It was how they had lived and how they had died. Surely that was not all foolishness, as Tatiana claimed. Surely it was not a meaningless life.

Jesse noticed her odd expression but didn't press her to tell him what she was thinking. Instead he went on making his point. "What if one day we were attacked by demons? Someone would have to protect our family."

"Will you train me, too?" Grace said, in a rush, and her brother broke into a smile that made her burst into tears, overwhelmed by the sudden feeling of being cared for. Of being cared about. Of belonging to something larger than herself.

They started with the knives. They didn't dare train during the day, but when their mother was asleep, she was far enough away not to hear the thunks of the blades into the backstop. And Grace, to her own surprise, did well at the training, learning fast. After a few weeks, Jesse gave her a hunting bow and a quiver of beautiful red cured leather—he apologized that they were not new, but she knew he had scrounged them from the attic and spent weeks cleaning and repairing them for her, and that meant more than would have any expensive gift.

They began archery lessons. This was an altogether more dangerous prospect, involving sneaking out of doors in the middle of the night to practice at the old range behind the house, almost to the walls. Grace would get into bed in all her clothes, wait until the moon was visible through her window, and descend the house's unlit gloomy stairs to join her brother. Jesse was a patient teacher, gentle and encouraging. She had never thought of having a brother, but now she was grateful every day to have one—and not only grateful in the dutiful way she was grateful to her mother.

Before she came to live with Tatiana, Grace had never understood how potent a poison loneliness could be. As the months passed, she realized that loneliness had driven her adoptive mother mad. Grace wanted to love Tatiana, but her mother would not allow such love to grow. Her loneliness had become so twisted up on itself that she had grown afraid of love, and rejected the affections of anyone besides Jesse. Slowly Grace came to understand that Tatiana did not want Grace's love. She wanted only her loyalty.

But that love had to go somewhere, or Grace might explode, like a river bursting a dam. So she poured all her love into Jesse. Jesse, who taught her to climb trees, to speak and read French, who finished every evening by her bedside, reading to her from works as diverse as the *Aeneid* of Virgil and *Treasure Island*.

When their mother was distracted by other matters, they would meet in the disused study at the end of the hall, where there were bookshelves floor-to-ceiling on all sides and several large decaying armchairs. This, too, was part of their training, Jesse told her, and they would read together. Grace never knew just why Jesse was so kind to her. She thought perhaps that he understood from the start that he and Grace were each other's only true allies, and that their survival depended on one another. Apart they might fall into the same pit that had claimed their mother; together they might even thrive.

When Grace was ten, Jesse convinced his mother to allow him, at long last, to take a rune. It was unfair, he said, to live in Idris without even so much as a Voyance rune for the Sight. It was understood that anyone who lived in Idris was Sighted, and it might even be dangerous for him not to be. Their mother scowled, but she gave in. Two Silent Brothers came. Grace barely recalled her own rune ceremony, and the sight of the scarred, drifting figures in the dark halls of Blackthorn Manor made her skin crawl. But she summoned her courage and was with Jesse when a Silent Brother inscribed the Voyance rune on the back of Jesse's right hand. She was there to see him hold up his hand, to regard it in wonder, to thank the Brothers profusely.

And she was there that night to see him die.

3

BITTER AND SWEET

Ah well, well, well, I may be beguiled
By some coquettish deceit.
Yet, if she were not a cheat,
If Maud were all that she seem'd,
And her smile were all that I dream'd,
Then the world were not so bitter
But a smile could make it sweet.
—Alfred, Lord Tennyson, "Maud"

You don't have to marry a man who doesn't love you.

The faerie's voice echoed in Cordelia's mind as she turned to face the mirror in her bedroom. She appeared almost a ghost to herself, despite the vivid gold of her wedding dress—a floating spirit, tethered to this reality by a thin ribbon. *She* wasn't the one about to marry a man who didn't love her. This day couldn't be the last time she'd stand in this bedroom, rise from sleeping under the same roof as her mother and brother, look out her window on the row houses of South Kensington, pale in the winter sun. Her life couldn't be about to change that much at just seventeen.

"*Dokhtare zibaye man.* My beautiful daughter," said her mother, wrapping her arms around Cordelia from behind in an awkward hug, careful of her pregnant belly. Cordelia regarded them both in the mirror: the similar shapes of their hands, their mouths. She wore a gold necklace that had been part of her mother's own dowry. Her skin was a few shades lighter than her mother's, but their eyes were the same black. And when had she gotten taller than Sona?

Sona clucked. A lock of hair had escaped the jeweled golden bandeau that encircled Cordelia's head; she moved to smooth it back in place. "Layla, *azizam*. You seem worried."

Cordelia exhaled slowly. She couldn't even imagine Sona's reaction if she told her the truth. "It is just quite a big change, *Mâmân*. To move out of this house—and not back to Cirenworth, but to quite a strange house—"

"Layla," Sona said. "Don't fret. It is always difficult to face a change. When I married your father, I was terribly nervous. Yet all anyone talked about was how lucky I was, because he was the dashing hero who had slain the demon Yanluo. But my mother took me aside and told me, 'He's indeed very dashing, but you must not forget your own heroism.' So all will be well. Only do not forget your own heroism."

The words gave Cordelia a start. Sona rarely mentioned her family, except as an ideal of heroism—a family whose lineage stretched far back among the Shadowhunters of Persia. Cordelia knew that her grandparents were no longer living—they had died before her birth—but there were aunts and uncles and cousins in Tehran. Sona barely spoke of them, and hadn't invited them to James and Cordelia's wedding, saying it would be rude to expect them to travel so far and that they did not trust Portals.

It was as though when she'd married Elias, she'd separated herself from her old life completely, and now Risa was the closest thing she had to her Persian family. And Sona's isolation was not the only matter that troubled Cordelia. Elias, after all, had not been a dashing hero in many years. What did Sona think of that? What did she think of her heroism, put aside to raise her children and wander always, never settling down, because of her husband's "health"?

"Sona *khanoom*!" Risa suddenly appeared in the doorway. "He has come," she went on, casting an urgent glance over her shoulder. "Just now—with no warning at all—"

"Alastair! Cordelia!" a familiar voice bellowed up from downstairs. "Sona, my love!"

Sona paled and laid a hand against the wall to steady herself. "Elias?"

"It's *bâbâ*?" Cordelia picked up the heavy skirts of her dress and rushed out into the hall. Risa was already headed downstairs, her expression stormy. Elias passed her without a glance, racing to the top of the steps with a smile on his face, a hand on the newel post.

Cordelia came to a dead stop. A wave of joy had gone over her when she heard her father's voice, but now—now she couldn't move as her mother hurried past her to embrace Elias. Cordelia felt oddly far away, as her father embraced and kissed her mother, then stood back to lay a hand on her rounded stomach.

Sona dipped her head, speaking softly and rapidly to Elias. Though he was smiling, he looked exhausted, deep grooves lining his face, gray stubble in patches on his jaw. His suit was threadbare, as if he'd been wearing it every day since he was taken away.

He put his arms out. "Cordelia," he said.

She broke out of her paralysis. A moment later she was in her father's embrace, and the familiar feel of him, the rough scrape of his stubble as he kissed her forehead, soothed her despite everything. "*Bâbâ*," she said, tipping her head back to look up at him. He looked so old. "Where have you been? We've been so worried."

The scent of his clothes and hair—smoky, like tobacco—was familiar too. Or was there a sweet rot underneath? Was she smelling alcohol on him or imagining things?

Elias held her at arm's length. "I appreciate the welcome, my dear." He looked her up and down and, with a twinkle in his eye, added, "Though you didn't need to dress up so much just for me."

Cordelia laughed and thought, *My father is back. He will be at my wedding. That is what matters.* "It's my wedding dress," she started to say, just as Elias interrupted her with a smile.

"I know, child. It's why I returned today. I wouldn't have dreamed of missing your wedding."

"Then why didn't you return when the Basilias released you?" They all turned to see Alastair, who had just emerged from his room. He had clearly been in the process of getting dressed for the ceremony—his cuffs were unfastened and he was jacketless. He wore a black waistcoat, traced with golden runes for Love, Joy, and Unity, but his expression was anything but celebratory. "We know they let you out a week ago, Father. Had you returned earlier, it would have eased Mother's mind. Layla's, too."

Elias looked at his son. He did not hold out his arms, as he had to Cordelia, but his voice was thick with emotion when he spoke. "Come and greet me, Esfandiyār," he said.

It was Alastair's middle name. Esfandiyār had been a great hero from the *Shahnameh*, a Persian book of ancient mythical kings who could bind any demon with an enchanted chain. Alastair had loved to hear stories from the *Shahnameh* when he was small; he and Cordelia would curl up by the fire with Elias while he read.

But that had been a long time ago. Now Alastair didn't move, and Elias began to frown.

"Yes, they did release me some days ago," he said. "But before I returned, I went into the wilds in France, west of Idris."

"To do penance?" Alastair's voice was sharp-edged.

"To fetch Cordelia's wedding gift," said Elias. *"Risa!"* he called down the stairs.

"Oh, no, we can exchange gifts later," protested Cordelia. She could feel the tension rising, her mother looking anxiously back and forth between her son and husband. "When I open them with James."

"Risa," Elias called down the stairs again, "can you retrieve that oblong wooden box from my things? And nonsense," he said to Cordelia. "It's not a gift for your household. It's a gift for *you*."

Risa soon appeared with the box balanced on her shoulder, a thunderous look on her face. Ignoring her scowl, Elias took it from her and spun to present it to Cordelia. She looked at Alastair, leaning against the wall. She raised her eyebrows as if to ask him what he thought she should do. He only shrugged. She wanted to shake him a little: Would it hurt to pretend to be happy?

She turned back to her father, who held the box as she unsnapped the brass latches and swung it open.

She gasped.

Laid on a bed of bright blue velvet was a scabbard—one of the most beautiful scabbards Cordelia had ever seen, worthy of being displayed in a museum. It was forged of fine steel, as bright as silver, its surface elaborately inlaid with gilt and etched with delicate patterns of birds, leaves, and vines. As she looked closer, she could glimpse tiny runes like butterflies among the leaves.

"The only gift worthy of my daughter," Elias said, "is the gift worthy of the sword that has chosen her."

"Where did it come from?" Cordelia asked. She couldn't help but be moved. What Alastair had told her about the many times he had needed to rescue their father—and himself and Cordelia and their mother—from the consequences of his drinking . . . it had—she had been angry. How could her father be so selfish, so indifferent to his family's needs?

But he had also been there for her, many times, helping her to climb trees, to train, teaching her the significance of Cortana and the responsibility conferred on the one who wielded it. And he had come to her today, her wedding day, and brought this gift. Would it be so wrong to think he meant well?

"The faerie folk of northern France are famed for their exquisite workmanship," said Elias. "It is said this scabbard was made by Melusine herself. I knew it had to be yours. I hope you will accept it as a token of my love, child, and—as a promise to do better."

Sona smiled tremulously. Elias set the box carefully down on the hall table. "Thank you, Father," Cordelia said, putting her arms around him. As he hugged her tightly, she caught a glimpse of movement out of the corner of her eye, and glanced up to see Alastair head back to his room without a word.

The bloody bracelet was still on his wrist, James thought, as he paced up and down the carpet in his bedroom. He had been meaning to remove it for days. In fact, he was fairly sure he *had* tried to remove it, but the fastening had been stuck.

He was halfway to his desk in search of a letter opener he could use to poke at the latch when he caught sight of himself in the mirror. He stopped to make sure everything was in place; for Cordelia's sake, he had to look his best.

He smoothed down his hair—hopeless, as it sprang up again immediately—and did up the last button on the gold brocade frock coat made for him by his father's tailor, an ancient man named Lemuel Sykes.

He thought of his father's excitement when he'd presented James to Lemuel: "My boy's getting married!" Sykes had angrily muttered his congratulations. Given his amount of ear hair, James put it at even odds that he was a werewolf, but he thought it impolite to ask. In any event, Will turned out to have been right to overlook Sykes's off-putting manner and the constant fear that he would drop dead of old age right in front of them. James felt he wasn't the best judge of his own appearance, but even he was taken by the way his suit, rich gold coat and all, made him look *serious*. Like a young man with intent, who knew what he was doing. Given the situation, he could use even the illusion of confidence.

He had just started toward the desk again when there was a knock on his door. James opened it to find his parents, elegant in their own formal attire. Like James, Will was dressed in a frock coat and black trousers, but his coat was cut from ebony wool. Tessa wore a simple dress of blush-colored velvet, adorned with tiny seed pearls. They both looked grave.

James's stomach dropped. "Is something wrong?"

They've found out, he thought. *About my burning down Blackthorn Manor—Cordelia stepping in to protect me—the sham of this marriage, meant to save us both.*

"Don't be alarmed," Will said soothingly. "There's a bit of news."

Tessa sighed. "Will, you're terrifying the poor boy," she said. "He probably thinks Cordelia's broken off the engagement. She *hasn't*," she added. "Nothing like that. Only—her father's come back."

"Elias is home?" James stepped out of the way, letting his parents into the room; the halls were full of maids and footmen rushing about getting the place ready, and this seemed the sort of discussion better had in private. "When did he return?"

"Just this morning, apparently," said Will. There were three chairs arranged near the window. James joined his parents there. Outside the glass, ice-laced tree branches shimmered in the winter wind. Pale sunlight streamed onto the carpet. "As you know, the Basilias let him out some time ago, but apparently he claims he went to get Cordelia a wedding present. Thus his delayed arrival."

"Doesn't sound like you believe him," said James. "Where do you think he's been?"

Will and Tessa exchanged a look. The fate of Elias Carstairs had become a lively part of Clave gossip only a week or two after he had been sent to the Basilias to be "healed." Most knew, or suspected, that he had found his illness at the bottom of a bottle. Cordelia had been painfully honest about it with James: that she had not known, growing up, that her father had a problem with alcohol, and that she both hoped the Basilias would cure him and feared that they could not.

When Tessa spoke, her words were careful. "He is Cordelia's father," she said. "We must trust he means what he says. Sona seems delighted to have him back, and Cordelia will no doubt be relieved that he's at her wedding."

"So they're here?" said James, with a pang of concern. "Cordelia and her family? Does she seem all right?"

"She was smuggled up the back stairs to prevent anyone glimpsing her," said Will. "She seemed—well, quite puffy and golden, from what I could see."

"You make her sound like a Yorkshire pudding," said James darkly. "Should I go to her? See if she needs me?"

"I don't think so," said Tessa. "Cordelia is a clever, brave, resourceful girl, but this is her father. I imagine the matter is quite sensitive, especially with so many of the Clave knowing about it. The best you can do is stand by her side, and by Elias's side. Make it clear we are delighted he is here, and that it is an occasion for happiness."

"This is part of being a husband," said Will. "You and Cordelia are one now. Your goals, your dreams, will all be shared, as well as your responsibilities. My understanding is that Elias hid his condition for many years; if he had not, things might be quite different. Might I give you a bit of marital advice?"

"Would wild horses be able to stop you?" said James. *Please, don't,* he thought. *The last thing I want is for you to think my marriage failed because your advice was flawed.*

"That depends," said Will. "Do you currently have access to any wild horses?"

James had to smile. "Not at the moment."

"Then no," said Will. "So here it is: always tell Cordelia what you feel." He looked James in the eye. "You may fear what will happen if you speak your heart. You may wish to hide things because you fear hurting others. But secrets have a way of eating at relationships, Jamie. At love, at friendship—they undermine and destroy them until in the end you find you are bitterly alone with the secrets you kept."

Tessa laid her hand quietly over Will's. James just nodded, feeling sick. *Secrets. Lies.* He was lying to his parents now—lying to everyone about his feelings. What would they say when he and Cordelia divorced in a year's time? How would he explain? A picture rose to his mind of his father, striking through James's marriage runes with a look of devastation on his face.

Will looked as if he were about to say something more when a rattling, crunching sound came from outside: wheels on snow and stone. Someone shouted a greeting. The first of the guests had begun to arrive.

They all rose, and Will reached out to brush a light hand through James's hair. "Do you need a moment? You're quite white-faced. It's natural to have nerves before such an event, you know."

I owe Cordelia a better performance than this, James thought. Oddly, the thought of Daisy strengthened him: he forgot sometimes, it was *Daisy* he was marrying, Daisy with her light laugh, her gentle, familiar touch, her surprising strength. It was not some stranger. If it were not for the thought of how disappointed his parents would be when it all came apart, he might be quite content.

"No need," he said. "I am only excited—that is all."

His parents broke into relieved smiles. The three of them made their way downstairs, through the brightly decorated Institute. Will opened the door, letting in a gust of sparkling ice crystals along with the first of the guests, and as James prepared to greet them, he realized that he was still wearing Grace's bracelet. Well, there was no time to remove it now. Cordelia would understand.

* * *

James was in the midst of greeting what seemed like every Shadow-hunter in London (and a good number from elsewhere), when he saw Lucie appear across the room.

He excused himself from the line of guests and hurried toward her. They had moved to what Tessa called the Long Hall, the rectangular room that separated the entryway from the chapel. Through the wide double doors of the chapel itself, James saw that it had been transformed. The beams were festooned in garlands of chrysanthemums woven with winter wheat and tied with gold ribbons, the aisle strewn with golden petals. The ends of the pews were decorated with sprays of yellow-hearted lilies, Welsh daffodils, and marigolds, and gold velvet banners hung from the ceiling, stitched with designs of birds and castles—the symbols of the Herondale and Carstairs families, united. On either side of the altar—*the altar where you will be standing, soon enough*, murmured a voice inside his head—huge crystal vases stood, overflowing with more flowers. Candles glowed from every niche and surface.

His mother and Sona had planned it all, he knew; they had truly outdone themselves.

"Where have you been?" James whispered, catching up to his sister. She was wearing a peach-colored silk dress with a chiffon overlay and gold satin bows at the sleeves. The gold locket she was fond of glittered at her throat. He'd asked her before where she'd acquired it: Lucie had told him not to be silly, she'd had it for a long time, and indeed he recalled her pressing it to his lips the night he'd nearly died in Highgate Cemetery. For good luck, she'd said afterward. "Matthew's not here yet and I've been greeting a thousand strangers all on my own. Including the Pangborns from the Cornwall Institute."

Lucie made a face at him. "Even Old Sticky Hands?"

James grinned at their nickname for Albert Pangborn, who had taken over the running of the Cornwall Institute from Felix Blackthorn in 1850. "I believe Father required me to refer to him as 'sir.' *And* shake his sticky hand."

"Alas." Lucie gazed at him loftily. "I," she said, "must be by Cordelia's side today, James. Not yours. I am her *suggenes*. She's getting ready in my room."

"Why can't I get ready in peace too?" James wondered—reasonably, he thought.

"Because you are not the bride," Lucie said. "You are the groom. And when you see her for the first time, in the chapel, in all her wedding attire, is meant to be magical."

They were silent for a moment. Lucie knew the truth perfectly well, but there was a stubborn set to her mouth that made James suspect now was not the time to point out that it wasn't that sort of wedding.

"Who lit all the candles?" James said. "It must have taken them an hour."

Lucie had sidled into the chapel and was gazing around. "Honestly, James. Not the thing you should be thinking about now. I suppose it could have been Magnus; he's been very helpful." She popped back out of the chapel, holding a fistful of yellow roses. "There we go. Good luck, James. I have to get back to Daisy." She glanced behind him, brightening. "Oh, look, Thomas and Christopher are here. Matthew can't be far behind."

James started across the room toward his friends, only to be descended upon by a whirl of aunts and uncles—Aunt Cecily and her husband, Gabriel Lightwood; Gabriel's brother Gideon and his wife, Sophie, and with them, a woman he didn't know.

Gideon clapped James on the shoulder. "James! You're looking splendid."

"What an excellent coat," Gabriel said. "Did my daughter help you find that?"

"Alas, this isn't Anna's work," said James, straightening his cuffs. "My father took me to his ancient tailor—who absolutely couldn't understand why I wanted a coat in gold and not a more gentlemanly color, like black or gray."

"Shadowhunters do not get married in gray," said Cecily, her eyes sparkling. "And Will has been using that tailor for so long I have begun to wonder if perhaps he lost a bet to him at cards. Have you met Filomena yet?"

James glanced over at the woman standing beside his uncles. She was probably about Anna's age, with smooth dark hair caught up at the nape of her neck. Her lips were very red, her eyes dark and heavy-lidded. She glanced at him and smiled.

"I haven't had the pleasure," James said.

"By the Angel, where are our manners?" Gabriel said, shaking his head. "James, may I present Filomena di Angelo? She has just arrived from Rome, on her travel year."

"Are you the groom?" said Filomena, in heavily accented English. "What a waste. You are very handsome."

"Well, you know what they say," said James. "All the best men are either married or Silent Brothers."

Cecily burst into giggles. James was spared from further discourse by the sudden appearance of Charles Fairchild, who cut into the conversation with a loud "Congratulations!" He slapped James enthusiastically on the back. "Have you seen either of your parents lately?"

Luckily, Will appeared, having apparently seen Charles's bright red hair across the room. "Charles," he said. "You were looking for us?"

"I wanted to confer with you about Paris," Charles began, and pulled Will aside to speak in hushed but intense tones. The Lightwoods had fallen into a discussion with Filomena about the long absence of demons from London, and the Clave's annoyance that their numbers were climbing back up again now, necessitating nightly patrols. Feeling there was little he could add to the conversation, James turned, intending to search for Matthew.

Standing in front of him, as if she had emerged, ghostlike, from a nearby wall, was Grace.

A flash of Tennyson went through James's mind. *My heart would hear her and beat, were it earth in an earthy bed.*

He couldn't remember what happened in the poem after that, just the poet dreaming of the girl he loved walking over his grave.

Other than at Enclave parties, when he had spotted her from afar and not approached, it had been months since James had seen Grace. It had certainly been that long since he had spoken to her. He had kept to his vow. No communication with Grace. No contact.

If he had hoped it would change the way he felt, he knew in this moment it hadn't. Her dress was cloudy gray, the color of her eyes: there was a little color in spots on her cheeks, like drops of blood tinting pale wine. She was as beautiful as a dawn that came without color, a sweep of gray sea unmarred by whitecaps or waves. She filled up his vision like a lamp blotting out the stars.

Somehow he had caught her wrist; he had drawn her behind a pillar, out of sight of the rest of the guests. "Grace," he said. "I didn't know if you would come."

"I could have no reasonable excuse to stay away." Everything about her—the way she looked, the clear sound of her voice, her small wrist under his grasp—went through him like a knife. "Charles expected me to accompany him."

He released her wrist, glancing around hastily. The only person nearby was a freckle-faced housemaid, who edged away awkwardly. James didn't recognize her, but then, he didn't know most of the servants in the Institute today; they'd been brought in by Bridget to help with the wedding. "I would rather you hadn't."

"I know." She bit her lip. "But I must speak with you alone before the ceremony. I *must*. It is important."

James knew he should refuse. "The drawing room," he said quickly, before his own better sense could kick in. "In ten minutes."

"Oh, no you *don't*." It was Matthew: James looked up in surprise. How his *suggenes* had found them, he had no idea, but found them he had. He was glowering at the both of them like an owl who had been mortally offended by another owl. "Grace Blackthorn, it is James's *wedding day*. Leave him alone."

Grace did not look in the least intimidated. "I shall quit James's company if *he* asks me to do it, not if you ask me to do it," she said. "I owe you nothing."

"I'm not sure that's true," Matthew said. "If nothing else, you owe me for the pain you have put my *parabatai* through."

"Ah, yes," said Grace, a light, mocking tone to her voice, "you feel his pain, don't you? If his heart shatters, does yours shatter? Does he feel what you feel? Because I can see how that might be awkward."

"Grace," James said. "Enough."

She looked startled; he supposed it was rare enough that he'd spoken to her harshly. "I have never meant to hurt you, James."

"I know," James said quietly, and saw Matthew shake his head, his cheeks flushed with anger.

"*Ten minutes*," Grace murmured, slipping away; she crossed the room, returning to Charles.

Matthew was still glowering. He was splendidly dressed in a morning coat over a stunning brocade waistcoat of Magnus Bane levels of magnificence, embroidered with a spectacular battle scene. He had a gleaming silk ascot at his throat that looked to be woven of pure gold. But the effect was somewhat spoiled by his tousled hair and look of fury. "What did *she* want with you?"

"Congratulations on your wedding day to you, too," James said. He sighed. "Sorry. I know why you're concerned. She said she needed to speak with me before the ceremony, that's all."

"Don't," said Matthew. "Whatever she has to say will only hurt you. It's all she ever does."

"Math," said James gently, "she is hurting too. This is not her fault. It is my fault, if it's anyone's."

"To feel hurt, she'd have to have feelings," Matthew began; seeing James's expression, he visibly bit down on the words.

"Perhaps if you got to know her better—" James started.

Matthew looked fleetingly, genuinely puzzled. "I do not believe I have spoken to her alone," he admitted. "Or if I have, I do not recall it." He sighed. "Very well. As your *suggenes*, it is my job to help you. I will withhold my judgment. Whatever you may need, I can see it is not that."

"Thank you." James laid his palm against Matthew's chest and found it surprisingly hard and metallic. He tapped Matthew's lapel with his fingers; with a sideways smile, Matthew reached into his jacket and James glimpsed his silver flask.

"Dutch courage," Matthew said.

"I'm the one who ought to need that, aren't I?" James said lightly. He hoped Matthew wouldn't drink too much before the ceremony, but he knew better than to say that. Sometimes he felt foolish for worrying—Anna was famous for her absinthe parties, and they all drank at the Devil Tavern. And yet.

But mentioning alcohol to Matthew would only earn a glib remark, and a blank stare if James persisted. Instead he smiled and withdrew his hand. "Well, then, as my *suggenes*, try to draw Inquisitor Bridgestock into conversation, will you? I think he's yearning to impart some manly advice to me, and I'm not sure I can keep a straight face."

The voices around Grace were beginning to blend together into an unpleasant roar. She had been half listening to Charles's conversation with James's parents—something about vampires—and watching the hands crawl slowly on the face of a grandfather clock against the wall.

She waited nine minutes exactly. When they had passed, she whispered to Charles, "If you'll excuse me a moment—I see the Wentworths have arrived, and I should say hello to Rosamund."

Charles nodded absently and returned to his conversation with Will Herondale. Not that Grace minded. Better he was distracted, and she had hardly chosen him for his devotion to her.

She slipped away, through the crowd of wedding guests, heading for the stairs that led to the main part of the Institute. It felt good to be away from the clamor. Most of the members of the London Enclave looked at Grace oddly, with the exception of the Lightwoods, and their friendly attentions were even worse than the sidelong glances.

Gideon and Sophie Lightwood offered her a room in their house practically every time they saw her, saying that as their niece and Thomas and Eugenia's cousin, she was always welcome. Cecily and Gabriel Lightwood had made the same offer, though they weren't as inclined to repeat it as Gideon and his wife were. Grace, for her part, felt no relationship to any of them at all. She supposed that was Tatiana's doing. She had characterized her brothers as monsters, though it seemed they were quite ordinary men.

Ordinary as they were, they could never be made to understand that for Grace to take shelter with her uncles would be the worst betrayal of her mother that she could think of. And Grace didn't believe for a moment that Tatiana would remain in the Adamant Citadel forever, regardless of the Clave. She would find a way out eventually, and there would be hell to pay.

Having reached the next floor, Grace heard footsteps behind her and turned—James, perhaps, catching up to her? But it was Lucie, carrying a bunch of yellow flowers. The Blackthorn locket—Jesse's locket—glittered at her throat; Lucie always wore it with the inscribed side against her skin, the telltale circlet of thorns safely hidden. But Grace knew the truth.

"Grace?" Lucie said in surprise.

An accidental meeting, but perhaps a convenient one, Grace thought. She always feared sending messages to Lucie, lest they be intercepted. Better to talk in person. "Lucie," she said. "You said you wanted to consult a warlock about our—project. What about Malcolm Fade?"

The flowers wobbled in Lucie's hands; she nodded enthusiastically. "Oh, indeed. He's easy enough to find—he's always at the Hell Ruelle— and the Enclave trusts him. But do you think that he'd be willing to help us with this . . . particular matter?"

"Ordinarily, perhaps not," Grace said. "But I think I know something that could persuade him to aid us."

"My goodness, what?" Lucie looked intrigued, but before she could insist on more information, a voice down the hall called her name. "You'll have to tell me later," she said, and dashed off in the direction of the wedding preparations, her flowers waving like yellow banners.

Excellent, Grace thought. With any luck, she'd kill two birds with one stone on this little excursion. It was odd, this business with Lucie— odd to find herself so deep in a partnership with someone she could not influence or control. But it was for Jesse. She would do anything for him.

It was easy to find the drawing room. It was the room in which, four months ago, Grace had taken her silver bracelet back from James and told him she would not marry him. It had been summer then, and now white gusts ghosted past the windows. Otherwise, not much had changed: here was the same flowered wallpaper, the velveteen settee and wing chairs, the faint scent of ink and writing paper.

It brought back that day to her, too sharply. The stricken look on James's face. The things he had said to her.

She knew there ought to have been pleasure in causing him pain.

There would have been for her mother, but there was none for her. For years she had lived with the knowledge of James's love like a weight on her shoulders. She thought of it as chains—iron chains that bound him to her. *The Herondales are made to love,* her mother had said. *They give all they have and keep back nothing.*

She did not love him. She knew he was beautiful—she had watched him grow into himself, every summer, as if she were watching a painting by Rossetti turn from a sketch into gorgeous, vivid art—but what did it matter? It seemed it had never occurred to her mother—and would not have mattered to her if it had—that just as it was a torment to love, it might be a torment to *be* loved. To be loved, and to know it was not real.

She had tried to release him from the chains once before, in this very room. She had seen the way he looked at Cordelia, and she had known: the chains would break, and he would hate her as a monster. Better to let him go, while her mother slept. Better to do a deed that could not be undone.

It is impossible between us, James.

She had thought there would be nothing her mother could do. She had been wrong, then. And perhaps she was wrong, now, to try again—but it had been four months. Four months in which she had not approached James, had barely spoken to him, and no message from her mother had come. With every week that passed, hope had risen in her heart: Surely she was forgotten? If she were to tell James—well, surely such power would not work if one were aware of it?

The door rattled; Grace turned quickly. She had expected James, but it was the young housemaid she had seen downstairs, the one with light brown hair and freckles on her nose. She was carrying a small whisk broom and dustpan. She looked at Grace in surprise, no doubt wondering how she had managed to wander away from the party. "Can I help you, miss?"

Grace tried not to scowl. "I had been hoping to find the library."

The maid moved toward Grace. Now that she was closer, Grace could see she had an odd, fixed smile on her lips. "Lost, then, are you?"

Unsettled, Grace started to move toward the door. "Not at all. I'll just return to the party."

"Oh, *Grace*." The whisk broom dangled at an odd angle, Grace realized. As if there were something wrong with the girl's hand. Her eyes stared, unfocused. "Oh, you *are* lost, my dear. But it's all right; I've come to find you."

Grace made for the door, but the maid was faster. She darted in between Grace and the exit. "Don't you know me, dear?" The maid giggled, a sound that grated like an out-of-tune piano chord, discordant and strangely hollow.

Four months. *Four months.* Grace swallowed the bile rising in her throat. "Mama?"

The maid giggled again; her lips moved out of sync with the sound. "Daughter. Are you truly surprised to see me? You must have known I'd wish to see this wedding day."

"I did not know you had the power to possess people, Mama," said Grace wearily. "Is *he* helping you?"

"He is," breathed her mother. "Our patron, who gave you your gift, very kindly helped me into this body, though I doubt it will hold up for long." She eyed the housemaid's trembling hands critically. "He could have sent a shape-changing Eidolon demon, of course, or any of his other servants, but he wished me to see to this personally. He does not want his gift squandered. And you would not wish to anger him. Would you?"

His gift. The power that allowed Grace to control the minds of men, to make them do as she wished. Only men, of course—Tatiana would never have thought of women as having power or influence worth bothering to subvert.

"No," Grace said dully. It was the truth. One did not lightly anger such a powerful demon. "But if you—and your patron—wished to prevent this wedding, you should have acted earlier than this."

Tatiana sneered. "I trusted you would act on your own. It seems that was foolishness. You have known how to contact me, with the *adamas*, but you have never bothered. As always you disappoint."

"I was afraid," Grace said. "The Bridgestocks—he's the Inquisitor, Mama."

"It was your choice to live in that lions' den. As for the wedding, it hardly matters. Making Herondale betray his vows is a delicious prospect. He will hate himself even the more for what our power has wrought." Tatiana's face split into a rictus grin; it was terrifying, *wrong*, somehow, as if the human face she had borrowed were about to come apart at the seams. "I am your mother," she said. "There is no one in this world who knows you as I do." *Jesse*, Grace thought, but she said nothing. "I saw the look on your face, downstairs. You intended to release him again, didn't you? You intended to confess?"

"There is no point to all this," Grace said. "The magic is not strong enough. I *cannot* bind him forever. He will see through it, you know, through the falsity."

"Nonsense." Tatiana made a dismissive gesture, the housemaid's wrist flopping bonelessly as she moved. "You understand nothing of the greater plan, girl. James Herondale is a piece on a chessboard. Your duty is to keep him in place, not tell him secrets he has no business knowing."

"But he will not do as I say—"

"He will do what we need him to, if you bend your will to it. It matters only that you do as you are told." Her shoulders twitched, violently; Grace was reminded of stories she had heard about animals, still alive, writhing inside the bodies of snakes who had swallowed them. "And should you think of disobeying, our patron is prepared to cut you off from any access to Jesse. His body will be taken to where you can never see him again."

Terror went through Grace like a knife. The demon could not know, could he, what she had been planning, hoping to do to help her brother? "You cannot," she whispered. "You cannot let him, Mama—I am so close to helping Jesse—you would not separate us—"

Tatiana laughed; just then the door rattled in its frame. The housemaid's face contorted; she gave a violent shudder and collapsed to the ground. Her broom and dustpan went flying. Grace raced to her side as the door flew open and someone said, "Miss Blackthorn! Miss Blackthorn, what happened?"

It was Christopher Lightwood, of all people. Grace knew him mainly as James's friend; he seemed the least alarming of the three. "I don't know," she said frantically. "She had only just come in when she collapsed in front of me."

"James sent me to tell you to return to the Long Hall." Christopher knelt and put two fingers to the maid's wrist, taking her pulse. A faint line of concern appeared between his brows. He scrambled back to his feet. "Wait here. I'll be right back."

Grace could only stare at the limp housemaid—she seemed to be breathing at least, thankfully—and wait. In a moment or so Christopher returned, along with the Herondales' cook, Bridget, and two footmen.

Bridget, wearing a musty black frock and a hat with an artificial yellow flower tilted sideways on her head, knelt down and turned the maid's head to examine her. "She's breathing normally. And her color is good." She gave Grace a wry look. "Malingering, maybe, to get out of all the work this wedding has brought."

"I believe her right wrist is broken, probably hurt in her fall," Christopher said. "I do not think she is pretending."

"Humph," said Bridget. "Well, we'll help Edith—don't you worry. You two get back to the chapel. The ceremony's about to start, and the young master will want you there."

Christopher laid a hand on Grace's arm and began to steer her from the room. Normally Grace heartily disliked being steered, but Christopher did it in a kindly, not a domineering, sort of way. "Are you all right?" he said as they reached the staircase.

"I was startled," Grace said, which she supposed was truthful enough.

"Is there a message you wished me to give to James?" Christopher asked. "He said you had wanted to speak with him, but that there was not time."

Ah, the irony, Grace thought. James, loyal and dutiful James, had decided not to meet her alone in the drawing room anyway. It had all been for nothing.

"I only wanted to wish him a happy day," she said. Then, after a moment's hesitation, she added more quietly, "And to tell him to look after his bride well. Love is a rarity in this world, and true friendship, too. That was all."

4

A GOOD NAME

May this marriage be a sign of compassion,
a seal of happiness here and hereafter.
May this marriage have a fair face and a good name,
an omen as welcome
as the moon in a clear blue sky.
—Rumi, "This Marriage"

James stood at the altar, looking out over the gathered crowd.
He felt a little dizzy to see the pews so completely filled with wedding guests—the Wentworths and Bridgestocks, the Townsends and Baybrooks sat alongside people he barely knew. Then there were his parents in the front pew, their hands tightly clasped. Cordelia's family—Sona in ivory silk with gold and silver embroidery; Elias looking tired, and years older than James remembered. Alastair, his face haughty and unreadable as ever. James's aunts and uncles, clustered together. Henry, a broad grin on his face, his Bath chair drawn up beside the pew where Charles sat. Thomas and Anna, smiling encouragingly.

Everywhere were pale flowers from Idris, garlanding the aisles and spilling over the altar, their delicate scent filling the chapel. The room glimmered in the soft golden haze of the candlelight. James had walked the flower-strewn aisle with Matthew's hand steady on his arm. Matthew had murmured to him—light, funny comments about the guests and a few harsh words for Mrs. Bridgestock's hat—and James had thought how lucky he was, to have a *parabatai* who was always there for him. He could never truly fall with Matthew to hold him up.

The chapel doors opened a crack—everyone looked up, but it was not Cordelia; it was Grace, escorted by Christopher. She made her way quickly to Charles's pew and slid in beside him, while Kit hurried to join Thomas and Anna.

James felt Matthew's grip tighten on his arm. "Well done, Kit," he murmured.

James had to agree. He had made a vow to himself that he would not spend time with Grace alone, and his wedding day seemed hardly the time to break it. Once she had left the Long Hall, he could no longer imagine what had induced him to say yes to meeting her.

Matthew had said not to worry, he would send Christopher to let Grace know the meeting was off. Feeling a little guilty, James had thrown himself into greeting guests—chatting with Anna and Thomas, welcoming Ariadne, introducing Matthew to Filomena and watching their flirting with amusement. Eventually Bridget had appeared, slightly grim-faced, and demanded that the last of the guests be ushered into the chapel. It was time for the ceremony.

James knew that at mundane ceremonies there was often music, and it was the case at Shadowhunter weddings as well sometimes, but it was dead silent now. One could have heard a pin drop. The palms of his hands itched with nervousness.

The doors opened, thrown wide this time. The candles flared up; the guests turned to stare. A soft exhale went round the room.

The bride was here.

Matthew moved closer to James, their shoulders touching. James knew Matthew was staring too; they were all staring, and yet he felt as if he were alone in the room, the only one watching as Cordelia entered, Lucie at her side.

Daisy. She seemed to blaze like a torch. James had always known she was beautiful—*had he always known? Had there been a moment he had realized it?*—but still the sight of her hit him like a blow. She was all fire, all heat and light, from the gold silk roses woven into her dark red hair to the ribbons and beads on her golden dress. The hilt of Cortana was visible over her left shoulder; the straps that secured it had been fashioned from thick gold ribbons.

"By the Angel, she is brave," he heard Matthew murmur, and he could not help but agree: technically, this wedding existed to correct a terrible social violation. Cordelia was a compromised bride, and to some it would seem quite daring that she went to her wedding in full gold, a Shadowhunter bride in all her glory, her sword at her back, her head held high.

If there were ever to be an expression of disapproval from the more ancient and pigheaded of the Enclave, it would be now. But there was nothing—only little gasps of appreciation, and the delighted look on Sona's face as Cordelia took her first step onto the aisle, the froth and gold of her dress parting for a moment to reveal a gold-and-ivory brocade boot.

Something chimed in James's ear. At first he thought he was hearing the sound of the wind in the icy branches outside. But he saw Lucie smile and glance behind her—it was indeed music, growing closer, rising in volume. A sound delicate and crystalline as winter, touched with an almost melancholy sweetness.

The sound of a violin, audible even through the thick stone walls. The guests looked about them, startled. James looked at Matthew. "Jem?"

Matthew nodded and indicated James's parents: Will and Tessa were both smiling. James thought there were tears in his mother's eyes, but it was natural to cry at weddings. "Your parents asked him if he would play. He's outside in the courtyard. He wouldn't come in— said Silent Brothers had no place at weddings."

"I'm not sure that's true," James murmured, but he recognized it for what it was: a gift from the man who had always been like an uncle to him. The music rose, as exquisite as Cordelia, as pure and proud as the look on her face as she stepped up to join him at the altar.

Cordelia had not expected to feel as odd as she did: both extraordinarily present and distant, as if she were watching the proceedings from a faraway place. She saw her family, saw Alastair glance at her and then over at the front pew, saw the look on her mother's face. She had not expected the scent of the flowers, or the music, which seemed like a carpet unrolling before her, urging her down the aisle, lifting her to the altar.

And she had not expected James. She had not expected that his eyes would fix on her the moment she entered the room, watching her and nothing else. He was beautiful enough to take her breath away, his dark gold coat the same color as his eyes, his hair wild and crow's-wing black. He looked dazed, a little stunned as she joined him at the altar, as if the breath had been knocked out of him.

She could not blame him. They had both known this day was coming, but the reality of it was staggering.

The violin music softened as the Consul rose to join them. Charlotte Fairchild took her place behind the altar. She smiled warmly, and Cordelia stepped away from Lucie; James took her hands, and they faced each other. His grasp was warm and hard, his fingers calloused. He had bent his head; all she could see was the fall of his curling black hair against his sharp cheekbone.

"Welcome, all." Charlotte's commanding voice filled the room. Lucie was vibrating with excitement, fairly bouncing up and down on her toes. Matthew's gaze wandered the crowd, a small ironic smile pulling at his mouth. "Twenty-three years ago, I married Will and Tessa Herondale in this very chapel. How proud and grateful I am to be here now to marry their son, James, to a woman whose family is also close to my heart. Cordelia Carstairs."

Charlotte turned her steady gaze on Cordelia, who felt immediately uneasy. Surely Charlotte of all people would see through them. But she only smiled again and said, "We come together, Clave and Enclave, children of the Angel and the ones they love"—she dropped a wink and Cordelia realized, with some surprise, that Magnus Bane had joined Will and Tessa among the guests—"to celebrate the joining together of lives under Raziel's auspices. We walk a lonely road and a high one, we Nephilim. The burden Raziel has laid upon us is a heavy one, as we have had recent cause to remember." Her gaze moved for a moment to Gideon and Sophie. "But he has given us many gifts to balance our responsibilities," Charlotte went on, and now her gaze rested tenderly

James Herondale

on her husband, Henry. "He has given us a tremendous capacity to love. To give of our hearts, to let them be filled and filled again with the love that consecrates us all. To love one another is to come as close as we ever can to being angels ourselves."

Cordelia felt a light squeeze to her hand. James had raised his head; he was looking at her with a level gaze and an encouraging smile. *Steady on*, he mouthed soundlessly, and she couldn't help but smile back.

"James Morgan Henry Herondale," said Charlotte. "Hast thou gone among the streets of the city and the watchmen there, and found the one thy soul loves?"

Cordelia heard Lucie catch her breath. She didn't release it until James responded in a firm, clear voice that echoed through the chapel.

"I have," he said, then seemed slightly startled, as if surprised at the strength of his own conviction. "And I will not let her go."

"Cordelia Katayoun Carstairs," said Charlotte. "Hast thou gone among the streets of the city and the watchmen there, and found the one thy soul loves?"

Cordelia hesitated. James's hands were firm and gentle on hers; she knew he would always be this way, gentle and determined, kind and thoughtful. Her heart beat hard and treacherous inside her chest. He had not been gentle in the Whispering Room. Not gentle with his hands on her body and his lips on hers. That had been the James she wanted, her one glimpse at the James she could not have.

She had told herself she could get through this time easily, that at least she would be close to James, be beside him, see him sleeping and waking. But she knew now, looking at his face—the curves of his mouth, the arch of his eyelashes, sweeping down to hide his thoughts—that she would not walk away at the end of this year unscathed. She was agreeing to have her heart broken.

"Yes," said Cordelia. "And I will not let him go."

There was a flourish of violin music. Charlotte beamed. "It is time for the exchange of the first runes, and the second vows," she said. Shadowhunters generally placed two runes upon each other when they were married: a rune upon the arm, given during the public ceremony, and a rune over the heart—done later, in private. One rune for the community, and one for the privacy of marriage, Sona had always said.

Matthew and Lucie turned to the altar, returning with two golden steles. "Set me as a seal upon thy heart, as a seal upon thy arm," said Lucie, handing the first stele to Cordelia with an encouraging smile. The ritual words were ancient, freighted with the gravity of years. Sometimes they were spoken by the bride and groom, sometimes by their *suggenes*. In this instance, James and Cordelia had wanted Matthew and Lucie to speak.

"For love is strong as death," said Matthew, placing the second stele in James's hand. His tone was uncharacteristically somber. "And jealousy cruel as the grave."

James pushed up the left sleeve of his jacket and shirt, revealing more of the runes placed on his arms earlier that day. Runes for Love, Luck, and Joy. Cordelia leaned in to place the marriage rune on his upper arm—a few quick, fluid strokes. She had to steady his arm with her free hand to do it, and she shivered a little at the contact: the hard muscle of his bicep under her fingers, the smoothness of his skin.

Then it was James's turn; he was gentle and quick, placing the first of the marriage runes on her forearm, just below the lace edging of her sleeve.

Charlotte bent her head. "Now will you each repeat after me: 'For I am persuaded, that neither death, nor life, nor angels, nor demons, nor principalities, nor powers, nor things present, nor things to come, nor height, nor depth, nor any other creature, shall be able to separate us.'"

"For I am persuaded," Cordelia whispered, and as she spoke the words aloud after Charlotte, she glanced sideways at James. His profile was sharp, the curve of his lips determined as he said the words after she did: "Neither death, nor life, nor angels, nor demons, nor principalities, nor powers, nor things present, nor things to come . . ."

Cordelia thought, *It's happening. It's really happening.* And yet, for all that, she was unprepared for what came next. The words spoken, she and James looked at each other in relief. But it was short-lived.

"You may now kiss," said Charlotte cheerfully.

Cordelia stared at James, openmouthed. He looked just as surprised; it seemed they had both forgotten that this would be part of the ceremony.

I can't do it, Cordelia thought, half panicking. She could not press an unwanted kiss upon James, and certainly not in public. But he was already drawing her into his arms. His hand cupped her cheek, his lips brushing the corner of her mouth. "We've come this far," he whispered. "Don't back out on me now."

She raised her chin, her lips grazing his. He was smiling. "I would never," she began indignantly, but he was already kissing her. She felt the kiss, and the smile it carried, all the way down through her body and her bones. Helplessly, she caught at him, holding his shoulders. Though he kept his mouth decorously closed, his lips were incredibly soft, so soft and so warm against hers that she had to bite back a soft moan.

He drew back, and Cordelia smoothed down her dress with shaking hands. Almost before they were finished, a cheer went up from the congregation, applause punctuated with a few whistles and the stamping of feet.

The cheering continued as they linked hands and began to make their way down from the altar. Cordelia saw Lucie smile at her—and then Matthew's face, grim and set. His expression jolted her. He must be worried about James, she realized. She couldn't blame him. No amount of preparing for this day could have readied her for the real thing.

She was married.

She was married, and she was absolutely terrified.

They walked out of the chapel into a burst of applause and cheers that followed them into the Long Hall, and upstairs into the ballroom, where the tables had been set for the wedding feast.

Cordelia, still hand in hand with James, looked around in wonder. The ballroom had been transformed into a glittering fantasia. Sona had worked tirelessly with Tessa to plan the party, and they'd left no corner of the ballroom untouched, from the candles winking from hundreds of brass sconces to the swaths of gold silk draped at the windows. The golden hues of Cordelia's gown were echoed again and again, in shimmering pennants and gleaming bells strung from the ceiling. Gold glinted from the ribbons that twined through garlands of tansy and Welsh poppies, and gilded the apples and pears nestled in arrangements of evergreen and white-berried quickbeam. Even the two huge tiered cakes at the center of the lavish spread were iced in gold and ivory.

There was a truly impressive spread laid out: steaming platters of roast lamb and chicken, thin pounded mutton chops, beef tongue, goose-liver pâté. Another long table was bedecked with cold salmon in a cucumber sauce; a salad of lobster and rice and another of boiled potatoes and pickles; and plump eggs suspended artfully in aspic. Interspersed among the dishes were towers of brightly colored jellies in amber, fuchsia, and green.

Cordelia exchanged amazed glances with James as their friends crowded around them. Christopher had nicked a pear from a display and seemed disappointed to discover that it was made of wax.

"Goodness, it's magnificent," Cordelia said, gazing around the room.

"You flatter me, darling," Matthew said mildly. "I *have* been saving this waistcoat for a special occasion, though."

Cordelia laughed just as James's parents descended on them—wishing to congratulate them and also, Cordelia suspected, to protect them from being overwhelmed by eager members of the Enclave. Cordelia caught Will's eye as he beamed at his son, and felt her smile slip. Of all those who believed the fiction of her marriage to James, betraying Tessa and Will was the most difficult to bear.

"I'm famished," James whispered to Cordelia as Lucie tried to shoo their well-wishers toward the tables—as the bride and groom, they could not stop to eat until all the guests were settled. She could see the small group of her own family toward the far end of the room, Alastair and Elias helping Sona carefully into a chair. She would have liked to join her family, but Sona had already made it clear that once the ceremony was over, she would expect Cordelia to remain by James's side. "It's cruel to have to gaze upon a feast like that and not be able to nab so much as a biscuit."

"Is Christopher *eating* his wax pear?" she whispered back. "That can't be healthy."

Cordelia gave up trying to keep track of all the guests; it was hard even to remember which of them she'd met before and which she hadn't. James, presumably from years of attending Institute functions, knew almost everyone at least by name. Cordelia found herself relieved by the appearance of anyone she actually knew: Gabriel and Cecily and their toddler son, Alexander, who had been retrieved from the nursery and remained amazingly asleep through the raucous congratulations and cheers. Rosamund Wentworth, who wanted to talk about wedding cakes since "as of course you know, I am also to be married soon. Thoby, stop that and pay attention." Thomas's elder sister, Eugenia, recently back from Idris. Henry Fairchild, who simply held Cordelia's hands and wished her happy with a straight-forward sincerity that made her want to cry.

With help from Lucie and Tessa, the guests were steered into their seats, and James and Cordelia were able to sit down. Lucie had managed to arrange it so most of the friends were sitting together in a cheerful group. Only Anna—off in a corner looking glamorous and chatting to Magnus Bane about Ragnor Fell's sojourn in Capri—had not joined them. (Cordelia had suggested asking her, but Matthew had said, "Anna is like a cat. You have to let her come to you," which Christopher had confirmed as true.)

Serving staff crowded around, bringing them plates piled with bits of everything. Cordelia popped a fig into her mouth, savoring the sweetness spreading across her tongue. She thought of her mother, the figs and honey they had often had on special occasions.

"Welcome to the family," Christopher said to Cordelia. "You're our cousin-in-law now. I've never had one of those before."

"All Shadowhunters are related already," Matthew said, tucking his flask into his breast pocket and deftly intercepting a passing waiter with a tray of champagne flutes. He abstracted two and passed one to James with a flourish. "You were already ninth cousins once removed, most likely."

"Thank you for that distressing analysis," Cordelia said, raising her own glass in a mock formal toast. "I shall be an honorary Thief, I hope."

"Well, we'll have to see," said Matthew, his eyes twinkling. "How you are at thievery and such."

"It really is excellent, all this, you know," Christopher said. "I mean, even though the whole wedding is . . . you know . . . because . . ."

Thomas jumped in before Christopher could find his words. "Expensive, yes," he agreed loudly. "But it's well worth it, I say."

"Anyway, it'll be quite a lark that you have your own house now, James," Christopher went on. "No more drafty Devil Tavern rooms."

"The Merry Thieves gathering in respectable surroundings," said Matthew. "Who would have thought?"

"I like the Devil Tavern rooms," protested James.

"I like a fire in the grate that doesn't get rained out," said Thomas.

"You are *not* to send your things from the Devil Tavern to my new house," James said sternly. "It is not a storage facility for my misbegotten friends."

Cordelia said nothing as the boys burst into protests and chatter. She was grateful to them all for taking everything in stride, for not hating her for marrying James. They seemed to understand the situation despite its complexities.

On the other hand, they were all going on about the new house, and not for the first time today, she thought, *At the end of this party, I don't go home with my mother and father and Alastair. I go home with my husband to our house.* Their house. The house she knew nothing about at all, not even its location.

Her mother had been impatient with Cordelia's decision to let James handle the purchase and readying of the house. Gentlemen, Sona had said, had no idea about decorating things, and didn't Cordelia want to put her own stamp on it? Make sure it would be a house she'd be willing to live in the rest of her life?

Cordelia had just said she was content to let James make it a surprise. His parents were buying it, she had thought to herself, and it would be his after the divorce. Perhaps he would want to live in it with Grace.

She glanced down the row of tables, unable to help herself. Grace was there, seated beside Charles, silent and beautiful as always. Ariadne sat on her other side—Cordelia had nearly forgotten that Grace was now living with the Bridgestocks. It was all very odd.

Suddenly Charles rose to his feet and headed toward them, looking worryingly pleased with himself.

Matthew had seen him too. "My brother heaves into view on the horizon," he said to James in a low voice. "Careful. He looks very happy about something."

"The new Mr. and Mrs. Herondale!" Charles called out, and Matthew rolled his eyes. "Might I be the first to offer my congratulations?" He extended his hand to James.

James took it and shook. "You are not the first, Charles, but we appreciate it no less."

"What an excellent wedding," Charles went on, looking up at the rafters of the Institute above them as if taking in the room for the first time. "We'll have quite the wedding *season* this year, what?"

"What?" said James, and then, "Oh, of course, yourself and . . . Miss Blackthorn."

Matthew took a long sip of champagne.

Cordelia studied James's face, but James betrayed nothing. He smiled pleasantly at Charles, and as always Cordelia was both impressed by and a little frightened by the impenetrability of the Mask—her name for the unreadable, blank expression James deployed to great effect whenever he wished to disguise his feelings. "We shall look forward to toasting your health and happiness in this very hall soon enough, Charles."

Charles departed. Matthew raised a glass. "That is what in Paris they call *sang-froid*, Monsieur Herondale."

Cordelia privately agreed. The Mask frightened her sometimes, when she could not tell what James was thinking, but it certainly had its uses. Wearing it, James seemed invulnerable.

"Is that a compliment?" Christopher asked curiously. "Doesn't it mean 'cold blood'?"

"Coming from Matthew, it is definitely a compliment," Anna said with a laugh; she'd appeared at the table quite suddenly, Magnus Bane in tow. He was wearing a light blue tailcoat with gold buttons, a gold waistcoat, taupe knee breeches, and buckled boots. He looked like pictures Cordelia had seen of men at the court of the Sun King.

"You all know Magnus Bane, of course?" Anna gestured to the tall figure standing next to her.

"It's my understanding," Cordelia said, "that the question is never whether *you* know Magnus Bane. The question is always whether Magnus Bane knows *you*."

"Oh, I like that," Anna said, clearly pleased. "Very clever, Daisy."

Magnus, to his credit, looked a bit abashed. It was a strange effect alongside his general level of glamorousness; he and Anna—in a polished black suit and sky-blue waistcoat, her family's ruby necklace at her throat—made quite a sartorial pair. "Congratulations. I wish you and James all the happiness in the world."

"Thank you, Magnus," Cordelia said. "It's good to see you. Do you think there's any chance you'll be staying in London permanently?"

"Perhaps," said Magnus. He had been in and out of London for the past few months, sometimes present, often away. "First I must depart for the Cornwall Institute, to undertake a project there. Tomorrow, in fact."

"And what project is that?" Matthew asked. "Something glamorous, secret, and admirable?"

"Something dull," Magnus said firmly, "but well paying. I've been assigned the task of conducting a survey of the spell books at the Cornwall Institute. Some may be dangerous, but others could be indispensable in the hands of the Spiral Labyrinth. Jem—Brother Zachariah, I should say—will be accompanying me; it seems he is the only Shadowhunter trusted by both the Clave and the Spiral Labyrinth."

"You'll be in good company, then," Cordelia said. "But I'm sorry that you'll be leaving London. James and I were hoping to invite you to dinner at our new house."

"Not to worry," Magnus said, "you will not be without my radiance for long. I should be back in a fortnight. And then we celebrate."

Matthew held up a hand. "I demand to also be invited to dinner with Magnus. I will not be scorned."

"Speaking of scorning," murmured Lucie. Out of nowhere had appeared Ariadne Bridgestock, looking quite lovely in a rose-colored dress with gold passementerie braiding.

"There you are," Ariadne said. "James, Cordelia. Congratulations." Then, without pause, she turned to Anna. "Would you take a turn about the room with me, Miss Lightwood?"

Cordelia exchanged a look of interest with Matthew, who gave a tiny shrug. His ears had perked up, though, like a cat's.

Anna's posture changed; she had been lounging with her hands in her pockets, but now she straightened up. "No one else is wandering about the ballroom, Ariadne."

Ariadne worried at a fold of her dress with her fingers. "We could talk," she said. "It might be nice."

Cordelia tensed; Ariadne was opening herself up to a cutting riposte. But instead Anna only said, "I don't think so," her tone very flat, and walked off without a word.

"She's a more complicated person than she pretends," Magnus offered to Ariadne.

Ariadne didn't seem to welcome the sympathy. Her eyes flashed. "I know that better than almost anyone." She nodded stiffly at James and at Cordelia. "Again, I wish you all the happiness in the world."

Cordelia felt an odd urge to wish her luck in battle, but there was no time: she had departed, her head held high in the air.

"Well," Magnus said, toying idly with the gold flower tucked into his buttonhole. A peony, Cordelia noted, dipped in gold. "It's hard not to admire her spirit."

"She is very determined," said Lucie. "She approaches Anna at every dance and party, always with some sort of request."

"Has Anna been responsive?"

"Not judging by her social calendar," James said. "Every time I see her, she's squiring some new lady about the town."

"She and Ariadne certainly have a history," said Thomas. "We just don't quite know what it was."

Cordelia thought of Anna kneeling by Ariadne's sickbed, murmuring softly, *Please don't die.* She had never mentioned the moment to anyone. Anna, she felt, would not like her to do so.

Magnus didn't comment; his attention had been caught by something else. "Ah," he said. "Mr. Carstairs."

It was Alastair, determinedly approaching Cordelia and James. Magnus, as if sensing the advent of an awkward situation, excused himself and slipped away smoothly into the crowd.

Cordelia regarded Alastair worriedly—did he really feel obligated to brave the den of Merry Thieves to offer his congratulations? It appeared that he did: spinning toward his sister with a near-military precision, he said sharply, "I'm here to offer my felicitations to both of you."

James regarded him. "I suppose you at least have enough social grace to know the right things to say," he said quietly, "even if you can't bring yourself to sound like you mean them."

Alastair's mouth set in a hard line. "No credit for the attempt, then?"

Stop, Cordelia thought. She knew Alastair was not always like this—she knew he could be kind, sweet, vulnerable even. She knew her father had broken his son's heart a dozen different ways, and Alastair was doing the best he could with the pieces. But it didn't help for Alastair to behave like this, to retreat behind a cold facade as cutting as glass.

The way James retreated behind the Mask.

"We are brothers now, Alastair," James said, "and you are welcome in our house. I will be civil to you and I hope you will be civil to me, for Cordelia's sake."

Alastair looked a little relieved. "Of course."

"But you had best be good to her," James said, still in an even, calm tone. "Because my hospitality lasts exactly as long as Cordelia finds your presence pleasing."

"Of course," Alastair said again. "I would expect nothing else." He turned to Thomas, who had been staring fixedly down at his plate. "Tom," he said carefully. "If I could talk to you for a moment—"

Thomas stood up, almost knocking over the table. Cordelia looked at him in astonishment.

"I told you before that if you spoke to me again, I would throw you into the Thames," said Thomas. His normally open, friendly face was twisted into an expression of fury. "You might at least have chosen a warmer day to take your plunge."

"Stop." Cordelia threw down her napkin. "Alastair is my brother, and I love him. And this is my wedding day. No one will be throwing my family members into the Thames."

"*Honestly*, Thomas," said Lucie, looking at her friend with disappointment. Thomas clenched his fists at his sides.

"Now," said Cordelia. "Will someone tell me what this is all *about?*"

There was an awkward silence. Even Alastair didn't look at her. He made an odd sort of sound, in the back of his throat. "This is—unbearable," he said. "It is not to be endured."

"It is what you deserve," said Matthew, his eyes flashing; James held out a hand toward his *parabatai*, as if to calm him—just as a loud crash came from the far end of the room.

Without another word, Alastair broke into a run. Knowing what that meant, Cordelia pushed back her chair and dashed after him. Her heavy velvet skirts hampered her, and she reached her parents some moments after Alastair. Her father was on the floor by his chair, clutching his knee and moaning in pain.

Sona was struggling to rise from her chair. "Elias—Elias, are you—"

Her father's face was beet red, and he seemed to have worked himself up into something of a lather. "I tell you, I should have been my daughter's *suggenes*," Elias snapped. "To be cut out of the ceremony as if I were a shameful secret, well, I can only imagine she was persuaded, but it is an outrage—a deliberate humiliation, and you cannot convince me otherwise!"

He slammed his hand against the floor.

Cordelia's heart sank into her brocaded boots. She glanced at Alastair, already trying to help Elias to his feet. Quickly, she moved to block the scene from the wedding guests—the ones near enough to see the messy goings-on were staring. Fury went through Cordelia like a lance. How *dare* her father suggest that he had not had enough of a role in her wedding—they'd had no idea he'd even be attending until his arrival this very morning.

"I'm here," said a voice at her shoulder. It was James. He touched Cordelia's arm lightly, then knelt down beside Alastair and seized Elias's other arm, raising him to his feet.

Elias glared at James. "I do not require your help."

"As you say," said James equably. Sona had her face in her hands; Cordelia stopped to touch her mother's shoulder lightly before glancing after James and Alastair, who were walking Elias away as fast as their feet could take them.

"Father, I think you need a bit of a rest," Alastair was saying. He spoke evenly, his expression matter-of-fact and calm. *This is how he's managed all these years*, she thought.

"Right this way, sir," James said, and mouthed *games room* at Alastair, who nodded. Sona had sunk back into her chair; Cordelia hurried after the boys, who were heading for the double doors at the other end of the room. She kept her gaze fixed straight ahead as she went—surely everyone was staring, though she could hear Will and Gabriel chatting loudly, their voices raised, doing their best to distract the guests.

James and Alastair had already disappeared with Elias. She slipped through the double doors after them and found herself in the narrow hallway outside the games room. It was a relief to be alone, if only for a moment; she leaned against the wall, saying a quiet prayer to Raziel. *I know I don't deserve it, but please give me strength.*

Voices rose from behind the games room door. She paused; did James and Alastair not realize she'd followed them?

"I suppose," said Alastair, "that you and your friends will have a great laugh about this later." He sounded defeated, rather than angry. As bothered as Cordelia often was by Alastair's stubbornness, the fight being drained from him was worse.

"No one blames you for your father, Alastair," she heard James respond. "Only for what you yourself have done and said."

"I have tried to apologize, and to change," Alastair said, and even through the door Cordelia could hear his voice shake. "How can I make amends for my past when no one will let me?"

When James replied, there was real kindness in his voice. "You must give people time, Alastair," he said. "We are none of us perfect, and no one expects perfection. But when you have hurt people, you must allow them their anger. Otherwise it will only become another thing you have tried to take away."

Alastair seemed to hesitate. "James," he said. "Does he—"

There was a sharp sound, as of something being knocked off a table, and then the familiar noises of Elias retching. Cordelia could hear Alastair telling James to go, that he would manage it. Not sure what else to do, Cordelia made her way soundlessly back to the ballroom.

The wedding luncheon was back in full swing. Glancing around, she saw that the Merry Thieves had all left their table. They were making their way up and down the room, greeting people, fielding congratulations for her and James. Matthew and Anna had a group of guests in fits of laughter; Will was regaling another table with a lengthy, and heavily embroidered, synopsis of a Dickens novel.

She leaned back against the wall. They were doing this for James, she knew, but also for her—distracting people, keeping them amused, making them forget about Elias. It felt such a relief, not to be facing it all alone.

She made her way into the room, smiling as she was stopped again and again to be congratulated. The string quartet was playing softly; most people seemed to have finished eating and were relaxing with glasses of port (for the men) and ratafia (for the ladies). Eugenia and Ariadne were playing with Alex. Matthew had begun singing, and Lucie and Thomas appeared to be trying to convince him to stop. Charlotte glanced over at them—Cordelia couldn't help but wonder what Charlotte thought of her younger son, with his bohemian yearnings, the restless dissatisfaction that seemed to drive him, the way he had of being very sad, or very happy, with little in between.

And there was her own mother—Sona was on her feet, chatting brightly to Ida Rosewain and Lilian Highsmith, as if nothing had happened. Cordelia realized she was watching her mother do what she had always done: pick up the pieces and move on. How had Cordelia been so blind for so long?

She took a deep breath, plastered a smile on her face, and went to join her mother. She saw Sona's quick look of relief as she approached, and thanked her mother's companions for attending. Ida Rosewain complimented her dress; Lilian Highsmith admired Cortana's new scabbard.

"Thank you," Cordelia said. "It's lovely too, isn't it? A wedding gift from my father."

She smiled; they all smiled; if anyone had anything to say about her father, they kept silent. Sona touched Cordelia's cheek, and Cordelia went on, going from group to group of guests, thanking them for attending, for making her wedding happy. All one had to do was pretend, she realized, marveling a bit, and everyone else would fall into line pretending along with you.

As she turned away from the Wentworths, who wanted to know who had provided the champagne, a gentle hand came down on her shoulder. "My dear." She turned; it was Tessa. "You're doing marvelously."

Cordelia only nodded; Tessa deserved better than a false smile.

Guests were beginning to take their leave, she noticed with relief, filing out in groups of two and three.

"So much of managing in society is keeping one's chin up," Tessa added carefully, and Cordelia thought of what Tessa and her family had put up with through the years: mutters and whispers about Tessa's warlock blood, her demon father. "And disregarding the ignorant things people say."

Cordelia nodded, wordless. She knew that Will and Tessa were fully aware of Elias's time in the Basilias, and what it had been about. But still, how humiliating, to have James's parents see her family like this.

"I ought to start bidding the guests goodbye," said Cordelia, "but James is in with—with my father."

"Then I'll accompany you," Tessa said, and gestured for Cordelia to follow her. Together they made their way to the ballroom's main doors, where Cordelia smiled again and again as guests departed. She thanked them for coming, and promised to invite them over the moment she and James were settled in their new house. She could see Lucie and Will out of the corner of her eye, circulating in the ballroom, handing out boxes with pieces of wedding cake in them for the guests to take home for good luck.

"Supposedly I'm meant to wait a year and then eat this," Christopher said, waving his box of cake at Cordelia as he took his leave. His family surrounded him; Cecily and Gabriel, a sleeping Alexander, even Anna, though she was heading out with Magnus Bane—perhaps to the Ruelle, or parts unknown. "It should have grown some very interesting mold cultures by then."

"I look forward to the results," said Cordelia solemnly. Thomas, leaving with Eugenia, smiled. At least he wasn't angry at her, even if he was furious at Alastair. Which, she thought, was not a situation that could be allowed to go on; she had to at least discover *why* the Merry Thieves were so angry at her brother.

When only a few guests remained in the ballroom, Cordelia spotted Alastair and James emerging from the games room. They headed in opposite directions—Alastair joined Sona, and James scanned the room, obviously searching for someone.

He caught sight of Cordelia then and waved, and she realized with a startled jolt that he had been looking for *her*. He hurried over and took her hands, bending to speak quietly in her ear. Cordelia glanced around, blushing, but no one was sparing them a second glance. (Tessa, discreetly, had melted back into the crowd.) Of course not, she thought: they were newlyweds, meant to be whispering in each other's ears.

"Sorry to abandon you," he murmured. "Your father kicked up a bit of a fuss." She was glad he was making no attempt to ignore or pass off what had happened. "We got him a cold flannel for his forehead and put out the lights in the games room. He said he needed to be alone until his headache cleared."

Cordelia nodded. "Thank you," she said. "The Basilias was supposed to have cured him, but—"

James cupped her face in one hand, his thumb brushing her cheek. "He was under a lot of stress. This might not happen again. And if he sleeps in the games room until morning, it'll do him no harm."

She glanced at Alastair. He was talking calmly with her mother. Cordelia had always thought that Alastair's moodiness was the result of their odd, lonely upbringing. Now she knew it was more. How often had Alastair had to deal with their father like this? What kind of toll had it taken on him?

I'll speak to him about it at home, I'll make some tea and we—

But no. She wasn't going home to Cornwall Gardens. She would not be sleeping in the same house as Alastair. She was going to go home with James. To their own house.

She raised her chin. James's face was just above hers: she could see the amber flecks in his eyes, the small white scar on his chin. His full lower lip, which she had kissed only a few hours before. His gaze clung to hers, as if he did not want to look away, although she knew it was only her imagination.

She felt tired. So extraordinarily tired. All day, she had played a part. All she wanted was to be at home, whatever that meant now. And if home meant James, well then, she could no longer pretend to herself that it was something she did not want.

"Let's go home, James," she said. "Take me home."

5

The King Is Dead

'Tis all a chequer-board of nights and days
Where Destiny with men for pieces plays:
Hither and thither moves, and mates, and slays,
And one by one back in the closet lays.
—Edward FitzGerald (trans.),
The Rubaiyat of Omar Khayyam

They managed to depart the Institute with a minimum of fuss, bidding goodbye to their families and their *suggenes*. Lucie hugged Cordelia tightly, speechless for once. Over her shoulder, Cordelia saw Matthew whisper something in James's ear. James smiled.

"Take good care of my boy," Will said to Cordelia, looking as if he wanted to ruffle her hair but was stumped by the sheer number of flowers and seed pearls in it.

Alastair touched Cordelia's cheek. *"Agar oun ba to mehraboon nabood, bargard khooneh va motmaen bash man kari mikonam ke az ghalat kardene khodesh pashimoon besheh."*

If he ever hurts you, come home, and I will make him regret it.

It was Alastair's way of telling her he would miss her. Cordelia hid a smile.

As they left the Institute, everything felt echoing, vast, and strange to Cordelia, as if she were dreaming. In the entryway, James paused at the door, pretending to busy himself with pulling on his gloves while he took a lingering look at the grooves worn in the stone floor by hundreds of years of visitors, the staircase with its wooden banister smoothed by countless hands. It felt peculiar enough to Cordelia to leave her house in South Kensington forever, though she had lived there only four months. How much stranger it must be for James to be leaving behind the only home he'd ever known.

"Are you going to tell me where our new house is?" she asked, hoping to distract him. "Or is it still a secret?"

He glanced over at her and she was relieved to see there was a spark of wicked humor in his golden eyes. "I've kept the secret this long. Might as well keep it an hour longer."

"Well, it had better be quite spectacular, James Herondale," she said with mock sternness as they descended the icy steps. The last of the sun was a faint yellow band in the east, the city having descended into the quiet of a winter evening.

Bridget had had their carriage sent around: a gift from Tessa and Will along with the new house. It was a sturdy brougham with extra fold-down seats for when they traveled with friends. The coachman, inherited from the Institute, tipped his hat to them. Hitched to the carriage was a horse called Xanthos, which had been Will's when he was young; he had a sweet, speckled white face and an even temperament. Xanthos was to belong to James and Cordelia from now on, and when Lucie married, his brother Balios would be hers.

Probably due to Cordelia's habit of feeding Xanthos carrots, Will had deemed him to be the horse with the best opinion of Cordelia, and she'd merely nodded and asked James later whether his father had been joking.

"It's often difficult to say," James had said. "Sometimes he's just pulling your leg, but then sometimes it's mysterious Welsh business. I think where horses are concerned, it's probably the latter."

Cordelia found herself grateful for the familiarity of the carriage and horse both. She had been trying to get into the spirit of the thing and let herself be surprised by the house, though due to her mother's warnings, she couldn't help but fear damp rooms, no heat, perhaps no furnishings. What if the house didn't have a roof? No, surely James would have noticed the lack of a roof. And Risa would be there; she had gone ahead of them, to get the place ready for their arrival. Cordelia tried not to smile, imagining Risa cursing angrily while snow fell into the coal scuttle.

As they rattled through the streets, she found herself trying to guess the house's location by the carriage's direction. They traveled west along the Strand, through the chaotic traffic of Trafalgar Square, and headed down Pall Mall past the War Office, its gates flanked by royal guards in bearskin hats. A few more quick turns followed, and Cordelia saw they were on something called Curzon Street, outside a pretty white town house on a quiet block. Cordelia was relieved to see it indeed seemed to have a roof on it, and all the other necessary outside bits to match.

She turned to James, astonished. "Mayfair!" she said, poking an accusing finger into his chest. "I was never expecting such a posh address!"

"Well, I'd heard the Consul lives near here, with her ne'er-do-well sons," James said. "Wouldn't want them lording it over us." He disembarked from the carriage and offered her a hand to help her down.

"By which you mean you wanted to live near Matthew." Cordelia laughed, looking up to take in the house's four stories. Warm light spilled from the windows. "You ought to just say so! I wouldn't blame you."

The front door opened and Risa stepped out. She had been in more formal clothes earlier, for the wedding, but she had changed into a plain dress and apron, and clutched her cotton *roosari* at her chin against the wind. She waved them inside. "Come in out of the snow, silly children. There is hot food for you inside, and tea."

She had spoken in Persian, but James seemed to understand well enough. He bounded up the front steps and quickly took control of the logistics, directing the coachman to take their valises upstairs.

Cordelia came inside more slowly. Risa helped her with her velvet sacque coat, and then with Cortana, taking the sword carefully as Cordelia stared around in surprise. The entryway was lit with a soft glow from the ornate brass sconces that lined the walls. There was wallpaper in a pattern of birds and passiflora on a deep emerald-green background. "So pretty," she said, grazing the outline of a golden peacock with her fingertips. "Who chose it?"

"I did," James said. At her surprised look, he added, "Perhaps I should show you around the house? And Risa, perhaps Effie could set out a simple supper? I believe you said something about tea."

"Who's Effie?" Cordelia whispered, while Risa, Cortana in hand, led the coachman upstairs with the bags.

"New maid. Risa hired her. Apparently she used to work for the Pouncebys," said James, as Cordelia followed him into a large dining room with a thick carpet, a marble fireplace, and tall windows overlooking Curzon Street. Her eye was immediately drawn to a set of four illuminated drawings arranged on the wall. James watched her nervously, the fingers of his right hand tapping against his leg, as she approached them.

They were Persian miniatures done in richly pigmented shades of scarlet and cobalt and gold. She spun to look at James in astonishment. "Where did you find these?"

"An antiquities shop in Soho," James said. She still couldn't quite read his expression. "They were selling off the estate of a Persian merchant living abroad."

Cordelia leaned close to examine the beautiful *nasta'līq* calligraphy above the images of prophets and acolytes and musicians, birds and horses and rivers. "This is by Rumi," she whispered, recognizing a verse: *The wound is the place where the Light enters you.* It had always been one of her favorites.

Her heart beating quickly, she turned to take in the rest of the room, with its silk-covered walls, its elaborately filigreed chandelier and rosewood table and chairs with carved details.

"The table expands to seat sixteen," James said. "Though I'm not sure I know that many people I'd want to have dinner with. Come see the rest of the house."

Cordelia followed him into the corridor, her full skirts barely fitting through the doorway. There was a beautiful drawing room, papered in blue and white, with a massive piano; skipping the study, they headed downstairs to a kitchen full of warm yellow light. A small door in the wall led out to a patch of garden—snow-covered now, but there were rose trellises whose flowers would bloom in summer.

A maid in a black dress—Effie, Cordelia assumed—marched into the kitchen, an empty tray in her hand. She eyed James and Cordelia speculatively, as if sizing them up for sale. She had steel-gray hair swept up in a pompadour, and a gimlet eye. "I've laid on some food for you in the study," she said, without bothering to introduce herself. "It won't be nearly so good when it's cold."

The corner of James's mouth twitched. "Then I suppose we'd better eat it now," he said to Cordelia, with an expression of great seriousness, and led her upstairs.

She had expected the study to be a small room, perhaps with a desk in it, but like everything else in this house, it surprised her. It was a big and graceful space lined almost entirely with bookshelves and stuffed with comfortable furniture, including a cozy Knole sofa. Its damask upholstery matched the curtains of the street-facing windows. A writing desk Cordelia recognized from the Institute anchored one corner of the room, and a beautiful table took pride of place in the center, its surface inlaid with a chessboard of polished ebony and mother-of-pearl. On it, a chess set had been arranged for a game, the pieces intricately carved of ivory, half of them stained black, the other rich red.

"You told me you love chess," James said. "Remember? At the Townsends' party?"

She did remember. It was one of the many events he'd squired her to, a forgettable ball during a damp October. She recalled chatting to him as they danced, but could not have imagined that he would have remembered what she said.

She found herself wandering the room in a sort of daze, reading the titles on the spines of books, picking up a brass mantel clock and setting it down. Over the hearth hung a gorgeously flowing painting of the Lady of Shalott, adrift in her boat, her long hair tumbling around her in a curtain of scarlet. On a wooden stand near the window was a massive leather-bound volume.

"This can't really be the New English Dictionary?" she exclaimed.

"Only through the letter *K*, I'm afraid," James said. "I ordered it as soon as they released the latest bit. We can only hope it isn't another twenty years before they release the rest. For now let's hope you don't need to look up words starting with *L* or *M*."

"It's wonderful, James. Lucie will be desperately jealous."

"Lucie can come over and consult it whenever she likes," James said. "But don't let her start bringing her books over here or she'll fill up the shelves I've left for you."

Cordelia hadn't noticed the empty shelves below James's enormous collection of books, many of which she had seen him carrying around at one time or another. There seemed to be no subject James wasn't interested in, and she spied volumes on topics ranging from naturalism to seafaring to *The Wonders of Britain* and a handful of Baedekers.

But he had left space for her. And the things he had picked out—the dictionary, the miniatures, the chess set—were thoughtful, beautiful. No wonder she had hardly seen James for the past few months. It must have taken him an incredible amount of time to create such a lovely space. It was perfect, everything she would have dreamed of and chosen for herself.

Though there were still the parts of the house she had not seen. The most intimate part, in fact. The bedroom.

She imagined a massive room, and smack in the center, a bed big enough for two people. Her blood seemed to fizz in her veins. How would she ever sleep, lying next to James in her nightgown? What if she were to reach for him in her sleep, unable to stop herself? Would James be horrified? Would he push her away?

Or . . . what if he expected a real wedding night? Cordelia had heard things whispered among other girls, had pored over a much-thumbed copy of *The Lustful Turk* she had filched from her parents' study, but she still had little idea what happened in the marriage bed. Lucie seemed to know no more than she did: when she reached the parts of *The Beautiful Cordelia* where such things might credibly happen, she inevitably invoked the weather—curtains billowing in strong winds, storms raging, lightning splitting the sky. Maybe Cordelia should hope for rain?

"Do you like it?" James had wandered over to a low table by the sofa where Effie had laid on the food: tea, butter, bread, and hot game pies. "The house, I mean."

"So far it's perfect," she said. "Is there a horrible secret I don't know about? A lunatic in the attic? Demons in the cellar?"

James chuckled. His cheeks were flushed, probably from the warmth of the room. The firelight brought out glints in his black hair, and sparked off his silver bracelet.

It was the first time that day she'd noticed he was still wearing it. She bit down on the pain. She had no right to demand he remove it. Few people knew it was a sign of the bond between himself and Grace. She had the right to demand not to be humiliated by an unfaithful husband, but no right to claims on his thoughts, or his heart. Still, the bracelet was a reminder of the way his emotions were parceled out on the scales of friendship and love and longing.

That's right, she thought. *Don't let yourself forget.* She cleared her throat. "We could play a game. Of chess."

James looked intrigued. "The lady of the house requests a game?"

"She demands one." Cordelia settled herself carefully on the sofa. Her dress really was vast.

"The first move goes to the lady of the house," he said, sinking onto the sofa beside Cordelia.

You may regret giving me that advantage, she thought. They executed their first few moves in silence, but soon the game took on an easy rhythm and they were able to chat. James explained the situation with the house staff: Effie came from a long line of mundanes with the Sight, as did the two footmen and another maid who would come in on occasion to "do the rough." Risa would remain at Curzon Street until Cordelia was settled before returning to Cornwall Gardens in time to help Sona with the new baby.

"My mother absolutely insisted Risa remain at least a few weeks," said Cordelia, nibbling a slice of buttered bread. "Risa accompanied her when she first got married, and I suspect she believes that left to my own devices, I will be found drowned in a pot of stew or crushed under a pile of dresses."

James moved a bishop. "Risa really doesn't understand a word of English?"

Cordelia relocated a pawn. "Oh, she understands everything we say. She pretends not to, when it suits her purposes. Whatever Risa hears, you can assume my mother will hear as well. We will need to be careful what we say and do in her presence."

James took a sip of tea. "So we must keep up the fiction that we are blissful newlyweds."

Cordelia felt herself turn scarlet. She supposed it ought to be a relief that James didn't find the situation as mortifying as she did. "Yes," she said. "And we should probably discuss, er, how we might go about that. Specifically."

James moved his rook so it threatened Cordelia's queen, taking advantage of her inattention. "Like rules for the game of chess, only our rules will be for the game of our marriage."

"Yes, exactly."

"Well, I suppose the first thing to consider is that we must be careful about who comes and goes from the house," James said.

"The Merry Thieves and Lucie are always welcome, of course," said Cordelia. "But for everyone else, we must each seek permission in advance. No unannounced guests who might catch us ..."

"*Not* in flagrante?" said James with a grin that made her think of the wicked sparkle she'd seen in his eyes earlier.

"Not being domestic," she said primly, and moved another chess piece. A rook, this time.

"I ought to be sitting about with my slippers before the fire, and you ought to be nagging me about leaving my poetry books in the bathtub?"

"And . . ." Cordelia hesitated. Perhaps she shouldn't say it. But abandoning her dignity had never been part of this scheme. "If you are going to see Grace Blackthorn, I ask that you tell me beforehand, so it doesn't look like you are going behind my back. I wish to be prepared."

"If I am going to—" James broke off, almost angry. "I had no intention of seeing her, Daisy. What do you take me for? I will not be alone with her, with your permission or not, not for this year. I wouldn't do that to you."

"Of course you wouldn't." She reached up to fiddle with one of her pearl combs; it was beginning to hurt. "We will be invited to parties and other public events," she added, working it free. "We must accept one out of each two invitations—"

"Done."

"—and when we attend one, you must appear to be wildly devoted to me the entire time." She had finally gotten the comb untangled, and pulled it free. It must have been holding up more of the architecture of her coiffure than she'd imagined: her hair came tumbling down, brushing her bared shoulders. "All right?"

She had expected James to laugh, but he didn't. He was staring at her. She felt herself blush—had what she said been too audacious? She had only meant to joke, but James looked as if she had mortally surprised him. His eyes had gone a dark gold.

She glanced down at the chessboard and saw that James had left himself open. She quickly moved her queen into a position that threatened both a knight and his king.

"Check," she said.

"So it is," James said, his voice oddly rough. "Cordelia, I—"

"You had better make your move," she said. "It's your turn."

"Right." He studied the board before moving a knight. "I was thinking—our best chance of success is to share everything with each other. Perhaps every night, we should each be able to ask the other a question. Something we want to know about the other, and the question must be answered truthfully."

Cordelia felt a little short of breath. What if he asked—? No. He wouldn't. "Or," she said, "what if only the winner could ask a question?"

"The winner?"

"Every night we play a game," she said, indicating the chessboard. "The winner of each game should earn something. Not money, but the right to ask something of the other."

James tented his hands and looked at her thoughtfully. "I'll agree on one condition. The loser gets to choose the next game. Chess, or draughts, or cards. Whatever they like."

"Fine. I'll match my wits with yours at any game you choose. Though I prefer chess. It was invented in Persia, you know."

His eyes lingered on her mouth for a moment. Then he looked down, returning his focus to the board. "I hadn't heard that."

Cordelia examined the placement of a rook on the board. "Do you know the *Shahnameh*?"

"The Book of Kings," said James. "Persian legends."

"All the stories are true," she reminded him. "And there is a story in the *Shahnameh* about two princes, Gav and Talhand. Talhand died in battle, but when they recovered his body, it had no wound on it. The queen, his mother, went mad with grief—she accused Gav of poisoning his brother, for how could a man die in battle with no injury? To convince her it was not so, the sages of the court created the game of chess, showing how the battle unfolded by moving the pieces on the board. Talhand had died of exhaustion, surrounded by enemies. From this we get the expression *shah mat*, meaning 'the king is dead.'" She quickly darted out a hand and made the move she'd been planning for most of the game, a classic epaulette mate. "*Shah mat*. Otherwise known as 'checkmate.'"

James sucked in his breath. "Bloody hell," he said, and burst out laughing. Cordelia let herself float in that laughter for a moment—he laughed so freely very rarely, and it transformed his whole face. "Very well done, Daisy. Excellent use of distraction."

"And now you're trying to distract me," she said, folding her hands demurely.

"Oh?" His gaze slid over her. "From what?"

"I won. You owe me an answer."

He sat up straight at that, tossing back the hair that had fallen in his eyes. "Well, go ahead," he said. "Ask me what you like."

"Alastair," she said immediately. "I—I want to know why everyone hates him so much."

James's expression didn't change, but he took a long, slow breath. "It's not true that everyone hates Alastair," he said finally. "But there is bad blood between him and Matthew and Thomas. When we were all at school, Alastair was—unkind. I think you know that. He also spread a terrible rumor about Gideon and Charlotte. He wasn't the one who started it, but he did repeat it. That rumor caused a great deal of pain, and Matthew and Thomas are not in a forgiving mood about it."

"Oh," Cordelia said softly. "Has Alastair—apologized? For that, for—for all of what he did at the Academy?" *Oh, Alastair.*

"To be fair to him, I don't think Matthew and Thomas have given him a chance to do so," said James. "He was not the only one who was unkind to me, to us, but—we had higher hopes of him, and I think thus a greater disappointment. I'm sorry, Daisy. I wish the answer was easier."

"I'm glad you told me the truth. Alastair—he has always been his own worst enemy, seemingly determined to ruin his own life."

"His life's not ruined," James said. "I believe in forgiveness, you know. In grace. Even for the worst things we do." He stood up. "Shall I show you upstairs? I imagine you are as exhausted as I am."

Upstairs. There it was. Cordelia was thrown right back into confusion as she followed James up the stairs, presumably to *their* bedroom. A space that belonged to just her and James, where no visitors could or would come. An intimacy she could not fathom.

All the lights were lit on the second floor. Gleaming sconces ran along a short corridor; James opened the first door, and indicated that Cordelia should follow him inside.

The blue-painted room faced the back garden. Cordelia saw white branches and a sliver of moon through the windowpanes before James turned a switch mounted on the wall. Twin lamps glowed to life on either side of a beautifully dressed bed that was certainly big enough for two.

Cordelia focused on the first thing her eye fell on, a carved panel over the fireplace. Worked into the marble were the crenellated towers of the Carstairs crest. "Is this . . . ?"

"I hope it's all right," James said quietly behind her. "I know that to the rest of the world, you are a Herondale now, but I thought you might like to have a reminder of your family."

She took another look around the room, taking in the quilted velvet coverlet, the silk canopy, the jacquard curtains in her favorite jewel tones of emerald and amethyst. The colors were echoed in the thick Kerman carpet beneath her feet. Risa had hung Cortana on gilded brass hooks next to the bed, clearly intended for just that purpose. A window seat big enough for two was piled with tasseled silk pillows and flanked with shelves bursting with books . . . her books. James must have arranged in advance to have Risa unpack them as a final surprise for her. "The room," she said. "It's—you picked out everything just for me."

But where are your things? Where are you, James?

He had taken off his gold jacket; it was folded over one arm. His hair was mussed, a smudge of pollen from the wedding flowers on one cheek, a spot of wine on his cuff. If she kissed him, he would taste like sugared tea, that sharp-sweet taste. Her insides felt muddled with uncertainty and desire.

"I thought your bedroom ought to be a place you could go just to be yourself," he said. "Where you wouldn't have to pretend anything." He crossed the room, throwing open a smaller door: through it was a gleaming modern bathroom with an enameled tub and shiny nickel-plated fixtures. On the far side of it was another door, painted emerald.

"The green door goes to my room," said James, "so if you need anything, and you don't want to wake the staff, you can always knock."

A terrible sense of shame washed over Cordelia. "Very sensible," she heard herself say, her voice tinny and distant. Many married couples kept separate rooms with a shared bathroom in between. What on earth had made her think James planned to share a bedroom with her? Her own parents had shared a bedroom, but that was unusual. Every bit of this house had been customized: of course he would want his own room.

She realized that James was staring at her, waiting for her to speak.

"I'm very tired," she said. "I ought to—"

"Yes, of course." He headed to the bedroom door but paused there, his hand on the doorknob. When he spoke again, his tone was gentle. "We did it, didn't we, Daisy? In the eyes of the Enclave, we are now married. We got through today. We will get through all the other days as well." He smiled. "Good night."

Cordelia nodded mechanically as he took his leave. She could hear his footsteps in the hall, the door to the other room opening and then closing again.

Very slowly, Cordelia shut the door to the bathroom, then turned off all the lamps but the witchlight on her bedside table. One of the drawers in the armoire was slightly ajar, and Cordelia knew her night-gown was waiting there for her, neatly folded and scented with linen water by Risa. There was a bell by the door; Cordelia had only to ring it, and Risa would appear to help her—

To help her out of her dress. Cordelia froze. She could not possibly call for Risa. If she did, Risa would know that the person who was sup-posed to be getting her out of her dress tonight—James—was asleep in another room, and certainly not planning to spend the night with his new bride. The news would be reported to Sona. There would be concern. Horror, even.

Cordelia tugged at the dress, trying to pull it off her body. But it was fitted tightly to her with a hundred little buttons, tiny and far out of her reach. She spun around frantically. Perhaps she could cut the dress off her body with Cortana. But no, Risa would find the ruination of the dress and she would know.

Heart slamming in her chest, Cordelia threw the bathroom door open. Her heels clicked on the parquet as she crossed the room. She had to do this now, right now, or she would lose her nerve.

She raised her hand and knocked on James's door.

There was a rustling on the other side, the door opened, and James stood in the doorway looking puzzled. He was barefoot, his waistcoat open, and a few buttons at the top of his shirt undone as well. His jacket had been tossed over a nearby chair.

Cordelia fixed her gaze in the middle distance, though that didn't quite work—she found she was staring directly at the hollow at the base of his throat, usually covered by a shirt button. He had a strong, slender neck, and the hollow was really very fascinating, but she couldn't allow herself to go to pieces over parts of James Herondale right now. She set her jaw and said, "You are going to need to help me with my dress."

He blinked, his long eyelashes flickering against his cheekbones. "What?"

"I cannot get the dress off without the help of a maid," she said, "and I cannot call for Risa, or she will know we are not spending the night together, in the marital sense, and she will tell my mother, who will tell everyone else."

He stared.

"There are buttons," she said evenly. "Many buttons. You need not help with my corset. I can manage that. You will not need to touch my bare skin. You will be touching only fabric."

There was a long, painful pause, during which Cordelia wondered whether it was possible to die of humiliation.

Then he swung the door wide. "All right," he said. "Come in."

She came into the room, trying to focus her attention on the decor.

Books, of course, everywhere. This was where he had put his beloved poetry books—Wordsworth and Byron and Shelley and Pope, next to Homer and Wilde.

The room was decorated in shades of warm ochre and red. She gazed down at the dark crimson carpet as James said, "I suppose you had better turn around."

Turning around was a relief, actually. It was much worse to have to look at him and know that he could see her blushing. She felt him come up behind her, felt his hands touch her shoulders lightly.

"Where should I start?" he said.

"Let me move my hair out of the way," she answered, reaching up to sweep the heavy mass of it over her shoulder. James made a funny sort of sound. Probably stunned by the sheer number of buttons on the dress.

"Just start at the top," she said, "and if you need to tear the fabric a bit, it's all right. I won't be wearing this again."

She had tried for a bit of humor, but he was utterly silent. She felt his hands move to brush the back of her neck. She closed her eyes. His fingers were light, gentle. He was close enough for her to feel him there, feel his breath against her skin, raising all the tiny hairs along her arms.

His fingers moved down. The dress was loosening, beginning to sag. His palm slid across her shoulder blade. She felt her eyelids flutter. She still thought she might die, but not of humiliation now.

"Daisy," he said, and his voice was thick, almost slurred. He must be horribly embarrassed, she thought. Perhaps this might even feel like infidelity to Grace. "There's . . . something else we need to discuss. The matter of the second runes."

Oh, Raziel. The second runes . . . the ones a bride and groom inscribed on each other's skin in private. Was James suggesting that since her clothes were coming off anyway, they do it now?

"James," she said, her throat dry. "I don't have my stele with me—"

He paused. If she hadn't known better, she'd have said his hands were shaking. "No, not now," he interrupted, "but we will have to mark the runes sometime. If someone were to learn that we don't have them . . ."

She could feel the first rune he had given her that day, burning on her arm. "We'll just have to try," she said, her teeth clenched, "not to get undressed in front of other people."

"Very funny." His fingers were moving again, sliding down her back. "I was thinking of Risa." She heard him draw a breath in, sharply. He must have reached the last button, for the top of the dress crumpled like a wilted flower, sagging down to her waist. She stood frozen for a moment. All she was wearing on top now was her corset, and the thin chemise under it.

There was nothing in any etiquette book to cover this. Cordelia tugged the front of the dress up, holding it against her chest. The back of the dress slipped farther down, and she realized with horror that James could likely see where her hips flared beneath the corset, curving out from her nipped-in waist.

Her gaze fixed on the Oscar Wilde books propped next to Keats on the bookshelf. She thought of The Ballad of Reading Gaol: "Each man kills the thing he loves." Cordelia wondered if it was possible to kill the thing you loved with embarrassment.

"Please go," James said. His voice was nearly unrecognizable. What had she done?

"I really am—awfully sorry," she said breathlessly, and fled. She had barely made it to her own bedroom when she heard the click of his door as it shut, and locked, behind her.

LONDON:
48 CURZON STREET

Huddled in the lee of a wall, he had watched them go in—James Herondale and his red-haired bride, the bearer of Cortana. They had climbed down from their carriage in Shadowhunter gold and splendor, both of them glimmering like precious trinkets in the fading light of the winter sun.

It was nearly dark now. Yellow light sprang into life at one upper window, then another. He knew he could not wait here much longer; he was risking frostbite, or some other sort of damage. Human bodies were cruelly frail. Trinkets indeed, he thought, huddling deeper within his coat. When the time was right, they would come apart so easily in his hands—like shiny, worthless baubles. Like broken child's toys.

6

THINGS TO COME

Do you not see how necessary a world of pains and troubles
is to school an intelligence and make it a soul?
—John Keats, *Letters*

James never mentioned the episode with the wedding dress, much
to Cordelia's relief. Other than making sure Risa would always be
around to assist her when she dressed, Cordelia was very content to go
on as if nothing had happened.

She found it easier than she would have guessed. On the day of her
wedding, she had been certain a year of horrible awkwardness lay before
her. But to her surprise, as the next two weeks passed, the question of
awkwardness never seemed to come into it. She was not reminded of
Grace; in fact, she found herself forgetting, sometimes for hours at
a time, that James's sentiments were engaged elsewhere. Being with
other people was easy, even enjoyable—she and James went out, had
suppers with friends and at the Institute, though they had not yet been
invited to Cornwall Gardens. Magnus had not yet visited—from Anna,
they learned that he and Jem had encountered problems with the books
at the Cornwall Institute, and had brought them to the Spiral Labyrinth
for further investigation. It was not yet certain when they'd return.

However, the Merry Thieves came over to carouse and to eat Risa's
cooking nearly every day. Will, Tessa, and Lucie visited frequently.
Anna stopped by in the evenings, once ending up in a four-hour

conversation with James about draperies, during which Cordelia fell asleep on the divan.

Being alone with James, Cordelia discovered to her surprise, was just as easy.

It did not happen all at once, of course. They relaxed into it: often reading together, in opposite chairs by the fire in the drawing room. Other nights, they ate dinner in the study and played games: draughts, chess, backgammon. Cordelia couldn't play cards and James offered to teach her, but she demurred; she preferred the physicality of the board games, the way they played out like a battle, in real space.

Each night, after the game was won, the winner would ask a question. It was how Cordelia discovered that James didn't like parsnips, that he sometimes wished he were taller (though, as she reminded him, he was a very respectable six feet), that he'd always wanted to see Constantinople. And how she told James that she was afraid of snakes even though she knew it was silly, and that she wished she could play the cello, and that she thought her best feature was her hair. (James had only smiled at this, and when she tried to make him tell her what he was thinking of, he waved it away.) The teasing and laughter after was often the best part; Cordelia had loved James as a friend before she'd ever loved him another way, and this was when she was reminded why.

She liked the way conversation would fade and slow as they both became sleepier, but neither wanted to stop talking about anything and everything. She talked about traveling the world, and what she had seen: chained Barbary apes in Marrakech, the lemon trees of Menton, the Bay of Naples after a storm, a procession of elephants at the Red Fort in Delhi. James spoke longingly of travel: how as a boy he had kept a map on his wall with pins stuck into the places he hoped to one day go. Since neither had ever been to Constantinople, they spent a night pulling books and maps off the shelves, reading accounts of travels to the city aloud, discussing the sights they'd want to see—the minarets of mosques illuminated at night, St. Sophia, the ancient port, the city divided by its river. James lay on the rug with his arms crossed behind his head as Cordelia read aloud from an old travel memoir: "*The Queen of Cities was before me, throned on her peopled hills, with the silver Bosphorus, garlanded with palaces, flowing at her feet.*"

He chuckled, only a sliver of gold visible beneath his half-closed eyelids. "You're better than a Baedeker," he said. "Go on, then."

And she did, until the fire burned down and she had to rouse him, and they crept upstairs together. They parted at their separate doors. Sometimes she thought his hand lingered at her shoulder as he kissed her good night, chastely, on the cheek.

She had dreamed of all this, in a half-guilty way—living with him, being so close, so often. But she had never imagined the reality of it. The sweet, piercing intimacy of ordinary married life. Of James making her giggle while teaching her slang words (considered too rude for ladies) over breakfast—a "donkey's breakfast" was a straw hat, and "half-rats" was being mostly intoxicated. Of wandering into their shared bathroom while he was shaving, shirtless, a towel around his shoulders. She had nearly fled, but he'd only waved at her amiably and struck up a conversation about whether they needed to attend Rosamund Wentworth's engagement party.

"Oh, we might as well, I suppose," she said. "Lucie's going, and Matthew, too."

He went to rinse the soap off his face, and she watched the smooth slide of muscles under the skin of his arms, his back. She had not known men had such deep grooves above their hip bones, nor did she know why the sight made the back of her throat feel odd. She glanced up hastily, only to notice that there were light freckles at the tops of James's shoulders, like golden starbursts against his skin. There wasn't a part of him she'd seen yet that she didn't think was beautiful. It was nearly unfair.

He was most beautiful when he was in motion, she'd decided. It was a conclusion she'd come to while they trained together—another part of married life she'd never considered, but found she liked very much. The training room James had installed on the upper floor was small but comfortable, with a high enough ceiling to swing a sword around, a climbing rope, and platforms to create makeshift terrain. Here she and James sparred and went through forms, and she could really see him, the actual beauty of him in motion, the long line of his body extended in a lunge or graceful in a controlled fall. She wanted to believe that, when she wasn't paying attention, he was sneaking looks at her just as she was sneaking looks at him. But she never caught him, and she told herself it was wishful thinking.

Sometimes Cordelia wondered if her unrequited love was a sort of third member of their household, present even when she was not—haunting James's steps, wrapping ghostly arms about him as he tied his tie before the mirror, curling up insubstantially beside him as he slept. But if he felt any such thing, he certainly gave no sign.

"Daisy," James said. He was in the corridor, outside Cordelia's half-open door; Risa was nearly finished helping her dress. "Can I come in?"

"One moment," Cordelia called; Risa was just doing up the last buttons on her gown.

"*Bebin ke mesle maah mimooni,*" said Risa, stepping back, and Cordelia glanced hastily at herself in the mirror. *Look how you are beautiful like the moon.*

Cordelia wondered dryly if Risa was referring to the fact that the dress was low-cut enough to reveal the tops of her breasts: swelling crescents above the dark green silk. She supposed it *was* true that a married woman could wear clothes that were far more daring than a single girl's. Every seam in her dress had been designed to emphasize her curves; every inset panel of lace offered a trompe l'oeil hint of her bare skin beneath. The effect, as Anna had explained to her when she chose the material, lay in the eye of the beholder: even the most ardent gossip could not fault its cut, but an admirer could easily imagine what lay underneath.

But will James imagine it? said a small voice in the back of her mind. *Will he notice the dress? Compliment it?*

She didn't know: it had been two weeks since her wedding to James and he was sometimes entirely opaque. Still, they had been two weeks so happy they had surprised her. Maybe this mad gamble would pay off. She would have this to look back on when she was old and gnarled like a tree trunk—a year of happiness married to a boy she adored. Some people never had so much as that.

"Maybe the dress is too much," Cordelia said, tugging at the neckline.

"*Negaran nabash.*" Risa batted her hand out of the way, tsking. "Don't worry. This is your first real night out before the whole Enclave as a married woman. Show them you are proud. Show them you will not be made to feel small. Show them you are a Jahanshah." She made a shooing motion. "Now I shall go." She winked. "You must not keep *Alijenab* James waiting."

Risa slipped out, leaving Cordelia to stand there feeling rather foolish. James rarely came into her room; she sensed he wanted her to have her privacy. He knocked once now before coming in and closing the door behind him.

She tried not to stare. James was wearing a black tailcoat and white waistcoat. His father's mad werewolf tailor had done another excellent job: James's clothes fitted him perfectly, dark broadcloth shaping his shoulders and long legs, white linen shirt showing the lean strength of his chest and throat. His gaze fell on her, his body going utterly still. There was a dull flush of color along the tops of his cheekbones.

"Daisy," he said. "You look—" He broke off, shaking his head, and fumbled something out of his pocket. It was a simple black velvet box. He held it out to her and she took it, quite surprised.

"Our two-week anniversary," he said, in answer to her quizzical expression.

"But—I didn't get *you* anything." She took the box, the velvet nap soft against her fingers. "I didn't know I was supposed to."

"You weren't," said James. "Sometimes I have foibles. This is one of them." He grinned. "Open it."

She did, revealing, nestled on a bed of more dark velvet, a glimmering gold pendant on a chain. She drew it out of the box, exclaiming as she realized what it was—a small, round globe, the faint outline of seas and continents etched onto its surface.

"We have talked so much of travel," James said. "I wanted to give you the world."

"It's perfect." Cordelia felt as if her heart might flutter out of her chest. "Here—let me put it on—"

"Hold on, hold on." James laughed, coming up behind her. "The clasp is small. I'll help you."

Deftly, he found the clasp at the back of her neck. She froze. His fingers slid lightly across the delicate skin at the top of her spine, where her dress dipped down. He smelled delicious, like bay leaves and clean masculine skin. There was a click as the necklace fastened; he breathed in deeply as he reached around to straighten the pendant and she *felt* it, felt his chest expand as he breathed, the linen of his shirt against her back, making the hairs rise all along the back of her neck. His hands drifted for a moment, inches from green silk, from bare flesh.

He stepped back, clearing his throat. She turned to look at him. The Mask had slid into place, and she could read nothing in his expression but an amiable blankness. "It looks lovely," he said, taking a folded piece of paper from his pocket. "And I nearly forgot—Neddy came with notes for the both of us, from Lucie. I didn't open yours, despite my obvious burning curiosity."

Darling Cordelia, the note read, in Lucie's familiar sprawling hand, *I am so, so sorry to miss tonight's party and leave you to the depredations of Society, but I'm feeling quite fishy about the gills. Should anyone trouble you, keep your head high and remember what the Beautiful Cordelia would say: "I shan't, and you can't make me!" I shall expect to hear everything about it tomorrow, especially what everyone was wearing and whether Thoby has grown another door knocker. All my love, LUCIE.*

Cordelia handed the note to James to read while they headed downstairs and out into the night. The footman had already brought the carriage around. It was a sharp, cold evening: the air was dry as chalk and the snow wore a top layer of ice that snapped and broke like glass under their feet. There were heavy fur rugs inside the carriage, and boxy foot warmers; Cordelia snuggled down with a sigh.

"Door knocker?" James inquired, as the carriage began to crunch forward over the icy road.

"It's a sort of beard," said Cordelia with a smile. "I'll point one out if I see it." Though beards were rare among Shadowhunter men: harking back to the armies of Rome, Nephilim regarded facial hair as something an enemy could potentially grab onto in battle. There were no such prohibitions for women's hair, likely because the Romans would never have imagined women fighting.

"Well, if Thoby is sporting one, that leaves me two choices," said

James. "Challenge him to a duel, or grow one even bigger."

"I hope you won't do either." Cordelia made a face.

"I suppose as my wife, you do get some say in my appearance," said James. Cordelia looked at him through her eyelashes, but he was only gazing out the window at the black-and-white night. "The Wentworths don't entertain often. I'm looking forward to your first glimpse of the Pastry."

"The Pastry?" she echoed.

"You'll see."

She did, the moment they pulled in through the gates. The house was a ridiculously ornate mansion with towers and turrets, like a castle, but plastered in pale ivory, so that it resembled a cross between the Taj Mahal and a wedding cake. With lights blazing from its windows and the grounds surrounding it covered in snow, the effect was blinding.

The carriage stopped in front of a green carpet, which led like a forest path up gleaming white steps to a massive faux-medieval door. The steps were lined with footmen in ivory livery, all standing stiffly to attention as James and Cordelia passed them. She couldn't help but giggle as they arrived in a very grand foyer with an elaborately tiled pink-and-white marble floor. It really did look like a cake.

James winked at her when they entered the ballroom, another massive space with ornate ceilings, slathered with gilding and boasting pastel paintings of clouds and cherubs. The edges of the room were crowded with people: Cordelia recognized Will and Tessa chatting in a corner with Gabriel and Cecily Lightwood. The Merry Thieves were there as well, sprawled at a table in one corner with Anna. Matthew raised a glass of champagne as he spotted them; Anna waved indolently. The dancing had not yet begun: guests milled around a long banquet table loaded down with enough food to feed a small town. Silver towers of pastries and sandwiches made a backdrop to huge glazed hams and fish the size of small children in gleaming aspic, staring balefully with boiled eyes from their silver platters.

In the center of the ballroom Martin Wentworth and his wife, Gladys, were admiring a large ice sculpture of Rosamund and Thoby, both in flowing robes. There was a small dove on Rosamund's shoulder.

James stared at it openly. "Would you say the theme of this party is 'Cold Reception'?" he whispered to Cordelia.

She clamped her lips shut but could not prevent herself from shaking with silent giggles. James gazed innocently at the cherubs on the ceiling as the real Rosamund and Thoby swept up to welcome them. "Oh, you both look lovely, *such* a beautiful couple I was saying, wasn't I just saying that, Thoby?" Rosamund exclaimed.

Thoby looked startled. "Were you?"

Rosamund gave James a hungry look, as if he were a delicious cream scone she couldn't wait to slather in blackberry jam. Feeling a need to rescue her husband, Cordelia said, "And how wonderful that everyone has come out to celebrate! James, we must greet your parents—"

"Not everyone," said Rosamund, with a heavy sigh. "Amos Gladstone had to go and get himself killed, and quite a few people felt attending was in poor taste, which is very unfair, because we *obviously* planned this event before he died. And we would have canceled it, but we'd already ordered the ice sculpture."

"That was an extraordinary speech, Rosamund," said James.

"Thank you," said Rosamund, seeming pleased. "I mean, how were we to know he'd get topped on patrol?"

"When did this happen?" said Cordelia. She glanced at James, who shrugged. "We hadn't heard—?"

"Oh, it was just the night before last," said Thoby, a tall, weak-chinned young man with pale blond hair.

"Was it a demon attack?" asked James.

"Well, clearly," said Rosamund. "What else would it have been? Now, Thoby, do show James the billiards room. It's *new*." She giggled and clasped Cordelia's arm. "We ladies have somewhere to be."

As Thoby led James away, Rosamund steered Cordelia toward a group of women in pastel dresses stationed near the refreshments table. Among them was Thomas's sister Eugenia, wearing a pale yellow dress and matching gloves.

"Here you go," Rosamund said with some satisfaction. Her hair had been dressed very high and studded all over with flowers. Petals rained down as she tossed her head. "This is where the *married* ladies are," she added in a stage whisper.

Of course, Cordelia realized belatedly. Married women tended to group together at dances: after all, they were no longer looking for husbands. She looked hopefully at Eugenia, but Rosamund had already bustled over to her. "*Eugenia.* You oughtn't be here. Come back to where the young ladies are—there are quite a few gentlemen here tonight eager to dance—"

"Shan't," said Eugenia, looking mutinous, but she was no match for Rosamund. A moment later she was a yellow speck disappearing into the crowd.

"Cordelia Herondale, is it?" said an angular woman in apricot silk. Cordelia recognized her as Eunice Pounceby, Augustus Pounceby's mother. It seemed Rosamund had left her with not just the married ladies but the matronly ones—mothers and grandmothers. "You look rather tired."

There was a gale of laughter; Cordelia stared.

"Eunice is only teasing you," said Vespasia Greenmantle, a comfortable-looking woman in purple velvet. "Newlyweds and their late nights, eh?"

Cordelia felt her cheeks turn crimson.

"Enjoy it while you can," said Eunice. "Soon enough you'll be readying the nursery."

"Babies are dull, Eunice," said Lilian Highsmith, who looked magisterial in an old-fashioned blue dress and sapphires. "Now weapons, on the other hand, are interesting." She reached out a hand toward Cortana. "I, for one, have been admiring your blade, my dear. May I?"

Cordelia nodded, and Lilian touched the hilt of Cortana, smiling wistfully. "As a girl, all I wanted was a weapon made by Wayland the Smith. When I was twelve, I ran away from home and my parents found me wandering the Ridgeway Road, looking for the smith's barrow. I'd brought a penny, just as the stories said I should, and was absolutely positive I'd get a sword in return!" She chuckled. "Yours is lovely."

"Thank you," said Cordelia, but behind her she could hear some of the other ladies whispering—someone wondering aloud why she wasn't on her honeymoon, and someone else, probably Eunice, replying that James and Cordelia hadn't had the luxury of waiting and planning. *A matter of her reputation, you know.*

Ugh, this was unbearable. And the music was about to start too: soon all Cordelia's friends would be dancing, so she could hardly escape to their company. She saw that James had returned to the ballroom, but he had been drawn aside by his parents, with whom he was engaged in intense conversation. It wasn't as if he could ask her to dance, she reminded herself. Husbands weren't meant to dance with their wives at balls.

"If the honor of the first dance is still available, Mrs. Herondale?"

There was a little rustle of astonishment among the married ladies. Cordelia looked up in surprise, recognizing the lazy, indolent drawl: Matthew stood in front of her, looking inquiring and colorful—his waistcoat was decorated with embroidered peacocks, his blond hair shining brilliantly under the lights of the chandeliers.

Gratefully, she let him lead her out onto the floor. "Well, *that* will be the most exciting thing that's happened to that lot in ages," she said. "Oh dear, I suppose that's rude, isn't it? I'm married too; I can't be finding married people boring."

"Most people are boring," said Matthew. "Being married or not has little to do with it."

The first dance was a polonaise, and couples were coming from all over the room to join the procession onto the floor. Cecily and Gideon, Catherine Townsend and Augustus Pounceby, Filomena di Angelo—Cordelia recalled meeting the dark-haired Italian girl at her wedding—and Albert Breakspear. Christopher had partnered with Eugenia, and there was Alastair, dancing politely with Ariadne.

"Why come to parties, then?" Cordelia demanded. "If you find everyone so dull."

"*People* are dull. Gossiping about them is *never* dull. Look—there's Thoby and Rosamund, already arguing. I wonder what about? Lilian Highsmith hit Augustus Pounceby with her umbrella earlier: What could he have done? Did he insult her? Esme Hardcastle is telling Piers Wentworth all about the book she's writing on the history of the London Enclave, but he only has eyes for Catherine Townsend. And the lovely Eugenia, rejecting every suitor. Possibly due to bad past experiences."

"What happened to Eugenia?"

Matthew Fairchild

"Augustus Pounceby." Matthew scowled. "He led her to believe they had an understanding." Cordelia was surprised; an understanding could be quite a serious thing. It meant a girl was confident of an offer of marriage. "So she behaved rather freely with him—going for walks with him without a chaperone, all very innocent—but when he proposed to Catherine Townsend, who refused him, Eugenia was made to look a fool. She went off to Idris to get away from the Enclave's gossip."

"How rotten," said Cordelia. "But surely someone must have a bigger secret than all that? Skeletons under the floorboards and such?"

"You mean is anyone a murderer?" Matthew turned her in a swift circle: the dozens of candles seemed to blur into a stream of light all around them. "I am."

Cordelia laughed, a little breathless. They had spun toward the outer edge of the dance floor. She caught sight of James; he was still in animated conversation with Will and Tessa.

"What if I told you I could lip-read?" said Matthew. "That I knew every word James and his parents were exchanging? And that the news they share is shocking?"

"I would tell you to stop eavesdropping. Also, I wouldn't believe you. It takes ages to learn lipreading. In fact, what I would say is that you are telling frightful bouncers to make yourself seem more interesting, when the truth is that if there is shocking news, you probably heard it from your mother."

Matthew mimed being stabbed in the heart. "Doubted! Unmanned! Cruelty, thy name is woman." He peered at her out of a narrowed eye. "Does that mean you don't want to know what they're talking about?"

"Of course I do, you oaf." She hit him lightly on the shoulder. The polonaise was not as intimate a dance as the waltz, but she was still close enough to Matthew to note the faint lines around his eyes when he *really* smiled. She didn't see them that often. He smelled of brandy, frangipani, and cigars.

"Well," he said, lowering his voice. "You know Charles has been in Paris, working at the Institute."

"I heard the head of the Paris Institute was ill, and Charles was pitching in."

"And quite a help he's been," said Matthew. "There was a meeting with all the vampire clans of France, and Charles neglected to invite the clan from Marseilles. Probably just forgetfulness, but they took mortal offense."

"Surely he could just explain and apologize?"

Matthew snorted. "Have you met Charles? He doesn't apologize. Besides, the vampires aren't inclined to trust him. They feel, not unreasonably, that in any serious disagreement, the Consul would side with her son. So Uncle Will and Aunt Tessa are going back with him to Paris tomorrow to help smooth things over quietly." Matthew's eyes danced. "Downworlders tend to look favorably on them, since Tessa is herself a Downworlder, and Will saw fit to defend her against the Clave, and even marry her."

They raised their hands up and placed them palm to palm. Cordelia could see the black Voyance rune shimmer against the back of her hand as her fingers twined lightly with Matthew's. "Well, I say they sent the wrong Fairchild brother there in the first place," she said.

They began to turn in a slow circle, keeping their hands clasped. "What do you mean?"

"*You're* the one who loves France. You're always talking about Paris," she said. "And you're devilishly charming—you know you are. You would have made a much better ambassador than Charles."

Matthew looked—well, "stunned" might be the best description. She had the feeling he was rarely compared favorably to his brother when it came to professional matters. They made one more turn in silence. Without the bulwark of light conversation, the dance seemed suddenly far more intimate. She could feel his movements beside her, feel the warmth of his hand, the cool press of his signet ring. The one James had given him.

She had seen couples like that on the dance floor before: utterly silent, drinking in the sight of each other, the rare opportunity to touch and be close without scandal. Not that she and Matthew were like that—she had only said something that made him feel awkward, was all. *Well, too bad,* she thought. *He ought to hear it.* He was worth a hundred of Charles.

The music stopped. Amid the bustle of dancers leaving the floor, they lowered their hands. "Alas," said Matthew, in his familiar bright tone, "I shall have to return you to durance vile, I fear. I would ask for a second set, but it is frowned upon for single men to dance too much with married ladies. We are meant to be hurling ourselves at unattached females like cannonballs."

Cordelia chuckled. "That's all right. You've spared me an otherwise dull ten minutes. I was about to throw myself into the trifle."

"Terrible waste of trifle," said a familiar voice, and Cordelia turned in surprise to see James. In the gilded light, his eyes were a startling gold.

"Freed yourself from the clutches of your parents, have you?" said Matthew, after a hesitation so brief, Cordelia wondered if she'd imagined it. "Heard about Charles?"

James mimed a whistle. "Indeed. Much to be said on that topic, but for the moment—" He turned to Cordelia. "Mrs. Herondale, would you do me the honor of dancing the first waltz with me?"

Cordelia looked at him in surprise. "But husbands aren't supposed to—I mean, they don't dance with their wives."

"Well, this one does," said James, and whirled her away across the floor.

GRACE:
1896

Jesse's was not a clean death. He had begun screaming in the night, and Grace had rushed in, to find her brother already a grotesque horror, a tangle of linens and blood, so much blood, screaming, inhuman in his torment. Grace shouted for her mother, her cries joining Jesse's. She knew there were healing runes, Shadowhunter magic that could help, but she didn't know how to draw them. Besides, she had no stele.

She held her brother, his blood soaking her nightclothes, and when she let go of him he was dead. In between she had a vague awareness of Tatiana's arrival, of her own wailing, there next to Grace. At one point her mother held a gold locket to her son's lips, sobbing violently, for what reason Grace did not then know, though she was to find out soon enough.

Grace had wanted her mother there, but she felt only more alone. Tatiana broke down, screaming, tearing at her clothes, crying prayers and imprecations to entities unknown to Grace to save him, save her boy, and once he was gone she sat on the floor, her legs splayed like a little girl, crying to herself. She didn't show any awareness of Grace at all.

In the days after, if Grace had hoped to find comfort in her common grieving with her mother, she was to be disappointed. In the wake of Jesse's death, her mother vanished further into herself, and often went long periods without acknowledging Grace or reacting when she spoke. While Grace sought to understand how to go on in the face of her desolation, her mother spat imprecations about the corruption of the Shadowhunters, their determination to ruin her, her unwilling-ness to go quietly without a fight. She even managed to throw blame in the direction of the Herondale family, though Grace could not see any connection between them and Jesse's death.

In truth, while some part of her would have happily clung to the idea that someone was at fault for Jesse's death, she knew that some-times Shadowhunters could not take runes and died in the attempt. It was terrible—unfair, meaningless—but it was true. And so Grace found no comfort in her mother's rage.

Nor was it comforting when her mother began disappearing into the manor's cellar and emerging with the reek of sulfur on her, mut-tering to herself in strange languages. When she did talk to Grace, it was mostly on the topic of the treachery and ill-intent of the Nephilim. These lectures would start and stop seemingly at random, picking up in the middle of a thought as though the days since the previous talk hadn't passed at all, and this was all one long continuous lesson.

Grace hadn't thought anything evil of the Shadowhunters as a whole—she had lived among them for her first years of life, after all—but Tatiana illustrated her lessons well, delving into the dark corners of Blackthorn Manor and finding all manner of gruesome his-tory there. In a dusty chest in the cellar, a collection of Downworlder spoils—vampire teeth, a desiccated preserved werewolf paw, what seemed to be an oversize moth's wing floating in a clear, viscous liquid. These spoils had been illegal to take for the past thirty years, Tatiana admitted, but for the nine hundred years of Shadowhunter history prior to that, they were common. A diary entry, detailing the stripping of the Marks of someone's insubordinate youngest son. "'They threw him into the road,'" Tatiana read aloud, "'for the good of the family and Clave.'"

The pièce de résistance of her collection, hidden in the study at Chiswick Manor, was an *aletheia* crystal, a faceted stone, enchanted to preserve a person's memories. Grace would have thought that families would use such magic to record joyful events, but this one contained a short, grisly scene in which one Annabel Blackthorn, who had lived a hundred years ago, was tortured by the Inquisitor for consorting with a Downworlder and sentenced to be exiled to the Adamant Citadel.

"These are the Nephilim," Tatiana said, "these are the ones who seek to destroy us. These are the ones who killed our Jesse."

She broke down then, sobbing and collapsing onto the floor, and Grace snuck away to bed once she realized her mother would demand no more of her that evening. But though Grace closed her eyes, the image of the long-ago Blackthorn girl stayed in her mind for many hours. Her helplessness. Her terror. She had made one decision for herself, Annabel, and for it she lost everything. Grace wondered, then, whether her mother had intended a somewhat different lesson than the one she'd given.

One night, still only days after Jesse's death, a black carriage pulled up to the front of the manor, and Grace was ordered to open the gates. It was a muddy, rainy evening, but she did as she was told, trudging down the gravel drive and pulling the heavy iron gates open; they groaned a keening wail from long disuse. The carriage passed through, and she followed, studying it curiously. There were strange symbols carved all over its surface—not Shadowhunter runes, and nothing she recognized.

The carriage came to a stop at the front door, and when Grace caught up to it, a figure emerged. It was a man—in her memory he was very tall, but perhaps that was only because she was still a child—wearing a black cloak with a hood pulled up, shadowing his face. He spoke in a deep, gravelly voice, harsher than Grace would have expected. "Where is Tatiana Blackthorn?"

"My mother," she said quickly. "I'll go and find her. Whom shall I say—"

"No need," the figure rasped. "I am expected." He brushed past her and went into the house, turning down the first hall as though he knew the way.

Grace had thought to follow him, but once he passed by her, she found she was shivering so hard that she could not walk. She clutched her arms around her waist, trying to warm herself, her teeth chattering, and after a minute she was able to make her way back to her bedroom. There was a small fire, and she built it up as best she could, though the shiver would not leave her bones.

Time seemed to lose all meaning after Jesse's death. Grace woke, and went about her business mechanically, and slept at night without dreaming. The color of the leaves changed in the gardens, and the briars grew higher. Tatiana wandered from room to shadowy room, not speaking, often staring at the broken clocks on the walls, which always showed the hour of twenty to nine.

They did not comfort each other. Grace knew herself to be alone, so alone that she was nearly not surprised when she began to hallucinate that Jesse was there. She had woken up in the depths of the night, gasping for air. And there he was, still wearing the clothes he had died in. He seemed to float just out of the range of her vision, at the other end of the room. And then all at once he was there next to her, a full, detailed apparition of her dead brother, faintly glowing, smiling just as he would when he was alive.

It was too much to bear, the cruelty of death and the cruelty of her own mind. She screamed.

"Grace!" her brother said in alarm. "Grace, don't be frightened! It's only me. It's me."

"You're not real," Grace said, numb. She forced herself to look up at him.

"I am," Jesse said, sounding a little offended. "I'm a ghost. You know about ghosts. You weren't hallucinating that time you saw that fellow drinking blood, either. He was a vampire."

Grace gave out a sound that was half laugh, half sob. "By the Angel," she said—an expression forbidden in the house, but she could not help herself. "You are real. Only the real Jesse could be so vexing."

"My apologies. I suppose it's hard for me to be sensitive to your mourning. Since I'm right here."

"Yes, but a ghost," Grace said. She allowed the meaning of this to penetrate her mind and, feeling a bit sharper, allowed herself to look curiously at her brother's spirit. "Have you been a ghost all this time? Why did you wait so long to come see me?"

Jesse looked grim. "I didn't. I tried, but—you didn't hear me. Until now." He shook his head, puzzled. "Maybe it takes some time for ghosts to return fully. Perhaps there's paperwork that needs to go through."

Grace hesitated. "Perhaps," she said. "Jesse—Mama is up to something. Something secret. I don't know what it is, but she's been digging books out of dark corners of the house, and a gentleman came to . . . assist her with something. Who is he?"

"I don't know," Jesse said, his voice thoughtful. He reached out and stroked Grace's hair, almost absentmindedly. She could feel his touch like cobwebs brushing her. She leaned into him, determined to take what comfort her brother could still offer. "I'll find out, Grace," he said. "After all, I can come and go as I please in the house now."

"No chance of waking Mama up, anymore," Grace said. "Come back soon, Jesse. I miss you."

When she woke the next morning, she was half convinced that the whole encounter had been a dream, that it was only a trick of her mind, fevered with sorrow. But Jesse came back the next night, and the night after that—and only at night. And finally, on the fifth night, he explained.

"Mother can now see me as well," he said in an odd, flat tone. "And she is determined to bring me back from the dead."

Grace felt a surge of conflicting emotions within her. She could understand why her mother would be driven to do so—the thought of Jesse returned whole to her filled her with such intense hope that she could hardly bear it. And yet. "That man who came—was he a necromancer?"

"A warlock versed in dark magic, yes." Jesse looked grim. "I have been . . . preserved," he said, pronouncing the word with distaste. "That is what she hired him to do. There is a glass coffin in the cellar, with my body in it, unchanging, as if I were some sort of—vampire. Around its throat—my throat—is a gold locket that holds my last breath."

Grace wasn't sure whether to feel relieved or disturbed. "So she will have all the time she needs to—to try to bring you back."

"Yes," he said. "In the meantime, I remain trapped here, in between life and death, sun and shadow. Haunting the house at night, when I am awake, and vanishing when the sun rises. At sunset, I awake to find I have slept unaware all day in my coffin." Grace could not imagine how terrifying that must have been, must still be. "Even without necromancy, it is still dark magic that keeps me in this state. It cannot stand like this forever."

She knew that Jesse was right. And yet a curl of happiness had twisted in her stomach, a guilt-inducing happiness maybe—but having Jesse with her, even only at night, was so much better than being alone forever. Alone with her mother, in a dark, cold house.

7

TREAD LIGHTLY

Faintly I met the shock of circling forms
Linked each to other, Fashion's galley-slaves,
Dream-wondering, like an unaccustomed ghost
That starts, surprised, to stumble over graves.

For graves were 'neath my feet, whose placid masks
Smiled out upon my folly mournfully,
While all the host of the departed said,
"Tread lightly—thou art ashes, even as we."
—Julia Ward Howe, "My Last Dance"

The sight of Anna was a pleasant hurt in Ariadne's chest.

Pleasant, because Anna had only grown more beautiful since the first time Ariadne had seen her, when she'd been all long dark hair, ill-fitting dresses, flaming blue eyes, and terrifying scowls. Now her beauty shone through how at home in her skin she was—the scowls were gone, her lips curved red and smiling as she took a sip from her glass of champagne.

And hurt, because Ariadne could not touch her. Anna was a fortress surrounded by her friends: tall, handsome Thomas; Christopher, who shared his sister's stern delicacy of features; peacock Matthew, who always looked as if he'd just rolled out of an unmade bed piled with silks and velvet. If James and Cordelia hadn't been waltzing on the dance floor—Cordelia looking lush as a flower in a dress Ariadne was sure had been Anna's suggestion—she was positive they'd have been surrounding Anna too.

The group eyed Ariadne suspiciously as she approached Anna. Anna didn't seem to see her at all; she was leaning against the wall, one booted foot up behind her. She was all lean black-and-white lines, her close-fitting jacket following the outline of her slim curves, her head thrown back as she laughed. Her ruby pendant, which Ariadne knew was sensitive to demonic energies, glimmered in the hollow of her throat.

"Hello, Anna," Ariadne said.

Anna flicked a lazy glance in her direction. "Miss Bridgestock."

Ariadne raised her chin. She was wearing her newest dress—a midnight-blue confection with matching ribbon strung through her hair. The color of Anna's eyes. She knew Anna would take note. "Would you honor me with this dance?"

Anna sighed and gestured to her cohort: they scattered just enough distance to give Anna and Ariadne some space. "Once more unto the breach, eh?" Matthew said in a low voice as he passed Ariadne, and dropped a wink.

"Ariadne," Anna said. "Do you really mean to dance with me? Here, in front of all these people?"

Ariadne hesitated for a moment. She'd waited until her parents had gone into the withdrawing room, but still, plenty of her family's friends were here and watching. The Rosewains, the Wentworths, Lilian Highsmith with her sharp old eyes . . .

It didn't matter. She firmed up her jaw. All that mattered was Anna.

But Anna was already looking at her skeptically, having noticed her hesitation. "Of course not," Anna said. "Nothing's really changed with you, Ari, has it? How many times are you going to ask me to dance when you know there's no point?"

Ariadne crossed her arms over her chest. "A thousand times," she said. "*Infinity* times."

Anna set her glass of champagne down on a windowsill. "This is ridiculous," she said, and Ariadne saw with surprise that her eyes were blazing. "Come on, then."

Picking up her heavy skirts, Ariadne followed Anna through a pair of sliding pocket doors into a deserted dining room. White cloths covered the furniture. Anna continued confidently down the length of the room, opening a narrow door and disappearing through it.

Ariadne slipped through after her, only to discover that they were not in another room at all, but in a small space—a pantry, she thought, just as Anna closed the door behind them, plunging them into near darkness.

Ariadne yelped. She heard Anna chuckle as witchlight began to glow, illuminating their little space. It was coming from the scarlet pendant around Anna's throat. Ariadne hadn't known it could do that.

She glanced around: they were indeed in a pantry. The shelves were mostly empty save for a few scattered items, rags that had probably once been used for polishing furniture. The floor was bare and clean. There was little enough room for movement that one of Ariadne's slippered feet was resting on Anna's left boot; she had to lean back to avoid bumping directly into her.

She was sure her cheeks were dark red. Hopefully Anna couldn't see her properly. Ariadne took a deep breath.

In years past, Anna had smelled of lavender water—now there was a different scent to her, shed by her clothes and skin as she moved. Something rich and dark, like tobacco and sweet resin. The red-tinged light of the pendant turned her eyes to a color more like her brother's, a sort of purple. Her cheekbones stood out like the blades of knives. Her mouth was rich and lush and full, the dark red color of berries. Ariadne's throat tightened.

"Listen to me," Anna said. There was nothing urgent in her voice, only a flat finality. "It has been four months since you told me you would win me back. I am not to be won, Ariadne. Love is a prison, and I have no desire for shackles. They would clash with my outfit."

"But I love you," Ariadne said, "and I do not feel shackled."

"It has led you to imprisonment in this pantry," Anna pointed out.

"With you," Ariadne said. She raised a hand slowly, moving as if she were trying not to scare off a wild animal. Her fingertips grazed Anna's cheek. Anna caught her wrist in a hard grip. She inclined her head; she was ever so slightly taller than Ariadne, especially in boots. "So I am happy."

"Then you're a fool," Anna said. "Do you want to know why?"

"Yes. Tell me. Tell me why I'm a fool."

Anna put her mouth to Ariadne's ear. She spoke in a near whisper, her warm breath stirring the hair at Ariadne's temples, her lips grazing Ariadne's skin. "Because I will never love you," Anna murmured. "I will never be with you. We have no future together. None. Do you still want me to kiss you anyway?"

Ariadne closed her eyes. "Yes. *Yes.*"

Anna's mouth captured hers in a hard, bruising kiss. Ariadne gasped as Anna's hand came up to tangle in her hair. Ariadne had never kissed Charles save for a few stiff pecks on the lips in public. She had tried, before him, kissing other boys and had found it seemed ridiculous to her. Two people mashing their faces together for no good reason.

With Anna it had been different. It *was* different. How had she nearly forgotten? The heat of Anna's mouth, the wine-and-roses taste of her. Ariadne surged up onto her toes; she bit and licked at Anna's lower lip and felt Anna's arms go around her, tightening. Lifting her.

Anna was strong, as all Shadowhunters were strong: she lifted Ariadne as if she weighed no more than a handkerchief and deposited her on the edge of a shelf. Now that her hands were free again, Anna returned to her task with redoubled attention. Ariadne whimpered, arching back, as Anna ravished her mouth, parting her lips—licking and sucking, kissing and biting, a masterful whirlwind that left Ariadne breathless and frantic.

She had not been wrong, this past four months. It was worth anything, everything to have this. And she had never felt a shadow of it with anyone but Anna. She recalled with tenderness their first time together, how inexpertly they had touched each other, how they had laughed and tried this and that to find out what each of them liked.

There was much Ariadne still didn't know. But Anna had outpaced her like a motorcar outpacing a carriage. Her hands were on Ariadne's knees, sliding up, finding the bare skin above her stockings. Slipping under her jaconet muslin petticoat. Ariadne's hand tightened in Anna's hair. She knew she was making little whimpering noises as

Anna's fingers found their way unerringly to the heart of her. She dropped her hands, flailed for a moment before grasping the shelf tightly. She felt as if she were falling, flying off the edge of the world. She dragged her eyes open, desperate to see Anna's face. In the scarlet light, her eyes were darkly blue, her lips parted. For the first time in two years, Anna was concentrating entirely on Ariadne.

It was too much. Ariadne gasped and shuddered as the world came to pieces around her. *"Anna, Anna, Anna,"* she whispered, the word losing itself against the broadcloth of Anna's jacket. Somehow, she had pressed her face into Anna's shoulder.

When she turned her head, she could hear Anna's heartbeat. It was racing.

She drew back, her hands stroking down the front of Anna's shirt, soft material over warm skin. . . . "Anna, come here. Let me—"

"Oh, there's no need." Anna stepped back. "Really, Ariadne, you should have told me *that* was all you wanted. We could have done it a long time ago."

Anna cracked the pantry door open as Ariadne hastened to straighten out her skirts. She jumped down from the shelf, her shaking legs barely able to hold her. "Anna, we cannot just—"

"Walk back into the party together? I agree. There will be talk," Anna said. "I'll go first; you follow some minutes later. And we should avoid each other for the rest of the evening, I'd say. Don't look so worried, my dear. I'm quite sure nobody saw us."

Cordelia could hear the murmurs as she and James spun around the ballroom. Not that she minded. Let them all mutter about how he was being rude, dancing with his wife when surely he got enough of her conversation at home. She didn't care what anyone said; she felt delighted, triumphant. She was not a fool who had been compromised into a marriage with an unwilling man. James cared for her.

She knew that he did. Her fingers were entwined with his, his other hand on her waist. The waltz was a far more sensual dance than the polonaise, and James wasn't bothering to keep his distance. She was pressed against him, making the starch of his shirtfront crinkle.

The corner of his mouth curled into a half smile. "I see Matthew has filled you in on all the gossip regarding Charles. How was your sojourn among the matrons of the Enclave?"

"Well, they are all looking over at us now," said Cordelia. "They seem scandalized."

"That's because all their husbands are off drinking port and playing billiards."

"Don't you want to go drink port and play billiards?" she teased.

"When you dance as well as I do, you have a responsibility to set an example," said James, swinging her in an exaggerated turn. She laughed, spinning back toward him. He caught her, his fingers splayed at her waist.

"I heard a bit more about what happened to Amos Gladstone the other night," he said. "He was found with his throat slit. Frozen in an alley. No ichor, or any demon traces, but it's rained since, so . . ."

Cordelia shuddered. "I can't help but be uneasy. The last time Shadowhunters were dying . . ."

"Those were attacks in full daylight," said James. "This is normal, or as normal as things get for Nephilim. We've stopped being used to it, but people die on patrol. Not that I advocate pretending it didn't happen because you've ordered an ice sculpture, mind you—"

He broke off. Two guests had entered the room, and Rosamund and Thoby had already rushed to greet them. Even through the crowd, Cordelia knew who they were: there was Charles, his red hair set off by his black tailcoat, and beside him, Grace. Her dress was a cloud of ivory net, worn over an ice-blue satin underskirt.

She looked at Cordelia for a long moment, her gray eyes wide. Then she glanced away.

"I wouldn't have thought Charles would have come," Cordelia said, struggling to seem unaffected. "Isn't he being packed off to Paris tomorrow?"

"First thing in the morning, along with my parents, but Charles is determined to put on a good face." James was no longer looking at Grace and Charles. He had practice, Cordelia supposed; it was not the first time she and James had seen Grace at a party, though it had not happened since their wedding. He never looked at her long, nor went to speak to her, but Cordelia, tuned as she was to his moods, could always sense his distraction. "My apologies—we have quite lost the thread of the dance."

"And you were doing such a good job setting an example," said Cordelia. James laughed, but it sounded brittle as glass. Cordelia glanced back: Rosamund seemed to be gesturing for Grace to come with her to join some of the other unmarried girls, but Grace only shook her head and turned to Thoby.

A moment later Thoby had taken Grace by the hands and spun her out onto the dance floor. Rosamund looked after the two of them, her mouth open. Charles shrugged and walked off.

Cordelia couldn't help but stare—there was nothing in the etiquette books that said one couldn't dance with the host of a party, be he engaged, married, or single. But to enter a dance in the middle was odd, and for Grace to have asked Thoby—as she clearly had—was a startling breach. It would certainly win her no friends among Rosamund's set.

And the look on Thoby's face wouldn't help. He was gazing down at Grace as they floated across the floor as if he had never beheld a more enchanting creature. If Charles minded, it wasn't apparent: he was heading determinedly across the room toward Alastair, who stood alone by a pillar, looking weary.

"What's wrong?" said James. "Daisy?"

It was a great irony, she thought, that he knew her so well. And a greater one that he had once left her on a dance floor and now she was going to leave him, even though it was the last thing she wanted to do.

"Alastair," she said, drawing her hands from James's. She hurried away, not looking back, darting through the maze of dancers till she burst out the other side.

Charles had already reached Alastair and was leaning casually against the pillar beside him. Alastair looked—well, Alastair looked expressionless, or would to someone who didn't know him. Cordelia knew by his slumped posture—he was nearly sliding down the pillar— and the tightly fisted hands in his pockets that he was quite upset.

"I know you read mundane newspapers too," Charles was saying, as Cordelia approached. "I wondered if you noticed the recent murder in the East End. It's the sort of thing that seems as if it shouldn't inter-est us, but on closer examination—"

Cordelia stepped up to Alastair, blinking demurely. She knew people were watching. She wanted to give them no reason to talk. "Charles," she said, smiling with too many teeth, "I believe that you agreed to stay away from my brother."

Charles raised a superior-looking eyebrow. "Cordelia, dear. Men have disagreements among themselves sometimes. It's best to leave them be to sort it out."

Cordelia looked at Alastair. "Do you wish to converse with Charles?"

Alastair shuffled upright. "No," he said.

Charles flushed. It made his freckles stand out like angry dots. "Alastair," he said. "Only a coward needs to be rescued by his little sister."

Alastair's expressive eyebrows flickered. "And only an ass puts other people into situations in which they need to be rescued at all."

Charles took a deep breath, as if he were about to shout. Cordelia moved swiftly between him and her brother; her smile was starting to make her face ache. "Charles, go away now," she said. "Or I will tell *everyone* how your aunt and uncle must go rushing off to Paris to rescue the Clave from your blunder."

Charles's lips tightened. And somehow, oddly, in that moment, she saw Matthew in him—she could not imagine why. They could not have been two more different people. If Charles were only kinder, more understanding, perhaps Matthew would not—

Cordelia blinked. Charles had said something, undoubtedly something cutting, and stomped off. As he did, she noticed that they were indeed being watched—by Thomas. He was gazing at them from across the room, seemingly arrested in mid-motion. Behind him, James had rejoined his friends and was chatting with them, one hand lightly on Matthew's shoulder.

Several things happened at once. Thomas, seeing Cordelia looking at him, blushed and turned away. The music ended, and the dancers began to stream off the floor. And Grace left Thoby without a word and came up to James.

Matthew and Christopher had been laughing together; Matthew stopped, staring, as Grace said something to James and the two of them stepped a bit apart from the others. James was shaking his head. The silver bracelet glimmered on his wrist as he gestured.

"Do you want me to go over and break your husband's legs?" Alastair said quietly.

"He can hardly run away screaming if Grace approaches him," Cordelia said. "He must be polite."

"As you were polite to Charles?" said Alastair, smiling crookedly. "Don't take it the wrong way, Layla, I'm grateful. But you don't need to—"

Out of the corner of her eye, Cordelia saw James break away from Grace. He came toward her, pausing only to nod a greeting at a few passersby. He was white as a sheet, but otherwise the Mask was firmly in place. "Alastair," he said, coming close. "Good to see you. Are your parents well?"

Alastair had told her she didn't need to be polite. But politeness had its uses. James wore his manners like a suit of armor. A suit to match the Mask.

"Well enough," said Alastair. "The Silent Brothers recommended my mother rest at home after all the excitement of the wedding. My father did not want to leave her."

Some of this was doubtless true, and some of it wasn't. Cordelia didn't have the heart for investigation. She no longer had the heart for the party at all. James hadn't betrayed their agreement, but it was clear that it caused him pain to be in the same room with Grace.

The worst part was that she could sympathize. She knew what it was like to be near to the person you loved yet feel as if you were a million miles away.

"James," she said, laying her hand on his arm. "I find I have rather a desire to play chess."

That brought a smile from him, though only a slight one. "Of course," he said. "We shall depart at once."

"To play chess?" Alastair muttered. "Married life sounds thrilling."

Cordelia kissed Alastair goodbye on the cheek as James went to offer the necessary excuses to their hosts. They collected their things in silence, and soon found themselves on the front steps of the Wentworths' house, waiting for the carriage to be brought around.

It was a lovely night, the stars water-clear, like diamonds. Grace had watched them go, a thoughtful expression on her face. Cordelia could not help but wonder how much Grace concealed. It was not like her to approach James. Perhaps she had felt desperate. Cordelia could not blame her if she did.

She could not ask James, though, because they were not alone on the steps—Tessa and Will were there. Tessa was smiling up at Will as she tucked her hands into fur-lined gloves; he bent to brush her hair from her forehead.

James cleared his throat loudly. Cordelia glanced up at him. "Otherwise they'd start kissing," he said matter-of-factly. "Believe me, I know."

Tessa seemed delighted to see them. She beamed at Cordelia. "Don't you look lovely. Dreadful we have to leave the party so early—fortunately, Miss Highsmith has offered poor Filomena the use of her carriage later—but we're meant to Portal to Paris early tomorrow morning." She did not, Cordelia noted, mention Charles.

"We tried to approach you inside but were cut off by Rosamund chasing Thoby around because their ice sculpture had melted," said Will. "What does it mean for the youth of today, that they don't know that ice melts? What are we teaching them in the schoolrooms?"

James looked amused. "Is this another 'youth of today' speech?" He dropped his voice into a passable imitation of Will's. "Running about, no morals, using ridiculous words like 'barmy' and 'brinkets'—"

"Even I know 'brinkets' is not a word," said Will, with great dignity. He and James bantered back and forth as the Institute's carriage rolled around the corner and stopped at the foot of the steps, driven by a skinny footman in silver and ivory. Cordelia could not help but think how different James's relationship with his father was from Alastair's with Elias. She wondered, sometimes, what Elias would say if he knew about Alastair and Charles. If he knew Alastair was different. She wanted to think he wouldn't care. Months ago she would have been sure of it. Now, she was sure of nothing.

Her reverie was broken by a sudden shout. The skinny footman had leaped to his feet, balancing on the seat of the carriage. He looked about, wild-eyed. "Demon!" he shouted hoarsely. "*Demon!*"

Cordelia stared. Something that looked like a spinning wheel covered in wet red mouths shot out from under the carriage and rolled about in a circle. She reached back for Cortana—and flinched, her palm stinging.

Had she cut herself on it, somehow? That couldn't be possible.

James laid a hand on Cordelia's shoulder. "It's all right," he said. "There's no need."

Will was looking at Tessa, his blue eyes wide. "Can I?"

Tessa smiled indulgently, as if Will had asked for a second helping of cake. "Oh, go ahead."

Will made a whooping sound. As Cordelia stared in puzzlement, he leaped down the stairs and raced off, chasing the wheel-demon. James and Tessa were both smiling. "Should we help him?" Cordelia asked, utterly bewildered.

James grinned. "No. That demon and my father are old friends. Or rather, old enemies, but it amounts to the same thing. It likes to chase him around after parties."

"That is very peculiar," said Cordelia. "I see that I have married into a very peculiar family."

"Don't pretend you didn't know that already," James said.

Cordelia laughed. It was all so ridiculous, and yet so very much the way James's family always was. She felt as if things were almost normal again by the time their carriage came around and they clambered into it. As they rolled off into the night, they passed Will, brandishing a seraph blade as he happily chased the wheel-demon through the Wentworths' rose garden.

"You must be so terribly disappointed to miss the party tonight," Jessamine said as she drifted past the bookcases in the drawing room. "You must be absolutely *crushed.*"

Lucie had been in the middle of reading *Kitty Costello*, or trying to, when Jessamine had appeared, looking for company. Normally Lucie didn't mind Jessamine, but her bone-jarring headache had only just faded, and she simply felt weary.

With a sigh, she folded down a page to mark her place and closed the book. "Honestly, I'm not sorry to miss the party."

"Even though that Italian girl got to go?" Jessamine inquired.

"Filomena?" Lucie felt she hardly knew Filomena; the older girl, though nominally living at the Institute, was always rushing around London, going to museums and exhibitions. Lucie hardly saw her.

"No, I'm glad she'll be having some fun. It's just that I don't really want to see Rosamund and Thoby being smug, but I *am* sorry not to be a support for Cordelia. Rosamund will doubtless cloister her away with the married ladies and she'll be terribly bored."

Jessamine had drifted down to sit on the desk's edge, swinging her insubstantial legs. "At least her marriage is publicly recognized. When I married Nate, no one even wanted to hear about it."

"Well, that's probably because he was a murderer, Jessamine." Lucie set her book aside and stood up, tightening the sash on her flannel dressing gown. She had already let her hair down for the evening, and it spilled to the middle of her back, making her think nostalgically of being a little girl—she had spent so many evenings in this room, curled up by her mother's side as Tessa put her hair into bows and plaits, and Will read aloud. She would miss her parents while they were in Paris with Charles, Lucie thought; them leaving so soon after James had moved out was a blow, though they had reassured her they would certainly return in time for the Institute's annual Christmas party. At least Aunt Cecily and Uncle Gabriel would be keeping her company, as they were stepping in to head the Institute while the Herondales were gone. Christopher and Alexander too, though she suspected Christopher would spend most of his time in the cellar blowing things up.

Jessamine sniffed but said nothing. Occasionally she romanticized her past, but she knew the truth as well as Lucie did. Not, Lucie thought as she headed back down the corridor toward her room, that Jessamine had deserved to die for the mistakes she'd made, or deserved to become a ghost, either, always trapped between life and death, haunting the Institute and unable to leave it.

It really made one quite melancholy to think about. Reaching her room, Lucie wondered if she ought to seek out Bridget and wheedle a cup of hot milk, lest she be unable to sleep—then the door swung wide, and suddenly hot milk was the last thing on her mind.

Bright moonlight spilled into the room, illuminating the carefully laid-out lilac dress she'd picked out for tonight, which had gone unworn. Low-heeled ivory kid boots stood under the window; her necklaces and rings were spilled across her vanity table, glittering like ice in the cold light. At her paper-strewn desk sat Jesse, the pages of

The Beautiful Cordelia spread out in front of him.

Lucie felt a rush of panic. She had intended to show Jesse *The Beautiful Cordelia*, but she had also planned to curate which pages he saw. "Jesse!" she said, slipping into the room and closing the door firmly behind her. "You shouldn't be—"

"Reading this?" he said. There was an odd note in his voice, and an odder look on his face. A look she hadn't seen before, a sort of shadow cast across his fine features. "I can see why."

"Jesse—"

She reached out a hand, but he'd already picked up a page. To her horror, he began reading aloud from it, his voice stiff:

> "*The Brave Lucinda clasped her hands before her. Did her eyes deceive her? But no! It was indeed her beloved, Sir Jethro, returned from the war. Truly he seemed weary and war-torn, his brightly blazoned armor daubed with blood—no doubt the blood of the innumerable poltroons he'd slain upon the battlefield. But these marks of battle only made his beauty shine more brightly. His black hair gleamed, his green eyes shone as she ran toward him.*
>
> *'My darling, you are alive,' she cried.*
>
> *He clasped her face between his cold hands. 'I am not alive. I am a ghost, and only you can see me.'*
>
> *'It does not matter!' cried Lucinda. 'Alive or dead, I love you still!'*"

Lucie snatched the page out of his hand. She was breathing hard. "Stop," she said. "Stop reading."

He rose to his feet. "I see why you didn't want me to see this. I suppose it could be that you are mocking me—"

She stared at him. There was an angry shape to his mouth that seemed to change his whole face—or was it just that she had never seen him furious before? "No—how could you think that?"

"Clearly I am something of a joke to you, or my situation is." There was still that awful curl to his mouth. That cold note in his voice. Yet through her humiliation, Lucie felt a spark of anger light.

"That is *not* true," she said. "It is a story. And while there are—similarities—between Lord Jethro and you, it is only what writers do. We model bits and pieces of characters on what we see in real life. It means nothing."

"You are right," he said harshly. "That boy in the book is not me. I don't know who he is—he is your imagined fantasy, Lucie."

With shaking hands, Lucie crumpled the page of her book into a ball and threw it to the floor. "It's just writing. Making a story."

"It is quite clear that if I were not a ghost, I would be of little interest to you. Just a boy who hadn't lived much, and died unheroically," he said. He began to pace, his footsteps utterly soundless. She could see through him partially, through his shoulder as he turned. As if he were losing strength, she thought, chilled; losing the ability to appear solid and whole. "You want to create a story in which I died in battle, or perished nobly. Not foolishly, weakly, getting my first Mark."

She glanced at the glass over her vanity table: she saw herself, very pale, her dressing gown wrapped tightly around her. And where Jesse stood, not even a ripple in the air. She tore her eyes away from the reflection.

"No," she said. "I care for you just as you are, the way you are. The book is a kind of truth, but is not what we are. Cruel Prince James isn't *James*. Matthew isn't a collection of ice goblins in spats. And Princess Lucinda isn't me. I made her far braver, more clever, more resourceful than I am." She took a deep, terrifying breath. "Princess Lucinda would have told you she loved you, a long time before now."

"Don't," he said. "Don't confuse what you feel with the stories you're writing. You do not love me. It is not possible."

Lucie wanted to stamp her foot on the floor but restrained herself. "I know what I feel," she snapped. "You cannot dictate such things, nor tell me what is possible!"

"You don't understand," he said. "When I am with you, I imagine that my heart is beating, though it has not beaten for seven years. You give me so much, and I can give you nothing at all." He caught up a handful of papers from her desk. "I told myself you felt nothing for me, any more than you would feel for—for a portrait, or a photograph of someone who had once lived and breathed. If I told myself lies, then this is my fault. All of it. And I must put an end to it."

Lucie reached out, as if she could catch at his sleeve. "What if I commanded you?" she said, her voice harsh in her own ears. "To forget you'd ever read the book? What if—"

"No," he said, and now he looked absolutely furious. "You must *never* command a ghost unless they ask you to do so!"

"But, Jesse—"

She could hardly see him clearly now: he had begun to fade, to blur around the edges. "I cannot, I *will* not stay," he snapped. "Unless you command me, of course. Is that what you want? To force me to stay?"

Wordless, Lucie shook her head. And Jesse vanished, leaving the white pages of her book to flutter slowly to the floor.

James sat before the fire in his bedroom, letting the light from the flames play over his hands, creating pattern and shadow.

He could not sleep; Cordelia had begged off chess the moment they'd returned home, and indeed, she'd looked strained and exhausted. James felt bitterly angry with himself.

He had not broken his agreement with Cordelia—he had spoken to Grace briefly, and only about Amos Gladstone's death. She had told him to be careful. All perfectly proper, but he knew he must have seemed stricken when Grace had walked into the room. Cordelia had been stunned. He must have looked awful; she was usually so cheerful and unflappable.

He hadn't even wanted to go tonight: it had been three full days that he'd hardly ventured out the door of his own home. Nominally, the weather had kept him inside; it had been blowing freezing sleet since Tuesday. But he had to admit: had he still lived at the Institute, he would have dragged himself out of doors, grumpy as a wet cat, to join his friends in the damp rooms above the Devil.

But staying at home with Daisy—he'd told her marriage would be a lark, and meant it, but he was enjoying it more than he'd imagined he would. He found he looked forward to seeing her at breakfast so as to tell her what he'd thought about during the night, and at night to hear what she'd thought about since breakfast. They saw their friends during the day, but he loved their evenings alone together, when they matched their wits over games, made and lost bets, and talked about anything and everything.

He recalled, when he was a boy and the whole family had gathered in the drawing room, seeing an expression on his father's face that James always thought of as the Quiet Look. Will's blue gaze would travel over his wife—tracing every line of her as if he were memorizing her all over again—and then his children, and a look of happiness that was sharp and gentle at the same time would come over his face.

James knew now, though, what his father had been thinking when he got the Quiet Look. It was the same thought he had in the study at night, watching the light of the fire pass through Cordelia's unbound red hair, listening to her laugh, seeing the graceful movements of her hands in the warm lamplight. *How do I live in this moment forever, and not let it go?*

Would it be like that with Grace, when they were married? James wondered. He had never felt comfortable around Grace as he did around Cordelia. Perhaps that was the difference between love and friendship. Friendship was more easy, more relaxed.

Though, whispered a treacherous voice in the back of his mind, it was not relaxation he was feeling when he let his gaze roam over Daisy as she sat before the fire. He noticed everything about her as if he had been given a divine mathematical assignment intended to total up her charms: the shape of her mouth, the smooth skin of her throat and forearms, the curve of her neck, the soft swell of her breasts under her nightgown. She had been stunning tonight; he had caught quite a few men staring at her, at her curves poured into that green dress, at the graceful tilt of her head when she danced, at his gold pendant glimmering against her skin. . . .

A sharp pain twinged behind his eyes. He'd been having bad headaches lately. Maybe due to lack of sleep. He rubbed at his temples. He would certainly not get any rest sitting here, staring into the fire. As he rose to his feet, he recalled that he'd intended to look for a pocketknife earlier. Perhaps it could undo the latch of his bracelet. But he was too tired to venture down to the study, and by the time he climbed into bed, he no longer remembered what he had meant to do.

London:
Finch Lane

Fog came stealthily in the small hours, settling in every doorway and alley of Bishopsgate *and obscuring the outlines of buildings and trees. As dawn approached, the costermongers were the first to break the silence, the fog muffling the sounds of their carts as they wheeled them into the streets to display their wares. A faint red glow between the buildings heralded a weak sun just as the Shadowhunter patrols trudged through the backstreets on their way home, invisible to the mundane merchants they passed.*

And on Threadneedle Street, a killer went in search of a victim.

He moved like a wraith, slipping soundlessly from the cover of one awning to the next, nearly invisible in a dark cloak that blended with the soot-covered stone. He darted past the statue of the Duke of Wellington and behind the white columns of the Bank of England. All around him, well-dressed bankers and brokers on their way to work took no note of him as they streamed through the doors of London's financial institutions like fish spawning up a stream. The killer mused that those pathetic mortals might as well be fish, they were so weak, so mindless, driven by no more noble pursuit than the exchange of currency.

But the killer's quarry was not just any mortal. He had more potent prey in mind.

There—that figure in black, gray-haired, exhaustion showing in the sag of his shoulders as he stepped off the main thoroughfare onto Finch Lane, the kind of quiet side street no one takes any note of as they hurry past. The killer followed a few paces behind his quarry, marveling that this was the best the Nephilim had to offer, this weary hunter who didn't even realize that he was the one who was being hunted now.

He wondered if the demons were disappointed in their prey; surely over the past thousand years they had grown used to the Nephilim putting up a better fight. This one, for example, didn't even notice the killer gaining on him. Didn't notice the blade until its cold edge was pressed against his throat. Adamas to flesh, the razor edge the work of the Iron Sisters at their forges, working adamas into killing tools.

He sliced again and again, blood sluicing over his blade and drenching his fist, falling onto the stones beneath their feet, pooling in the crevices. Rage rose within him and soon he was stabbing harder, bringing down the knife over and over again, his other gloved hand over his victim's mouth, muffling the screams until they were no more than bubbling gasps.

When there was nothing left of the Shadowhunter but limp flesh, the killer loosened his grasp. The body slid to the cobblestones. He knelt and carefully, almost tenderly, rolled up the dying man's sleeve and held his own bare arm close to the Shadowhunter's.

The killer produced an object from his jacket, a slim metal shaft that did not reflect the light, its surface crisscrossed with etched lines. He ran his fingers over his victim's Swiftness rune, tracing the marks on the dead man's flesh, feeling the energy just below the surface, the power of the rune itself.

The killer smiled.

The rune was his now. He had earned it.

8

To Bring a Fire

I have come to bring fire on the earth, and how I wish it
were already kindled! But I have a baptism to undergo,
and what constraint I am under until it is completed!
Do you think I came to bring peace on earth?
No, I tell you, but division.
—Luke 12:49–51

After waking late the next morning, Cordelia dressed in a warm wool skirt and white high-necked blouse and made her way downstairs and into the dining room, where she found James seated at the table with an open copy of Housman's poems at his left elbow and a breakfast plate at his right.

He offered her a tired smile. He didn't look much better than she felt—there were crescent moons of darkness under his eyes. As she sat down across from him, she couldn't help but notice his poetry book was upside down.

Risa bustled in with tea and breakfast for her. James stayed silent, his face closed, his eyes half-lidded. As soon as she was gone, he said, "Daisy, there's something I've been wanting to tell you. It's about what happened the night before our wedding."

Cordelia attacked her boiled egg with vigor. She wasn't sure she wanted to know what had gone on at the Devil. "I . . . believe I heard something about a reverse mermaid?"

"Ah," said James, sitting back in his chair. "That was Matthew's fault, and truly one of the strangest things I've ever seen. Anyway, it seems Claribella has found true love in the arms of a gin-soaked kelpie, so I suppose no one was harmed too badly."

"Really?" Cordelia was amused, but James went on, his expression darkening.

"It's not that. All I'd really wanted was to spend some time with the Merry Thieves that night. But I'd only just got to our quarters when—I found myself in that other world." His left hand, with its long, elegant fingers, played with the fork by his plate. He'd eaten very little. "Belial's world."

The name seemed to fall between them like a shadow. Belial. When Cordelia had seen him, he had taken the form of a beautiful man, icy-pale. It had been hard to look upon him and imagine him as anyone's grandfather, much less Lucie and James's.

"But—that's not possible," Cordelia said. "Belial's realm was destroyed. We saw him shatter and vanish—Jem said it would take a hundred years for him to regain enough strength to return!"

James shrugged unhappily. "And yet . . . it was so real. I felt it, Cordelia—I felt his presence. I may not be able to explain it, but—"

"Did you say anything to Jem?"

"Yes. I sent him a message this morning. Or at least, I tried." James released the fork. He had bent several of the tines. "It seems he's still in the Spiral Labyrinth with Magnus; I cannot get through. I'll try again, but meanwhile, we must do everything we can to understand what's going on, how it's possible that I could be sensing Belial nearby when he could not possibly be there."

A look flickered at the back of James's eyes—a look that made Cordelia sit up straight, suddenly very worried indeed. But before she could respond, they heard the doorbell ring.

Risa hurried in from the front hall. *"Oun pessareh ke tou Sirk bazi mikoneh, injast,"* she told Cordelia, rolling her eyes.

James looked inquiring.

"She said, 'The one from the circus is here,'" translated Cordelia, giving Risa a mock-stern look. "She means Matthew. She disapproves of his waistcoats."

James started to grin as Matthew swaggered into the dining room, a spring in his step. He wore burgundy-and-olive spats with a matching waistcoat, and folded gracefully into a seat at the head of the table. He helped himself to a kipper from James's untouched plate before announcing, "I have news."

"Please make yourself at home, my delinquent friend," James said. "I'm sure the lady of the house won't mind."

"Do you mind?" Matthew asked Cordelia, his fork halfway to his mouth.

"No," said Cordelia decidedly. "Come whenever you like."

"Oh, good. Then do you think I could have some coffee? With milk, and an exceptional amount of sugar?" Risa, who had been lurking in the corner of the room, gave him a suspicious look and departed for the kitchen. Matthew leaned forward. "All right. Do you want to hear the news?"

"Is it good news?" said Cordelia.

"No," said Matthew, and James groaned. "But I think it's important. I heard Charles talking to Mother this morning, before he Portaled to France with your parents. He was on patrol late last night, and he came in with the dawn contingent. One of their number was missing—Basil Pounceby. Augustus's father. Charles went with the search party and was there when they found his body. It seems he was killed while on patrol last night."

James and Cordelia exchanged a glance.

"Do they suspect the same demon that killed Amos Gladstone?" Cordelia asked.

"They're thinking it wasn't a demon at all," Matthew said as Risa appeared with coffee. "The wounds were made with a knife—a very sharp blade that was used to poke a lot of holes in the senior Pounceby. Demons tend to slaughter, like animals do. Pounceby was stabbed by a thin metal blade, Gladstone had his throat slit, and there were no traces of demonic presence at either murder site." He tipped his head back to smile at Risa like a Botticelli angel. "You are as beautiful as all the stars," he told her, "but better, because you have coffee."

"*Dary mano azziat mikoni*," Risa said, threw up her hands, and stalked from the room.

"My attempts to charm her have not been successful," Matthew observed.

"Risa is a sensible woman," said James. His eyes were fixed on the middle distance. He seemed almost unbearably tense; Cordelia could see it in the set of his shoulders, the hard line of his mouth. "Was Pounceby killed someplace near white pillars? And a statue, perhaps of someone on a horse?"

Matthew set his coffee cup down with a slow deliberation. "Near a statue of the Duke of Wellington, in fact," he said. "Close to the Bank of England."

"Which has a colonnade of white pillars," said Cordelia, looking at James in surprise. "How did you—?"

James had the look of a man who had suspected a deadly diagnosis and had just had it confirmed by his doctor. "He was near Threadneedle Street, correct?"

"Have you been in touch with Uncle Gabriel, or Aunt Cecily?" said Matthew, clearly puzzled. "You should have stopped me if you knew all this already."

"I didn't." James pushed his chair back from the table and went to stand by the window, staring out at the frost-covered hedges. "Or at least, I didn't realize what I knew."

"James," Cordelia said. "What is going on?"

He turned back to face them. "This is—more than it seems, I think. It would be best if I spoke to everyone together. We should gather the other Thieves."

"That'll be easy enough," Matthew said casually; Cordelia had the clear sense that he was holding off peppering James with questions. "Lucie and Christopher are already at the Devil, reasoning with Thomas."

James's black eyebrows lifted. "Why does Thomas need to be reasoned with?"

"Well, if you come to the Devil, you'll find out," said Matthew. "I've got my carriage waiting; we can be there in a quarter hour. Do you think Risa would mind if I brought a plate of buttered toast with me?"

*　*　*

"I will not bow out of patrol," Thomas was saying as James, Matthew, and Cordelia entered the room. Faint cheers had greeted Matthew and James as they crossed through the pub below, but the mood at the Devil seemed muted. News of murders and the like tended to travel swiftly through Downworld. "It's a ridiculous suggestion and there's nothing you could say to convince me!"

He broke off as he caught sight of Cordelia and the others. He had one hand upraised, his finger jabbing the air as he spoke, as if to punctuate his sentences. He was flushed, his light brown hair in disarray. Cordelia was surprised—kind, calm Thomas rarely got out of temper.

Though there had been that moment with Alastair at the wedding.

Lucie and Christopher sat side by side on a sofa in front of Thomas, like two small children being scolded by their parents. Both had their hands folded in their laps, though when she caught sight of Cordelia, Lucie couldn't help but wave. "Thank the Angel, you're all here! Isn't it awful?"

Cordelia joined Lucie and Christopher on the old sofa. When she sank gratefully into the well-worn feather cushions, a puff of dust drifted into the air to join the comforting smells of old books and incense. Despite the circumstances, it was good to be back in these familiar rooms. Cordelia watched James take a seat in one of the sagging brocade armchairs and Matthew his usual spot in the corner. While they were settling in, Lucie touched Cordelia's hand.

"We were just telling Thomas he oughtn't patrol," she said earnestly. "At least not alone. Not with what happened to Basil Pounceby."

"And Amos Gladstone," said Christopher. "Two deaths in such a short time, both killed on patrol—it seems reasonable they might be connected."

"Or it might just be bad luck." Thomas threw up his arms. "Patrol is always going to be dangerous. That's just part of the job, like demons and Alastair Carstairs—" He broke off, turning bright red. "Ah, Cordelia, I—"

She smiled pleasantly. "Did you just remember that Alastair is my brother?"

"Yes. No," Thomas said. He looked around at his friends beseechingly.

"Oh, no," said James. "You have to get yourself out of this one, Tom."

Thomas turned to Cordelia, making her suddenly aware how very tall he was. She had to stretch back her neck to look up at him. "Cordelia, I—I have owed you an apology for some time. I may have my own issues with Alastair, but I'm sorry I was rude to him at your wedding. It was unforgivable. I like you very much and consider you a friend. Though I cannot forgive Alastair, I will treat him politely for your sake. I should never have suggested otherwise."

"Well," Cordelia said. "Thank you. Though I agree that you shouldn't be patrolling alone right now."

Thomas opened his mouth, closed it, and opened it again. "May I have your permission to shout, keeping in mind I am not shouting at you?" he said to Cordelia.

"Oh, quite," she said. "I like a good shouting in general."

"Yes," agreed Lucie. "Shout at Matthew if you like."

"Thank you very much, Luce," said Matthew.

"*Stop*," said James. They all looked at him in surprise. "We need to discuss what we're dealing with before we argue about who's going on patrol and when. Patrol is meant to be about demons, and Math told me the Enclave is already thinking this wasn't a demon's doing—"

"WHAT?" said Thomas, so loudly they all jumped. "Sorry," he said. "I was all prepared to shout and I hadn't got a chance yet."

"What makes them say it wasn't a demon?" Christopher asked thoughtfully.

"Pounceby was stabbed at least thirty times with a sharp blade," Matthew said. "Demons don't carry weapons."

"It could have been a demon with very pointy talons," Christopher argued, "or—it could have been a demon with a knife face." He looked around eagerly.

"Knife face?" Matthew echoed. "That's your argument?"

"Yes," said Christopher stubbornly. "It could have some sort of facial protuberance. Maybe several. Like a long, pointy nose with a sharp edge."

"There wasn't any residue of demonic activity, either, on the bodies or at the sites," said Matthew. "A demon would leave behind some kind of trace."

"What about a Sighted mundane?" suggested Lucie. "Maybe he didn't even know what he was seeing. He could have been drunk. Or mad. Maybe he was stumbling about in the dark, saw a Shadowhunter, and perceived he was some kind of threat."

"Or it could be another Shadowhunter," Matthew said. "Don't look at me like that—we have to consider the possibility. After all, people commit murder for all kinds of reasons."

"Like what?" James said skeptically.

"I don't know—maybe Basil was a rival for someone's affections, or the object of a grudge. Or someone resented him for creating Augustus. No one would be surprised. For that matter, it could have been Alastair."

"Matthew," Cordelia said furiously. "Must we keep bringing up my brother? Alastair may be many things, but he is not a murderer."

"I just like to blame him for things," Matthew said a bit sheepishly.

"None of this makes any sense anyway," said Cordelia. "If someone murdered Basil Pounceby for revenge, or love, or any such thing like that, why would they also murder Amos Gladstone? And we would be foolish to assume the deaths are not connected."

"I believe they are connected," James said. He looked tightly drawn; he seemed to be steeling himself, as if to deliver bad news. "I had a dream last night," he added abruptly. "A ghastly awful dream that felt so real—"

"Real like—like traveling into the shadow realm?" Lucie looked alarmed. Matthew and the others were exchanging worried glances as well.

"Not at all like falling into shadow," James said. "I was very much here, in London. I *saw* the murder."

"You saw it?" echoed Matthew. "What do you mean?"

"It was a dream, but not at all like an ordinary dream," said James. "I was there—I felt the cold of the air, the cobblestones under my feet. I recognized Threadneedle Street. I saw a knife—I saw a body falling— and I saw hands. Hands covered in blood. They were—human hands."

"The murderer's hands?" Thomas said.

"I don't know," James said, "but I felt such hate, hate like I've only felt before in Belial's realm. It did not seem like a human hate."

"Who was it that you hated?" Cordelia whispered. "In the dream?"

His eyes fixed on hers. His voice was a whisper. "Everyone."

"So you witnessed the murder in your sleep," Lucie said, worry etched on her face. "But here, in London, not in the shadow realm, or through it. If you understand what I mean."

"Not the shadow realm," agreed James. "This was London, not some blasted landscape of hellish death and destruction."

"Unless you are talking about Piccadilly Circus when the traffic's bad," said Matthew.

"I am going to ignore that comment," said James, "as it is not helpful. All I can say is that I do not believe Pounceby was killed by a demon—or by a jealous husband, or a vampire, or a vampire's jealous husband. I cannot say, but what I do believe is that the same entity that killed Amos Gladstone killed Pounceby, too."

"Did you dream about that as well?" Cordelia asked. "But that was only a night or so before last, wasn't it?"

"I had what I assumed was a nightmare," said James. "Nothing like as clear and detailed as the dream I had last night. But I recall a suffocating sense of horror. It simply didn't occur to me that there was any connection to what happened to Gladstone—not until I dreamed of Pounceby's death last night."

"Jamie," Lucie said. "When the Khora demons were attacking, before they even claimed a victim, you had a vision of what was coming. Is it possible perhaps you have the ability to somehow see when bad things are going to happen to Shadowhunters?"

"Not before they happen, unfortunately," said James. "I had only just woken up from the nightmare perhaps a half an hour before Matthew arrived to tell us that Pounceby was dead and the whole Clave knew."

"And that was already ten o'clock in the morning," said Matthew. "Could you tell what time it was in your dream?"

James shook his head. "Around dawn, I think."

"So not much of an early warning," said Thomas. "And no way to know if it'll happen again."

"We ought to tell someone," said Christopher. "Not just sit here coming up with theories. Though I do love coming up with theories." He looked wistful.

"Our parents—" Lucie began.

"No," James said. "We are absolutely not dragging our parents back from Paris for this. They only just left. I'll try again to get a message to Jem."

Matthew frowned. "My mother said something about him—whatever he and Magnus are doing in the Spiral Labyrinth, it seems to be important. I get the sense they're both cloistered there; she said there was no reaching Magnus, for now."

"If we were to say to the Enclave—" Thomas began.

"We cannot," Matthew said. "They already think that the two deaths are connected. There's nothing new we could tell them except that James has been having these dreams, and for them to think the dreams had any relevance or meaning . . ."

"We'd have to tell them about Belial," said Cordelia.

"And that would potentially be disastrous," said Matthew. "For Jamie, for Lucie, for Will and Tessa—for all the reasons we decided not to tell them in the first place."

Thomas had sat down on the edge of the sofa. He laid a hand on James's shoulder. "Of course. We weren't suggesting we tell them any of *that*."

"I would be prepared to tell them about Belial if it affected only me," said James, "but it would put my mother and Lucie under the Clave's microscope too." He turned to Thomas. "Now. Tom, no one's saying you can't patrol. Just not by yourself. I'll go with you."

"I wish you could," said Thomas. "But they're setting a curfew for everyone under eighteen. None of you will be allowed to patrol at all, and if I can't patrol with you, I'd rather be on my own. Last time they paired me with Augustus Pounceby. It was torture."

"Speaking of Pouncebys," said Lucie. "What could Amos Gladstone and Basil Pounceby have had in common, besides both being out on patrol?"

"I imagine that's what the Enclave is looking into right now," said Matthew. "As for us, perhaps we ought to concentrate on preventing James from being tormented in his dreams."

"There are tinctures and things that are meant to offer dreamless sleep," said Christopher. "I'll ask Uncle Henry about them."

"Oh, that would be wonderful," said Lucie, looking relieved. "I'm sure these are just bad dreams—some remnant of the shadow power tormenting you, James."

"No doubt," said James, but Cordelia could tell from the look on his face that he had many doubts indeed.

As they collected their coats and gloves, Lucie watched her brother carefully, looking for clues to how he was holding up, but his face was impassive. She wondered if it bothered Cordelia, how little emotion James could show sometimes. But then, Cordelia probably did not expect much, or even want much, from James. It was a dispiriting thought.

"I'm going to visit the Pouncebys," James said, wrapping his scarf around his neck. "I ought to go offer condolences."

Matthew made a face. "I'm sure they're being well looked after by the Enclave," he said. "You needn't trouble yourself, Jamie."

"And yet I shall trouble myself," James said, squaring his shoulders. "It's what my mother and father would do if they were here. With them in Paris, it's my responsibility to pay respects to the Pouncebys."

"You're a good man, James," Thomas said sympathetically.

"Capital of you to step in for Uncle Will and Aunt Tessa," Christopher added. "Please send the condolences of us Merry Thieves as well."

"Yes," agreed Matthew. "Whether they want them or not."

Lucie admired her brother's resolve but did not share it. "I'd join you," she said, "but Cordelia and I were meant to train today. We've fallen dreadfully behind, and we must catch up if we're going to be ready for our *parabatai* ceremony in January. Are you coming back to the Institute with us, Kit?"

"No—I'm off to Henry's lab."

Lucie couldn't say she was surprised—despite the fact that Christopher was in principle residing at the Institute, she expected he'd be nearly always away: either at the Devil Tavern or at his beloved laboratory at the Consul's house.

Christopher turned to James. "If you're going to the Pouncebys' anyway, come to Grosvenor Square afterward. There's something I want you to have a look at in the lab."

As James and Christopher fell into a discussion of the laboratory, Matthew took Thomas aside. Lucie perked her ears up. She suspected Cordelia was eavesdropping as well, though she was drawing on her napa leather gloves and looked perfectly demure.

"Do, please, be careful, Tom," Matthew advised. "I know you're eighteen and you can do what you like, but don't take foolish chances."

Thomas drew the hood of his gear jacket up, covering his light brown hair. "You, too, Matthew. Be careful."

Matthew looked puzzled. "What's that supposed to mean?"

Thomas sighed. Lucie could not help wondering if he, too, had noticed what she had noticed about Matthew. What everyone else seemed determined not to see or address. "Just take care of yourself."

Outside, they all scattered to their respective carriages. All save Lucie. "I'll just be a moment, Daisy," she called to Cordelia, then darted to Christopher's carriage and yanked open the door.

"What on earth—?" He gazed at her through his spectacles. "Is something wrong, Luce?"

"No!" She dropped her voice to a whisper. "You were meant to have more thorn-apple for me—don't you remember?"

"Oh. Yes," Christopher said, digging in his pocket for a small parcel. "But Henry is getting more suspicious about why you're asking for all these things."

Lucie took the packet of dried flower heads, holding it delicately by the corners, and tucked it into her skirt pocket.

"It's really nothing," she said. "I'm only working on a beauty potion—but you can imagine that my brother would give me no peace if he found out."

"You should have said so," Christopher said, brightening. "Henry has some sperm whale oil. It's supposed to be good for your complexion if you put it on your face."

"No, thank you," Lucie said with a shudder. "I think this thorn-apple will do the trick."

"Just be careful with it," Christopher said, as she stepped back from the carriage. "It's very poisonous. Don't swallow any of it, or drink it, or anything like that."

Lucie gave him a reassuring smile. "I wouldn't dream of it."

And she wouldn't. She wouldn't dream of making a beauty potion either, but even Christopher—who, among all the boys in the world, was surely one of the best and kindest—found it an easy enough excuse to believe. *Gentlemen*, Lucie thought, hurrying to catch up with Cordelia.

It was one of those days when nothing seemed to be going right in the training room.

Cordelia had caught a ride to the Institute with Lucie. Usually she found her best friend an excellent sparring partner. But neither of them seemed to be able to concentrate properly today. They had ducked where they should have dodged, missed their targets when knife throwing, and Cordelia had pivoted where she should have lunged, bruising her hip against a post. Worse, she had fumbled Cortana twice, letting it slip out of her hands in a way that had startled and alarmed her.

"Today is just not our day, I'm afraid," said Lucie breathlessly, her hands splayed in the middle of her back. "I suppose we can't help being distracted."

"Is it awful if I wasn't thinking about the murders at all?" said Cordelia.

"That depends on what you *were* thinking about," said Lucie. "New bonnets might be bad, the meaning of the universe less so."

"I was thinking about my father. We're meant to all have dinner at Cornwall Gardens tomorrow night. It'll be the first time we've seen him since the wedding." She pushed back her damp hair impatiently. "I tried so hard to make this happen," she said. "I did everything to get my father back, and now that he's here, I don't know at all how to feel."

"They sent him to the Basilias because you defeated the Mandikhor demon," Lucie pointed out. "Otherwise he'd have gone to jail, Daisy, and he'd still be there. You don't have to know how to feel, but it's because of you that there's a chance for reconciliation. I'm sure he knows that."

"I suppose," said Cordelia, with a wan smile. "Only I don't know what to say to him, and I don't have time to think of it. And it seems an awful thing to do, to make James attend this awkward family dinner—"

"He is your family," said Lucie firmly, "just as I am; you are my sister now, and you will be my sister forever after. We will always be sisters and *parabatai*. That is what matters. In fact—" She glanced around. "Why don't we practice the ceremony?"

"The *parabatai* ceremony?" said Cordelia. She had to admit, the thought had a certain appeal. "Do you know all the words?"

"I watched James and Matthew's ceremony," said Lucie. "I think I remember. Here, pretend where you're standing is a circle of fire, and I'm standing in a different circle of fire."

"Hopefully we will be wearing gear," said Cordelia, arranging herself in the imaginary circle. "Our skirts would quite go up in flames."

Lucie thrust out her hands and indicated Cordelia should do the same. They clasped hands, and Lucie, an intense look of concentration on her face, began to speak: "Though most *parabatai* are men, the ceremony uses words from the scriptures that were spoken by Ruth to Naomi. By one woman to another." She smiled at Cordelia. "'Entreat me not to leave thee, or to return from following after thee, for whither thou goest, I will go—'"

Lucie suddenly jumped as if stung and dropped her hands. Alarmed, Cordelia moved toward her, forgetting about the imaginary fire rings in her concern. "Lucie, is everything all right—?"

The door opened and Filomena di Angelo came in. She wore a bored, sulky sort of expression—she had very dark eyebrows and red lips, and it made everything she did seem dramatic.

"Ah, Lucie, I did not realize you would be in here," she said, looking around without curiosity. "Mr. Lightwood suggested I take a look at the training room, as I had not yet seen it. I admit," she added, "I have more interest in examining the art and culture of London than discovering whether British Shadowhunters stick demons with pointy things in decidedly different ways. I suspect not. What do you think?"

Lucie seemed to have recovered herself. She gave a too-bright smile and said, "Do you recall Cordelia, Filomena? She was the one who was getting married a few weeks ago—"

"Ah, yes, to the young man, the one who looks *magnifico* in *abiti formali.*" Filomena sighed. *"Quelli sì che sono un petto su cui vorrei far scorrere le dita e delle spalle che mi piacerebbe mordere."*

Cordelia burst into giggles. "I'm afraid that if you went up to James and—what was it?—bit into his shoulder, he would be very alarmed."

"I didn't know you spoke Italian!" Filomena seemed delighted. "I actually said I wanted to run my hands over his chest and bite his shoulders—"

"Filomena! That's my brother we're discussing!" Lucie protested. "And Daisy's husband. I promise you, there are many other handsome men in the Enclave. Thomas has very nice shoulders. Legendary shoulders, in fact."

Filomena looked surprised. "Thomas? Yes, but—" She looked from Lucie to Cordelia and shrugged. "I suppose that Fairchild boy seems interesting. Not the redheaded one, obviously."

"Anna Lightwood is throwing a party at her flat tomorrow night," Lucie said. "You must come! All the young people from the Enclave will be there. Matthew, too."

"L'affascinante Anna is hosting a party?" Filomena clapped her hands. "Now that seems like something I might well enjoy."

"Oh, if you like art and culture—and attractive shoulders—you certainly will," Cordelia assured her. She couldn't wait to tease James about the pretty Italian girl who admired him so much. "And find many beaux there, I suspect."

"Of course," Filomena said, tossing her dark head as she prepared to leave the room. "Rome conquered the world in six hundred years. I shall conquer the Enclave in one night."

James's visit to the Pounceby household had been grim and difficult. The drawing room had been dim, the curtains pulled to keep out the harsh winter sun. Augustus had glared the entire time, as though James had tied all his shoelaces in knots, and Basil's widow, Eunice, had cried on James's shoulder at great length, telling him that he was a good boy and had grown into a thoughtful young man.

James longed to extract himself and sprint for Mayfair on the double. But his loyalty to his parents won out, and he had stayed with the Pouncebys for nearly an hour, until blessedly Gideon, Sophie, and Eugenia had shown up and provided him an opening to escape.

It was a relief when James arrived at the Consul's house in Grosvenor Square. The place itself was a comfort to him. He had whiled away many happy afternoons there during his life. Not five minutes after he arrived, however, he was already beginning to suspect this was not going to be one of them.

He had intended to head directly to the laboratory, under the assumption that his friends were there. Alas, he found his progress blocked by the flung-open doors of the study, where Matthew was draped across a settee like Cleopatra, blandly regarding his nails as Charlotte paced the floor worriedly. Oscar the dog was asleep in the corner, snuffling as he dreamed.

"The Enclave is putting together a day patrol to search the area Basil Pounceby's body was found. Your name came up, Matthew, but I took you off the list, explaining that you are not well," Charlotte said. She sounded less than happy about it.

James would have tried to sneak past unnoticed, but Matthew had seen him. Matthew began gesturing frantically but subtly (the sort of trick really only he could pull off) for James to stay. James glared, but remained.

"Why would you do that?" Matthew demanded. "I'm fit as a fiddle, Mother."

"I said it because it was true." Charlotte's voice shook. "Matthew, you *aren't* well. You are always drinking, and when you are not drinking, your hands are shaking. Neither condition is conducive to patrol."

Matthew rolled his eyes, sitting up a few degrees and rearranging the cushions. "It's not my fault that you and Father were the most boring people alive when you were adolescents. I'm not like you. I want to *enjoy* being young. I want to drink and stay up late. There's nothing wrong with it. You are over-worrying."

"There is an old saying." Charlotte's voice had gone very quiet. "First a man takes a drink, then the drink takes the man."

James thought of Cordelia's father and winced. However well intended, Charlotte was taking exactly the wrong tack with Matthew, mistaking his blasé attitude for indifference. He had resettled himself in a position of even more louche inactivity than before; Charlotte might take the gesture for scorn, but James knew that underneath Matthew's lassitude was fury—the same fury that drove him to brazen the situation out in front of James, as if to say: *See how ridiculous this all is, see how foolish they're being.*

"So would you rather I was more like Charles, then?" Matthew demanded. "He wants everyone to know how very important and capable he is. And yet Will and Tessa have had to rush off to Paris to smooth over his latest catastrophe. And if they are successful in preventing war from breaking out over the mess he made, he'll have to hurry back to his loveless alliance with Grace Blackthorn—"

"*Don't* try to change the subject, Matthew." Charlotte was clearly struggling to stay calm. "We weren't talking about Charles. We were talking about you—"

James could stand it no more; he cleared his throat and took a few steps into the room. Matthew made a show of sitting up in surprise. "Look who's here, Mother—*James* has come for a visit."

Charlotte gave James a strained smile. "Hello, darling."

"Mother and I were just discussing why your parents have had to hurry off to France."

"Don't let me interrupt." James made a face at Matthew in response to his glare; he felt a *parabatai*'s duties ended where arguments with one's mother began. "I thought I would say hello before I go down to the lab to see what Christopher is up to."

Matthew collapsed back onto the cushions. James could hear his voice, and Charlotte's, too, rising as he descended the stone spiral staircase to the cellar. It had been dubbed "the Dungeon" when Henry first took it over as a place to conduct his experiments many years earlier. James was struck, as always, by a vague smell of rotten eggs emanating from the collection of stoppered tubes, sample jars, and labeled boxes.

The lab was brightly lit with witchlight, but Henry's workbench was empty save for a neat stack of notes. In the fireplace, which had long ago stopped working, was propped a straw dummy covered in stains and tears: the victim of countless past experiments.

Christopher's corner was piled with its usual research in progress and piles of books with scrawls in the margins. An alabaster statue of Raziel, upon whose nose someone had placed a pair of spectacles, looked on benignly from the mantel as Thomas, seated on a stool beside Christopher, examined something in his hands.

As James drew closer, he saw that the object Thomas held was a nickel-plated handgun. Shadowhunters couldn't use firearms; weapons had to be runed to be any use against demons, but runes also prevented gunpowder from igniting. Christopher had been long convinced that there must be some way to fix this problem, and this particular gun had been in the lab for some time; the plating was covered in runes. Christopher had never been able to make it work.

"Hullo, James," Christopher said brightly. "You're just in time."

"What's the idea, Kit?" James asked. "Have you made a break-through?"

"Not quite—but I had an idea for some adjustments I could make to the revolver. After what happened to poor Basil Pounceby, I decided to set aside my message-sending project and turn my attentions back to the firearm. Think how useful it could be! If one were able to develop a runed gun that would work on demons and other creatures alike, they could be issued to everyone who goes on patrol. It could be an invaluable tool for defeating Knife Face—or whoever the killer turns out to be."

James couldn't help smiling at Christopher's enthusiasm. His cousin's violet eyes were shining, his hair was sticking up, and he was gesturing wildly as he spoke. Thomas was also smiling, though he looked a little skeptical.

"So I wanted help from you, James," Christopher went on. "Obviously I've never fired a gun, and neither has Thomas, but you have. We want to make sure we're doing it right. It *is* loaded," he added, rather as an afterthought.

James went over to Thomas. "It isn't hard," he said. "You push down the hammer, like this, and sight down along your arm. Aim and pull the trigger."

With an intense look of concentration, Thomas followed James's directions, the hammer clicking as he cocked the gun and aimed at the statue of Raziel. James hurriedly backed away as Thomas clamped down on the trigger.

There was a loud click. Christopher's face fell. Thomas gave the gun a shake, as though it were a cart whose wheels had gotten stuck in snow.

"Don't wave it about, Tom, even if it isn't working," James warned, and Thomas handed the revolver quickly to James. James examined it, taking care to keep the muzzle pointed at the wall, away from the others. The gun was heavier than he had expected, its river-gray barrel etched with the inscription LUKE 12:49.

"Where did you get that thing, anyway?" said Thomas.

"It's from America," Christopher said, looking discouraged by the failure of his experiment. "Henry acquired it years ago. It's a Colt Single Action Army revolver. Mundanes call it a 'Peacemaker.'"

James wrapped his hand around the grip, finding it fit his hand comfortably. Experimentally he pushed down the hammer with his thumb. He squinted down the barrel, lining up the dusty alabaster statue with the sight. "But runes prevent it from firing."

Christopher sighed. "They do. Only I thought I'd found a way around the problem. I tried different mixes for the gunpowder, different runes, I even said the protection spell over the gun—you know, 'Sanvi to the right of me, Semangelaf behind me—'"

"That's part of the protection spells they say over Shadowhunters when they're born," said James. "It's a gun, not a baby, Kit. And besides," he added, resting his finger on the trigger experimentally, "it doesn't—"

The gun bucked in James's hand. A deafening crack echoed in the small room, followed by a muffled explosion. In the stunned silence that followed, the three of them watched a small cloud of blue smoke drift away from the gun.

The statue of Raziel was now deprived of its left wing. Bits of alabaster skittered off the mantel onto the worktable below.

James looked down at the gun in his hands with wonderment and not a little apprehension.

"Mundanes call that a Peacemaker, you say?" Thomas asked indignantly. "Mundanes are even odder than I thought."

But Christopher gave a triumphant crow. "By the Angel, James, this is tremendous. Tremendous! You've made it work! Let me see."

James held the gun out to Christopher, grip first. "It's all yours." He listened for hurried footsteps above, but none came. Henry had mentioned that he was improving the soundproofing of the laboratory—or maybe it was just that the residents were so accustomed to occasional explosions that they no longer batted an eyelash.

Christopher cocked the hammer with more assurance than James would have expected and pointed the gun at the dummy in the fireplace. James and Thomas both hastily covered their ears, but when Christopher pulled the trigger, there was only the click of the hammer returning to its starting position, and the cylinder revolving. Christopher tried twice more, then shook his head in frustration.

"Maybe it was just a fluke that it fired that one time," he said, his disappointment evident.

"May I?" James took the gun back from Christopher. "I wonder . . ."

This time he aimed at the straw dummy in the fireplace, and this time he was ready for the gun's strong recoil. With another almighty *bang* it jumped in James's hand, and the dummy's chest burst, straw exploding in all directions. Thomas inhaled a stray bit and fell into a coughing fit. James set down the revolver carefully on its side and knelt in the fireplace, searching for the slug, which he found embedded in a neat hole in the mortar.

"Maybe only *you* can fire it," Christopher said, after thumping Thomas on the back until he could breathe again. "Because of your—your lineage. Interesting."

Thomas picked up the gun and gave it one last curious look before handing it back to James. "Perhaps James should keep it."

"As long as you're willing to come back over for some experiments with it later, Jamie," Christopher said. "We'll try to find a safer place to test it out."

James hefted the Colt in his hands, balancing its weight. He had heard other Shadowhunters talk about discovering the weapon that would become their favorite, the one they were never without, the one they reached for first in battle. James had always assumed his weapon was knives—he was good with them, but it was true there had never been a particular blade that had caught his fancy. That he might have just discovered his weapon of choice because of his heritage was not an altogether welcome thought.

"If it works on demons," Thomas said, as though he guessed what James was thinking, "it could change things. Change the way we fight. Make it safer for Shadowhunters. That's worth the risks."

"Yes—you're probably right." James carefully settled the revolver in his jacket. "Kit, I'll keep you informed of any—developments."

He could have stayed longer, he supposed, but he found he wanted to be back at Curzon Street when Cordelia returned from the Institute. She couldn't be training too much longer—it was nearly dusk. Christopher had packed up a few tinctures meant to promote sleep: sliding them into his pocket, James hurried upstairs, where he found Charlotte's study door closed. He could hear her voice, blended with Matthew's and now Henry's, rising and falling behind the door. It was too bad, he thought; he would have liked to tell Matthew about the gun, but Christopher and Thomas would have to catch him up.

As he set out for home, he thought of the inscription on the barrel of the gun—LUKE 12:49. He knew the Biblical verse; any Shadowhunter would.

I have come to bring fire on the earth, and how I wish it were already kindled.

9
THE SCARS REMAINING

But never either found another
To free the hollow heart from paining—
They stood aloof, the scars remaining,
Like cliffs which had been rent asunder;
A dreary sea now flows between;—
But neither heat, nor frost, nor thunder,
Shall wholly do away, I ween,
The marks of that which once hath been.
—Samuel Taylor Coleridge, "Christabel"

"Tell me, James," Elias said with a gleam in his eye, **"have you ever** heard of the fearsome demon Yanluo?"

Papa, of course he's heard of Yanluo, Cordelia wanted to say, but she held her tongue. From the moment they'd arrived at the door, it had been clear that her mother had put an enormous amount of effort into making the evening special. Their most beautiful china, from Paris, was on display, as was the damask table linen with delicate floral sprigs. Epergnes of expensive hothouse flowers—jasmine and heliotrope— decorated the table, and the house smelled of spices and rose water.

At first it was all a relief—Cordelia had been more worried about this dinner than she'd wanted to admit to herself. Lying to Will and Tessa about her marriage had been terrible, but for them, at least, this relationship had been a complete surprise. Lying to her own family was different. For Sona, and no doubt Elias, this outcome had been a dream. Not only had Cordelia gotten married, but she had married into a powerful and influential family (however Elias might have felt about the Herondales). She'd given them what they'd hoped for, but now that she'd taken the marriage oaths before the Enclave and the Angel, the lie of it seemed to loom much larger. Her parents knew her better than almost anyone: she had been half-certain that when she and James walked in, her parents would look at them and say, *We see. You obviously don't love each other and this is clearly some strange kind of marriage of convenience.*

Instead everyone had been as polite as possible. Sona had fussed over James, Alastair had gazed thoughtfully at the ceiling, and Elias had been his most charming self—expansive, generous, welcoming, and full of war stories.

James set down his forkful of *ghormeh sabzi* and nodded easily. "A very famous demon," he said. "I know of the evil he brought to the Shanghai Institute."

"Perhaps this is not an appropriate discussion for dinner," Sona said. Though she was lovely in a velvet tea gown trimmed with lace and sable, and a black *roosari*, she looked tired. She must have been crafting this meal since yesterday, ensuring the cook had the recipes and knew how to prepare everything from the *fesenjoon*, sweet with lamb and pomegranate paste, to the hot *kaleh pacheh*.

Ignoring Sona, Elias leaned over to James and raised his eyebrows. In a dramatically grim voice he said, "He's the demon that killed my brother Jonah and his wife, Wen Yu, but only after torturing their son, my nephew Jem, in front of them. Have you heard the story of how I came to kill Yanluo?"

James smiled; if there was a little strain in it, Cordelia was sure her father didn't notice. "Only that you did. And never firsthand. I would, of course, be eager to hear the story from you."

Cordelia met Alastair's eyes across the table. He raised one eyebrow as if to say, *Well, well.*

She only shrugged. She didn't know what had gotten into James either. Since it was just family at home, he had dressed casually— she had even teased him that his midnight-colored velvet jacket was something Matthew might wear—but the moment that they had crossed the threshold, his manners had been nothing short of exquisitely formal. He had complimented Sona on the beautiful flower arrangements and the deliciousness of the food, and even told Alastair that his hair looked nice. Now he had drawn out Elias by insisting on hearing his stories of past heroism.

"When I found out that Jem had been orphaned, I came to Shanghai straightaway, of course," Elias said. "The Shanghai Institute wanted revenge just as badly as I did, and they partnered me with the fiercest warrior they had: the legendary Ke Yiwen."

James murmured some sort of acknowledgment or agreement, but Elias didn't seem to need his input; by now he was off and running. "For two years Yiwen and I tracked the demon across the world. The passage to Yanluo's own realm was in Shanghai, so he never strayed too far for too long, but he eluded our grasp. Until one day . . ."

The story went on. Cordelia had heard it so many times she had ceased to really hear the words, but she grasped that her father was going over his most impressive feats of tracking, the terrible conditions he'd endured, and several dramatic hairbreadth near misses with lesser demons. The story grew a little more embellished each time it was told. Cordelia looked to Alastair, hoping to share a long-suffering look.

But Alastair looked more than long-suffering. His gaze was focused on their father with a barely contained loathing. Finally he gulped down his wine in a single swallow and interrupted Elias midsentence:

"Father, I've wondered: Are you still in touch with Ke Yiwen? Or is she too busy to write letters these days, given that she's the head of the Shanghai Institute?"

There was a moment of awful silence. Nothing Alastair had said was truly that bad, but it was impossible to miss the implication. Everyone at the table was now thinking about the difference in the current status of Yanluo's killers: one an Institute head and celebrated hero, one who had been imprisoned by the Clave for drunken incompetence and now hoped only to return to being a Shadowhunter in good standing at all.

James looked from Alastair to Elias. Not much showed on his face; in that moment, Cordelia was grateful for the Mask. Then he smiled, that smile that lit his face up, transformed it into something luminous. He inclined his head to Sona. "Truly," he said, "*to bayad kheili khoshhal bashi ke do ta ghahraman tooye khanevadat dari.*"

Truly, you must be happy to have two such heroes in your life.

Cordelia gaped. She'd had no idea James knew any Persian beyond a few words for food, "thank you," and "goodbye." Even Alastair was staring at him with a mixture of surprise and respect.

Sona clapped her hands together in delight. "Have you been learning Persian, James? How wonderful!"

"It was a wedding surprise for Cordelia," said James. He turned to Elias, still seeming perfectly at ease. "Cordelia tells me you taught her chess," he said, as if there were no tensions roiling beneath the surface of the dinner. "She is a fierce player. She has beaten me every time we've had a match."

Elias chuckled; the maid had come around to clear the plates, and he was on his fourth glass of wine. There was a red stain on his lapel. Alastair stared at him stonily, but he didn't seem to notice. "Well, chess is a Persian game, you know, according to the Book of Kings," he said. "Have you heard the story of how it originated?"

"Not at all," said James with a straight face. "Do tell."

He kicked Cordelia lightly under the table. It was fortunate they didn't play cards more, she thought; he had a perfect face for bluffing.

"*Mâmân,*" she said, rising from the table. "Let me help you with the *chai.*"

It was a bit unorthodox for a lady to have anything to do with the preparation of food, but Cordelia knew her mother: no matter how strict the instructions, she would never trust someone else to make tea for her family. It had to be steeped for hours, and spiced with the right blend of saffron, cardamom, cinnamon, and rose water. Water would then be added from the samovar; water from a kettle simply *would not do.* Sona insisted it made all the difference.

In the kitchen, Cordelia saw with a touch of homesickness that the desserts had already been laid out on a silver tray: sweet *sohan assali,* and chunks of fried *zoolbia bamieh* soaked in rose syrup. She came up behind her mother and gently laid an arm about Sona's shoulders, the silk sleeve of her lace-and-chiffon tea gown fluttering gently. "*Mâmân,*" she insisted. "You shouldn't be on your feet so much."

Sona ignored this and gave a look in the direction of the dining room. "James and your father seem to be getting along."

Cordelia made an impatient noise. "Father's rewriting what happened. Every time he tells that story it gets more elaborate and he gets more heroic."

Sona added a bit of water to the red-brown tea in the pot and eyed it critically. "We're all allowed to embroider stories a bit. It's harmless." She turned to Cordelia. "Layla," she added, her voice softening, "so much has changed so quickly. You and your brother must give him a chance."

"But don't you wonder where he was all those days? He was released from the Basilias and instead of coming home he just . . . wandered around?"

Sona sighed. "He's told me all about his travels. If you want to know about them, you could simply ask him yourself. Honestly, it saddens me to think how much he put himself through—but I believe the experience has changed him for the better. What he has survived has made him whole again."

Cordelia wished she could believe it. Whatever her mother saw in her father since his return, Cordelia was blind to it. He seemed the same as he had always been—and now that she knew that all that time he had been drunk, or hungover from being drunk, rather than chronically ill, the sympathy she'd felt for him seemed like a cruel trick he'd played. She didn't want to be like her mother—telling herself a story that made it all right, when it obviously wasn't. But she also didn't want to be like Alastair, angry all the time, unable to make peace with the reality of who their father was, butting his head against it over and over, though it would never budge.

Cordelia picked up the tray of desserts and carried it into the dining room. James was laughing. Alastair made eye contact with her, and she could decode the complexities of his look perfectly well: he thought he knew exactly what they had been discussing in the kitchen, and she was sure he was correct.

Fortunately, everyone managed to get through dessert with no further discord. Sona excused herself, saying she was tired, and seeing that her father was fading quickly himself, Cordelia announced that they too should be going, as the hour had grown late.

This left Alastair to see them out. He went with Cordelia into the vestibule as James, faultlessly polite as always, lingered to thank Elias for the evening.

"Well, *he* was in rare form tonight," Alastair said with disgust.

Cordelia had no need to ask who "he" was. "It's so different," she said as Alastair helped her on with her coat. "Spending time with him, knowing he's . . . he's not ill at all. Was it always like this for—"

She broke off as James appeared, pausing to retrieve his coat and gloves. He took one look at Cordelia and Alastair and said, "I'll just step outside. I need a breath of fresh air, and to check on Xanthos."

Cordelia knew perfectly well that it was freezing outside and that Xanthos was probably asleep, but she appreciated that James was leaving her a moment to talk to Alastair alone. After James slipped out, she reached up to pat her brother's cheek. "Alastair, *dâdâsh*," she said. "Are you all right? If you ever want to stay at Curzon Street—"

"With you and James?" Alastair raised an eyebrow, glancing out the window. Cordelia could see James standing by the snowy curb, stroking Xanthos's nose. "I was worried that he would never move on from Miss Blackthorn. But from all appearances, he seems not to be moping."

It was a relief to be able to talk about it out loud. "I don't know— when he saw her at Rosamund's party, he looked as if he were going to be ill."

"That doesn't signify. Whenever I see Charles, I feel like I'm going to be ill. But that doesn't mean I still . . . Contrary to what your beloved poets say, unrequited love doesn't last forever. And being treated badly by someone doesn't make you love them more."

"Alastair," she said softly. "I don't regret my marriage, but there is a part of me that feels terrible for leaving you alone just as Father came back. Is every night as awkward as this one?"

Alastair shook his head. "Never feel that way, Layla. One of the things that makes all this"—he gestured, as if to encompass the whole living situation at Cornwall Gardens—"livable for me is knowing that you aren't here, having to endure his moods and his demands and his very selective amnesia." He smiled. "And maybe it's selfish of me, but now that you know the truth, and I can speak of it to someone, it is an easier burden to bear than I would have imagined."

It was late when Lucie left Anna's party. She had spent a restless evening there, unable to lose herself in the champagne or the conversation. She kept looking toward the windows, watching the fat white flakes of snow come down and wondering how cold it had grown tonight in a roofless shed in Chiswick.

She knew that Jesse didn't care. Couldn't feel the cold. She worried, nonetheless.

Finally she had given up and headed home among cries for her to stay and join another round of games and chatter. Despite her vow to conquer the Enclave, Filomena had spent most of the night in animated conversation with a vampire who shared her admiration for the art nouveau movement sweeping through Europe. After Filomena promised she would find someone to see her safely home, Lucie had maneuvered her way through the room—someone had turned a table over, and people were using it as an impromptu dance floor—toward Matthew, meaning to ask him to take her home in his carriage.

He had smiled at her, then stumbled and nearly knocked over Percival, Anna's stuffed snake. He was obviously drunk, and Lucie preferred her own company to that of an inebriated Matthew, which hurt her heart and made her want to shake him and ask him why he couldn't treat himself better. Why he couldn't see himself the way her brother saw him. Why he was so determined to harm himself and harm James in the process.

As Lucie made her way down Percy Street, a few snowflakes chased each other lazily in the glow of the gaslights, the streets empty and quiet at this hour. London wrapped in snow was a hushed promise of a city, gas lamps strung like a chain of pearls across the sky. Lucie snuggled deeper into her astrakhan coat. At her waist clinked the daggers and seraph blades she'd brought with her tonight. One could never be too careful.

After walking a few blocks, she took out her gloves. She had to

Lucie Herondale

admit it was cold, despite the heat rune she'd put on before she left the party. It had been awfully warm inside Anna's apartment, and as the evening wore on, things had become ever more riotous as the crowd danced and drank and flirted, Anna perched atop the sound-board of the piano, watching them all with her *La Gioconda* smile. Thomas's sister Eugenia had danced with Matthew, tossing her long dark hair. At one point Lucie talked briefly to a wide-eyed mundane girl who proclaimed the party the wildest she'd ever attended, and asked Lucie in a rather astonished tone if everyone present were bohemians.

Lucie considered replying that they weren't bohemians, they were vampires, werewolves, and demon hunters, but she didn't want to shock the poor girl to death. "Yes," she'd said. "Bohemians."

"Goodness," the girl had exclaimed. Later Lucie saw her kissing Anna in a window seat and decided the bohemian lifestyle must have grown on her.

The snow began coming down harder as Lucie passed the silent, deserted bulk of the British Museum. It gleamed palely behind its railings, the stately columns of its entrance frosted all over with a thin layer of ice. A tickle started at the base of her spine. The feeling of being watched. Her breath puffed out in a cold white cloud as she spun around, her hand going to a dagger at her waist.

He was there, a dark shape against a background of white snow and ice-frosted buildings. The snow fell all around him but did not touch him—not his dark hair, or his perennial costume of white shirt and black trousers.

"You startled me!" she cried, her heart pounding.

Jesse smiled thinly. "Well, I am a ghost. I could have jumped out from behind the museum and shouted 'boo,' but I restrained myself."

She had begun to shiver. "I thought you didn't want to see me again."

"I never said that." It was as if he stood beneath a shield of glass, she thought, the snow drifting away from him as though he and the space he occupied were not really *there*. His eyes, though, were as keen and thoughtful as ever. "In fact, I was curious as to how Princess Lucinda and Lord Jethro were getting along."

Without looking at him, Lucie started off at a brisk walk. "Don't make fun of me."

"I wasn't," he said mildly, joining her as they made their way down High Holborn, picking through slush churned up by the last few home-bound carriages, and turned down Chancery Lane. There was no traffic at all here; the silent pavements sparkled with a white, fragile layer of snow. "I'd just like to see you for a bit."

Lucie rubbed her hands together. They were cold even through the gloves. "I can't imagine why. You made it very clear how you felt."

"Did I," he said in a low voice, and then, "For that, I need to apologize."

Lucie brightened up. "Oh, well, if there are going to be *apologies . . .*"

His green eyes flashed with amusement. "Surely you aren't out on patrol, dressed like that?"

Lucie looked down at the pale green chiffon peeking from under her coat. "I dressed this way for a party," she said lightly, "and I went to a party, and now—like a proper young lady—I am being escorted home from a party."

"Was it a proper party, then?"

"Certainly not! There's nothing wholly proper about any event hosted by Anna Lightwood. But that's what makes her parties so good."

"I've never been to a party," Jesse said. "I would have loved to have attended one of hers."

"You were at the ball when you first came to London," Lucie reminded him.

"True. But I couldn't dance, couldn't taste the food or the wine." He cocked his head to the side. "You're the writer," he said. "Describe the party to me."

"Describe it?" They had turned onto St. Bride's Lane. The neighbor-hood was smaller, cozier; the snow gave the cobbled streets a fairy-tale feel. Icicles hung from the corners of half-timbered houses, and through leaded glass windowpanes glowing fires could be seen. Lucie put her chin in the air. "I will take your challenge, Jesse Blackthorn. I shall describe tonight's party to you in such detail, you will feel as though you had been there."

She launched into a description, painting the scene as if she were writing in her novel. She embroidered on conversations, making them funnier than they had been; she described the taste of everything on offer from the flakiness of the pastries to the fizziness of the punch. She wove a picture of the outrageous polka-dotted cravat Matthew had paired with striped silk trousers and a magenta vest. She remembered that Jesse hadn't met Filomena, and she told him all about the young Italian girl and her vampiric admirer.

"She's a very good dancer," said Lucie. "She taught us a new waltz that she learned in Peru."

The gates of the Institute rose before them, its spire piercing the clouds overhead. Lucie paused at the gates, turning to Jesse. "Thank you for walking me home. However, I did not hear the apology I was promised. You should not have read my book without asking."

He leaned against the gatepost. Or at least, he seemed to: Lucie knew that he was insubstantial, and the gatepost solid. "No," he said. "I shouldn't have."

There was something about him, she thought; he was the opposite of Matthew, in his way. Matthew put a bright face on every situation, even if it was dreadful. While Jesse spoke directly, never deflecting.

"And you should not have said I thought of you as a joke, or of your situation that way," she said. "All I want is to help you. To repair this."

"To repair death?" he said softly. "Lucie. You *were* wrong in what you said—but only when you claimed you are not like Princess Lucinda. Not brave or resourceful or clever. You are a thousand times those things. You are better than any imagined heroine. You are *my* heroine."

Lucie felt herself blush. "Then why—"

"Did I get so angry? It must have seemed to you that I hated the book," he said, his voice low and rapid, as if he wished to get to the end of what he had to say before his nerve failed him. "Or hated your writing, or hated that character—Jethro—but it was nothing of the sort. If anything, I was jealous of the bastard. His one purpose is to say exactly what he feels." He looked up at the sky, the snow. "You have to understand that I always, *always* assumed that you could never feel anything for me. And that is why I thought that it was safe that I felt the way I did about you."

Lucie stood motionless. She couldn't have moved had a charging

Shax demon suddenly appeared. "What do you mean?" she whispered. "What do you mean, the way you felt?"

He pushed himself away from the wall. He was truly agitated now, she realized, so much so that when he gestured, the movement of his hands seemed to shimmer in the air. It was something she had seen before, when ghosts became desperately upset—not that she wanted to think of Jesse as an ordinary sort of ghost like Jessamine, or Old Mol. "It's almost a joke," he said, and the bitterness in his voice surprised her. "A ghost falling in love with a living girl and pining away in a dusty attic while she lives her life. But I could survive that, Lucie. It would just be a tragedy for me."

A ghost falling in love.

A small flame lit in Lucie's chest. An ember, the beginning of a blaze. "It's never a tragedy to love somebody."

"I think Romeo and Juliet would disagree with you on that." His voice shook. "And don't you see? If—if you loved me back, then that is not just a tragedy for one of us; it's a tragedy for both of us. For there can be no future in it."

"Jesse," she said. "Jesse, are you shivering?"

He looked up and around him with a sort of amazement. For a moment she saw the boy who'd saved her in Brocelind Forest when she was a child, the one she'd thought was some sort of changeling prince—pale-skinned and green-eyed. "I think," he said, in a hushed voice, "that at this moment, perhaps, I am able to feel the wind."

"See?" She caught hold of his hand; it was neither warm nor cold, but seemed to catch warmth from her own skin, his fingers curling over hers. "We have a future. I promise you we do—"

He stroked his free hand down the side of her cheek. "Command me, Lucie," he said roughly. "I am asking you: command me to dance with you. Show me this waltz from Peru."

Very slowly, her eyes never leaving his, Lucie unbuttoned her coat, slipping each circle of leather out of its buttonhole with gloved fingers. At last she stood before him, the coat hanging from her shoulders, the wind plastering the lacy scraps of her dress to her body. Jesse could not seem to look away; she could feel the gold locket at her throat rise and fall with her breath.

"Dance with me, Jesse Blackthorn," she said. "I command you."

He reached out, sliding his arms inside her coat, pulling her against him. She laid a palm against his shoulder; his free hand spanned the side of her waist. She fitted her body to his, and color swept into his face, flushing his cheeks. She did not question it. One should not, she felt instinctively, question miracles too closely.

The night was hushed, enchanted. They danced, with only the sound of the softly falling snow as music. It dusted Lucie's cheeks, her eyelashes. She couldn't stop looking at Jesse. He was so beautiful, so awfully, terribly beautiful, like a marble carving of an angel—but no carving had such dark, tumbling hair, such secretive eyes. He held her tight against him as they danced, and for the first time she felt his body close to hers, the shape of him, the strength in his arms, the lean hardness of his chest beneath his too-thin shirt.

Her skirt brushed a path in the snow, though when she looked down, she could see only her own footsteps, crisscrossing each other. There was no sign at all of where Jesse had walked. She tipped her head up and found him watching her, his gaze slipping from her eyes to her mouth. It was as if his fingertips brushed her lips, shaping them; his gaze clung, neither of them looking away—

The front door of the Institute slammed in the distance. As if the music had stopped, they stilled, both frozen, gazing toward the courtyard.

"Don't go," she whispered—but there were footsteps on the path coming toward them. Reaching out, Jesse plucked a gold comb from Lucie's hair, closing his hand around it. His eyes burned like stars against the night.

Lucie heard her uncle Gabriel's voice, calling out her name, and then the rattle of the gate. Turning away, Jesse vanished, melting into the darkness like snow.

James was uncharacteristically quiet when they returned to the house after the dinner party. Cordelia could not help but worry that after a night spent with her family, he was regretting marrying her, even if it was only for a year. Once they'd dispensed with their coats, she thought he might make a break for the stairs, so he could be alone with his thoughts about his bizarre in-laws, but instead he turned to her, his gold eyes unreadable.

"I'm not ready to go to sleep just yet," he said. "Would you like to join me in the study?"

Definitely. Anything was better than going back to her room alone and worrying she'd horrified James permanently.

The study was snug and cozy as always; Effie had built up the fire, and a plate of chocolate biscuits had been set out on the chess table. Cordelia curled up in a brocade chair beside the hearth, sticking her cold feet and hands out toward the fire like a little girl. James, more decorous as always, sank onto the sofa, looking thoughtful.

"Are you all right?" Cordelia asked, as the fire crackled into the silence between them. "I cannot imagine tonight was enjoyable for you."

James looked surprised. "For *me*? I'm not the one who suffers when there is tension in your family, Daisy. I was only there to make it easier for you. If I didn't help—"

"Oh, but you did. You absolutely charmed my mother. She would marry you herself if she could. And my father was delighted to have someone to tell the old stories to. And—I hadn't known you were learning Persian."

"I remember Lucie studying it to impress you," he said, with a sideways grin. "I thought it was the least I could do."

"Lucie only ever managed to memorize a few sentences," Cordelia laughed. "She's much better in English." She cocked her head to the side. "So you aren't looking so—so serious—because you had an awful evening?"

James gazed into the flames. They danced, moving gold inside his golden irises. "You told me before that Alastair kept your father's condition from you during your childhood. That you never knew about it."

"That's true."

"I suppose I never realized until tonight what a great effort that must have taken. It is not an easy thing to hide. And not an easy thing to confront someone about, if you fear they have—such an illness."

"I have felt guilty since Alastair told me," Cordelia said. "When I was young, I believed Alastair was jealous when he scowled to see me with my father, but I know now he only feared I would realize the truth, and be hurt."

"I can see how your father can be very charming when he is drinking," said James. "Like Matthew."

Cordelia looked at him in surprise. "Matthew isn't like my father. Matthew drinks to amuse himself and be amusing—my father drinks to sink deeper within himself. Matthew is not . . ." *Ill*, she wanted to say, but it seemed wrong to even bring the word that close to Matthew, to his situation. "Bitter," she said instead.

"I sometimes wonder," James said, "if we can ever quite understand other people." He ran a hand through his hair. "All we can do is try, I suppose."

"I am grateful to you," she said. "For trying tonight."

He smiled unexpectedly. Mischievously. "I know of a way you can repay me. One I would greatly appreciate."

She indicated he should continue.

"I want you to read to me from *The Beautiful Cordelia*."

"Oh, by the Angel, *no*. James, it's not a real book. Lucie just wrote it to amuse me."

"That's why I want to hear it," James said, with a disarming straightforwardness. "I want to know what she thinks makes you happy. Makes you laugh. I want to know more about you, Daisy."

It was impossible to say no to *that*. Cordelia went and fetched the book; by the time she returned, James had pulled a lap rug onto the sofa and was half under it. He was shoeless, his tie gone, his hair a soft halo of dark flames.

Cordelia sat down beside him and opened the bound book Lucie had given her for her wedding. "I'm not going to start at the beginning," she said. "It wouldn't make any difference, and that was when I was thirteen—so it's quite different now."

She began to read.

"The brave princess Lucinda raced through the marble halls of the palace. 'I must find Cordelia,' she gasped. 'I must save her.'

'I believe the prince holds her even now, captive in his throne room!' Sir Jethro exclaimed. 'But Princess Lucinda, even though you are the most beautiful and wisest lady that I have ever met, surely you cannot fight your way through a hundred of his stoutest palace guards!' The knight's green eyes flashed. His straight black hair was disarranged, and his white shirt was entirely undone.

'But I must!' Lucinda cried.

'Then I will fight at your side!'

Meanwhile, in the throne room, the beautiful Cordelia struggled against the terrible iron shackles chaining her to the floor.

'I really do not see why you don't want to marry me,' said Prince Augustus in a sulky manner. 'I would love you forever, and give you many jewels and a herd of stallions.'

'I want none of those things,' said the noble and beautiful Cordelia. 'I only wish you to release my true love, Lord Byron Mandrake, from durance vile.'

'Never!' said Prince Augustus. 'For he was an evil pirate. And before that, you were entangled with a highwayman, and before that, there was the band of smugglers. . . . Really, if you agreed to marry me, you would finally be making yourself respectable.'

'I do not want to be respectable!' cried Cordelia. 'I only care for true love!'"

Hardly daring to look, Cordelia glanced up at James—and realized he was laughing so hard he seemed to be having trouble breathing. "Many jewels," he gasped, "and a herd—a herd of stallions."

Cordelia stuck her tongue out at him.

"Do you *want* a herd of stallions?" he inquired, struggling to get his laughter under control.

"They would be terribly inconvenient in London," said Cordelia.

"Not as inconvenient as Lord Byron Mandrake," said James. "Is he fictional Cordelia's true love? Because I don't think I like him."

"Oh, not at all. Cordelia has many suitors. She meets them, they woo her, they kiss, and then they usually die a horrible death to make way for the next suitor."

"Jolly hard on them," said James sympathetically. "Why so much death?"

Cordelia set the book aside. "Probably because Lucie doesn't know what happens after the kissing bit."

"Quite a lot," said James absently, and suddenly the room seemed slightly too warm. James must have been thinking the same thing, because he kicked the rug off and turned his body so that he was facing her. Though the Mask had gone, she still couldn't quite read his expression. His gaze traveled over her, from her eyes to her lips, to her throat and down, like a hand tracing the curves and hollows of her body. "Daisy," he said. "Have *you* ever been in love?"

Cordelia sat up. "I have had—feelings for someone," she allowed, finally.

"Who?" he demanded, rather abruptly.

Cordelia smiled at him with all the unconcern she could muster. "If you want the answer," she said, "you'll have to win a chess game."

Her heart pounded. The air between them felt charged, like the air during a lightning storm. As though anything could happen.

Suddenly James winced and put his hand to his head, as though in pain.

Cordelia caught her breath. "Is something wrong?"

The strangest look passed over James's face—half surprise and half almost confusion, as though he were trying to remember something he'd forgotten.

"Nothing," he said slowly. "It's nothing, and you're tired. We'd better get to bed."

LONDON:
SHOE LANE

Morning came, spilling blood and flame across the sky like the fruits of a great massacre.

The killer chuckled a little at his fanciful thoughts. London in winter was surely worthy of poetry. The temperature had fallen, last night's snow giving way to a freezing mist that drifted through the icy gray streets. His strength had grown, leaving him feeling impervious to the elements, and he moved with a new confidence, daring to walk among the mundane businessmen on their way to work, rather than crossing the street to avoid them. He passed merchants and deliverymen and the occasional drunkard frozen in the lee of a building. None of them held any interest for him.

He was stronger—stronger by far than any of these mortals—but not yet strong enough. Not for what he intended to do.

The killer could afford to be choosier now, and he passed over several possibilities before spotting the dark-haired girl tottering home in a party dress, her long hair mussed, ice crystals sparkling among the strands.

Others saw her too. But he did not want what other men wanted from her. Even from a distance he could sense her strength.

The girl turned a corner onto High Holborn, a broad boulevard lined with law offices. He kept his distance, blending in with the clerks and shopkeepers hurrying past. When she turned down a narrow, quiet lane, he drew closer once again.

She didn't notice him. She didn't know that she was breathing her last breaths.

He was ready when she passed into the shadow of a church. He fell on her like a wolf.

To his surprise, she tried to fend him off. No, she did more than try—she fought ferociously, spinning and kicking and punching as he stabbed clumsily with his blade, the angle all wrong, barely nicking her. Droplets of blood fell to the snow-covered street, but it was not enough to kill.

He drew back his hand to slash wide, but she ducked under the blade and kicked at his shin, unbalancing him. She ran before he could react, heading for the dark mouth of an alley.

The killer, knife still in hand, plunged after his prey.

10

The Damned Earth

"Avaunt! to-night my heart is light. No dirge will I upraise,
"But waft the angel on her flight with a Pæan of old days!
"Let no bell toll!—lest her sweet soul, amid its hallowed mirth,
"Should catch the note, as it doth float up from the damnéd Earth.
"To friends above, from fiends below, the indignant ghost is riven—
"From Hell unto a high estate far up within the Heaven—
"From grief and groan, to a golden throne, beside the King of Heaven."
—Edgar Allan Poe, "Lenore"

"James!"

Someone was on top of him, holding him down. James thrashed and kicked, trying to shake them off. The claws of the dream were still in him: not a real memory, but a feeling, a feeling of hatred and darkness, a choking sense of horror—

"James, *please!*"

His eyes flew open.

The world spun around him. He was on his bed, tangled in a snarl of blankets. Most of his pillows were on the floor, and the window had been cracked open—the air in the room was cold. There were hands on his shoulders—Cordelia's hands. She had clearly climbed on top of him in an effort to control his thrashing. Her chemise was slipping off her shoulder, her red hair undone, spilling down her back like a river of fire.

"James?" she whispered.

He had dreamed something, something awful, but it was fading, gone like morning mist. This was the real world. His icy bedroom, the air so cold his breath puffed out in white clouds. The empty tincture bottle on his nightstand, the bitter taste of its dregs still on his tongue. Cordelia above him, her dark eyes wide. She was shivering.

"I'm all right." His voice was rough, husky. "Daisy . . ."

He sat up, drawing her into his lap, trying to pull the blankets up around them both. He meant to warm her up. He realized how foolish that was the moment she slid against him. He was freezing, but she was radiating heat: suddenly he was hot everywhere her skin touched his. She was all warm softness under her thin chemise. He had never seen a girl in this state of undress at any point in his life, and certainly never imagined what one would feel like in his arms.

She felt perfect.

He settled his hands at her waist. She was still, looking at him with surprise, but no nervousness. There was nothing shy about Daisy. She was impossibly soft and curved. She moved, settling her weight against him, and he could not help but remember the night she'd asked for help with her wedding dress. He'd tried not to stare, but he could still recall the shape of her body under the fabric. Now he could feel it: the indent of her waist, her hips just below his hands, flared like the body of a violin.

"You're so cold," she whispered, looping her arms around his neck. Her voice shook slightly. She settled more closely against him, her hand stroking the back of his neck. He was helpless to stop his hands; they smoothed up and down her back, on either side of her spine. Her breasts were round and firm, pressed against his chest. He could tell she was wearing nothing under the chemise. He could feel the arches and hollows of her, and every touch seemed to unravel another strand of the thin thread of control binding his good sense. Blood pooled, hot and low in his belly. The fabric of her nightgown bunched up in his hands. His fingers curved over the shape of her, brushing the silk of her bare thighs, sliding up—

Something echoed through the house.

It was the doorbell ringing. James quietly cursed himself for having a doorbell put in at all. He heard hurrying feet, and cursed himself for having hired domestic staff too. He and Cordelia would have been better off alone, on top of a mountain perhaps.

More footsteps, and voices now, coming from downstairs.

Cordelia was scrambling off him, off the bed, smoothing down her hair. Her cheeks were flaming red. The little globe necklace he'd given her bounced as she moved, sliding down under the neckline of her chemise. "James, I think we'd better—"

"Get dressed," he said mechanically. "Yes. Probably."

She hurried out of the room, not looking at him. He scrambled to his feet, furious with himself. He had lost control of himself, and quite possibly horrified Cordelia. Swearing viciously, he slammed the window closed so hard that a crack spidered across the glass.

Despite feeling like her whole body was blushing, Cordelia dressed hastily and raced downstairs, where she found Risa in the foyer, looking puzzled and worried. *"Oun marde ghad boland injast,"* Risa said, which translated roughly to "The very tall man is here."

Indeed, Thomas was hovering uncertainly on the doorstep. In the summer, Cordelia had thought him nearly blond, but she realized it had been sunlight, bleaching the strands of his hair. It was nut-brown now, rather straggly and damp with snow. He was breathless, seeming almost frozen, as if he could not think of what to say.

"Has something happened?" It was James, having just arrived downstairs. Cordelia looked at him out of the corner of her eye; thinking about the way she'd last seen him made her feel like feathers were tickling her from the inside. James, though, did not look flushed, disheveled, or undone at all: he was still buttoning his jacket but seemed otherwise tranquil. His golden eyes were fixed on Thomas.

"I was at Matthew's," Thomas said. He seemed too distracted to come inside, though his rapid breath was making white clouds in the cold air. Cordelia could see no carriage behind him. He must have walked here, or run. "At least, I went to see Matthew. But Henry said Matthew wasn't at home and he didn't know when he'd be coming back. He took Oscar with him, too. Henry seemed grumpy. I thought that was odd. Henry's hardly ever grumpy. It is odd, isn't it? I should have asked more, but I couldn't, not after I heard—"

"*Tom*," James said gently. "Slow down. What happened?"

"I was meant to meet Matthew this morning," said Thomas. "But when I got to the Consul's, only Henry was there. He didn't want to talk about Matthew, really, but he said Charlotte was called to the Institute—that someone else had died—" He rubbed at his eyes with the heels of his hands, almost violently.

"Someone was killed last night?" said Cordelia. "Another Shadowhunter on patrol?" She could not help but think of James's screaming—she had burst into the room because the sound was so awful, and he had been thrashing, crying out in his sleep.

What had he dreamed?

"Not on patrol," Thomas said. "Henry says they think it was someone coming back from Anna's party. A girl."

"Lucie was at Anna's party," Cordelia breathed. "Thomas—"

"It wasn't Lucie. It seems Uncle Gabriel saw her come home last night. This girl was out much later, close to dawn. The patrol who found her body just said it was a girl with dark hair. And—Eugenia—I didn't see her this morning. I know she was at the party last night, but I didn't think anything of it until Henry told me what happened," Thomas said quietly. "I should have gone straight home once he did, I know, but—after Barbara, I can't—I need you with me. I need you with me, James."

Thomas had lost one sister already that year, in the Mandikhor attacks. No wonder he looked so sick with terror. James went to put an arm around him as Cordelia turned to Risa.

"Please call the carriage," she said. "We must get to the Institute, as fast as possible."

There was already a crowd at the Institute when they arrived. The gates had been propped open, and Xanthos sped cheerfully below the arch, as if glad to be home.

A small crowd had gathered at the base of the front steps. Among the group, Cordelia recognized many of the older Shadowhunters—the Inquisitor and Charlotte, Cecily Lightwood—along with Lucie, Anna, and Matthew. (Cordelia was glad to see he'd turned up, though Oscar did not seem to be with him.) All of them looked shocked, their expressions grave.

As their driver pulled the carriage to a stop in the courtyard, the crowd parted and Cordelia saw a pale bundle lying at the foot of the steps. Thomas threw the carriage doors open and she realized: no, not a bundle. A body, covered in a white sheet. The sheet was stained red with dried blood. From one corner of the sheet, a hand protruded, as if reaching out for help.

At the edge of the sheet was a spill of dark hair.

Thomas leaped down to the ground. He looked frantic. James followed; as he stepped off the running board, Lucie bolted over. Anna, wearing a caped greatcoat and a grave expression, followed more slowly with Matthew. Cordelia found herself wondering where Christopher was, especially since he was currently residing at the Institute. Perhaps inside, with his father?

Lucie threw her arms around James. "I should have waited for her," she sobbed, her small body shaking. "It's my fault, Jamie."

James held his sister tightly. "Who was it?" he demanded. "Who's dead?"

"Please," Thomas said, looking sick. "Just tell me—"

"Filomena di Angelo," said Anna. "Stabbed to death, just as Basil Pounceby was. The Silent Brothers are on their way to bring her to the Ossuarium."

"I thought—" Thomas began, and broke off. Shock, relief, and guilt at that relief played across his face. Cordelia could not blame him—she too was glad it was not Thomas's sister. And yet Filomena had been so young, so lively—so excited to be on her travel year, so in love with art and culture.

"Were you worried about Eugenia?" Anna said, laying a hand on Thomas's shoulder. "Poor darling. No, Eugenia is still quite peacefully asleep on my sofa. She *may* have been sick in a plant pot last night, but she is perfectly well."

"My parents," Thomas began. "Do they know—?"

"My mother sent a runner to them with a message," said Matthew. "They ought to be on their way."

"When did Filomena leave the party?" Cordelia asked. "Did she depart with anyone?"

"She was at my flat until almost dawn," Anna said. "She left then—insisted on going home alone." She scowled. "I should have gone with her. *Someone* should have gone with her."

"So close to sunrise," James said thoughtfully. "So this must have happened sometime in the last few hours."

"Anna, this isn't your fault," Cordelia said. "You couldn't have known."

"I ought to have waited and made sure to take her home—" Lucie began.

James swung about with a stern look. "You shouldn't have walked home by yourself, Luce, not in the middle of the night. Promise me you won't again. It's too dangerous."

"But I—" Lucie clamped her mouth shut. After a moment she tried again: "None of us should be out alone, I suppose. Poor Filomena."

"Where's Christopher?" Thomas asked.

"Apparently Father set up a patrol to search the neighborhood for any evidence," said Anna. "Christopher volunteered. They're still out looking."

"Poor Kit, he was distraught," said Matthew. "Said he'd had quite a nice chat with Filomena at the Wentworths' party, about botany. I didn't even know you could *have* a nice chat about botany."

"I volunteered as well, but Uncle Gabriel said if anything happened to me he'd never hear the end of it from Mam," said Lucie, looking disgruntled.

A Silent Brother—Enoch, Cordelia thought—had emerged from the Institute. He knelt down, his parchment robes brushing the snow, and peeled back a corner of the sheet to examine the body. Cordelia looked away.

"Where was she killed?" she asked. "Near Anna's?"

"No," James said quietly. He had pulled off his gloves and was worrying them with his bare fingers. The day had warmed, the bright sunlight falling through the bare branches of the nearby trees making a delicate pattern of latticework across his face. "She was killed somewhere else. Close to here."

Anna looked at him in surprise. "Yes, on Shoe Lane," she said. "She almost made it all the way back to the Institute."

James was crushing his gloves in his hands. Lucie stared at her brother, a peculiarly blank look on her face, as if she didn't quite recognize him, or were looking past him at something else. But there was nothing else there.

"I'm starting to remember," James said.

Matthew laid a hand on James's shoulder. Cordelia could not help but wonder if she should have done that—surely she should be comforting James? But the thought of touching him in public frightened her. Not because it was inappropriate, but because of what it might reveal. Surely her emotions would be written on her face. "Jamie," Matthew said, in a low voice. "Did you have another dream?"

"I didn't remember it when I first woke up," James said, not meeting Cordelia's eyes. "But now—it's coming back in pieces." He dropped the gloves into the melting snow, stark black against the white. "There was a girl, she was singing—singing in Italian—Raziel, and there was blood—so much of it—"

"*James*," Anna said sharply, moving to block him from the view of those crowded around Filomena's body. She glanced around at their small group. "We need to get inside."

James nodded, white-faced. He was leaning quite hard on Matthew, who had an arm around him. "Yes. I'll take us through the Sanctuary."

"I'll catch you up," Lucie called as James led the others toward the nearly hidden entrance to the Sanctuary—the one chamber in the Institute where Downworlders could comfortably come and go, since it was without wards against them. It was often used as a meeting room, and in a pinch, a holding cell for troublemakers, since there was another set of doors inside that kept it secure from the rest of the Institute. Cordelia glanced back worriedly, but Lucie made a gesture that she hoped communicated *Don't fret. I'll be there in a moment.*

She bent down to pick up James's gloves, just to seem as if she was doing something; by the time she straightened, the others had disappeared through the Sanctuary door. She edged around the side of the Institute, just out of sight of the front steps. Gazing directly at an odd patch of shadow, between two bare trees, she said, "All right. You might as well show yourself again."

Slowly, the ghost began to coalesce out of shadows and air, darkening to an appearance of solidity. She had seen him in the courtyard first, just past James's shoulder—for a moment she had thought he was Jesse, and nearly panicked.

But Jesse could not appear during the day. Most ghosts took no notice of sunrise or sunset, though, and this one was no exception. He did appear to be a young man, but looked nothing like Jesse: he was sandy-haired and short, with a sharp, pointed face. He wore the clothing of the Regency era—breeches and boots and a wide cravat, like a portrait of Mr. Darcy. There was a desperate look about him as he drifted a little closer to her, twisting his insubstantial top hat between his hands. "Miss Herondale," he said, his voice a low whisper. "I have heard that you listen to the dead. That you can help us."

There was a rattling sound: more carriages, arriving in the courtyard. Lucie shook her head slowly. "I can see and hear the dead," she said. "But I do not know what I could do to help you. I don't think I've ever been very helpful in the past."

The ghost's eyes were entirely colorless. He blinked at her. "That is not what I've heard."

"Well," said Lucie, "I cannot help what you've heard." She started to move away. "I ought to go inside."

The ghost held up a transparent hand. "I can tell you that the ghost of the young lady whose body lies in the courtyard has already awakened," he said. "She is filled with the grief and terror of the newly dead."

Lucie sucked in a breath. Not all the dead became ghosts, of course. Only those who had unfinished business in the land of the living. "Filomena? She—she didn't pass on?"

"She screams, but she is alone," said the ghost. "She cries out, but none can hear."

"But I ought to be able to hear her," Lucie cried. She turned back toward the courtyard—spun in a circle, looking about wildly. "Where is she?"

"She barely knows," the ghost whispered. "But I know. And she remembers. She remembers who did this to her."

Lucie narrowed her eyes. "So take me to her, then."

"I will not. Not unless you do something for me."

Lucie put her hands on her hips. "Truly? Blackmail? You're a *blackmailing* ghost?"

"Nothing so untoward as that." The soft-spoken ghost lowered his voice even further, in a way that made the hair on the back of Lucie's neck rise. "I have heard that you can command the dead, Miss Herondale. That threescore of the Thames's drowned souls rose at your bidding."

"I should not have done it." Lucie felt a little sick. She could still remember that night, the ghosts rising from the river, wearing the uniforms of prisoners, one carrying Cordelia in his arms. "I could command you to leave me alone, you know."

"Then you will never know where the girl's ghost is," the ghost said. "And it is only a small thing I want from you. So very small." In his urgency he had grown more solid. Lucie could see that he wore a stylish fawn-colored jacket, and that the lapel of the jacket was pocked with charred black holes. Bullet holes. She was reminded suddenly of the ghost of Emmanuel Gast, a warlock who had appeared to her after his murder, covered in blood and viscera. This at least seemed to have been a cleaner death. "You would have my consent, and also my gratitude, if only you would command me to forget."

"Forget what?"

"The reason that I cannot rest," he said. "I murdered my brother. I spilled his blood in a duel. Command me to forget my last sight of his face." His voice rose. "Command me to forget what I have done."

Lucie had to remind herself: no one could hear the ghost but her. Still, she was shivering. The force of grief around him was almost palpable. "Don't you see? Even if you did forget, that wouldn't free you. You'd still be a ghost. And you would not even know why."

"It matters not," the ghost said, and his face had changed. Behind every ghost's face, it seemed to Lucie, there lay the mask of death, the shadow of the skull beneath the phantom skin. "It would be better. What I endure now is torment. I see his face, every waking moment I see his face, and I *can never sleep. . . .*"

"Enough!" There were tears on Lucie's face. "I will do it," she said. *It's all right*, she told herself. *If I can speak to Filomena's shade, perhaps she can tell me who murdered her. It will be worth it.* "I will do it. I will make you forget."

The ghost let out a long sigh—a sigh without breath; it sounded for all the world like wind through broken boughs. "Thank you."

"But first," she said, "tell me where Filomena is."

They found their way to the library. The world was swaying around James like the rolling deck of a ship. He staggered over to a long table and braced his hands on it; he was dimly aware of Matthew beside him, of Cordelia's soft voice as she spoke to Anna. He wanted to go over and put his head in Cordelia's lap. He imagined her stroking his hair, and pushed the image away: he already owed her an apology for earlier that morning.

Memories of his dream were pouring into his mind like water through a smashed dam. London streets—light glinting off a blade. Red blood, red as roses. The recollection of a song, sung in delicate Italian, verses turned into screams.

And that hatred again. That hate he could not fathom or explain.

"Math," he said, rigid with strain. "Tell—Anna. Explain to her."

Voices swirled around James, Anna's calm and measured, Matthew's urgent. Thomas and Cordelia chiming in. *I have to get hold of myself,* James thought.

"Daisy," he said. "Constantinople."

"Oh God, he's raving," said Thomas dismally. "Perhaps we ought to get Aunt Charlotte—"

"He's not," said Cordelia. "He's just having an awful time—Thomas, *do* move out of the way." James felt her cool hand on his shoulder. Heard her soft voice as she bent toward him. "James, just listen for a moment. Focus on my voice. Can you do that?"

He nodded, grinding his teeth. The hatred was like knives in his skull. He could see hands scrabbling at cobblestones, feel a sick sort of pleasure that was the worst bit of all.

"Once Constantinople was called Basileousa, the Queen of Cities,"

Cordelia said, in a voice so low he suspected only he could hear it. "The city had a golden gate, used only for the return of emperors. No one else could pass through it. Did you know the Byzantines created Greek fire? It could burn underwater. Mundane historians have lost the source of the fire, the method of its making, but some Shadowhunters believe it to have been heavenly fire itself. Imagine the light of angels, burning beneath the blue waters of the Stamboul port. . . ."

James closed his eyes. Against the back of his eyelids, he could see the city take shape—the minarets flung darkly against a blue sky, the silver river. Cordelia's voice, low and familiar, rose above the clamor of his nightmare. He followed it out of the darkness, like Theseus following the length of thread out of the Minotaur's labyrinth.

And it was not the first time. Her voice had lifted him out of fever, once, had been his light in shadows. . . .

A sharp pain spiked through his temples. He blinked his eyes open: he was firmly back in the present, his friends all looking at him worriedly. Cordelia had already moved away from him, leaving behind the lingering scent of jasmine. He could still feel where her fingers had rested against his shoulder.

"I'm all right," he said. He stood up straight; there were lines across his palms where the edge of the table had cut into his skin. His head ached abominably.

"You dreamed of Filomena's death?" said Anna, perching on the arm of a chair. "And this has nothing to do with your visions of the shadow realm?"

"I did dream of her death. Pounceby's, too. But they're not dreams of a different world," James said, drawing out his stele. An *iratze* would fix his headache, at least. "I dream of London. The details are real. The only death I didn't see was Amos Gladstone's, and I still had a nightmare that night, a sort of vision of blood."

"The Enclave is fairly certain that he was also murdered," said Thomas. "His throat was slashed roughly—they had assumed by a demon talon, but it could have been someone with a serrated blade."

"Perhaps the murderer was still working out his technique," said Matthew. "I suppose even killers have to practice."

"He certainly seemed to be taking more pleasure from killing

Filomena," said James. Having sketched a quick healing rune on his wrist, he put his stele back in his pocket. "It was sickening."

Lucie appeared in the doorway, giving them a start. She was very pale. "I'm sorry," she began. "I stayed behind—"

"Lucie!" Cordelia exclaimed, hurrying over to her friend. "Are you all right?"

Lucie rubbed at her eyes, the same gesture she'd once made as a tired little girl. "I saw a ghost," she said, without preamble.

"Doesn't that happen rather often?" said Matthew. Cordelia shot him a quelling look. "Sorry—I just didn't think it was too out of the ordinary."

"This one was," said Lucie. "He told me that—that Filomena's ghost is already risen, and where she might be found. He seemed to think she might know who killed her."

"Odd that I didn't see him," said James. He could usually see ghosts, though he had long harbored the suspicion that Lucie saw more of them. She would never admit it, though.

"Well, you were staggering, rather, and Matthew was holding you like a sack of oats," pointed out Anna. "So where is Filomena's ghost, Lucie?"

"Limehouse. An old factory," said Lucie. "I wrote down the address."

"I'm all for conversing with the dead and gathering clues," Thomas said, "but what if this is a trap?"

"It's true that when mysterious spectral figures appear in novels telling the hero to visit a certain place, it's always a trap," Lucie admitted. A little of the color was coming back into her cheeks. "But it could also be true. We can't afford not to go—Filomena might be able to point us directly at the murderer."

"Still a trap," said Matthew.

"A trap is a surprise attack," said James. "We won't be surprised, will we?" He winked at Lucie.

"Exactly," she said. "This ghost—and he didn't seem a bad sort, he was rather stylish, even—approached me alone. He has no reason to think that if I went to the place, I'd bring all my friends along."

"We should go," James said, his thoughts coming fast, almost too fast to track. "If we assume this ghostly advice is a trap, and ignore it, then we have no clues. If we assume it means something, and follow it up, we might discover something useful. Do you see what I mean?"

"You mean that we have a choice," said Anna. "Go to the Limehouse docks, and perhaps learn something, or do nothing, and certainly learn nothing."

"If there's really a chance we could speak to Filomena's ghost, we have to try." Cordelia spoke firmly.

"And if it's an ambush, there will be more than enough of us to handle it," Anna said. "We can't just roll up to the docks in the Consul's carriage, though. We'll have to glamour ourselves and keep a low profile."

"Delightful!" said Matthew. "We'll take the train. I love the train. The little tickets are so amusing."

As they made their way into the chilly, bustling interior of Fenchurch Street Station, Cordelia could not help but wonder quite what it was about the place that enchanted Matthew so. She'd taken plenty of trains in her life, with her family, so perhaps they'd lost their charm. This station seemed like many others: flower sellers, newsstands, telegraph offices, passengers rushing to and fro in the fog of steam from the engines, the smell of burning coal strong on the air. Dim light seeped through grimy panes in the arched ceiling high above, illuminating a large sign reading CHARRINGTON ALES. Below it hung the big station clock.

They were all in gear and heavily glamoured, save Matthew. He had thrown on a long coat to cover his Marks, but he insisted that they pay for their train tickets, regardless of the fact that James, Thomas, Anna, Cordelia, and Lucie were entirely invisible to the mundane eye. Luckily, the queue at the ticket office was a short one. Lucie rolled her eyes at him as he carefully fished out six threepenny bits from a pocket and handed them over. Their train was departing in just a few minutes, and as they followed Matthew to the platform, an engine heaved into place, disgorging smoke and steam. It was a small train, with just three carriages, and not many passengers in the middle of the day. They found themselves a conveniently empty third-class compartment and piled in.

They spread themselves over the brown plush seats—all except Anna, who remained standing. Matthew had slumped into a seat by the window. James eyed him; there was always love in the way he looked at

Matthew, but it was mixed now with worry. "Did you move out of your parents' house, Math?"

Matthew looked up, flushing slightly. "Leave it to you to guess, I suppose—or did someone tell you?"

"Your father rather hinted at it to Thomas," said James. "And I know you've wanted to for ages."

"Well, yes." Matthew sighed. "I've been eyeing this mansion flat in Marylebone for quite a few months. I'd even put a deposit on it some time ago, but had been rather waffling on it. Yesterday afternoon I decided it was time." He met James's gaze with his own. "Independence! Hot and cold running servants and my own teakettle! I'll have you all around to *pendre la crémaillère* when things are a bit more cheerful."

"You should have told us," said Thomas. "We would have helped you move your things. I'm exceptionally good at carrying large objects."

"And think of all those hairbrushes you would have had to relocate," Lucie said. "Haven't you got six or seven?"

Matthew glowered at her affectionately. "I try to be at least as stylish as our local ghosts—"

The whistle blew loudly, drowning out the rest of his sentence. The carriage doors slammed and the train chuffed away from the station in a cloud of black smoke.

Thomas was looking thoughtful. "I wonder why that ghost approached Lucie, rather than one of the older Shadowhunters of the Enclave? Most Nephilim can see ghosts if the ghosts wish to be seen."

Lucie shrugged. "Maybe because I was the last one into the Institute this morning."

"It could be," said James. "Or it could be that there are certainly many Enclave members who wouldn't be all that keen on receiving information from a ghost."

The compartment was stuffy and smelled of damp woolen over-coats. Outside the sun had vanished behind clouds. A drizzling rain hazed the outlines of rows of grimy little terraced houses backing directly onto the tracks, with the vague outlines of factory chimneys in the distance. The train stopped briefly at Shadwell. It was raining harder now and the long, wet platform with its dripping wooden canopy was completely deserted. As the train pulled away, live sparks from the coal shot past the window like fireflies, oddly beautiful in the mist.

"Shadowhunters are being killed," Anna said grimly. "We should be glad that anyone cares enough to pass along a clue, ghost or no. I believe the popular attitude among most of Downworld is that we can take care of our own problems, since we meddle in everyone else's."

Now the train was running alongside a looming row of tall black warehouses, the spaces between them briefly giving fog-blurred glimpses of an expanse of water on the right, crowded with the tall, ghostly masts of Thames barges, bringing in cargoes from the river.

"That's Regent's Canal Dock," said Matthew. "We're almost there."

Everyone got up as the train pulled into Limehouse station. A guard in a peaked cap and dripping overcoat eyed Matthew curiously as he held out his ticket for punching. The others slipped by invisibly and started down the wooden stairs behind him.

It was still raining as they emerged from the station under the railway bridge onto a narrow, cobbled street. In front of them, looming through the mist, was the dim bulk of a huge church with a tall square tower. They started for the address given by the ghost, following the churchyard wall along the street until they reached a quiet little lane crowded with small houses. At the end of the alley was a low wall, from beyond which came the faint sound of something large slicing through water: a barge on a canal.

"This is the Limehouse Cut," said Matthew. "It ought to be just up here."

It was a working day; the canal was busy with watermen shouting to each other, their voices echoing oddly across the water as they maneuvered heavily laden barges in both directions, barely visible through the fog, which seemed even thicker down here. The Shadowhunters slipped down the narrow towpath silently, passing the high walls of warehouses until Lucie came to a stop beside a doorway set into a high fence.

The corners of the door were coated heavily in spiderwebs; it had clearly not been used in years. A rusty padlock hung ineffectively from an even rustier hasp. Across the warped and rotten boards, peeling paint spelled out the ghosts of faded letters, unreadable except for the last row: ILMAKERS.

James raised an eyebrow. "Thomas?" he said.

Thomas turned sideways and slammed his shoulder into the door. It promptly collapsed. The Shadowhunters piled through and found themselves standing in a tiny yard filled with a tangle of weeds and rubble, looking at the back of a building. It might have been painted white, once. Now its bricks were green with mildew, its windows cracked and blind with dust. A set of rotting wooden steps led up to a gaping doorway into darkness.

"If I were writing a novel in which someone set up a headquarters for their criminal enterprises," Lucie said, "I would describe a place just like this."

"Wishing you had your notebook?" said Cordelia, checking to make sure Cortana was firmly strapped to her back. Her fingers brushed the new scabbard her father had given her, and she sighed inwardly. She was not sure she could quite love it, just as she was no longer quite sure how she felt about her father.

Lucie winked. "You know me too well."

The steps, surprisingly, held their weight as they climbed carefully and lightly up one by one. James led the way, laying a finger to his lips, and the other five followed through the doorway and down a low-ceilinged, pitch-black, spidery corridor. Webs brushed unpleasantly against Cordelia's face as they moved silently along, and she could hear the scrabbling of rats inside the walls.

Suddenly they were in a wide-open space, no doubt the main factory floor, with iron pillars all around it like a cloister in a cathedral. A peaked glass roof with iron ribs arched high above, and a gallery circled the room halfway up. Large metal hooks dangled from iron chains attached to gantries overhead. ILMAKERS, the sign outside had said. It must have been a sailmaker's factory, where swaths of canvas would have been hung up to dry. Now, the empty hooks spun lazily in the dusty air; beneath them, dimly lit by the roof-light, lay the ruins of an enormous, splintered loom.

Lucie looked around, her face tight. "She's here," she said.

James shot her a curious, sideways look. "Filomena? Where?"

Lucie didn't answer. She was already scrambling past a number of rusting iron machines whose purpose was unclear, picking her way over the cluttered floorboards. "Filomena?" she called. She kicked aside a chunk of rotting plaster. "Filomena!"

The others exchanged glances. Anna took out a witchlight rune-stone, sending up a flare of light; the others fell into step, following Lucie. She seemed to be making her way toward the center of the room, where debris lay in dark heaps. She made a strangled sound. "Come here!"

Cordelia leaped over a piece of broken floorboard, finding Lucie standing white-faced and ill-looking over a pile of what looked like discarded rags. The floor was stained with a dark sludge. "Luce?"

The others had arrived, bringing with them the comfort of witch-light. Anna prodded the rags with her boot, then knelt to look more closely, using the tip of her finger to lift a corner of the fabric. Her face tightened. "This is the shawl Filomena was wearing when she left my flat."

Thomas speared another dark piece of clothing with a dagger, holding it aloft. "And this is someone's cloak. Stained with blood—"

Lucie held her hand out. "Could I see the shawl—please?"

Anna handed it to her. The shawl was of a pale cashmere, torn and ragged now. James stood back as Lucie bunched the fabric up in her hand, her lips moving, though she was making no sound. Cordelia had thought she knew all Lucie's moods, but she had not seen her like this—so intent, so inward in her concentration.

Something glimmered in the air. Lucie looked up, and in her eyes Cordelia could see a reflection of the growing light, as if two lamps glowed within her pupils. "Filomena?" Lucie said. "Filomena, is that you?"

The shimmer resolved itself, like a sketch being filled in around the edges, taking form and shape. A long yellow dress, a blood-splattered white shoe on a slender foot. Long dark hair, catching the faint breeze, swaying like black sailcloth. The ghost of a girl, hovering above them, wrapped in the translucent ghost of a shawl.

Filomena di Angelo.

"*Mi sono persa. Ho tanto freddo,*" the ghost whispered, her voice desolate. *Oh, I am lost. And so cold.*

Cordelia glanced around at the others' puzzled faces; it seemed she was the only one who spoke Italian. "You are among friends, Filomena," she said gently.

"I drifted in shadow," said the ghost-girl, in English. "Now you have called my name. Why?"

"To secure justice," said Lucie. "You should not have died. Who did this to you?"

Filomena gazed down at them. Cordelia felt the hairs along the back of her neck rise. She had never thought closely about how eerie it must be for Lucie, for James, to be able to see the dead. They were not simply insubstantial people. They were very alien indeed. Filomena's eyes, which had been so dark, were entirely white now— no iris at all, only two single black pinpoints of pupils. "He came out of the shadows. There was a blade in his hand. I fought him. I cut him. He bled. Red blood, like a man. But his eyes . . ." Filomena's mouth twisted, elongating strangely. "They were filled with hate. Such hate."

Cordelia glanced at James. *I felt such hate. It did not seem like a human hate.*

"His blood is here," Filomena whispered. Her gaze had fallen on Thomas. "I spilled it, but not enough. I was not strong enough. He took from me. My strength, my life." Dark hair drifted across Filomena's face. "I could not withstand him."

"It's not your fault, Filomena," Cordelia said. "You fought bravely. But tell us who he was. Was he a Shadowhunter?"

Filomena's head whipped toward her. Her gaze fixed on Cordelia, her eyes changing shape, widening into impossible circles. *"Per quale motivo sono stata abbandonata, lasciata sola a farmi massacrare?"* she whispered. *Why did you leave me alone to be slaughtered?*

Filomena's voice rose to an eerie singsong, the musical Italian words skipping over each other in her haste to say them: *"Cordelia, tu sei una grande eroina. Persino nel regno dei morti si parla di te. Sei colei che brandisce la spada Cortana, in grado di uccidere qualunque cosa. Hai versato il sangue di un Principe dell'Inferno. Avresti potuto salvarmi."*

Stricken, Cordelia could only stammer, "Filomena—I'm so sorry, Filomena—"

But Filomena had begun to twist and jerk, as if a strong wind were blowing through her. A network of lines appeared on her face, splintering with lightning speed into a web of cracks throughout her whole body. She moaned, a sound of terrible pain. "*Lasciami andare* . . . let me go. . . . There, I have told you. . . . I cannot bear it any longer. . . ."

"Go, if you wish it." Lucie spread her hands out. "Filomena, I will not hold you here."

The Italian girl went still. For a moment, she looked as she had in life—her face full of hope and thought, the tension of her body gone. Then she shuddered and crumbled apart like dust, vanishing into nothing among the particles in the air.

"By the Angel," said Anna, gazing at Lucie. "Is it always so harrowing, speaking with ghosts?"

Lucie was silent; it was James who replied. "No," he said. "But ghosts remain on Earth to fulfill unfinished business. I think Filomena's was telling us what she knew. Once she'd done that, she was desperate to rest."

"I'm not sure she knew that much, poor girl," Matthew said.

"What did she say to you, Cordelia?" Thomas asked. "That was a great deal of Italian."

Before Cordelia could respond, a loud noise echoed from deeper within the factory. The small group of Shadowhunters spun around. Cordelia caught her breath—the dangling chains were whipping back and forth overhead, the hooks suspended from them swinging wildly.

"We're not alone," Anna hissed suddenly, angling her witchlight toward the gallery above. The ruby necklace at her throat was pulsing with light like a second heart.

Dust and grayness, the humped shapes of broken machines; then Cordelia spotted a shadow moving along the underside of the gallery railing, scuttling on what seemed like countless thick grayish limbs.

Cordelia whipped Cortana from its sheath. All around her, the others were arming themselves: Anna with her whip, Thomas his Argentinian *bolas*, James with a throwing knife, Matthew with a seraph blade, Lucie her axe.

Spider, Cordelia thought, backing up with Cortana held out before her. The demon was indeed arachnoid: its row of six eyes gleamed as it leaped to a dangling iron hook and swung out into the open space, chittering wildly. Its front four legs ended in claws with long, curved talons. The additional legs protruding from the back each ended in a hook. Mandibles jutted from either side of its fanged mouth.

The demon sprang from the hook.

"*Anna!*" Cordelia screamed.

Anna ducked just in time. The demon flew past her, landing atop the broken loom. Anna came out of her crouch into a full spin, sending her whip whistling toward the demon. It reared up to avoid being hit, its back four legs clinging to the loom as the whip slashed through the air.

"Ourobas demon!" James called. He flung his knife, but the Ourobas had already scuttled down from the loom and under a piece of broken machinery. The knife buried itself in the opposite wall.

"You know it personally?" Matthew had his blade at the ready. Lucie was beside him, her axe out, clearly waiting for an opportunity to engage the creature at close quarters.

James leaped atop a nearby pile of rusted metal, flicking his gaze over the factory floor. "Never had the pleasure, but they're meant to be fast and agile. Not too clever, though."

"Sounds like some people we've met," said Anna.

James yelled a warning. Lucie lashed out with her axe as the demon hurtled past her, barreling straight for Thomas. He was ready with his *bolas*: the flexible leather thong shot out and doubled back, emitting a deafening crack as it encircled one of the demon's legs and pulled tight. The leg was wrenched off: with a spray of ichor it fell to the ground, where it twitched like a dying insect.

The demon howled and leaped for a dangling hook, catching it and swinging away fast. James swore, but there was no point chasing it; it had already pushed off one of the gantries and was flying, ichor dripping from its injured leg, directly at Cordelia.

She raised Cortana, the arc of the blade golden and beautiful in the ugly factory light—

A sudden, blinding pain shocked her palms. With a gasp, she dropped the sword. The demon was nearly on her: she could see its ugly black mouth, its glittering, nested eyes. She heard Lucie scream, and her training took over: Cordelia flung herself to the ground and rolled, the Ourobas's claws narrowly missing her.

The Ourobas yowled, dropping to the debris-strewn floor. Lucie's throwing axe had buried itself deep in the demon's side, but it didn't even slow down. It sprang toward Cordelia. She could smell the stink of ichor as she scrambled backward, fumbling at her belt for a seraph blade—

A blast ricocheted through the room, echoing off the walls. Something punched through the Ourobas, leaving a smoking wound behind. Jittering, twitching, the Ourobas gave an unearthly shriek and vanished.

Lucie's axe fell to the floor, where it stuck, blade-down.

Cordelia scrambled to her feet. She could see the others all turning to stare at a spot just behind her. There was smoke in the air, and the unmistakable smell of cordite.

Gunpowder.

Cordelia turned slowly. Behind her was James, his arm extended, a revolver gleaming in his right hand. A wisp of smoke rose from the barrel. His gaze locked with Cordelia's, and he slowly lowered the gun to his side. There was a look in his eyes she could not read.

"James," said Anna, brushing dirt from the sleeves of her gear jacket. "Explain yourself."

"Christopher made it," Matthew said, breaking the shocked silence. "He wanted to make a runed gun that could fire. But only James can shoot it."

"Are you sure?" Anna said. She approached James, holding out her hand. "Let me try."

James handed the gun over. Anna pointed it at a window and pulled the trigger; everyone winced, but nothing happened. She handed it back to James with a curious look.

"Well," she said. "That *is* interesting."

James looked at Lucie. "It might work for you, as well," he said. "I'm not the only one—you know."

But Lucie held her hands up, shaking her head. "No. I don't want to try, James."

"But you ought, Luce," said Matthew. "What if Christopher could make a second one? Think what we could do against demons with two of them. Two of *you.*"

"Oh, all right," Lucie said crossly, and went toward James, taking the gun from him. As he started to show Lucie how to use it, Cordelia took the opportunity to move away from the others. There was her sword—Cortana, gleaming like lamplight among the rubble and dust. Cordelia bent to retrieve it, touching the hilt tentatively, half expecting it to burn her again.

Nothing happened. With shaking hands, she sheathed the sword. She could not help but remember the moment at the Wentworths' when she had reached for Cortana. It had stung her palm. She had not thought about it then, but the memory was vivid now.

She glanced down at her palm. There was a red mark across it, almost in the shape of an L, where the crosspiece had burned her. Had *rejected* her.

But Cortana is my sword, whispered a small voice in the back of her head. *It chose me.*

Could a sword of Wayland the Smith change its mind?

With a shudder, Cordelia returned to the others: they were crowded around Lucie, who was shaking her head and handing the revolver back to James.

"Nothing," Lucie said. "It doesn't appear to be a talent we share, James. Like seeing the shadow realm." She glanced around the factory. "Speaking of which, this place gives me the creeps. I'd rather be elsewhere, gun or not."

No one disagreed. As they headed back out of the factory, into the grim drizzle, Cordelia could not help but hear, over and over, the last words Filomena had spoken to her. She thought she would hear them for the rest of her life.

Cordelia, you are a great heroine. Even in the realm of the dead they speak of you. You are the bearer of the blade Cortana, which can slay anything. You have spilled the blood of a Prince of Hell.

You could have saved me.

GRACE:
1897

Some time after Jesse's death, Tatiana told Grace that she had a surprise for her, and that she would take her to Brocelind Forest to receive it. But, she added, Grace must be blindfolded for the whole trip, as she was not permitted to know where in the forest she was going, or who she was meeting there.

For some reason the excursion had to happen in the dead of night, and Grace was sorry to have to miss her appointment with Jesse that evening. He always managed to get away from Tatiana—who liked to weep over his ghost when the mood took her—long enough to spend some time reading aloud to Grace. They were halfway through Mr. Stevenson's *The Strange Case of Dr. Jekyll and Mr. Hyde*. Grace found it deliciously frightening in a way that had nothing to do with the terrors of her everyday life.

The trip into the forest in the pitch dark was eerie. Grace, blindly following her mother, tripped over roots and lost her balance stepping into unexpected divots, sending unpleasant jolts up her legs. Tatiana did not hurry her, but nor did she break her stride. And when they did stop, she did not remove the blindfold, but let her daughter stand in confused silence as minutes passed.

Grace wasn't sure if she would be in trouble if she spoke, so she kept her silence and quietly counted to herself. When she got to about two hundred, a voice spoke out of the darkness, though there had been no sound to indicate someone approaching.

"Yes," the voice said consideringly—a man's, with a dark, sweet timbre. "She's just as beautiful as you said."

There was another silence, and then her mother said, "Well, go on, then."

"Little one," said the voice. Grace couldn't tell where the man was standing, how close or how far, ahead of her or to her side. His voice seemed to be everywhere at once. "I've come to give you a great gift. The gift your mother asked for you. Power over the minds of men. Power to cloud their thoughts. Power to influence their opinions. Power to make them feel what you wish them to feel."

Hands were suddenly at her temples, only they were not human hands, they were burning-hot pokers. Grace started in pain and alarm. "What—"

The world turned white, and then pure black, and Grace awoke with a shriek, disoriented, in her own bed, as if from a dream of falling. Light shone through the dingy lace curtains, casting yellow stripes on the coverlet, and she was even more disoriented until she realized that she must have slept the whole night and it was now the next day.

Shakily, she emerged from bed and found her slippers. There was no way to call for her mother; their bedrooms were too far apart and the walls too thick for her mother to hear such a call. So she padded through the stone halls of the manor in her dressing gown, feeling the wet draft chill her ankles and wishing Jesse were there to talk to. But of course he wouldn't appear until the sun set again.

"You seem to have come through all right," her mother said, when Grace found her in the old office, studying a parchment with a magnifying lens. She looked at Grace appraisingly. "None the worse for your new gift."

Grace wouldn't dare argue otherwise; she only said, "What is the gift, Mama?"

"You have been given power over men," Tatiana said. "You have the power to make them do whatever you ask, only to please you. To fall in love with you, if that is your desire."

Grace had never given much thought to love—not that kind of love, anyway. She understood that grown-ups fell in love, and even people as young as Jesse had. (But Jesse had never been in love, and now he was dead, and never would be.) "But if I can get them to do what I want regardless," Grace said, "why would I require them to love me?"

"I forget how little you know," her mother said thoughtfully. "I have kept you here to protect you, and it is good that you've encountered so little of the wickedness that pervades the world outside this house." She sighed. "My child, as a woman, you will be at a disadvantage in this cruel world. If you marry, your husband will own everything and you nothing. Your very name will go away, in favor of his. See how my brothers flourish, where we crouch in penury. See how the word of Will Herondale is taken as more credible than the word of Tatiana Blackthorn."

That is not an answer. "But who was the man? The one who bestowed the gift?"

"The point is," Tatiana said, "we must take all power that is available to us, for we are so far below others. We must take it just to have a chance to survive at all."

"The power to . . . make men do as I wish," Grace said, uncertain. "And to make them love me?"

Tatiana smiled like the blade of a knife. "You will see, Grace. Love leads to pain, but if you are careful with the way you wield it . . . you can use it to wound, as well."

The very next morning Grace awoke to find that her mother had packed her a trunk in the night, and that they were leaving that afternoon for Paris. She didn't want to go, for Jesse couldn't accompany them. It was too risky, Tatiana said, to attempt to move his body, and previous experiments had indicated he could not travel far from it. Grace was horrified that she wouldn't have a chance to say goodbye or explain where they were going, so Tatiana allowed her to leave him a note. Grace wrote it in a shaky hand, with her mother watching, and left it on her bedside table for Jesse to find. And then she was whisked away to Paris.

In that glittering city, Grace was dressed in fine gowns and brought to mundane balls. She was swept from ballroom to ballroom, introduced to bejeweled strangers who complimented her roundly. "What a beautiful child!" they would exclaim. "How enchanting she is—like a princess from a fairy tale."

The change in her life staggered her. In a short time, she went from speaking to no one but her mother and her spectral brother in a dark, silent house, to chatting with sons of Europe's noble families. Grace learned that it was best to say little and appear to be transported to ecstasy by whatever it was these stuffy adults and boring boys had to say. In any event, her mother had made it clear that they were here for practice. And so Grace practiced.

When she tried her power on grown men, they thought she was a delightful curiosity, like a beautiful vase or a rare flower. They wanted to give her gifts—toys, dolls, jewelry, and even ponies. Grace found using her power on boys her own age more annoying, and yet Tatiana insisted she do so. The problem was not that the boys didn't like her— it was that they liked her too much. They invariably hoped to kiss her or propose marriage—preposterous, when they were only children and marriage wouldn't even be possible for years at least. They seemed desperate to do whatever they could to make her love them back. In an effort to steer them away from kisses, Grace asked for gifts, and she reliably received them.

The youngest son of a German duke gave her the necklace, a family heirloom, off his own neck; the third younger brother of the Austro-Hungarian emperor sent her home one night in a carriage and four horses that were hers to keep.

Despite the attention, Grace felt staggeringly alone without Jesse. She began to feel the poison of loneliness cutting into her, as it had hollowed out her mother. These boys would do anything for her, but none of them knew who she truly was. Only Jesse knew that. Grace went to bed every night feeling desperately lonesome, without Jesse to sit with her until she fell asleep.

And so her requests grew stranger. She asked the nephew of a Czech viscount for one of the two horses attached to his carriage, and he gallantly untethered it for her before awkwardly riding off with only his left horse. She took to eccentric dietary habits that changed at every event: a tall glass of cold milk for her meal, or fifty of one kind of canape. And this way she learned more than her own power. She learned how power worked within the halls of the upper classes. It was not enough to be able to cloud men's minds—she had to understand which of those men had the power to produce what she desired.

For once, Grace had a way of earning her mother's approval, however unethical the method. During their time in Paris, Tatiana was often in great spirits, finally pleased with Grace. She would smile at Grace in the carriage as they returned home from a particularly successful night. "You are your mother's blade," she would say, "cutting these arrogant boys down to size."

And Grace would smile back, agreeing. "I am my mother's blade indeed."

11

CROWNS AND POUNDS
AND GUINEAS

When I was one-and-twenty
I heard a wise man say,
"Give crowns and pounds and guineas
But not your heart away;
Give pearls away and rubies
But keep your fancy free."
But I was one-and-twenty,
No use to talk to me.
—A. E. Housman

Cordelia rose the next day to find that it had snowed during the
night, wiping the world clean. The streets of London sparkled, not yet
turned to churning mud by carriage wheels. Roofs and chimneys were
wreathed in white, and snow sifted gently down from the boughs of
the bare trees along Curzon Street.

She shivered her way out of bed and into her dressing gown.
Cortana hung by its gilded hooks on the wall of her room, the scabbard gleaming, the hilt like a wand of gold. She slipped past it on her
way into the bathroom, trying to concentrate on how pleasant it was
to be able to wash her face in hot water instead of needing to break
through a layer of ice in the washstand jug on her night table—and

not on the fact that her sword seemed to be staring at her, posing a question.

After they'd left the sailcloth factory the previous day, it had been decided that there was no way around it: the adults would need to be told about the factory, the bloody cloak. Concealing the information would only interfere with the investigation into the murders. Cordelia had pled a headache, hoping to simply return home and not bother the others, but desperate for some time alone to think about Cortana. It had worked only somewhat. James had insisted on returning with her to Curzon Street, where he had gone straight to Risa for headache remedies. Risa had fussed over Cordelia half the evening until she hid under the covers of her bed and pretended to be asleep.

Now, having pinned her hair into a twist, she slipped a burgundy wool dress over her chemise and petticoats and took Cortana down from the wall. Sliding it from its scabbard, she gazed at the weapon. It bore a pattern of leaves and runes on the hilt—Cortana was unusual in having no runes upon its blade, only words: *I am Cortana, of the same steel and temper as Joyeuse and Durendal.*

She lifted the blade, half expecting another shot of pain through her arm. She spun, slicing at the air—spun again, a double feint, step back, blade raised.

There was no pain this time. But there was an odd sensation, a feeling of wrongness. She was used to Cortana fitting perfectly in her hand, as if shaped to be hers. She had always felt a whispered communion with the sword, especially when heading into a fight, as if they were telling each other that they would win together.

She felt only silence now. Dispirited, she hung the sword back on the wall. "Ugh," she muttered to herself, lacing up her low boots. "It's a sword, not a pet hedgehog. Have sense."

After making her way downstairs, she found the dining room empty. She went out into the hall, where she saw Risa carrying a tray with a silver coffee service on it and looking extremely put-upon.

"All your friends are in the drawing room, and the circus boy spent the night sleeping on the piano bench," she said, in Persian. "Really, Layla, this is most improper."

Cordelia hurried along the hall to find the drawing room door flung open. Inside, a fire was roaring in the grate. Lucie sat in a velvet armchair, and sprawled on the rug were the Merry Thieves—James with his long legs stretched in front of him, Thomas spooning porridge from a bowl, Christopher munching blissfully on a lemon tart, and Matthew sunk into a massive pile of cushions.

James looked up as she came in, his golden eyes sleepy. "Daisy," he said, waving an empty coffee cup in her direction. "Please don't blame me—these young roustabouts appeared at an unseemly hour and refused to leave without infesting our house."

Cordelia felt a flush of pleasure. *Our house.* Risa had come in after her, and the boys—overjoyed to see coffee—burst into a rousing rendition of "For She's a Jolly Good Fellow." Matthew leaped up from the cushions to cajole Risa to dance, but she simply smacked him smartly on the wrist with a spoon and withdrew from the room, dignity intact.

"In case you are curious," James said, as the other boys fought over the coffeepot, "Christopher is utterly furious to have been left out of the goings-on yesterday and has decided to have revenge upon us with a large pile of books."

"If he wishes to revenge himself with books, he has picked the wrong audience," said Cordelia, taking a seat on an ottoman beside Lucie. "Where's Anna, by the by?"

"On patrol," said Lucie. "We elected her to tell Aunt Charlotte exactly what happened at the factory yesterday—and Aunt and Uncle, too, since they have charge of the Institute while Mama and Papa are in Paris."

"*Exactly* what happened?" Cordelia raised an eyebrow. "Every bit of it?"

Lucie smiled primly. "Quite. She told them she was wandering in Limehouse yesterday, when her necklace alerted her to demons nearby. She followed its warning to the abandoned sailcloth factory. Upon entering, she was accosted by an Ourobas demon, which she destroyed. Further investigation revealed Filomena's shawl, and the bloody cloak."

"Quite a coincidence," said Cordelia, accepting a cup of coffee from James. He had put milk into it, no sugar, as she liked. She smiled at him, a little surprised.

"Chance *is* a fine thing," said Lucie, her eyes sparkling.

"I assume she didn't say anything about the—about Filomena's ghost? Either of the ghosts, in fact?"

"It would have strained credibility, I think, to try to explain that Anna had happened on the demon, the cloak, *and* Filomena's ghost," said Thomas.

"What about the factory?" said Cordelia. "Has the Enclave searched it?"

"Yes—there was a meeting last night, and then a group went over to Limehouse," said Thomas.

"Father went with them," Christopher added, taking off his spectacles and cleaning them on his shirt. "They turned the place upside down, but they didn't find anything but an abandoned Ourobas nest. They'll keep an eye on it, but . . ."

"No one really thinks the killer's likely to return," James said. "Why he dumped the cloak there, we don't know—presumably he didn't want to be caught wandering about London in bloody clothes."

"They've tried Tracking the killer with the cloak, but no luck, even with the blood on it," Thomas said. "They'll probably hand it over to the Brothers for further investigation."

"I can't help wondering, ought we to tell the Enclave about the other ghost? The one who guided us to the factory?" asked Lucie. She was twisting her skirt around one hand anxiously.

"No," James said firmly. "Ghosts talk to each other, don't they? There's no reason to think that your Regency gentleman had anything to do with the murders. And if the Enclave finds out that ghosts are appealing to you, Luce . . ." He sighed, leaning his back against the frame of the ottoman. His hair was even untidier than usual, his eyes a dark, somber gold. "I don't like the idea. They'll start poking and prodding at you, seeing if you can get other ghosts to approach you, seeing if they can use you to get clues. And not all the dead are friendly."

Lucie looked horrified. "You think they'd do that?"

"Bridgestock would certainly want to," said Matthew. "James is right."

"Then let's think about something else instead," said Cordelia. "What of the killer's motive? Filomena was barely known by anyone, and why would anyone who wanted Pounceby or Gladstone dead have something against her as well?"

"Your brother, Alastair, said something last night, at the meeting," said Thomas reluctantly. "I gather he reads mundane newspapers. Among mundanes, there are mad people who kill just to kill. Perhaps there *is* no motive."

"When there is no motive or personal connection, only indiscriminate hate, it may be nearly impossible to find a murderer," said Matthew.

"But the killer *isn't* being indiscriminate," Lucie said. "He killed three Shadowhunters. We're a specific group. Mundanes don't know about us, so it can't be one of them killing randomly. Though I suppose . . . I suppose it could be someone with the Sight killing within Downworld."

"If that were the case, Downworlders would turn up dead as well," said James. "As for Shadowhunters, we kill for our livelihood. They put weapons in our hands when we are children and tell us, 'Kill monsters.' Such violence might make anyone mad."

"What about a possessed Shadowhunter?" said Lucie. "Under a warlock's control or—"

"We cannot be possessed, Lucie," said Christopher. "You know that. We have the protection spells we are given at birth."

"If Filomena returned as a ghost to tell us what she knew about her murder," said Thomas, "isn't it a bit odd she didn't really tell us very much?" He looked at Cordelia apologetically. "What she said in Italian—"

Cordelia froze. She could hear Filomena's eerie voice in her mind. "She spoke about how I stabbed Belial." She tried to keep her voice steady. "She wanted to know why, if I did that, I couldn't help her. She asked why I didn't save her."

She did not mention Cortana. She couldn't bear to. What if Filomena had been wrong? What if she was not a heroine, not the true bearer of Cortana? What if the sword had decided she didn't deserve it?

Cordelia looked down at her hands. "I failed her."

There was a murmur of dissenting voices; she felt a hand brush her arm. She knew it was James, without having to look. "Daisy," he said. "We are Nephilim, not angels themselves. We cannot be where we do not know we are needed. We cannot know all things."

"I, for instance," said Matthew, "know very little."

"And I do not know why I am seeing these deaths in dreams." James set down his cup. "There is some reason I am connected to all this. Though I could quite understand if none of you wanted to be involved."

"I believe the spirit of our organization is that we do want to be involved," said Matthew, "when it comes to each other."

"That is why we should be looking into oneiromancy, the study of dreams," said Christopher brightly. "I have brought quite a few books on the topic, to be distributed among us."

"Do any of them have love scenes?" inquired Lucie. "I've been working on mine."

"If they do, I am sure they are quite disturbing," said James.

"These books are *very interesting*," said Christopher sternly. "There are stories of necromancers who have traveled in dreams, even killed and collected death energy in dreams."

"What exactly do you mean when you say 'death energy'?" Lucie asked. If Cordelia wasn't mistaken, she looked a little pale. "You mean, what necromancers use to raise the dead?"

"Exactly that," said Christopher. "There are ways to raise the dead using a catalyst—an object imbued with collected power by a warlock—but most involve using the life force released when someone dies to power a corpse's rising."

"Well, if the killer were a Shadowhunter, he or she could have no use for death energy," said Matthew, nibbling the edge of a pastry. "Unless they were in cahoots with a warlock, I suppose—"

"Oh, bother," said Thomas, rising to his feet and brushing off his waistcoat. "I promised to get home by noon. My parents are fussing, and they keep threatening to ask Charlotte to strike me off the patrol lists if I don't sign up for a partner."

"Don't be silly, Tom," said Lucie. "Go with Anna, at least. Or I hope they *do* strike you off the lists." She made a face at him.

"*I* hope I run into the killer," Thomas said grimly. "So far he hasn't attacked anyone who was expecting him. But I will be."

He blushed as this announcement was greeted by a round of amiable cheers. The others were getting up too, save James and Cordelia—taking copies of the books Christopher had brought, chattering about who was going to read what, joking about the oddest dreams they'd ever had. (Matthew's involved a centaur and a bicycle.)

Despite everything, despite Cortana, Cordelia felt a wash of happiness. It wasn't just that she loved James, she thought. She loved his friends, loved his family, loved their shared plans, loved Lucie being her sister. She would have felt guilty being so happy, had it not been for the hollow place in the deepest part of her heart—the small, echoing space that held the knowledge that all this was temporary.

Matthew's carriage was waiting at the curb; he had nearly reached it when James caught up with him. Matthew turned in surprise, his expression changing quickly to amusement: James had left the house with his coat half on and was struggling to button it with gloved hands.

"Let me do that," Matthew said, pulling his right glove off with his teeth. He shoved it in his pocket and went to work on James's Ulster coat, fingers slipping the leather circles through the buttonholes with practiced ease. "And what are you running about for in this weather half-dressed? Oughtn't you to be curled up by the fire with Cordelia, reading *Dreams in Which I Have Been Chased and the Things That Chased Me* by C. Langner?"

"That one does seem to have dubious informative value," James admitted. "Math, I didn't know you'd gone and gotten a flat. You didn't tell me."

Matthew, having finished buttoning James's coat, looked slightly abashed. He ran a hand through his hair, which was already tumbling about his head like unkempt sunshine. "I'd been considering the idea for some time, but I never thought I'd move so suddenly. It was an impulse—"

"Nothing to do with that argument you were having with Charlotte the other day?"

"Perhaps." Matthew's face took on a guarded expression. "And living with Charles had become all a bit much. I bristle when he speaks of his upcoming marriage."

"I appreciate the loyalty," said James. "And it is, of course, entirely your decision what you do. But I don't like the idea of not knowing where you live."

"I didn't want to trouble you," Matthew said, with uncharacteristic shyness.

"Nothing you do troubles me," said James. "Well, that is not precisely true. You are quite troublesome, as you well know." He grinned. "But that doesn't mean I don't want to know what's happening in your life. I'm your *parabatai*."

"I know. And I had rather thought—I suppose I had thought, since you had just been married, that you would want to spend time alone with Cordelia. That there was some chance your marriage might become a real one."

There was a look close to distress on Matthew's face. It startled James—Matthew, who so rarely showed distress even if he felt it. Perhaps, James thought, he had been worrying that things might change between them with James a married man. That their closeness might be diminished.

"Cordelia and I are friends only," he said, with more surety than he felt. "You know I am pledged to Miss Blackthorn."

"She cannot hold a candle to Daisy," Matthew said, then looked utterly horrified. "My apologies—it is absolutely none of my business. I ought to get back to my flat, before I cause any more trouble."

James was startled, though he supposed he shouldn't be. Matthew had nearly bitten Grace's head off at the wedding. Certainly James felt no resentment at Math's dislike of Grace: he understood that Matthew did not want him to be hurt.

"Let me come with you," James said.

Matthew shook his head, opening his carriage door. "I ought to be alone—settle myself—"

"No one need be alone to settle themselves," said James quietly. "All I want for you, Math, is that you love yourself as much as I love you."

Matthew took a shaking breath. "Cordelia doesn't mind you coming to my flat?"

"She suggested it. She loves you too," James said, and glanced up at the sky. Dark, snow-laden clouds were rolling in, obscuring the blue. He did not see Matthew close his eyes and swallow hard.

A moment later Matthew had flung the carriage door all the way open and was gesturing James inside. "Well, come on then," he said. "If we hurry, we can get there before it starts to snow."

Cordelia spent the afternoon curled up in the study, reading *A Thaumaturgy of Dreams*. Christopher had been right—the book was very interesting, though it was entirely about how one might direct the dreams of others and very little about what to do if one found oneself being visited by violent, unpleasant dreams that turned out to be true.

As the day wore on, groups of men came down the streets with shovels and brooms, and scraped and cleaned the night's snow from the walkways; children emerged from houses, too, wrapped up like little packages, and proceeded to pelt each other with snowballs. She remembered, long ago, doing the same with Alastair. She hoped he was managing all right at Cornwall Gardens.

As the sun dimmed outside the window, snow began to fall again. It sifted down from the sky like flour, covering the world in a layer of powdered glass. The children were ordered inside, and the streetlamps glowed through a haze of fine white crystals. Cordelia found her mind wandering from the book: she could not help but think about Cortana again.

If you had any thought of meeting Cortana's maker, I could take you. Past the great white horse and under the hill.

She bit her lip. Trusting faeries was one thing, but Lilian Highsmith had mentioned Wayland the Smith as well.

When I was twelve, I ran away from home and my parents found me wandering the Ridgeway Road, looking for the smith's barrow.

Cordelia scrambled off the couch and headed for the bookshelves. The section devoted to volumes on travel was rather haphazardly knocked about—she and James had gone through half the books—but she found what she was looking for easily enough: *The Wonders of Ancient Britain*.

She found the Ridgeway Road in the index and flipped to the page, illustrated with a pen-and-ink drawing of a dark barrow piercing the side of a hill. *Wayland the Smith's cave lies Wiltshire way, along the Ridgeway Road, that highway of vanished races which runs end to end of the Downs. The fields are cultivated now, but the place still has a strange look. A fitting place to possess one's soul in silence after a pilgrimage to White Horse Hill—*

The sound of carriage wheels on icy pavement cut into Cordelia's thoughts. Hearing the front door slam, she set the book aside hastily; a minute later James came into the study, hatless, his tumbled dark hair feathered with snow.

She took down a book on Constantinople as he came over to the fire and held out his hands to the flames. "How was Matthew's?" she asked.

"Nice enough," James's sharp cheekbones were flushed with the cold. "Whitby Mansions, I think it's called, all very posh—they've got a motorcar he can use when he likes, which seems a recipe for disaster, and a cook and cleaners on the premises. Not that I think the Enclave would be too thrilled if they knew where he was. They don't like us having servants who don't know about Downworld, lest they see something untoward. I've warned him not to bring home any tentacles."

"He's more likely to burn the flat down trying to make tea," Cordelia said with a smile. "Do you want supper? Risa's been cooking all day, and muttering about it. We could eat in here," she added. "It's cozier."

He gave her a long, measuring look. The kind that made her heart thump harder for no real reason. The snow in his hair had melted, and the damp strands were curling at the ends. "Why not?"

She went to talk to Risa; by the time she returned, James had sprawled on the couch with *A Thaumaturgy of Dreams*, leafing idly through the pages. "Anything useful in here?" he asked.

"Not really," said Cordelia, settling onto the couch beside him as Risa came in with a tray full of dishes. She left them to serve themselves: soup and rice, spiced vegetables, and tea. "Mostly about how to give other people dreams, not what to do if you're having them yourself."

"Matthew went into greater detail about his centaur dream," said James, spooning up the soup. "It was very troubling."

"Was *he* the centaur, or was someone else? Or do I not want to know?" asked Cordelia. James stared at his spoon. "Is the soup all right? It's *ash reshteh*. Risa cooked it for you when you had scalding fever."

"Did she?" he said slowly.

"We were both fourteen," she said. He *had* to remember. "You had come to Cirenworth; Alastair wasn't there, and you and Lucie and I played all through the gardens. Then one day you collapsed; you were burning up. Do you recall any of that?"

James rubbed at his eyes. "It's strange. I ought to remember more about the fever. It's the most ill I've ever been."

"They sent Lucie away, but I'd already had the fever. They let me stay and sit with you," she said. "Do you remember me reading to you at all?"

James rested his chin in his hand. "Well, I remember stories of some kind, but I don't know if it was something I dreamed, or a real memory. There was a tale like *Romeo and Juliet*, perhaps? Something melancholy and romantic?"

"Yes," Cordelia said slowly. Could he really have forgotten? It seemed to her that months ago, when they had spoken of the tale, he had remembered it well. Had she been mistaken? "The story of Layla and Majnun—you liked that one quite a bit. We talked about it afterward. We talked a lot, actually, because it seemed to take your mind off how badly you felt. You really don't remember?"

"I'm sorry, Daisy. I wish I did."

There was a copy of the book upstairs, Cordelia knew, in among the volumes that had been brought from her old house. She stood up, suddenly determined. If she couldn't jog his memory, maybe Nizami could. "Then there's only one thing to be done. I'm going to remind you."

James rose and paced the room the moment Cordelia left. He wished he could remember what she so clearly badly wanted him to recall. He felt as if he were disappointing her, letting her down somehow. Yet when he reached back into his mind, it was as if a curtain had been drawn across that time at Cirenworth, and he could see only in glimpses through gaps in the fabric.

The smell of jasmine and woodsmoke.

The length of a body, warm and solid, all along his own.

Her husky voice: *I sought not fire, yet is my heart all flame. Layla, this love is not of earth.*

He took a deep breath. His head ached. He had come into the study earlier preoccupied, thinking of Matthew, worried about him alone in his new flat. And then he had seen Cordelia—her head bent over her book, her hair shining like a new penny; she had been wearing a soft woolen dress that clung to her body, outlining every curve. He had nearly gone to her and kissed her, as any man coming home to his wife might do. Only at the last minute had he recalled himself, and turned toward the fire instead.

And still his body ached, as if it yearned for something entirely separate from what his mind knew was good for him. Long ago—he was almost sure of it—Cordelia had put her arms around him while he burned with fever. Yesterday morning, he had held her, soft and pliant against him, and he had burned with another sort of fever.

He wanted her. It was something he had to face. She was beautiful and desirable and they were cooped up in the house together. It was bound to happen. He recalled the Whispering Room at the Hell Ruelle. He had kissed her there, though it also seemed faded in his memory, like the time at Cirenworth. He rubbed at his right wrist, which ached; he knew he must have been out of his wits, then—Grace had just ended things with him. He had sought comfort with Cordelia, which was not fair to her. In fact he had behaved like a starving animal: seizing her up, throwing her down on the desk, clambering on top of her. . . .

He put his hand to his head. It was splitting. Desire and love were not the same, he reminded himself, and Cordelia was innocent. He could not take advantage of her. He would have to control himself better. He would have to—

There was a noise at the door; he looked up, expecting Cordelia.

A harsh astonishment went through him. Risa was there, a look of consternation on her face, but it was not Risa who had surprised him. Standing behind her was Elias Carstairs, wearing a threadbare brown coat of a style that had not been in fashion for years.

The shock that went through James was nearly painful. Whatever he had been thinking about was entirely derailed; fortunately, a lifetime of control and good manners asserted itself. He stepped forward, holding out his hand. "Good evening, sir."

Elias returned the handshake, glancing past James at the food spread across the low table. "Ah—you are at dinner? My apologies."

"Is everything all right with Mrs. Carstairs?" James asked, wondering what could have brought Elias calling with no notice.

Elias seemed unconcerned. "Of course. Never better. I don't wish to keep you, James, and I require only a moment of your time. But perhaps we could retire somewhere briefly to discuss an important matter? Between father and son. Between men."

James nodded and led Elias to the drawing room with a whispered aside to Risa. He didn't want Cordelia wondering where he had gone.

Upon reaching the drawing room, Elias closed and bolted the door. James stood before the cold fireplace, hands locked behind his back, puzzling through the situation. He supposed he shouldn't be quite as surprised as he was. It was natural for a father to want to talk to his son-in-law—there were all sorts of ordinary things that weren't considered women's business: finances, politics, mortgages, horses, carriage upkeep . . . not that he could imagine that Elias had ventured out on a snowy night to discuss carriage upkeep.

Cordelia's father roamed the room slowly, taking his time, squinting owlishly at the fine paintings. As James watched Elias knock over a small ceramic figurine—then try to right it, before giving up and turning away—his heart sank. If Elias was attempting to seem sober, he had chosen the wrong person for his performance. The past years with Matthew had taught James well: Elias was quite drunk, indeed.

After his little tour, Elias rested a hand on the piano lid and regarded James appraisingly. "So richly appointed, your new home. What wonderfully generous people your parents are! We must seem beggarly in comparison."

"Not at all. I assure you—"

"No need to assure," Elias said with a chuckle. "The Herondales are wealthy, that's all! It's hard for me to ignore, I suppose, after all I've recently been through."

"A difficult time, indeed," James said, casting about for the proper response. "Cordelia is so happy to have you back home."

"Home," Elias said, and there was a faintly ugly tone to his voice. Something almost mocking. "Home is the sailor, home from the sea, eh, James? Home, with a new brat on the way and no way to feed it. That's home, for me."

A new brat. James thought of Cordelia, so determined to save her father, her family. If it hadn't been for her bravery, Elias would have gone to trial, not the Basilias. And yet nothing in his father-in-law's behavior—at the wedding, at dinner, now—betrayed even the slightest sense that his daughter deserved his admiration. His gratitude.

"What do you want, Elias?" James said flatly.

"I am, if I may be frank, in debt. Cirenworth, you see, was an investment in my legacy. It was far too expensive, but I thought, quite reasonably at the time, that given my history I would soon be promoted within the Clave." Elias leaned against the piano. "Alas, I have been passed over for promotion multiple times, and due to my recent troubles, I have no longer been drawing a salary at all. I do not wish to rob my children or my wife to pay down my debts. Surely you can see that."

Surely you can see that. And James could, though he could see just as clearly that Elias wasn't telling him the full truth. He made a noncommittal noise.

Elias cleared his throat. "Let me come to the point, James—we are family now, and I need your help."

James inclined his head. "What kind of help?"

"Five thousand pounds," Elias announced in a tone he might have used to call the winner of a horse race. "That is the sum that would set me right again. You can manage that much, surely—you'll barely miss it."

"Five *thousand*?" James couldn't keep the shock from his voice. He knew no one who would not have struggled to produce such a sum. "I don't have that kind of money."

"Perhaps you don't," said Elias, though he didn't sound as if he believed it. "Perhaps you might speak to your parents? Surely they could sell something, help me in my time of need."

Elias was drunker than James had realized. Unlike Matthew, he did not hide his liquor well; it made him both more ebullient and more unreasonable. Maybe time, and the consequences of Elias's poor decisions, had weakened him—a thought that worried James greatly, not on his father-in-law's behalf, but on Matthew's.

"I cannot help you, Elias," James said, more forcefully than he intended.

"Ah," Elias said, fixing his bleary gaze on James. "Can't, or won't?"

"Both. It's wrong of you to come to me in this way. It will only poison your relationship with Daisy—"

"Do not use my daughter as an excuse, Herondale." Elias slammed his hand down on the piano lid. "You have everything, I have nothing; surely you can give me this—" With a visible effort, he forced his voice to be steady. "There are those in the Enclave who do not believe your mother belongs among the Nephilim," he said, and now there was a different look on his face—a sort of drunken cunning. "Or that you and your sister do either. I could put a word in the Inquisitor's ear, you know—if I failed to give my approval, it's unlikely they would allow your sister's *parabatai* ceremony with my daughter to go forward—"

Rage drove through James like an arrow. "How dare you," he said. "You would not just be hurting me and my sister, but the damage you would do to Daisy—"

"Her name is Cordelia," snapped Elias. "I let you marry her, despite the rumors that swirl around your family, because I thought you would be generous. And this is how you repay me?"

James felt his mouth twist violently. "Repay you? You claim you do not want to rob your family, yet you speak of robbing Cordelia of the most precious hope in her life. And she above all people would be ashamed of you, trying threats where begging won't do the job—"

"All I've told you is the truth," Elias snapped, his face contorted. "There are many—many who don't trust you. Many who would be glad to see you and your whole family burn."

James caught his breath. In that moment, he hated Elias Carstairs, hated him so much he wished he could strike him dead where he stood.

"Get out of my house," he snarled; it was all he trusted himself to say.

Elias turned and stormed out of the drawing room, nearly colliding with an astonished Cordelia in the hall. "Father?" she said in surprise.

"Your husband is a very selfish man," Elias hissed. Before she could respond, he shoved roughly past her and let himself out, slamming the door behind him.

Lucie huddled in a sheltered doorway next to the Hell Ruelle, pulling her coat tightly around her, a shield against the icy air while she waited for Grace. It was a moonless night, the stars hidden behind thick clouds. The alley was a churned-up mess of mud and slush that stained Lucie's kid boots.

Furtive figures slipped by her, heading for the Hell Ruelle. Lucie looked after them longingly. Whenever the nondescript door opened to a Downworlder's knock, golden light flared from the darkness like a match being lit inside a cave.

"There you are," said Grace, as if Lucie had been hiding. She stepped into view under the light spilling from the Ruelle's upper windows. She wore a pale woolen cape trimmed with fur at the throat and carried a matching fur muff. Her hair was pinned up in an arrangement of tiny plaits threaded with silver ribbons. She looked like the Snow Queen in a book of fairy tales.

"Are you sure this is a good idea?" Lucie said. "They just put the curfew into effect, and we're already breaking it."

Grace shrugged. "You're the one who's insisting we do this the 'proper' way. So, here we are."

She had a point: breaking curfew was better than doing evil. The brief discussion of necromancy in James's drawing room earlier that day had sent shivers up Lucie's spine.

"Have you been here before?" Grace asked.

"Just once." Still, Lucie was feeling a bit smug about her prior experience. She sauntered up to the door and knocked; when a faerie with purple hair, dressed in spangled pantaloons, answered the call, she gave her most charming smile.

"I've come by to see Anna Lightwood," she said. "I'm her cousin."

"Humph," said the faerie. "Anna's not here, and we don't like Nephilim, neither. Go away."

"Oh, brilliant," Grace muttered, casting her gaze upward in exasperation. The faerie seemed about to slam the door in their faces.

"Wait!" called a voice. It was Hypatia Vex, her hair pinned up with elaborate porcelain flowers, her brown skin dusted with glittering powder above the neckline of a ruby velvet dress.

"She is Anna's cousin," Hypatia said to the door faerie, indicating Lucie. "She was here a few weeks back. As for the other one—" She shrugged. "Oh, let them in. It's still early. I doubt even a Herondale could stir up trouble at this hour. And call my carriage, Naila. I'm ready to go out."

Lucie and Grace slipped past the departing Hypatia and found themselves in a maze of rooms connected by cramped hallways. Following the sound of voices, they reached the large central chamber; it looked entirely different than it had the last time Lucie had been here. Then, it had been full of revelers. Tonight seemed quieter—lamps were shaded in cream-colored velvet, casting a softened glow. Jewel-toned couches were scattered about the room, and on them were crowded all manner of vampires and faeries, even a werewolf or two, as well as creatures Lucie could not identify. They spoke to each other in low voices as satyrs carrying silver trays of iced drinks passed between them.

"Hardly the bacchanal I expected," Grace said coolly. "I can't imagine why people are so desperate to be invited."

Lucie spotted Malcolm Fade first, sprawled on a settee alone, his arm behind his head, his purple gaze fixed on the ceiling. He sat up as they approached, his expression frankly skeptical.

"Is this how it's to be, then? Shadowhunters showing up here every night?" Malcolm sighed. He was wearing a formal white frock coat, the same color as his hair. "My patience begins to fray."

"I'm glad it's only begun," Lucie said, "because we need to speak with you. In private. I'm Lucie Herondale, and this is Grace Blackthorn—"

"I know who you are." With a sigh, Malcolm rolled off the settee. "You get five minutes of my time, less if you bore me. Come to my office."

They followed him down a narrow hall to a private room papered in a William Morris pattern and outfitted with a writing desk and several amber-colored brocade chairs. He gestured impatiently for them to sit. Grace perched coquettishly on the edge of her seat, tilting her head so that she gazed up at Malcolm through fluttering lashes. Grace really was awfully odd, Lucie thought, sitting down in another brocade chair. Did she think flirting with a century-old warlock would work? Then again, any port in a storm.

Malcolm, leaning back against the wall beside a painting of a stormy sea, seemed amused—and entirely unmoved. "Aren't you children supposed to be home at this hour?"

"You mean," Grace said, quick as a whip, "you know about the murders, then?"

Malcolm sank down into a leather chair behind the desk. Something about him reminded Lucie of Magnus, though Magnus had kinder eyes. By contrast, there was something remote about Malcolm, as if he were walling some part of himself away where it could not be touched. "I am the High Warlock. Things like Shadowhunter curfews fall under my purview. Though I've already told the Clave: I have no idea who killed those three Nephilim."

"We understand," Lucie said. "And we truly are sorry to interrupt your evening. I was hoping you might be able to help us with something else. Something we're trying to learn more about. It has to do with raising the dead."

Malcolm's eyes widened. "How refreshingly candid," he said, running a finger over the ebony inlay on his desk. "It's always nice to see the youth of today thirsting for knowledge. Do you think the murderer is trying to raise the dead?"

"It's not about that," Lucie said carefully, "but rather, whether there are ways to raise the dead that don't involve so much . . . er, death. Ways that don't require evil deeds."

"There is no way to raise the dead without doing great evil," Malcolm said flatly.

"That can't be true," Grace said. Her gaze was still fixed on Malcolm. "I beg you. Help us. Help *me*."

Malcolm's gaze darkened. "I see," he said, after a long moment, though Lucie wasn't sure what he saw. "Grace—your name is Grace, isn't it?—I am helping you already, by telling you the truth. Life is in balance, just as magic is in balance. And so there is no way to grant life without taking life."

"You are very famous, Mr. Fade," said Grace. Lucie looked at her in alarm: What *was* Grace playing at? "I remember hearing that you were once in love with a Shadowhunter. And that she became an Iron Sister."

"What of it?" Malcolm said.

"My mother just joined the Iron Sisters in the Adamant Citadel, but she is not one of them. She is not bound by their rules of silence. We could ask her to find out how your beloved fares in the Citadel. We could tell you how she is."

Malcolm froze, the color draining from his already pale face. "You're serious?"

Lucie wished she had asked Grace for more details about her plan. Somehow she'd imagined they'd simply approach Malcolm and ask for help. This was entirely unexpected; she wasn't at all sure how she felt about it.

"We are serious," said Grace. "Lucie would agree with me."

Malcolm turned his gaze to Lucie. His eyes had darkened; they looked nearly black. "Is this indeed your offer, Miss Herondale? I assume you make it without the knowledge of your parents?"

"Yes, and yes," said Lucie. "But—my parents have always taught me to right injustice. That is what I am trying to do. Someone is dead who should—who should never have died."

Malcolm laughed bitterly. "Determined, aren't you? You remind me of your father. Like a dog with a bone. Here is what you must know: even if it were possible to raise the dead without also taking life to restore balance, you would need a body for the departed to occupy. A body that hasn't rotted away. But alas, as you surely must know by now, it is in the nature of the dead to rot."

"But what if one had a body that was still in perfect condition?" Lucie said. "Unoccupied, as it were, but still, um, pristine?"

"Really?" Malcolm's gaze moved from Lucie to Grace and back again. He sighed, as if in defeat. "All right," he said at last. "If what you say is true—and you can bring me word of Annabel—then return when you have a message from her. I will be here."

He rose, inclining his head curtly. It was clear their interview was over.

Lucie got to her feet, discovering she felt quite shaky. Grace had already risen, and made as if to stalk from the room, but as she passed Malcolm, he caught her arm and spoke in a deadly quiet voice.

"Miss Blackthorn," he said. "In case you haven't realized it already, the kind of enchantment you employ doesn't work on those like me, nor do I consider it a frivolity, a harmless bit of magic. Try such tricks in the Ruelle again, and there will be consequences."

He flung her arm away; Grace darted from the room, her head down. For a moment, Lucie thought—but no. It wasn't possible. She could not have seen tears shining in Grace's eyes.

"What do you mean by enchantment?" Lucie said. "Grace can't cast a spell to save her life. I ought to know."

Malcolm looked at Lucie for a long time. "There are different sorts of enchantments," he said at last. "Miss Blackthorn is of the sort who know that men like to be needed. She plays at helplessness and flirting."

"Humph," said Lucie. She forbore to point out that given the limits placed on women by the world, they often had no choice but to seek assistance from men.

Malcolm shrugged. "All I am saying is that you should not trust that girl," he said. "The decision, of course, is up to you."

"It's the *most* extraordinary thing," Ariadne said, closing the door of the Whispering Room behind her and locking it for good measure. "Grace Blackthorn just burst out of Malcolm Fade's office and went running out of the Ruelle. Do you think I should go after her?"

They had lit a fire in the grate; Anna was lounging in front of it, wearing only a man's white button-down shirt. Her long bare legs, extended toward the flames, were elegant as a poem. She rolled over onto her stomach, propping her chin on her palms, and said, "No—she's made it quite clear that she doesn't care much about you. Perhaps you should extend her the same consideration. Besides," Anna added, her red lips curling into a smile, "you're not thinking of charging out into the night wearing *that*, are you?"

Ariadne blushed; she'd nearly forgotten she was only in her shift—white muslin with an olive-green ribbon threaded through the bodice. The rest of her clothes—dress and shoes, petticoats, drawers, tapes, and corset—were scattered around the room.

She started back toward Anna, dropping down on the rug beside her. It was Ariadne's third trip to the Whispering Room to meet Anna, and she had grown quite fond of the place. She liked the silver paper on the walls, the copper bowl always kept full of hothouse fruit, the smoke from the fire that always smelled like roses. "She isn't rude to me," she said thoughtfully. "She's polite and mouths responses when she's asked questions, but she's just not really *there*."

"Probably busy thinking about how she can ruin James's life," said Anna, rolling onto her back. Her ruby pendant gleamed at her throat. "Do come here," she said languidly, reaching up her arms, and Ariadne slid on top of her.

Anna was all length and loose limbs, every gesture a sensual sprawl. Ariadne's heart fluttered as Anna reached a pale hand up to tug gently at the straps holding up Ariadne's shift. It slid down to her waist. Anna's eyes darkened to sapphires.

"Again?" Ariadne whispered, as Anna's hands worked their magic. It still amazed her how fingers brushing her throat, even her shoulders, could make her ache all over, setting off a storm of longing. She tried to do the same things to Anna, and sometimes Anna allowed it. She preferred, though, to be in control. Even when Ariadne was touching her, she never quite lost herself.

"Do you mind?" Anna said, in a tone that indicated she knew perfectly well the answer.

"No. We're making up for lost time."

Anna smiled and drew Ariadne down. Her hands found Ariadne's thick, dark, unbound hair, her tongue the hollow of Ariadne's throat. Her fingers worked music from her body as if it were a violin. Ariadne gasped. This was what she was living for, every long, dark winter day as she waited to see if the invitation from Anna would come in the evening. The folded piece of paper slipped through her window, the message scrawled in Anna's strong, elegant hand.

Meet me in the Whispering Room.

Her body felt as out of control as a train that had jumped its tracks. She found the buttons on Anna's shirt, undid them, pressed her bare skin to Anna's. She knew she was in love with Anna again, just as badly as she had been before, but she didn't care. She didn't care about anything but Anna.

Anna Lightwood
&
Ariadne Bridgestock

When the world had come apart and together again like the fractured glass in a kaleidoscope, they lay before the fire, Ariadne curled against Anna's side. Anna's arm was crooked behind her head, her blue eyes fixed on the ceiling.

"Anna," Ariadne said tentatively. "You do know that what happened with Filomena—even if she was coming home from your party, it wasn't your fault."

Anna glanced over. "What brought that thought into your head?"

The way you kissed me. Like you were trying to forget something.

Ariadne shrugged.

"Ari," said Anna in her low, husky drawl. "I appreciate the effort, but if I have concerns about my feelings, I have many friends to talk to."

Ariadne sat up, drawing her arms through the straps of her shift. "Are we not even friends?"

Anna put both hands behind her head. In the rose-scented light, the dips and hollows of her slender body were described softly by light and shadow. "I think I was very clear the first time we spoke," she said calmly. "I choose not to have my emotions bound up in romances. When you give people your heart, you deliver them the opportunity to hurt you, and it leads to bitterness. You would not want us to be bitter with each other, would you?"

Ariadne had risen to her feet. She began to look about for her discarded clothes. In the past, when she had not dressed quickly enough, Anna—whose masculine attire was much easier to don and doff—had departed without her, leaving her to find her own way out of the Ruelle. "No."

Anna sat up. "I'm not being dishonest with you, Ari. I've told you exactly what I have to offer. If it's not enough, I won't blame you if you leave."

Ariadne stepped into her petticoats. "I'm not leaving."

Anna looked at her with real curiosity. "Why not?"

"Because," Ariadne said, "when you want something very much, you are willing to accept the shadow of that thing. Even if it is just a shadow."

London:
Shepherd Market

It was a grimy dawn, yellow light beginning to seep through the cracks in the heavy gray clouds, when the man half tumbled out of the pub and into the square. He limped along toward Half Moon Street, past the hodgepodge of shops—greengrocers, butchers—that lined the central square. The neighborhood had its charms despite the close quarters and grime, but the man took no notice. He had not been the last patron in Ye Grapes, but the others had drunk themselves unconscious and would soon be treated to a complimentary trip out the back door, where they would be unceremoniously deposited on the pavement to await the coming day.

The killer slipped from one doorway to the next, trailing his prey more for sport than necessity. Stealth was hardly needed here. The man was staggering drunk, singing a tuneless little song, his breath puffing out in white clouds as it met the icy air. He did not seem to feel the cold in his battered coat.

The girl had been too ready, too quickly. She had turned the killer's own blade on him, sinking it deep into his shoulder. Her death had been messy, fast and brutal; afterward he had been forced to slip away and hide, abandoning the bloody evidence in an empty factory in Limehouse. As he swiftly healed, he had heard the scrape and chitter of an Ourobas demon nearby, drawn by the scent of murder and blood. He did not fear it; demons knew him as kin now.

But he was angry. There would be no more such accidents.

The killer quickened his pace. One, two, three strides and he was upon the man. He grabbed his shoulder roughly and spun him around, shoving him up against a cold brick wall. The man blinked in anger, then confusion. His mouth opened, and a single word passed his lips just before the knife went into his chest:

"You?"

12

REQUIEM

This be the verse you grave for me:
Here he lies where he longed to be;
Home is the sailor, home from sea,
And the hunter, home from the hill.
—Robert Louis Stevenson, "Requiem"

The knife went in, grinding past bone, sinking into soft tissue, blood pulsing
up and around the blade, the stench of it, hot and coppery, thickening the air. . . .

James sat up in bed, pain shooting through his chest. His heart
was slamming against his ribs. He choked, memories flooding back—
the empty streets, the shops and stalls of Shepherd Market. The man
leaving the noisy, bright pub, heading for the narrower streets, perhaps hoping to find an unwatched mews house to sleep in.

The killer, the blade, the hate again, that hatred hot as fire.

I have come to bring fire on the earth, and how I wish it were already
kindled.

He pushed himself upright, dread growing like a cancer in the pit
of his stomach. He had thrashed about in the bed hard enough to tear
his pajama top; his shoulder and arm were bare, freezing in the cold air
coming from the open window.

It was cold, so cold; he gripped the man's brown coat with one hand,
driving the knife in with the other—

James was suddenly unable to breathe. "No," he gasped, throwing off the bedcovers, sucking in lungfuls of air. He staggered to the window—he *knew* he hadn't left it open; he had checked twice last night—and slammed it shut.

He could see the man on his back, staring up at the sky. He knew him. His brown coat, his face, his voice.

Elias.

He threw on his trousers, buttoned up his shirt with shaking hands. Let it have been a nightmare, a meaningless dream and not a vision. Maybe he had only had a dream because he and Elias had fought last night; maybe he'd dreamed of Elias only because he was angry with him. Such things happened.

A pounding started up downstairs, someone knocking over and over on the door. James raced out of his room, barefoot, and tore down the stairs. Cordelia was already in the entryway, her hair a loose red river, a dressing gown thrown on over her nightclothes. Risa was there with her; she tore open the door, and Sona Carstairs stumbled inside.

"Mâmân?" he heard Cordelia say, her voice rising with panic. "Mâmân?"

Sona gave a keening wail. Risa caught her in her arms, and Sona buried her face against her old nursemaid's shoulder, weeping as if her heart would break.

"He's dead, Layla," she sobbed. "They found him this morning. Your father is dead."

Though Cordelia had visited the Silent City before, she had never been inside the Ossuarium. She had been lucky, she realized numbly, as she, James, Alastair, and Sona filed along a narrow corridor, following the light of Brother Enoch's witchlight torch. She had not encountered death so close to her before.

Alastair had come into the Curzon Street house after Sona and explained with surprising calm that Elias's body had been discovered by a morning patrol and already brought to the Silent City. If the family wished to see him before the autopsy began, they would need to hurry to the Ossuarium.

Cordelia recalled what happened next only in bits and pieces. She had gone to get dressed, feeling as numb as if she had fallen through Arctic ice into a black and frozen sea. When she emerged from the house to join her mother and brother in the carriage, she had been distantly surprised to find that James was beside her. He had been absolutely insistent on coming to the Silent City, though she had told him it wasn't necessary. "Only family need go," she told him, and he had said, "Daisy, I *am* family."

In the carriage, he had murmured words of condolence in Persian: *Ghame akharetoon basheh.*

May this be your last sorrow.

Sona had wept steadily and silently all the way to Highgate Cemetery. Cordelia had half expected Alastair to react to Elias's death with the blazing rage he often showed when he was hurt. Instead he seemed stiff and hollow, as if he were being propped up inside by wires. She could hear him, as if from a distance, saying all the correct things as they met Brother Enoch, who was waiting for them at the entrance to the Silent City.

Cordelia had felt a pang inside for Jem. If only he were not in the Spiral Labyrinth. If only he could be here for them: he was family, and Enoch was not. Did Jem even know? How long would it be before he was told that his uncle, the man who had slain his parents' murderer, was dead?

There would be a funeral eventually, she supposed now, her eyes fixed on Brother Enoch's witchlight torch, bobbing ahead of them. It would have to wait. Elias's body would be studied and then preserved until the murderer had been caught: they would not burn it and destroy potential clues. Jem could be with them then, but she found she could not imagine the scene—the fields of Alicante, her father's body on a pyre, the Consul speaking soothing words. It seemed like a horrific dream.

She felt James take her hand as they came into a stone square, the iron entrance of the Ossuarium rising up before them. Words were inscribed above the doors:

TACEANT COLLOQUIA. EFFUGIAT RISUS.

HIC LOCUS EST UBI MORS GAUDET

SUCCURRERE VITAE.

Let conversation stop. Let laughter cease. Here is the place where the dead delight to teach the living.

The doors opened before them, the ancient iron hinges groaning. Sona walked ahead, seemingly oblivious of everything but what was waiting inside the large, windowless room.

Inside the Ossuarium, walls of smooth white marble rose up to an arched ceiling high above them. The walls were bare save for a series of plain iron hooks from which various instruments of autopsy hung: shining scalpels, hammers, needles, and saws. Jars of viscous liquid lined a series of shelves; there were folded piles of white silk—bandages, Cordelia thought, before she realized: there was no reason to bandage the dead. The white silk strips were for binding the eyes of Shadowhunters before they were laid on the pyre to be burned. It was tradition.

At the center of the room was a row of high marble tables where the bodies of the deceased were laid out for examination. Here Amos Gladstone and Basil Pounceby had been brought to be examined, Cordelia thought, and Filomena as well. Only one table was occupied now. Cordelia told herself that lying there, draped in lengths of pristine white fabric, was what was left of her father, but she could not quite make herself believe it.

Shall we begin? asked Enoch, approaching the table.

"Yes," said Sona. She stood close to Alastair, his arm around her for support, her hand on her rounded belly. Her eyes were wide and haunted, but when she spoke, her voice was clear. She kept her chin level as Enoch slowly drew back the long white sheets to reveal Elias's body. He wore his old brown coat, the lapels peeled back to show a shabby white shirt beneath, stained heavily with blood. His skin was ashen, as if drained of blood: his hair and stubble looked dirty gray, like an old man's.

"How did he die?" said Alastair, his gaze fixed on his father's body. "Like the others?"

Yes. He was stabbed repeatedly with a sharp knife. His wounds are identical to those we discovered on the bodies of Filomena di Angelo and Basil Pounceby.

Alastair stared stonily at Elias. Cordelia said, "Was it a fight? A battle between him and his attacker?"

His attacker approached from the front, as deduced from a study of his wounds. There is no sign that a fight took place. There were no weapons at the scene, and there is no evidence on the body to suggest that Elias Carstairs drew a weapon.

"He was probably too drunk," Alastair muttered.

Perhaps. There was no kindness in Enoch's voice, and also no cruelty. There was no emotion at all. *Or perhaps he knew the person who attacked him. We see from wounds on his hands that he raised them to protect himself, but by then it was too late, as he had already received a mortal wound.*

"I don't understand," Sona said in a hoarse whisper.

"He means," Cordelia said, "that Father waited until the last moment to defend himself."

"But why?" Sona's voice rose in anguish. She caught at the material of Elias's coat, fisting it in her hand. "Why did you not fight, Elias? You, who slew a Greater Demon—"

"Mother, don't," Alastair said. "He isn't worth it—"

Cordelia could bear it no longer. Wrenching her hand free of James's, she hurried out of the Ossuarium: away from the gray wax figure of her dead father, away from her sobbing mother.

Just past the stone square outside the Ossuarium was a narrow corridor. Cordelia turned down it, only to find herself confronted by the sight of a long, thin passage, twisting away into utter blackness. It was foreboding enough to stop her in her tracks. She slumped against one of the walls, the cold from the stone seeping through the wool of her coat.

Sometimes, she thought, she wished she could pray, as other Nephilim did, to Raziel, but she had never learned quite how. Her parents had not been observant of the religion that bound all Shadowhunters together: the worship of the angel who had made them who they were, who had committed them to a destiny as harsh as beauty, as unforgiving as goodness itself. To remember that you worshipped Raziel was to remember that you were separate, for good or ill, from those you were sworn to protect. That even in a crowd, you might be alone.

"Daisy?" It was James, having made his way almost silently into the corridor. He leaned against the opposite wall, his eyes fixed on her.

"You didn't have to follow me." Her voice was a whisper, echoing down the hall. The ceiling above them rose into shadow: it could have been a foot above their heads, or a thousand feet.

"I'm here because of you," he said. Her eyes flicked up to him: he was a poem in black and white in the shadows, his hair like streaks of dark paint across the pale canvas of his skin. "And I want to be here. Because of you."

She took a shuddering breath. "It's just—I've been angry at him since he came back from the Basilias." If she were truthful with herself, she had been angry with him since she had first learned the truth from Alastair. "I never welcomed him home. Never accepted him. Now that he's dead, I've lost the chance to reconcile with him, to forgive him, to understand him."

"My father," James said, and hesitated. "My father used to tell me that sometimes you cannot reconcile with someone else. Sometimes you have to find that reconciliation on your own. Someone who broke your heart is often not the person who can mend it."

Someone who broke your heart. Cordelia thought of her father. They would never have a good moment between them again. If only she had let him walk her down the aisle. Lucie would have understood. If only she had given him a chance.

She should have stopped him from running out of her house last night. The awful truth was that she'd been glad to see him go, and worried, not on his behalf, but on James's. All she'd been able to think was that somehow, her father had humiliated her again. *What did Father do to James? What had he said?* James had insisted steadfastly it had been nothing, but he had looked sick to his stomach and had gone to bed early.

"Did you see it?" she whispered.

It was so quiet she could hear the scrape of James's jacket against the stone wall as he moved. "See what?"

"Did you dream it? Him dying?"

James put a hand up to cover his eyes. "Yes."

"It was the same killer?" Her voice sounded tiny and dry. "The same murderer, the same hate?"

"Yes. But Daisy—"

She put her hand over her stomach, feeling the urge to wrap her arms around herself, to keep herself from breaking apart. "Don't tell me. Not now. But if there's anything—"

"That might tell us who did this? I've been racking my brain, Daisy. If there was anything, anything at all, I would tell you, I would message Jem, my parents—" He shook his head. "There's nothing more than before."

"Then tell me why he came to our house last night." She gave a dry little laugh. "Pretend I've won a chess game. I can owe you an answer. But tell me the truth. What did he want?"

There was a pause before James said, "He wanted money."

"Money?" she repeated, incredulous. "How much money? What did he need it for?"

James was very still, yet oddly, the Mask had not gone up. Cordelia could see what he was thinking, feeling. The agonized look in his eyes. He was letting himself feel all of it, she thought, and more than that. He was letting himself *show* it.

"Your father asked me for five thousand pounds," he said. "Where he thought I would get it, I can't imagine. He told me I should ask my parents. He insinuated that they had so much money they would not even notice it. He said it was for Cirenworth. That he could not afford the costs of the house. I don't know whether that was the truth."

"I have no idea," Cordelia whispered, though plenty of alternate possibilities presented themselves. Gambling debts. Unpaid loans. Unsettled scores. "Why didn't you tell me?" Her body felt like fire and ice—burning and freezing with rage and despair. "If I had only known he was in trouble, I could have helped him."

"No," James said quietly. "You couldn't have."

"I could have stopped him from going out into the streets, in the snow—"

"He didn't die from lack of money," James said. "Nor did he die from the cold. He was *murdered*."

Cordelia knew that James was being reasonable, but she had no use for reason. She wanted to explode with fury, wanted to destroy something. "You didn't need to give him five thousand—you could have given him a little bit, a little money to get him safely home."

Something flickered in James's eyes. Anger. She had never seen those golden eyes furious before, not at her. She felt a sick sort of gladness: now, instead of feeling nothing, she felt rage. She felt despair. She felt the agony of hurting James, the last thing in the world she wanted to do.

"Had I given him any money at all, he would have gone out to spend it at the pub, and he still would have been staggering drunk and he still would have been killed. And you would still be blaming me, because you don't want to think that his own choices—"

"Cordelia."

She turned, saw Alastair standing at the entrance to the narrow corridor. He was backlit by witchlight; it turned the edges of his hair to light, reminding her of the time he'd dyed it. "Brother Enoch says if you wish to say goodbye, it has to be now."

Cordelia nodded mechanically. "I'm coming."

She had to edge past James before she turned to go; as she did, their shoulders brushed. She heard him sigh in frustration before following her. Then they were back out in the square and trailing Alastair into the Ossuarium, where Sona stood by Elias's body. Brother Enoch was there, too, motionless, his hands folded in front of him like a priest's.

James had paused by the double doors. Cordelia didn't look at him; she couldn't. She took Alastair's hand and crossed the marble floor to where her father lay. Alastair drew her close against his side. Her mother stood very still, her eyes red and swollen, her head bent.

"*Ave atque vale*," Alastair said. "Hail and farewell, Father."

"*Ave atque vale*," Sona echoed. Cordelia knew she should say it too, the traditional farewell, but her throat was too tight for words. Instead she reached out and took her father's hand, exposed where the sheet was turned back. It was cold and rigid. Not her father's hand at all. Not the hand that had lifted her up when she was small, or guided her bladework as she trained. Gently, she set it on his chest.

Her body stiffened. Elias's Voyance rune—the rune every Shadowhunter had on the back of their dominant hand—was missing.

She heard Filomena's voice again, echoing through the empty sail-cloth factory. *He took from me. My strength. My life.*

Her strength.

Enoch, she thought. *Do you know if Filomena di Angelo had a Strength rune?*

Silent Brothers couldn't look surprised. Still, Cordelia sensed a sort of startlement radiating from Enoch. He said, *I do not know, but her body is in Idris, with Brother Shadrach. I will ask him to examine her, if this is important.*

It is very important, she thought.

Enoch nodded almost imperceptibly. *The Consul will be here soon. Do you wish to remain, and to receive her?*

Sona passed a hand across her eyes. "Honestly, I cannot bear it," she said. "All I wish is to go home, and to have my children with me—" She broke off, smiling weakly. "My apologies, of course, Layla. You have your own home."

"James won't mind if I stay with you tonight, *Mâmân,*" said Cordelia. "Will you, James?" She glanced over at James, wondering if the traces of their argument would show in his eyes. But he was expressionless, the Mask firmly in place.

"Of course not. Whatever will make you comfortable, Mrs. Carstairs," said James. "I will have Risa come to you, as well, and bring any of Cordelia's things that she wishes."

"There is only one thing I want," Cordelia said. "I just want to see Lucie. Please—please let her know."

When James left the Silent City, he did not immediately return home. He had planned to flag down a hansom cab, but something about the idea of returning to Curzon Street without Cordelia was darkly painful. He could not help but feel he had failed her.

He found himself wandering the snowy aisles between the headstones of Highgate Cemetery, recalling the last time he had been here—when he had made his way to Belial's stolen realm with the help of Matthew and Cordelia. He had nearly died among these mausoleums, these leaning trees and solemn stone angels. Even now he sometimes wondered how he had survived, but one thing he knew without a doubt: Cordelia had saved his life.

He should have told her the truth. He struck savagely at a low branch above his head, showering himself with silvery particles of snow. Snow and ice had obscured the faces of most of the headstones, leaving only the occasional word visible: DEARLY, and CHERISHED, and LOST.

It was bad enough that he and Cordelia had exchanged sharp words. It was far worse that he hadn't found a way to tell her, somehow: *As I dreamed of your father's death, he looked at me. He seemed to recognize me, my dream-self. He knew who I was.*

I fear there was a reason for it. I am afraid these dreams are more than just dreams. More, even, than visions.

She had said she did not want the details, and he had let himself hold back the truth. But now he could think of nothing else. His memory of Elias, his face twisting with surprise and fear, the recognition in his eyes, sent James pacing through the snow, kicking up white clouds with his boots. In his mind, he pleaded with Cordelia:

My nightmares come only on the nights that there are killings. When I awake, my window is open, as if I unlocked it in my sleep and threw it wide. And why? So someone could come in? So I myself could get out?

There were facts that argued against the idea. Was he moving barefoot through the streets of London, in his nightclothes? If so, he would surely have frostbite. Was he washing the blood from his hands when he came home? How was that possible, without his mind being even a little aware of it? And Filomena had not seemed to recognize him as her killer—but they had found that bloody cloak in the factory; if her attacker had been wearing it, his face might have been hidden by the hood.

What if it is me, Daisy? What if Belial is somehow controlling me, making me into a murderer, bloodying my hands?

But Belial is gone, James. Cordelia's voice, that voice that made him want to tell her everything, that voice that promised no judgment, only kindness. *For a century at least,* Jem said.

James stopped, leaned against the wall of a marble mausoleum, decorated with carvings of Egyptian sarcophagi. He put his face in his hands. *He is a Prince of Hell. Who knows what he can do? I cannot live my life wondering, nor can I let myself be free if I am some kind of threat. I need to know.*

I must know.

*   *   *

Grace gazed out the window of her small room at the Bridgestocks' town house. She had waited many hours for everyone in the house to be gone. The Inquisitor had gone to the Institute for a meeting; Ariadne and her mother were out paying calls. They had invited Grace to come with them, but she had declined, as she always did. She did not care for company and loathed meals with the Bridgestocks, where the four of them made strained conversation. She could rarely wait to get to her room, where her books waited for her—books on magic, on necromancy and science.

Her room was small but prettily furnished. There was even a little view through the window: the tops of the trees in Cavendish Square, swaying bare and black against the gray sky. She had already made sure the door was locked; she had put on a plain white dress and let her hair down. Best she look as innocent as possible.

From the top drawer of her vanity she drew a witchlight rune-stone. She had asked Charles to give her one, and of course he had had no choice but to do so. She held back from asking him for more, not wanting to raise suspicions.

The *adamas* felt cool and smooth as water in her hand. She held it up to her lips, watching her reflection in the vanity mirror. The *adamas* was white, shot with bits of silver: the same color as her hair. Her eyes were wide and frightened. There was nothing she could do about that, and perhaps it was better.

She raised the stone to her lips and spoke. "Mama," she said, her voice low and clear. "*Audite*. Listen."

Her reflection rippled. Her long pale hair turned iron-gray, her eyes darkening to a muddy green. Lines crept across her face. She wanted to shudder, to flinch away, but she held still. It was not her own reflection she was looking at, she told herself. She was gazing through a window, opening a pathway.

Tatiana Blackthorn smiled back at her from the glass. She wore a simple gray dress, and her hair was bound into long braids in the style of the Iron Sisters. Her eyes had not changed: they were sharp, calculating.

Tatiana smiled mirthlessly. "I thought you might have forgotten about your poor mother, trapped in the Adamant Citadel."

"I think of you often, Mama," said Grace. "But they watch me, you know. It is difficult to be alone."

"Then why are you reaching out now?" Tatiana frowned. "Do you want something? I settled with the Inquisitor before I was exiled: there should be plenty of money for the Bridgestocks to buy you new dresses. I will not have it said my daughter is poorly outfitted."

Grace did not try to protest that she had not asked her mother for money; there was never any point. "It is about Malcolm Fade," she said. "I am close to getting him on our side."

"What do you mean?"

"That he will help us," said Grace. "With Jesse. Do you recall that *aletheia* crystal in the study at Chiswick House? The one that shows the trial of Annabel Blackthorn?"

Tatiana indicated impatiently that she did.

"She was exiled to the Citadel," Grace said. "Because of her relationship with Malcolm. But if you could speak to her—perhaps get a message to him—"

Tatiana burst out laughing.

Grace sat very still, feeling cold and small, as she often had when she was a child. Her mother's mocking laughter was as brittle as the cracking of melting ice.

"A message," Tatiana said at last. "From *Annabel Blackthorn*. Grace, she's been dead for nearly a century." She smiled; there was real delight in her eyes. "The Blackthorns killed her. Her own family. The story that she had become an Iron Sister was only a lie to beguile Malcolm. They didn't care what *he* did—a warlock can always be useful. But Annabel was their daughter. They were an old Nephilim family. They ran the Cornwall Institute. She had shamed them, so she had to die." She looked gleeful. "I told you the Nephilim were savages."

Grace's stomach dropped. "Are you sure?"

"The proof is in the crystal," said Tatiana. "Watch it, if you like; you know where it is. I never showed you all of it before, but since you've managed to stir up this trouble, you might as well know everything."

"But we need Malcolm's help, Mama. He can show us how to raise Jesse—"

"Well, you should have thought ahead, then, shouldn't you," said

Tatiana dryly. "All these years the truth has been concealed from Fade, by the Clave, by other warlocks—who knows what the Spiral Labyrinth could have told him, if they'd wished? He won't thank you for being the one who tells him. I can promise you that."

Why don't you care more? Grace thought. *Don't you want Jesse back?*

But all she said was, "I'm sorry, Mama."

A slow smile spread across Tatiana's face. "Now, now. I had begun to worry that you had given up on your brother. On your family. That you had forgotten us in your rush to become the Consul's daughter-in-law."

"I could never forget you," said Grace. It was the truth. "Mama— where is the crystal?"

Tatiana's eyes gleamed. "I can tell you exactly where to find it," she said. "In exchange, I ask only that you pay a visit to James Herondale at his new house on Curzon Street. I am ever so curious about his life with his new bride. Satisfy an old woman's curiosity, won't you, my dear?"

When James finally returned to Curzon Street, it was nearing sunset: the sky was sapphire shot through with amber. He found Effie waiting for him, looking put out: she told him that the Merry Thieves had all been in the drawing room for hours, demanding innumerable cups of tea. At last the Consul had arrived, bearing flowers and condolences, and demanded that the boys return home, as curfew was coming. Matthew (for whom Effie seemed to have a slight fancy) had left a note, which was waiting for James in his room. Risa had gone to Kensington with a packed valise, and also without explaining herself, which Effie thought was very rude, and she didn't mind saying so.

James nodded, barely listening, and finally gave her his coat to put away so she'd have something to do. All he wanted was to be alone. What he needed to do required it. He was almost guiltily glad he had missed his friends, that they had gone before he had returned. If he had told them of his suspicions, they would have insisted on remaining with him. He knew it, even before he made his way upstairs and sat wearily on his bed, unfolding Matthew's note.

Jamie bach—

I would stay if I could, you know that, but it is impossible to fight the Consul single-handedly, especially if she is one's mother. I left a shilling on the piano bench in case you want to send Neddy with a note, and if you do, we shall all rally around you directly. Knowing you, I suspect you wish to be on your own, but do not expect me to accept that for more than a day's time. Also, I shall expect the shilling back, you parsimonious bastard.

Yours,
Matthew

James folded the note up and placed it in his shirt pocket, close to his heart. He glanced at the window. Darkness was coming. He could no longer trust the night, or his own mind. His resolve had only hardened as he'd made his way home: he would test himself. Once he knew, he could face his friends, whatever the truth was.

He went upstairs and, in the training room, found a length of densely woven rope. He returned to his bedroom, closed the door firmly, and lay down—barefoot and jacketless, but otherwise fully dressed—on his bed. He proceeded to use the strongest knots he knew to tie his legs and one arm to the bedposts. He was trying to puzzle out a way to tie the other arm with the use of only one hand when Effie bustled into the room, carrying a tea tray.

When she saw the ropes, she froze for a moment before settling the tray carefully on the small table next to his bed.

"Ah, Effie, hello." James tried to nudge the bedcovers over the ropes, but it was impossible. He waved his one free hand airily. "I was just—I'd heard this was good for the circulation."

Effie sighed. "I'll expect a rise in my wages, I will," she said. "And I'm takin' the evenin' off. Just try and stop me."

She stalked out of the room without another word. Unfortunately, she had set the tray just out of reach, and unless James wanted to go through the business with the ropes a second time, he would simply have to make do without tea tonight.

The lamp was also out of reach, but that was not a problem as

James intended to keep it on all night. He had made sure that his knife was close by, and his plan was to hold it lightly in his fist. If he became sleepy, he would squeeze the blade hard enough to wake himself up with the pain.

A little blood was nothing if it meant proving to himself that he was not a murderer.

Much of the afternoon was a blur. Cordelia returned to Cornwall Gardens and helped Alastair get Sona into bed, a pillow propped behind her back, cool cloths for her eyes. She held her mother's hands while Sona cried and repeated over and over that she could not bear to think that Elias would now never see his third child. That he had died alone, without his family, without knowing he was loved.

Cordelia tried not to look too much at Alastair; he was her big brother, and it pained her to see him as helpless as she was. She nodded along as Sona spoke, and told her mother it would all be all right in the end. At some point Risa arrived with a small valise holding a few of Cordelia's things and took over. Cordelia could only be grateful as Risa gave Sona tea laced with laudanum. Soon her mother would sleep, and forget for a while.

She and Alastair went into the drawing room and sat side by side on the divan, silent and shocked, like the survivors of a shipwreck. After some time, Lucie arrived, breathless and tearful—it seemed James had indeed sent a runner to the Institute carrying Cordelia's request. Alastair told Cordelia that he could remain and receive visitors, if any came; she and Lucie should go upstairs and rest. They all knew few would come to pay condolences: Elias had been neither well known nor well liked.

Lucie went to get tea while Cordelia changed from her dress into a nightgown—quite a few of her old clothes were still folded away in drawers. She clambered into bed. Though the sun had not yet set, she felt exhausted.

When Lucie returned, Cordelia cried a bit on her warm, ink-smelling shoulder. Then Lucie poured her tea, and together they reminisced about Elias—not Elias as Cordelia had come to know him, but the father she'd always thought she had. Lucie recalled the way he had shown them where the best berries were to be found in the hedges at Cirenworth, or the day he had taken them horseback riding on a Devon beach.

When the sun began to slip below the rooftops, Lucie rose reluctantly and kissed the top of Cordelia's head. "I am so sorry, my dear," she said. "You know if you need me, I will always be here."

Lucie had only just gone when Cordelia's door opened again, and Alastair came in; he looked immensely tired, fine lines drawing down the corners of his mouth and eyes. Some of the black dye had faded out of his hair, and there were still bits of blond in it, incongruous among the darker strands. "*Mâmân* is finally asleep," he said, sitting down on the edge of her bed. "She kept weeping over and over to Risa about how this child will never know its father. I say: lucky child."

Another Cordelia, at another time, might have scolded him for saying such a thing. Instead she sat upright against the pillows and reached out to pat his cheek. It was a little rough—she struggled to remember when Alastair had started shaving. Had her father taught him how to do it? How to tie a tie, put on cuff links? If he had, she couldn't recall. "Alastair *joon*," she said. "The child will be lucky, but not because our father is dead. Because it will have you for a brother."

Alastair turned his face into her palm, gripping her wrist with one hand. "I can't mourn," he said in a choked voice. "I cannot mourn my own father. What does that say about me?"

"That love is complicated," said Cordelia. "That it lies beside anger and hatred, because only those we truly love can truly disappoint us."

"Did he say anything to you last night?" Alastair said and, when she widened her eyes, added gruffly, "He died in Shepherd Market, a few blocks from Curzon Street. It wasn't a great leap to assume he was visiting your house."

"He didn't say anything to me," said Cordelia. Alastair had let go of her wrist; she laced her fingers together thoughtfully. "He spoke to James. Asked him for money."

"How much money?"

"Five thousand pounds."

"Bloody hell," said Alastair. "I hope James sent him packing with a flea in his ear."

"You don't think he should have given him any money?" said Cordelia, though she knew the answer. "He said it was for Cirenworth."

"Well, it wasn't," said Alastair. "Our mother's money paid for Cirenworth. Our father, on the other hand, owed money at bars and gaming hells all over London—he has for years. It simply would have gone to paying down those debts. Good for James, which are words I never thought I would speak during my lifetime."

"I'm afraid I wasn't as understanding," Cordelia admitted. "I snapped at him about sending Father out in the snow, though I knew it wasn't at all his fault. What does that say about *me?*"

"That grief makes us mad," said Alastair quietly. "James will understand that. No one is expected to be on their best behavior the day their father dies."

"It's not so simple," Cordelia whispered. "Something is wrong with Cortana."

Alastair blinked. "Cortana? We *are* talking about your sword?"

"The last time I tried to use it in battle—and don't ask for the details, I can't tell you—suddenly the hilt went burning hot, as if it had been lying in coals. There was no way to hold on to it. I dropped it, and if James hadn't been there, I would have been killed."

"When was this?" Alastair looked shaken. "If this is true—"

"It is true, and it wasn't long ago, but—I know why it happened," Cordelia continued, not looking at him. "It's because I'm not worthy of it anymore."

"Not worthy? Why on earth would that be?"

Because I am living a lie. Because my marriage is a sham. Because every time I speak to James and pretend I do not love him, I am lying to his face.

She said, "I need *you* to take Cortana, Alastair. It no longer chooses me."

"That's ridiculous," Alastair said, almost angrily. "If something's wrong, it's the sword, not you."

"But—"

"Take the sword to the Silent Brothers. Have them look at it. Cordelia, I will not take Cortana. You are the rightful owner of the sword." He stood up. "Now get some sleep. You must be exhausted."

GRACE:
1899

"I'm going to ask the Herondale boy to come cut our briars,"
Tatiana said casually one day after breakfast.

Grace said nothing. It had been two years, but she sometimes missed
the approval her mother had once shown her in Paris. When they had
returned, Tatiana had forbidden Grace to tell Jesse the details of their
activities, and Grace had not needed persuasion. She didn't want Jesse to
know what she had done. He might have thought she was a terrible person, and Grace couldn't bear that. She knew Jesse would never compel
someone's will, even if Tatiana bade him to. But there was no comparison to be made. Tatiana would never have lifted a hand against her boy,
and she would never have willingly infused him with sorcery, either.
Tatiana had different rules for her son and her daughter. There was no
point in questioning them.

Tatiana looked out the window at the manor walls. "The thorns
have overgrown the gates. We can barely open and close them without
cutting ourselves to ribbons. It's badly needed."

Grace was taken aback. Her mother did not normally act familiar
with the idea that a house needed to be maintained, or even repaired
when broken. Grace knew that the hated Herondales had come to stay
at their own family manor, not too distant, for the summer, and that

there were a boy and a girl, both near her age. They'd come in summers before, and Tatiana had always forbidden her to meet them. "I thought you didn't want us to have anything to do with them," she said carefully.

Tatiana smiled. "I want you to bring the boy, James, under your spell."

That was even more puzzling. "What do you want me to ask of him?" What could her mother possibly want with James Herondale?

"Nothing," said Tatiana, looking shrewd. "Nothing yet. Simply make him love you. It will amuse me."

After all her mother's curses and fussing over the family, Grace half expected something monstrous to come loping over the horizon with the name Herondale. James turned out to be an entirely normal boy, however, much more friendly and easy than the boors she'd met in Paris, and not too bad to look at either. And though she knew it was only in service of her mother's orders, she was starved for company, and James seemed to welcome hers. It was nice to have someone to talk to who was not a ghost. Soon they were chatting every evening, and she could tell that James was shirking on his briar-cutting duties in order to extend the number of days he would be needed at Blackthorn Manor.

Was it her power? She wasn't exactly sure. She had asked nothing more of James than that he visit her, and he was willing, but she thought he might have done so without any ensorcelling at all. He must also be lonely, with no friends nearby, and he had a kind soul.

At one point she said, casually, "Will I see you here tomorrow night?" It was the sort of question she'd asked a dozen times before.

James frowned. "No," he said. "I am summoned to a reading tomorrow night, of the latest installment of my sister's ongoing masterpiece about Cruel Prince James."

"Oh?" said Grace, not entirely sure what this meant.

"Evidently," James said, his mouth quirking on one side, "in this chapter the Cruel Prince James tries to keep the Princess Lucie from her true love, the Duke Arnoldo, but he falls into a pig bog. Riveting stuff."

Grace pouted—an expression she hadn't used with James before, but she had much practice from her time in Paris. "But I'd so like to see you," she said in sorrowful tones. She leaned toward him. "Come see me tomorrow night anyway. Tell your family my mother has threatened you, and you have to work or risk her wrath."

James laughed. "Tempting as that may be—I'm so sorry, Grace, but I really must be there, or Lucie will fashion me into a large hat. I'll see you the day after next, I promise."

Grace waited until the very end of the summer to speak to her mother about the situation. James and his family had already left for London. It was so strange to think of them as the same Herondales her mother railed against; to go by James's descriptions, they seemed to resemble Tatiana's sworn enemies not at all. She had been fairly certain what was happening for a few weeks, but she had decided to give it the season. "My power wasn't working on James."

Tatiana's eyebrows went up. "Is he not fond of you?"

"He is fond of me, I think," Grace said. "But sometimes I've made requests—unreasonable requests, things he wouldn't ordinarily do, to see if I could make him. And I can't."

Her mother had a sour look. "The crowned heads of Europe come at your beck and call," she said, "but the son of a Welsh mud farmer eludes your grasp."

"I have been trying, Mama," Grace said. "Maybe it's because he's a Shadowhunter. Maybe they have more resistance to the magic."

Tatiana didn't say anything further then, but a few weeks later she abruptly announced that they were departing for Alicante in an hour, and Grace should ready herself to go out.

13

THE WINTRY WIND

No boughs have withered because of the wintry wind;
The boughs have withered because I have told them my dreams.
—William Butler Yeats, "The Withering of the Boughs"

Once Alastair was gone, the room seemed terribly quiet. Cordelia glanced at the door—she was used to falling asleep with James but a few feet away. Now he was miles away, and likely going to bed assuming she was furious with him.

James. She had grown accustomed to seeing him first thing in the morning, and last thing at night. It still felt very strange to undress in the bathroom knowing he was just a few feet away, but . . . Now she was alone. Not alone—her brother was down the hall, her mother asleep downstairs—but she missed James.

Cordelia sighed. She wasn't going to get to sleep anytime soon, whatever Alastair had said. She was about to find a book to pass the time, when her window flew suddenly open with a crash, and someone hurtled through the gap, landing on the floor next to her bed in a hectic tumble of freezing-cold air, blond curls, and bright orange spats.

"*Matthew?*"

He had landed awkwardly on the floor. He sat up, rubbing his elbow and cursing softly. "That was the first decent thing Alastair ever did in his life. And to think I was here to see it. Well, spy on it, technically."

"Go and close the window," Cordelia said, "or I *will* throw the teapot at you. What are you doing here?"

"Visiting," he said, dusting himself off and going to close the window. "What does it look like?"

"Most people use the front door," Cordelia said. "What did you mean about Alastair?"

"Cortana. I'm talking about Alastair refusing your ridiculous offer. I agree with him, by the way: that sword can't un-choose you and it has no reason to do so. Probably it's broken."

"It's a mythical sword. It can't be *broken*." Cordelia tugged her covers up; it felt very odd indeed to be sitting in front of Matthew in her nightgown. "Were you really out there listening?"

"Yes, and you might have been quicker about sending your brother off. I was freezing."

Matthew's utter lack of repentance made it impossible to be angry at him. Cordelia hid a smile—her first smile of the day. "And why, pray tell?"

"When I heard what happened, I went to pay my respects at Curzon Street, but neither of you were there—"

"James wasn't at home?"

"I suspect he was having a wander. He likes to walk about when he feels troubled—apparently Uncle Will used to do the same thing," said Matthew. "I guessed you might be here, but I was afraid if I knocked on the door, your family wouldn't let me see you, not at this hour."

She looked at him, puzzled. "You could have waited until tomorrow."

He sat down on the end of her bed. It was most improper, Cordelia thought, but then again, she was a married woman. As Anna had said, she was free to do as she liked, even to let young men in orange spats sit on the end of her bed. "I don't think I could have," he said, avoiding her gaze by prodding gently at her coverlet. "There was something I needed to tell you."

"What?"

Very quickly, he said, "I know what it is to be in pain, and not to be able to seek comfort from the one you love the most, nor to be able to share that pain with anyone you know."

"What do you mean?"

He raised his head. His eyes were very green in the dim light. "I mean," he said, "this may be a false marriage, but you're truly in love with James."

Cordelia stared at him, horrified. His hair was madly tousled, damp with melting snow. The cold had whipped sharp color into his cheeks, and his eyes were bright with—nervousness? Could Matthew actually be nervous?

"Does James know?" she whispered.

"No," Matthew said, forcefully. "Lord, no. I love James, but he's blind as a bat where it comes to matters of the heart."

Cordelia gripped the blanket in both hands. "How long? How long have you known, and how—how did you guess?"

"The way you look at him," Matthew said simply. "I know you did not mean for this marriage to happen, that you did not scheme for it. Indeed, it must be a special sort of torture for you. And I am sorry for it. You deserve to be happy."

Cordelia looked at him in surprise. She had, she realized, never thought of Matthew as enormously insightful. She had not thought he took things seriously enough for that.

"I know what it's like to hide what you feel," he said. "I know what it's like to be in pain and not be able to explain why. I know why you're not with James tonight. Because when we are in pain, we are flayed open, and when we are flayed open, we cannot hide our true selves. And you cannot bear for him to know that you love him."

"How did you learn all this?" Cordelia demanded. "When did you become so wise?"

"I have known unrequited love myself, in the past."

"Is that why you are so very sad?" Cordelia said.

Matthew was silent. "I did not know," he said, after a moment, "that I seemed sad, to you."

Cordelia shivered a little, though it was not cold in the room. "There is something weighing on you, Matthew," she said gently. "A secret. I know it, as you knew I was in love with James. Will you tell me what it is?"

She saw his hand go to his breast pocket, where he often kept his flask. Then he lowered it stiffly to his side and took a deep breath. "You do not know what you are asking."

"Yes, I do," she said. "I am asking for the truth. *Your* truth. You know mine, and I do not even know what makes you so unhappy."

It was as if he had frozen, sitting there at the end of her bed, a Matthew-statue. Only his fingers moved, tracing the embroidery on a pillow. When he spoke, finally, his voice sounded almost like a stranger's—not Matthew's usual bright, water-swift tones, but something much deeper, and more still. "I have told no one this story," he said. "Not in all my life. Jem knows it. No one else. It is perhaps the very height of foolishness to tell you, and to ask you to keep it from James. I have never told him myself."

Cordelia hesitated. "I cannot promise to hide it from him."

"Then I can only leave it to your judgment, and hope you will share my opinion that it would do him no good to know," Matthew said. "But beware. This story is also about Alastair, though I do not think he knows all of it."

"James told me some of it, then. The rumors Alastair spread. Perhaps you think I am terrible, still loving him."

"No. I think you are his saving grace. If you know about the rumors, you know some of it, but not all."

"I want to know it all," Cordelia said, and Matthew, staring at the wall next to her bed, said in the same low, toneless voice, "All right, then. We were at school. Too young to know the power of words, perhaps. When Alastair came around, saying things about my mother . . . saying Henry was not my father, that instead I was Gideon's bastard . . ." He shook his head, his entire body tensing. "I thought I would kill Alastair right there. I didn't, of course, but—" He cast the pillow aside. "The awful thing about it was that once I had the idea planted in my brain, I couldn't stop thinking about it. My father was injured before I was born; I had only ever known him confined to his chair. Nor do I resemble him at all. It began to consume me, the wondering . . . and one day I gathered my courage and went to the Shadow Market. I didn't know exactly what I was looking for, but in the end, I bought a bottle of 'truth potion.'

"The next morning I put some in my mother's food. I thought

I would ask her to tell me who my father was, and that she would either not realize she was under a spell, or she would forgive me and understand that I deserved to know."

Matthew let his head fall back. He stared at the ceiling as he said, "It wasn't a truth potion at all, though I suppose you could have guessed that. Whatever it was, it was poison, and . . . my mother was pregnant. I didn't know it, of course, but whatever I gave her, it caused her agony, and she—she lost the baby."

Horror jolted through Cordelia. "Oh, Matthew," she whispered.

He didn't pause, his breath catching on his words. "The Silent Brothers were able to save my mother, but not my sister. My mother has not been with child since, though I know my parents have hoped and tried.

"That very day, I learned the truth—that I was without a doubt my father's son. It had all been a stupid rumor. I was drowning, speechless, shattered. My father assumed I was struggling to make sense of the loss. The truth was that I was horrified by my own actions, disgusted by my lack of faith in those closest to me. I swore to myself that I would never tell anyone, not even James. And I decided that I would never forgive Alastair, though I blamed myself so much more than I ever blamed him."

At last, he looked at her. "That's the story, Cordelia. That's my secret. You hate me now, and I can't blame you. I can't even ask you not to tell James. Do whatever you must. I will understand."

Cordelia pushed her coverlet down. Matthew watched her with some apprehension—perhaps he thought she was going to throw him out of the house. Instead she reached out, nearly toppling over, and put her arms around him.

She heard him inhale sharply. He smelled of snow, of soap and wool. He was stiff as a board, but she held on, determined.

"Cordelia," he said in a choked voice, at last, and put his head down on her shoulder.

She held him as close as she could, feeling his heartbeat against her chest. She held him the way she wished she could have asked James to hold her, that morning in the stone corridor outside the Ossuarium. She stroked the soft hair at the nape of his neck. "You never meant to harm anyone, though you did cause harm," she said. "You must forgive yourself, Matthew."

He made an incoherent noise, muffled against her shoulder. Cordelia couldn't help thinking of Alastair. He could not have known, of course, what would come of his rumor-spreading—but neither could Matthew have known what the result of his truth potion would be. They were more alike, she thought, than either would want to admit.

"Matthew," she said gently, "you must *tell* your mother. She will forgive you, and you will no longer carry this bitter weight alone."

"I can't," Matthew whispered. "Now she grieves for one child. After that she would grieve for another, for she and my father would never forgive me." He raised his head from her shoulder. "Thank you. For not hating me. I promise you, it makes a difference."

Cordelia drew back, squeezing his hand.

"Now that you have heard what I have done," said Matthew, "perhaps you will stop thinking you are not worthy of Cortana. For there is nothing *you* could have done to deserve such treatment, even from an inanimate object." He smiled, though it was not Matthew's usual sunshine smile, but something altogether more tense and strained.

"Then perhaps it is a flaw with the sword, as Alastair says, though—" She broke off, eyeing Matthew thoughtfully. "I have an idea. And it involves another secret. If I asked you to go somewhere with me—"

He smiled crookedly. "I would do anything for you, of course, my lady."

"Don't play about," she said, waving off his theatrics. "James told me your new flat has a motorcar they let you use. And I have some distance I need to travel. Fetch me tomorrow morning, and we will go together." Quickly, she told him what the faerie woman in the Hell Ruelle had said to her of Wayland the Smith. "If anyone can tell me what's wrong with Cortana, he can. If he even exists, but—I have to do *something*. I must at least try to find him."

"And you want me to take you?" Matthew looked both surprised and pleased.

"Of course I do," Cordelia said. "You're the only person I know who has a motorcar."

* * *

Alastair stood in the parlor, staring blankly out the window at the house next door. He had been watching two little boys playing on the floor of their living room while their mother worked at her embroidery and their father read the newspaper. He could not help but hear his mother's words as she'd wept, *The child will never know his father.*

Lucky child, he'd said to Cordelia, but under the flippancy, there was a hard, cold sorrow, a sorrow that felt like a blade of ice cutting through him. It was hard to breathe around the loss. It had been a long time since he had felt an uncomplicated love for his father, but there was no ease in knowing that. If anything, it made the blade of ice inside him twist harder with every breath, with every thought of the future. *Never to see him again. Never to hear his voice, his footstep. Never to see him smile at the baby.*

Pulling the curtains shut, Alastair told himself the baby would have everything he could give it. A presence in its life of someone who could not quite be a parent, but who would try to be a better brother than he had been to Cordelia. Someone who would tell the child he or she was loved, and perfect, and need not change for anyone or anything.

There was a knock at the door. Alastair started—it was late, too late for anyone paying their respects to stop by. Not that many people had. Even the older Shadowhunters who knew Elias as the hero who slew Yanluo had forgotten over the past decades; his death was a ghost's death, the vanishing of someone who had barely been there at all.

Risa had long gone to sleep; Alastair went himself to answer the door. When he flung it open, he found Thomas Lightwood standing on the doorstep.

Alastair couldn't think of a thing to say. He just stared. Thomas, like all his fool friends, went without a hat: his hair was wet, and the damp ends kissed the angles of his face. His features were surprisingly refined for all that he was so enormous—well, "enormous" wasn't really the word for it. It didn't capture Thomas's compact way of moving. He was tall, but unlike some other tall men, he carried himself with a quiet authority that matched his height. His body was perfectly proportioned too, from what Alastair recalled—it was hard to tell when someone was bundled up in an overcoat.

Thomas cleared his throat. His hazel eyes were steady as he said, "I came to tell you that I'm sorry about your father. I really am."

"Thank you," Alastair whispered. He knew he had to stop staring at Thomas, but he wasn't quite sure how to manage it, and in a moment, it didn't matter anyway. Without another word, Thomas turned on his heel and strode quickly away.

"What did you do with my gold comb?" Lucie said.

Jesse, who had sprawled on her bed with a most unghostlike aplomb, smiled. He was leaning back against her pillows, looking rather pleased with himself. She had been sitting at her desk in her nightgown, scrawling notes, when he had appeared, causing her to blot her page. He seemed pleased to have managed to surprise her.

"Hidden it away safely," he said. "It reminds me of you when you are not there."

She sat down on the edge of the bed. "Perhaps you should haunt me more often."

He touched a wisp of her hair, which she had taken down for the evening. She wished sometimes she had radiant hair like Cordelia, who always looked like a sunset. Instead hers was plain brown, like her mother's. "But then you would not be able to see your friends in the evening, which would be a shame," he said. "It sounds as if you are having quite a lively time. Though," he added with a frown, "I wish I knew who this Regency gentleman was who importuned you. I don't like the idea of you seeing other ghosts."

Lucie had told him all about the murders, their visit to the factory, and her conversation with Filomena. The only thing she had not told him was the favor she had done for the Regency ghost. She did not think he would like it.

"What's wrong?" Jesse inquired. "You seem plagued with dark thoughts."

Uncle Gabriel, Aunt Cecily, and Christopher had all surrounded Lucie when she returned from Cordelia's, wanting to know how the

Carstairs were managing. Lucie had felt too exhausted to say much then, but talking to Jesse was different.

"I am worried about Cordelia," she said. "I cannot imagine losing my father."

"Yours seems to be a very good father," said Jesse. He was looking at her with that level, serious gaze that always made her feel as if he were listening to her, thinking about her above all other things in the world.

"I always thought he was perfect," she confided. "Even now, when I am old enough to realize no human being is perfect, I can say with confidence that as a father, he has never disappointed me or left me in doubt of how much he loves me. But for Daisy . . ."

"Her father was gone," said Jesse. "And when he came back, any joy she might have felt was complicated by his behavior."

"And now she will never have a chance to confront him, or to make peace with him, or even to forgive him."

"She can forgive him regardless," said Jesse. "My father died before I was born. I loved him nonetheless. And forgave him, even, for leaving me. One can reach peace on one's own, though it is difficult—but Cordelia has you. That will make it easier." Seeing her worried look, Jesse held his arm out. "Come here," he said, and Lucie clambered onto the bed and curled up against his side.

As he had when they had danced, he felt solid. She could feel the fabric of his shirt, even, see a tiny cluster of freckles on the side of his neck.

He touched her hair again, smoothing his hand down the strands. "I feel lucky to see you like this," he said, his voice low. "With your hair loose. As if I were your husband."

She felt herself blush. "It's such dull hair. Just brown, not an interesting color like Grace's, or—"

"It's not 'just brown,'" he said. "It glows like polished wood, and it has all sorts of colors in it—bits of gold where the sun's touched it, and strands of chocolate and caramel and walnut."

She sat up, reaching for her hairbrush where it lay on the nightstand. "What if I were to command you," she said, "to brush out my hair? Jessamine does it sometimes—"

His smile was long and lazy. "I am yours to command."

She handed him the brush and turned around, dangling her legs off the end of the bed. She felt him move behind her, kneeling, his hand lifting the heavy coil of her brown hair to loosen it over her shoulders.

"Long ago," he said in a low voice, "when Grace first came to us, I used to brush her hair out at night. My mother had no interest in doing it, and otherwise it would tangle and snarl, and Grace would cry."

Lucie leaned back as the heavy brush slid through her hair, followed by his fingers. It felt decadent, luxurious to be touched like this. His hand grazed the nape of her neck, sending shivers up her spine. Not at all like when Jessamine did it.

"Grace must have been just a child when she first came to you," she said.

"She was a slip of a thing. Terrified. Remembered almost nothing about her parents. I think, if my mother had loved her, Grace would have devoted herself entirely to my mother's wishes and goals. But—" She sensed him shaking his head. "I was all Grace had. Sometimes I think that's why I came back as I did. I do not remember death itself, but I do remember waking out of it. I had heard Grace crying in her sleep and knew I must go to her. I have always been all she has. It is why I cannot bear to tell her—"

He broke off. Lucie turned; he was kneeling on the bedcovers, the brush in one hand, his expression frozen between guilt and alarm.

"That you are fading," she said quietly. "That you have been, slowly, since you gave your last breath to save my brother."

He set the brush aside. "You know?"

She thought of the way his hand had faded against hers in the carriage, the way he had gone part-transparent when he was angry, as if he lacked the energy to appear whole.

"I guessed it," she whispered. "It is why I have been so desperate— I am afraid. Jesse, if you fade, will I ever see you again?"

"I don't know." His green gaze was stark. "I fear it as anyone would fear dying, and I know as little about what waits on the other side of the great gate."

She laid her hand on his wrist. "Do you trust me?"

He managed a smile. "Most of the time."

She turned fully, so that her hands were on his shoulders. "I want to command you to live."

He jerked in surprise; she felt the movement under her hands. She was as close to him as she had been the night they danced. "Lucie. There are limits. I cannot be commanded to do what is impossible."

"Let us forget, just for a moment, what is possible and impossible," Lucie said. "It may do nothing; it may make you stronger. But I cannot live with myself if I do not try."

She did not mention the animals she had tried this experiment on, or her unsuccessful attempts to call back Jesse himself while he slept in his coffin. But—unlike the animals—Jesse occupied a place between life and death and was therefore unpredictable; perhaps she needed him there, consciously alongside her, to raise him properly. She thought of the Regency ghost again, after she had commanded him to forget. There had been a look of peace on his face that had startled her.

There was a long pause. "All right," Jesse said. There was uncertainty in his eyes, but his cheeks were flushed; she knew it was not real blood, real heat, but it made her spirits lift nevertheless. Other ghosts did not blush, or touch, or shiver. Jesse was already different. "Try."

She settled back on her heels. She was quite a bit smaller than he was, and felt slight indeed as she laid her palms against his chest. She could feel the fabric of his shirt, the hard solidity of him.

"Jesse," she said softly. "Jesse Rupert Blackthorn. I command you to breathe. To return to yourself. *Live.*"

He gasped. She had never heard a ghost gasp, or imagined it, and for a moment her heart soared. His green eyes widened, and he caught at her shoulder—his grip was hard, almost painful.

"Knit your soul with your body," she said. "Live, Jesse. Live."

His eyes went black. And suddenly she was falling, struggling in a complete, choking darkness. There was no light—no, there was light in the distance, flickering, the wan light of an illuminated doorway. She struggled to catch at something to arrest her fall.

Jesse. Where was Jesse? She could see nothing but darkness. She thought of James: Was this what it was like to *fall into shadow*? This terrible, alien, unmoored feeling?

Jesse! She reached out for him—she could sense he was there with her, somehow. She was touching mist, shadow, and then her hands

Jesse Blackthorn

closed on something solid. It writhed in her grip. She held on hard; yes, it had a human form. They were falling together. If she held on tight enough, she could bring him back, she thought, like Janet had done for Tam Lin in the old story.

But there was something wrong. A terrible pressure of wrongness, invading her chest, stealing her breath. The shadows around her seemed to break into pieces, each one a snarling, twisting monster—a thousand demons born of darkness. She felt a barrier, unbreakable, terrible, rise up before her, as if she had arrived at the gates of Hell. The form in her arms was spiky-sharp, burning and stabbing her; she let go—

And hit the ground, hard, knocking out her breath. She moaned and rolled over, retching dryly.

"Lucie! *Lucie!*" Jesse was hovering over her, an expression of terror on his face. She was on the wooden floor of her room, she realized dazedly. She must have tumbled off the bed.

"I'm sorry," she breathed, reaching out to touch him, but her fingers glided through his shoulder. They both froze, staring at each other. "No, no," she said. "I've made it worse—"

"You haven't." He closed his hand over her reaching one. His fingers were solid. "It's the same. Nothing's changed. But we can't try that again, Lucie. There are some things, I think, that cannot be commanded."

"Death is a jealous mistress," Lucie whispered. "She fights to keep you."

"I am not hers," he said. "I am yours for as long as I can be."

"Stay," she said, and closed her eyes. She felt more drained than she ever had before, more exhausted. She thought again of James. She should have been more sympathetic, she thought, all these years. She had never understood before: how bitter it was to have power, and not be able to turn it to any kind of good.

Thomas almost welcomed the bitter cold, the crunch of ice underneath his boots, the aching stiffness in his fingers and toes. All day he had waited for this, for the solitude of patrolling alone late at night, when all his senses seemed heightened, and the melancholy that followed him everywhere was replaced—if only for a few hours—by a sense of purpose.

Thomas missed the weight of the *bolas* in his hand, but even his tutor in Madrid—Maestro Romero of Buenos Aires—would have agreed it wasn't the best choice for stalking a killer on the streets of London. Such a weapon wasn't easy to hide, and he had to be stealthy.

He knew that if anyone found out what he was doing, there would be trouble. He had never seen his parents as stern as they had been when they explained the new rules the Enclave had decided on. And he agreed with them: the curfew absolutely made sense, as did the rule against anyone patrolling alone.

Except him.

Earlier in the evening, Thomas had been in South Kensington and could not resist paying a visit to the Carstairs. He had half hoped Cordelia would be there—he liked her, and truly felt for her. But it had been Alastair who had answered the door. Alastair, looking strained and tense, as if grief had tightened his skin over his bones. His lower lip was red, as if he'd bitten it, his fingers—*fingers that had run so gently over the inside of Thomas's forearm, where a compass rose now unfurled its inked lines*—twitching nervously at his side.

Thomas had nearly run away on the spot. The last few times he had seen Alastair, rage had successfully blinded him to any other feeling. But it had deserted him now. It had been only a few months since Barbara had died, and there were times when the pain of losing her was just as great as it had been during the first hours after she was gone.

He could see that same pain on Alastair's face. Alastair, who he had told himself had no feelings. Alastair, who he had been trying so hard to despise.

He had managed only a few clumsy words of condolence before turning and walking away. Since then he had simply kept going, covering miles and miles of London, keeping to the smaller streets and alleys where the killer would be likely to hide himself. Now he found himself in the area around Fleet Street, its newspaper offices and restaurants and shops shuttered, the only light coming from the windows of the buildings that housed the presses hard at work printing copies of tomorrow morning's paper.

Pounceby had been killed only blocks from where Thomas now walked. He decided to turn down Fleet Street, to see the scene of his death. If Thomas retraced Pounceby's steps, maybe he could discover something the others had missed. Or, if the killer was a creature of habit, Thomas might even draw him out. The thought did not make him afraid; on the contrary, it made him determined and hungry for a fight.

Thomas turned down the side street where Pounceby's body had been found. It was snowbound, quiet, no hint that anything dreadful had happened here. Only a sense of tension in the air—a prickle at the back of Thomas's neck, as if he were being watched—

A footfall crunched on packed snow. Thomas tensed and spun around, landing in a defensive stance.

There, in the shadow of an awning, a dark figure froze, face obscured by a hood. For a moment neither moved—and then the stranger bolted. He was fast—faster than Thomas expected. Even as Thomas broke into a run, the stranger was already putting distance between the two of them. Thomas sped up as the figure cut nimbly into an alley.

Swearing, Thomas ducked under a railing; he thundered into the alley, but the figure had already vanished around a distant corner. Thomas jogged to the alley's end, already knowing what he would see. Nothing. His pursuer had vanished, his footprints indistinguishable from dozens of others in the much-trodden snow.

14

THE FLAMING FORGE

Thus at the flaming forge of life
Our fortunes must be wrought;
Thus on its sounding anvil shaped
Each burning deed and thought.
—Henry Wadsworth Longfellow, "The Village Blacksmith"

Cordelia was waiting early the next morning, when Matthew arrived in his shiny Ford Model A. It was quite cold; despite her heavy coat and wool dress, the wind seemed to cut through to her skin. Cortana was strapped across her back; she had not glamoured herself to be invisible to mundanes, but she *had* glamoured the blade.

She had slipped out before breakfast, leaving a note for her mother saying that she had to return to James and Curzon Street. Her mother would understand that; demands of home and hearth were paramount for Sona. As for Alastair, Cordelia had left him a separate note, repeating firmly that he was welcome at her house and begging him to visit whenever he wanted. She was worried about him; she could tell from signs around the house that he had been up all night.

Thinking about their father, she assumed. She felt a little unreal as Matthew gave her a tour around the little car, absently admiring its gleaming red paintwork and shiny brass rails while he talked excitedly about the finer points of its engine, including something called a crank chamber. Though she tried to stop them, every once in a while pain-dark thoughts would intrude:

My father is dead. My father is dead. This is the first morning of my life when I will wake up knowing he is gone.

". . . and there's a combined epicyclic gear and clutch mechanism mounted on the crankshaft," Matthew went on. Cordelia distantly noted that the car's slender wheels with their matching red spokes seemed barely attached to the rest of it; that its padded leather seat was only just wide enough for two. The folded-down canopy behind it was not likely to provide much in the way of coverage if it rained, and the whole contraption looked flimsy enough to blow away in a strong wind.

"This is all very nice," she said finally, pushing her darker thoughts away again, "but I can't help noticing that there is no roof on this car. We're both likely to be frozen stiff."

"Not to worry," Matthew said, rummaging behind the seat and producing a pair of magnificent fur-lined traveling rugs. He was dressed immaculately in a smart, also fur-lined leather duster coat and boots polished to a high shine. He looked remarkably awake, considering.

"Does anyone know where we're going?" she asked, taking hold of his extended hand and climbing up into the car.

"I didn't tell anyone *where*," Matthew said, "but I let Thomas know that we were going for a drive. We'll be back in time to meet the others at Curzon Street this evening."

The others, Cordelia thought. Which included James. She pushed the thought of him away determinedly as she settled herself under the traveling rug. Glancing back at Cornwall Gardens, her eyes caught a flicker of movement. Alastair stood at an upper window, looking down at her; she raised a gloved hand to him tentatively—the last thing she could bear at the moment was an altercation between Matthew and her brother—and he nodded, flicking the curtain back into place.

"What was that?" Matthew asked.

"Alastair," said Cordelia. "Just—waving goodbye."

Matthew cranked the starting handle, and Cordelia settled gratefully back as the Ford roared to life. She couldn't help thinking, as they pulled out onto the street, how much her father would have loved to see the car.

* * *

James blinked his eyes open; his room was full of sunlight. If he had dreamed, he did not remember it: his mind was blissfully free of the recollection of screams, of darkness, of hatred and the flashing of a knife. He glanced down: he was still in his clothes, wrinkled after a night's sleep. It was icy cold.

He looked around, shivering; the window was cracked open several inches.

Swearing, James sat bolt upright. The ropes lay in pieces around him, the knife beside his hand. Somehow, during the night, he had cut himself free.

He rolled out of bed and stalked to the window. He reached up to slide it closed—perhaps it was time to nail the thing shut—and paused.

In the ice on the windowsill had been traced an odd mark. He stood for a moment, studying it. Who had scratched it there?

Dread rose in the pit of his stomach. He had not been still while he slept. He'd cut himself free. Anything could have happened. And the symbol, on the window—

He had to talk to Daisy. He was halfway to her room when he remembered, his brain clearing: she wasn't there. She was at her mother's. He wanted to rush to Kensington, wanted to beg Cordelia to come home. She lived *here*, belonged here. But he couldn't blame her if she didn't want to see him. He had been the last person to speak to her father, and their exchange had been ugly and vicious. And what was he proposing to confess? That he thought he might be the reason her father was dead? That his might have been the hand that held the knife?

And God knew what he had done last night.

Nausea stabbed through him. Downstairs, he thought. That was where the books he'd brought from the Institute were. He needed to look, to be absolutely sure. He threw on a jacket and shoes and clattered down the steps—

The doorbell rang.

No Effie appeared to answer it; she must not have returned from her night off. Praying it wasn't some half stranger bearing condolences,

James flung the door open. A werewolf boy of eight or nine occupied the stoop outside, his dirty hair tucked under a worn woolen cap, his face grimy.

"Neddy," James said, surprised. "What are you doing here?" His hand tightened on the doorknob. "Has there been another murder?"

"No, sir," the boy said, digging in his pocket for a crumpled note, which he handed to James. "No reports of any Shadowhunter deaths."

No deaths. The killer had not struck. There was relief—no one had been hurt—as well as apprehension: he was no better off than he had been the day before. The deaths were occurring sporadically, not every night, but close together. He could not assume there would not be another. What could he do tonight, if tying himself to the bed hadn't worked?

James unfolded the note and immediately recognized Thomas's handwriting. He scanned the brief lines quickly: Matthew had taken Cordelia for a drive to cheer her up; the other Thieves, Thomas and Christopher, would be coming to Curzon Street shortly. *I know Elias's death has been a shock,* Thomas had written. *But brush your hair. Risa said you looked as if you'd been electrocuted.*

"Everything all right, then?" Neddy said. "Right enough for me to get my tip?"

As James turned up a shilling for Neddy, he found the boy gawking curiously at the large, glossy carriage that had just drawn up before the house. James frowned. It was the Fairchild carriage, marked on the side with its pattern of wings. Had Charlotte come to pay her respects?

James pressed the money into Neddy's hand and sent him on his way, just as the door to the carriage opened, and a slim hand in a dove-colored leather glove appeared, followed by sweeping ivory-colored skirts and a short coat of pale mink, topped with a head of upswept silver-blond hair, glimmering like metal in the sun.

It was Grace.

Cordelia fished a long woolen scarf from her handbag and wrapped it around her hair, securing her hat firmly to her head to keep it from flying off in the wind. Even slowed down by the London traffic, the little car felt wildly fast; it was able to nip in and out of spaces that a carriage would never have been able to navigate. Feeling somewhat windblown, she tied her hat down more firmly with her scarf as they zipped between two horse-buses and a milk cart and narrowly missed swerving onto the pavement. Several workmen by the side of the road cheered.

"Apologies!" yelled Matthew with a grin, spinning the wheel deftly to the right and shooting across another junction.

Cordelia eyed him severely. "Do you actually know where we're going?"

"Of course I do! I have a map."

He produced a slim red clothbound book from a pocket and handed it to her. *The Bath Road,* read the cover.

"We'll definitely need a bath, by the time we get there," she said, as the car splashed through a muddy puddle.

Their route took them through Hammersmith, roughly following the course of the Thames, visible in glimpses through the factories and houses of the outer suburbs. As they passed a sign for the turning toward Chiswick, Cordelia thought of Grace, a sort of humming discomfort behind her ribs.

Once they were through Brentford, its busy high street clogged with buses, the traffic thinned out and the buildings gave way to a more rural landscape. Open fields stretched out in front of them, pale with frost tinged pink by the early-morning sun. Matthew, hatless and grinning, his hair whipped back by the wind, beamed at her.

She had never experienced anything like this before. The world was unfolding before them, promising the unknown. Every mile they drove made the ache in her chest recede further. She was not Cordelia Herondale, who had just lost her father, who loved a man who would never love her. She was someone free and nameless, flying like a bird above the road that blurred beneath their wheels.

As the countryside hurtled by, the green hills mottled with melting patches of snow, the little villages with smoke drifting from chimneys, Cordelia imagined what it must be like to be Matthew—living on his own, able to go wherever he liked, whenever he liked. Always keeping some part of himself separate, slipping in and out of events and parties, never committing to being anywhere, disappointing hosts by not showing up, or arriving late to the undimmed delight of everyone who knew him. She wasn't sure anyone had a true hold on Matthew, save James.

Of course Matthew would be the one among all of them to take up motoring, she thought. He diligently sought out exactly the feeling it provided, of nothing under your feet, of speed and purpose, of noise too loud to think. For perhaps the first time she realized that a small part of her sought it too.

She kept the little map on her lap and checked off the towns and villages as they passed through them. Hounslow, Colnbrook, Slough, Maidenhead. At Maidenhead they stopped briefly for a cup of tea in a hotel beside the Thames, next to the pretty seven-arched stone bridge. The decor and the atmosphere was rather Victorian; a pair of break-fasting old ladies stared disapprovingly at their somewhat disheveled motoring outfits. Matthew deployed the Smile at them, causing them to flutter like alarmed sparrows.

Back in the car, the villages whirled past like stage sets. Twyford, Theale, Woolhampton, Thatcham, Lambourn. There was an inn at Lambourn, in the village's tiny market square. It was called the George, and it had a place to leave the car and a dim, cozy interior of which Cordelia—freezing by now—noticed nothing at all apart from a huge fireplace with a beautiful, roaring fire and two armchairs at a table beside it, which were wonderfully vacant. Cordelia suspected that not many travelers passed by this part of the Downs in deep winter.

A young woman in a sprigged cotton dress and white apron hurried to serve them. She was pretty, with auburn hair and a lush figure. Cordelia didn't miss the way the girl looked at Matthew, who was handsome indeed in his leather coat, his goggles pushed up into his tousled blond hair.

Matthew didn't miss the glance either. He ordered ale for himself and ginger beer for Cordelia, then inquired—with a rather shocking wink—what was good to eat. The girl flirted back as though Cordelia wasn't there, but she didn't mind; she was enjoying watching the other patrons, mostly farmers and tradesmen. She wasn't accustomed to seeing Londoners drinking in the middle of the day, but she suspected these men had been working since well before dawn.

When the barmaid went off to the kitchen to see to their steak pies, Matthew turned his charming smile on Cordelia. But she was having none of it.

"Goodness," she said. "You're an awful flirt."

Matthew looked offended. "Not at all," he said. "I'm a diabolically excellent flirt. I've learned from the best."

Cordelia couldn't help but smile. "Anna?"

"And Oscar Wilde. The playwright, that is, not my retriever."

The barmaid returned with their drinks and a sparkle in her eye. She set them down before scampering off behind the bar. Cordelia took a sip of her ginger beer: it was spicy-hot on her tongue. "Do you know anything of Anna and Ariadne? There is clearly a story there, history between the two of them, but I have always felt awkward inquiring. Anna is so private."

"It was some years ago. Anna was in love with Ariadne—very much so, I gather—but Ariadne did not return the feeling. It seems the tables may have turned, but . . ." Matthew shrugged. "It took quite a bit of asking for me to learn that much. Anna has mastered being entirely open without ever revealing anything significant about herself to anyone. It is why she is an excellent shoulder to cry on."

"And have you made use of it?" She studied him: his dark green eyes, a faint scar on his cheek, the wisps of blond hair that curled at his temples. It was rare he stayed still enough for her to really look at him. "Anna said you had a habit of getting your heart broken."

"Crikey," said Matthew, turning his half-empty glass in his hand. "How unfeeling. She probably means Kellington." He looked at her sideways, as if gauging how she'd react to this news. Cordelia wondered what Matthew would say if she told him in turn about Alastair and Charles. It was odd to know something so personal about Matthew's brother, and not be able to say so. "Not long after my first visit to the Ruelle, Kellington offered me a private concert in the Whispering Room."

Cordelia felt her cheeks turn pink. "And that became a broken heart?"

"That became an affair, and the affair became a broken heart. Though I am, as you see, entirely recovered."

Cordelia remembered Matthew in the Ruelle, Kellington's hands on his shoulders. She remembered the look on Lucie's face too, when Anna had said, *Matthew seems to prefer a hopeless love.* "What about Lucie, then? Did she break your heart? Because she wouldn't have wanted to."

Matthew rocked back slightly in his chair, as if she'd pushed him. "Does everyone know about that?" he said. "Does Lucie?"

"She has never told me anything indiscreet on purpose," Cordelia reassured him. "But in her letters, she has often revealed more than I think she meant to. She has always . . . fretted over you."

"Just what every gentleman wants," Matthew muttered. "To be fretted over. One moment." He stood up and went to the bar; Cordelia felt a twinge of sympathy for the barmaid as Matthew leaned over the polished wood, flashing his charming smile. She hoped the girl understood that Matthew's flirtation was only a game, a mask he wore without thinking of it. It should never be taken seriously.

Matthew returned with a new ale of a much darker color and flopped back into his chair.

"You haven't finished the other," Cordelia said, gesturing to the glass. She could not help but think of her father—he, too, would often start a new drink without finishing the old one. But Matthew was not like Elias, she told herself. Elias hadn't been able to make it through her wedding without falling to pieces. Matthew drank more than he should, but that didn't mean he was like her father.

"Since we are apparently unburdening ourselves, I decided to switch to something stronger," Matthew said. "I believe you were scolding me for flirting?"

"We were talking about Lucie," said Cordelia, who was beginning to regret she had brought it up. "She does love you—just—"

He smiled, a crooked but real smile. "You needn't console me. I *did* think I cared for Lucie romantically, but that is ended. I promise I am not nursing a broken heart and covering it up with wild flirting."

"I don't *mind* the flirting," Cordelia said, nettled. "It just keeps you from being serious."

"Is that so bad?"

She sighed. "Oh, probably not—you're awfully young for serious, I suppose."

Matthew choked on his ale. "You make it sound as if *you* are a hundred."

"I," said Cordelia, with dignity, "am an old married woman."

"That is not what I see when I look at you," Matthew said.

Cordelia stared at him in surprise. He had finished his glass; he set it down on the table between them with a decided thump. She could have sworn there was a flush along his cheekbones. *More flirting,* she thought. *Meaningless.*

He cleared his throat. "So, given what you told me in Maidenhead, we're looking for a mythical barrow somewhere on the Ridgeway Road. How are we meant to find it, exactly?"

"According to the book I read, it's near the Uffington White Horse."

"It's near a *horse?* Don't they move about?"

"Not this one," said Cordelia. "It's a massive drawing of a horse, on a hillside—well, not quite a drawing, really. It's cut out of the hill in chalk trenches, so it shows very white against the earth."

"Is it the Uffington Horse you're talking about?" said the barmaid, who'd snuck up on them with their steak pies.

Matthew and Cordelia exchanged a look. "That's the one," said Matthew, fixing the barmaid with his most angelic look. "Any help you could give us in finding it?"

"It's just down the road a bit. You can see it for miles on the hillside, and folk come from all around every year to help scour the horse— keeping the chalk white, like. There's a path up the hill leads to the chalk trenches. People climb it every so often, and they leave offerings, too—flowers and candles. It's a witchy kind of place."

Matthew's eyes were sparkling as the barmaid left them alone to dig into their lunch. "You think the barrow's there?"

"There, or near there." Cordelia was beginning to feel real excitement. It had been a desperate gesture, coming out here in hopes of finding out what was wrong with Cortana. A method of seizing her fate with her own hands, even if it meant finding out something she did not want to know. "Perhaps it was once known that Wayland the Smith had a forge there, and the white horse was created as a sort of—"

"Shop sign?" said Matthew, grinning. "Get your enchanted swords here?"

"As a way to let people know it was a powerful, protected place. Though," she added, "bet you a shilling there's a stall selling hot cider once we get there."

Matthew laughed. They hurried to finish their food and pay the bill before departing. They left the barmaid gazing longingly at Matthew and got back in the car. Cordelia crawled under a multitude of blankets as the car started up with a roar and they trundled out onto the road.

"Grace." James blocked the door with his body. "You shouldn't be here."

She looked up at him, her small face shaded by her hat, her expression invisible. "But I need to speak to you," she said. "It's important."

He curled his hand around the doorframe. The pressure was there in the back of his brain, the whisper that said, *Let her in. Let her in. You want to see her. You need to see her.* "Grace—"

She was past him somehow, and inside the house. Thank the Angel that Risa had gone to the Carstairs' house to help Sona. James slammed the door shut—no point making a scene the whole of Curzon Street could see—and turned to see Grace already halfway down the hall.

Shah mat, he thought, and hurried after her. She always managed to get past him somehow. His emotional walls. The actual walls of his house, apparently. He could hear her skirts swishing down the corridor; he caught up with her as she was about to turn into the study.

"Not in here," he said. Somehow this room was his and Cordelia's place. It was bad enough having Grace in his home the day after Elias's death. There had to be limits. "The drawing room."

She gave him a lingering, curious look but went where he indicated, her delicate boots clicking on the parquet floors as she walked.

James locked the drawing room door behind them. He hadn't been in here since the argument with Elias. He could still see a small porcelain figurine tipped sideways on one of the shelves, where Elias had knocked it over.

He turned to Grace. "We had an agreement."

She had shrugged off her heavy cape; under it she wore a cream wool dress embroidered with blue. It was tight around the waist and hips, narrowing to a swirl of lace panels below the knee. "You told me how things were going to be," she said, "but I don't recall agreeing."

He leaned back against the side of the piano. "I don't mean to be unkind," he said. "But this is not fair on either of us. Nor is it fair on Daisy. I made her a promise, and I intend to keep it."

"Daisy," she echoed, laying her gloved hand on the back of a chair. "Such a pretty nickname. I don't think you have one for me."

"Cordelia is a much longer name than Grace," he said shortly. "You said you had something important to tell me."

"I have a question, really. About Lucie."

James didn't bother to hide his surprise. "You've never shown much interest in Lucie." Every summer in Idris, he had offered to introduce her to his sister, but Grace had refused, saying sometimes that she could not bear to part with a moment of her time alone with James, saying other times that she wished to meet Lucie when she was free of her mother and could speak of her love for James openly. James happened to think that the last thing Lucie wanted to hear about was a strange girl's passion for her older brother, but Grace would not be moved.

"It is about her power," Grace said. "I know Lucie, like you, can see the dead—but you can also travel in shadows. Can Lucie do the same?"

"Why do you want to know?" James asked. "And why now?"

"The murders, I suppose," Grace said, looking away. "They've been so awful—and I know of your shadow power, but few others do, and I suppose I wondered if you and Lucie had any way of—of perhaps seeing the ghosts of those who had been murdered? Of knowing who might have done this?"

This was rather awkwardly close to the truth, James thought, though he could not share that thought with Grace. Certainly nothing he knew currently would comfort her. He couldn't help but feel sympathy; she had always been so sheltered in Idris—from demons, from the ordinary violence of a mundane city.

"We can only see ghosts who linger on this Earth because they have unfinished business, or are tied to a place or object," he said gently. "I can only hope the murdered dead will have passed on to peace, and so no—we will not see them."

He could not imagine telling Grace about the Regency ghost, the factory, Filomena's ghost. Not the way he told things to Cordelia. "Grace," he said, "is that truly what is bothering you? Is something else wrong? Are you not happy at the Bridgestocks'?"

"Happy?" she echoed. "It is all right, I suppose. I do not think they like me much—but consider my position. Ariadne wishes to befriend me and exchange confidences, but how can I? I cannot tell her of my situation without revealing yours; I cannot speak of my pain without revealing your secrets, and Cordelia's. I can confide in no one, while you can confide in any of your friends."

James opened his mouth, and closed it again; she was right, in her way, and he had not thought of it—not thought of her isolation, only her impending marriage to Charles.

She stepped closer, raising her eyes to his, and James felt his heartbeat quicken. "I cannot speak to Charles, either," she said. "He is in Paris, and besides, we are not given to confidences with one another. I suppose I thought you would find some way to get messages to me— some way to let me know you still loved me—"

"I told you I couldn't," James said, blood singing in his ears.

"You said you *wouldn't*. Duty, you said, and honor." She laid her gloved hand lightly on his arm. "But do we not also owe a duty to love?"

"Is that why you came here?" James said hoarsely. "To hear that I love you?"

She placed her hands against his chest. Her face was almost waxen in its pallor—beautiful but still, like a doll's. James could feel the weight of the bracelet, heavy on his wrist. A reminder of all he had sworn, all he and Grace had felt for each other, must still feel for each other. "I don't have to hear it," she whispered. "Just kiss me. Kiss me, James, and I will know you love me."

Love me. Love me. Love me.

A force that seemed imprinted on every corner of his soul flared to life, burning up his blood: he could smell her perfume, jasmine and spice. He closed his eyes and took hold of her wrists. Some small part of his brain was crying out in protest, even as he pulled her up against him—she was slight and slender; why had he remembered her as soft and curving? He crushed his lips to hers and heard her make a muffled sound, a gasp of surprise.

Her hands looped around his neck; her lips answered his as he kissed and kissed her. The hunger inside him was desperate. It was as if he were at a faerie feast, where the more mortals consumed, the more intense their hunger became, until they starved to death among the plenty.

When he abruptly released her and staggered backward, she looked as stunned as he felt. A vast emptiness ached inside him. He was drowning in it: it was a physical, almost violent pain.

"I should go," she said. Her cheeks were flushed. "I can see—perhaps I should not have come here. I will not—I shan't come again."

"Grace—"

Halfway to the door, she whirled to look at him, an accusation in her eyes. "I do not know who you were kissing just now, James Herondale," she said. "But it certainly wasn't me."

Before long the little village of Uffington came into view, the hill rising sharply behind it, and Matthew and Cordelia could see the white horse—like a clumsy child's drawing splayed across the mountainside. Nearby, a flock of sheep grazed placidly, apparently unimpressed at being in the presence of a famous historical artifact.

Matthew took the road up as far as it went, leaving the Ford next to a path that took a jagged route to the top. They walked the rest of the way, Cordelia glad that she had brought her thickest woolen coat; the wind over the downs was sharp as a knife. Matthew's cheeks were scarlet by the time they reached the top of the scarp, a few feet from the chalk-filled trenches that formed the horse—up close, they were startlingly white.

"Look." Cordelia pointed. She felt an odd surety, an instinctive sense that she was right deep in her bones. "The horse is facing that way, almost pointing with its nose. Down to that copse, you see, there's a path—an old road, I think."

Matthew seemed a little startled, but he joined her on the descent to the path, occasionally stopping to help her when her skirts made walking tricky. Cordelia half wished she'd worn her gear, though it likely wouldn't have kept her as warm.

"Look," Matthew said as they reached the path, and indicated a wooden post sunk deep into the earth. A rectangular sign had been nailed to it, proclaiming the path to be THE RIDGEWAY. "So this is the Ridgeway," Matthew said, sounding subdued. "The oldest road in Britain. Not a Roman road—older than that."

"I suppose it would be." Cordelia's excitement had faded; something more serious gripped her now. As if she were going to the Silent City, or the Hall of Accords. As if this were not a journey but a pilgrimage.

They passed in silence over the next hill, and there it was, unmistakable. A number of slabs of stone, framing the dark entrance to a barrow. The barrow itself seemed little more than a grass-covered swell in the ground, its entrance—a dark hole tunneling into the rise of earth—half the size of an ordinary door.

Cordelia removed her heavy coat. She drew Cortana from the scabbard on her back and laid it on the grass, then took a penny from her pocket and knelt to place it before the barrow's entrance.

Matthew cleared his throat. "And now what?"

"I'm not sure. According to Lilian Highsmith, the myths say one must leave a penny by the barrow."

"Perhaps there's been inflation?" Matthew suggested. "I could lend you a sixpence."

Cordelia shot him a dark look. "If you cannot stop joking, Matthew . . ."

He held up his hands innocently, backing away. "All right, all right. I'll go keep an eye out. There's a farmer coming over yonder hill, and woe if he finds us trying to catch the attention of ancient smiths on his land."

He headed back the way they had come, keeping her within eyesight. She saw him stop at the summit of the hill and lean his back against a tree, reaching into his coat for his flask.

Cordelia returned her attention to the matter at hand, looking from the sword to the barrow; the entrance into the barrow's underground space was black as night. She would have crawled into it anyway, but something told her that that was not what was being asked of her.

She reached out and drew Cortana toward her, laying it across her lap, the blade sparking in the sun.

"Wayland the Smith," she whispered. "I am a chosen bearer of the sword Cortana. I have borne it always with faith, with courage. I have carried it into battle. I have spilled the blood of demons with it. Bearing it, I have slain even a Prince of Hell."

"Daisy," she heard Matthew call, and turned to see a man walking in their direction. It must be the farmer he had mentioned before, she thought, and was about to rise to her feet when she went cold all over.

The man was no farmer. He was a blacksmith.

He was plainly dressed in a rough cotton shirt with a soot-stained leather apron tied over it. He could have been any age—he had the young-old features Cordelia associated with warlocks. He resembled a slab of the barrow's sarsen stone—broad-shouldered and thick-handed, with a short fair beard and close-cropped hair. Around his neck was a band of twisted metal, set with a deep blue stone.

"You summoned me, bearer of the blade Cortana?" said the man—Wayland the Smith; it could be no one else. "You cannot imagine I would not know a Prince of Hell cannot be truly slain, though your nerve in claiming such a deed is admirable."

"I slew him in *this* world," said Cordelia, raising her chin. "Wounded and weakened, he was driven from our realm."

"And that wound still bleeds," said Wayland the Smith, his teeth gleaming in a grin. "A great slash in his side, spilling his demon's blood. It may be decades before he heals."

Cordelia tilted her head back. "How do you know all this?"

"I know the actions of every sword I have ever forged. Ah, my children of steel and iron, how they cut pathways through this world." His voice was a deep rumble. "Now, give me your blade."

Cordelia swallowed hard and handed Cortana to Wayland. As he took it in his massive hands, the world around her seemed to change. Still kneeling, she looked around in amazement—the sky had darkened, the hills putting on a coat of blue-black ash. Matthew was gone. All around her were the noises of a smithy—the clang of hammer on steel, the crackle of fire. Copper-red sparks sprang to life inside the barrow, rising up like fireflies, claiming the dark.

"Ah, my child, my child," Wayland crooned, holding Cortana up to the strange new light. "Long has it been since I forged the steel that made you and your brothers, Joyeuse and Durendal." His gaze snapped back to Cordelia. "And long has your bloodline borne my blades. When you plunged this sword into the body of Belial, did you not think there might be consequences?"

"That's why?" Cordelia thought back frantically; it was true she had not had cause to use Cortana since she had stabbed Belial. Not until the warehouse fight. "The contact with Belial—it harmed Cortana?"

"This blade was forged in heavenly fire and bears within its hilt the feather of an angel," said Wayland. "When it touched the blood of Belial, it cried out. You did not hear it. You are only a mortal," the smith relented. "And it has been a long age since mortals knew to see to the soul of their swords."

"Tell me what to do," Cordelia said fervently. "Whatever I need to do for Cortana, I will do it."

Wayland turned the sword over in his hands. His eyes were coppery embers, and his fingers seemed to sing up and down the blade as he stroked it. The sword gave a single, ringing note—a sound Cordelia had never heard before—and Wayland smiled.

"It is done," he said. Cordelia stared at him, astonished that it could be so simple. "Cortana is healed. I have granted back its seraphic essence. Keep it with that scabbard you wear on your back—whoever gave you such a gift clearly meant for you to be protected. There are strong spells upon it that will guard you and Cortana both."

The only gift worthy of my daughter is the gift worthy of the sword that has chosen her.

It seemed her father had given her one true thing. Cordelia bit her lip. "I did not realize it would be so simple," she said.

"It may be simple, but I shall ask for something in return. And it will not be a penny."

Cordelia hugged Cortana to her. She could feel, already, the change in the sword—it fit in her hand as it always had, familiar and beloved. "Anything."

Wayland seemed to smile. "You are familiar with Joyeuse and Durendal?"

"Yes—the sword of Charlemagne and the sword of Roland. The brothers of Cortana, as you said."

"And do you know the sword Caliburn?" he asked, and when she shook her head, he sighed. "You may know it," he said, "as Excalibur."

"Yes," Cordelia said, "of course—"

"Charlemagne, Arthur, and Roland were paladins," said Wayland. "The blades I have crafted sing with their own souls. They must find matched souls among the gods and mortals of the world. But the strength of those swords, the power of the bond between the blade and bearer, can be made greater when the bearer has sworn fealty to a greater warrior, as Lancelot did to Arthur."

"But Arthur had not sworn fealty to anyone," said Cordelia. "He was king himself, as was Charlemagne."

"Arthur had sworn fealty," said Wayland. "He had sworn it to me."

"My father told me long ago that you were a Shadowhunter," said Cordelia, her mind whirling. "But all you speak of happened before Raziel created the Nephilim, nor do Shadowhunters live forever. And you bear no runes."

"Many claim me. I have been called one of the fey. Some call me a god," said Wayland. "In reality, I am beyond and above such things. In the early days of the Nephilim, I came to Shadowhunters in their own form, that they might know me as one of their own and trust my making of weapons. In truth, I am far older than they. I recall a time before demons, before angels." His gaze was steady, but his ember eyes shone intently. "And now a darkness walks among Shadowhunters, striking at will. This death will only spread. If it falls upon your shoulders to stop the killings, Cordelia Herondale, can you bear it?"

If it falls upon your shoulders. Her heart began to beat more quickly. "You—are you asking me to be your paladin?"

"I am."

"Truly? Not the bearers of Excalibur, or Durendal?"

"Excalibur lies far beneath the lake; Durendal is trapped in rock," growled the smith. "But Cortana is free, and burns for battle. Will you take up your blade? For I believe you have within you the soul of a great warrior, Cordelia Herondale. It but demands an oath of fealty to be truly free."

Distantly, Cordelia wondered how Wayland the Smith knew she had married—she was still not accustomed to hearing her new name.

But then, he seemed to know everything. He was, as he had said, very nearly a god.

"Yes," she said, "yes, I will take up my blade."

He smiled, and she realized each of his teeth was forged of bronze, glimmering in the dark light. "Raise your blade. Hold it before you."

Cordelia raised the sword, the tip pointing toward the heavens. The hilt was a narrow streak of golden fire, burning before her eyes. Wayland the Smith moved so that he was standing in front of her. To her surprise, he caught the unsheathed sword in his enormous right fist, wrapping his hand around it. Blood dripped from his fingers, streaking the blade.

"Now swear," he said. "Swear you will be loyal to me, that you shall not falter—and when you draw a blade, you will draw it in my name."

"I swear my loyalty," Cordelia said fervently. His blood continued to run down the blade, but as soon as the drops struck the hilt, they became sparks that lifted, gold and copper and bronze, into the air. "I swear my courage. I swear neither to falter nor to fail in battle. Whenever I draw my sword, whenever I lift up a weapon in battle, I shall do it in your name."

Wayland released the sword. "Now rise," he said, and Cordelia stood for the first time. She had not realized until this moment how very big the great smith was: he towered over her, his massive bulk a dark shadow against the stormy sky. "Go forth," he said. "And be a warrior. I will find you again."

He touched her, once, on the brow—and then he was gone. In a single blink, the world changed again: there was no more storm, no more embers, no more ringing sound of the forge. She stood on an ordinary hill under an ordinary blue sky, the sun bright as a golden coin. She took one last look at the barrow and was not surprised to see that the opening was dark again, half-hidden by moss.

Cordelia started back up the hill and saw Matthew, at the summit, raise his hand to greet her. Her heart rising in triumph, she ran toward him, Cortana held aloft, its blade shedding golden sparks in the sunlight.

15

WALK BY DAYTIME

Dreams that strive to seem awake,
Ghosts that walk by daytime,
Weary winds the way they take,
Since, for one child's absent sake,
May knows well, whate'er things make
Sport, it is not Maytime.
—Algernon Charles Swinburne, "A Dark Month"

It was sunset, and Berwick Street was lively with foot traffic: tradesmen going home from work, rouged ladies already plying their trade from doorways, and laborers in high spirits arriving at the Blue Posts pub.

Leaning against the wall by the entrance to Tyler's Court, Lucie sighed. Fog softened the edges of the city, turning the lights of salesmen's naphtha flare lamps into shimmering, heatless bonfires. Balios, waiting at the curb with the carriage, stomped his feet and neighed softly, his breath a white plume in the air.

"Lucie Herondale?"

She whirled, about to snap at Grace for being late—and froze. Behind her stood a girl in a thin muslin dress, far too lightweight for the winter weather. Scanty blond hair was scraped back under a white cap. She was bone-thin, her arms and neck pitted with black sores. Through them, Lucie could see the street beyond, as if she looked through cracks in a brick wall.

"I'm Martha," the girl whispered. "I heard you could help folks like me." She drifted closer: her skirts seemed to end in a kind of white smoke that floated just above the pavement. "That you could command us."

"I—" Lucie took a step back. "I shouldn't. I oughtn't. I'm sorry."

"Please." The girl moved closer: her eyes were white, as Filomena's had been, though they were blank and pupil-less. "I want to forget what I did. I shouldn't have taken the laudanum. My mam had the greater need. She died screaming 'cause I took it. And then there was no more for anyone."

"You want to forget?" Lucie whispered. "Is—is that it?"

"No," said the girl. "I want to feel again what I felt when I took the laudanum." The girl bit at her insubstantial thumb, her white eyes rolling. "All those lovely dreams. You could command me to have them again." She drifted closer; Lucie stumbled back, almost catching the heel of her boot on the pavement. A strange feeling arrowed through her—a sort of ice, sizzling in her veins.

"Leave her alone."

Jesse stood at the alley's entrance, looking so real it was hard even for Lucie to recall he wasn't exactly *there*. His gaze was fixed on Martha.

"Please," the ghost-girl whined. "She helps *you*. Don't be selfish—"

"You know what you were doing," Jesse said. His green eyes were burning; Lucie realized, at the look of fear on Martha's face, that Jesse must be a terrible oddity to her. He was not alive enough to be among the living, nor dead enough to seem natural to the dead. "There is no excuse to harm the living. Now go."

The ghost bared her teeth—a sudden, savage gesture. They were black, ragged stubs. "You can't always be with her—"

Jesse moved lightning fast. He was no longer at the alley's entrance; he was next to Martha, his hand closing on her shoulder. She gave a little shriek as if the touch had burned her, and pulled back—her body seemed to stretch out like taffy, strands of white ghost-matter clinging to Jesse's hand as Martha twisted away. She gave a little hiss as she came apart in strings of ropy white stuff that drifted away like fog.

Lucie gasped. A moment later Jesse was beside her, leading her under the overhang of a market stall shuttered for the night.

"What—what was that?" she demanded, angling her hat to protect her from the dripping awning. "Is she—dead? I mean, more dead?"

"Not at all. She'll re-form again somewhere tonight, just as bitter and vengeful as always. But she'll stay away from you now."

"Because she's afraid of you?"

"As you've said before, ghosts gossip." His tone was very flat. "I cannot harm them, not really, but I can make them uncomfortable. And they always worry if it might be more. Most ghosts are cowardly, afraid to lose the ragged little bits of life they have left. I am not one of them exactly, but I can see them, touch them. That makes them afraid. They know who I am—hopefully Martha will let them know to stay away from you unless they wish to deal with me."

"They are not afraid of *me*," Lucie said thoughtfully, "though I have always been able to see them—"

Though, she had to admit, that was not entirely true. She remembered the shade of Emmanuel Gast, the dead warlock, hissing at her—*truly, you are monsters, despite your angel blood.* But he had been a criminal, she reminded herself, and a liar.

"Oh, they likely are afraid," Jesse said grimly. "But they are also greedy. The ghost who gave you the location of that factory—others are starting to hear what you did for him. That you made him forget what tormented him."

Lucie clasped her gloved hands together. "He asked me to do it. I did not command him without his request—"

"And I'm sure he would not tell you where Filomena's ghost was unless you helped him," Jesse said. "Ghosts can be as unscrupulous as the living. But you didn't tell me about it, did you—"

"Because I knew you would take on like this," Lucie snapped—she was cold, worried for James, and most of all she could not bear the disappointed look on Jesse's face. "This is my talent, my power, and I can decide when to utilize it."

"You can," he said, in a low voice, "but there are consequences, and I cannot help you with them if you do not tell me—I will not always be waiting in the shadows, Lucie. It was only an accident that I was here to stop Martha."

"Why *were* you here?"

He set his hands on her shoulders. There was no warmth where his fingers touched her, yet there was weight there, and realness. "I know you have been trying to—to help me. To raise me." She wanted to lean into his touch. "When I rise at night, I see where you and Grace have left the marks of your works behind—the ashes, the scattered bits of potion ingredients. But now blood—blood magic is dark stuff, Lucie."

Lucie frowned inwardly. *Grace, what are you doing?* "You have been fading," she said softly. "I worry that there is not much time. I think Grace feels it too, in her way."

"As do I," he said, a deep ache in his voice. "You think I do not want to live again, truly? To walk with you by the river, hand in hand in the sunlight? And I have had hopes. But after what we tried last night, Luce—you cannot keep putting yourself in danger. That includes seeking out dangerous people as though you're at some—some garden party."

To walk with you by the river, hand in hand. Words she would store away and take out later to turn over in her memories as someone might take out a beloved photograph to study its details. Now, however, she only said, "Jesse, I am a Shadowhunter, not some mundane girl you need to shelter from the riffraff."

"We're not talking about riffraff. We're talking about necromancers. Real danger, for you and for Grace."

"We have hardly done anything that serious. Why don't you speak to Grace about this? Why am I the only one scolded?"

"Because I can say to you what I cannot say to her." He hesitated. "Remember, I have witnessed this journey before. I cannot bear the thought of you—either of you—drawn into dark magic as my mother was."

She stiffened. "Tatiana and I are nothing alike."

Jesse flashed a bitter smile. "Certainly you are not alike now. But I think my mother might have been a whole person once, a—an ordinary person, maybe even a happy person—and I do not know how much of that life was taken away from her by bitterness, and how much was because she lost herself to this sort of shadowy magic and necromancy—all the forces that you and Grace are dabbling in."

The hollowness in his eyes when he spoke of Tatiana broke her heart. How deep were the scars his mother had given him?

"Do you—hate her now? Your mother?"

Jesse hesitated, glancing over her shoulder at the street beyond. A second later Lucie heard the sound of wheels, and turned to see the delicate faerie wings of the Fairchild family crest painted on the side of a carriage. Grace had finally arrived.

She knew without looking that Jesse was already gone by the time Grace joined her under the awning. His voice still rang in her head: *I can say to you what I cannot say to her.*

He had disappeared into the night as if he were part of it. And maybe he was, she thought. It was almost a comfort to imagine Jesse as a part of the stars and shadows, always around her, ever-present even if he could not be seen.

"*Lucie,*" Grace said, and it was clear she was repeating herself. "Goodness, you're in a brown study. What were you thinking about?"

"Jesse," Lucie said, and saw Grace's expression change. Was there anything in the world Grace cared about as much as she cared about her brother? In fact, was there anything else in the world she cared about at all? "I—saw him a bit earlier. He said you'd been experimenting in the shed. Do be careful. Blood necromancy is nasty stuff."

Something flickered in Grace's eyes. "It's rabbit's blood," she said. "I didn't tell you. I knew you'd want nothing to do with it." She headed for the entrance of the Hell Ruelle, forcing Lucie to scramble after her. Grace's heels clicked on the pavement; she wore delicate boots under a narrow blue-and-ivory skirt frothed with lace. "You'll be pleased to know it seemed to have no effect. The rabbit population of Chiswick House is safe from my further depredations."

Lucie was mildly horrified; she was quite sure she could never have harmed a rabbit. "Did you get the information about Annabel that we promised to Malcolm?"

Grace's shoulders seemed to tighten. "Yes, but I'm not going to tell you. I'm only going to tell *him.*"

Humph, Lucie thought, but there was no point arguing. At least getting into the Hell Ruelle was easier this time; the door guardian recognized them and, with a sideways smile, sent them on their way.

Inside the large central chamber, a relaxed crowd of Downworlders chatted at small tables scattered throughout the room. Lucie searched for Hypatia but did not see her, though she saw a number of other familiar faces, including Kellington, who was playing violin among a string quartet onstage. The women were dressed in the height of fashion—narrow skirts and pagoda sleeves, the sort of thing one might see in Paris—which was only fitting, since the walls had been painted with scenes of Parisian life. The theme had been extended to the waiters serving *moules frites* and ham sandwiches with tiny cornichons. Bottles of French wine and absinthe lined the bar. The guests seemed to be thoroughly enjoying themselves, gossiping and laughing. The liveliest were attempting to learn the beguine on a makeshift dance floor in the corner.

Grace looked astonished. "What is *she* doing here?"

Lucie followed her gaze and saw—to her surprise—Ariadne Bridgestock, sitting at one of the tables by herself. She looked very pretty in a dark green gown, her black hair held back by a yellow silk bandeau. "I've no idea," she said. "Has she ever mentioned the Ruelle before?"

"No. We hardly talk," said Grace. "I am keeping rather too many secrets to be anyone's confidante right now."

"We ought to go speak to her, don't you think?"

"We *ought* to go find Malcolm," said Grace. "We can't keep him waiting—Lucie!"

For Lucie was already halfway across the room. She slid into a chair across from Ariadne, who looked up in surprise as she recognized her visitor. "Lucie, dear. I heard you frequented this place."

"'Frequented' seems an exaggeration," Lucie said. "But what of you? What brings you tonight?"

Ariadne tucked a dark curl behind her ear. "Everyone made it sound so exciting. Since my engagement ended, I've realized how—restricted—my life has been. I've seen so very little, even of London."

Lucie smiled to herself; though Ariadne was looking at her with sincerity, she couldn't help but wonder how much this interest in the Ruelle had to do with a certain blue-eyed Lightwood. "It's quite a quiet night this evening. You may not be seeing the Ruelle at its liveliest."

Ariadne shrugged philosophically. "Well, I can always come another time." She looked around. "I was hoping to see the famous Hypatia Vex, at least, but she isn't here either."

"She's opening her new magic shop in Limehouse soon."

"And the rumor is she's got a new admirer. One of the werewolves told me. I hope you girls have a good time," she added, with a glance toward Grace, "and if you haven't tried absinthe before, you might want to start with a very *little* bit."

Lucie thanked Ariadne for the advice and returned to the main part of the room to find Grace examining a guillotine that had been brought in, minus its blade, and propped next to a marble bust of a beheaded man. "How odd," Lucie said, eyeing the statue. "A bust without a head is really more just a *neck*, isn't it?"

"Thank goodness you're back," said Grace. "Can we go meet the warlock now?"

The door to Fade's office, at the end of the narrow corridor, was ajar. Lucie pushed it open with her gloved fingertips; inside, Malcolm Fade sat in a brocade chair gazing thoughtfully into the glowing fireplace, an unlit burled-wood pipe in his hand.

He glanced over at them. There were lines of tension around his eyes and mouth. Lucie had always thought he looked young, twenty-four or -five perhaps, but at the moment it was impossible to put an age to his face. His dark amethyst eyes regarded them coolly.

"Come in," he said. "And lock the door behind you."

They did as he asked before taking their seats, side by side on a tapestry sofa.

"Did you get the information from the Adamant Citadel?" Malcolm asked, not bothering with pleasantries.

"Yes," Grace said, her gray eyes serious. "I can tell you about Annabel. But you may not like it."

"Yes, well, you might not like everything that I know either," he replied, drumming his fingers on the arm of his chair. "That doesn't mean it isn't worth knowing."

"I'm not sure I should tell it to you," Grace said, without emotion. "It is often true that people resent the bearer of bad news."

"*Grace*," Lucie hissed. "This is why we're here."

"Perhaps you should listen to Miss Herondale," Malcolm told Grace. "I shall tell you one thing I know: I know who it is you're trying to raise from the dead. It's your brother, isn't it? Jesse Blackthorn.

I should have recalled the story earlier. He died receiving his first rune. A tragedy, but not one unheard-of among the Nephilim. What makes you think it entitles him to another chance at life?"

"My brother is not fully dead," Grace said, and Lucie looked at her in surprise: there was real emotion in her words. "My mother preserved his body using dark magic. Now he is trapped between life and death, unable to experience either the joy of living or the release of dying. He hovers between two worlds. I have never heard of anyone else forced to endure such a torment."

Malcolm did not look entirely surprised. "I had heard there might be a warlock involved in that story. That Tatiana Blackthorn had hired someone to assist her in—unorthodox magic."

This was not news to Lucie. She recalled the first time Jesse had told her about his death, and what had happened after. *I know she brought a warlock into the room in the hours after I died, to preserve and to safeguard my physical body. My soul was cut free to wander between the real world and the spirit realm.*

It had not occurred to her, though, that Malcolm would be aware of it, or know which warlock Tatiana had hired. And the warlock who had preserved Jesse, who had arranged for him to remain in this half-alive state—well, who better to know how to bring him back?

"Which warlock?" she demanded. "Do you know?"

Malcolm templed his fingers. "We had an agreement," he said. "Tell me what you know of Annabel. Then we will discuss what I know, and not before."

Grace hesitated.

"If what you need to tell me is that Annabel wishes to hear nothing from me, then say it," said Malcolm. His voice was calm, but his face was strained, his fingertips pressed so hard together they had gone white. "You think I have not already thought of that, resigned myself to it? Hope is a prison, truth the key that unlocks it. *Tell me.*"

Grace was breathing very fast, as if she had been running up a hill. "You wanted to know what news I have from my mother, from the Adamant Citadel?" she said to Malcolm. "Well, here it is: she is dead. Annabel Blackthorn is dead. She was never an Iron Sister."

Malcolm flinched back in his chair, as if he'd been shot. It was very clear he had been braced to hear one thing—that Annabel wanted nothing to do with him—and entirely unprepared for this. *"What did you say?"*

"She never became an Iron Sister," Grace repeated. "That was a lie you were told, to let you believe she still lived, to make you think she didn't *want* to be with you. Nearly a hundred years ago, the Clave tortured her until she was nearly mad—they planned to ship her to the Citadel to rave out her remaining days. But her family murdered her before she ever arrived there. They murdered her because she loved *you*."

Malcolm didn't move, but the blood seemed to drain from his face, leaving him a living statue with burning eyes. Lucie had never seen anyone look quite like that—as if they had been dealt a mortal blow but had not yet fallen. "I do not believe you," he said, his hand closing tightly around his pipe. "They—they could not have lied to me about this. About *her*." There was an intonation to Malcolm's voice when he said "her" that Lucie knew: it was the way her own father spoke of her mother. As if there could be no other "her." "And how could you know what happened? No one would tell you these things, or tell them to your mother."

Grace reached into her handbag. She removed an object and held it up between her thumb and forefinger—a round, multifaceted crystal about the size of a cricket ball. "This is an *aletheia* crystal."

"I know what it is," Malcolm whispered. So did Lucie: she had read of them. *Aletheia* crystals were carved of *adamas*. In past years, the Clave had used them to contain information in the form of memories that could be viewed again if the viewer had the power to see them. As far as Lucie knew, only Silent Brothers could release the image contained in such a crystal—though it made sense that a warlock or magician might have that same ability.

Grace placed the crystal on the desk in front of Malcolm. He made no move to touch it. "It was stored in Chiswick House. It contains memories that will prove the truth of what I'm saying."

Malcolm spoke in a low, guttural voice. "If any part of what you are telling me is true," he said, "I will kill them. I will kill them all."

Lucie surged to her feet. "Mr. Fade, please—"

"It does not matter to us," said Grace, quite coldly, "what you do for revenge." In the firelight, her silver-spun hair gleamed like ice. "We have done what you asked; we have provided you word of Annabel Blackthorn. I have told you the truth. No one else would tell it to you, but I did. That must matter. It must count for something."

Malcolm looked at her blindly. Fury had made his expression a near blank; only his eyes moved, and they were like wounds in his face. "Get out," he said.

"We had an *agreement*," said Grace. "You must tell us—"

"*Get out!*" Malcolm roared.

Lucie caught at Grace's arm. "No," Lucie said through her teeth. "We are *going*."

"But—" Grace clamped her mouth shut as Lucie dragged her out of the room and into the corridor. A second later, Malcolm's door slammed shut; Lucie heard the lock click.

She stopped short and whirled on Grace. "Why on earth did you do that?"

"I told him the truth," Grace said defiantly. "You said I should tell him the truth—"

"Not like *that*. Not told in a way that's—that's so cruel."

"The truth is better than lies! However cruel it may be, it is crueler still for him not to know—*everyone* knew when it happened, and no one told him, and even now he's been allowed to believe she's still alive all this time—"

"Grace, there are *ways* of telling the truth," Lucie protested, glancing back and forth to make sure no one was approaching. "You didn't have to throw it in his face. You've made him hate the Blackthorns even more; how could you think he'll still want to help Jesse?"

Grace's lips trembled. She pressed them together. "Betrayal and pain are facts of life. He doesn't get to escape them just because he's a warlock."

Lucie knew that Grace had suffered, that Tatiana had likely made her childhood nearly unbearable. But had she entirely forgotten what people were *like*? Had she never known?

"I shall never understand my brother," Lucie said, without thinking. "Why on earth does he love you?"

Grace looked as if Lucie had slapped her. She seemed about to lash out—then turned without a word and raced down the corridor.

After an astonished pause, Lucie gave chase, following Grace into the main room of the salon. It was crowded now, the floor seething with partygoers: she caught a glimpse of a blond head as Grace pushed past a group of werewolves. A moment later, she'd vanished.

Lucie stared glumly at a juggling phouka. She'd argued with Jesse, she hadn't gotten a whit of information from Malcolm but merely angered him, and she'd upset Grace. And Jesse was fading—their time was running out. She needed to do more, know more. Perhaps if she went back in to talk to Malcolm on her own—

"Lucie?"

Lucie turned in surprise. Behind her was none other than Ariadne Bridgestock, her emerald silk dress catching the light from the wall sconces. Ariadne put a finger to her lips. "Come with me," she said in a low voice, gesturing for Lucie to follow her.

They made their way down another corridor, this one papered in damask. Ariadne paused before a wooden door and gave it a quick knock. A plaque on the door proclaimed it the Whispering Room.

Ariadne stepped back to usher Lucie into the room and followed her inside, closing the door carefully behind them. It was rather dizzying, the number of rooms there were in the Hell Ruelle. This one was lined with bookshelves, scattered with comfortable-looking armchairs and settees. A fire, purple and sweet-smelling, burned in the grate.

Nor was the room empty. Lounging on a chaise by the fireplace was Anna. She wore black trousers and a sapphire-blue waistcoat unbuttoned over a fine-milled linen shirt. Her legs were crossed, a glass of red wine in one of her hands. "Glad to see Ariadne found you," she said. "Is there a reason you and Grace Blackthorn keep having fraught meetings with Malcolm Fade? Something scandalous I ought to know?"

Lucie glanced back and forth between Anna and Ariadne, who had seated herself atop a large walnut desk. She was swinging her legs, her petticoats rustling around her ankles.

So Ariadne had been expecting to see Anna. Lucie had been right. But she'd imagined that Ariadne had simply been hoping to bump into

Anna by mischance. It was clear, however, that a prior assignation had been made. *Well, that's an interesting development.*

"And where *is* Grace?" Anna said, and took a sip of wine.

"She bolted," said Ariadne. "I never knew she could run so fast."

Anna gave Lucie a sharp look. "This is beginning to sound familiar," she said. "Isn't this the second time you've appeared at the Hell Ruelle with Grace Blackthorn and she's run off like her hair was on fire? I hope this isn't going to become a pattern."

Lucie raised her eyebrows. "You saw us the last time?"

Anna shrugged. "Lucie, ducks, you don't have to tell me anything you don't want to tell me. Your secrets are yours. But Malcolm Fade is a powerful man. If you're going to have dealings with him . . ."

"I was trying to help," Lucie said. She stuck her hands out to the purple fire. Her mind was spinning. What could she tell, and what must she hold back? "To help Grace."

"That's awfully odd," said Ariadne. "She's never mentioned you. In fact, I have never seen her meet a single friend, and when she takes the carriage—Charles lent her his, for her use while he is in Paris—she is always alone. I don't think she likes me much."

"I don't think she likes anyone much," Lucie said. "At least, not anyone living." A story was spinning itself into being in her mind, one that might do nicely. "But she's not all bad. As you've probably noticed," she added, looking back up at her cousin, "Grace was raised by a delusional monster, and as such has had a miserable life. I don't think she ever experienced a whit of caring from any part of her family save her brother."

"Jesse, you mean?" said Anna. "My cousin?"

Lucie looked at her with a little surprise; it had not quite really occurred to her before that Anna, being older, might remember Jesse. "Did you meet him?"

"Not properly," Anna said. "My father wanted us to meet, but Aunt Tatiana forbade us to see him. One day I do recall, though; I must have been around eight years old. Aunt had come to our house to retrieve a pair of candlesticks she insisted were family heirlooms." Anna rolled her eyes. "She didn't come inside, but I looked out the window because I was curious. I saw Jesse sitting in the open carriage. A skinny thing, like a little scarecrow, with that straight black hair and sharp little face. Green eyes, I think."

Lucie started to nod, and stopped herself. "He was kind to Grace," she said. "She remembers it as the only kindness she ever knew." She took a deep breath. She knew she could not tell Anna and Ariadne the full truth: they could not know of her hopes to raise Jesse, or about the preservation of his body. But if they knew just enough to wish to help . . . well, there were other warlocks besides Malcolm Fade. "What I am about to say must stay between the three of us. If Grace finds out I told you, she will be very upset."

Ariadne nodded, her amber eyes catching the light of the hearth. "Of course."

"Jesse died when his first rune was placed on him. It was an awful thing," said Lucie, letting a little of the real grief she felt creep into her voice. Anna and Ariadne might think it was empathy for Grace, and a bit of it was. But it was also sorrow for Jesse, for all the days he had not lived, the sunrises he had not seen, for the quiet hours trapped in an empty house all the years since his death. "And—well, let us say, there were mysterious circumstances surrounding the event. Now that Tatiana is in the Adamant Citadel and can no longer control her daughter's movements, Grace has become obsessed with finding out the truth."

Ariadne looked intrigued. "She's playing detective?"

"Er," said Lucie, who had not expected quite this reaction. "Yes. We went to see Malcolm Fade to ask if he knew anything of Jesse Blackthorn. He *is* High Warlock, after all; he knows a great deal. He implied that there was more to the story of what happened to Grace's brother than what the Clave believed. And that a warlock was somehow involved."

"Involved in what manner?" Anna demanded.

"And who was the warlock?" asked Ariadne.

Lucie shook her head. "He wouldn't say."

Anna gazed into the fire. "I would not normally feel much sympathy for Grace Blackthorn. But I do remember when Tatiana adopted her. I was only ten or so, but there were . . . rumors."

"What kind of rumors?" Lucie asked.

Anna set her wineglass down. "Well, you know that Grace was

orphaned. Her parents were slain by demons." She cast a quick look at Ariadne, who had been another such orphan. "Ordinarily, a surviving child would have been sent to live with a family member. If there were no family members who could take an orphan in, they would be sent to the orphanage in Idris, or placed in an Institute, as happened with Uncle Jem. There *are* living Cartwrights. Grace was to be sent to live with her father's cousin, until Tatiana intervened."

"What do you mean, 'intervened'?" Lucie asked.

"Tatiana bought her," Anna said flatly. "The Cartwrights were already overstretched with their own children, and she apparently offered them quite a handsome sum. The story is that she'd been skulking around the orphanage for years, claiming she wanted a daughter, but she hadn't found any child to her liking. Until Grace."

Lucie was horrified. "Does Grace know? That she was a—a transaction?"

"I rather hope not, for that would be a monstrous thing to face," Anna said. "Though perhaps it is better to know the truth."

The echo of Grace's own words gave Lucie a start.

Ariadne said, "I wish there was some way we could help her."

"I think there might be," Lucie said, choosing her words with care. "Only she mustn't know we're doing it. Perhaps we could . . . *inquire* into the circumstances of Jesse Blackthorn's death. We are better connected than Grace; we might be able to learn things she hasn't."

"Do you really think it would help her, to know the truth about her brother's death?" Ariadne asked. "It does not always do good, to dig up the past."

"I think any sort of resolution about the matter might bring her peace," Lucie said.

For a few moments, the only sound was the crackling of the flames. Anna gazed restlessly into them; it was always a paradox, Lucie thought, the way Anna—generous, openhearted Anna—could be as opaque as clouded glass.

When she looked up at Lucie, her eyes were thoughtful, a little curious. "So what did you have in mind for this investigation?"

"We must find someone to talk to," Lucie said, "someone who might know if there really was a warlock involved in Jesse—in what happened to Jesse Blackthorn. Ragnor Fell is in Capri, Malcolm Fade will not speak of what he knows, Magnus Bane is close with my parents. . . . We need to find another source. I thought perhaps you might speak to—Hypatia Vex?"

She tried not to look too eager. As far as they knew, this mystery mattered to Grace—not to her. Anna raised her eyebrows. Ariadne said nothing, though she didn't look at all thrilled with the idea.

"Hypatia remains somewhat displeased with me about the way our last encounter ended," said Anna. "Though not displeased enough to bar me from the Ruelle." She stood up, stretching like a cat. "I suppose the question is whether I wish to test her patience again or not—"

There was a knock at the door. Jumping down from the desk, Ariadne went to get it. "Oh, goodness," Lucie heard her say, "and who are you, little man?"

"That's Neddy," said Anna, with a wink at Lucie. "Runs about delivering messages for the Merry Thieves and their sundry friends. What is it now?"

"Message from James 'erondale," said Neddy, ducking into the room. "'E wants you at 'is house, soon as possible, and 'e wants you to give me a half crown, for my troubles." He squinted at Lucie. "Same message for you, too, miss," he said. "Only now as I don't 'ave to go to the Institute to deliver it, I s'pose that saves me an errand."

"But not me a half crown," said Anna, producing the coin as if by magic; Neddy took it with an air of self-satisfaction and scampered out of the room. "What could James want? Do you know, Lucie?"

"No—not at all, but he wouldn't call us there if it wasn't important. We can take my carriage; it's just around the corner."

"All right." Anna shrugged on her jacket. Ariadne had returned to sitting on the desk. "Ari, get yourself added to my next patrol. I've an idea about Hypatia."

"But if you're going to talk to Hypatia, I want to be there too," Lucie protested. "I know the right questions to ask—"

Anna shot her an amused look. "Don't fuss, pet. I'll let you know where we're meeting Hypatia."

"Oh, good, a secret message," Lucie said, pleased. "Will it be in code?"

Anna did not reply; she had started out of the room—then paused in front of Ariadne. She slid a finger under Ariadne's chin, raised the other girl's face, and kissed her, hard—Ariadne's eyes flew wide with surprise before she closed them, surrendering to the moment. Lucie felt her cheeks turn pink.

She looked away, fixing her gaze on the amethyst fire. She could not help but think of Grace, bought and sold as a child as if she'd been a porcelain doll, not a person at all. No wonder she seemed to know so very little about love.

16

DARK BREAKS TO DAWN

And here, as lamps across the bridge turn pale
In London's smokeless resurrection-light,
Dark breaks to dawn.
—Dante Gabriel Rossetti, "Found"

"This is absolute madness, James," said Anna, slamming her teacup down on the saucer with enough force to send a crack spidering through the china. She must be quite upset, James thought: her appreciation for fine china was well honed. "How could you even *think* such a thing?"

James looked around the drawing room. His friends were staring at him from chairs pulled close to the cozy fire. Anna—dapper in a blue waistcoat and black spats—Christopher, wide-eyed, and Thomas, his mouth set in a grim line. Lucie, her hands in her lap, clearly struggling with her emotions and determined not to show it.

"I hadn't planned to tell you at all," James said. He had sat in an armchair on the theory that one might as well be comfortable when telling one's friends one might be engaged in murdering people in one's sleep. "If there hadn't been that mark on my windowsill—"

"Is that supposed to make us feel better?" demanded Thomas.

"You didn't want to tell us because you knew that we would say it was ridiculous," said Lucie. "You and Cordelia already rid us of Belial."

"But a Prince of Hell cannot be killed," James said wearily. He was exhausted down to his bones: he had barely slept the night before, barely eaten, and Grace's visit had shaken him. He pushed away from thoughts of her now, returning determinedly to the matter at hand. "We all know it. Belial may be much diminished after being wounded by Cortana, but that does not mean his sphere of influence has ended. Something made that mark on my windowsill this morning."

"You mentioned the mark before," said Christopher. "What was it? What makes you so sure it has to do with Belial?"

James rose and took the *Monarchia Daemonium* from where he had placed it on the piano bench. It was a tall volume, bound in dark purple leather. "This is where I first read about Belial and the other eight Princes of Hell," he said. "Each has a sigil, a sign by which he is known." He sat down and opened the book to the two-page section on Belial. "This is the symbol I saw in the ice."

The others crowded around, Anna leaning over the back of James's chair. There was a silence as they took in the illustration of Belial— he was facing away, his head turned to the side, his profile razor-sharp. He wore a dark red cloak, and a single clawed hand was visible at his side. Not quite the elegant gentleman James had met in Belphegor's realm, though there remained the same aura about him of leashed menace.

"So Belial left you a calling card," Anna murmured. "Rude of him not to wait until the footman was at home."

"So is it meant to be a message?" said Thomas. "A way of saying, 'Here I am'?"

"Perhaps a way of saying he is me," said James. "Perhaps he has found a way to possess me when I am unconscious—"

"You are not a murderer or possessed," snapped Lucie. "In case you've forgotten, demons cannot possess Shadowhunters. You don't think our parents forgot our protection spells when we were born, do you?"

"Lucie," James said. "I don't blame them or expect they forgot. But this is Belial. He's a Prince of Hell. Half my life, he's reached into my waking dreams. If anyone could break through the protection spell, a Prince of Hell—"

"It should protect against any demonic interference," said Christopher. "The spell was originally intended to keep Lilith away specifically. The angels Sanvi, Sansanvi, and Semangelaf are her mortal enemies. But the full ritual, performed by the Silent Brothers, should be strong enough to keep away even Belial, or Leviathan."

"An excellent reminder it could be worse," said James. "Our grandfather could have been Leviathan. We'd both have tentacles."

"So hard to find clothes that would fit," said Christopher sympathetically.

"So what do these sigils do?" wondered Thomas, settling back into his chair. "Do they just serve as elaborate signatures?"

James set the book down on the inlaid table by the fire. "They are more than symbols. They can be used in summoning. Ancient cults used to create massive sigils with standing stones or marks on the ground, which would serve as gateways for demons." He paused, arrested by a sudden thought. "Christopher, do you have a map of London?"

"I am a scientist," said Christopher, "not a geographer! I don't have a map of London. I do have a beaker of Raum venom," he added, "but it's in my shoe, and will be difficult to reach."

"Does anyone have questions about that?" James said, glancing around. "No? Good. All right, a map—"

Anna clambered lightly onto an upholstered chair and reached for a high shelf of books. She drew down a volume of maps. "How fortunate that you have a well-stocked library, James."

James took the book and set it down on the table, flipping through the pages. The map of London was easy to find: no Londoner did not know the shape of his city, with its crowded banks, its bridges, its river winding past wharves and docks.

Over Thomas's protests, James flicked a pen from his friend's pocket. He began to mark spots on the map, counting them off in order. "Clerkenwell, Fitch Lane, Shoe Lane, Shepherd Market—"

"I think he is possessed," said Thomas. "He's defacing a *book*."

"Desperate times call for desperate measures." James squinted. Splashed across the map were his marks, one for each address where a body had been found. He had connected them with his pen, but they formed nothing resembling Belial's sigil. "I had wondered—"

"If someone was trying to draw the sigil, so to speak, with the locations chosen for the murders," said Christopher, his face alight with thought. "I realized what you were doing—it's very clever, but

I don't see how that could even be the beginning of Belial's sigil. It's all circles, and this is more like a line that hooks at the end—"

James tossed the pen onto the table. "It was just a theory. But that doesn't mean that Belial isn't working his will through me while I sleep. Think of what Filomena's ghost said to Cordelia, that she had wounded Belial and should have been able to help her. Perhaps because she knew her murderer was also one of Hell's princes? Maybe even the same one?"

"We can't know that's what she meant," said Thomas. "And if Belial is influencing you—you know none of this would be your fault, don't you?"

They were all silent for a moment. James took a deep breath. "Would you feel that way?" he said. "If you were me?"

"Well, you can hardly never sleep again," said Christopher. "Studies have shown that is quite unsafe."

"Be reasonable," said Anna. "How would you come and go in the middle of the night, knocking about and bumping into things because you're not even awake, and not raise—not raise the whole house?"

"I'm not sure it's the same as sleepwalking," James said. "Maybe I wouldn't be bumping into things. Maybe I'm more aware than that and the dreams are a kind of memory of what I've done. And—" His throat felt desert-dry. "And the night Elias died, when I dreamed—it was different from the others. He seemed to see me. He *recognized* me."

Anna, who had been pacing, stopped in her tracks. "He said your name?"

"No," James had to admit. "I saw recognition spark in his eyes—he said something, I think it was, 'It's you.' But he didn't say my name."

His friends exchanged worried glances. "I see why you didn't want Cordelia here," Anna said finally. "To tell her you think you were responsible for the death of her father—"

"Though you *weren't*, James," Lucie put in.

"I do want her here, actually," James said. "I thought she and Matthew would be back by now. I can't keep this from her. A conspiracy of silence like that—" He shook his head. "No. If she despises me after, then I will need you to be there for her. Her friends."

"She will not," Anna began, "despise you, James—"

As if on cue, they all heard the sound of a motorcar coming to a stop in front of the house. His friends' voices rose in a murmur behind James as he went to open the front door.

He was in shirtsleeves, and the cold air outside cut sharply through the cotton. It was not snowing, but a fog had come in with the setting sun, softening the edges of the city, making the motorcar look like a faerie carriage drawn by invisible horses.

He leaned against the doorjamb as Matthew, a shadow in the fog, came around the car to help Cordelia out. The blanket wrapped around her started to slip down as she stood, but Matthew caught it before it reached the ground and carefully rearranged it around her shoulders. Even through the fog, James could see her smile.

He felt an odd sensation, a sort of tingle between his shoulder blades. Apprehension, perhaps; he was not looking forward to telling his tale to Cordelia. She and Matthew were making their way toward the house, their booted feet silent on the snowy pavement. Cordelia's hair was loose, its brilliant red the single focal point of color in the monochrome fog.

"Daisy!" James called. "Math! Get inside. You'll freeze."

A moment later they were hurrying past him into the entryway, Matthew reaching to help Cordelia off with her coat before James could think to do it. They both looked windburned, high color in their cheeks. Matthew was chattering about the car, and how James should have a try at driving it.

Cordelia, though, was quiet, drawing off her gloves, her wide, dark eyes thoughtful. As Matthew took a moment to breathe, she said, "James—who's here?"

"Anna, Lucie, Thomas, and Christopher are in the drawing room," he said. "I asked them to come."

Matthew frowned, pulling off his goggles. "Is everything all right?"

"Not quite," said James, and added, as they both turned apprehensive faces toward him, "There hasn't been another death—nothing like that."

"But things are not all right?" Matthew said. "Has something else happened? The Enclave done something dreadful?"

"The Enclave is torn between thinking it's a warlock gone rogue and thinking it's a Shadowhunter," said James. "But Thomas and Anna can tell you more about that. I need to talk to Cordelia for a moment. If you don't mind, Math."

A flicker of emotion crossed Matthew's face but vanished before James could identify it. "Of course," he said, sliding past James to vanish down the hall.

Cordelia looked up at James inquiringly. Her hair was damp; it curled around her face like the buds of roses. A whisper pressed at the back of his mind: *You have to tell her you kissed Grace.*

He told the whisper to be quiet. What he had to tell her first was so much worse.

"I've missed you," he said. "And before we go into the drawing room, I wished to apologize. What I said about your father in the Ossuarium was unforgivable, and my sending him away was something I will always regret—"

But she was shaking her head. "I have been wanting to apologize to *you*. You have nothing to be sorry for. You could not have saved my father. By awful luck, you were the last one to see him, and he was— oh, the *shame* of him demanding money from you." There was a cold passion of anger in her voice. She shook her head, her hair straining against the few pins still confining it. "Alastair set me right, of all people. You did what you should have, James."

"There's more," he said, forcing the words past his dry throat. "More that I have to tell you. I do not know if you will still feel as kindly toward me when I am done."

He saw her flinch, saw her steel herself. It was a reminder of how much her childhood must have taught her to brace for bad news. "Tell me."

In a way, it was easier to tell her than it had been to explain himself to the others. Daisy already knew of his screaming awakenings from nightmare, of the open window in his bedroom, the things he saw when he dreamed. Daisy, like him, had met Belial. It was one thing to imagine you could face down a Prince of Hell. It was another entirely to stand near one, to feel the freezing blast of their hatred, their evil, their power.

He forced himself through the last of it—explaining his

experiment, the ropes, the mark on the sill—as she stared at him, her expression very still.

"I see," she said, when he was done, "that I should not have left you alone last night."

His hair was in his eyes; he raised a shaking hand to push it back. "The worst of it is, I know precious little more now than I did then. And we may need to hire another maid to replace Effie."

"And what do the others say?" she asked.

"They refuse to believe it—any of it," he said. "They may think the shock of what happened with your father has turned my brain." His breath caught. "Daisy. The hate I have felt, every time I have dreamed, I cannot but imagine it is anything but Belial's hate. And your father—" His breath caught. "If you want nothing to do with this, with me, I would never blame you."

"James." She took hold of his wrist; the small gesture went through him like an electric shock. Her face was set, determined. "Come with me."

He let her pull him down the hall, into the drawing room, where the others had congregated. Matthew was seated on the back of the sofa; he turned toward James as he entered the room, his eyes dark with worry.

Anna's blue gaze flicked to Cordelia. "Did you tell her?"

Cordelia released James's wrist. "I know everything," she said. Her voice was very level. There was something different about her, James thought, something he could not quite put his finger on. She had changed—since yesterday, even. But then, she had lost her father. Her family would never be the same.

"It's ridiculous," Matthew said, sliding off the sofa back. "James, you can't really believe—"

"I understand why he believes it," Cordelia said, and Matthew stopped mid-motion. Every face in the room was turned to Cordelia. "There were two things I thought when I met Belial. First, that I would do anything in the world to get away from him. And second, that it would not matter what I did, because his focus was entirely on James. It has been for some time now. If there is a way he can reach him . . . he will."

"But James is not a murderer," said Lucie. "He would never—"

"I don't think he's one either," said Cordelia. "If Belial is control-ling him, then none of this is *his fault*. He cannot be blamed. Any of us would do the same, for the power of a Prince of Hell—" She shook her head. "It is unstoppable."

"I tried to stop myself, last night," James said. "And still somehow I woke with the ropes in pieces all around me."

"You cannot do this alone," said Cordelia. "In fact, if we are to prove anything at all about what is really going on, you cannot be alone for a moment."

"She is right," Anna said. "We will remain here tonight, keeping watch. If you try to leave the house, we will know."

"Not if he tries to get out the window," Christopher pointed out, reasonably.

"We nail it shut," said Thomas, getting into the spirit of the thing.

"And someone sits with James. Lets him sleep, but watches what happens," said Matthew. "I'll do it."

"It might be better if Cordelia did it," James said quietly.

Matthew looked a little hurt. "Why?"

"Because I have Cortana," said Cordelia. "I have wounded Belial with Cortana before; if necessary, I suppose . . ." For the first time she looked doubtful. "I could do so again."

"Indeed," said James. "She can strike me down if necessary."

"Certainly not!" exclaimed Lucie, bolting to her feet. "There will be no striking down of anyone!"

"Except Belial," remarked Christopher. "If he makes an appear-ance—on his own, you know, not inside James, as it were."

"Just wound me, then," James said to Cordelia. "Stab me in the leg if you need to. The left one, if you can—I'm fonder of my right."

"Just promise you'll call out, if you need us," Matthew said. He exchanged a long look with James. It said all the things Matthew would never say in front of all these people, no matter how he cared for them: it said that he loved James, that he would be here all night, if James needed him, that he believed in James as he believed in himself.

"So it's decided," said Anna. "We will wait down here tonight and make sure James never leaves his room; Cordelia will stand guard upstairs. And I will raid the larder, since we are likely to get hungry. An army marches on its stomach, as the saying goes."

"So how are we planning to stay awake all night?" Thomas inquired.

"I could read to you all from *The Beautiful Cordelia*," Lucie suggested. "I have some pages in my handbag. One never knows when inspiration may strike."

"Oh Lord," said Matthew, reaching for his flask. "In that case, I'll be needing brandy. What was it Lord Byron said? 'Man, being reasonable, must get drunk; the best of life is but intoxication.'" He raised the flask in a salute. "Lucie, begin. As the demons of Hell are battled upstairs, so we shall battle the demons of romantic prose in the drawing room."

James retired to his room with Thomas, who helped nail the window shut before heading back downstairs to play cards. Cordelia, after visiting her own room to change into a comfortable tea gown, joined James, who locked the connecting door firmly after her and moved a chair in front of it for good measure.

Then he began to get undressed.

Cordelia supposed she should have expected this. The whole idea was that James would go to bed, after all, and he couldn't be expected to sleep with his shoes and jacket on. She pulled a chair up beside the bed and settled herself on it, Cortana across her lap.

"Your drive today," he said, undoing his cuff links. His shirt sprang apart at the wrists, revealing the strong line of his forearms. "Did it lift your spirits?"

"Yes," she said. "There's a fanciful story of a barrow in the Berkshire Downs where if you leave a coin, Wayland the Smith will mend your sword. I brought Cortana there, and it does seem to be sitting easier in my hand now."

She wanted to tell him the rest—of Wayland the Smith, of her swearing fealty as a paladin. She had not told Matthew. It was too new, then, and there was too much wonder in it. And now, she found, she could not tell James, either; it was too much, too strange a tale for tonight. If all went well, she would tell him tomorrow.

"They say Wayland the Smith made the sword Balmung, which

Sigurd used to kill the dragon Fafnir," James said, stripping off his jacket and braces. "A king imprisoned Wayland, to try to force him to forge weapons. He killed the king's sons in revenge, and made goblets from their skulls and a necklace from their eyes."

Cordelia thought of the blue stone necklace Wayland had been wearing and shivered a little. It had not looked even a bit like eyes, but nothing about the man she had met made her believe him incapable of the deeds in the story James was telling.

"They say all swords have souls," she said. "That makes me feel slightly uneasy about Cortana's."

He smiled crookedly, unbuttoning his shirt. "Perhaps not *all* the stories are true."

"We can hope not," she said, as he clambered onto the bed in trousers and undershirt; there were already pillows stacked against the headboard, and a coil of rope on the coverlet. The undershirt left his arms bare from the elbows down, traced with black Marks and the pale scars of faded runes. "I will tie my wrist to the bedpost, here," he said, "and then, if you could tie the other wrist, it would be safest, I think."

Cordelia cleared her throat. "Yes, that—that does seem most secure."

His glanced over at her, his hair ruffled. "What was the trouble with Cortana?"

"It had not felt quite right in my hand since we fought Belial," Cordelia admitted; that much was the truth. "I think that his blood might have affected it somehow." *Which Wayland himself explained to me, but I cannot tell you that.*

"Belial." James took the rope, carefully looping it around and around his left wrist and binding himself to the bedpost. His head was down; Cordelia watched the muscles in his arms flexing and relaxing as he secured himself. Though it had been months since the summer, there was still a visible line where his skin was browner, then whiter, below the sleeves and collar of his shirt. "That is why I wanted you in the room with me." His voice was low, almost rough. "The others know Belial is a Prince of Hell, but only you and I have *seen* him. Only we know what it means to confront him."

Finished with the knot, he sat back against the stacked pillows. His hair was very black against their whiteness. For a moment, Cordelia saw again that blasted place where they had fought for their lives: the sand flaming into glass, stark trees like skeletons, and Belial, with all his beauty, and every bit of humanity burned from him.

"You don't believe the others would be willing to stop you if it meant harming you," she said. "But you think I would be."

James gave the ghost of a smile. "I have faith in you, Daisy. And there is one more thing I must tell you." He squared his jaw, as if he were steeling himself for something. "I kissed Grace today."

The night lay before James in all its possible horrors, yet at this moment, his whole world seemed to have narrowed down to Cordelia. He knew he was staring at her, and could not stop himself. He did not know what he had expected—she did not love him, that he knew, but he had broken their agreement, his promise to respect her dignity.

In a way it would be easier if she did love him, if he had broken a romantic agreement. He could throw himself at her feet, beg and apologize. She could weep and make demands. But this was Daisy; she would never do either of those things. She said nothing now, only her eyes seemed to have gotten a little bigger in her face.

"She came here," he said finally, unable to bear the silence. "I did not invite her. You must believe me; I would not have done that. She came unexpectedly, and she was upset about the murders, and—I kissed her. I don't know why," he added, because he could not explain to Cordelia what he could not explain to himself, "but I will make no stupid excuses."

"I noticed there was a crack," Cordelia said, in a low, expressionless voice, "in the metal of your bracelet."

The rope looped James's right wrist, partially concealing the bracelet. Glancing down, he saw Cordelia was right: a hairline crack ran along the metal. "I may have punched the bookcase, after she left," he admitted. His hand still ached from the impact. "It may have split the metal."

"May have?" she said, in the same low voice. "And why are you telling me this now? You could have waited. Told me tomorrow."

"If you are to watch over me all night, you should know who you're watching," said James. "I let you down. As a friend. As a husband. I didn't want to compound that by keeping secrets from you."

She gave him a long look. A considering look.

"If you wish to leave," he said, "you can—"

"I am not going to leave you." Her voice was measured, even. "On the other hand, you have broken our agreement. I would like something in exchange."

"As if I had lost at chess?" She never failed to surprise him. He almost smiled. "You might want to ask me at a different time, when I am not tied to a bed. The services I can render you at the moment are limited."

She stood up, leaning Cortana against the wall. The red tea gown she wore was loose but of clinging silk material, with bands of black velvet ribbon at the hem and sleeves. Her hair was a shade darker than the silk, her eyes the same color as the velvet, and fixed on his as she climbed onto the bed. "Adequate to what I need, I think," she said. "I want you to kiss me."

His blood seemed to speed up in his veins. "What?"

She was kneeling, facing him; their eyes were on a level. The gown spread around her as if she were a water lily, rising from leaves. Its deep collar plunged low, edged with white lace that feathered lightly against her brown skin. There was a look on her face that reminded James of her expression the night she'd danced at the Hell Ruelle. A determination close to passion.

"You will one day find your way back to Grace, who knows of our situation," she said. "But I will marry some other man, and he will know I was married to you. He will expect me to know how to kiss, and—do other things. I do not expect a complete tutorial, but I think I could reasonably ask that you show me how kissing is done."

He remembered Cordelia dancing, all fire. He remembered the moments after that, in the Whispering Room. He could say to her that she hardly needed any teaching from him; she knew how to kiss. But his mind was consumed with the thought of this man, some man she would marry in future, who would kiss her and expect things from her—

James hated him already. He felt dizzy with it—with rage toward someone he did not know, and with how near she was to him.

"Get on top of me," he said, his voice barely recognizable to his own ears.

It was her turn to look surprised. "What—?"

"I am tied to the bed," he said. "I cannot get up and kiss you, so I will have to sit here and kiss you. Which means I need you"—he held out his free arm, his gaze never leaving hers—"closer."

She nodded. A flush had spread across her face, but otherwise she watched him, wide-eyed and serious, as she moved across the bed toward him, crawling a little awkwardly into his lap. His blood was already running hot and fast through his veins as she settled her knees on either side of his hips. Her face was close to his now: he could see the dark individual lines of her eyelashes, the movement of her lower lip as she took it between her teeth.

"Tell me again what you want me to do," he said.

The smooth column of her throat moved as she swallowed. "Show me how to kiss," she said. "Properly."

He put his free arm around her, angling his knees up so that her back was against his legs. The tea gown rustled, the material tightening as she moved, molding to her shape. He could smell the scent of her perfume: smoky jasmine. His hand slid into her thick, satiny hair, cupping the back of her head. She sighed, settling more closely against him; the feel of her sent a jagged shard of desire up his spine.

Her lips were heart-shaped, he thought: that dent in the top lip, the circle formed by the lower. She was no longer biting her lip, only looking at him, her eyes filled with the same cool challenge with which she'd faced down the Hell Ruelle. There was no reason to treat her as if she were afraid, he realized: this was Daisy. She was never afraid.

"Put your hands on my shoulders," he said, and when she leaned forward to do just that, he kissed her.

Her grip on him tightened immediately; she exhaled against his mouth, surprised. He swallowed her gasp, parting her lips with his tongue, until her mouth was hot and open under his. He teased the corner of her mouth with butterfly kisses, sucked and licked at her bottom lip as she gripped his shoulders harder. She was trembling, but she had asked him to teach her and he intended to be complete.

With his free hand, he stroked her hair, pulling the last pins from it, tangling his fingers in the thick strands. Her hands moved to cup either side of his neck, her fingers in the curls at his nape. His tongue teased hers, showing her how to return the kiss—how the exchange could be a duel of lips and tongue, of breath and pleasure. When she sucked at his bottom lip, he surged up against her, deepening the kiss ruthlessly, his free hand fisting in the back of her dress, crushing the material.

Oh, God. Thin silk made hardly any barrier; he could feel her body all up and down his own, the shape of her: breasts, waist, hips. He was drowning in kissing her, would never get enough of kissing her. The softness of her mouth, the noises of pleasure she made in between kisses—she moved to get closer to him, her hips rocking against his. A sharp hiss escaped between his teeth. His arm ached; he had been pulling and pulling against the rope restraining him, his body operating by its own set of needs and desires now.

Cordelia moaned and arched against him. Sparks shot through his veins; the need to touch her was blinding, searing, the ache growing in his blood to do more, to have more of her. She probably had no idea what she was doing to him—he barely knew himself—but if she kept moving like that—

She was his wife, and she was adorable, incredibly desirable. He had never wanted anyone like this. Half out of his mind, he moved his lips across her jaw, down to her throat. He could feel the beat of her pulse, inhale the scent of her hair, jasmine and rose water. He kissed his way down, teeth grazing her collarbone; his lips grazed the hollow of her throat—

She drew away swiftly, scrambling off him, her face pink, her hair tumbling freely down her back.

"That was very instructive," she said, her calm voice at odds with her flushed face and rumpled dress. "Thank you, James."

He let his head fall back against the headboard with a thump. He was still dizzy, blood slamming through his veins. His body ached with unexpressed desire. *"Daisy—"*

"You should sleep." She was already gathering up Cortana, already sitting back down in the chair by his bed. "You *must*, in fact, or we will never know."

He struggled to regulate his breathing. Bloody hell. If she were anyone else, he'd have said she'd intended this as revenge: his body felt ravaged by wanting her. But she had settled herself calmly in her chair, her sword across her lap. Only the slight disarrangement of her hair, the red marks on her throat where his lips had been, showed that anything had happened.

"Oh," she said, as if just recalling an item of shopping she'd forgotten. "Did you need your other wrist tied as well?"

"No," James managed. He was not about to explain why further proximity to Cordelia seemed like a bad idea. "This is—fine."

"Do you want me to read to you?" she said, picking up a novel from the nightstand.

He nodded very slightly. He was desperate for a distraction. "What book?"

"Dickens," she said primly, opened the volume, and began to read.

Thomas was buttoning his coat as he crossed the kitchen—dark, now, as midnight had come and the place was blissfully free of domestic staff. He had crept out of the drawing room without the others noticing, caught up as they were in their chatter and card games. Even Christopher, on watch by the door, hadn't noticed as Thomas had gathered up his gear jacket and *bolas* and crept down the hall.

Feeling rather proud of himself, he soundlessly unlatched the back door to the garden and threw it open. He had just slipped outside into the chilly darkness when a light flared in front of him. The burning tip of a match illuminated a pair of sharp blue eyes.

"Close the door behind you," Anna said.

Thomas did as requested, silently cursing himself. He could have sworn that ten minutes ago Anna had been asleep in a chair. "How did you know?"

"That you'd be sneaking out?" She lit the tip of her cheroot and tossed the match. "Honestly, Thomas, I've been waiting for you so long

Thomas Lightwood

out here I was afraid my waistcoat would go out of style."

"I just wanted some air—"

"No, you didn't," she said, puffing white smoke into the frigid air. "You had that look in your eye. You're going to go out and patrol alone again. Cousin, don't be foolish."

"I have to do what I can, and I'm of better use out there than I am in the drawing room," Thomas said. "James doesn't need five of us to make sure he doesn't leave the house."

"Thomas, look at me," she said, and he did. Her blue gaze was steady. His cousin Anna: he remembered when she had worn petticoats and dresses, her hair long and braided into plaits. And always in her eyes a look of discomfort, of sadness. He remembered, too, when she had emerged like a butterfly from a cocoon, transforming into what she was now—a vision in gleaming cuff links and starched collars. She lived her life so boldly, so unapologetically, that sometimes it made Thomas's stomach hurt a little, just to look at her.

She laid a gloved hand on his cheek. "We are special, unusual, unique people. That means that we must be bold and proud, but also careful. Don't think you have so much to prove that it makes you foolish. If you must patrol, go to the Institute and ask to be assigned a partner. If I discover that you are out on your own, I will be very angry."

"All right." Thomas kissed the palm of Anna's gloved hand and returned it to her gently.

She watched him with troubled eyes as he scrambled over the back garden wall.

He had, of course, no intention of seeking a patrol partner. He disliked misleading Anna—but this madness of James's had to end. James was one of the best, kindest, and bravest people Thomas had ever known, and for James to doubt himself like this was painful— for if James could doubt himself like this, what did it mean for those like Thomas, who already doubted themselves so much?

He was determined to put a stop to it, he thought, as he strode out onto Curzon Street, deserted under the moon. He would find the real killer if it was the last thing he ever did.

* * *

"After I had turned the worst point of my illness, I began to notice that while all its other features changed, this one consistent feature did not change. Whoever came about me, still settled down into Joe. I opened my eyes in the night, and I saw in the great chair at the bedside, Joe. I opened my eyes in the day, and, sitting on the window-seat, smoking his pipe in the shaded open window, still I saw Joe. I asked for cooling drink, and the dear hand that gave it me was Joe's. I sank back on my pillow after drinking, and the face that looked so hopefully and tenderly upon me was the face of Joe."

James did not know how long Cordelia had been reading: he had kept his eyes shut, his free arm flung across his face, willing himself to sleep. But sleep had not come. It seemed an impossibility. He could not stop thinking of Cordelia, though she was beside him. Of the feel of her, her heavy hair gathered in his hands, her body against his. But not just of that—memories of all their minutes together came like flashes of lightning, illuminating the darkness behind his eyes: the nights they'd spent game playing, the times they'd laughed, exchanged glances of understanding, whispered secrets. The bracelet on his wrist felt as heavy as a two-ton weight. *But you love Grace,* whispered the unwelcome voice at the back of his mind. *You know that you do.*

He pushed back against the thought. It was like pressing on a bruise, or a broken bone. He had kissed Grace that day, but the memory of it felt faded, like old parchment. Like the shadow-memory of a dream. His head throbbed, as if something hard were pressing at his temples; the voice in his mind wanted him to think of Grace, but again he pushed against it.

He thought of Daisy. He had missed her when she was gone; when he woke this morning, he had thought first of her, of laying his troubles before her so they could be shared and sorted out together. That was something more than friendship, and besides, friendship did not make you want to seize someone the moment you saw them and ravage them with kisses.

But he owed Grace. He had made promises to her for so many years. He could not recall specifically what they were, but the certainty was as real as an iron bar rammed through his heart. He had made them because he loved her. Loyalty bound him. His wrist ached where the rope crisscrossed her bracelet, sending a cold pain up his arm. *You have always loved Grace*, came the voice again. *Love is not to be abandoned. It is not a toy to discard by the roadside.*

You have never loved anyone else.

There was a soft murmur in his head. It was Daisy, reading Dickens.

> "*Of late, very often. There was a long hard time when I kept far from me, the remembrance, of what I had thrown away when I was quite ignorant of its worth. But, since my duty has not been incompatible with the admission of that remembrance, I have given it a place in my heart.*"

A real memory came then, strong and dark as tea, of another room, a time when he had tossed and turned, and Daisy had read aloud. The memory was like the surge of a wave; it lifted and broke under him, and was gone. He reached for it, but it had evaporated in the darkness; exhausted, he could no longer push against the force of his own mind. The voice in the back of his head returned like a flood. He had seen Grace that day, and he had not been able to stop himself from kissing her. He *did* love her. It was a surety that felt like the closing of a cell door.

"James?" Cordelia had paused in her reading; she sounded worried. "Are you all right? No bad dreams?"

The night was a canyon, black and depthless; James ached for things he could not name or define. "Not yet," he said. "No bad dreams."

London:
Golden Square

The killer could move so swiftly now that mundanes did not see him; he was a shade, flickering past them on the streets. No more would he have to hide, or discard his bloody clothes in abandoned buildings—though it amused him no end that the Shadowhunters had kept a watch on the abandoned Limehouse factory as if they expected his return.

He brushed past crowds like the shadow of a passing cloud. Sometimes he paused, to look around and smile, to gather himself. There would be blood at dawn, but whose would spill? A group of patrolling Shadowhunters moved past him and onto Brewer Street. He grinned ferociously—what fun it would be to separate one from the pack and take him down, leaving him dead in his own blood before the others had even noticed.

Even as he reached for his blade, another Shadowhunter passed—a young one, tall, brown-haired. This one was alone, watchful. Not part of a patrol. He was walking into Golden Square, his back straight, head held high. A voice whispered in the back of the killer's mind: a name.

Thomas Lightwood.

PART TWO

- ❧ -

BY THE SWORD

In a dream, in a vision of the night, when deep sleep
falleth upon men, in slumberings upon the bed,
Then He openeth the ears of men,
and sealeth their instruction,
That He may withdraw man from his purpose,
and hide pride from man.
He keepeth back his soul from the pit, and
his life from perishing by the sword.

—Job 33:15

17

PROPHET OF EVIL

Prophet of evil I ever am to myself: forced for ever into
sorrowful auguries that I have no power to hide from my
own heart, no, not through one night's solitary dreams.
—Thomas De Quincey, *Confessions of an English Opium-Eater*

The city slept, beneath its blanket of snow. Every footstep Thomas took seemed to echo down empty streets, beneath the awnings of shops, past houses where people lay warm and safe inside, never knowing he paced past their thresholds.

He had walked up from Mayfair through Marylebone, past closed shops whose windows glittered with Christmas displays, until he reached Regent's Park. The freezing rain had turned the trees into elaborate ice sculptures. There were a few carriages on the Euston Road as the hours turned toward dawn; doctors making emergency calls, perhaps, or traveling to or from late-night shifts at the hospitals.

It had been a long night, both because of the rain that had begun shortly after midnight, and because as he passed along Brewer Street, he had nearly run into a patrol of Shadowhunters: four or five men bundled in gear and heavy coats. He slipped away from them, through Golden Square. The last thing he wanted was to be caught, and likely censured. He could not—would not—rest until the killer was apprehended.

He could not have entirely explained what drove his restless determination. James was certainly a part of it—James, tied up in his own bedroom all night while their friends stood guard downstairs, prepared for something none of them believed possible. James, who bore the weight of a heritage darker than any shadows. It never seemed to touch Lucie, but James's eyes were always haunted.

There was only one other person Thomas had known with eyes like that. Not golden eyes, but dark, and so sad—he had always been drawn to that dichotomy, he thought, of the cruelty of Alastair's words, and the sadness with which he said them. Sorrowful eyes and a vicious tongue. *Tell me,* he had always wanted to say, *what broke your heart, and let such bitterness spill out?*

On and on Thomas strode, down through Bloomsbury, barely noticing how numb and cold his feet had grown, driven on by the feeling that just around the next corner, his quarry would be waiting. But there was nobody about except for the occasional bobby on his beat, or cloaked and bundled night workers trudging home, their faces invisible but no sense of threat coming from them. He passed the Covent Garden market, just beginning to open, tall stacks of wooden crates lining its colonnades as the wagons rolled in and out, carrying flowers, fruit, and even Christmas trees, whose boughs filled the air with the scent of pine.

As Thomas began to loop back west again toward Soho, the sky seemed to be growing perceptibly lighter. He stopped short in front of the statue of King George II at the center of Golden Square, its pale marble almost luminous under the deep, just-before-dawn blue of the sky. Somewhere, an early riser was playing the piano, and the mournful notes echoed through the square. Dawn was moments away. Back at Curzon Street, they would soon have their answer. Either there had been no deaths tonight—in which case James would still be a suspect—or the killer would have struck again, in which case they would know James was innocent. How strange, not to know what to wish for.

Suddenly Thomas wanted nothing more than to return to his friends. He started walking more briskly, rubbing his gloved hands to warm his stiff fingers as the glow of yellow and pink over the treetops signaled the sun's approach.

Then a scream shattered the stillness. Thomas broke into a run without thinking, his training propelling him toward the sound before he had a moment to hesitate. He prayed that it was a fight, maybe drunks stumbling out of a pub, or a thief snatching a handbag from an early-morning commuter—

He skidded around a corner onto Sink Street. A woman was sprawled across the threshold of a terraced town house, half in and half out of the iced-over garden. She was facedown on the ground, her garments streaked in blood, gray hair spilling onto the snow. He looked wildly around, but saw no one else. He knelt and gathered the woman into his arms, turning her head to see her face—

It was Lilian Highsmith. He knew her—everyone did. She was an elder of the Clave, a respected figure—and kindly, too. She had kept peppermints in her pocket to give to children. He remembered her handing them to him when he was a little boy, her thin hands ruffling his hair.

She wore a morning dress, as if she had not expected to be outside. The fabric was slashed, blood pouring from multiple gashes in the material. Bloody foam flecked her lips—she was still breathing, he realized. With shaking hands, he drew out his stele, desperately carving *iratze* after *iratze* onto her skin. Each flickered and vanished, like a stone sinking into water.

He desperately wished, now, for the patrol he'd seen earlier. They'd barely been a few blocks from here. How could they have missed this?

Lilian Highsmith's eyelids flickered open. She caught at the front of his coat, shaking her head, as if to say, *Enough. Stop trying.*

His breath hitched. "Miss Highsmith," he said urgently. "It's Thomas—Thomas Lightwood. Who did this to you?"

She tightened her grip on his lapels, pulling him closer with surprising strength. "*He* did," she whispered. "But he was dead, dead in his prime. His wife . . . she wept and wept. I remember her tears." Her eyes fixed on Thomas's. "Perhaps there is no forgiveness."

Her fingers loosened their grip and slowly trailed down his coat, leaving a bloody smear behind. Her face went slack as the light left her eyes.

Numbly, Thomas laid her limp body on the ground. His mind whirled. Should he bring her inside? Someone might come along soon, and she was not glamoured—mundanes should not see her like this, and yet perhaps the Enclave would not want him to move her?

At least he could arrange her as a Shadowhunter should be laid out in death. He shut her eyes with his thumb, and reached for her hands to fold them on her chest. Something rolled free of her left hand, clanking gently against the icy ground.

It was a stele. What had she been doing with it? Trying to heal herself?

Thomas heard footsteps approaching and lifted his head, dazed. Could the murderer be returning, worried that Lilian might survive— and determined to come back and make certain she hadn't? Quickly, he stuffed the stele into his pocket and drew a knife from his belt.

"Oi! There! Don't you dare run!"

Thomas froze. It was the Shadowhunter patrol he'd seen earlier. Four men rounded the corner, Inquisitor Bridgestock in the lead. They slowed as they approached, staring in shock at Thomas, and at Miss Highsmith's body.

He realized in a split second how it must look. A Shadowhunter dead beside him, and him with a knife in his bloody hand. Worse yet, he wasn't scheduled for patrol—no one knew about his nightly outings. No one could vouch for him. His friends could say they knew he was patrolling on his own, but that wasn't much, was it?

A clamor of voices started up as the Inquisitor moved toward Thomas, his face set, his black cape swirling around his legs. Thomas dropped the knife and let his hands fall to his sides, knowing it would be pointless to speak. He didn't bother to try to understand what they were all saying. Everything felt slow and surreal, like a terrible dream that was trying to pull him under. He watched from what felt like miles away as Bridgestock spoke in a triumphant voice.

"Gentlemen, we have found the murderer," he said. "Arrest him at once."

Having set the book aside, Cordelia was watching James sleep. She had an excuse, she supposed, beyond unrequited love. She was watching over him. Protecting him, from the terrors of the night, from the threat of Belial. She felt the weight of Cortana in her hands, as she felt the weight of the trust Wayland the Smith had placed in her.

Go forth. Be a warrior.

Not that it was a hardship, watching her husband sleep. She had thought when they first became engaged that she would lie beside James at night, hearing his breaths even out into slumber. When she had realized they would have separate bedrooms, it had felt like a loss of that dream.

She would have liked to say the real thing was a disappointment. But it would have been a lie. She had watched him toss and turn and finally fall asleep, his free arm bent behind his head, his cheek resting almost in the crook of his elbow. The lines of worry on his face had smoothed out into clarity and innocence. His cheeks flushed with his dreaming, his black eyelashes fluttering against his high cheekbones. Watching him, she thought of Majnun from Ganjavi's poem, a boy so beautiful he illuminated the darkness.

When he moved in his sleep, his thin shirt slid up, showing the ridges of his stomach. She had blushed at that, and looked away a little, before asking herself fiercely, *Why?* She had kissed that soft mouth, the lower lip fuller than the upper, dented slightly in the center. She had felt his body all up and down her own, the heat of him, his muscles straining to pull her closer.

She knew he wanted her. He might not love her, but from the moment she had asked him to kiss her—to teach her—he had desired her, and she had felt powerful. Beautiful. She was a paladin, a warrior. When he told her he had kissed Grace, she had felt shock and hurt, and then an absolute refusal to cry. She would *not* be weak. She would demand a kiss, demand that he show his desire. They could not always be on unequal footing.

It had worked better than she had ever imagined. So well she knew it could easily have gone on, have tumbled over the edge of restraint into territory that was unknown, irrevocable. And though she had wanted that, she had been the one to pull away in the end, to put a stop to it.

Because you know it would be the end of you, whispered a small voice in the back of her mind. *Because if you fell even a little more in love with him, the fall would break you.*

It was true. She knew that if she gave even one more bit of herself to

James, she would go up like a bonfire lit by a thousand torches. There would be nothing left of her but ash. In desire they could be on equal footing, but in the matter of love, they were not.

Something had been brightening at the edge of her vision for some time now: she glanced out the window and saw the faint seashell glow of dawn. Relief flooded through her. They were safe, for the moment. It was morning. The sun was rising and nothing had happened.

James's head turned fretfully on the pillow. Setting down Cortana, Cordelia moved closer, wondering if the light was waking him. She could draw the curtain—

He gasped, his body arching suddenly backward, shoulders and heels digging into the mattress. "Not the garden," he gasped. "No—get back inside—no—*no!*"

"*James!*" She unlocked the door, threw it wide, and called down the corridor for help. When she turned back, James was thrashing, his wrist bloody where the rope tore against his skin.

She flew to his side as he cried out, "*Let her go! Let her go!*"

She scrabbled at the rope around his wrist, bloodying her fingertips as she worked to untie him. He sprang up suddenly, tearing free of the headboard. He scrambled to his feet and, barefoot, staggered to the window, catching hold of the frame. Cordelia realized he was trying to force it open.

Footsteps were pounding up the stairs. Matthew burst into the room, rumpled-looking, green eyes dark with sleep and worry. Seeing James at the window, he caught hold of him by the shoulders, spinning him around. James's eyes were wide, staring, blind.

"*Let—her—go,*" James gasped, struggling.

"Wake up!" Matthew demanded, forcing James's body back against the wall.

James was still pushing against him, stiff-armed, but his movements were slower now, his chest no longer heaving. "Matthew," he whispered. "Matthew, is that you?"

"Jamie *bach*." Matthew dug his fingers into James's shoulders. "It's me. *Look* at me. *Wake up.*"

James's eyes focused slowly. "Perhaps there is no forgiveness," he whispered, his voice oddly hollow.

"Probably not," said Matthew, "and we'll all go to Hell, but what matters now is that you are all right."

"James," Cordelia said. He stared at her; his black hair was wet with sweat, and there was blood on his lower lip where he'd bitten it. *"Please."*

James shuddered and went limp against the wall. Looking exhausted, he nodded. "I'm all right." He sounded breathless, but the hollow edge was gone from his voice. "It's over."

Matthew relaxed, lowering his hands. He was in his vest and trousers, Cordelia realized, and blushed slightly. She could see an *enkeli* rune on Matthew's bicep, part of it disappearing under his sleeve. Matthew had very nice arms, she realized. She'd never noticed before.

Oh, dear. If her mother knew Cordelia was in a bedroom with two such scantily clad men, she would faint.

"So you dreamed," said Matthew. He was looking at James, and there was such affection in his voice that it broke Cordelia's heart cleanly in half. Dear God, if only she and Lucie could become *parabatai*, she hoped they would love each other nearly as much. "A nightmare, we assume?"

"You assume correctly," James said, his fingers going to the knot of rope still around his wrist. "And if my dream was accurate, someone else is dead." His tone was bleak.

"Even if that's true, you didn't do it," Cordelia said fiercely. "You've been here all night long, James. Lashed to the bed."

"That's true," said Matthew. "Cordelia has been with you, she never left your side, and we've all been downstairs—well, except Thomas, he buggered off on patrol again, but the rest of us. No one came in or out the door."

James untied the rope still trailing from his wrist. It fell away, revealing a circle of bloody skin. He flexed his hand and looked from Matthew to Cordelia. "And I tried to get the window open," he mused. "But it was after my dream, not before. I don't know—" He looked frustrated. "It's like I can't *think*," he said. "Like there's a fog in my brain. But if it isn't me doing this—who is it?"

Before either Matthew or Cordelia could answer, a noise echoed from downstairs. Someone was pounding on the door. Cordelia was up in a flash, racing down the steps in her stockinged feet. She could hear movement from the drawing room, but she reached the door before anyone else, and threw it open.

On the threshold stood a figure in a parchment-colored cloak. Glancing behind him, Cordelia could see that his boots had left no traces on the snow that frosted their front walk; he seemed to carry quiet with him, a sense of hushed spaces and echoless shadows.

For a moment Cordelia was filled with a wild hope that Jem had come to see her. But this Silent Brother was more stooped, nor did he have thick, dark hair—or any hair at all. When he looked down at her, his sewed-shut eyes visible beneath the shadow of his hood, she recognized him. It was Brother Enoch.

Cordelia Herondale, he said, in his silent voice. *I must speak with you on several matters. First, I bring you a message from Brother Zachariah.*

Cordelia blinked in surprise. James had said there had been another death—but maybe that was not why Enoch was here, after all? His face was as expressionless as ever, though his voice in Cordelia's mind was surprisingly kind. She had never quite thought of the other Silent Brothers, those who were not Jem, as being kind or unkind, any more than trees or fence posts were kind.

Perhaps she had been unfair. Finding her voice, she ushered Brother Enoch into the entryway, murmuring a welcome. She could hear the noises of the others inside the house, their voices raised in the drawing room. It was still quite early, and the sky outside had just begun to steady into blue.

She closed the door and turned to look at Enoch. He stood, seemingly waiting for her, marble-pale and silent, like a statue in an alcove.

"Thank you," she said. "I am glad to hear from Je—from Brother Zachariah. Is he all right? Is he returning to London?"

There was a noise of footsteps. Cordelia glanced up the stairs and saw James and Matthew descending. They saw her and both nodded, passing the entryway and heading to the drawing room. She realized they were giving her a moment alone with Enoch. He must have silently communicated to them as well.

Brother Zachariah is in the Spiral Labyrinth and cannot return, said Enoch.

"Oh." Cordelia tried to hide her disappointment.

Cordelia, said Enoch. *For years now I have watched Brother Zachariah grow into his role in our order with increasing respect. If we were allowed to have friends, many of us would count him as such. For all that, we know he is unusual.* He paused. *When a Silent Brother joins the ranks of the order, he is meant to give up his life, even his memories of who he was before he became a Silent Brother. This was more difficult for Zachariah, given the unusual circumstances of his transformation. There are those from his former life that he still considers his kin, which as a general rule is forbidden. But in his case . . . we allow it.*

"Yes," said Cordelia. "He thinks of the Herondales as family, I know—"

And you, said Enoch. *And your brother. He knows about Elias. There are things happening in the Spiral Labyrinth that I cannot tell you of, things that prevent his departure. Yet he wishes above all to be with you. He cannot lie to me, nor I to you. If he could be beside you in this time, he would.*

"Thank you," Cordelia said quietly. "For telling me, I mean."

Enoch gave her a sharp nod. She could see the runes of Quietude carved into the hollows of his cheeks; Jem had been marked that way too. Certainly it must have been painful. Knowing it likely violated some kind of rule, Cordelia laid a hand on his arm. The parchment robe seemed to crackle when she touched it: it was as if suddenly she could see down the span of many years, see the curve of the past, the silent power of a life spent among history and runes. "Please," she said. "Has there been another death? I don't know if you're allowed to tell us, but—but the last death was my father. We have all been up all night, worrying there would be another. Can you set our minds at rest?"

Before Enoch could respond, the door to the drawing room opened, and James, Matthew, Christopher, Lucie, and Anna piled out. Five anxious faces fixed on Enoch—six, Cordelia supposed, if she counted her own. Five pairs of eyes made the same demand, asked the same question: *Has anyone else died?*

Enoch's answer flowed calmly, without sentiment or bitterness. *If another Shadowhunter has been struck down, I do not know about it.*

Cordelia exchanged an uneasy look with James and Matthew. Could James's dream have been wrong? None of the others had been.

I have come here to speak to Cordelia, Enoch went on, *on a subject related to the murders and their investigation.*

Cordelia stood up straighter. "Anything you want to say to me privately, you can say to all of my friends."

As you wish. In the Ossuarium you asked me a question about Filomena di Angelo's Strength rune.

The others were looking at Cordelia in confusion. "I had asked," Cordelia explained, "whether she had one."

She did, Enoch said. *She wore a permanent Strength rune on her wrist, according to her family, but that rune is missing now.*

"Missing?" Christopher sounded baffled. "How's that possible? Scarred over, you mean?"

There is no scar. A rune can be used up, leaving only a phantom of itself behind, but it cannot vanish from one's skin entirely once it has been drawn. Enoch's focus shifted to Cordelia. *How did you know?*

"I saw my father's Voyance rune was missing," Cordelia said, "and in the courtyard, when Filomena's body was there, I thought I noticed her Strength rune missing from her wrist. It could have been nothing, my own memory playing tricks—but after I noticed my father's rune, I had to ask. . . ."

She could feel the weight of Brother Enoch's gaze, as if he were staring at her, though she knew he did not see as ordinary people did. She tried to keep her face expressionless. She hoped the others were doing the same. Lying to a Silent Brother was more than difficult: if Enoch chose to rummage in her mind, he'd see easily enough that it had been Filomena's ghost herself who'd hinted at the truth.

He took my strength.

If she told the truth, though, there would be inquiries—prodding—questions that might turn toward Lucie. She willed herself to look pleasant and blank, as James did when he wore the Mask.

"But what could it mean?" James said, the sharpness in his tone cutting the tension like a knife. "The fact that two of the victims are missing runes? It's not possible to steal runes, and even if one did, what use would they be?"

"As some sort of trophy, maybe?" Lucie said, with a grateful look in Cordelia's direction.

Christopher looked slightly ill. "Jack the Ripper took . . . parts . . . of the people he killed."

Lucie said, "Or as proof the person is dead? If the killer was acting at the behest of someone else—if he had hired himself out, perhaps, and had to prove he'd done the deed—"

That could not be. It is not that the skin where the rune is inked has been cut away, said Enoch. *The rune itself has been taken. Its spirit. Its soul, if you will.*

Anna was shaking her head. "But what could one do with a rune that's been removed? It's bizarre—"

She broke off as Enoch went suddenly, perfectly still. He held his hands up, as if to stop all noise. He was speaking with the other Silent Brothers in his head, Cordelia realized. She knew they were all connected, a strange and silent chorus bound together across the globe.

After a long moment, Enoch lowered his hand. His blind gaze swept over the group. *I have received a message from my brothers. Lilian Highsmith has been murdered, and an arrest made. The Inquisitor believes he has found the murderer.*

Cordelia could not prevent herself from shooting a quick look at James. Someone had been murdered while James had been literally bound and imprisoned: it was impossible for him to have done it. Relief went through her in a wave, followed immediately by horror and shock: horror that someone had died, shock that the culprit might have been found.

"Who have they arrested?" Anna demanded. "Who did this?"

I believe it is someone you know, said Enoch, his silent voice grim. *Thomas Lightwood.*

The carriage hurtled through the streets of London, whipping in and out of traffic: thank Raziel it was a Sunday, and the roads were not crowded. It had barely come to a stop in the Institute courtyard before James had flung open the door and leaped down onto the flagstones.

There was already a crowd in the courtyard: Shadowhunters milling about, murmuring among themselves and stamping their feet in the cold of the morning. Some were in gear, others in their normal day dress. Cordelia and Lucie were scrambling down after James; the second carriage pulled in after them, disgorging Anna, Matthew, and Christopher. Everyone looked as stunned as James felt. It was some kind of thundering, bitter irony, like an awful revenge of the angels, he thought, giving the crowd a wide berth as he headed to the front door of the Institute. No sooner had it been proven that he was not guilty of the murders than Thomas was falsely accused.

And James knew it was false. Someone was playing a trick, a horrible trick, and when James got ahold of them, he would slice off their hands with a ragged seraph blade.

As he careened up the steps, the others quick on his heels, someone in the crowd shouted out, "*You!* Lightwoods!"

Christopher and Anna both turned, Christopher with an inquisitive look on his face. It was Augustus Pounceby, who had been muttering with the Townsends, who had called out. Anna gazed at him as if he were an insect she planned to feed to Percy.

"What?" she demanded.

"Get your parents to open up the Institute!" Augustus yelled. "We've heard they caught the murderer—we deserve to know who it is!"

"The Institute's locked?" Lucie whispered. Usually anyone with Shadowhunter blood could open the front doors of the cathedral. Institutes were locked only in times of emergency. James took the remaining steps two at a time and seized the heavy door knocker.

The sound echoed through the Institute. Anna continued to look at Augustus as if he were a bug. A few moments later the front door of the cathedral opened a crack, and Gabriel Lightwood ushered them all inside.

"Thank the Angel it's you. I thought I might have to chase off more nosy Enclave members." Gabriel looked haggard, his brown hair sticking up in spikes. He hugged Anna and Christopher before turning to the rest of the group. "Well, this is a fine mess, isn't it? How'd you find out?"

"Brother Enoch told us," Matthew said shortly. "We know they found Thomas with Lilian Highsmith's body, and they've arrested him."

"Brother Enoch?" Gabriel looked puzzled.

"He'd dropped by with a recipe for mince pies," said James. "How are Aunt Sophie and Uncle Gideon? And Eugenia?"

"They raced here as soon as they found out," said Gabriel as they reached the second floor. "Just ahead of the crowd, thankfully. They're frantic, of course—Thomas wasn't just found *with* the body; he was covered in blood and holding a knife. And of all people to find him, it had to be Bridgestock."

"The Inquisitor?" Cordelia looked dismayed. Come to think of it, James *had* seen Mrs. Bridgestock outside, though there had been no sign of Ariadne—or Grace, either, for that matter.

"He happened to be on patrol in the area," said Gabriel. They had reached the library; they all spilled inside to find James's aunt Sophie pacing back and forth across the polished wood floor. Lucie raced over to her. James stayed where he was; he felt wound impossibly tight, as if he might explode with rage if he touched anyone.

"Where is he?" James demanded, as Lucie seized their aunt's hands and squeezed them. "Where's Tom?"

"Oh, darling. He's in the Sanctuary," Sophie said, looking as warmly as she could at all of them. Her forehead was furrowed deeply with worry. "Bridgestock brought him back here and insisted he be locked up and the Council notified. Gideon went straight off to fetch Charlotte, and as soon as the Inquisitor got wind of that, he hared off to try to get to Mayfair first." She passed a hand across her forehead. "I don't know how word gets around so fast. We had to lock the doors— we were afraid we'd be mobbed by Enclave members who heard rumors that a suspect had been apprehended."

"Will the rest of the Enclave be informed?" James asked, thinking of the angry crowd in the courtyard. "That Thomas is the suspect?"

"Not yet," Sophie said. "Bridgestock grumbled, but even he saw the sense in keeping quiet until Charl—until the Consul arrived. He swore his patrol partners to secrecy too. There's no reason to raise everyone's ire, since Thomas is obviously innocent."

Gabriel turned away, swearing quietly under his breath. James knew what he was thinking. Sophie might be convinced of Thomas's innocence, but not everyone would be.

"We need to see Thomas," James said. "Before everyone else gets here. Especially the Inquisitor. Aunt Sophie," he said, seeing the uncertain look on her face. "You *know* he'll want to see us."

Sophie nodded. "All right, but only you, Christopher, and Matthew. And be quick. I expect Charlotte will be arriving shortly with her entourage, and the Inquisitor won't want to find anyone in the Sanctuary. The rest of you will have to wait here—"

"Well, *I* shan't be doing any waiting," Anna said, in a voice like ice crystals. "Were there any witnesses to what happened, Aunt Sophie? Lilian's death, or why Thomas was there?"

Sophie shook her head. "He says he heard her screaming when he passed by, but she was already dying when he reached her. There were no witnesses."

"That we know of," Anna said. "I have my own ways of discovering information. Aunt Sophie, Father, I'd rather make my own inquiries than remain here and have to see Bridgestock's face." She glanced at Christopher. "And if he is rude to you, let me know. I will cut his sneering nose off."

Anna turned without waiting for a reply and stalked out of the room. James could hear her boots clattering away down the hall. A moment later, Matthew and Christopher headed for the door; James paused to glance back at Lucie and Cordelia, who were watching them with grim expressions.

"Tell Tom we all know he's innocent," said Lucie.

"Yes," Cordelia agreed. Her expression was fierce. James knew she couldn't be pleased about being left behind in the library, but she gave him an encouraging nod nevertheless. "We'll stand by him."

"He knows," James said.

He caught up with Christopher and Matthew in the corridor, and together they raced downstairs, hurrying through the sloping hallways of the Institute until they reached the recessed vestibule outside the Sanctuary. The passageway ended here in a high pair of doors made of blessed iron, studded here and there with *adamas* nails. The keyhole in the left-hand door was carved in the shape of an angel. The key itself was currently in the hand of a dark-haired girl in a green dress, standing beside the doors and scowling.

It was Eugenia, Thomas's sister. "Took you lot long enough to get here," she said.

"What are you doing down here, Genia?" Matthew asked. "Surely Bridgestock wouldn't have asked you to guard the door."

She snorted. "Hardly. I'm worried for Thomas. I'm here to keep other people out, not keep him in. The whole Enclave has been walking on eggshells since these murders began; it wouldn't surprise me if an angry mob showed up with torches and pitchforks now that there's a suspect." Her eyes flashed. "Go on, tell me I'm being foolish."

"On the contrary," said James. "I'm glad you're here. We all are."

"Indeed," said Christopher. "You're very frightening, Eugenia. I still remember the time you tied me to a tree in Green Park."

"To be fair, we were playing pirates, and I was eight," said Eugenia, but she smiled a little. She held out the angel key to James. "Tell him we'll get him out," she said fiercely, and James nodded and unlocked the doors.

Inside, the large stone room was dim, lit only by the light of a row of burning candelabras. The windowless walls were hung with long tapestries, each featuring the intricately woven image of a Shadowhunter family crest. A mirror nearly the size of one wall made the room seem larger still. In the middle of the room was a massive stone fountain, dry of water, an angel rising from its center. Its eyes were closed, its blind face sorrowful.

The last time James had been in this room, it had been at the meeting where Cordelia had stood up to declare that he was innocent of burning down Blackthorn Manor—that she had spent the night with him and would vouch for his whereabouts. He still remembered the moment. He had been stunned, not so much by what she had said, but that she had said it at all: he had never imagined anyone making such a sacrifice for him before.

The traces of that meeting were still here, in the family crests on the tapestries, the black velvet chairs scattered about the room, the lectern still in one corner. On one of the chairs, by the dry fountain, sat Thomas. His clothes were creased and spotted with blood, his hands pulled behind the chair, his wrists tied. His eyes were closed, his head hanging.

Christopher gave an indignant gasp. "He's already locked up. They didn't need to tie him up as well—"

Thomas lifted his head, blinking. Exhaustion showed in his sunken eyes. "Kit?"

"We're here," Christopher said, racing across the room toward Thomas. James followed, joining Christopher in kneeling down before Thomas's chair, while Matthew went behind, sliding a dagger from his belt. With one slash, the rope parted and Thomas pulled his arms free with a gasp of relief.

"Don't be angry," he said, looking at his friends. "I told them it was all right to tie me up. Bridgestock insisted, and I didn't want my parents to have to keep defending me."

"They shouldn't have to defend you at all," said James, catching at Thomas's free hands. He could see the dark shadow of Thomas's compass rose tattoo where it showed through the sleeve of his shirt. It was supposed to lead Thomas to love and safety, James thought bitterly; in this case, it had failed. "This is ridiculous—"

"Thomas," said Christopher, with uncharacteristic firmness. "Tell us what happened."

Thomas made a sort of dry gasping noise. His hands were ice-cold. "You'll think I'm mad. Or a secret killer—"

"I should remind you," said James, "that yesterday, I thought I was a secret killer, and you told me that was ludicrous. And now I'm telling you that you, out of all of us, are *least* likely to be a secret killer."

"I, on the other hand, am the *most* likely to be a secret killer," said Matthew, throwing himself into one of the chairs. "I wear peculiar clothes. I come and go as I please and do mysterious, illicit things in the night. None of the rest of you are like that at all. Well, Christopher might kill someone, but he wouldn't mean to. It would be an accident resulting from an experiment gone horribly wrong."

Thomas let out a shuddering breath. "I know," he said, "with crystal clarity, that I did not harm Lilian Highsmith. But Bridgestock and his cronies are acting as though they believe I did—they believed it *immediately*. Nothing I said made any difference. And these are people I've known my whole life."

James chafed Thomas's hands between his, getting the blood flowing. "Tom, what *did* happen?"

"I—I was walking through Golden Square when I heard someone scream. I ran toward the sound and saw the body lying there, and I turned her over so I could see her face and . . . and it was Lilian, barely alive. There was no sign of the murderer. I tried . . ." Thomas put his hands over his face. "I tried to heal her but I couldn't; she was too close to death. And then the next thing I knew, I heard shouting and then the Inquisitor and some others were standing over me. I was covered in Lilian's blood by then . . ."

"Did you see anything?" said James, sitting back on his heels. "Anyone else, someone running away?"

Thomas shook his head.

"Did Lilian see her killer?"

"I asked her who attacked her." Thomas's hazel eyes burned with frustration. "She said something like 'He did it. He was dead in his prime. His wife wept for him.' None of which makes sense."

"You think she recognized her killer as someone who was already dead?" echoed Matthew, looking puzzled.

"I think she was probably delirious," said Thomas. "And there's something else a bit odd. When I reached her, she was clutching her stele. I put it in my pocket without thinking." He reached into his trouser pocket and extracted something that gleamed in the candlelight. "At least, I thought it was her stele. But it isn't, is it?"

He handed it to James, who turned it over curiously between his fingers. It was a hard square of whitish-silver material, carved all over with runes. "It's certainly *adamas*," said James. "But you're right, it's not a stele. It's a sort of box, I think."

"And I don't recognize the runes," said Matthew. "Are those, you know, ours? Good runes, I mean."

"Ah, yes," said James. "Long ago, the Angel gave unto the Shadow-hunters the Book of Good Runes."

Thomas choked out a laugh. "Glad to know my horrid imprisonment hasn't depressed you all too badly."

"We know it's horrid, Tom," James said. "But it's temporary. No one's going to believe you really did this, and if it comes to that, the Mortal Sword will prove it."

"But if they try me by the Mortal Sword, they might learn about everything we've been doing," Thomas said. "They might learn about your connection with Belial. I'd end up betraying you all, especially you, Jamie."

James, already kneeling, laid his head on Thomas's knee for

a moment. He could hear Christopher and Thomas breathing, sense their worry; he felt Thomas's hand rough against his hair—Thomas was trying to comfort *him*, James realized, though Thomas was the one in trouble. *These are my brothers, he thought, all around me; I would do anything for them.*

"Tell them what you need to tell them," he said, raising his head. "I'd never be angry at you for such a thing, Thomas, and I'll manage—we all will—"

Voices rose outside suddenly, Eugenia saying very loudly, "WELL, HELLO, INQUISITOR BRIDGESTOCK. MADAME CONSUL. LOVELY TO SEE YOU."

"They're here." James stood up, slipping the *adamas* box into his pocket. Matthew glanced up as Charlotte entered the room with Inquisitor Bridgestock and Gideon Lightwood. The two men were arguing furiously.

"This is a travesty," Gideon snapped. "You must release Thomas at once. You've got no real evidence against him—"

"What is this?" Bridgestock bellowed when he saw the Merry Thieves. "How did you lot get in here?"

"I live here," said James dryly. "I have all the keys."

"Actually, you live on Curzon Street—all right, never mind," said Christopher. "It was a jolly good answer."

"Thomas is being held on suspicion," said Charlotte, glancing at Matthew, who half turned away, hunching his shoulders. James couldn't blame him. There had always seemed to him to be two Charlotte Fairchilds—one, the aunt he loved, and the other, the Consul, dispensing law and justice with a cool, unemotional hand. "He is not forbidden to have visitors. Nor," she added, glancing at Gideon, "can we dismiss the suspicions against him without any investigation. You know what the Enclave will say—that we are showing favoritism, releasing a suspect because he is a family member, not because he has been cleared of any part in the crime."

"You make it very difficult sometimes, Charlotte," said Gideon in a low, angry voice. "All right. Go ahead, Thomas; tell them what happened."

Thomas repeated his story, leaving out only the curious *adamas* box. Gideon crossed his arms over his chest, glowering at the Inquisitor. Bridgestock, whose face had gone purple with the effort of not interrupting, objected immediately when Thomas was finished.

"This story is nonsense," he hissed. He turned on Thomas, who had sagged back in his chair. "You're asking us to believe that all this was just a coincidence, when by your own admission you've been breaking the rules every night? Patrolling on your own? Have you *any* alibi for where you were the night Basil was killed? Or the Italian girl?"

"Her name was Filomena," Thomas said quietly.

Bridgestock scowled. "Irrelevant."

"It probably wasn't irrelevant to Filomena," said James.

"That's not the *point*," Bridgestock roared. "Lightwood, you were not scheduled for patrol and you had no reason to be in Golden Square."

"Thomas has explained that already." Gideon was white-faced with fury. "And he cares more to know the name of a dead Shadowhunter than you do, Maurice, because none of this matters to you except what you can get out of it. If you manage to convince the Clave you've caught a killer, you think they'll shower rewards on you. But you will look like a *fool* if you cast him into prison and the murders continue."

"Not as much a fool as you'll look, having a murderer for a son—"

"There's an obvious solution here," James interrupted. "I'm sure you know exactly what I'm talking about. What I'd like to know is, what's stopping you from suggesting it?"

Bridgestock glared at him with such pure hatred that James was taken aback. It was true that James had sometimes clashed with the Inquisitor, but he had no idea what would cause the man to despise him.

"The Mortal Sword," James said. "Thomas isn't afraid of it. Why would you be?"

"That's enough out of you," Bridgestock snarled, and for a moment, James was half-sure the Inquisitor was actually going to hit him. Charlotte caught Bridgestock by the arm, real alarm on her face, just as the doors slammed open once again.

They all stared in utter surprise. It was Alastair Carstairs, striding into the room like he always did—as if he'd bought the place and sold it at a handsome profit. He wore a black suit, and his weapons belt glittered where it was visible beneath his jacket. James could see Eugenia in the doorway, looking after Alastair with a thoughtful expression.

Why did she let him in?

"Dear God," said Matthew. "Could this day get worse? What the hell are you doing here, Carstairs?"

"Alastair," said Charlotte, "I'm afraid I must ask you to go. These are private proceedings." She frowned at Gideon. "Has the front door become unlocked?"

Alastair's chin was up, his expression haughty. A terrible tension knotted James's stomach. He could see Thomas looking at Alastair with an expression almost of panic. After Elias's death, James had begun to think Alastair had changed—he loved his sister, at least—but was he actually here to *gloat*?

"No," Alastair said. "The door was not unlocked, at least not when I came in. Which was some time ago. You see, I followed Thomas here and came in with the Inquisitor and his patrol. I witnessed Miss Highsmith's death—the entire incident."

Matthew came to his feet. "Alastair, if you're lying, I swear on the Angel—"

"Stop!" Charlotte held up a commanding hand. "Alastair. Say what you mean. *Now.*"

"As I said." Alastair's lip was curled, his head back; he looked every inch the arrogant bastard he'd been at the Academy. "I was in Golden Square when Thomas was passing through. I also heard Lilian Highsmith scream. I saw Thomas run to help her. She was already dying when he got there. He never harmed her. I'll swear to it."

Matthew sat back down with a thump. Thomas stared at Alastair with a dazed expression. Gideon looked pleased, if not a little bit baffled by everyone else's stunned expressions.

"Er—what?" said Christopher—speaking for them all, James felt.

Bridgestock sneered. "So it's coincidence on top of coincidence, then. Tell me, Carstairs, what possible reason could you have had to be in Golden Square at the same time as Thomas Lightwood?"

"Because I was following him," Alastair said, raking the Inquisitor with a disdainful gaze. "I've been following Thomas for days. I knew he was going out on these insane night patrols by himself, and I wanted to make sure that he was safe. Cordelia is fond of him."

"*You're* the one who's been following me?" Thomas said, astonished.

"You *knew* someone was following you?" Matthew demanded. "And you didn't say anything? *Thomas!*"

"Everyone be *quiet*," said Charlotte; she didn't raise her voice, but something in the pitch of it reminded everyone why she'd been elected Consul.

Thomas was still looking as if he might faint. Alastair was studying his nails. It was Bridgestock who broke the ensuing silence first. "This is preposterous, Charlotte. Carstairs is lying to cover up for his friend."

"They're not friends," said James. "One of us might lie for Thomas. Not Alastair."

"Then he's probably mad with grief over his father's death. Either way he's not credible," Bridgestock snarled.

"And yet we are going to hear him out, and Thomas as well, because that is the task that is appointed to us," Charlotte said icily. "Thomas and Alastair *both* will be held here in the Sanctuary until they can be tried by the Mortal Sword."

"You cannot make that decision without me," Bridgestock objected. "I would try them right now, if not for the fact that the Mortal Sword is currently in *Paris*." He said the word "Paris" with surprising loathing.

"Fortunately, Will and Tessa will be here tomorrow morning, *with* the Sword," said Charlotte, exchanging a swift look with Gideon. "Now, Maurice, I fear your eagerness to make your arrest known has only stoked panic. You had best come with me to the courtyard, to communicate that the Enclave has the matter well in hand. The identity of the accused will not be released until after the Mortal Sword is employed tomorrow."

Bridgestock gave Charlotte a long, furious look, but he had no choice. She was the Consul. With an oath, he stalked from the room; he would have slammed the doors behind him, James was sure, if not for the fact that Cordelia had shoved herself through the gap. She raced past the Inquisitor without a glance and threw her arms around Alastair. "I heard," she said, pressing her forehead to her brother's shoulder. "I was outside with Eugenia. I heard everything."

"*Ghoseh nakhor, hamechi dorost mishe,*" Alastair said, stroking his sister's back. James was surprised to realize he understood. *Everything will be all right.* "Listen to me, Layla." Alastair lowered his voice. "I haven't wanted to fret you, but *Mâmân* has been told by the Silent Brothers to keep to her bed, for the sake of her health and the baby's. I do not think we should worry her more. Tell her I'm spending the night at the Institute to keep Christopher company."

Cordelia blinked back tears. "Yes—I'll send a runner with a message, but—will she believe that? You hardly know Christopher."

Alastair kissed Cordelia's forehead. As he did, he closed his eyes, and James felt the strange sense that he was getting a rare glimpse at the intensity of Alastair's true feelings. "She'll just be glad to think I have a friend, I suspect."

"*Alastair—*"

"This room has become entirely too crowded," said Charlotte, looking worriedly after the Inquisitor. "All of you, save Alastair and Thomas, clear out—you, too, Gideon. We must be seen to be cooperating. You *do* understand that."

"Indeed," said Gideon, in a tone that indicated that he very much didn't. He smiled at Thomas, who was still looking dazed. "But it's ridiculous just leaving them here—they need blankets, food—they're not being *tortured*, Charlotte."

Charlotte looked indignant. "Indeed not. They'll have everything they need. Now, Gideon, Christopher, Matthew, James—and you, too, Cordelia—you *must* go."

Reluctantly, the Merry Thieves began filing out of the Sanctuary, each of them stopping to lay a hand on Thomas's shoulder and murmur an encouraging word. As Cordelia released her brother reluctantly, joining her friends, she murmured—loud enough for James to hear, "If they don't have the Mortal Sword here by tomorrow morning, I'll break you out with Cortana."

"I *heard* that!" Charlotte scolded. She held herself very straight, as befitted a Consul, but James could have sworn her face wore the faintest trace of a smile as she closed the iron doors of the Sanctuary behind them, locking Thomas in with Alastair Carstairs.

18

GOBLIN MARKET

One set his basket down,
One rear'd his plate;
One began to weave a crown
Of tendrils, leaves, and rough nuts brown
(Men sell not such in any town);
One heav'd the golden weight
Of dish and fruit to offer her:
"Come buy, come buy," was still their cry.
—Christina Rossetti, "Goblin Market"

"So what *is* this contraption?" Christopher wondered aloud,
prodding gingerly at the *adamas* object Thomas had retrieved from
Golden Square. It sat squatly in the middle of the round table in the
upstairs room of the Devil Tavern; around the table were ranged James,
Matthew, Christopher, Lucie, and Cordelia. Anna sat on her own in
a wing-backed chair with stuffing sprouting from its arms. Several
bottles of whiskey stood half-empty on a windowsill.

Anna had arrived at the Devil sometime in the afternoon, only
waving away the question when the others asked her whether she had
learned anything. "I warned him," she'd said, sinking down into the
armchair and declining offers of tea or sherry. "I knew Thomas was
going out on his own last night, and I warned him not to do it. I must
not have been convincing enough."

Anna so rarely expressed self-doubt that the others, including

Cordelia, stared in amazement for a moment. It was Matthew who broke the silence. "We all warned him, Anna, but Thomas is a bloody-minded stubborn bastard. Though quite tiny when he was young, and really," he added, "rather adorable, like a guinea pig or a mouse."

James thwacked Matthew gently on the back of the head. "I believe what he means to say is that it cannot be the responsibility of one's friends to prevent one from doing something one believes is right," he said. "It is, however, the job of one's friends to rescue one from the consequences of one's actions when it all goes skew-whiff."

Lucie clapped and called out, "Hear, hear!" With a half smile, Anna patted Lucie absently on the hand. Anna looked tired, though still perfectly coiffed, her hair a careful cap of finger-combed waves, her boots gleaming with fresh polish.

"All right," she said. "I did learn a few things, though not as much as I'd have liked. One fact that might prove of interest, though: Lilian Highsmith's body was missing a Precision rune."

"So that settles it," said Matthew. "Someone's murdering Shadowhunters to steal their runes. And we know for certain that James isn't the murderer," he added. "Or Thomas, either."

"No," said James, "but Belial is involved somehow. That sigil on my windowsill—I think I drew it myself, without realizing I was doing it, just as I opened my window. I think there was a part of my mind, a hidden part, that knew, and was trying to warn the conscious part of me. Belial has certainly been sending me these dreams, these visions. I cannot for the life of me guess why."

"Do you think he wanted Thomas arrested?" Christopher asked.

"No," James said slowly, "though I cannot be sure, but it seems—small, for Belial. Most human beings are beneath his notice, unless they get in his way. And I cannot see how Thomas was in his way."

Maybe just to hurt you, Cordelia thought, but she did not say it; it would not help for James to think Thomas's arrest was his fault. "Perhaps he simply wanted the Enclave's attention averted," she said, "from whoever is really doing this, and their connection to Belial."

"As far as the Enclave goes, the news has started to leak out that it's Thomas who's suspected. About half of those who know think he did it, and the other half still think it's a warlock, or a Downworlder who's hired a warlock," said Anna.

"Perhaps it would help if we figured out what *this* does," Christopher said, indicating the *adamas* object. "Then we might know if it was Miss Highsmith's, or the killer's, or something else entirely. Oh—I've decided to call it a *pithos*. It's a sort of container in Greek mythology."

"But we can't be sure there's anything inside it, Kit," said Matthew. "It could be one of Miss Highsmith's paperweights. She might have had a tremendous collection."

"I don't believe it was hers. I think the killer dropped it at the murder scene. It certainly isn't a Shadowhunter object—not with runes like this on it." Christopher sighed, his lilac eyes mournful. "I just don't like it when I don't know what things do."

"I don't like it that Bridgestock seems to have it in for Thomas," Matthew said. "He seems desperate to see him convicted."

"I've always had the sense," said James, "that Bridgestock was none too fond of any of us—our parents, really. I don't know why. He's older; perhaps he finds them irresponsible. He probably thinks that if he's the one to catch the killer, he might get promoted, or win the next Consul term."

"Over Charles?" said Matthew. "I will enjoy watching that punching match."

"Enough about politics," said Cordelia. "Thomas is languishing in jail—I know it's the Sanctuary, but it's still jail—and so is my brother. I know you don't care particularly what happens to Alastair, but *I* do."

She hadn't meant the words to come out quite so pugnaciously. After a moment, James said, "Daisy, what Alastair did was quite brave. Not in the least because he did it for someone he knows dislikes him."

"It was rather selfless," said Lucie. "Honestly, we *do* care what happens to Alastair."

"We do?" Christopher sighed. "I feel as if I can never quite keep up. Why was he following Thomas again?"

"For me," Cordelia said firmly. "So I wouldn't worry."

Christopher looked as if he had another question. Quickly, Anna interrupted, "One thing I feel has not been mentioned is that these killings have all happened near dawn. As if for some reason, the murderer is waiting for the night to near its end."

"Thinner patrols, perhaps," James suggested. "Shadowhunters starting to head home."

"Truly, our knife-faced demon is a clever fiend," Christopher said, causing Matthew to gaze at his flask.

James looked thoughtfully at the *pithos*. "One of these runes resembles a rune for 'dawn,'" he observed.

Cordelia picked the box up, turning it over in her hand. Like all *adamas*, it was smooth and cool to the touch, humming with a sense of potential power. At first glance, the etched designs on the object resembled a matted tangle of yarn, individual runes indistinguishable from each other. But as she gazed at them, she began to detect a pattern of jagged, branching designs, as if additions and modifications had been made to familiar runes. It was like nothing else she had quite seen before.

"There must be someone who can tell us what this is," she said. "I agree with Christopher. It *feels* quite unlikely to be anything a Shadowhunter would have owned."

"It is very odd that it's *adamas*," said Matthew. "Only the Iron Sisters mine it, and only Shadowhunters can use it."

"Technically, but there is quite an underground trade in the stuff," said Anna. "Old steles and the like fetch a price at the Shadow Market. Not many can work the material, but it has potency as a catalyst for magic."

"Well, there it is," James said. "We must go to the Shadow Market. It's in Southwark, isn't it? Near St. Saviour's?"

Lucie winked at Cordelia across the table. Cordelia had always wanted to go to a Shadow Market—transitory bazaars where Downworlders gathered to hawk enchanted wares, conduct business, and gossip. Many different cities had Shadow Markets, but Cordelia had never had the opportunity to visit one.

Matthew took a long drink from his flask. "I despise the Shadow Market."

James looked puzzled. Of course, Cordelia recalled with a jolt. The potion Matthew had bought, which had nearly killed his mother—it had come from the Shadow Market. But James didn't know that. No one else knew but her.

"Besides," said Matthew, "if we go around asking who sells demonic *adamas*, I'm sure that won't bring us any unwanted attention."

"Well, we'll need to be careful about it," said James. "But *adamas* is valuable. And where else are valuable magical items bought and sold and appraised? I can't think of anywhere else we might find someone with that sort of expertise, not on such short notice."

Christopher brightened, excited by the prospect. "Capital idea. The sun's nearly down; we can go straightaway."

"Alas, I cannot join you," Anna said, rising gracefully from her chair. "I have patrol tonight."

As the rest of them gathered their things to leave, Cordelia noticed Lucie giving Anna an odd look. It was the sort of look that meant Lucie knew something that she wasn't saying. But what on earth could she know about Anna? Cordelia wondered briefly if she should ask, but she was distracted by Matthew, who was refilling his flask from one of the bottles on the sill.

His hands trembled slightly. Cordelia wished she could approach him, say something comforting, but what he had told her was a secret. She must pretend as if she saw nothing wrong.

Troubled, she followed the others out of the tavern.

Lucie leaned out the window of the carriage she was sharing with Cordelia as they approached the southern end of London Bridge. The scent of the Market was on the air: incense and spices, hot wine and a charred smell like burning bone. Night had only just fallen, and the sunset brushed the sky with copper and flame. It was one of those times, Lucie thought, when the world seemed improbably big, and full of possibilities.

She sprang out of the carriage as soon as it drew up, Cordelia following after her. The stalls and stands and carts of the Shadow Market snaked away beneath an arched, glass-paned ceiling supported by tall iron girders, tucked between Southwark and Borough High Streets. Stands that held fruits and vegetables and flowers during the morning had been transformed by Downworlder merchants into a colorful, noisy bazaar, the stalls lit by sparkling lights and decorated with painted signs and lengths of colored silk.

Lucie took a deep breath of the incense-scented air as James's carriage rattled up and he, Christopher, and Matthew spilled out, James brushing off Christopher's coat where he had somehow managed to spill powder on it. A roar of sound rose up from the bazaar, like soft thunder: *Come buy! Come buy!*

"No running off into the Shadow Market alone, minx," James said, coming up behind Lucie. His black wool coat was buttoned to his chin, hiding his runes. They had agreed there was no point trying to disguise that they were Shadowhunters—Shadowhunters were no more welcome in the Shadow Market than they were in other Downworlder haunts, unless, of course, they had money to spend—but there was no point calling attention to it either. "It may look like a harmless fair, but there's quite a bit of danger down those narrow aisles."

He glanced at Cordelia—perhaps to see if she'd heard him as well, but she was busy putting on her gloves. Some of her red hair had come free beneath her velvet cap and was curling against her cheek. She seemed lost in thought. As Matthew and Christopher came toward them, she hurried toward Matthew, saying something to him in a low voice Lucie couldn't hear. *Odd,* Lucie thought.

James offered Lucie his arm. "Cruel Prince James at your service."

Lucie giggled; it was a nice reminder of times past, when she and James had been playmates who teased and protected each other in turns. Taking his arm, she passed into the Shadow Market proper, beneath the glass roof. A railway viaduct ran by far ahead, and the distant rumble of trains was just audible over the sound of the Market itself: tinny enchanted music played from various stalls, the tunes clashing loudly with each other. Downworlders crowded the aisles looking for a bargain, an illicit trade, or something in between. Silk banners flew, and sparkling baubles of light drifted like will-o'-the-wisps through the air.

Lucie caught one as they passed an apothecary stall with tins and jars set up on wooden shelves, a warlock with a double set of curving horns calling out the virtues of his potions. The bauble was like a child's ball made of thin glass. Inside it glowed with a deep violet light. When Lucie opened her fingers it flitted away, seeming glad to be free.

Matthew said something, and Cordelia and Christopher laughed. Lucie was too entranced to ask what the joke was. She had spied a pair of carts painted in scarlet and gold and green; a mustachioed troll standing on a raised platform expounded on the scientific properties and dubious claims of his medicinal remedies. At the heart of the Market, where the larger stalls were located, there were tailors catering to faeries and werewolves, selling clothes with holes for wings and tails. Nearby was a tiny cart operated by a vampire modeling her line of cosmetics: fine powder to cover any imperfections and lipsticks guaranteed to give one's lips "that bloodred tinge coveted in Europe's most cosmopolitan cities."

The group convened in a central space, where the stalls were arranged around them in a square. Lucie released James's arm so he could consult a hand-lettered directory nailed to a post. Matthew gazed warily at a vampire selling bottles of "special" ginger beer as Christopher produced a long scroll of paper from his pocket. Cordelia had darted off to examine a stall selling hand-tooled leather scabbards and wrist gauntlets.

"What have you got there?" Lucie asked Christopher, peering over his shoulder at a list of unfamiliar terms.

"Oh, this? It's my shopping list," Christopher said. "What with the curfew business, I haven't been able to attend the Market for quite some time, and I've got ingredients to acquire."

He set off briskly along a winding path between the stalls. Lucie followed; to her amusement, the vendors greeted him enthusiastically:

"Mr. Lightwood! A new shipment of marrubium has just come in. Would you be interested?"

"Christopher Lightwood! Just the man I was hoping to see! I've got the materials we discussed last time we spoke—top grade, very rare. . . ."

As Lucie watched, Christopher paused to haggle with a werewolf who was selling dried roots and fungi, eventually walking away empty-handed, only to return when the werewolf called after him to accept the price he'd offered.

"Christopher haggles like an expert!" Cordelia exclaimed, appearing at Lucie's side with two bottles of fizzy pink liquid. "He could hold his own in the souks of Marrakech. Here, try this—I'm told it makes the cheeks rosy."

"Oh, no you don't," James said, swooping in and taking the bottles from her hands. "Daisy, Lucie, do not eat or drink anything that is being sold here. At best, you might get a mild stomachache. At worst, you will wake up as a pair of otters."

"Otters are lovely," said Cordelia, her eyes dancing.

"Your cheeks are rosy enough as is," said James firmly, tossing the bottles on a trash heap behind the stalls before joining Matthew to look at a display of swords with dubiously sparkling "gems" decorating the hilts.

"Speaking of brothers," said Lucie. "Not that we were, exactly, but—I am so sorry that Alastair was arrested. I think what he did was exceedingly brave."

Cordelia looked surprised. "I knew you would understand," she said, laying a hand on Lucie's arm. "And Lucie . . ."

Lucie glanced about. Cordelia had the air of someone wanting to confide a secret. James and Matthew were deep in conversation with a werewolf—a woman with long, gray-brown hair and a necklace of teeth, presiding over a glass case full of colorful crystal bottles from which perfumed scents wafted. A hand-lettered sign on a shelf declared WILL COVER UP THE SMELL OF WET FUR.

"I know that you've been doing something—something you're keeping secret. I'm not angry," Cordelia hastened to add. "I just wish you'd tell me what it is."

Lucie tried to cover her surprise; she had thought that—busy with marriage and a house to keep up—Cordelia hadn't been paying her any mind. "I'm sorry, truly," she said slowly. "What if I told you . . . that I am trying to help someone, someone who is very deserving of help, but for their safety I cannot share the specifics at this point?"

Cordelia looked hurt. "But . . . I'm your *parabatai*. Or I will be, very soon. We are meant to face our challenges together. If there is someone who needs help, I could help them as well."

Oh, Daisy, Lucie thought. If only it were that easy. She thought of Grace—her bluntness, her maddening secrecy—and knew that Cordelia would not understand Lucie's decision to work with her. "I can't," she said. "It is not my secret to tell."

After a moment Cordelia withdrew her hand. "I trust you," she said, but her voice sounded a bit . . . small. "I hope you can tell me sometime soon, but I understand you're trying to protect someone. I won't push any further. Now, let's get back to the others, shall we?"

Surely I could have managed that better, Lucie thought, as they rejoined their companions. James and Matthew were speaking to a gentry faerie wearing a fur cap in the Russian style, the flaps covering his ears. He was shaking his head: no, he didn't know anyone buying or selling *adamas*. As the girls started toward them, a pixie brushed by Lucie's ear and whispered, "Malcolm Fade wishes to see you. Find him in the blue tent."

Startled, Lucie stopped in the middle of the aisle, causing a collision with a selkie loaded down with shopping bags. "Watch where you're going, *Shadowhunter!*" the creature hissed, making a gesture with her flipper-like hand. It was a rude gesture, to be sure, but it also clearly indicated a stall in the distance—one draped with swaths of cheap blue velvet.

"Luce, are you all right?" Cordelia asked.

"Yes . . . I just remembered something. Something I need to tell Christopher. I'm just going to find him—I'll be right back."

"Lucie—*wait!*"

But Lucie had darted away before Cordelia could stop her—or before James caught sight of her; he'd made his position clear on wandering off alone. Pushing through the crowd until it swallowed her, Lucie bit her lip, guilt and regret weighing like a stone in her chest. Keeping secrets from James, hiding from Daisy—she hated every bit of it. But Malcolm Fade might be Jesse's only chance. Glancing behind her once to make sure she was out of sight of her friends, she slipped inside the blue tent.

"Well, that was a waste of time," Matthew said, giving the side of the stall they had just left a lingering kick.

"Nonsense," said James. "No time spent playing bridge whist with Welsh slate-mine goblins can be truly said to have been wasted. Besides, if I ever want to buy a werewolf-hair rug, I will know exactly where to come."

The truth was that he was just as discouraged as Matthew. They'd spoken to dozens of vendors and turned up nothing useful yet, but as his *parabatai* seemed nervous and unhappy tonight, James was treating him with kid gloves. Earlier, James had left Matthew alone for a moment to read a sign directing customers toward UNTOLD MIRACLES OF NATURE, PRESERVED IN THE MOST LIFELIKE MANNER, only to turn back around to see Matthew swiping a bottle of wine from behind the counter of a Sighted mundane who was showing a bottle of horn polish to a faerie customer. By the time James caught back up with him, Matthew had stowed the entire bottle in his coat.

Matthew obviously did not want to be here. He seemed brightly, cheerfully miserable, alternating between chatter and silence. He was drunk already, having emptied his flask and started in on the wine bottle. It was puzzling; James had always wondered why Matthew didn't seem to care to visit the Market. The Market-goers were a motley and disreputable lot, but Matthew enjoyed nothing more than the company of the motley and the disreputable, in James's experience at least. Perhaps he was simply worried about Thomas? Especially since Thomas was locked in a room with Alastair Carstairs; James felt Thomas could fend for himself, but he didn't dislike Alastair as much as Matthew did.

James stopped to consult the directory once again. It had begun to snow—thick flakes drifted down as Matthew wandered over to a display of potions that promised to attract unicorns, whether you were "virginal" or not. He was examining them when Cordelia appeared, white crystals of snow caught like delicate flowers in her red hair.

It reminded James of their wedding day. He leaned back against the post to which the directory had been nailed, heedless of the snow that tumbled lightly down the back of his collar. He had been trying not to think of the night before—it felt far away and so close, all at the same time. He had been in Hell, thinking of Belial, and yet in the middle of it all there had been that space with Cordelia—a space of quiet and tumult, utterly intense yet somehow peaceful. The memory of her perfume, smoke and jasmine, heated his blood, making the cold of the snow a relief.

Through the white fall of it, he saw Cordelia go up to Matthew. He wasn't sure whether they could see him: he was likely a shadow among shadows, half-concealed by snow.

Cordelia laid her hand over Matthew's and leaned in to say something to him. The sight sent a jolt through James, as if his hand had brushed a live wire. He supposed Matthew had taken her for a drive the day before to cheer her up—and many times, when James had been getting the Curzon Street house prepared, Matthew had gone around to keep Cordelia company—but he had not thought Cordelia and Matthew were such good friends as to have secrets. Yet everything in the way they leaned into each other bespoke confidences.

Cordelia stroked Matthew's hand gently and walked away; James could hear her inquiring about the *adamas* from a satyr manning a stall that sold faerie fruit. A snowy owl perched atop a bowl of white peaches hooted gently at her, and she smiled.

Pulling the wine bottle out of his coat, Matthew trod a meandering path toward James, squinting at him through the snow. "So it *is* you," he said, as he drew closer. "If you keep standing about letting the snow fall on you, you'll wind up as the ice sculpture at the Wentworths' next party."

"Seems a relaxing existence," James said, still looking at Cordelia. "Where's Lucie? Weren't she and Cordelia together?"

"Went off to find Christopher, apparently," said Matthew. "No explanation why. Maybe she remembered something."

"She's been acting peculiar lately," said James. "Grace even asked me about her—"

He broke off, but it was too late. Matthew's eyes, which usually grew wider and more liquid green as he drank, had narrowed. "When did you see Grace?"

James knew he could say *at the Wentworths' party* and put an end to the questioning. But it would feel like lying to Matthew. "Yesterday. When you and Daisy were out driving."

Matthew stared. There was something alarming in his total stillness—despite his tousled hair, his bright waistcoat, the bottle in his hand.

"She came to Curzon Street," said James. "She—"

But Matthew had caught hold of his arm with a surprising strength and was steering James through a gap between two stalls. They found themselves in an alley—barely an alley, really: more a narrow space between the wooden side of a stall and the brick wall of a railway arch.

Only when James's back hit the brick wall did he realize Matthew had shoved him. It hadn't been a hard shove, especially one-handed—Matthew was still gripping the neck of his wine bottle with a white-knuckled hand. But the gesture alone was enough to startle James into an exclamation of annoyance: "Math, *what* are you doing?"

"What are *you* doing?" Matthew demanded. The air was full of the thick smell of incense, and glassy bubbles floated past them, illuminating the space in star-bright shades of emerald, ruby, and sapphire. Matthew pushed one away impatiently. "Having Grace to your house while your wife is away mourning the death of her father is hardly in the spirit of the agreement you have with Daisy."

"I *know* that," said James, "and so I've told Cordelia all that happened, even that I kissed Grace—"

"You did *what?*" Matthew threw his hands in the air, splattering wine onto the snow. It stained the white crystals red. "Are you mad?"

"Daisy knows—"

"Cordelia has far too much dignity to show that you have hurt her, but she also has honor. I know you have an agreement with her that you will not see Grace while you're married—to save Cordelia from ridicule, from the Enclave gossiping that you were forced to marry her after you compromised her. She deserves better than to be seen as an anchor around your neck."

"An anchor around my—I didn't *invite* Grace over. She appeared at my door and demanded to talk to me. I cannot even recall why I kissed her, or if I even bloody wanted to—"

Matthew gave James an odd look—more than odd; it seemed as if he were trying to make sense of something he could not quite remember. "You shouldn't have let her into the house, James."

"I have apologized to Daisy," James said, "and I will do so again—but what difference does this make to you, Math? You know the circumstances of our marriage—"

"I know that ever since you met Grace Blackthorn, she has been a misery in your life," said Matthew. "I know there was a light in your eyes, and she puts it out."

"It is being separated from her that makes me miserable," James said. Yet he was keenly aware, as he had been the night before, that there seemed to be two James Herondales. The one who believed what he was saying, and the one torn by doubt.

The doubts never seemed to last for more than a moment, though. They would slip away until he barely remembered them, just as he barely recalled kissing Grace the day before. He knew that he had. He could remember kissing Daisy—in fact, the memory was so sharp-sweet it was difficult to think of other things. But he could not recall why he had kissed Grace, or what it had been like when he had.

"You have always believed love came at a cost," said Matthew. "That it was torment and torture and pain. But there should be some joy. There is joy in being with someone you love, even knowing you can never have them, even knowing they will never love you back." He sucked in a ragged breath of cold air. "But even the moments you are with Grace, you don't look happy. You don't seem happy when you talk about her. Love should bring you happiness, at least in the imagining of what your lives will eventually be like when you are together. What will your future with her be like? Tell me how you think of it."

James knew it was impossible. All his dreams of a future with Grace had been abstract, none concrete. When he thought of her in the house on Curzon Street, he realized suddenly that he had chosen nothing in the house with Grace in mind. He had considered his own wants and Cordelia's. He had never thought of Grace's, for he had no idea what they might be.

He felt the bracelet cold against his wrist, the metal picking up the chill of the snow. "Enough," he said. "We shouldn't be discussing this now. We should be looking for answers."

"I will not continue to watch you make yourself miserable," said Matthew. "There is no point to it—if you will never see reason or good sense—"

"Because you're a bastion of reason and good sense?" James snapped. He knew he had a temper, just like his father; his anger spilled past everything else now, tasting of copper and fury. "Matthew, you are drunk. For all I know, you mean nothing you are saying right now."

"I mean all of it," Matthew protested. *"In vino veritas—"*

"Don't you quote Latin at me," said James. "Even if you were sober, which would be a fine chance, *you've* never taken love seriously enough to lecture me about this. Your passions have been a series of dalliances and ill-conceived attachments. Look at me and tell me there is someone you love more than that bottle in your hand."

Matthew had gone very white. James realized with a distant dismay that he had broken a pact between them, unspoken, that he would not speak to Matthew about his drinking. That if it remained unmentioned, it might vanish.

Matthew turned then, raising his arm—James stepped forward, but Matthew had already violently slammed the bottle against the brick wall. Glass sprayed in all directions; Matthew flinched back. A flying bit of glass had scratched his face, just beneath his eye. He wiped at the blood on his face and said, "I don't want to see you ruin your life. But if you don't love Cordelia, you should let someone else love her."

"I could hardly stop them, could I?" said James. "Now let me see your hand—Matthew—"

"There you two are," a voice called. Cordelia was approaching, picking her way through the slippery new snow. "No luck, I'm afraid; I tracked down a faerie smith who sometimes worked with other metals but not *adamas*, it seems—" She stopped, looking between them, her lips pressed together worriedly. "What's going on?" she demanded. "What's wrong with you two?"

Matthew held up his left hand. James heard Cordelia make a sound of distress; she hurried toward them. James started, feeling sick: glass from the bottle had gone into Matthew's hand, and blood seeped out from the cuts on his palm.

Mechanically, James fumbled for his stele. Matthew turned his hand over, looking at it curiously; the blood was running fast, no doubt mixed with wine. Fat red drops splashed onto the snow.

"I was playing around," Matthew said, sounding drunker than James suspected he was. "I cut myself and James brought me back here for a healing rune. So silly of me. Who knew toys had sharp edges?"

James began to draw the healing rune onto Matthew's hand, as Cordelia searched in her bag for something with which they could bind up the wound. It had stopped snowing, James realized; he wasn't sure why he was so very cold.

The blue tent opened into a much larger space than Lucie would have guessed from its outer appearance. Malcolm was seated in an armchair next to a long table that had been set up on a threadbare carpet laid out on the ground. On the table were books, stacks and stacks of them: histories of Shadowhunter families, books of fairy tales, necromantic texts.

"Is this where you live?" Lucie demanded, looking around. "How lovely—so many books! Though what do you do during the day?"

"Of course I don't live here." Malcolm did not appear especially pleased to see her, though he was the one who had summoned her. "I keep some of my books here. A few that I would not like discovered in my flat should the Shadowhunters choose to raid it." Rising, he gestured toward the armchair, the one seat in the room. "Please, make yourself comfortable."

Lucie sat as Malcolm picked up his pipe. "I must apologize for how I behaved at the Ruelle," he said without preamble. He leaned back against the book-strewn table. "For the past ninety years I have believed that Annabel—" His voice cracked; he cleared his throat and went on. "That my Annabel was content in the Adamant Citadel. She was not with me, but I dreamed she might be happy. Might even come back to me. Even if she did not, had she died as Iron Sisters and Silent Brothers die—fading into silence, their bodies preserved forever in the Iron Tombs—I should have gone to lay down near her resting place, that I might sleep by her side for eternity."

Lucie wondered if he had been up all night—he seemed exhausted, his sleeves rolled up to the elbow, the shadows beneath his eyes as purple as the eyes themselves. Long ago, she recalled, when she had been a child, she had thought Malcolm quite thrilling—a dashing and beautiful warlock, with his stark white hair and fine hands. Now he looked as if he had aged twenty years in the past day. As if grief had ravaged his face.

"I'm so sorry," she said. "I—I never would have told you of Annabel's fate in the way Grace did, and if I'd known she was going to do so, I would never have brought her to see you."

"To be honest," Malcolm said as he lifted the lid from a tin of tobacco, "I appreciate her bluntness. It is better to know the truth."

Lucie could not help the surprise that went through her. She recalled Grace at the Hell Ruelle: *I told him the truth. Shouldn't he know the truth?*

"That is why I summoned you. I thought you deserved to hear my decision from me." Malcolm filled the bowl of his pipe with tobacco and tamped it down gently. "I will not help you. Necromancy is inherently evil, and notoriously difficult. Even if I could assist you in compelling Jesse Blackthorn to rise again, I fail to see what would be in the bargain for me."

It had begun to snow outside; Lucie could hear the soft brush of the flakes against the tent fabric. "But if you could help me raise Jesse, I could—I could help you do the same with Annabel."

"You told me that Jesse Blackthorn's body has been preserved using magic. Annabel died a century ago, and I have no idea where she was buried." Bitterness sheathed the rage in his voice, like a brittle scabbard over a blade. "She is lost to me. I've read over the texts, I've studied what there is to know. It might be one thing with Jesse, as he is an . . . unusual case. But with Annabel—" He shook his head. "To compel the dead back into a mortal body requires necromancy, and necromancy carries too heavy a price. And without the original body—to take a body from another living human would be a terrible act."

Lucie took a deep breath. She could get up and walk out of this tent and resume her normal life, with no one the wiser. But she thought of Jesse— of Jesse dancing with her in the snow outside the Institute. Of Jesse vanishing as the sun touched him. Of Jesse in his coffin, with the snow falling all around him, never feeling the cold. "Mr. Fade, I am able to speak with the dead, even those who are not restless. I could summon Annabel's ghost for you, and we could ask her where to find her body—"

Malcolm went rigid, the pipe unlit in his hand. He turned slowly; Lucie could only see his profile, sharp as a hawk's. "Annabel is a ghost? She haunts this world?" His voice was ragged. "That is not possible."

"Mr. Fade—"

"I said it is not possible." His hand shook, loose tobacco spilling from the bowl of the pipe. "She would have shown herself to me. She would *never* have left me alone."

"Whether they are ghosts or not . . ." Lucie hesitated. "I can reach the dead."

Slowly, Malcolm sat up straighter. Lucie could sense his desperation; there was something almost brutal about it, about the intensity of his need. "You could speak to Annabel? Bring her ghost to me?"

Lucie nodded, lacing her cold fingers together. "Yes, and if you help me reunite Jesse's soul with his body, I will do whatever you need. I will summon Annabel, and find out where she is buried."

A few minutes later, Lucie stepped out of the blue tent. She felt nearly dazed, almost incredulous, as if it had been someone else in there with Malcolm Fade, making deals, swearing promises. Pretending to a confidence she did not really feel. Agreeing to let Malcolm take Jesse's body out of London, to his country house near Fowey, as if she had the authority to countenance such a thing. She did not yet know what she would say to Grace, or to Jesse either—

"Lucie?"

The snow was falling thick and light, laying its gauzy veil across the Market. She squinted through the flakes and saw a boy with dark hair. James, she assumed, and hurried toward him, her hand up to shield her face from the snow. She hoped he would not ask her what she had been doing. His protectiveness could turn quickly to scolding, as was, she suspected, the nature of older brothers—

But it was not James. Out of the hazy white night, he evolved like a shadow: a slim boy in shirtsleeves, the snow falling around him, but not *on* him.

"Jesse," she breathed. She hurried up to him, the hem of her skirt dragging in the snow. "Is everything all right? Can anyone here *see* you save me?"

A small smile touched the edge of his mouth. "No. You will look as if you are talking to yourself. Fortunately, that is not an unusual occurrence in the Shadow Market."

"Have you been here before?"

"No. I've seen pictures, but the reality is far more interesting. As always, Lucie, following after you has opened up my world."

She kicked at a bit of snow, wondering if she should mention her conversation with Malcolm. "I thought you were angry at me."

"I'm not angry. I'm sorry about what I said outside the Ruelle. I know you are doing what you are because you care about me. It is only that—I am fading faster, I think. I forget, sometimes, where I have just been. I know Grace will have come to talk to me, but I will not recall it. I find myself in the city, and its roads seem like foreign passages."

Panic jangled her nerves. "But I am getting so close—to finding someone who can help us. To finding out what happened to you, what enchantments were put on you, so they can be reversed, undone—"

Jesse closed his eyes briefly. When he opened them, all pretense of smiling or lightness was gone; he looked unguarded and vulnerable. "You have already done so much. If it were not for you, I would have faded a long time ago. I knew something was keeping me anchored here, when by all rights I should have vanished. For these past months, I have been able to see the moonlight reflected on the river, feel the wind and rain against my skin. I remember what it is to be hot or cold. To want things. To need things." He looked into her eyes in wonderment. "All those things are real for me again, as nothing else has been real to me since I died—except for you."

There was a hot ache in Lucie's throat. "Those feelings are the proof that you belong here, with the living."

He inclined his head toward her. "Command me to kiss you," he whispered urgently. "Tell me to do it. Please."

She looked up at him, her hands clasped, shivering. "Kiss me."

He dipped his head. A cascade of sparks danced across her skin: he feathered kisses across her cheek before seeking her mouth. Lucie inhaled sharply as he captured her lips, his arms drawing her against him.

Despite everything, she drowned in the delight of it.

I didn't know. She had not considered the softness of his mouth contrasted with faint roughness, the nip of his teeth, his tongue stroking along hers. She had not realized she would feel his kisses all through her, a delicious tension she had never imagined. His hands were in her hair, cradling the back of her head, his mouth learning hers, leisurely, carefully. . . .

She whimpered low in her throat, her hands on his shoulders, steadying herself. *Jesse, Jesse, Jesse.*

A train roared over the viaduct overhead, its lights illuminating the darkness, turning night to sunrise. Jesse let her go, his dark hair unruly, his eyes sleepy and stunned with desire.

"If I must fade," he said, "I would like to fade remembering this as my last waking dream."

"Don't go," she whispered. "Hold on, for me. We are so close."

He touched her cheek. "Only promise me one thing," he said. "If I do go, give us a happy ending, will you? In your book?"

"I don't believe in endings," she said, but he only smiled at her, and faded slowly from view.

19

THINE OWN PALACE

And seeing the snail which everywhere doth roam,
Carrying his own house still, still is at home,
Follow (for he is easy paced) this snail,
Be thine own palace, or the world's thy jail.
—John Donne, "To Sir Henry Wotton"

Thomas had no idea what time it was. There were no windows in
the Sanctuary, for the comfort of vampire guests. The tapers in the
candelabras burned on, their level never seeming to drop.

Charlotte hadn't been untruthful when she'd said Thomas and
Alastair would have whatever they needed. Warm bedding had been
provided, and a stack of books (chosen by Eugenia), not to mention
food. Thomas could tell that Bridget felt sorry for him, because she had
brought some of his favorite things: besides a platter of cold chicken,
there was bread still warm from the oven, a wedge of yellow sheep's-
milk cheese, sliced apples, and a salad with absolutely not one speck of
celery. Thomas hated celery.

Bridget had set the tray down without a word, scowled at Alastair,
and left.

Alastair had seemed unmoved. He hadn't said a single word to
Thomas since the door had closed and locked behind the Consul for
the last time. He'd wandered over to one of the "beds" provided—a
mattress with a pile of blankets and pillows, sat down with a book

(Machiavelli's *The Prince*, which he must have produced from a coat pocket—did he carry it around everywhere with him?), and stuck his nose in it. And there he still was, hours later, not even looking up when Thomas accidentally knocked over a candelabra while pacing the room.

Thomas eyed the "bed" Alastair wasn't currently occupying, wishing he knew whether it was time to go to sleep yet. Although if their confinement were to continue, he supposed it didn't matter; he and Alastair would become like stable cats, sleeping whenever they felt like it.

The notion of spending even another hour in this room made Thomas so despondent that he walked to the door and shook it, on the very remote chance that for some reason the lock and wards had failed.

Naturally, nothing happened. Alastair's voice pierced the silence, nearly making Thomas jump. "A little menacing that the Sanctuary bolts shut from the outside, isn't it? I never thought about it much before."

Thomas turned around to look at him. Alastair had shrugged off his jacket, of course, and his shirt was rumpled.

"I, er, suppose one might have to keep an unexpectedly dangerous Downworlder out, or something," Thomas said awkwardly.

"Maybe." Alastair shrugged. "On the other hand, it does give the Institute a makeshift prison."

Thomas wandered a little closer to Alastair, who was looking at his book again. It was unusual to see Alastair with a hair out of place—he was like Anna that way—but it was tousled now, and fell in soft, thick locks over his forehead. At least they *looked* soft; Thomas supposed he wasn't sure. What he did know was that he liked Alastair's hair much more now that he had dyed it back to its natural color.

Unfortunately, he reminded himself, he didn't much like *Alastair*. Despite what Alastair had done for him, just a few hours ago.

Which had been as impressive as it had been surprising.

"Why have you been following me around?" Thomas demanded.

Alastair's breath seemed to hitch, though Thomas knew he might have been imagining it. "Someone had to," he said, still staring at *The Prince*.

"What on earth does that mean?" Thomas said.

Alastair Carstairs

"Don't ask questions you don't want the answer to, Lightwood," said Alastair, with a flash of the old arrogance he'd had at school.

Thomas sat down with a thump on Alastair's mattress. Alastair looked at him in surprise. "I do want the answer," Thomas said. "And I will not get up until you tell it to me."

Slowly and decidedly, Alastair set his book aside. There was a pulse beating at the base of his throat, just at the notch above his collarbone. It was a location Thomas had stared at before—he thought of the time in Paris when it had been just him and Alastair, wandering the streets, going to a moving picture, laughing together. He thought of Alastair's fingers on his wrist, though that was dangerous territory.

"I knew you were taking extra patrols," Alastair said. "And more than that—going out by yourself with a murderer on the loose. You were going to get yourself killed. You're meant to take someone with you."

"No, thank you. All these people going out in pairs, announcing themselves every time they speak, unable to make a move without consulting each other—they might as well ring a bell to let the killer know they're coming. And meanwhile, if you're not on the schedule, you're supposed to just sit around on your arse doing nothing. We'll never catch the murderer if we avoid being out on the streets. That's where the murderer *is*."

Alastair looked amused. "Never before have I heard such a concise statement of the ludicrous philosophy with which you and your school friends go through the world, running toward danger," he said, stretching. Raising his arms lifted his shirt free of his trousers, leaving a strip of stomach briefly visible. Thomas determinedly did not stare. "But that's not why you were doing what you were doing," Alastair added. "There's a little truth to what you just said, but not the heart of it."

"What do you mean?"

"You couldn't save your sister. So you want to save other people. You want revenge, even if this isn't the same evil that took Barbara— it's still evil, isn't it?" Alastair's dark eyes seemed to see into Thomas and through him. "You want to behave recklessly, and you don't want your reckless behavior to compromise a patrol partner's safety. So you went alone."

Thomas's heart gave a slow, solid thump. It was unnerving in a way he could not quite get his mind around that Alastair Carstairs seemed to understand his motivations when no one else had been able to guess at them.

"Well, I don't believe you really think that we're stupid," Thomas said, "or that we willingly court danger for danger's sake. If you believed that, you would do more to stop Cordelia spending time with us."

Alastair scoffed.

"My point," Thomas went on, an edge to his voice, "is that I don't think you believe the rude things you say. And I don't understand why you say them. It doesn't make any sense. It's as if you want to drive everyone away." He paused. "Why were you so awful to us in school? We never did anything to you."

Alastair winced. For a long moment he was silent. "I was awful to you . . . ," he said at last, "because I could be."

"Anyone can be a bastard if they want to be," said Thomas. "You had no reason to do it. Your family are friends with the Herondales. You could at least have been kinder to James."

"When I got to school," said Alastair slowly, the effort clearly costing him, "loose talk about my father had preceded me. Everyone knew he was a failure, and some of the older students decided I was an easy target. They . . . let's just say that by the end of the first week, I had been made to understand my place in the hierarchy, and I had the bruises to remind me should I ever forget."

Thomas said nothing. It was bizarre to think of Alastair being bullied. He had always seemed like a prince of the school, striding about with his hair perfect and his chin in the air.

"After about a year of being knocked around," Alastair went on, "I realized I could either become one of the bullies, or suffer for the rest of my school days. I felt no loyalty to my father, no need to defend him, so that was never a problem. I wasn't very big—well, you know what that's like."

He eyed Thomas for a moment, speculatively. Feeling self-conscious, Thomas shrank back a bit. It was true that his muscles had come with his growth spurt, and he still wasn't entirely comfortable taking up so much space in the world. Why couldn't he have turned out more like Alastair—elegantly made and graceful?

"What I did have," said Alastair, "was a savage tongue and a quick wit. Augustus Pounceby and the others would collapse laughing when I cut some poor younger student down to size. I never got my hands bloody, never hit anyone, but it didn't matter, did it? Soon enough the bullyboys forgot they'd ever hated me. I was one of them."

"And how did that turn out for you?" Thomas said in a hard voice.

Alastair looked at him matter-of-factly. "Well, one of us has a close-knit group of friends, and the other one has no friends at all. So you tell me."

"You have friends," Thomas said. But as he thought about it, he realized that whenever he saw Alastair at parties, he was either alone or with Cordelia. Or Charles, of course. Though that hadn't been the case since Charles's engagement . . .

"Then you lot arrived, a bunch of boys from famous families, too well brought up to understand at first what went on far from home. Expecting the world would embrace you. That you would be treated well. As I never had been." Alastair pushed back a lock of hair with a shaking hand. "I suppose I hated you because you were happy. Because you had each other—friends you could like and admire— and I had nothing like that. You had parents who loved each other. But none of that excuses the way I behaved. And I do not expect to be forgiven."

"I've been trying to hate you," Thomas said quietly, "for what you did to Matthew. You richly deserve to be hated for what you have done."

Alastair's dark eyes glittered. "It wasn't just his mother I slandered. It was your parents, too. You know it. So you don't have to—to act all high-minded about this. Stop pretending you are only upset on behalf of Matthew. Hate me on your own behalf, Thomas."

"No," Thomas said.

Alastair blinked. His whole body seemed tensed, as if he were awaiting a blow, and part of Thomas wanted to deliver it—to say, *Yes, Alastair, I despise you. You will never be anything but worthless.*

But throughout the conversation, something had been building inside Thomas, having nothing to do with Alastair's behavior at school and everything to do with events that had come later. All of Thomas's instincts bade him to stay silent, to push these emotions back in the recesses of his being as he always did. But they had spoken more truthfully to each other in the last few minutes than they had in their entire lives, and Thomas suspected that if he did not say the rest now, he never would.

"The reason I cannot hate you is because—because of those days we spent in Paris together," he said, and saw Alastair's eyes widen. "You were kind to me when I was very alone, and I am grateful. It was the first time I realized you could be kind."

Alastair stared at him. Why had Alastair ever dyed his hair? The contrast of his dark eyes and hair with his brown skin was beautiful in the candlelight. "It is my favorite memory of Paris as well."

"You don't have to say that. I know you were there with Charles."

Alastair stiffened. "Charles Fairchild? What about him?"

So Alastair really was going to make him say it. "Wouldn't *that* be your best memory of Paris?"

Alastair's jaw was rigid. "Exactly what are you suggesting?"

"I'm not suggesting anything. I've seen the way you look at Charles, the way he looks at you. I'm not an idiot, Alastair, and I'm asking . . ." Thomas shook his head, sighing. Nothing about this conversation had been easy—it had felt like a sort of footrace, and now Thomas could see the finish line up ahead. Alastair might prefer to keep lying to himself, but Thomas would not. "I suppose I'm asking if you're like me."

It took two *iratzes* to heal Matthew's hand, which had the side effect of somewhat sobering him up. Cordelia had been able to tell, the moment she caught sight of him, that Matthew was quite drunk, and that he had been arguing with James. She knew the look from Elias, recognizing what it was now, as she had not years ago.

Now Matthew's hand was wrapped in a handkerchief—a makeshift bandage in case the wound reopened. He seemed to have forgotten all about the argument and was deep in conversation with Lucie and Christopher, examining the purchases clanking in Christopher's market bag.

"I happened on some powdered hemlock root that was being offered at a terrific bargain—even better after I got him to throw in an adder's tongue." Christopher pulled it out to show them—a tiny, leathery strip in a glass vial. "Have you lot turned up anything?"

"Nothing worth pursuing," James said. "No one's willing to talk about *adamas* to a pack of Shadowhunters. They assume we're trying to shut someone down, so they close ranks."

Whether he had forgotten the argument or not, Cordelia couldn't tell. The Mask was firmly in place, hiding his thoughts. She wondered if they had been arguing about Thomas—or perhaps the bottle of wine that had lain in shards around their feet? She felt a stir of unease, recalling Matthew's shaking hands at the Devil when he'd filled his flask. *Matthew is not your father*, she reminded herself. *This is a place of terrible memories for him, that is all, and the others cannot understand.*

"The shopkeepers have reason to keep their counsel," said Christopher. "Nephilim raids have nearly wiped out the Market in the past."

"Perhaps we ought to start showing people the box," said Cordelia. "Seeing if they can say anything about the runes."

"What about someone who deals strictly in real, powerful magical artifacts?" Lucie asked. "There's quite a bit of junk here but also some real, expensive items. I could have sworn I saw a copy of the Red Scrolls of Magic."

"Or what about searching for warlocks for hire?" Matthew suggested. "What about—" He pointed. "Hypatia Vex?"

"Hypatia's here?" Lucie looked puzzled. "But how—?"

They had reached a part of the Market where caravans were set up in a loose circle. In the center of the circle a bonfire of enchanted flames burned: as the sparks rose up, they took on different shapes— roses, stars, towers, crescent moons, even a coach-and-four. Ahead of them, freshly painted in purple and gold, was a caravan with an elaborately lettered advertisement on the side for Hypatia Vex's new magic shop in Limehouse.

"Can we *trust* Hypatia?" said James. "She does seem to like Anna, but I'm not sure how far that liking stretches where we're concerned. Especially since we stole her Pyxis."

"She did mention that when Cordelia and I were at the Ruelle," said Matthew, shooting Cordelia a rueful look. "She seemed to have come to terms with it. And she likes *me*."

"Does she?" said Cordelia. "I really couldn't tell."

"Shadowhunters!" called a voice, rising above the noise of the Market. Cordelia turned to see Magnus Bane standing in the doorway of the purple-and-gold caravan. He wore a fitted silver frock coat, brilliant peacock-blue trousers, and a matching embroidered waistcoat, with a watch on a glittering chain tucked into one pocket. Silver cuff links glittered at his wrists, and he wore a silver ring set with a luminous blue stone. "What on earth are you doing, wandering around the Shadow Market like chickens waiting to get your heads cut off? Come inside immediately."

He shooed them in, shaking his head as they spilled into the caravan. Inside, Hypatia had left her mark on every surface: jewel-toned velvet cushions were piled on the fringed carpets; gilded mirrors and exquisitely framed Japanese illustrations lined the walls. Lamps glowed from coved niches, and in the center of the room was a small table covered in papers—scribblings about the Limehouse magic shop, from what Cordelia could see.

"Magnus!" Lucie said, delighted, as she and the others found places on the scattered cushions. It was delicious to be in the warmth after the icy night outside. Cordelia sank into a massive blue velvet cushion, wiggling her toes inside her boots as they began to thaw. James settled beside her, his shoulder warm against her side. "Are you and Uncle Jem back, then? From the Spiral Labyrinth?"

"I'm only in London for tonight," Magnus explained, settling into a brightly painted rattan chair. "Hypatia has kindly allowed me to hole up here, as my flat is full of ice trolls. It's a bit of a long story. Brother Zachariah, alas, is still in the Labyrinth. His work ethic is unimpeachable."

Cordelia cast a sideways glance at James. Did it bother him that Jem was so out of reach? If so, she could not tell; his expression was unreadable.

"Perhaps my information is out of date," Magnus went on, setting out a tray laden with small dishes of biscuits, nuts, and sugary jellies. "But isn't there a murderer on the loose in London? Should you lot really be out on your own? Not to mention the Shadow Market isn't that welcoming of Nephilim."

"Dealing with monsters is what we do," James said, reaching for a biscuit. "It's our job."

"And all the murders have happened in the early morning," Cordelia said. "So it doesn't follow that it's not safe in the evening."

"Besides, the killer wouldn't dare strike here, not with so many Downworlders around. The murders have been happening in the shadows, on deserted streets," said Christopher. "Drawing from a sample set of five, the logical conclusion—"

"Oh dear, not logic, please." Magnus held his hands up in a conciliatory fashion. "Well, you certainly aren't the first generation of young Nephilim to decide saving the world is your responsibility," he said. "But what are you doing in the Market?"

James hesitated only a moment before taking the *pithos* out of his coat pocket and handing it to Magnus. He explained as quickly as he could the situation: Thomas mistaking it for a stele, James taking the object before the Inquisitor arrived, their suspicion that it might have something to do with the murders, Christopher giving it its name.

"I am not sure your friend Thomas was as mistaken as he thought," said Magnus. He pressed down on a particular rune with a well-manicured finger. With a faint *click*, the box elongated and rearranged itself into a new, familiar shape.

"It *is* a stele," Christopher said in amazement, leaning in close to stare.

"It is certainly modeled on one," said Magnus. "And I would say this was Shadowhunter work, but . . . all magic has a kind of alliance. The tools of the Nephilim are angelic. *Adamas* itself has a seraphic alliance, while objects from the realms of demons are demonic in their very nature. This"—he nodded at the object in his hand—"is demonic. And the runes bear a resemblance to the runes of the Gray Book, but they have been altered. Changed. Rendered in a demonic script. A demonic demotic, if you will." He wiggled his eyebrows. "All right, no one got that joke. Over your heads, I suppose. The point is, this is a demonic artifact."

"Might I examine it again?" Christopher asked.

Magnus handed it over, his eyes betraying a flicker of concern. "Just be careful. It's certainly not a toy."

"An Iron Sister couldn't have made it?" asked Matthew. "Gone a bit barmy on the crumpet in the Adamant Citadel and started up production of evil objects?"

"Certainly not," said Lucie. "The Iron Sisters take their job *very* seriously, and even if they didn't, you can't make demonic objects in the Adamant Citadel. The wards won't let you. I used to want to be an Iron Sister," she added, as everyone looked at her in surprise, "until I found out how cold it gets in Iceland. Brr."

"Could someone else have taken a stele and reversed its alliance?" James asked. "Made it demonic?"

"No," said Magnus. "It was never a real stele. It was made the way you see it now, I'm sure of it. Very unlikely to have been Lilian Highsmith's. I would agree—that object belongs to whoever has been committing these murders."

"Could a demon shape *adamas*?" said James. "We believe a demon is connected to these murders somehow. Not perhaps that he is *committing* the murders, but that his—will—is somehow involved."

"No idea *which* demon?" Magnus asked casually, selecting a biscuit from the platter.

James exchanged a quick look with the rest of the group. Matthew shrugged and nodded, speaking for them all: it was James's secret to tell.

"Belial," James said. "Somehow, he seems to have regained enough strength, even after his wound, to return to me in dreams. I have been having . . . visions, it seems, of the murders. I see them happen. I almost feel as if I'm the one—the one doing the killing."

"You *feel* as if you're the one . . . ?" Magnus narrowed his cat's eyes. "Would you care to elaborate?"

"James is definitely not committing the murders," Cordelia said hotly. "Do you think we'd be foolish enough not to think of that? We tested him—he's innocent."

"They tied me to a bed," James said, examining a piece of Turkish delight.

"Charming." Magnus waved a hand in mock alarm. "There's no need to tell me anything else about that part."

"It has to be my connection to Belial that's causing these visions," James said. "There's just no other reason I'd have them. They're like the ones I've had in the past, when I was in his realm. My grandfather must be involved somehow."

"Have you seen his world again?" Magnus asked quietly. "His realm?"

"Not quite." James hesitated. "I fell into shadow once—the night before my wedding—but the realm didn't resemble the one Cordelia and I destroyed." He glanced at her. "It was no place I'd seen before. There was a huge, empty heath, and beyond that—ruins—the remains of towers and canals. There was a dark fortress with a gate—"

Magnus sat forward, his eyes alight. "Edom. The realm you saw is Edom."

"Edom?" Matthew rubbed the back of his neck. "The name is familiar. Probably a class I largely slept through."

"'The wild beasts of the desert shall also meet with the wild beasts of the island, and the demons shall cry to each other; Lilith also shall come there, and find for herself a place of rest,'" said Cordelia, recalling the party at the Hell Ruelle the night before her wedding. "It's a demon world, ruled by Lilith."

"That's right," said Magnus. "I have heard rumors that she was cast out of it, that it had been taken over—but not by whom. It seems it may have been Belial."

"So Belial has a new realm," said Christopher. "Could that be making him stronger? Could he be able to walk in our world?"

"Unlike his brethren, Belial cannot walk upon Earth, no matter what realm he controls. It is the curse he is always trying to circumvent."

"What if he's possessing mundanes, or Downworlders?" said Matthew. "Using them as tools?"

"A demon as powerful as Belial cannot possess a human body—not even the body of a vampire, or one of the fey. It would be like putting a bonfire in a shoebox. Such power as he possesses would literally tear the body apart."

"But couldn't he just possess someone long enough to commit a murder before the body falls apart?" Lucie asked.

"Then we'd be finding two bodies," Cordelia pointed out. "The murder victim *and* the body Belial had possessed."

"Though remember what Lilian Highsmith said when she was

dying," Christopher said. "Thomas told us. He asked her who attacked her and she said someone who was dead in his prime, and that his wife was crying—"

"Corpse possession? Those would fall apart even faster than live bodies," Magnus said. "It doesn't make sense."

Christopher looked glum. "Thomas did say she might have been delirious."

"Perhaps," said James thoughtfully. "Elias, too, seemed to recognize his killer, and I don't think he was raving. He seemed sane enough, which supports the idea that it's a Shadowhunter."

"A Shadowhunter who has summoned up a demon to help him? Belial, perhaps?" suggested Lucie.

"No one *summons* a Prince of Hell and controls him." Magnus shrugged. "The point is—there are a million possible theories. And every night and dawn bring with them the possibility of another death." He scrubbed his hands over his face. "Perhaps it is time for you to use your power, James," he said. "Not just to fear and avoid it."

James's face went blank. Cordelia thought of the way he had torn Belial's realm apart with his power, the way he had seemed to turn the earth inside out, shredding rocks and hills and trees. "He has used it," she said. "It is not easy to control—though I should not speak for him. James?"

"I suppose it depends what you mean," James said. "Use it how?"

Magnus rose from his chair and went to a gilded cart on which an array of bottles and decanters was arranged, and selected a bottle of deep gold spirits. "Would anyone care to join me in a bit of port?"

Matthew drew his empty flask from his pocket and held it out. The bandage on his hand seemed to glow whitely in the lamplight. "If you wouldn't mind, I could use a top-up."

Magnus gave him a look that said expensive port didn't belong in pocket flasks, but he complied. He poured himself a measure and sat down again, the glass of rose-gold liquid balanced between the fingers of his left hand. "You know the ways of shadows, James. Did Belial *show* you his new realm of Edom, or did you somehow force your way into it? Do you remember?"

"Not consciously," said James. "I was—upset at the time." *I made a promise to Daisy, and I will keep that promise. If you wanted to prevent me from doing the right thing, you should have started the campaign quite a bit earlier than the night before my wedding.*

"If you are suggesting he enter the shadow realm of his own will, the last time he did that, he nearly destroyed the Institute ballroom," said Matthew.

"And I almost shot him with an arrow," said Christopher sorrowfully.

"Surely you could refrain from doing that again, er, which one are you? Cecily's son? Try not to shoot arrows at James," said Magnus. "Look, when he went into the shadow realm from the ballroom, did he disappear, or was his body still present in this world?"

"I can answer that," said James. "It was the former. I disappeared."

"But earlier, when you envisioned Edom," said Magnus. "Did you actually travel there?"

"No," Matthew said. "He remained in the room with us. Quite present."

"I have spoken about this with Jem," said Magnus. "Most of your travels, so to speak, James, have taken place within a dream-realm. Only when you have physically removed yourself to a dimension controlled by Belial has Belial been in a position to hurt you. He is spying on you, in his nasty little way—I say spy on him right back. In dreams."

"Dream-magic," said Christopher, pleased. "I told you those onei-romancy books would be helpful."

"You saw Edom once in a dream," said Magnus. "You can see it again."

"But what is the importance of seeing Edom?" said Cordelia. "What will it tell us?"

"Whether Belial is indeed there," said Magnus. "Even what his plans are. Is he building an army? Hiding and licking his wounds? What demons follow him? What are his vulnerabilities? Think of it as spying on the camp of the enemy."

James shook his head. "I have never done anything like that before, in practice with Jem or by accident," he said. "I am not sure I would quite know how."

"Fortunately, I am an expert at dream-magic," said Magnus. "I will accompany you—I would do it myself, but I do not have your power. I can pass through with you, but I cannot open the door."

Cordelia felt a prick of unease. Magnus spoke matter-of-factly, but he had not been with them in Belphegor's realm, had not made the terrifying journey there and back. "If James is going to do this, I would like to remain in the room with him, with Cortana drawn," she said. "In case we catch Belial's attention somehow, or the attention of some other unpleasant individual."

"Oh, indeed," said Magnus. "One cannot be too careful, and Belial fears Cortana as he fears little else." He swirled his port, watching it coat the sides of the glass. "The great powers, the archangels and the Princes of Hell, are playing their own game of chess. They have their own alliances and enmities. Azazel and Asmodeus have worked together, as have Belial and Leviathan, while Belphegor hates his brethren. But all that could change should a new power emerge." He shrugged. "Mortals cannot see the greater movements of the game, the strategy or goals. But that does not mean one need be a pawn on the board."

"*Shah mat,*" said Cordelia.

Magnus dropped a wink in her direction. "That is correct," he said, rising to his feet. "Alas, I must leave you, or at least, encourage you to leave me. I must be here when Hypatia returns, and you lot must be absent. She won't like it that I let you into the caravan." He smiled. "It's always better to respect a lady's personal space. James, Cordelia, I'll meet you at Curzon Street at midnight. Now off you all go—no more shopping, dallying, or skulking about. The Shadow Market's a dangerous place, especially after moonrise."

20

EQUAL TEMPER

One equal temper of heroic hearts,
Made weak by time and fate, but strong in will
To strive, to seek, to find, and not to yield.
—Alfred, Lord Tennyson, "Ulysses"

By the time they reached the carriages waiting for them outside the Market, Matthew had produced his refilled flask from inside his coat and was drinking steadily. He stumbled getting up into the carriage and refused James's offer of help, batting his hand away before collapsing onto the velvet seat and breaking into a rousing chorus of "I Could Love You in a Steam Heat Flat."

Cordelia and Lucie exchanged a worried look before clambering into their own carriage. Balios started off through the thinly powdered snow, and they rattled away from the Market. Outside the windows, London had been transformed into a winter fantasia, fat flakes of snow settling prettily on bare tree branches and dancing in the light cast by the gas lamps. Candles flickered in the windows of St. Saviour's Church, and the distant hum of trains was muffled and almost pleasant.

"I *hate* this," Lucie burst out, wiggling her fingers inside their damp gloves. "I hate the idea of James going into the shadow realm. I know—if Magnus says it's all right, I'm sure it will be, but I hate it."

"I hate it too," Cordelia said. "But Luce, I'll be there with him—as much as I can be—"

"I know. But it seems dreadful, and I hate that—that Matthew is—"

"Miserable?" Cordelia said, trying hard not to think about the broken bottle in the snow.

Lucie glanced at her, biting her lip. "I know none of us talk about it. We can't. I don't even know how much Christopher and Thomas are aware of it. But he's been like this for ages now. He must be awfully unhappy. But I don't know why. We all love him, and James loves him so terribly much. When we were younger—James had this shirt, just an ordinary shirt, you know, and Mam threw it away because he'd outgrown it and he was so furious and went to fetch it from the rubbish. It was the shirt he was wearing when Matthew asked him to be *parabatai*. He wouldn't get rid of it."

Cordelia hesitated. "Sometimes," she said, "it is not enough for others to love you. I do not think Matthew loves himself very well."

Lucie's eyes widened. "What is there about him he could possibly not love?" she said, with such sincerity it made Cordelia's heart ache. She would try to convince Matthew to tell his friends his secret, she thought. They loved him so. They would never judge him as he feared.

The two carriages clattered noisily under a railway viaduct and down a narrow backstreet toward a courtyard surrounded by Georgian row houses. A peeling sign declared it to be Nelson Square. They were cutting along one corner, wheels crunching on gravel and ice, when Balios whinnied loudly, rearing up.

The girls' carriage stopped so abruptly that Cordelia and Lucie nearly toppled out of their seats. The door was ripped open, and a taloned hand reached inside, snatching a screaming Lucie out into the night.

Cordelia whipped Cortana from its sheath and launched herself out into the darkness, her boots crunching on snow, her skirts swirling. Outside, the blank faces of the row houses surrounded a patchy and dilapidated garden, edged with a few leafless plane trees. A dozen small demons were scampering around it, frightening Balios, who stamped and snorted. Lucie, half-covered in snow where she had fallen, had already yanked herself free of them. Her hat was gone, and she stood bareheaded and furious, brandishing her axe.

Cordelia looked around, Cortana in her hand. The sword sat perfectly, any feeling of wrongness banished. It hummed with the rightness of being wielded, of being one with her. She saw that the boys had already spilled from their carriage some distance away; they were bright shadows in the darkness, Christopher with a glowing seraph blade, Matthew with gleaming *chalikars* in his hand. There were dozens of small, gray-skinned, trollish demons charging about Nelson Square like mad things, hopping on top of the carriages, hurling snowballs at each other.

"Hauras demons!" called James, who wore an expression that mingled annoyance and anger. Hauras demons were pests. Sometimes called scamp demons, they were fast and ugly—scaled and horned, with vicious talons—but only about the size of small wolves.

James let a blade go. Cordelia had seen him throw before but had nearly forgotten how good he was at it. The knife flew like silver death from his hand, severing a Hauras demon's head from its body. Ichor splattered, and the two halves of the demon puffed into nothingness; the other scamp demons shrieked and laughed.

"Ooh! *Pests!*" Lucie cried in outrage as two of the creatures caught at her skirts, tearing at the velvet rosettes. With no room to swing her weapon, she began to club at them with the handle of her axe. Cordelia sliced out with Cortana, a bright golden line of fire against the night. She saw one demon puff into ash; the other, squealing, released Lucie's skirts and darted into the center of the square, where it joined the rest of the scamps in trying to trip and unbalance the Shadowhunters— lunging and jabbing them with sharp little talons, laughing and cackling all the while.

One leaped at Matthew, who jammed a *chalikar* into its throat with both hands, not even bothering to throw it. The demon crumpled, gurgling, and disappeared. Another came from behind; Matthew turned—stumbled, and slipped. He went down, slamming hard into the icy ground.

Cordelia started toward him, but James was already there, hauling his *parabatai* to his feet. She caught a glimpse of Matthew's white face before he drew a seraph blade from his belt: it blazed up, its brightness searing a line across Cordelia's vision. She could see Christopher laying about with his blade, James with a long knife. The night was filled with shrieks and hissing, their feet churning the snowy ground into a stinking mess of ice and ichor.

It all seemed almost silly—the Hauras were ridiculous-looking creatures—until Lucie screamed. Cordelia whipped around and ran toward her, only to see the ground between them, all ice and dirt, erupt. Something long, slithering, and scaled burst from it, scattering clods of earth.

A Naga demon. Cordelia had seen illustrations of them in India. This one had a long snake's body and a flat, arrow-shaped head, split by a wide mouth lined with yellow, spiky teeth. Its eyes were black saucers.

Cordelia heard James give a hoarse shout: she looked over to see the boys trapped behind a wall of Hauras demons. The Naga hissed, curled, and lunged toward Lucie, who leaped aside just in time, her hand axe going flying; she fumbled for a seraph blade—

A bolt of energy thrummed up Cordelia's arm; she leaped forward as the whole world seemed to turn to molten gold. Everything had gone slow and still—only she was striking like lightning, like a rain of gold. Cortana described a fiery arc against the night; the Naga writhed as the blade stabbed into its side. Ichor flew but Cordelia felt no burn, no sting: she no longer even felt the cold of the air. She felt only a savage triumph as the Naga howled, dropping to the ground to slither behind her.

She spun as it rose above her, its flat head outspread like a cobra's. It swayed back and forth, then plunged its head toward her, faster than sparks rising from a fire. But Cordelia was quicker still: she whirled as it opened its saw-toothed mouth, and plunged her blade upward, stabbing through the roof of its mouth. It reared back, spraying ichor: it turned to slide away through the snow, but Cordelia gave chase. She shot after the slithering demon, the ground blurring under her feet. She drew alongside it, lifted the ichor-soaked sword, and brought it down in a last clean sweep that cut through scale and bone, severing the Naga's body in half.

A gush of steam rose from the body. The head and tail twitched before dissolving in a wet, stinking mess that soaked into the ground. Cordelia lowered the sword, gasping; she had crossed Nelson Square in what felt like only a few seconds, and she was quite a distance from the others. She could see them—shadows, pushing against the mass of Hauras demons. James broke away from the others, angling toward her just as a shrill scream split the air.

Cordelia stared. It was not a human noise, nor was a human making it. One of the larger Hauras demons stood a few feet away, goggling at her with its gray-white eyes.

"*Paladin!*" the Hauras demon wheezed. "*Paladin! We dare not touch!*"

Cordelia stared. How could the demon know she was a paladin of Wayland the Smith? Had he marked her in some invisible way?

A cry rose from the other Hauras demons. They began to scatter. Cordelia could hear her friends' shouts of surprise; James vaulted a low hedge, heading straight for her.

"*Paladin.*" The Hauras demon held out its gnarled hands toward Cordelia. Its voice had taken on a whining quality. "*Forgive. Tell your master. We did not know.*"

With a quivering bow, the demon turned and ran, joining its fellows in slinking retreat. A few yards away, Matthew, Lucie, and Christopher were looking around in puzzlement as their attackers vanished. Cordelia barely had time to sheathe her blade before James was beside her. She started to open her mouth, to explain, but he was staring at her—at the terrible ichor burns up and down the front of her dress, on her sleeve. In a strangled voice, he said, "Cordelia—"

Her breath went out of her in a gasp as he caught her in a hard embrace. Despite the cold night, his shirt was damp with sweat. His arms around her were strong and solid; she could feel the swift hammering of his heart. He pressed his cheek against hers, chanting her name, *Daisy, Daisy, Daisy.*

"I'm all right," she said quickly. "It got on my dress, is all, but I'm perfectly all right, James—"

He let her go, looking almost abashed. "I saw that Naga demon rear back to attack you," he said, his voice low. "I thought—"

"What was that about?" said Christopher, who had just arrived with Lucie. "I saw that Hauras demon shout at Cordelia, and then they all raced off like the devil was after them."

"I—I've no idea," Cordelia said. "I suppose it was Cortana. The Hauras demon looked terrified of it."

"Perhaps word has spread that Cortana dealt a wound to Belial,"

Lucie said, her eyes sparkling like they did when she was working on *The Beautiful Cordelia.* "Your sword's reputation precedes you!"

Only James said nothing as they made their way back across the square, seeming lost in thought. Matthew had returned to the carriages to soothe the horses' nerves. As though he could feel Cordelia's gaze on him, he turned and looked at her, his green eyes dark. She couldn't help but wonder if he'd seen more back at the barrow than he had let on, but no: surely he could not have seen Wayland, could not have heard the smith speak the word "paladin" as Cordelia knelt before him.

But it was all Cordelia could think about. Around the edges of her astonishment, a wild joy was beginning to fizz upward. *You have the soul of a great warrior,* Wayland the Smith had said. She was a paladin now, the champion of a legendary hero, and even demons were taking notice. Suddenly she hoped that these scamps were the gossipy sort. She hoped that word would travel through the ranks of demons all the way up to Belial himself, and that he would understand that Cordelia and her sword would stand between the Prince of Hell and all her friends, defending them to the death.

It had been decided that Christopher would ride home with Daisy and James, as the Consul's house was only a few blocks from Curzon Street and Kit wished to use the lab there to study the *pithos.* Lucie would go with Matthew, which suited her excellently. James tended to ask questions. Matthew, however, did not.

Lucie settled herself in Matthew's carriage as they rattled out of Nelson Square, Matthew complaining all the while that traffic in London was bad enough without demons leaping into perfectly decent people's vehicles. Lucie knew he was merely venting his feelings and didn't expect an answer, so she didn't provide one, just looked at him affectionately. His blond hair was disheveled from the fight, his jacket torn. He was looking the part of a romantic hero, if a slightly dissipated one.

The carriage lurched as they turned a corner, and Lucie realized that while she'd been lost in thought, Matthew had dropped his face into his hands. That *was* troubling, and not within the usual range of his moods.

"Matthew, are you quite all right?" she asked.

"Right as rain," Matthew said unconvincingly, his words muffled by his hands.

"What are you thinking about?" Lucie asked lightly, trying a different tack.

"What it is like," Matthew said slowly, "to be entirely undeserving of the person you love most in the world."

"What a very sort of novelish complaint," Lucie said, after a moment. She had no idea what to make of this dramatic statement. Wasn't James the person Matthew loved most? Why would he have suddenly decided he didn't deserve James? "I don't suppose you want to tell me about it."

"Certainly not."

"All right, then, I have to tell *you* something."

Matthew looked up. His eyes were dry, if a little red-rimmed. "Oh, Raziel," he said, "that never portends anything good."

"I'm not going home," Lucie informed him. "I'd planned to stop there and then leave again, but there's no time now. I need to get to Limehouse, and *you're* going to take me there."

"Limehouse?" Matthew looked incredulous. He ran his fingers through his curls, making them stand out even more wildly than before. "Lucie, please tell me you aren't going back to that sailcloth factory."

"Fear not. I'm going to Hypatia Vex's new magic shop. I'm meeting Anna and Ariadne there, so you needn't trouble yourself that I'll be unattended."

"Limehouse isn't in the least bit on the way to Marylebone," Matthew said, but he was smiling a little. "By the Angel, you're a schemer, Luce. When did you make this plan?"

"Oh, sometime." Lucie gestured vaguely. The truth was that she hadn't been sure when they were meant to meet Hypatia until earlier at the Devil Tavern when Anna, under the pretense of patting her hand, had slipped her a folded note with instructions. "I suppose you don't *have* to drive me, Math, but if you let me walk to Limehouse on my own and I am murdered, James will be *very* annoyed with you."

Lucie had meant it as a joke, but Matthew's face fell. "James is already very annoyed with me."

"Why is that?"

Matthew leaned his head back against the seat, eyeing her speculatively. "Are you going to tell me what this magic shop business is about?"

"No," Lucie said pleasantly.

"Then I suppose we both have our secrets." Matthew turned and opened the window to tell the driver to head toward Limehouse. By the time he popped back into the carriage proper, he had a curious gleam in his eye. "Don't you think it's odd, Luce, that James is constantly tormented by Belial, and yet Belial doesn't seem to have any interest in *you*?"

"I do not believe that Belial has read and understood Mrs. Wollstonecraft's *Vindication of the Rights of Woman*. He is interested in James because James is a boy, and not interested in me because I am a girl. I suspect that Belial would rather possess a tortoise than a woman."

"In that case, you should count yourself fortunate to be a member of the fairer sex."

"But I am not fortunate," Lucie said, her joking tone gone. "I would rather have Belial's attention focused on me, for James always tends to blame himself for things, and I hate to see him in pain."

Matthew smiled at her tiredly. "You and your brother are lucky, Lucie. I fear that if Charles had to choose between me or him for possession, I'd be a very well-dressed demon."

The carriage was crossing the Thames, and the cold air outside brought with it the smell of river water. Lucie could not help but remember when Cordelia had been knocked into the river after wounding the Mandikhor demon. How Lucie, terrified for Cordelia's life, had summoned ghosts to rescue her friend from the Thames, without even knowing what she was doing. She recalled the terrible weakness that had swept over her after, the way her vision had darkened before she lost consciousness in Jesse's arms. Malcolm's words came to her, unbidden. *Necromancy carries too heavy a price.*

Lucie looked away from the window. She still hadn't told any of her friends what had truly saved Cordelia that night beneath Tower Bridge. Matthew was right, it seemed—she was keeping secrets, perhaps too many. James and Matthew were *parabatai*, and Cordelia and Lucie were meant to become *parabatai* as well. Yet it seemed to Lucie that none of them were being honest with each other. Was that what Matthew meant by "undeserving"?

By the time they returned to Curzon Street, Cordelia's ebullient mood had faded. Though Christopher and James kept up a steady stream of conversation in the carriage, she could not help but let her mind stray to thoughts of the night ahead, and the danger of what was being asked of James.

The windows of the house were dark; Effie must long ago have gone to bed. As they entered the hallway, cold and weary, Cordelia's hands slipped and fumbled at the buttons on her coat. "Here," said James, "let me do that."

When he leaned over her, she let herself breathe him in: the warmth, the smell of wet wool, a little salt, the fading sweetness of cologne. She studied the curve of his jaw where it met his throat, the steady beat of the pulse there. She felt her cheeks redden. Only the night before, she had kissed that spot.

James slid her coat from her shoulders and hung it on the rack by the door, along with her damp scarf. "Well, Magnus isn't getting here until midnight," he said lightly, "and I don't know about you, but I'm starving. Meet you in the study?"

A quarter of an hour later, Cordelia—in a new dress and dry slippers—entered the study with Cortana in one hand and a book in the other. She found James already on the sofa, a low fire burning in the grate, and a simple meal set out on the games table. She leaned Cortana against the hearth and came over to inspect the food. James had clearly raided the kitchen—arranged on a wooden platter was sliced cheese and bread, along with apples, cold chicken, and two steaming cups of tea.

"I had no idea you were so domestic," Cordelia said, sinking gratefully onto the sofa. Rest and warmth were bliss. She set the book she'd been carrying on the end table and reached for an apple. "Is this another inherited secret power?"

"No, just the result of providing food for the Merry Thieves. I got used to scrounging from the kitchen at the Institute. Christopher would starve if you didn't remind him to eat, and Thomas is so enormous he needs to be fed every few hours, like a captive tiger." He tore off a bit of bread. "I hope Thomas is managing with Alastair."

"Alastair will sit in a corner and read. It's what he always does when things are awkward," said Cordelia. "I *do* feel awful not telling my mother what's really happened, but what good would it do? She needs to rest and be calm."

"It is hard to keep secrets," James said. "Both for those who do not know the truth, but also those who keep them. Daisy . . ." He hesitated. "I'd like to ask you something."

When he said her name that way, she wanted to give him everything and anything he wanted. "Yes?"

"Tonight, in Nelson Square, I heard what the Hauras demon said to you. You have wielded Cortana before, many times. Even against Belial. But no demon called you 'paladin' then."

Cordelia lowered her hand with the apple in it. She'd been hoping he hadn't heard. "That isn't precisely a question."

"No," he said. "But I saw the way you were fighting—you have always been incredible with Cortana, but tonight you were different. Like nothing I've seen before." There was no Mask hiding his expression; it was open and clear. "If something has changed with you, you needn't tell me. But I would like it if you did."

She set her apple aside. "Do you know what a paladin is?"

"Yes," he said, "though from history class alone. In the time of Jonathan Shadowhunter, when I gather it was easier to meet a god or an angel, one might swear fealty to such a being to increase one's power and nobility. So goes the story."

"And all the stories are true," Cordelia said. She told him of her meeting with Wayland the Smith, of the change that came over the landscape, the clang of the forge, his words, the oath she had sworn. James watched her intently as she spoke.

"I did not know what effect the pledge would have," she finished. "But—I have never felt before what I did tonight, battling the Naga demon. It was like a bronze-gold light came down over me, was *in* me, burning up my veins, making me want to fight. And those demons fled from me."

"'Bronze gleamed around him like flashing fire or the rays of the rising sun,'" quoted James with a smile. "It *was* rather like Achilles had come to South London."

Cordelia felt a small, warm spark in her chest. For all the glory of fighting as a paladin, she had felt oddly invisible, separated from the others by a peculiar space. But James had seen her. "Still," he added. "It is such a great oath, Daisy. To be sworn to a being like Wayland the Smith—he could call upon you at any time, demand you face any danger."

"As you are doing tonight? I *want* to be called upon, James. I have always wanted this."

"To be a hero," James said, and hesitated. "Cordelia, have you told—"

A knock echoed throughout the house. A moment later Effie appeared, looking furious in a nightcap and paper curlers. She ushered Magnus into the room, muttering. He wore a caped greatcoat of blue velvet, and next to Effie, looked taller than ever.

"Magnus Bane here to see you," said Effie darkly, "and I must say, this is not at all the class of person I was led to believe I would be working for, not at all."

Calmly, Magnus doffed his coat and handed it to her expectantly. She stalked off, muttering about going back to sleep with a flannel wrapped around her head to block out the "unending clatter."

Magnus looked inquiringly at James and Cordelia. "Do you always keep a staff that insults you?"

"I prefer it," said James, rising to his feet. He had his revolver stuck through his belt, Cordelia realized. After what had happened in Nelson Square, perhaps he didn't want to be caught without it again. "It keeps me on my toes."

"Would you like some tea?" Cordelia asked Magnus.

"No. We ought to get started. Hypatia will be expecting me back." Magnus looked around the study, his eyes flicking over the windows; he gestured once with his fingers, and the curtains flew shut. "This room is as good as any, I suppose. Cordelia, can you guard the door?"

Cordelia stationed herself at the door, drawing Cortana from its sheath. It gleamed in the firelight, and for a moment, pulsing through her hand, she felt the same energy she had during the fight with the Naga—as if the blade were whispering to her. Asking her to wield it.

Magnus had moved James to stand before the fire. Cordelia had never noticed before how oddly alike their eyes were: Magnus's gold-green, slit-pupilled, and James's the color of yellow gold. Soft sparks of magic, the color of bronze, spilled from Magnus's hands as he pressed his fingers to James's temples.

"Now," he said. "Concentrate."

GRACE:
1899–1900

As it turned out, Grace's power worked on Shadowhunters. All male Shadowhunters except James. Tatiana drove home from the trip to Alicante with a carriage so laden with baked goods that it could barely get over the ruts in the road.

"Just tell the baker to give you everything he has," Tatiana had snapped, when they'd first arrived outside the shop in Alicante. Now she watched Grace stonily as the carriage bumped sluggishly back in the direction of Blackthorn Manor. She alternated her time between biting into an enormous flaky strudel and glowering in silence as stacks of cardboard boxes jostled unpleasantly into both of Grace's sides.

Back at home, her mother sized Grace up, and then, without warning, surprisingly quick, slapped her in the face.

Grace flinched and brought her hand up to her stinging cheek. Her mother hadn't slapped her since before the visit to Paris.

"James Herondale is a Shadowhunter like any other," Tatiana ground out. "He is not the problem." She glared. "Steel your nerve, girl. If ever I am able to teach you anything, let it be that you must steel your nerve. The world is hard, and it will work to destroy you. That is the nature of things."

She stalked off before Grace could speak, and Grace silently vowed to herself that when it was again summer, and the Herondales returned, it would be different. She would try harder.

Summer came, after a long winter of being quiet and obedient to her mother, having only her times with Jesse to feel like a real person. They had continued training, in a fashion, though it was rather one-sided now that Jesse was a ghost.

Grace steeled her nerve as requested and arranged to meet with James, but when she first saw him, she cursed herself for the immediate pang of sorrow she felt at what was being asked of her. James had just gotten over scalding fever, as it transpired—but though he looked pale and delicate, he was full of energy and enthusiasm. He was happy to see Grace—happy to tell her all about another Shadowhunter named Cordelia Carstairs, who had been his nursemaid and companion in his illness. In fact, Grace quickly found that James was unwilling to shut up about this Miss Carstairs for even one minute.

"Well?" her mother snapped when Grace came into her study that afternoon.

Grace hesitated. "James has fallen in love with someone," she said. "In the past months. I don't think he can fall in love with me if he is already in love."

"If there is a lack in you, it is a lack of will, not of power," Tatiana scoffed. "He can be made to forget that he is in love. He can be made to feel anything you wish."

"But—" Grace wanted to say that whether or not her power could make James forget this girl he loved, she was not sure whether she should do such a thing. James was, after all, her only real friend. Other than Jesse, who was her family and also a ghost, and thus doubly didn't count. But she didn't dare suggest anything of the sort to her mother. "Mama, my power doesn't work on him. I promise I have tried. With others, all the tests you made me do in Paris—the effect was instantaneous. And it took no effort at all. With James, even trying very hard led to nothing."

Tatiana looked at her wryly. "You silly girl. You think that your power doesn't work on him because he's in love with someone. But I have done some research these months myself, and in fact, it may be Herondale's unclean blood that is the trouble."

"What?" Grace said uncertainly.

"His mother is a warlock," Tatiana said. "She is the only warlock who is also a Shadowhunter to have ever lived, it seems. So she is doubly cursed."

She seemed lost in thought for a moment. Grace remained silent.

Then Tatiana's head snapped up and she again focused on her daughter. "Wait here," she said sharply, and went out of the room and down the corridor. Grace supposed she was going to the cellars, where Grace was forbidden to go. She sank down on one of the chairs by the fire, wishing the sun would hurry up and set so she could see Jesse. Her mother was always kinder to her if Jesse was about.

It seemed that hardly any time had passed at all when Tatiana reappeared, rubbing her hands together with excitement. Grace rose, wary. "One of my patrons," Tatiana said as she went around the desk, "has found a solution to your problem."

"Your patrons?" Grace said.

"Yes," said Tatiana, "a solution that will grant us even greater power over Herondale than you could wield over anyone else."

From her pocket she produced a bracelet, a band of sleek silver. For a moment, it reflected a glare of candlelight into Grace's eyes. Tatiana went on to explain her plan, the story she had crafted. Grace was to tell James the bracelet was an old heirloom of her birth parents, Tatiana said, and Grace felt a pang so deep within herself that, she was sure, no part of it was expressed on her face at all. Tatiana would hide the bracelet in a box in her study; next, Grace was to trick James into recovering the bracelet for her. "The moment he lays his willing hand upon it," her mother was saying, "he will be lost, for it is so powerful that even to touch it is to be overcome by its magic."

"Why make him retrieve the bracelet himself from the house?" Grace said, puzzled. "I'm sure he would simply accept it if I offered it to him as a gift."

Tatiana smiled. "Grace, you must trust me. The adventure of getting the thing will stick the bracelet in his mind. He will care about it—because he loves you, of course, but also because of the story it carries in his mind."

Grace knew there was no point resisting. There was never any point resisting. Her mother was all she had; there was nowhere else she could go. Even if she confessed everything to James, threw herself on the mercy of his infamously brutish parents, she would lose everything. Her home, her name, her brother. And her mother's wrath would burn her to nothing.

And there was another factor motivating her as well. All year, Tatiana had been dropping hints that this plan to enchant James Herondale was in some manner part of the plan to restore Jesse. She would not say so outright, but Grace was not so stupid that she could not put two and two together. Perhaps there were limits to what she would willingly do for the sake of her mother. But to have Jesse back in a physical form, alive and safe, would change Grace's life immeasurably. She would do whatever was necessary to save him, so that he might save her.

21

HELL'S OWN TRACK

"Turn again, O my sweetest,—turn again, false and fleetest:
This beaten way thou beatest I fear is hell's own track."
"Nay, too steep for hill-mounting; nay,
too late for cost-counting:
This downhill path is easy, but there's no turning back."
—Christina Gabriel Rossetti, "Amor Mundi"

Grace was weary of winter, weary of stepping into slush puddles
that stained her kid boots, weary of the cold that seeped into her thin
frame when she went out, finding its way under her skirts and into the
fingers of her gloves and to the very core of her, until it seemed she'd
never feel warm again.

She had lived through many other winters, huddled inside
Blackthorn Manor. But this winter she'd spent most of her nights
sneaking out. She'd return to the Bridgestocks' chilled to the bone,
only to find the bedcovers ice-cold, the warmth long gone from the
ceramic hot-water bottle at the foot of the bed.

Tonight, though, Grace would much rather have been in her small
room at the Bridgestocks', perhaps visiting with Jesse, than where
she was—working up the courage to break into the Consul's house as
a chill winter wind sliced through her coat, and night owls hooted in
the branches of the trees in the square.

She'd have thought everyone would be asleep at this hour, but annoyingly, light still glowed from the well windows below street level. Maybe Henry Fairchild had left them on by accident? He was certainly absentminded enough for that to be a possibility. Unless she wanted to freeze to death, she would just have to take her chances.

She slunk along the side of the building toward the stairs down to the furnace room, which connected to the lab via a narrow, dank passage that hardly anyone ever used. She had brought the master key to the house that she'd filched from Charles long ago. She was just glad he was still in France, in no position to find out what she was up to.

She slipped inside and crept along in the dark, following the weak light that spilled into the narrow passageway up ahead. The laboratory door had been cracked open slightly; she peered through the gap and saw the room empty, Henry's work area as untidy as usual.

She stepped inside—and jumped. There was Christopher Lightwood, perched in the corner on a wooden stool, turning a peculiar object over in his hand. *What is he doing hiding in a corner?* she thought furiously. Couldn't he sit at the table like a normal person, where she could have spied on him properly?

She smiled, opening her mouth to lie—she was on an errand for Charles, he'd left something in his old room—when Christopher turned and blinked at her.

"Oh! It's you," Christopher said with his usual sunny smile. "I thought it might be rats again. Hullo, Grace."

"It's awfully late," she said conversationally, as if she ran into young men in cellars every day. "Do the Fairchilds know you're here?"

"Oh, I'm here all the time," he said, holding the peculiar object up to the light. It looked like a strange stele. "Henry's got loads of equipment, and he doesn't mind if I use it."

"But—aren't you going to ask me what I'm doing here?" Grace asked, approaching the worktable.

"Why would I do that?" Christopher seemed genuinely puzzled. "You're affianced to Charles—surely you have a right to be here."

She cleared her throat. "It's a surprise for Charles. Could I convince you to take pity on me and help me find a particular ingredient?"

Christopher slid off the stool. "You're working on a scientific surprise for Charles? I never thought he had much interest in science."

Christopher Lightwood

He set his odd stele down on the workbench. "Would you like a quick tour of the laboratory? I daresay it's the best-equipped scientific workshop in London."

Grace was nonplussed. She hadn't compelled him to offer her the tour; he'd come up with that on his own. She could have reduced him to a babbling lump, she thought, saying things like *I would die in order to help you with anything you could possibly desire*, his eyes crossed with longing. But as Christopher seemed honestly chuffed at the chance to show off his beakers and tubes and vials, she found herself holding back.

She didn't like using the power, really, she thought, as he led her to a series of shelves containing tiny jars full of colorful substances and started telling her about a table of chemical elements invented by a scientist in Russia a number of years earlier. Using it made her feel tied to her mother. To the darkness her mother served.

As she studied the contents of the little jars, Christopher told her about the way magic and science could be combined to create something entirely new. She didn't quite follow, but she surprised herself by wanting to know more as he talked about the purpose of various objects and instruments, the experiments he and Henry conducted, the things they discovered.

Grace was reminded of the time he had given her a ride home from a picnic last summer during the demon attacks. He'd told her then about his love of science without being the least bit condescending, as her male admirers often were, or self-important in the way Charles always was. Christopher treated her as an equal whose enthusiasm for science was not only similar to his own but unsurprising.

"What were you working on when I came in?" she asked, truly curious, as he concluded the tour of the shelves and bins crammed with neatly labeled specimens and ingredients.

Christopher led her back to the stele and handed her a magnifying lens so that she could view the designs more closely. They were very odd—not quite the runes she was used to seeing on the skin of Shadowhunters, but not entirely *unlike* them either.

"It's not a real stele at all," he said. "I've been calling it a *pithos*, because it turns into a sort of box, too. I could try to melt down the material, see if it's really *adamas*, but the problem is that once you melt something down, you can't put it back the way it was."

"I suppose not," she said. "May I handle it?"

He passed it to her. Grace felt its weight in her hands, not quite sure what she was looking for. If she were an ordinary Shadowhunter, she would have handled plenty of steles, but Tatiana had always disapproved of her studying or training.

Christopher blinked his unusual violet eyes. "Just because it looks like a stele doesn't mean anything—especially if its purpose was meant to be disguised for some reason."

"Hold out your arm," Grace said impulsively.

Christopher pushed up his shirtsleeve, revealing a Mark on his inside left forearm. Craft, maybe? Or Technique? "Go ahead if you like," he said. "Draw something."

She touched the tip of the *pithos* to his skin and hesitated, suddenly unsure of herself. She momentarily wished she had used her powers on him; she was sorely in need of the confidence they would bring her. Slowly and awkwardly, she drew the *enkeli* rune, the rune most Shadowhunters learned to draw first. *Angelic power.*

To her amazement, the moment it was finished, it disappeared from Christopher's arm.

"Odd, isn't it?" Christopher examined his arm; he'd clearly tried this already. "You draw a rune and it vanishes."

"This Creation rune here on your arm," she said. "Are you terribly fond of it?"

"No, not really—"

Grace took the *pithos* and, with the tip, traced the Creation rune on Christopher's arm. He watched her with interest, and then some surprise as the Creation rune shimmered—and vanished.

Christopher's eyebrows shot up into his hair. "What ho," he said, sounding pleased. "Try to draw it on me again now."

But that wasn't what Grace had in mind. Experimentally, she touched the tip of the *pithos* to her own wrist—only to see the Creation rune leap into existence there, stark and black against her skin.

"Blimey," Christopher said. "So it can move runes from one person to another? I wonder if that's the purpose of it, or just one of its powers?"

"You don't seem that surprised," Grace observed.

"On the contrary. I've never heard of transferring a rune between Shadowhunters—"

"No, I meant—" Grace wished she hadn't said anything. "I only meant that you didn't seem surprised to see me put a rune on myself."

"Why would I be?" Christopher asked, obviously confused. "You're a Shadowhunter. It's what we do."

Grace's heart sank. Now Christopher probably thought she was completely peculiar—and for some reason, that bothered her.

But Christopher was focused on the *pithos* in her hands. "How might it work, I wonder?"

Grateful that the subject had been dropped, Grace handed it back to him. "All we know so far is that it can move runes from one person to another, right?"

"Indeed, but why? And just as importantly, how? Runes can't be contained in any metal, or any substance at all, that I am aware of. So is it sending the rune to another dimension for storage, and then bringing it back? Like a miniature rune-focused Portal?"

"A . . . rune-storage dimension?" Grace said doubtfully. "That seems unlikely."

Christopher gave her a sheepish grin. "I'm still in the early hypothesizing phase of my investigation." He gestured excitedly as he talked, his hands—covered in stains and burns and scars—slicing the air. "Different substances have different properties—density, for instance, or flammability, or dozens of other things. Magical things are no exception. As an example, I have been trying to determine what *adamas* is made of. All things in the world are made up of elements— like iron and oxygen and chlorine and so on—and there are only a discrete number of them. Yet *adamas* is not one of them. Surely it has magical properties separate from its physical makeup, but—" Suddenly he stopped, looking stricken. "I'm sorry, Grace, this must be tremendously boring for you."

Grace gathered that boredom was the reaction Christopher was accustomed to from most people. But Grace *wasn't* bored, not in the least. She wished he would keep talking. But Christopher was looking at her expectantly. If there was one thing she couldn't bear, it was other people having expectations. She would always disappoint them. "I—no, but you see, I was hoping to find some activated moth-wing powder."

The light in Christopher's eyes dimmed. Clearing his throat, he set the *pithos* on the worktable. "We only have the unactivated sort," he said in a businesslike tone, "but we could activate it here, I suppose."

Make him, a little voice whispered inside her, the same voice that had guided her to force all kinds of people to do her bidding.

"There's no need for that," she said, instead, staring down at her hands. "I can manage it myself."

"Very well," Christopher said. "I am in your debt for helping me discover this device's purpose, and happy to oblige. I'll get the powder for you, and then would you mind going back out the way you came? I'd let you out properly, but I rarely use the front door."

Hypatia Vex's magic shop was in a large, one-story brick building between a shipping concern and a damp little restaurant serving coffee and sandwiches to a clientele of longshoremen. The exterior of the shop resembled a small, disused factory; mundanes passing by along the Limehouse street would see only a padlocked door with brass letters above it, small windows filmed with dirt and grime.

Lucie knew that long ago, the place had been a curiosity shop owned by a faerie named Sallows. It had fallen into disuse after his death, but now the floors had been sanded and given a fresh coat of wax, and the walls were painted in scarlet and blue. A series of floor-to-ceiling shelves were already filled with merchandise, and a long display case served as the shop counter. Behind it stood Hypatia, dressed in a flowing purple gown with black silk frog closures. She had a pair of small spectacles perched on the bridge of her nose and was going through a stack of bills and invoices, muttering under her breath.

Anna and Ariadne had already arrived—Anna was leaning against the counter, examining her gloves as if searching for a flaw in the leather. Ariadne, dressed in gear, was looking in fascination at a dollhouse on one of the shelves in which small, living dolls—faeries, perhaps?—darted from room to room, playing tiny musical instruments and sleeping in Lilliputian beds.

"Lucie," Anna said, looking up with a smile. "I was beginning to wonder if you'd read my note."

"I did—only I was a bit delayed at the Shadow Market," said Lucie.

"What an exciting life you do lead," Anna said. "Now, mind your manners. Hypatia thinks the workmen have been cheating her, and she isn't in a good mood."

"I can hear you," Hypatia snapped, scowling. "Never hire gnome workmen, Herondale. They will overcharge you for lumber."

Being overcharged for lumber was *not* the sort of thing that happened to heroines in books. Lucie sighed inwardly—she'd hoped that by the time she'd gotten there, Anna would have charmed Hypatia into a good mood. Clearly, that hadn't happened. She hesitated, wondering how much she should say. Anna knew more than Ariadne about what Lucie and the others had been up to, but neither girl had any idea of the true purpose of Lucie's mission.

"Madame Vex," Lucie said, "we've come because we need your help."

Hypatia looked up from her bills. Some of her cloudlike hair had escaped the colorful scarf she'd used to tie it back, and there were ink stains on her hands. "Do you Shadowhunters ever come for any other reason? And I see you sent Anna to wheedle me." She eyed Anna. "While I am quite fond of her, the last time we dallied, your friends ran off with my Pyxis box. It was an antique."

"It had a demon in it," Anna pointed out. "We probably did you a favor taking it safely off your hands."

"The demon," Hypatia said, "was also an antique. Regardless, I am not available for dalliances at the moment. I have a gentleman caller."

Anna had finished her inspection of her glove. She smiled at Hypatia, and Lucie marveled—despite the Pyxis, despite Hypatia's gentleman caller, she could see the warlock soften just a bit. Anna's charm was a magical thing. "Speaking of gentleman callers," she said. "There's something I brought to show you." From inside her jacket, Anna produced a small silver snuffbox, engraved with the initials MB in blocky script. "This belongs to our mutual friend Magnus Bane. He has been looking for it for quite some time."

"You stole Magnus Bane's snuffbox?" said Ariadne. "Anna, that could not *possibly* be a good idea. He'll set you on fire. *Magic* fire."

"Of course I didn't," said Anna, turning the small box over in her hands. "As it happens, my boot maker—a fine gentleman, one of the Tanner family—once had *une liaison passionnée* with Magnus. Boot makers are a surprisingly tempestuous bunch. When things ended badly between them, the boot maker pinched Magnus's snuffbox, knowing he was fond of it." She smiled at Hypatia. "I thought you might like to give it back to him. I'm sure he would be most grateful."

Hypatia raised a dark eyebrow. "And how did you know that Mr. Bane is my gentleman caller? I thought we'd been rather discreet."

"I know everything," said Anna matter-of-factly.

Hypatia eyed the snuffbox. "I can see that you are not offering me something for nothing. What do you want?"

"To speak with you about an issue having to do with warlocks," Anna said. "An old issue, recently—disinterred, so to speak. The death of a Shadowhunter boy named Jesse Blackthorn."

Hypatia looked alarmed. "You think a warlock *harmed* a Shadowhunter child? You can't imagine I'd—"

Lucie winced inwardly. She almost wished she could explain to Hypatia that it was the nameless warlock's involvement in what had happened to Jesse *after* he died that she most needed to understand. She knew that was impossible, though: if anyone learned what she knew, what Grace knew, the danger to Jesse's continued existence would be immense.

"Please don't mistake our intent," Ariadne said in an even, soothing tone. "We are not looking to bring trouble to anyone. Jesse Blackthorn is long dead. We only wish to know what happened to him."

Hypatia stared suspiciously at the three of them for a long moment, then threw up her hands with a sigh. She pushed her papers aside, searching the counter until she found a dish of candy pastilles and selected one, not bothering to offer any to the others. "So tell me, what is it you think this warlock was hired to do?"

"You know about first runes?" Lucie said, and Hypatia nodded, looking bored. "Most children get through the procedure easily. A few suffer ill effects. Jesse Blackthorn died in agony." She swallowed hard. "And—we are told a warlock may have been involved in what happened to him."

Hypatia popped the sweet into her mouth. "Would his mother have been a woman with a peculiar Russian sort of name?"

"Yes," Lucie said eagerly. "Tatiana."

Hypatia regarded them over her tented hands. "Some years ago she sought a warlock's help in putting protection spells on her son. He had just been born, and she did not want to involve the Silent Brothers or Iron Sisters. She claimed she didn't trust Shadowhunters. Can't blame her, but none of us wanted to get involved—none of us except Emmanuel Gast."

Emmanuel Gast. A shudder ran through Lucie as she remembered Gast's body lying ruined on the bare floorboards of his flat. *Flesh and bone had been carved apart, ribs cracked open to show a collapsed red cavern. Blood had sunk in black grooves into the wooden floor. The most human-looking part of him left were his hands, his arms outflung with the hands turned palm up as if he were begging for mercy he had not received.*

Emmanuel Gast had done Belial's bidding, and been killed for it. A suspicion stirred in the back of Lucie's mind, though she kept her expression blankly curious.

"The warlock who was killed during the summer?" said Ariadne.

"That's the one." Hypatia seemed unperturbed. "He was quite corrupt—the warlock council eventually had to forbid him to practice magic."

"So is it possible," said Ariadne, "that he placed the protection spells on Jesse Blackthorn, but he did it incorrectly? They're meant to be done by the Silent Brothers."

"And that caused the first rune to malfunction somehow? A clever thought," said Anna, and the two girls looked at each other, seeming to enjoy a moment of shared detecting.

Maybe it was more than detecting. Ariadne gazed at Anna with unabashed longing, Lucie realized, and Anna—was there a softness in the way she looked back at Ariadne? It was not a look Lucie had seen on Anna's face before.

Lucie glanced away and caught Hypatia Vex smirking again. "There you go, Shadowhunters," she said. "A bit of assistance, in exchange for a snuffbox. Remember that I was helpful the next time the Institute needs to hire a warlock."

"Oh, we will indeed remember it," said Lucie, though her mind was still on Emmanuel Gast. *Why have you dragged me back to this place of agony? What do you want, Shadowhunter?*

Hypatia made a shooing gesture. "Now go. Having Shadowhunters about isn't good for business."

Lucie forced a pleasant smile onto her face as she followed Anna and Ariadne out to the street. She'd better hurry herself into a cab, she thought—her cousin Anna was a keenly perceptive person, and the last thing Lucie wanted was for anyone to guess the task that lay ahead of her tonight.

"Thomas Lightwood," said Alastair. "I am nothing like you."

All Thomas could do was stare. He had been so sure. But Alastair's gaze was steady, his voice resolute. Dear God, Thomas thought, about to rise to his feet, there was nothing for it now but to go and bury his terrible humiliation at the other side of the room. Perhaps he could hide behind a candelabra.

"I am nothing like you, Thomas," said Alastair, "because you are one of the better people I have ever known. You have a kind nature and a heart like some knight out of legend. Brave and proud and true and strong. All of it." He smiled bitterly. "And all the time you have known me, I have been a terrible person. So, you see. We are nothing at all alike."

Thomas's gaze snapped up. This wasn't what he was expecting. He searched Alastair's face, but his eyes were hard mirrors, giving nothing away.

"I'm not—" Thomas bit off the words before he could stop himself. He *was* kind; he knew that. Sometimes he wished he wasn't. "That's not what I meant."

"I know what you meant." The words hung between them, neither daring to move a muscle. After a moment Alastair added in a gentler voice, "How did you know about Charles?"

"You wouldn't tell me what you were doing in Paris," said Thomas. "But you mentioned Charles, over and over again, like you got pleasure out of just saying his name. And when you came to London this summer, I saw the way you looked at him. I know what it is to have to hide the—the signs of affection."

"Then I imagine you may have noticed I don't look at Charles that way anymore."

"I suppose I did," Thomas said, "though for the past four months, I've been trying not to look at *you*. I told myself I hated you. But I could never really make myself. When Elias died, all I could think about was you. What you must be feeling."

Alastair winced. "I insulted your father and blackened his name. You were under no obligation to care about mine."

"I know, but sometimes I think that it is much harder to lose someone who we are on bad terms with than it is to lose someone with whom all is well."

"Bloody hell, Thomas. You should hate me, not be thinking about what I must be feeling—" Alastair swiped at his eyes; Thomas realized with a stunned shock that they were bright with tears. "And the worst of it is, you're right, of course. You always understood other people so well. I think I partly hated you for it, for being so kind. I thought, 'He must have so much, to be able to be so generous.' And I thought that I had nothing. It never occurred to me that you had secrets too."

"You were always my secret," said Thomas softly, and Alastair turned a startled gaze on him.

"Does no one know?" said Alastair. "That you—like men? How long have you known?"

"Since after I came to school, I think," Thomas said in a low voice. "I knew what caught my eye, quickened my pulse, and it was never a girl."

"And you never told anyone?"

Thomas hesitated. "I could have told my friends that I liked men. They would have understood. But I couldn't have told them how I felt about *you*."

"So you did feel something for me. I thought—" Alastair looked away, shaking his head. "I didn't *see* you—you were this boy, following me around at school, and then I met you in Paris and you'd grown up and turned into Michelangelo's *David*. I thought you were beautiful. But I was still caught up with Charles—" He broke off. "Just another thing I've wasted. Your regard for me. I wasted my time and my affection on Charles. I wasted my chance with you."

Thomas felt light-headed. Had Alastair just said, *I thought you were beautiful?* Alastair, who was literally the most beautiful person Thomas had ever known? "Maybe not," he said. "About me, I mean."

Alastair blinked. "Speak sense, Lightwood," he said testily. "What do you mean?"

"I mean this," said Thomas, and leaned in to kiss Alastair on the mouth.

It was a quick kiss—Thomas had never kissed anyone before, really, just a few furtive moments in a shadowy corner of the Devil Tavern—and nearly chaste. Alastair's pupils flared; even as Thomas drew back hesitantly, Alastair caught hold of Thomas's shirtfront in a firm grip. He slid onto his knees so that they faced each other; with Thomas sitting back on his heels, their heads were at the same level.

"Thomas—" Alastair began. His voice was rough, unsteady; Thomas hoped he had something to do with that. Abruptly, Alastair let go of Thomas's shirt, started to turn his face away.

"Just imagine," Thomas said. "What if we'd never gone to the Academy together? What if none of those things had happened, and Paris was the first time we'd met? And this was the second?"

Alastair said nothing. This close, Thomas could see the gray flecks in his dark eyes, like delicate veins of crystal in black marble.

Then Alastair smiled. It was the ghost of his old arrogant smile, just touched with the lofty wickedness Thomas remembered from school. It had made his heart skip a beat then; it raced now. "Damn you, Thomas," he said, and there was resignation in his voice, but something else, too, something dark and sweet and intense.

A moment later he was pulling Thomas toward him. Their bodies collided, awkward and thrilling. Thomas closed his eyes, unable to bear so much feeling, as Alastair's lips touched his—gently, at first, but with growing confidence, he explored Thomas's mouth, and it was like flying, like nothing Thomas had ever imagined. The heat and pressure of Alastair's mouth, the softness of his lips and skin, the sheer intensity of breathing and moving together with *Alastair Carstairs*.

He had never imagined anything like this. Nothing like the soft growling noise Alastair made as his hands roamed Thomas's chest, his shoulders, as if they were places he'd been longing to touch for some time. Nothing like the feel of Alastair's pulse against his lips as Thomas kissed the arch of his throat. And in the moment, Thomas could only think that if he had to be arrested for murder for this to happen, it had been worth it.

Christopher carefully fitted a rubber stopper to the last of the test tubes. Since Grace left, he had busied himself recording the results of his experiments on the *pithos* so far, but it had been hard to stay focused. He'd been thinking about secrets, about how other people seemed to somehow know what was good to share with others and what should be kept to oneself, what words could encourage and which caused hurt, how some people surprised him by not grasping the simplest concepts, no matter how carefully he explained them, while others . . .

While others seemed to understand Christopher even without a considerable effort on his part. Not very many others: Henry, certainly; and Thomas, usually; and frequently—though not always—the rest of his friends.

But Grace, confoundingly, seemed to see Christopher clearly. Talking to her had been so easy that he'd forgotten to filter everything he said, going over it to make sure it would come out right before speaking.

He wouldn't tell anyone about her sneaking into the lab, not until he'd had more time to think about it. Was this why James had been drawn to Grace? But James wasn't interested in experiments and science—not the way Grace seemed to be. She'd been so eager to look through the microscope at the gunpowder compounds he'd been studying; so curious to see the contents of his journals.

But it was silly to dwell on it. Grace would likely never visit the lab again. It was too bad—many great discoveries had been made by teams working in tandem. Look at the Curies, who had just won the Nobel Prize for their experiments with radiation. Perhaps if he told her about the Curies . . .

Christopher's thoughts were interrupted by a banging at the front entrance. He hurried upstairs to answer it; the rest of the household must have gone to bed hours ago. He opened the door to find Matthew waiting on the stoop. He was bundled in a red wool coat, hatless and blowing on his hands for warmth.

Christopher blinked in surprise. "Why are you knocking on the door to your own house?"

Matthew rolled his eyes. "I think they've changed the locks. My mother, making a point as usual."

"Oh. Well, do you want to come in?"

"No need; I'm just on an errand. James sent me. You still have that *pithos*, don't you?"

"I do!" Christopher said, brightening. Excitedly he explained the discovery that the stele removed runes from one person and transferred them to another. Though—for reasons he couldn't entirely explain—he left Grace out of it. "I must say, I find it very strange," he concluded. "And inefficient! But the killer must be murdering people and taking their runes for some dark purpose that we do not yet grasp."

"Right, I see," Matthew said, though Christopher wasn't sure he did see, as he hadn't appeared to be paying attention. "Whatever its purpose, James needs it right away—so I had best take it to him now."

Of course James would already have a plan of some kind—James was always coming up with plans. Christopher felt around in his pockets and located one of the white rags he used for cleaning his instruments. He carefully wrapped the *pithos* in it and handed it to Matthew.

"It's just as well you take it," he said. "I'm completely exhausted anyway. I'm going to sleep in your room, if you don't mind, seeing as you've got a whole other flat."

"Of course," Matthew said, tucking the *pithos* into a pocket inside his coat. "My home is yours."

They said their goodbyes, and then Christopher went up to Matthew's room, which looked oddly bare since Matthew had taken many of his books and belongings with him when he moved. Something tickled the back of Christopher's scientific mind—something about Matthew, something he'd forgotten to tell him, perhaps? But he was too exhausted to think much on it. There would be plenty of time to sort things out tomorrow.

22

HEART OF IRON

And there the children of dark Night have their dwellings,
Sleep and Death, awful gods. The glowing Sun never looks upon
them with his beams, neither as he goes up into heaven, nor
as he comes down from heaven. And the former of them roams
peacefully over the earth and the sea's broad back and is kindly
to men; but the other has a heart of iron, and his spirit within
him is pitiless as bronze: whomsoever of men he has once seized
he holds fast: and he is hateful even to the deathless gods.
—Hesiod, *Theogony*

"Concentrate on what, precisely?" James said. He felt slightly nervous: Magnus's gaze was focused and intent, as if he were staring *into* James and through him.

"You truly have your grandfather's blood in you," Magnus murmured, still staring at James with a curious expression.

James stiffened. He knew Magnus meant nothing by it: it was a statement of fact and nothing more. Still, not pleasant words to James's ears. "There are doors in your mind that lead to other worlds," said Magnus. "A mind forever voyaging, as they say. I have never seen anything like it. I understand that Jem has taught you how to close them, but your control is not yet perfect." He dropped his hands with a smile. "Well, never mind, we shall voyage together."

Not entirely sure he wanted the answer, James said, "Are you not at all concerned what my parents will say when they find out we have risked this? And they *will* find out."

"Oh, undoubtedly." Magnus waved a breezy hand. James shot a look at Cordelia, who stood by the study door with her sword drawn, looking like a statue of Joan of Arc. She shrugged as if to say, *Well, it's Magnus.*

"James, I believe your parents will understand, once they have a grasp of the gravity of the situation," said Magnus. "Nor, considering their own past activities, do they have much of a leg to stand on." He laid a long-fingered hand over James's chest, atop his heart. "Now, no more of this trying to shock or upset you to bring you into the shadow realm. It isn't necessary."

James looked at him in surprise, but the world was already sliding away to grayness. The familiar walls of the study turned to monochromatic dust; the books and couches and chairs crumbled and vanished. James was rising, spinning into the void.

He had never experienced travel into the shadow realm like this before. The world hurtled away from James, as if he were rocketing down a tunnel. One moment the study was there, the fire, Cordelia, the London night beyond the window. The next his familiar world was flying away—he reached out to catch it, to grab on, but only darkness surrounded him; no moon, no stars, just a darkness that felt infinite, never-ending.

A light flared in the shadows, an amber glow that gradually intensified. Magnus stood a few feet away from James, yellow light playing around his right hand. He gazed about, frowning. "This," he said, "is not Edom."

James got to his feet, the world righting itself around him. Suddenly there was an up and a down, a sense of gravity absent a real sense of space. And there was ground underfoot, or something like it. It was not the dust of Edom, but a smooth and polished surface, stretching into the infinite distance, made up of alternating squares of dark and light. "Magnus," he said, "I think we may be standing on a chessboard."

Magnus muttered something under his breath. It sounded as if he were cursing in another language. James turned in a circle: he thought he could see glints above him, like pinprick holes in the black sky. A faint glow clung to everything: he could see it outlining his hands, his feet. Magnus seemed to be glowing slightly too. James moved his hand across the air and watched his bracelet glitter.

"James, think," Magnus said. "Can you picture Edom, the last time you saw it? Can you recall the dark fortress?"

James took a deep breath. The cold air tasted like metal, silvery-sharp. He had never felt so far away from home, yet he was not at all afraid. Somewhere, he thought, somewhere very close, if he could just reach out—

And then he saw it, a small whirlwind, like a miniature sandstorm. He stepped back as it grew, solidifying, taking shape.

It was a throne. The sort of throne James had seen in books, illustrating pictures of angels—ivory and gold, with gold steps rising up toward a massive seat. A peculiar symbol was carved repeatedly into the sides, spiky and odd-looking, and across its back were written the words: AND HE WHO OVERCOMES, AND HE WHO KEEPS MY DEEDS UNTIL THE END, TO HIM I WILL GIVE AUTHORITY OVER THE NATIONS; AND HE SHALL RULE THEM WITH A ROD OF IRON, AND I WILL GIVE HIM THE MORNING STAR.

This was an angel's throne, he thought, or at least it had been made to look very like one. And the words carved on the throne were in Latin, though the strange symbol carved across the sides and arms was nothing he recognized—

No, he thought. He did recognize it. He'd seen it in that book, just the other day. Belial's sigil. He glanced over at Magnus, who closed his fist, his expression wary. The amber light that had glowed from his fingers vanished.

"Grandfather," James said, looking at the throne. "Grandfather, show yourself."

James heard a low chuckle, very near, as if someone leaned close to his ear. He jumped back as Belial appeared on the throne, lounging rather casually. He wore the same pale suit he'd worn in Belphegor's realm, the color of mourning, with white lace at the cuffs and throat. His hair was that same mix of white and gray, like dove's feathers. "I'm surprised, James. I was left with the impression that you wanted nothing to do with me. Have you reconsidered my offer?"

"No," James said.

"I am abashed," said Belial, who looked no such thing. "It would seem you have sought me out, not the other way around. Did you come here to scold me?"

"Would you believe," James said, "I didn't come here for *you* at all?"

"Probably not," Belial said. "You must admit it does seem unlikely. I see you brought a warlock with you." His steel-colored eyes danced across Magnus. "And a son of Asmodeus at that. My *nephew*."

"'How art thou fallen from Heaven, O Lucifer, son of the morning,'" said Magnus, in a thoughtful sort of tone, and James realized he was quoting the Bible. "'For thou hast said in thine heart, I will ascend into Heaven, I will exalt my throne above the stars of God, I will ascend above the heights of the clouds; I will be like the most High.'"

Belial finished the quote. "'Yet thou shalt be brought down to Hell, to the sides of the Pit.'"

"Quite," said Magnus.

"You are very rude," said Belial. "Does your father enjoy being reminded of the Fall? For I doubt it."

"I don't much care what he enjoys," said Magnus. "My father is not a thief, however; he does not go about robbing others of their homes. Lilith is powerful. Do you not fear her wrath?"

Belial began to laugh. The sound seemed to echo off the polished floor, off the far points of light James had begun to suspect were very distant stars. "Fear *Lilith*? Oh, that is amusing."

"You should be afraid," said Magnus, very softly. "You have one. You only need three."

Belial's laughter stopped. The look he bent on Magnus was fleeting, but filled with a sudden, sour hatred. "I do not like trespassers," he said. "Or, for that matter, nephews."

He flicked his hand toward Magnus, and Magnus—with a shout— was lifted off his feet and flung bodily into the darkness. James gave a cry and ran toward the place where he'd vanished, but he was gone. There was no sign he'd ever been there at all.

You have one. You only need three.

James glanced back at Belial, who was regarding him with a cold calculation. It was clear Belial had not expected his presence here, and—like a chess master surprised by an unexpected move—was wondering how to turn the situation to his advantage.

"If Magnus is hurt," James said, "I will be very upset."

"Such an odd child you are," Belial said. "As if it would matter what you felt. I admit, though, I am curious: If you did not come here to seek me out, then why come?"

James considered. Belial was clever; it would take a careful lie to fool him. "I wanted to see Edom. It was there that I intended to travel."

"I see." Belial's eyes gleamed. "I had rather expected incursions into my new realm, so I set this gate here to stop intruders." He gestured airily at the chessboard darkness. "I did not expect *you* to be one of the intruders. What interest could you have in Edom?"

"Magnus had heard you stole the realm from Lilith, the mother of warlocks," said James. "I suppose I was curious what my grandfather could want with such a trackless waste. I was curious about you. Your plans."

"Bane pities Lilith, I imagine," said Belial. "Warlocks are taught she is their ancestor, and to worship her. But if you did the same, you would bestow your sympathy on the undeserving." He leaned back against the throne. "Lilith was Adam's first wife in Eden, you know, but she left the Garden to couple with the demon Sammael. The world's first unfaithful female." He smiled sourly. "She is known as a murderer of children, whatever the warlocks may tell you differently."

"I do not pity her," said James, "nor any of you ancient demons— for all your claims to royalty, your thrones and titles, for all your pride, you are nothing more than the first evil the world ever saw."

Belial narrowed his eyes.

"I see why you made this place a chessboard," said James. "Worlds, lives, all are a game to you."

"Might I remind you," said Belial, with a cryptic smile, "I did not seek you out. And here you come, fussing and angry, into *my* realm, *my* lands. I have left you quite alone—"

"You lie," James said, unable to help himself. "You have tormented me in dreams. Showed me every death. Made me live them." His breath came quickly. "Why are you murdering Shadowhunters and taking their runes? And why send me visions of what you're doing? Why would you want me to *know*?"

Belial's smile stayed fixed in place. He drummed his fingers—his hands were oddly curved, almost like claws—on the arms of his throne. "Visions, you say? I have not sent you any visions."

"And that is a *lie!*" James shouted. "Is this your game? If you cannot force me to obey you, you will drive me mad? Or do death and grief amuse you for their own sake?"

"Be *quiet*," said Belial, and his voice was like a slap. "Death and grief do in fact amuse me, but to assume you are worth my lies—that is arrogance indeed." He gazed down at James, and James realized with a spark of surprise that there was a red mark on the lapel of Belial's white suit. A red mark that was spreading.

It was blood from the wound Cortana had dealt him all those months ago. It was true then—he had not healed.

"You have one," James said, his voice ringing clearly through the darkness. "All you need is three."

Belial turned his burning eyes on James. "What did you say, child of my blood?"

"One wound," said James, gambling that he was right. "You already have one mortal wound from Cortana. All it takes is three—"

"*Be silent!*" Belial roared, and suddenly James could see *through* the beautiful human mask of his face to what lay within—a terrible pit born of fire and shifting shadows. James knew he was seeing Belial's true face, a burning scar across the skin of the universe.

"I am a Prince of Hell," said Belial, in a voice like flame. "Such is my power. You think your protection will save you? It will not. You are human, as is she who bears Cortana—maggots crawling across the Earth." He rose to his feet, the image of a human man, but James could see what lay behind and beyond the false image. A pillar of fire, of cloud, of lightning black as night. "I shall raise my throne above the stars of God! I shall walk upon the Earth and my reach shall exceed the heavens! And *you will not stop me!*"

He began to advance on James. There was a hunger in his gaze, a terrifying wordless appetite. James began to retreat, backing away from his grandfather.

"You have brought yourself to my place of strength," Belial said. "There is no land here for you to reach into and turn against me."

"It doesn't matter." James was still backing up, stepping carefully across the alternating squares: white, black, white. "You cannot touch me."

Belial grinned. "You think you are protected here, because you are protected on Earth?" he said. "I invite you to test that theory." He took another step forward and winced—he covered it quickly, but James had not missed it. Belial's wound was paining him still. "In fact, why have you not already tried to escape back to your little world?" Belial mused. "Are you unwelcome there? Tired of the place? Worlds are small things, aren't they?" He smirked. "Or is it that you don't know how to get back, without your warlock to help you?"

Picture Edom, Magnus had said. James now tried the opposite—he pictured his study, the familiar little room, the fire, the books, the painting over the mantel. But though he could conjure a memory of it perfectly well, it refused to take on life or realness. It was an image only, adrift against the back of his eyelids when he shut his eyes.

"As I thought," Belial said, reaching for James. His fingers seemed to have grown longer, like spindly crab's legs. They flexed, white and sharp-tipped. "You have no power here—"

The explosion rocked James back on his feet. He had moved so quickly he had barely felt it himself—his hand under his jacket, the metal against his fingers, the recoil of the gun. The scent of gunpowder mixed with the metallic scent of the air.

He looked at Belial wildly; he knew the shot had not gone wide. Belial hadn't moved. He stood with his teeth bared, his hand outstretched in front of him, closed into a fist. As James stared, Belial opened his hand slowly. James's heart sank. In the center of Belial's palm lay a bullet, glowing red.

"You *fool*," Belial said, and flung the bullet at James; James heard the sound of fabric tearing as the bullet grazed his upper arm. He staggered as something caught hold of him—it felt like a great, invisible hand—and sent him flying. He landed awkwardly on his shoulder, the gun spinning out of his grasp. He rolled over, agony shooting up his arm, and began to crawl after it.

The same invisible hand caught him again. He was flipped over onto his back, gasping; he stared up at the figure that towered over him.

Belial seemed to have grown to a height of ten feet. He was grinning, his face cracking like old wallpaper. Through the cracks James glimpsed a terrible infinity—flame and darkness, agony and despair. In a low, mocking tone, Belial said, "You truly sought to kill me, James? 'Behold, I am alive forevermore, and have the keys of Hell and of death.'"

"I have read that quote," James said, struggling up onto his elbows. "But I do not think it was about you."

Belial turned to look at the horizon, such as it was. It was a relief to James, if a small one, to no longer have to look at his grandfather's face. "They are meaningless words, James," he said. "The truth interpreted by humans is fact seen through a cloudy glass. Soon enough, you will agree to my terms. You will let me possess you. And I will rule the Earth—*we* will rule the Earth." He turned back to James; he looked fully human again, calm and smiling. "You like to save lives. A peculiar hobby, but I will indulge it. Join with me now, and there need be no more death."

James rose slowly to his feet. "You know I would rather die."

"Really?" Belial spoke mockingly. "It can be arranged, easily enough, but think of all you'd miss. Your *sweet* little parents. Your sister—how sad she would be to lose you. Your *parabatai*: I hear a wound like that will mark him for the rest of his life. And that adorable little wife of yours. I'm sure she would miss you."

James's hand tightened into a fist, sending a slow pulse of blood down his arm.

Daisy.

Like someone falling, reaching desperately for a handhold, his mind caught and clung to the thought of Cordelia. Cordelia picking strawberries at Cirenworth, dancing in her ashes-of-roses gown at the Institute ball, walking up the aisle of the Institute's chapel toward him, whirling with Cortana in her hand. Her face when she was reading: the bow of her mouth, curve of her throat, arch of her hand.

Cordelia.

"Come now, James," said Belial. "There is no need to be so stubborn. You can rest. Give yourself to me, be mine. I will let you sleep—"

Light burst into the darkness, illuminating shadows that had never seen illumination before, like the first sunrise of the world. Belial cried out; James threw up his arm, shielding his eyes as the brightness grew and grew, a lance of fire across his vision.

Cortana. A golden seam across his vision, widening. Images rose up to nearly blind him—he could see the skyline of London, the blaze of sunlight on ice, Thomas bound to a chair, the fiery baubles at the Shadow Market, green grass and Matthew throwing a stick for Oscar, the room above the Devil Tavern, Lucie and his parents turning toward him, Jem in the shadows. And there were hands on his shoulders, and they were hers, Cordelia's, and she said, in a voice of absolute determination:

"He is not yours. He is mine. *He is mine.*"

James's vision crackled out to blackness. There was the familiar twisting, whirling nothingness of the shadow realm, the great chessboard, Belial, the throne, all splintering into the void—and seconds later James landed hard enough to jar his bones.

Pain shot through his arm and he cried out. He heard someone say his name, and he opened his eyes: it was Cordelia. He was back in the study of the house on Curzon Street and she was standing over him, ashen, Cortana in her hand. "James," she gasped. "James, what did you—"

He sat up, looking around dizzily. Quite a bit of the furniture in the room seemed to have fallen over; a delicate occasional table lay in splinters before the hearth. Magnus Bane sat in the corner of the room, one hand knotted into the front of his brightly colored waistcoat, his face contorted with pain.

James used his right hand to brace himself on the chess table and lever himself upright. It took longer than he would have liked. Pain made him breathless as he said, "Daisy. You're all right—?"

She nodded. "Yes, but I don't know about Magnus." She started to pick her way through the tumbled furniture toward the warlock. "He just reappeared here and collapsed—and then I heard you calling—"

James puzzled at that, but there was no time to ask. "Magnus," he said. "If Belial did something to you, we'll have to call the Silent Brothers—Jem, maybe—"

Magnus had risen painfully to his feet. He held out a hand, shaking his head firmly. "I'm fine. Just stunned. I didn't realize Belial would be blocking the entrance to Edom."

"Belial was—" Cordelia swallowed down her questions, looking from James to Magnus and back again. "What do we do now?"

Magnus moved stiffly toward the door. "This is much worse than I'd thought. Do nothing, do you understand? Take no more risks. I must reach the Spiral Labyrinth and speak with the warlock council."

"Let us at least help you," said James. "You could take our carriage—"

"No." Magnus spoke sharply. "You must trust me. Remain here. Keep yourselves safe."

Without another word, he was gone. In the distance, James heard the front door slam. Bewildered and more than a little dizzy, James turned to Cordelia, only to realize she was staring at him in horror.

"*James*," she said. "You're bleeding."

To Cordelia's relief, James's wound was not as serious as it looked. He had stripped off his jacket with uncharacteristic obedience, making her wince—the sleeve of the shirt was soaked through with blood. She unbuttoned the shirt with shaking fingers—it seemed moments ago that James had helped her with her coat in the entryway—and hissed through her teeth. Something had dug a shallow groove along James's bicep.

"And Belial did this?" she demanded, reaching for a damp rag to sponge the blood away. It was generally better to get a look at a cut before using a healing rune on it, lest the *iratze* close up skin over dirt or debris in the wound. "By *throwing* a bullet at you?"

"Seems so," said James. "Oddly, not a power of his that was mentioned in the *Monarchia Daemonium*."

He'd told her what had happened in the shadow realm as Cordelia had gotten bandages and water, and somehow found her stele. She set the stele to his skin now, carefully etching *iratzes* onto the skin below the cut. James flinched and said, "And the bloody gun's gone. I lost it there. What a mess."

"It's not important," Cordelia said firmly. "You've other weapons, just as good."

He looked at her quietly for a moment. "How did you—come to me where I was?"

"I'm not sure," Cordelia said. "I heard you call out for me. It was as if I was pulled toward you—but all I could see was shadows, and then I knew you in the dark. That you were there. I lifted up Cortana so I could see, and I heard Belial's voice." *Give yourself to me, be mine. I will let you sleep.*

He glanced up at her; she was standing over him as he sat on the arm of one of the upholstered chairs. They had abandoned the study for the drawing room, where the furniture was still upright. Witchlight glowed from sconces above the mantel, softly illuminating the room.

"I was afraid," Cordelia said, "after Magnus came back without you, that you would be trapped there." "Afraid" seemed a pale word for it. She had been terrified. "Did you open a door to return? Like a Portal?"

His golden eyes searched her face. She moved the stele up his arm, to make a third Mark: the graze was already healing, closing into a scar. Dirt and blood stained his undershirt, and his cheekbone was scraped, his hair a wild explosion. She wondered if it was odd that in some ways she preferred this James—mess and blood and sweat and all—to the perfectly behaved gentleman with the Mask at the ready. "Perhaps Belial didn't want me there," he said, which was not quite an answer to the question. "He did say he never sent me any visions of the murders—never intended me to see them at all."

"Do you believe that?"

"Yes," said James, after a pause. "I know he's a liar, but he usually wants me to think he's all-powerful. I don't see the advantage of lying to me in a way that makes it seem as if he made a mistake."

"Then what does that mean?"

"I don't know," James said, though Cordelia suspected he had some guesses. "But I believe I do understand why he is so fearful of Cortana and of you. When we were in the shadow realm, Magnus said to him, 'You have one. You only need three.'"

"One what?"

"One wound, I think," said James. "From Cortana. It still hasn't healed. It's like the wound of the Fisher King; it bleeds and bleeds. I guessed that two more blows from the sword—mortal wounds, not scratches—could finish him. And when I mentioned that, Belial seemed terrified."

Cordelia stepped back to examine her handiwork. James's arm and shoulder were still bruised, but the cut was a thin white line now. She dropped the small towel she'd been holding into the copper bowl of pinkish water on the table and said, "But I don't understand. They say nothing can kill a Prince of Hell, so how could Cortana do it? No matter the number of blows?"

James's golden eyes shone. "I cannot say, not yet. But I believe all the stories are true, even the ones that contradict each other. Perhaps *especially* those." He reached out to take the stele from her hand; surprised, she let him do it. "You asked me before if I opened a door to return here. I didn't. I *couldn't*. Magnus was right—it's not something I ever practiced with Jem, or even considered that I could do: opening paths between worlds with my mind."

"Magnus seemed so sure—"

"Well, I tried. I thought of this house, the study, tried to picture every piece of it. Nothing worked. I might as well have been trapped in quicksand." He set the stele down. "Until I thought of you."

"Of me?" Cordelia said, a little blankly, as James rose to his feet. Now she was looking up at him, at his serious eyes, his thick lashes, the grim turn to the corners of his mouth.

"I thought of you," he said again, "and it was as if you were there, with me. I saw your face. Your hair . . ." He wound a finger through a dangling curl beside her face. She could feel the warmth from his hand against her cheek. "And I was no longer afraid. I knew I would be able to come home, because of you. That you would lead me back. You are my constant star, Daisy."

She wondered for a moment if he were light-headed—though she had given him a blood-replacement rune. "James, I—"

His fingers stroked down her cheek, slid under her chin. He lifted her face gently. "I only want to know one thing," he said. "Did you mean it, what you said?"

"Mean what?"

"What you said in the shadow realm," he murmured. "That I was yours."

Her stomach lurched; she'd fancied he hadn't heard her. She remembered shouting the words into the shadows; she had not been able to see Belial, but she had sensed him, all around, sensed his claws in James.

But clearly he had. His golden eyes were fixed on her, lovely as sunrise, fierce as a hawk's gaze. She said, "It doesn't matter what I said. I wanted him to leave you alone—"

"I don't believe you," he said. She could feel the slight tremors running through his body—tremors of stress, which meant he was forcing himself to otherwise hold very still. "You don't say things you don't mean, Daisy—"

"Fine." She jerked her chin up, away from his hand, her mouth trembling as she said, "I meant it, then—you belong to me and not to him—you will *never* belong to him, James—"

The breath went out of her in a gasp as his arms circled her and he lifted her off her feet. Cordelia knew she was no delicate little doll like Lucie, but James swept her up as if she weighed no more than a parasol. Her hands came down on his shoulders just as he clamped his mouth over hers, stopping her words, her breath, with one explosive kiss.

Blood sang in her ears. His mouth was hot and open over hers; she parted her lips as his tongue swept inside, stroking, caressing. She pressed against him, fingers digging into his skin, wanting more, running her own tongue over his lips, the soft inside of his mouth. He tasted like honey.

They sank to the floor, James still holding her; he let her down gently onto the carpet, arching over her, his expression drunk and dizzy. "Daisy," he whispered. "Daisy, my Daisy."

Cordelia knew that if she told him to stop, he would, immediately and without question. But it was the last thing she wanted. His body stretched the length of hers, pressing her into the yielding carpet; he was stripped to his undershirt, and she let her hands go free—sliding them up his biceps, feeling the swell of muscles there and in his back as he rose over her on his elbows.

"That's right," he whispered against her mouth. "Touch me—do what you want—anything—"

She reached down, tugging at his shirt, pushing her hands up under the fabric. She wanted to lay her hands on the place where his heart beat. She shimmied her palms up his bare chest, feeling the flutter in his belly as she skimmed its flat planes. Up over his rib cage, the smooth muscles of his chest—his skin was like silk, raveled here and there with the marks of old scars.

He pressed his forehead against her shoulder, shivering at her touch. "Daisy."

Cordelia felt again that power she had felt before. The knowledge that though James did not love her, he wanted her. Even despite himself, he wanted her. It was a shameful sort of power, stronger even for the guilt of it. "Kiss me," she whispered.

The words seemed to go through him with the force of lightning. He groaned, crushing his lips to hers before dragging kisses down her throat, over her collarbone. His hands found the buttons at the neck of her gown: he flicked them open one by one, pressing his lips to each inch of newly uncovered skin. Cordelia sucked in a deep breath of air—she had dressed herself, and there was no corset, no chemise under the gown. She heard his sharp inhalation as the fabric fell away, baring the tops of her breasts.

He splayed his hand wide, stroking over her skin, even as he surged up to press his lips to hers again. She kissed him back eagerly, winding her fingers into the silky tangle of his black hair. His hand shaped itself to cup her breast. He moaned softly against her mouth, murmuring that she was beautiful, that she was his—

Distantly, she heard something that sounded like the chime of metal, like the striking of a delicate, tiny instrument. . . .

James gasped and pulled away, half sitting up. His hand had gone to his right wrist; there was a red mark there, like a burn. But there was something else—something missing.

She looked down. His silver bracelet, the one he always wore, lay in two broken halves on the hearth.

Cordelia sat up, hastily buttoning her gown back up. She could feel her cheeks flaming red as James, on his knees now, reached to pick the pieces up, turning them over in his hands. Cordelia could see the long cracks that ran through the metal, as if it had been subjected to intense pressure and torsion. The words that had once been carved within the turn of the metal were nearly illegible now: LOYAULTÉ ME LIE.

Loyalty Binds Me.

James, she could say. *James, I'm so sorry.*

But she wasn't sorry. She crossed her arms over her chest; every piece of her body still felt alive, sparking with excitement. Her legs were shaking; apparently it took one's body a bit longer than one's mind to realize the state of current events. Her hair was a tangled mess, coursing down over her shoulders; she tossed it back and said, "James? What happened?"

He was still kneeling near the hearth's edge, his shirt rucked up where she'd half torn it off him. He turned the bracelet over in his hand and said, "Daisy, I think—"

His head snapped back. She saw his eyes—fully black, the whites gone utterly—as he spasmed once and crumpled, motionless, to the floor.

GRACE:
1903

Grace never mentioned a word about the bracelet to Jesse. He was
only present at night, of course, and avoided the Herondales on principle because they were apparently able to see ghosts, though James
had never seemed to glimpse him.

She told herself that there was no point in telling Jesse about the
spell. If she told him that James loved her, he would be encouraging
and happy for her, and she would feel terrible. And if she told him that
she and her mother controlled James's feelings, he would be horrified.

When they had moved to London in the summer, chasing James,
Tatiana desperate that the enchantment of the bracelet not be broken,
Grace had feared above all other things that now Jesse would find out.
That he would learn that she had exploited James, used him, tricked
him. That he would believe she was a monster.

And perhaps she was, but she couldn't bear to have Jesse think so.

23

A Silken Thread

I had a dove and the sweet dove died;
And I have thought it died of grieving.
O, what could it grieve for? Its feet were tied,
With a silken thread of my own hand's weaving.
— John Keats, "I had a dove"

"Jessamine," Lucie said crossly. "I *told* you, I am about to summon a ghost, and you won't like it at all. You don't even like other ghosts."

"But I do like *you*," said Jessamine. "And besides, your father told me to look after you while he was in Paris. I am quite sure he would not have approved of you summoning a ghost or other undead personage."

Lucie sank onto her bed with an exasperated sigh. Usually she didn't mind Jessamine floating about the place. When she was small, they'd had excellent games of hide-and-seek during which Jessamine continuously cheated by concealing herself in Lucie's shoeboxes or glove drawer (Jessamine saw no reason why she should be required to remain person-size just because Lucie was). Now that she was older, Jessamine often helped her find lost items or chatted with her while Tessa did her hair.

Now, however, having her here was decidedly inconvenient. Lucie had rushed home from the shop in Limehouse, entirely determined on what to do next, only to find Jessamine wafting about her bedroom with the curtains, complaining about being lonely. Getting rid of her without raising too much suspicion was turning out to be more difficult than she'd thought.

"See here," Lucie said. "I need to understand a—a thing that happened years ago. I can't get it out of the living, so . . ." She allowed her voice to trail off meaningfully.

"So you will go to the dead?" Jessamine said. "Lucie, as I have told you before, not all ghosts are like me, with kind eyes and a wonderful personality. This could turn out very badly."

"I know. I've met this ghost before. It's going to be extremely unpleasant," Lucie added, "and you won't like to see it. You should spare yourself and leave now."

Jessamine drew herself up. She had firmed up quite a bit around the edges and was giving Lucie her darkest glare. "I should say not. I will not leave your side. Whatever it is you have in mind, you should not be doing it without supervision!"

"I wouldn't do it at all, if it weren't absolutely necessary. But there is no need for you to trouble yourself over the matter, Jessamine."

"I *am* troubled over the matter," Jessamine said, making the lights flicker a bit for effect. "But I am not going anywhere." She crossed her arms over her chest and stuck her chin in the air.

Lucie sprang off the bed, brushing down her dress. She hadn't even had a chance to change clothes, and the hem of her skirt was still damp. "Stay, then, if you must."

She stood in the middle of her room and closed her eyes, then slowed her breath until she could count several heartbeats on every inhale and exhale. This was a process she had worked out for those times when she was having trouble focusing on her writing, but she'd found that it was useful for all sorts of things. It was what she'd done in the warehouse when she'd needed to reach Filomena, to summon her out of the shadows and air. . . .

She visualized a great darkness spreading around her, a darkness inhabited by points of light, scintillating like stars. This, she told herself, was the vast world of the dead. Somewhere, among these glimmering memories of what once was life, he was there.

Emmanuel Gast.

She felt a fluttering, as she had felt on a few occasions when she had tried to command the souls of animals. Gast's spirit was there—she felt it—but it did not want to come forth. She drew on him, feeling his soul's reluctance like the drag of a sleigh rail on a patch of earth.

Then, suddenly, it came free.

She gasped and opened her eyes. Gast's ghost hovered before her, glowering. The last time Lucie had encountered his ghost, he had borne the marks of his violent death—a slit throat and blood-soaked clothes. Now he seemed intact, though around him thrummed a violent tear in the world, a shimmer of darkness that vanished if looked at directly.

"I know you," Gast said. Dank hair straggled about his face, his rows of teeth showing in a scowl. "The girl in my flat. The one with the power to command the dead."

Jessamine shrank back, appalled. "Lucie, what is he—"

Oh no. Lucie had not expected Gast to spill the beans so quickly, or so thoroughly. She shook her head at Jessamine, as if to say that Gast didn't know what he was talking about.

"Emmanuel Gast," she said. "I summoned you because I need to know something about a Shadowhunter named Jesse Blackthorn. Do you remember him?"

Gast's mouth contorted in a sneer. "Yes, I remember him. Tatiana's whelp."

Lucie felt her heart skip a beat. "You *did* have something to do with what happened to him, then."

Jessamine made an uneasy noise. After a long pause, Gast said, "How would you know anything about that, Shadowhunter?"

"Just tell me what you know," Lucie said. "I won't ask you twice."

Gast crossed his arms and looked down his nose at her. "I suppose," he said finally, "it matters very little now."

"I already know about the protection spells," prompted Lucie.

"Indeed." The ghost seemed to be warming to his subject. "Tatiana Blackthorn didn't trust the Silent Brothers and Iron Sisters to do the work, of course. Didn't trust nearly anybody and least of all Shadowhunters. She hired me to work the spells instead."

"But when the Voyance rune was put on Jesse, he died," said Lucie. "Would that have something to do with the protection spells?"

Gast spit in disgust—a spark of white translucence that vanished before it struck the floor. "I am not the one who put the first rune on the boy. Your precious Silent Brothers did that. I did the protection spells by the book. The council may have scorned me when I was alive, but I was a perfectly capable warlock."

"So you did the protection spells just as a Silent Brother would have done them?" Lucie said. "You can swear to that?"

Gast stared directly at Lucie as a look of panic stole across his face. Abruptly he turned away from her, his hands clawing at the air as if he were trying to drag himself back into the darkness he'd come from.

"Stop it," Lucie said, and he stopped immediately. He hung in mid-air, glaring.

Jessamine whispered something; Lucie couldn't quite tell what, but she couldn't worry about Jessamine now.

"Tell me the truth," Lucie said.

Gast's face twisted. "No. There are worse things than death, little Shadowhunter, and more to fear on the other side than you might imagine. Do you think you are the only one who can control the dead? Where do you think that power comes from?"

"Enough!" Lucie snapped her fingers. "I *command* you to tell me."

"Lucie, stop!" Jessamine fluttered her hands in terror. "You mustn't!"

Gast's head snapped back with a sound like a stick breaking. He twisted, pushing back at her, scrabbling like a trapped rabbit. For a moment, Lucie pitied him.

Then she thought of Jesse, dying in agony when the rune was placed on him. Tangled in blood-covered sheets. Screaming for help when no help could be had.

A cold sweat broke out on Lucie's forehead. She bent her will on Gast, the force of her power and her anger.

Tell me. Tell me the truth.

"The anchor!" Gast cried, the words torn from his throat. "By God, the anchor, sunk in his soul! I didn't want to do it, but I had no choice!" His voice rose to a howl. *"Dear God let me go he'll tear me to pieces—"*

Jessamine screamed, just as Gast's translucent body ripped down the middle like a piece of paper. Lucie stumbled back as the ghost came apart, splitting into tattered pieces that sank to the floor and dissolved, leaving faint black stains behind.

Lucie sagged against the bedpost. Exhaustion freighted her limbs, as if she'd run a marathon. "Jessamine," she whispered. "Jessamine, are you all right?"

But Jessamine was staring at her, her ghostly eyes vast in her pale face. "You can command the dead," she choked out. "That means— every time you asked me to fetch your hairbrush, or asked me to tell you a bedtime story, or asked for the window to be opened—you were *commanding* me? I had no choice?"

"Jessamine, no," Lucie protested. "It's not like that. I didn't even know. . . ."

But Jessamine had vanished, between one breath and the next. Lucie slumped onto the bed, her face in her hands. The room stank like smoke and death. She had never thought that even Gast could resist her so hard he would rip himself to smithereens. Surely that would be like tearing one's own head off.

But he had clearly been terrified. Someone very much did not want him answering her question—perhaps to the point of placing a magical compulsion upon him. Torn between warring compulsions, Gast had been ripped apart.

Lucie went very still. Barely breathing, she thought back on what Gast had said. What Jesse had said.

Do you think you are the only one who can command the dead? Where do you think that power comes from?

The anchor, sunk in his soul.

I knew something was keeping me anchored here, when by all rights I should have vanished.

"The anchor," Lucie whispered.

She seized up her weapons belt and stele. Any thought of going after Jessamine had vanished. She scrawled a quick note to her aunt and uncle and made straight for the door; she had to get to Chiswick before anyone noticed she'd left.

She had to see Jesse.

A loud metallic rattle sounded through the Sanctuary, causing Thomas to scramble upright on the bed. Someone was unlocking the door.

Thomas had no idea how long he'd been kissing Alastair Carstairs, but he was fairly sure it had been hours. Not that he was complaining. They had stopped once to eat sandwiches and drink cider, laughing together until something about the way Alastair bit into a slice of apple made Thomas want to kiss him again. They'd rolled off the mattress several times, and Thomas had knocked his head fairly hard into the wall at one point, but Alastair had been very apologetic about it. He'd also been gentle and patient, refusing to take things any further than kissing. "If something serious is to happen between us," he'd said firmly, "it will not be because you were bunged into the Sanctuary on account of being suspected of murder."

Thomas supposed this line of reason had merit, but he'd rather thought something serious had already happened between them. He had been a bit crushed, but thought he had hidden it well.

Now he rushed to smooth down his clothes, throw on his jacket, and kick his feet back into his shoes. Alastair did the same, and by the time the door swung open, they were both standing on opposite sides of the room, fully dressed.

Which was a good thing, because into the room strode Thomas's uncle Will and aunt Tessa. Tessa wore a sea-green French silk dress, her long brown hair bound up in a chignon. Will had clearly discarded his coat somewhere and was carrying a long, heavily ornamented scabbard balanced jauntily on his shoulder. A hilt whose cross guard had been carved in the shape of an angel with outspread wings protruded from the scabbard.

"This thing," Will said cheerily to Thomas, "is bloody heavy."

"Is that the *Mortal Sword*?" said Alastair, looking incredulous.

"We had the Mortal Sword with us in Paris—we brought it as a show of good faith, to demonstrate that we would be nothing but truthful to the vampires of Marseilles. We hurried home as soon as we finished our business with them. Good to see you, young Alastair. I heard what you did for Thomas. Very thoughtful."

"Just reporting what I saw," said Alastair, who seemed in danger of retreating into his usual sulk.

"Oh, indeed," said Will, a gleam in his eye. "Now, for the bad news—"

"We asked if we could do this privately," said Tessa. "Just the four of us. But the Inquisitor wouldn't hear of it. He insists on being present."

"Technically, darling, being present during interrogations is his job," said Will.

Tessa sighed. "I'm sure at one point in history there's been a pleasant, grandfatherly sort of Inquisitor, and we've just never met them," she said. "Will, dear, I'm going to check in with Gabriel and Cecily. Lucie's off at James and Cordelia's—the minx ducked out last night and left a note. We'll have to remind her about showing proper respect to one's aunt and uncle and asking permission before disappearing in the middle of the night to pay social calls."

She smiled affectionately at Will and gave Thomas an encouraging look before letting herself out of the Sanctuary.

"Thanks for coming here straight from Paris," Thomas said, feeling grim.

"I thought, better to get it over with," said Will. "Bit of trial by the Sword before breakfast, what?"

Alastair looked dismayed; Thomas, who was used to his uncle's ways, shrugged. "You'll get used to it," he said to Alastair. "The more alarming the situation, the more frivolous my uncle's demeanor becomes."

"Is that right?" said Alastair bleakly.

"It is right," said Will. "I do not believe my nephew is a murderer; therefore, he has nothing to fear from the Mortal Sword."

"He might have something to fear from the Inquisitor," said Alastair. "Bridgestock desperately wants it to be a Shadowhunter. He needs it to be, so he can have been right about the whole situation. If you let him run the interrogation—"

"I won't," Will said quietly.

The door of the Sanctuary pushed open a bit, and Matthew poked his head through. Thomas could see that behind him there was a press of people: he thought he saw Christopher, and Eugenia behind him, stretching for a glimpse through the doors. He wondered what time it was—morning, he thought, but beyond that it was anyone's guess.

"Hullo, Thomas," Matthew said with a smile, then looked over at Alastair and added in an icy voice, "Carstairs."

"Fairchild," said Alastair in an equally cold tone. Thomas thought perhaps Alastair was relieved to have some normalcy in this situation, even if it was just his and Matthew's mutual contempt.

"Certainly not." Inquisitor Bridgestock stalked into the Sanctuary, followed by Charlotte. It was a jolt to see Charlotte in her formal Consul robes. Beside her, Bridgestock was wrapped in the official black and gray of the Inquisitor—a long black cloak, figured with gray runes, a silver brooch at his chest, black boots with metal buckles. Thomas's stomach swooped and fell; Bridgestock meant business. "Get out, Fairchild."

Charlotte shot a glare at Bridgestock and turned to Matthew. "You'd better go, darling," she said gently. "It'll be all right. Charles Portaled back home this morning too, if you want to see him."

"Not particularly," said Matthew, and gave Thomas a mournful look as the Sanctuary door was shut between them. He mouthed something at Thomas that could have been encouragement, or could have been a recipe for lemon biscuits. Thomas had never learned lipreading.

Charlotte looked after her son for a moment before turning her attention to the matter at hand. "Thomas Lightwood," she said. "Alastair Carstairs. This is to be a trial by the Mortal Sword. Do you understand what that entails?"

Thomas nodded. Alastair merely looked angry, which as Thomas would have guessed, earned them an explanation from the Inquisitor.

"The Mortal Sword is one of the gifts of Raziel," he said pompously. "It compels any Shadowhunter holding it to tell the truth. It is our great weapon against corruption and evil in our own ranks. Thomas Lightwood, come forth and take the Sword."

"I will bring it to him," said Will, and now he didn't sound jovial. His blue eyes were serious as he unsheathed the Sword from its scabbard and carried it to Thomas. "Lay your hands out palms up, my boy," he said. "You will not be wielding the Sword. It will be testing you."

Thomas held out his hands. He could sense Alastair watching him, tension stringing him tight. The whole Sanctuary seemed to be holding its breath. Thomas told himself he was innocent, but as the Sword descended toward him, doubts began to punch holes through his self-assurance. What if the Sword could see down into his soul, see every secret, everything he'd ever tried to hide?

Will placed the Sword, the blade flat, on Thomas's upturned palms.

Thomas sucked in a breath—the weight of the Sword was greater than he had imagined. It felt like a weight not just in his hands but dragging at his whole body, at his heart and blood and stomach. He wanted to gag but fought the feeling back.

He heard Bridgestock chuckle. "Look at him," he said. "Big as a horse, that boy, but even *he* can't withstand the force of Maellartach."

Will was very still. Thomas stared at him desperately. Will Herondale was a man who, though not directly related to Thomas by blood, was essentially his family—his uncle, someone who could be trusted, kind and funny. As Thomas had gotten older, he'd begun to understand that behind that kind exterior was a smart and strategic thinker. He wondered how Will was going to play this particular situation.

Will looked him straight in the eye. "Did you murder Lilian Highsmith?"

Matthew and Christopher were herded down the corridor by a gaggle of muttering Enclave members—Gideon and Sophie, Eugenia, Gabriel and Cecily among them. Matthew couldn't count the number of adults who had come up to him this morning and squeezed his shoulder, assuring him that everything would turn out fine for Thomas.

Of course, there were also the others—those who stared accusingly and shot dark, suspicious glances. Matthew was just glad that Christopher didn't seem to notice even when people glared at him.

"I can't say I care for leaving Thomas behind," Christopher said, casting a mournful look over his shoulder as they were shepherded into the Institute's main entryway. The double doors were open, and even more Enclave members were massed in the courtyard. Matthew could see the Pouncebys and Wentworths, all scowling.

"We've got no choice, Kit," said Matthew. "At least Will and my mother are there along with Bridgestock. And Tom's innocent."

"I know," Christopher said. He glanced around at the packed crowd and shivered a little. Maybe he noticed more than Matthew had thought. "D'you think James is all right?"

The thought of James opened up an ache in Matthew's chest. He'd argued with James the night before: they *never* argued. "Magnus wouldn't let anything happen to him," Matthew said. "I'm sure he'll be here any minute and can tell us all about last night." He dropped his voice. "Journeying into the dream-realm and all that."

"Well, I hope the *pithos* was helpful," Christopher said, shoving his hands into the pockets of his coat. "I still can't figure out why anyone would want an object that picks up runes and pops them onto someone else."

"What are you talking about?" Matthew often felt he'd missed something when he was talking to Christopher about his experiments, but this was even more confusing than usual.

"Well," said Christopher, "if you were a Shadowhunter, you could just draw your runes on yourself, and if you weren't, you couldn't have runes at all without becoming Forsaken—"

"Yes, yes, but what are you *talking about?*"

Christopher sighed. "Matthew, I know it was very late when you came to Grosvenor Square last night, but you must listen when I explain things. It's not all boring trivia, you know."

A faint spark of dread flared in Matthew's stomach. "I didn't come by the house last night."

"You did, though," Christopher insisted, blinking in puzzlement. "You told me that James needed the stele, so I gave it to you."

A spike of ice pierced Matthew's stomach. He recalled dropping Lucie off the night before and returning to his flat to spend the rest of the night drinking with Oscar by the fire. If he'd made a surprise visit to his father's lab at some point in the small hours, he was sure he'd remember it.

"Christopher, I don't know who you gave the stele to last night," he said urgently, "but it wasn't me."

Christopher went pale. "I don't understand. It was you, it looked just like you. If it wasn't you . . . oh, God, who did I give the stele to? And to what purpose?"

Thomas struggled for breath. The weight of the Sword spread through his chest, and it was more than weight, it was pain—a dozen, a thousand small needles stabbing and dragging at his skin. Words spilled from his mouth, uncontrolled and unpremeditated: he understood now the way in which Maellartach made it impossible to hold back the truth. "No," he gasped. "I did not kill Lilian Highsmith."

Charlotte exhaled with relief. The Inquisitor muttered something in a furious tone; if Alastair made a sound, Thomas couldn't hear it.

As though he were asking Thomas about his breakfast, Will said, "Did you murder Basil Pounceby? Or Filomena di Angelo? Or Elias Carstairs?"

Thomas was prepared for the pain this time. It came from resistance, he thought. From pressing back against the Sword's urging. He let himself relax, let the words come without fighting them. "No. I am a warrior. But I am not a murderer."

Will jerked his thumb in the direction of Alastair. "Have you seen that fellow murder any Shadowhunters? Alastair, I mean. He commit any murders to your knowledge? Amos Gladstone, maybe?"

"Excuse me," said Alastair, looking horrified.

"No," said Thomas. "I've never seen Alastair commit murder. And," he added, somewhat to his own surprise, "I don't think he would do such a thing."

At this, the corner of Will's mouth twitched almost imperceptibly. "Do you have any other secrets, Thomas Lightwood?"

The question caught him off guard. Thomas pushed back, swift and hard, before any of a number of secrets could come spilling out of his mouth—secrets about his friends, secrets about James's heritage. Anything at all about Alastair.

"*Will*," Charlotte scolded. "You have to ask about specific things! You can't just fish about. Sorry, Thomas."

"Question retracted," Will said, and the dragging weight of the Sword lightened immediately. Will gave Thomas a hard look and, after a moment, said intently, "Is Gideon aware that he still owes me twenty pounds?"

"Yes," said Thomas, without being able to stop himself, "but he is pretending not to remember."

"I knew it!" cried Will. He turned to the Inquisitor with a triumphant look. "I believe we're done here."

"*Done?*" Bridgestock barked. "We've hardly even begun! These two must be properly questioned, William, you know that."

"I have asked all the relevant questions, I think," Will said.

"You have asked Alastair no questions at all!" Bridgestock shouted. "Either boy could know more. They might know why, for example, no one has been murdered since they've been locked up here. That alone is cause for suspicion."

"Why would that be?" said Charlotte. "The murders aren't happening every night, and it's ridiculous to even think Alastair murdered Lilian. He came along after Thomas, there wasn't a spot of blood on him, and *he* came to *us*—an actual murderer would have washed his hands of the whole business once we had the wrong suspect in custody."

Bridgestock seemed to inflate like a toad. "The wrong suspect? I came across Thomas standing over Lilian, *covered in blood*—"

"In the wise words of someone or other," said Will, lifting the Sword from Thomas's grasp, "there are more things in heaven and earth than are dreamt of in your philosophy, Maurice."

"Shakespeare," said Alastair. "That's from *Hamlet*. Not the Maurice part, clearly, but the rest."

Will looked surprised, then amused. He turned to Thomas. "Tom," he said gently. "I know this has been rotten, but I was suspected of all sorts of shenanigans when I was your age. Once the word gets out about you being tried by the Sword, the Enclave will forget all about this. I promise." He paused. "Now, I see no need for further use of the Sword—"

"It is *not your decision!*" the Inquisitor roared.

The Institute rocked beneath their feet. Thomas looked around in disbelief as candelabras crashed to the ground around them and chairs toppled over. A thin crack splintered the floor underfoot as Alastair started toward Thomas—then froze, seeming uncertain. Bridgestock was clinging to a pillar, eyes wide. Will had pulled Charlotte to him and was keeping her steady, his arm around her shoulder as he gazed around, brow furrowed.

The tremors ceased.

"What—?" Bridgestock gasped, but there was no one to hear him: the other Shadowhunters had exploded into motion and were racing out the door.

* * *

Anna strode a little more forcefully than was strictly necessary, making Ariadne struggle to keep up with her long-legged stride as they crossed over Waterloo Bridge. The tower of the Institute loomed high across the river, dark against the lightening sky.

She was halfway across the bridge before she realized she was alone. Turning, she saw Ariadne standing some yards back, her hands on her hips. Ariadne had very pretty hips, curving into a neat waist, and her legs—as Anna had cause to know—were well-shaped. She even had attractive feet, which she had currently planted on the pavement, unmoving.

"I cannot walk as fast as you do," Ariadne said. "But I will not race to keep up. It is undignified. If you'd prefer to go alone, you merely need say so."

Even at this early hour, there was traffic on the bridge—clerks hurrying to work, costermonger carts on the way to the morning market at Covent Garden, milk vans rattling with bottles—but as Ariadne and Anna were glamoured, no one stopped to stare.

I have been running away from you for two years. Why should I stop now? Anna thought. Though if she had to admit it to herself, she'd been doing a poor job of running these past few weeks.

She gave a little mocking half bow but stayed where she was; in a few moments, Ariadne had caught up with her, and they made their way across the bridge together. The sky was beginning to turn copper-blue in the east. The wind tugged at Ariadne's dark hair. Anna had always thought that when it was unbound, it looked like a storm cloud.

"It's odd," Ariadne said. "Now that we have this information about Jesse Blackthorn, what do we do with it?"

"Nothing at the moment," said Anna. "Lucie wants to tell Grace first."

It was the last thing Lucie had said, an urgent request as she'd swung into a hansom cab, saying she desperately needed to get back to the Institute before Aunt Cecily noticed she was gone. Anna and Ariadne still had to finish their patrol; they were headed back to the Institute now, Anna determined to see if anything new had developed with Thomas.

"I'm rather surprised they're friends," said Ariadne. "I've never known Grace to have a plan to meet anyone, or a friend to visit at the house. She's a sort of ghost when Charles isn't about."

Anna was not entirely sure Lucie and Grace *were* friends. It was not in Lucie's nature to befriend someone who'd caused her brother grief. On the other hand, Lucie was always telling herself stories in which she was the heroine of grand adventures. Investigating the slightly romantic mystery of a boy's death certainly fell into that category.

They had reached the Victoria Embankment, which ran along the north side of the Thames. The wind off the river was bitter here, and Anna shivered. "Hopefully Grace won't be troubling you for too much longer," she said. "Eventually Charles will have to return from Paris and marry her."

Ariadne laughed softly. "Everyone thinks I should scorn Grace. For the insult of taking up with my former betrothed. But it was actually my idea to take her in."

"It was?" Anna was curious despite herself.

Ariadne shrugged. "I didn't want to marry Charles, you know. You *would* know. Better than anyone."

Anna didn't reply. *Perhaps you didn't want to,* she thought. *But you agreed to marry him, knowing it would break my heart. Knowing you would never love him. I would never have done such a thing.*

"When I woke up from being ill and found out that he had left me for Grace, I was more relieved than anything else," said Ariadne. "I was grateful to Grace, I think. I thought if we invited her to live with us, it would show the Enclave that I bear her no ill will."

After turning onto Carmelite Street, they passed a brick building with mullioned windows. The spire of the Institute loomed close above the nearby buildings, the warren of familiar streets around the cathedral welcoming them in. "Well, that's quite a sacrifice to make for the Enclave," Anna said.

"It wasn't just for the Enclave. I wanted to get to know Grace better, because of our shared experience."

Anna laughed shortly. "How are your lives at all alike, Ari?"

Ariadne gave her a steady look. "We're both adopted."

It was not something that had occurred to Anna. After a pause, she said, "I have not always seen eye to eye with your parents. But they love you. I think it is doubtful whether Tatiana has any gentle feelings toward Grace."

"My parents do love me," Ariadne conceded. "But they never acknowledge my past—the fact that I came here from India when I was seven—nor even that I had a different name when I was born." Ariadne faltered, seeming to search for the right words. "I feel as though I am always between worlds. As if I am glad to be their daughter, but I am someone else, too."

Anna heard a rumble in the distance, like the sound of a tram. "What was your name when you were born?"

They had almost reached the gates of the Institute. Ariadne hesitated. "Kamala," she said. "Kamala Joshi."

Kamala. A name like a flower.

"And there was no other family—no one who could help?" Anna said.

"An aunt and uncle, but there had been bad blood between them and my parents. They refused to take me in. I could have been raised at the Bombay Institute, but I—I wanted a mother and father. A proper family. And perhaps, to be far from those who had rejected me." Ariadne's lovely deep eyes with their flecks of gold were fixed on Anna's face. It was unnerving, being looked at like that—it made Anna feel *seen* in a way she rarely did. "Anna. Will you ever forgive me?"

Anna tensed, caught off guard by the question. "Ariadne—"

Lightning cracked through the sky. Anna spun in surprise. There had been no sign of storm, the dawn sky untroubled. But now . . .

"What is *that*?" Ariadne whispered.

A huge dark cloud had gathered over the Institute—but only over the Institute. It was massive, inky black, and billowing above the church as though propelled by internal gusts. All around it the sky spread dark blue and untroubled to the horizon.

Thunder rumbled as Anna stared around in perplexity. A mundane man in workman's clothes walked past, whistling to himself; it was clear that the storm was invisible to him.

Anna pushed open the gates, and she and Ariadne ducked into the courtyard. It was deep in shadow, the cloud billowing overhead. Lightning crackled around the Institute's spire.

Ariadne had a *khanda*—a double-edged blade—already in her hand.

Unfastening her whip from her belt, Anna turned in a slow circle, every sense on alert. Her eye caught a flicker of movement—something dark, like a spill of ink or blood, was moving in the center of the courtyard.

She took a step toward it—just as it surged up and outward: it wasn't a spill after all, but something slick and black and moving and alive. Anna leaped back, thrusting Ariadne behind her, as it smashed upward through the earth, sending cracks zigzagging through the flagstones. Water rushed up through the cracks, filling the courtyard with the stench of hot salt and brine. Even as Anna spun, lashing out at the darkness with her whip, she couldn't help but wonder: How on earth was the Institute's courtyard possibly filling with *seawater*?

Though initially reluctant to venture out of his warm stall and into the icy weather, Balios gained his energy back quickly, delivering Lucie to Chiswick House in the dark small hours. She dismounted and patted the horse's muzzle before tying him to a post near the gates with a blanket draped over his withers.

She moved cautiously over the ruined, winter-burned grounds. As always, Chiswick House seemed abandoned, only the whistle of the winter wind through the trees to accompany her. But she was determined to take no chances. If her guess about Jesse was even remotely close to the truth, then she had to be very careful indeed. She crossed the ruined garden, with the wry thought that she was becoming as familiar with the paths of the Chiswick grounds as she was with the streets of her own neighborhood. She wended her way past broken statuary and overgrown shrubbery until she arrived at the old garden shed.

She listened for several moments to reassure herself that no one had followed her. The scrape of bare branches against the slate walls of the shed jangled her nerves, but she pressed on and approached the door, which stood slightly ajar. She caught a bitter scent in the air—incense, perhaps, that Grace had been burning as part of some attempt to revive her brother.

Lucie slipped inside, and once her eyes adjusted, she saw Jesse's body, just as she'd last seen it, laid out peacefully in the glass coffin. His eyes closed, his hands folded on his chest.

Still, she had to make sure. With trembling hands she did something she had never done before, and raised the hinged lid to the glass coffin.

The body before her was not Jesse, she told herself. Jesse was her ghost, a spirit, and not this physical remnant. It still felt like a strange kind of violation as she pulled back the lapels of Jesse's white funeral jacket.

The broadcloth shirt beneath was spattered with blood.

Half holding her breath, Lucie began to unbutton the top of the shirt, peeling the cold fabric away, the gesture bizarrely intimate.

There, across the pale skin of his chest, was a Strength rune. On his left shoulder, Swiftness and Precision. Voyance on his left hand, though she knew it was not his dominant one. At the inner turn of his arm was the *enkeli* rune.

Lucie let the fabric slip from her fingers and stared at the black markings on Jesse's pale, waxy skin. It was as she had feared.

The anchor.

The runes. Jesse had never had any runes. Now he had five. One for each murdered Shadowhunter: Amos Gladstone, Basil Pounceby, Filomena di Angelo, Lilian Highsmith, Elias Carstairs.

Numbly, she went to the far wall and took down the Blackthorn sword. Her steps slowed as she returned to the coffin. The lid was still open, and inside, Jesse lay still—peaceful, and utterly unaware. It was unfair. Horribly unfair. Jesse was innocent.

But those who had been murdered—they had been innocent too.

Lucie had to do it now, before she lost her nerve. She gritted her teeth and raised the sword, gripping the hilt with both hands, ready to swing it down straight and true, as her father had taught her.

"Jesse," she whispered. "Jesse, I'm so sorry."

Light flashed off the blade of the sword, just as something slammed into the back of Lucie's head. The Blackthorn sword fell from her hands. As it glanced off the edge of the glass case and clanged to the hard earth, shadows crept in around the edges of Lucie's vision, washing her into the dark.

24

HE SHALL RISE

There hath he lain for ages, and will lie
Battening upon huge sea worms in his sleep,
Until the latter fire shall heat the deep;
Then once by man and angels to be seen,
In roaring he shall rise and on the surface die.
—Alfred, Lord Tennyson, "The Kraken"

James was in the shadows and they were around him; he was dreaming, though he had not been asleep.

He could hear his own breath, ragged in his ears. He was prisoned in the shadows, unable to move—unable to see save out of two holes torn in the darkness, like the eyes of a mask.

It was past dawn, the sky the color of cold blue glass. Arching above him as he lurched forward were plane trees, their branches outstretched to catch the attenuated sunlight. His body ached and burned. Dark hair fell across his vision; he reached to push it away. Glancing down, he saw his hands—narrow, pale white hands, clutching a silvery runed box.

His hand, which was not his hand, closed over the box. He was in a familiar space—gardens of some sort. There were hedges, and paths winding among wintry trees. Before him, a church's gothic spires rose against the clear sky; winding out from its door were footpaths that circled the bronze fountain in the center.

James could hear whistling. His vision was beginning to fade around the edges, but he could see someone—someone in a gear jacket—walking a path, among the laurels and holly bushes, their leaves seared with ice that glittered in the sun. . . .

Somewhere a hand closed itself around the hilt of a blade. Somewhere there was hatred, that bleak, pitiless hatred James had felt before, and contempt—contempt for the man in the jacket, the Shadowhunter, who he had waited for in the square, had followed from his house, driving him, unawares, toward this place, this confrontation. . . .

Stop, James whispered. *Don't do this.*

Sneering scorn. *Begone, child.*

And he was hurled free of the vision, crying out, his hands reaching for purchase, something to hold him to the world.

"*James!*"

It was Cordelia's voice. She was kneeling over him, and so was Matthew: he lay on the floor of the study, half-stunned, as if he'd been dropped from a great height. He jerked into a sitting position like a puppet yanked upright on too-tight strings. "It's happening," he said. "Another murder—"

"Here." Matthew reached out; James caught hold of his *parabatai*'s hand and hauled himself upright. He still felt dizzy, and somehow different—lighter, though he could not begin to explain why. He leaned back against the marble fireplace, catching his breath, Matthew's worried gaze fixed on him. "Steady on, Jamie *bach*."

James realized three things simultaneously. One was that he'd been kissing Cordelia what felt like moments ago, but no evidence of their embrace remained: Cordelia wore a gear jacket buttoned over her dress, and a watchful expression. He himself was wearing a clean shirt, which seemed an even greater mystery.

The second was that Matthew must have just arrived: he hadn't yet taken off his bright green brocade-and-velvet overcoat, and one end of his long ivory scarf trailed on the floor.

The third was that it was as if someone had unlatched a cage inside him, letting his mind run free. He very urgently needed several things at once: an answer, a map, and a book. "Math," he said. "The *pithos*— did Christopher lose it?"

Matthew's eyes widened. "It was stolen—by someone who looked like me. How did you know it was gone?"

"Because *he* has it," James said. "Belial. He must have sent an Eidolon demon to Christopher, to trick him." He took a deep breath. "I think—I think I may know what's happening."

Cordelia rose to her feet, Cortana gleaming where it was strapped to her back. She blushed a little as she looked at him. "What do you mean, you know? You know who's responsible for the murders?" she demanded. "I mean, Belial, of course—"

"I don't know all of it," said James, racing to the center table, where books on dreams and magic still lay scattered haphazardly. "But some of it. Why he's doing what he's doing. Maybe even how. Here—" He yanked the dark purple volume free. "The map," he said. "That map of London—where is it?"

"Here." Matthew slid the book toward him, open to the map in the center. Hurriedly James glanced at the *Monarchia*, then back at the map. He picked up a pen and made one last mark.

"Mount Street Gardens?" said Matthew, squinting at the new scrawl. "We've been there before. It's quite near here."

"But that still doesn't make Belial's sigil, does it?" said Cordelia, glancing over Matthew's shoulder. "It looks rather like Poseidon's trident. A sort of spear with three prongs."

"It is a sigil," said James. "Just not Belial's. It's *Leviathan's* sigil." He tapped the *Monarchia*, where Leviathan's sigil was scrawled across a full page, spiky and vicious-looking. "Thus the trident. He is a sea demon, after all."

Matthew and Cordelia exchanged a puzzled look. This was it, James thought; they were going to declare him mad and toss him in the attic.

"Magnus said the Princes had alliances," said Cordelia slowly. "Azazel and Asmodeus. Belial and—"

"Leviathan," said Matthew, who had gone a little white around the mouth. "James, you said the sigils can function as gates. If this murder happens—it will open up a gate for Leviathan to enter our world?"

"Do you think it's already happened?" Cordelia asked.

James glanced at the window. "No. In my vision it was just after dawn, and dawn is breaking now. Mount Street Gardens isn't far, but we have no time to waste. We must run—"

"Not like that, you're not," said Matthew sternly. "You need shoes, weapons, and a gear jacket at least. And Cordelia needs boots."

"And then?" said Cordelia.

"*Then* we run."

As Thomas barreled through the Institute and into the entryway, he heard someone calling his name. Everything was chaos, a seething mass of Shadowhunters surging to and fro, catching up weapons, throwing on gear, and charging out the open front doors into the courtyard beyond, from which the sounds of fighting were already audible.

"Thomas! Here!" It was Christopher, pushing toward him through the crowd; he was holding a gear jacket and a number of seraph blades. "Where's Uncle Will?"

"Went to find Tessa." Thomas took the jacket and threw it on, jamming some of the blades into his belt. "What's happening?"

"Some kind of attack. Your parents are out there already, joined the fighting. Mine, too—well, Father has. Mother's upstairs with Alexander. But the Institute's not safe. Do you want some seraph blades?"

Thomas was about to protest that he'd already taken several when he realized Christopher wasn't talking to him. He was talking to Alastair, who seemed to have remained at Thomas's side. Thomas determined to analyze this development at a later date.

Alastair nodded his thanks and took the weapons. He headed to the front doors while Thomas was still fastening his jacket. Christopher followed—he was saying something about the *adamas* object Thomas had found, and about Matthew having run to get James. His voice trailed off as he joined Thomas and Alastair at the front door.

The courtyard was in ruins. A massive black cloud hid the Institute and its surroundings in shadow: bright beams of witchlight lanced back and forth across the courtyard, illuminating scenes of battle—there was Gideon, sword in hand, climbing atop a pile of rubble. Anna, in gear, back-to-back with Ariadne, her whip tracing a thin gold line across the air.

"But what are they *fighting*?" said Alastair—for once voicing what everyone was thinking. "It's too bloody dark to see, and—" He wrinkled his nose. "It smells of fish."

"We need light!" It was Will, having returned to the entryway; he had Aunt Tessa with him, and they were both in gear. He was snapping out orders—everyone who could not join the battle was to fetch a witchlight rune-stone and head to an open window to direct the light down onto those fighting outside.

Thomas exchanged a quick glance with the others. He had no intention of being kept back so he could stand at a window with a witchlight. If the Institute was being attacked, he wanted to be out there, defending it.

It was Alastair who moved first. He started down the steps, Christopher and Thomas on his heels. Thomas coughed as the air thickened around them, suffused with the rank, damp smell of salt, fish, and rotting seaweed. As they reached the bottom of the steps, Thomas's boots came down in freezing water. He could hear Christopher exclaiming about scientific impossibilities.

"Well, it might be impossible," said Alastair, rather reasonably, "but it's happening."

"Whatever it is," Thomas said. The courtyard began to brighten—dozens of windows around the Institute were being flung open. Thomas recognized some of the faces there, hands holding out glowing rune-stones—there was Aunt Cecily, and Mrs. Bridgestock, Piers Wentworth, and several of the Pouncebys.

In the increasing light, Thomas could see that the entire courtyard was afroth with ocean, gunmetal-gray, sloshing chaotically back and forth as though caught in a windstorm. Shadowhunters had clambered atop heaps of piled flagstones and other rubble, hacking and slashing at the *things* emerging from the water. They were long, like sea serpents—a muddy shade somewhere between brown, gray, and green, but shining slickly as though metallic. One whipped through the air toward Anna; she flicked her whip, slicing it in half. The stump thrashed, spraying gray-green, watery ichor. Thomas heard Eugenia shout—he hadn't realized she was in the courtyard—and he spun, catching sight of the remains of the tentacle wrapping itself around Augustus Pounceby's waist.

Augustus screamed, dropping his seraph blade, and clutched desperately at the fleshy green appendage tightening around his body. It was clearly choking the breath out of him; his face had gone red and he was gasping for air. Thomas started forward, but Eugenia was already there, her longsword flashing. She brought it down at an angle, slicing through Augustus's gear jacket and then through the tentacle itself. It fell away in two spasming chunks and Augustus sank to his knees, clutching his midsection.

"Eugenia," he wheezed. "Please—I don't deserve—"

Eugenia shot him a disgusted look. "No, you don't," she said. "Now pick up your weapon and make yourself useful, for once."

She strode off, returning to the thick of the battle, pausing only to wink at Thomas as she hurried by.

"That was unexpectedly satisfying," said Christopher.

Thomas agreed, but there was no time to enjoy the moment. "*Midael*," he intoned, and his seraph blade blazed to life in his hand. He sloshed farther into the courtyard, through the ankle-deep water, Christopher and Alastair nearby. Something surged up out of the seafoam—another tentacle, this one thrashing and alive. It was as big around as a grown human and impossibly long, and as it reared back out of the waves, Thomas could see that its underside was covered with hundreds of hard, spiked black barbs.

It slammed down. Something caught hold of Thomas, yanking him savagely out of the way.

Alastair.

They half collapsed onto each other as the end of the tentacle smashed into the front of the Institute; when it dragged itself back into the water, a chunk of the wall came with it. Brick dust puffed into the air as Gabriel Lightwood leaped down from a teetering stack of flagstones, sword raised.

The tentacle whipped back and curled around Gabriel, wrapping his torso, pinning his arms to his sides. The sword flew out of Gabriel's hand, its blade smeared with ichor, the cross guard with blood.

Gabriel struggled, but the thing held him fast. Christopher shouted hoarsely and ran toward his father as shilling-size drops of scarlet blood pattered down around him. Thomas scrambled to his feet and dashed after Christopher, hurling himself at the massive tentacle. He plunged his seraph blade into the rubbery green-black flesh, over and over, dimly aware that beside him, Alastair Carstairs was doing the same.

Cordelia, Matthew, and James arrived at Mount Street Gardens at a run. The gate was open, the garden itself seemingly deserted. Cordelia slowed to a walk as they passed onto the footpaths that ran beneath the plane trees. She told herself that the silence—despite the red Jacobean primary school building looming up on the right—was due to the earliness of the morning. The schoolchildren wouldn't have arrived yet, and it was chilly weather for a walk.

And yet, she could not shake her feeling of prickly unease, as if someone were watching them. But the raked footpaths were bare. James ranged restlessly across the park, hatless, his dark hair whipping in the wind as he searched. They were all glamoured—they would certainly have alarmed the pedestrians on South Audley Street otherwise—but it seemed no one was here to see them. She was wondering if they were too late—or too early—when James gave a hoarse bark of alarm.

"Matthew! Come quickly!"

Matthew and Cordelia exchanged a quick look of puzzlement; James was over by a bronze statue in the middle of the garden, waving furiously. Matthew ran to him, and after a moment, Cordelia followed.

She saw immediately why James had called Matthew to him first. The statue surmounted a now-dry bronze fountain; slumped behind the fountain was the body of a Shadowhunter—a man in gear, with dark red hair. Not far away, an object glittered on the pathway, as if it had fallen or been tossed aside. The *pithos*.

Nearing the fountain, Matthew froze. He had gone an awful color, like chalk.

"*Charles,*" he whispered.

He seemed unable to move. Cordelia caught hold of his hand and half dragged him to where James was kneeling by the body—no, not a body, she realized with relief. Charles was alive, if barely. James had rolled him onto his back, and his blood-soaked chest rose and fell unevenly.

James had his stele out and was frantically drawing *iratzes* on Charles's skin, where a torn and bloody sleeve exposed his forearm. Cordelia heard Matthew suck in a ragged breath. He was staring intently at the runes, and Cordelia knew why: when a wound was fatal, *iratzes* would not hold their place on skin. They would vanish, overwhelmed by a level of damage they could not heal.

"They're staying," she whispered, though she knew it was not a guarantee. She squeezed Matthew's hand hard. "Go—Matthew, you'll hate yourself if you don't."

With a stiff nod, Matthew drew away and fell to his knees beside James. He laid his hand, long and slender, glittering with his signet ring, on his brother's cheek. "Charles," he said breathlessly. "Hang on, Charlie. We'll get you help. We'll—"

He broke off and sat motionless, one hand on his brother's face, the other arrested in the motion of reaching for his stele. The slow rise and fall of Charles's shallow breathing seemed to have stopped as well. They were frozen, like statues. Cordelia looked wildly at James, who was staring around them in amazement. The park was utterly silent, utterly still. Where were the sounds of birds—city starlings and sparrows? The sounds of London awakening: the cries of costermongers, the tread of pedestrians on their way to work? The rustle of leaves in the wind? The world felt still and frozen, as if pressed under glass.

But James—James could move too. Pocketing the *pithos*, he rose to his feet, seeking out Cordelia with his gaze. His golden eyes were burning. "Cordelia," he said. "Turn around."

She whirled to face the park gates and nearly jumped out of her skin: a young man was strolling toward them, whistling softly. The tune carried through the silent park like music in a church. The boy seemed familiar, though Cordelia couldn't have said why; he was dark-haired and smiling, carrying a heavy sword with an etched crosspiece in one hand. He was dressed in a pure white suit as if it were summer, his shirt and jacket spattered with bright red blood. He was handsome—striking, really, with dark green eyes the color of new leaves. Yet something about him made her skin crawl. There was something feral about his smile, like the grin of the Cheshire cat.

James was gazing at the boy in what seemed to be dawning horror. Beside him Matthew and Charles remained frozen in their strange tableau, their eyes blank and staring.

"But that can't be," James said, half to himself. "It's not possible."

"What do you mean? What's not possible?"

"That's Jesse," James said. "Jesse Blackthorn."

"Tatiana's son? But he died," Cordelia said. "Years ago."

"Maybe," said James, taking a knife from his belt. His gaze never left the boy—Jesse—as he approached, fastidiously skirting a border of holly. "But I recognize—I've seen his portrait in Blackthorn Manor. And a few photographs Grace had. It's him."

"But that's impossible—"

Cordelia broke off, her hand flying to Cortana. The boy was suddenly standing in front of them, twirling his sword in his hand like a music-hall singer with a cane. His jacket hung casually open, his smile widening as he looked from James to Cordelia. "Of course it's impossible," he said. "Jesse Blackthorn is long dead."

James cocked his head to the side. He was pale, but his gaze was steady and full of loathing.

"Grandfather," he said.

Of course. It was not the boy who had struck Cordelia as familiar, but rather his cruel smile, the way he moved, those pale clothes like the ones she had seen him wear in the hell-world where she had followed James. He wasn't looking at Cordelia—rather pointedly so.

Interesting.

"Indeed," said Belial, with an unexpected cheerfulness. "Even without *quite* the ideal vessel, I walk in your world freely. Feeling the sunshine on my face. Breathing the air of London."

"Calling a dead body 'not quite the ideal vessel' is rather like calling the sewers of London 'not that bad a holiday destination,'" said James, flicking his eyes over Jesse Blackthorn's admittedly well-preserved remains. "Indulge me a moment—the tale I heard of the manner and time of Jesse's death. Was all of it a lie?"

"My dear boy," said Belial. Cordelia unsheathed Cortana; she saw

Belial flinch almost imperceptibly, though he still refused to look at her. "My dear boy, there is no need to trouble yourself that your dear Grace lied to you." He gazed lovingly down at Jesse's left hand, where a Voyance rune gleamed, new and black. "There was a time, you know, when I feared your mother would never procreate. That there would never be a James Herondale. I was forced to make alternate plans. I placed an anchor in this world, sunk deep into the soul of a baby boy when his protection spells were placed on him. Little Jesse Blackthorn, whose mother didn't trust Shadowhunters but *did* trust warlocks. Emmanuel Gast was easy enough to threaten into obedience. He placed the protections on Jesse, as instructed, and a little something extra as well. A bit of my essence, tucked under the skin of the child's soul."

Cordelia felt sick. A Shadowhunter's protection spells were precious, almost holy. What Belial had done felt like a nauseating violation. "But James *was* born," she said. "So you didn't need Jesse after that, did you? Is that why he died?"

"I didn't kill him, if that's what you're asking," Belial said. "His own mother did. She let the Silent Brothers place a rune on him. I warned her not to let them interfere. The angelic runes of the Gray Book reacted quite badly with the demonic essence deep inside him. So . . ."

"He died," James said.

"Oh, yes, quite painfully," said Belial. "And that would have been that, really, but Tatiana is a stubborn woman. She called on me. I did owe her a favor, and I have my own sense of honor—"

James made a scornful noise. Belial widened Jesse's green eyes in mock horror.

"You forget," said Belial. "I was an angel once. *Non serviam* and all that. Better to reign in Hell. But we keep our promises." He stretched luxuriously, like a cat, though his grip on the sword—its hilt, Cordelia saw now, carved with a design of thorns—never faltered. "I ordered Gast to preserve Jesse's body. To keep him in a twilight state, not quite dead and not quite alive. During the day, he slept in his coffin. At night, he was a ghost."

Cordelia thought of Lucie. Lucie, who could see ghosts. Who had been so secretive lately. "All the necromancy Tatiana was doing," she said slowly. "The dark magic that got her exiled to the Citadel. It wasn't to raise Jesse—it was to keep him preserved like this?"

"Oh, she's always wanted him raised as well," said Belial. "But that didn't suit me. I've had to put her off for years. It wasn't until she was carted off to be watched over by the Iron Sisters that I was able to access her precious baby boy so that he could do what I needed him to do."

"So you made him a killer," said James flatly. "But why?" Cordelia loved that look on James's face—sharp, problem-solving, precise—it seemed the opposite of the Mask, somehow. He was seeing a pattern, one she didn't see yet, the way those with the Sight saw through glamours impervious to mundanes. "You woke his body at dawn—possessed it—walked him around London like a puppet. Had him use the *pithos* to take runes from dead Nephilim. Had him kill." Realization sparked in his eyes. "Not just to collect death energy, or to make Leviathan's sigil. You were making Jesse stronger. Strong enough to bear those stolen runes."

Belial smirked. "Ah, yes, and you saw it all. It's rude to spy, you know, even in dreams."

"You still deny you had anything to do with those dreams?" said James.

"I do indeed. It was not me who showed you those deaths. Perhaps someone else wished you to see them." He shrugged. "You can believe me or not. I have no reason to lie, and less reason to care what you think."

Cordelia exchanged a look with James; she sensed they both doubted they would get a better answer from Belial. "So Jesse isn't alive or dead," said James, "and your anchor inside him allows you to possess him without his body giving way and crumbling apart. You're even carrying the Blackthorn sword." He looked disgusted. "So why did you ask me again, outside Edom, if I would let you possess me? Why not give up on *me*?"

Belial only grinned his icy grin. "Perhaps I don't need you. Perhaps I only want to kill you. Your reluctance, your refusal to cooperate with me—they have vexed me very much. And one does not vex a Prince of Hell without consequences."

"No," James said. "That's not it. Jesse isn't your final goal."

"His body can only be used half the day," said Cordelia. "Isn't that right? At night he becomes a ghost and his body can't be used?"

"He *is* alive only half the day, and not even the amusing half," Belial agreed. "No, I have never thought of this body as a final destination for my soul. More a method of reaching that destination."

"Which is still James," said Cordelia. "But you will not touch him." She raised her blade.

And this time, Belial did not flinch. He began to smile—a manticore's smile, as if his jaw were not properly hinged, and the grin might take over his whole face, turning it to a mask of teeth.

"Cordelia, no." James flung out his hand, his arm across Cordelia's body. He was suddenly very pale. "The runes," he said. "When Jesse lost the *pithos*, you had to send an Eidolon to retrieve it from Christopher, even though it risked discovery of your plan. You needed it that badly. You've been making Jesse a warrior. Demon and angel, dead and alive. You think he can defeat Cortana. *That's* why you made him. To get Cordelia out of the way—to get at me—" He spun to face her. "Daisy—*run*—"

And leave you without protection? Cordelia shot James a single, incredulous look before she raised Cortana high above her head. "I said," she repeated, "you will not touch him—"

Belial charged at her. One moment he was lounging with the Blackthorn sword dangling from his hand. The next he was a streak of fire, a blaze tipped with silver.

James lunged at Cordelia, knocking her out of the way. They rolled across the packed dirt of the pathway; Cordelia somersaulted up and into a standing position, slashing out with Cortana. Her blade clanged against Jesse's—Belial's. She registered the pattern of thorns winding around the cross guard of the Blackthorn sword even as he spun, stabbed out at her again—the blade's tip parted the fabric at her collar with a whisper. She felt the burning sting, a hot spill of blood.

She heard James shout her name. But he seemed distant; the gardens and everything in them were far away. She was facing Belial as if on the vast chessboard James had described to her from his vision. There was nothing there but the two of them, and the next moves they would make.

She charged at Belial, leaping onto a nearby bench and pushing off it, spinning like a top as she whirled through the air, coming down with the sword. He sprang out of the way, but barely fast enough: the sword slashed a cut across the front of his shirt.

He bared his teeth.

Wound him, she thought. *Three mortal wounds from Cortana—*

Belial hissed and leaped at her, the Blackthorn sword dancing in his hand. Distantly, Cordelia was aware that she had never seen sword work like this before. She should have been cut to ribbons. A week ago she would have been, despite a lifetime of training.

But she was a paladin now. She let the power of it flow into her, igniting the marrow of her bones. Cortana was lightning in her hand: the blade slammed against Belial's, over and over, filling the gardens with the sound of ringing metal. Surely one of the blades would crack in half. Surely the *world* would crack in half, and she would spin across the gulf, carried by Cortana's whirling blade.

The Blackthorn sword swept by, dancing and slashing, but with every movement Cordelia was able to dart out of its way. She returned over and over, Cortana blazing in her hand, driving Belial backward on the path, even as his eyes widened with incredulity.

"This is *impossible!*" he hissed, the Blackthorn sword slicing through the air where Cordelia had stood a moment ago.

Cordelia exulted, raising Cortana overhead, then delivering a fast kick to Belial's abdomen. It propelled him back; his unbuttoned jacket flew open, and Cordelia saw James's gun, thrust through his belt.

Belial dropped into a crouch, slashing out with the Blackthorn sword; Cordelia leaped over the blade intended to slice her legs out from under her. She feinted, parried, and brought Cortana down in a long diagonal arc; it slammed against the cross guard of Belial's sword.

His right hand began to bleed.

He howled, a long scream of rage that seemed to shake the last leaves from the trees. It struck Cordelia as impossible all London could not hear it. Her heart pounded—had she wounded him? Would it be enough?—as Belial raised his raging eyes and barked out a vicious laugh.

"You think because you have scratched me, it will make a difference?" he snarled. He wiped the back of his injured hand across his face. It left behind a scarlet streak of blood. But he was smiling now. "You think so little of your grandfather, James?"

Cordelia froze, Cortana still upraised; she had not even realized James was beside her on the path, a seraph blade in his hand. She should be attacking, she thought, should be lunging at Belial—but there was something in his expression that held her back. Something in the way he smiled and said, "Did you not guess that I was delaying until my brother was ready?"

Cordelia felt James, beside her, stiffen.

My brother.

Belial laughed and raised his left hand. The air between the plane trees seemed to go white, and suddenly it was as if they were looking through an enormous window.

Through it, Cordelia saw a scene of chaos. It was the courtyard of the Institute, but barely recognizable. The flagstones had been smashed into heaps of rubble, around which gray-green water surged. Lightning crackled above, the air heavy and black.

Through the shadows, figures darted, illuminated by witchlight. There was Ariadne, standing over a crumpled body, holding off something Cordelia couldn't quite see—something that looked like a massive rubbery limb clustered with vicious suction cups. It was a tentacle, she realized, the waving appendage of something huge, and hidden.

And in among the tentacles were their family and friends: Anna, high atop a broken section of wall, intercepted a tentacle headed for Christopher with her whip. Henry, his chair backed up against a slab of rock, laid about him with a *sanjiegun*. Alastair clambered onto a pile of rubble, spear in hand, turning to help Thomas up after him. The windows of the Institute, full of faces—

Belial dropped his hand. The window blinked out of existence. Cordelia could hear her own panicked breathing.

Alastair.

Beside her, James was very still. She knew what he was thinking, his mind darting from name to name: Will, Tessa, Gideon, Gabriel, Sophie, Cecily. Cordelia hadn't seen Lucie, but she was almost certainly there as well, probably inside the Institute. Nearly everyone James loved in his life was there, facing obliteration.

"Your brother," said James, his voice barely recognizable. "Leviathan, the sea demon. You have called him up out of Hell."

"He owed me a favor," said Belial, his old insouciance returning. "And he enjoys this sort of thing. So you see, James, you really have no choice at all, regardless of Cortana."

"You are telling me that if I do not give up my body willingly, let you possess me, then you will have Leviathan kill them," said James. "All of them."

"Oh, yes, I'll make sure they all die," said Belial. "It's your choice."

"James," said Cordelia. "No. He's a liar—the prince of liars—no matter what you do, he'll never save them—"

The smile vanished from Belial's face. "I don't think you understand," he said. "If you do not consent to what I want, your family and friends will die."

"Cordelia is right," said James. "You will kill them anyway. I cannot save them. You are only offering me that illusion to compel my agreement. Well, you cannot have it."

Belial huffed out a sound that was almost like a laugh. "Spoken like the grandson of a Prince of Hell," he said. "How *practical*, James. How *logical*. Do you know it was logic and rationality that resulted in our casting out from Heaven? For goodness is not logical, is it? Nor compassion, nor love. But perhaps you need to be able to see the situation more clearly."

James glanced quickly at Cordelia. She knew what he was thinking, hoping—*let Belial not realize that Charles is still alive, that the sigil is not complete*—but feared her expression would give away her thoughts. She glanced down at the blade in her hand, smeared with Belial's blood.

"You mortals fear such small things," Belial went on. "Death, for instance. Merely the passage from one place to another. Yet you do all you can to avoid it. Now, torment—that is quite different. There is no reason for my brother to *kill* these acquaintances of yours, you know—not when more refined tortures are available and . . . infinite."

James looked at Belial, his gaze level—and desperate. Perhaps only Cordelia, who knew him as she knew the map of her own heart, could see it. But it was there: desperation, and worse than that, despair.

James, no. Don't do it. Don't agree.

"Only if you swear," James said, "that no harm or hurt will come to them—"

"James, *no*," Cordelia burst out. "He is lying—"

"And what of your brother, Carstairs girl?" Belial demanded, his green gaze fixed on her. "Leviathan could cut him down as I cut down your father—I could blight every root of your family tree—"

With a scream, Cordelia raised her sword. James moved toward her, flinging out his hand—just as a noise cut through the still gardens. A sound like a fire, crackling and hissing. Shadows whirled and sliced through the air like dark birds. Belial's borrowed eyes followed them, his expression wary.

"What mischief is this?" he demanded. "Enough! Show yourself!"

The shadows coalesced into a shape. Cordelia stared in utter astonishment as a figure took form, growing dark and solid against the sky.

It was Lilian Highsmith. Dead Lilian, in an old-fashioned blue dress. Sapphires sparkled at her ears. The same stones she had worn at the Wentworths' party.

"You disappoint me," she said, her voice low and even. "You found the Ridgeway Road, the forge and the fire. You call yourself paladin yet you cannot slay one measly Prince of Hell?"

"*Measly?*" echoed James, incredulous. "Ghost or not, how dare you speak to her like that?"

"Oh," said Lilian. "I am no ghost." She smiled—a smile not unlike Belial's. Cordelia's blood ran cold as Lilian broke apart into shadows again, then re-formed: she was gone and in her place was another familiar figure, the faerie woman with iridescent hair who Cordelia had spoken to at the Hell Ruelle, the one who'd first told her about Wayland the Smith.

"Is this better?" she breathed, her long fingers toying with her blue necklace. "Or perhaps you would prefer *this*?"

The faerie woman vanished, and in her place was Magnus Bane, dressed as he had been at the Market. *Peacock-blue trousers and a matching embroidered waistcoat, with a watch on a glittering chain tucked into one pocket. Silver cuff links glittered at his wrists, and he wore a silver ring set with—*

A luminous blue stone.

"Not Magnus," breathed Cordelia. "It was never—it wasn't Magnus." She felt sick. "James—"

"No," James whispered. "But who, then? This isn't part of Belial's plan. Look at his face."

Indeed, fury had twisted Jesse Blackthorn's features; he was barely recognizable. It was as if his human face was a skin stretched too tightly over the features below: Belial's true, monstrous face. "Enough!" Belial hissed. "Show me who you are."

False Magnus bowed low to the ground, and when he rose, he had transformed once more. Standing before them was a slender woman, her skin pale as milk, and her hair jet-black, falling down her back like dark water. She would have been beautiful but for her eyes: black snakes writhing from otherwise empty sockets. A rope of deep blue gems wound about her throat.

"Lilith," Belial said bitterly. "Of course. I should have known."

25

ARCHANGEL RUINED

His form had yet not lost
All her original brightness, nor appeared
Less than archangel ruined, and the excess
Of glory obscured.
—John Milton, *Paradise Lost*

There was a low moaning sound. It took Lucie a moment to realize it was coming from her. She was lying on her stomach, her cheek pressed to a cold, hard surface. She blinked her eyes open with effort and saw a thick layer of dust on a wooden floor, and ahead of her, a filthy, dark blue wall.

Her head ached so badly the pain sent spikes of nausea through her. Swallowing hard, she pushed herself up on her elbows and looked around.

She was in a long room, high-ceilinged and dancing with dust: above her sparkled a battered chandelier in the shape of a twisted spider. *Aha.* She was in the ballroom of Chiswick House, where she had once climbed through a window and met Jesse.

Jesse. More recent memories came back to her in a flurry—her rush to the coffin, the discovery of the runes on Jesse's body, taking the Blackthorn sword from the wall. The blow from behind and the darkness . . .

Lucie touched the back of her head and felt a painful lump where she had been struck. She twisted around another inch—and saw a froth of gray skirts, and a pair of dove-gray kid boots. She dragged her gaze up. Grace sat a few feet away on a splintered wooden chair, her ankles neatly crossed, her back straight. Across her lap she held a fireplace poker.

Lucie sat up hastily, ignoring the pain in her head. Her back hit the wall; she thrust out her hands defensively as Grace stared at her. "Don't you come near me with that thing again," Lucie gasped. "Why on earth would you—"

Grace looked incredulous. "How can you even ask? Lucie, you— you of all people, standing over my brother with a drawn sword! How could *you* do it? Did you think if you destroyed his body, I could never raise him? Why would you want such a thing?"

Despite everything, Lucie felt a twinge of guilt. In Grace's disbelief and horror, she felt her own horror: she had never wanted to be in that position, never wanted to be a danger to Jesse.

She scrubbed her dusty hands across her face. "You don't know the whole situation," she said. "There's more to it, Grace."

Grace looked skeptical. "More to what? Or do you stand over all your friends brandishing swords while they sleep?"

"Jesse isn't asleep," Lucie said in a low voice. "Grace, I need you to listen to me."

"No!" Grace's eyes flashed. "I shan't." Her hands tightened on the poker. "You've been reluctant for ages now—you haven't wanted to do everything we can to help Jesse. But I've kept trying things, even without you—"

"You mean that horrid incense you were burning out there?" Lucie demanded.

Grace glared. "Burning activated moth powder as a means of catching a wandering spirit is very well attested to by Valdreth the Unliving."

"Well, if Valdreth the Unliving says it'll work, I'm sure it will; necromancers are *notoriously* trustworthy." Lucie's voice dripped sarcasm. "You're right—I haven't wanted to have anything to do with this nonsense, because it can't work. There's no little, harmless way to raise the dead—"

"But it *is* working," said Grace.

Lucie stared at her.

"Jesse has runes now," said Grace, in a small voice. "They've begun to appear on his skin. Sometimes I can see his coffin's been disturbed. Like he's *moving* inside it. Jesse is getting better, Lucie. Ready to come back."

"No," Lucie said, shaking her head. "Oh, no, *no*. I'm sorry, Grace. But it's not your incense or spells or anything else like it that's making runes appear on Jesse." She took a gamble. "You said you'd sacrificed a rabbit out here," she said. "But that didn't happen, did it? You actually quite like animals. There was blood in the shed, but you didn't know where it came from, did you?"

"What are you suggesting?" Grace's voice rose, and Lucie knew she'd been right. "I—yes, I came one morning, and I saw him in the coffin, and there was blood on his clothes. I thought he must have risen and injured himself somehow; I thought—that's *good*, isn't it? Only living things bleed."

"Oh, Grace." Lucie felt immensely sad. "You thought he was coming back to life? I *wish* it was that. He isn't better. He's possessed."

Grace only stared at her. "What?"

Lucie brushed her palms down the skirt of her dress, leaving black smears of dust. "I raised the ghost of a warlock before I came here. Emmanuel Gast. Your mother might have mentioned him." Grace said nothing; undeterred, Lucie plowed on. "He placed the protection spells on your brother when he was born. He said he'd left an anchor in him. In his soul. I think it was—was an opening for a demon to get in and possess him."

There was no sound. No response from Grace. Only her harsh breathing.

"Jesse is not like other ghosts. He is awake at night," said Lucie. "During the day, he sleeps, or something like it. His ghost vanishes when the sun rises. He doesn't remember those hours. All the murders have taken place at dawn, when Jesse would be unconscious, unaware of what his body is doing. Unaware that he was being possessed and controlled."

Grace's lips trembled. "You're saying he's the killer," she said. "That a demon is *using* his body. Making him murder people. Shadowhunters."

"Not just any demon—"

"I know," said Grace. "You mean Belial."

The single word rocked Lucie back against the wall. "You know? *What* do you know?"

"Months ago, when you came here—when I realized you could see Jesse," said Grace. "There was a demon here. My mother had arranged for it to be sent, to threaten me. To demand I do what she wanted." Her voice was leaden. "Do you remember what it said to you?"

Lucie nodded slowly. "'I know you. You are the second one.'"

"I thought at first it meant only: the second Herondale," said Grace. "But I began to suspect more. I went through my mother's private papers. I had always known she dealt with demons, some very powerful indeed. But that was where I saw his name, and I understood. *Belial.* You are the second of his grandchildren."

"Does James know?" Lucie whispered. "About your mother, working with Belial?"

Grace shook her head. "I never wanted him to," she said. "After all, what else do my mother and Belial have in common but a hatred of your family? My mother hates so blindly she could tell herself there was no danger in tying herself to a Prince of Hell. But I never thought—" Her voice shook. "I thought there was one thing she cared about. Jesse."

"She may know nothing about this," said Lucie, a little reluctantly. She hardly wanted to defend Tatiana. "She hired Gast to put the protection spells on Jesse because she hates the Silent Brothers, not because of Belial. She may not even know Belial had left an opening there, a way for him to return and to possess Jesse."

"You think she didn't even guess at it when they put the rune on Jesse and he died?" Grace demanded. "She destroyed him. Her mistrust killed him. And she never took an ounce of the blame, never spoke a word of regret, only said it was the fault of the Nephilim. But it was her fault. Hers."

"You have to let me go," Lucie said. "I have to go after Jesse—stop him—"

"Stop him how?" Grace demanded. "I won't let you go if you might hurt him—he'll come back tonight, he has to come back—"

"And let someone else die? Grace, we can't do that."

It had been the wrong tactic to take. Grace's lips tightened. "I haven't even said I believe you. Just because there was blood in the shed—"

Lucie leaned forward. "Grace. Each Shadowhunter who has been killed is missing a rune, wiped away as if it were never drawn. Elias Carstairs lost his Voyance rune. Filomena di Angelo lost Strength; Lilian Highsmith, Precision. Swiftness, Angelic Power—these are the *same* runes that have appeared on Jesse. I know it seems impossible—"

Grace had gone a sickly gray color. "To move a rune from one Shadowhunter to another? No—not impossible," she said. "But *why?*"

"I don't know," Lucie admitted. "But everyone is looking for the killer, Grace. There are day patrols, dozens of Shadowhunters on the streets, all searching. They could find Jesse. The first thing they would do is destroy his body. I almost did it myself—"

"There are things you can do," Grace said, her pupils very wide. "You can see Jesse, but it's more than that. You can converse with the dead. Sense them, even. What is it, Lucie? What is your power?"

Something in Lucie rebelled. She could not tell her secret to Grace, not before she told Cordelia, before she told James and her parents. It was bad enough that she had told Malcolm. She already owed Cordelia so much more of the truth. "I cannot say. You will just have to trust me."

"I cannot trust you. I cannot trust anyone."

"You trust Jesse," said Lucie. "You *know* Jesse. Better than anyone, Grace. He's talked about you—he worries about you—he says you understand him. That without you, he would have gone mad alone in the house with Tatiana."

Tears welled up in Grace's eyes. Her gaze was fixed on Lucie. "I can't let you hurt him," she whispered.

"He is being hurt now," said Lucie. "He is being imprisoned. Controlled. Forced to do what he would never do if he had a choice. Grace, *please*. Imagine if Jesse knew."

Grace closed her eyes. Tears spilled from beneath her eyelids, tracking through the dust on her face. There was no sign she was aware of them. *Please understand,* Lucie prayed. *Please understand what this means and help me. Could* Grace understand? Grace, who had been brought up by a lunatic in a house of ruin and ghosts?

Grace rose from the chair. "Come with me," she said, and Lucie scrambled upright, desperate with hope. Grace gestured at her with the fireplace poker. "Go on, then," she said, sounding like a school headmistress. "We're going to see him. Jesse."

Using the poker as a sort of prod, she nudged Lucie down the stairs of the manor house, passing into an entryway lined with portraits of Blackthorns past: dark-haired men and women who gazed haughtily down from the walls. Tatiana must have placed them here at some point, to stake her claim on Chiswick House. Below the portraits were engraved copper plates bearing their names (and a thick coat of verdigris): Felix Blackthorn, John Blackthorn, Adelaide Blackthorn. Annabel Blackthorn, read one engraving, though the portrait above it had been slashed through with a knife, rendering the subject unrecognizable. Just the sort of decoration Tatiana would enjoy, Lucie thought.

"Hurry up." Grace brandished the poker like an angry old man with an umbrella. "Lucie!"

"But it's Jesse," Lucie said, stopping in front of another portrait—though he looked quite a bit healthier in it than she'd ever seen him. His skin was tanned, his green eyes bright.

"It isn't," Grace said crossly. "That's his father, Rupert. Now come along, or I shall hit you with the poker."

"You won't, though," said Lucie, with confidence. Grace muttered but didn't contradict her, and together they descended the front steps at a run. Outside it had grown warmer, the sun properly up now. Their feet crunched on the frost-scorched weeds as they crossed the garden and ducked into the shed.

Lucie had braced herself for what they would find. Still, she felt her heart give a painful thump: the coffin lid was open, the coffin itself empty. The Blackthorn sword was gone.

Grace made a despairing noise. Lucie wondered if she had quite believed the truth before this moment. "He's really gone," she whispered. "We're too late. We'll never find him—"

"Yes, we will," Lucie said. "*I* will. I can sense him, Grace. Just like you were saying in the ballroom—I can sense the dead. I'll locate him. And I'll take Balios; I'll be faster than Jesse could be on foot."

Grace nodded, but there was panic on her face. "What should *I* do?"

"Find Malcolm Fade. Tell him what's happening. Tell him I need his help."

Grace hesitated. Feeling as if she had done all she could do, Lucie turned to go—and froze. Grace's hand had shot out, clamping onto Lucie's wrist.

"I'll do it," she said. "I'll seek out Fade. But you must swear you won't let anything happen to Jesse. Swear you'll bring my brother back safe."

There was no artifice in Grace's eyes now, no cunning. Only desperation.

"I swear," Lucie whispered, and took off at a run.

Lilith. The First of All Demons, the mother of warlocks. She was beautiful as a work of art might be beautiful, her face a study in sculpture and symmetry, her hair a cloud that moved of its own accord despite the lack of wind. Cordelia recognized her now from her portrait in the Hell Ruelle, the woman with the serpent's body twined around a tree.

"Of course I am here," she said. Her gaze had flicked over James and Cordelia and rested now on Belial. "When you cast me from my realm, Prince of Hell, I came to this world. Beliya'al, liar, ruin-lover, I could not believe you would have broken the trust of millennia—would have tried to take from me the land granted to me by Heaven itself."

"Heaven," Belial sneered. "Heaven has no place in Edom, and no use for you, *Lilitu.*"

"I wandered the voids between the worlds," Lilith said. "And how the infernal realms were abuzz with the news that Belial had been brought low by his grandson, who could see the shadow realms. How the lower demons chattered that you had been wounded, truly wounded, by the blade Cortana. I realized then that your obsession with this world was an obsession with your own bloodline. That you had managed to sire grandchildren who combine your blood with the blood of Nephilim—and you would never leave that alone."

"Spoken like the barren creature you are," sneered Belial. "Your loins bring forth only monsters, thus you must batten on my offspring, Lady of Owls?"

Lilith curled her lip. "So what has prevented you from seizing your grandson and forcing him to your will? Cortana. You fear Cortana like you fear nothing and no one else. It bears within it a feather of the archangel Michael, who cast you down into the Pit. And the bearer of Cortana is the bride of your grandson. This world is rich in irony indeed."

Belial spat. "Scorn me as you will, Lilith; you cannot touch me. You swore the oath, and Hell's Oath binds you. You cannot harm a Prince of Hell."

James and Cordelia exchanged quizzical looks. Cordelia could not help but recall what Lilith herself, disguised as Magnus, had said at the Shadow Market: that Princes of Hell were engaged in battles with angels themselves, crossing and crisscrossing the chessboard of the universe, obeying and breaking rules no mortal could hope to understand.

"Indeed, I cannot harm you," said Lilith. "But my paladin can."

"*Paladin,*" Belial breathed. He turned to look at Cordelia, his expression half fury, half amusement. "That explains it. You are Nephilim, not an archangel. I should have been able to defeat you."

"Me?" Cordelia said. "No—I am not *her* paladin—"

"Foolish child," said Lilith. "You *are* mine. And while Belial, in his new form, might have been able to defeat a bearer of Cortana, he cannot defeat one who is my paladin."

"That is a lie. I swore fealty to Wayland the Smith—"

"You swore fealty to *me,*" said Lilith. Shadow passed across her, and she changed: a tall man, burly, with close-cropped hair, now stood on the frozen grass where Lilith had been. He wore a bronze torque, and blue fire burned in its center.

Cordelia's mind raced. *A bronze torque with a blue jewel. A blue necklace. Sapphire earrings. A ring with a blue stone. The same jewels. The same—*

Wayland smiled. "Do you not remember the oath you swore me?" Though Cordelia knew it was Lilith, had always been Lilith, the sound of his voice still moved her. "'Whenever I lift up a weapon in battle, I do it in your name.' It was as if you cried out to me, my paladin of the golden blade and the shining scabbard. All that power, bound to my name."

"*No,*" Cordelia whispered. It couldn't be true; she wouldn't allow it to be true. She couldn't look at James, even as the shadow passed again and Lilith was herself once more, the blue stones burning softly at her throat. She turned her serpent gaze on Cordelia.

"I am the Queen of Demons," she said. "In the shape of a Nephilim woman, I touched the hilt of your sword, causing it to burn you from that moment on. As a faerie, I came to you at the Hell Ruelle to tell you of the smith who might mend it. As Wayland himself, I took your oath as my own, made you my paladin, and removed my curse from your blade. As Magnus Bane, I brought you close to Edom. As myself, I sent the Hauras and Naga demons to entice you into battle, to show you what a paladin could do. I choreographed each decision you made, each step you took." There was pity in her voice. "Do not blame yourself. You are but mortals. You could never have known."

But Cordelia was beyond hearing her. Her heartbeat was loud in her ears, every pulse seeming to snap an accusation: *stupid, foolish, reckless, arrogant.* How could she have believed she would have been chosen as Wayland the Smith's paladin? That he would have offered such a gift so quickly, with so little consideration, simply because he liked the look of her? She had wanted to be a hero so badly it had blinded her, and now she was here, crushed and shamed, gazing into the dark.

Lilith said, "I cannot harm you directly, Belial, it is true. I am not an oath breaker. But as a woman I am well accustomed to using methods other than brute force. With a paladin and Cortana at my disposal, the oath cannot stop me. When I learned that you'd recruited your stupidest brother to invade this world, I knew you must be desperate, and that your confrontation with my paladin would happen soon. And here we are."

She spread her hands out, smiling a sideways catlike smile.

"What do you want, Lilith?" Belial demanded.

"Edom," said Lilith. "Return my realm to me and I will remove my protection and power from Cordelia. You can slay her and end this business as you see fit. I wish only my kingdom back."

"You would try to force me?" Belial demanded. His eyes were green fire. "You would try to make demands of me, you who never learned obedience? Who were cast out because of it?"

"I may have been cast out," said Lilith. "But *I* did not *fall*."

"You will never best me." Belial raised his blade, and for a moment, he seemed to be Jesse—a young Nephilim warrior with a shining sword, gleaming in the sunlight. "Send your paladin against me.

I shall give her back to you in pieces, and your realm in ruins!"

Cordelia felt James catch at her wrist; she thought he was trying to pull her away, perhaps to safety. She barely knew. There was no safety for her, would be none as long as she was the paladin of Lilith. There was only rage and emptiness.

"Cordelia," Lilith said, her voice a low flame. "Take up your sword. Kill Belial."

"No." Cordelia forced herself to break away from James. She ought to look at him, she thought, try to show him she realized he was trying to help, that she appreciated it even as she knew it was hopeless. But her body had already begun to move on its own; it was as if puppet strings were bound to her arms and legs, jerking them into motion. She watched her own hand lift Cortana into the ready position, unable to stop herself, even as she bit her lip savagely until she tasted blood.

The vow that she had made to Wayland the Smith came back to her, repeating itself tauntingly in her mind.

I swear my courage. I swear neither to falter nor to fail in battle. Whenever I draw my sword, whenever I lift up a weapon in battle, I shall do it in your name.

Something silver flashed past Cordelia; James had hurled a throwing knife, with his usual unerring accuracy; it shot toward Lilith, who raised a slim white hand and caught the knife by the blade.

James swore. Cordelia could not look to see Lilith's reaction: she was walking toward Belial, who stood smirking, his blade gripped in his hand. It was as if she were in a dream; she could not stop herself. She raised Cortana and, for the first time in her life, took no pleasure in the golden arc of the blade as it passed across the sun.

"*Kill him,*" Lilith hissed.

Cordelia flung herself at Belial.

Blade slammed against blade, metal grinding; Cordelia felt the same burning in her bones, the clang and crash in her heart that echoed the sounds of battle. But there was no joy in it now, not even that she could swing faster, leap higher, duck and parry and blow with the silent speed of a dream. Not even the dark joy of battling a Prince of Hell.

She raised her eyes and met the icy depths of Belial's gaze. Was this how it was to be an angel who fell? Cordelia thought. To have once served what was good, and radiantly beautiful, and to find instead that every gesture was turned toward the service of evil and the Pit? Was there a screaming hollow place in Belial's soul, the way there was now in hers?

Belial hissed, as if sensing her thoughts; the Blackthorn sword swept in from the right, slicing across her shoulder as she turned to duck it; she heard Lilith scream in rage, and suddenly she was spinning back, heedless of the danger, her sword whirling in her grasp—

James cried out. There was a flash of movement as something darted between Cordelia and Belial, arms outstretched wide to protect him.

Not something. Someone.

Lucie.

Cortana was already moving, ripping a path through the air that would cut Lucie apart. With a last, desperate convulsion, Cordelia wrenched her body sideways, against Lilith's will. Her sword thrust went wide as she staggered, collapsing to her knees before pushing herself immediately upright again. She turned back toward Lucie, pain shooting through her like daggers. Lucie's eyes were huge, pleading with Cordelia: *Daisy, don't do it. Daisy, no.*

But Cortana seemed to burn in Cordelia's hands, the blade whispering, demanding, telling her what to do.

It would be easy to make the pain stop. Just raise the sword and cut Lucie down.

It took everything she had to hold herself still. The pressure was brutal, pushing from the inside outward, clenching her hand around Cortana's hilt.

"Lucie!" James called, starting toward his sister. "Lucie, *get out of the way!*"

Lucie shook her head wildly. She looked impossibly small and fragile, her arms flung wide, shielding Belial. "I know why you want to hurt him," she said. "But you can't—I summoned Emmanuel Gast, he told me everything—Jesse is *innocent*—"

"There is no Jesse," James said, coming closer. "That's his body. What animates it is Belial. Jesse Blackthorn is *dead*, Lucie."

"No," Lucie said, "he isn't dead, not the way you think. He can be saved, he can be brought back—"

Belial chuckled. "I must say, this is *very* entertaining."

Lucie looked at Cordelia, wide-eyed and beseeching. "Daisy, listen to me—"

"No." Lilith's voice was low, throaty; it echoed in Cordelia's mind. "Listen to *me*, paladin. Rise and strike down Belial. If Lucie Herondale stands in your way, kill her, too."

Cordelia took a lurching step forward. Blood dripped down her chin. Her lip felt torn open, but the pain was a distant buzz. Far more intense was the pain of resisting Lilith's will. It felt as if her veins were burning. "Lucie," she gasped. "You have to get out of the way—"

"I won't," Lucie said defiantly. "Daisy, I know you wouldn't hurt me."

Energy was gathering in Cordelia's hands, wrapping them around the hilt of Cortana. Her arms ached with the effort of holding herself back; she knew if she let her control slip for even a moment, she would run Lucie through. "Lucie, please, for the love of the Angel, get out of the way—"

Belial snarled something in a language Cordelia had never heard; his free hand went to his belt, pulling the Colt pistol free. He aimed it at Lilith, his upper lip curled back, and pulled the trigger.

The hammer came down with a dry click.

Lilith laughed. "A *gun?*" she said. "Beliya'al, have you become foolish, demented in your old age? You, who brought nations into darkness? Shall I finally be able to tell the infernal realms you have gone mad, lost even the image of the Creator?"

"*Grandfather!*" James shouted. He flung a hand in the air. Belial, who had been glaring at Lilith, looked at him in astonishment. James stood straight as an arrow, his golden eyes blazing, his hand outstretched. He threw back his head and cried out, "*I have come to bring fire on the earth!*"

"Kill them!" Lilith shouted, her black hair whipping about her face, her serpent eyes darting. "Paladin, *now! Kill them both!*"

Cordelia felt her arm savagely jerked back, as if by invisible wires. She raised Cortana. Tears mixing with the blood on her face, she said, "Lucie, Lucie, please—"

Belial took a step back—and flung the Colt revolver to James.

It seemed to take an age to reach him, an age during which Cordelia struggled, the muscles in her body screaming as she fought not to move Cortana, not to slice the blade across Lucie's throat, where her gold locket glimmered. An age during which the gun flashed through the air, nickel and silver, turning end over end before it smacked into James's palm.

James pivoted. The gun seemed an extension of his own body as he sighted along his arm, aimed at Lilith—and pulled the trigger.

The gunshot was loud as a cannon in the still air. The bullet punched into Lilith with a force that lifted her from her feet. With a howl, she burst apart, scattering into a dozen black owls; they took to the air, circling and screeching.

The vise grip on Cordelia loosened; she crumpled to her knees, clutching Cortana. She gasped, breath sawing in and out of her lungs, black spots dancing in front of her eyes. *Lucie. I almost killed Lucie.*

The owls rose overhead, their awful screeches echoing in Cordelia's mind, becoming words that hung, silently, behind her eyelids.

Do not forget, paladin. You are mine to command.

The screeching faded. The air smelled of cordite and blood, and someone was laughing. Cordelia raised her head slowly and saw that it was Belial. He was chortling as if immensely amused, the Blackthorn sword dancing in his hand. "James, James," he said. "Do you see what we can accomplish if we work together? You have banished the Mother of Demons!"

"She's not dead," James said flatly.

"No, but gone and weakened," said Belial cheerfully. "Are you ready to fight again, Carstairs? For I think you will find it quite a different experience to battle me without the power of Lilith to protect you."

Shaking his head, James pointed the gun at Belial. "Let her alone," he said, sounding exhausted. "Go from this place. I will not try to follow."

Belial snorted. "You know you cannot harm me with that. I am not Lilith; I have no weakness where the Three Angels are concerned. Besides," he added with a twisted grin, "your sister does not want me hurt."

"My sister doesn't understand what you are." James gestured with the muzzle of the gun. "Lucie. Move out of the way."

"No." Lucie set her jaw stubbornly. "James. Jesse is still there, part of this body. He's inside. James, *he saved your life.* In Highgate Cemetery.

You were dying, and he gave me this locket"—she touched her throat—"because it had his last breath inside it. He gave it to me to save you."

In Highgate Cemetery. Cordelia remembered that night. The darkness, the pain she had been in, the terror that James would die. The shimmer of gold in Lucie's hand. She had asked Lucie many times what had happened in the graveyard that night, what had cured James, but Lucie had always shaken her head and said she didn't know. That it had just been luck.

So many secrets between them. So many lies.

"His last breath." James was still pointing the gun at Belial, his aim unwavering, but he spoke the words as if they had some puzzling, unknown meaning for him. "I saw him—"

"Enough. You dull, disobedient children," said Belial. "Shoot me if you like, James; it will make no difference. Nor can the paladin protect you now." He lifted the Blackthorn sword, moving easily, lightly, with no sign of weariness. "I shall cut down your wife and your sister as easily as scything grass."

"No," James said raggedly.

"You know what choice you have to make." Belial took a step toward James, shoving Lucie out of the way; she stumbled aside. "You know what you must give up. Your family, the Institute, all depends on you."

Lucie's eyes widened. "James? What does he mean?" She turned to Belial. "*Jesse,*" she said. "Don't do this—I *know* you're inside there, I know you don't want this—"

"Be quiet," Belial snapped. "You, girl, do not matter. Your little talent with ghosts does not matter. When I heard you were born, I wept tears of fire, for you were female, and you could not see the shadow realms. You are useless, do you understand? Useless to me, to the world."

But Lucie—slight and small, without a weapon in her hand—only looked at him steadily. "Talk all you want," she said. "*You* certainly don't matter. Only Jesse matters." She held out her hands. "Jesse," she said. "Be yourself and only yourself. Cast Belial from your body."

Belial burst into laughter. "Oh, granddaughter, that is adorable. But I am not so easily gotten rid of."

"*Jesse,*" Lucie whispered, and there was something about the way she said his name. *She loves him,* Cordelia thought, with a sudden astonishment. *She loves him, and I never even knew he existed.* "Jesse, I know you told me never to command you unless you asked me to. But this is different. A terrible thing was done to you." Lucie's voice shook. "You have never had any choice. But you can choose now. To trust me. To come to me. Please, Jesse."

"Ugh." Belial looked faintly nauseated. "This is quite enough."

"Jesse Blackthorn. I *command* you," Lucie said, her voice rising, "to cast Belial from your body. Be *yourself.*"

"I said *enough,*" Belial roared, and then his body jerked, the Blackthorn sword flying from his hand as he doubled over. He fell to one knee, his head thrown back. His mouth and eyes flew open, stretching impossibly wide.

Cordelia staggered to her feet, lifting Cortana. It felt heavy in her hand, as it had not before, but still familiar. Still powerful. She raised the blade.

"Not yet!" Lucie cried. "Daisy, wait—"

Belial spasmed. Dark light burst from his eyes, his mouth: a flood of blackness, pouring into the air like smoke. He turned, twisted, like a bug impaled on a metal spike. His body bent back, an impossible, awful curve, his shoulders nearly touching the ground as his hands flailed, reaching out to catch at nothing.

"*Deus meus!*" Belial screamed, and Cordelia understood: he was calling out for his Maker, the Creator he had rejected thousands of years ago. "*Deus meus respice me quare me dereliquisti longe a salute mea verba delictorum meorum—*"

There was the sound of a great tearing. The shadow that poured from Belial's eyes began to coalesce, a shower of darkness that swirled and turned in the air. Jesse's body crumpled to the ground, going limp as the animating force of Belial's spirit left it.

Lucie dropped to her knees next to Jesse, her hands on his chest. She made a little broken keening sound. More than anything, Cordelia wanted to go to her, but she stood where she was, gripping Cortana, knowing it was not yet over.

For above Jesse's body, his feet not touching the ground of Earth, hovered Belial.

Though it was not quite Belial. He was form and shape, but no substance—translucent as colored air. Cordelia could see *through* him: he wore a robe of white samite, edged with graphic black runes, jagged as lightning bolts. Behind him, she could see the shadow, the suggestion of wings: great, black, ragged wings, their edges as serrated as knives.

Darkness leaked from a slit in the material over his chest: the still-bleeding wound she had given him in the shadow realm. Malevolent eyes gazed from a face of thunder, fixed on Lucie with loathing. "Oh," he said, and his voice sounded different now that it was no longer emerging from Jesse Blackthorn's throat—darker, and freighted with the promise of a terrible threat, "how you do not know what you have done."

"Leave us," said James. He had come close to where Lucie and Cordelia were on the path. His eyes were blazing; his hand with the gun in it hung at his side. "This is over."

"This is no end," said Belial, "but a beginning you cannot even imagine." His voice rose, raggedly; it was like listening to the crackle of a fire burning out of control. "'For I will set my face against you so that you will be struck down before your enemies; and those who hate you will rule over you, and you will flee when no one is pursuing you. If also after these things you do not obey me, then I will punish you seven times more for your sins. I will break down your pride of power; I will make your sky like iron and your earth like bronze—'"

Cordelia's last thread of control snapped. She charged toward Belial, Cortana in hand; it made a beautiful golden arc through the air, with all her strength behind it—but the blade passed through him without resistance.

She staggered back, despair clutching at her heart. If Cortana could no longer harm him—if there was no substance of him she could strike at—

"Daisy!" Lucie cried. "Be careful!"

"Indeed, be careful," Belial sneered, drifting closer to her. There was a stench in the air around him, like old rubbish burning. "Little stupid child, little helpless human. You know where your power comes from now—from Lilith. Not from good as you thought, but from evil. She is off now licking her wounds, but she will return, and she owns you. Anytime you draw a weapon, she will be summoned. You will *never* escape her."

Cordelia cried out. She raised Cortana again, knowing there was no use, no point—

Suddenly James was there, throwing an arm around her from behind. He seemed heedless of Cortana as he drew her back against him, whispering in her ear, "'Neither death, nor life, nor angels, nor demons, nor principalities, nor powers, nor things present, nor things to come, shall be able to separate us.' Do you understand? Keep hold of me, Daisy. Keep hold of me and don't let go."

She heard Lucie cry out. Looking down, Cordelia saw that the arm around her had begun to fade at the edges. The tips of James's fingers turned black—the darkness spread, up his arm, *through* him. He was becoming a shadow.

But something more was happening. Darkness spread from him and into her at the point of contact between their two bodies. She watched her forearm, where his hand rested, go cloudy and dark. A strange sensation passed through her, a feeling of travel without movement, of transforming into something both less and more than herself.

Was this what it had always been like for James when he tumbled into the shadow realms? For the world had gone dark around her, the trees standing out stark white against a black sky, the paths branching like bones through the skin of a hazy, tenebrous world. The sun glimmered like a coin at the bottom of a murky pool. Lucie was a shadow; Belial a dim shade with gleaming eyes.

The shadows had spread up Cordelia's arm and down to her wrist, through her hand, passing into Cortana. The blade alone had color. The blade alone shone, golden, in the darkness.

Before Belial could react, Cordelia leaned forward—James's arm still around her—and plunged the blade into his chest, directly below the wound she'd given him before.

Belial twisted, impaled on her blade as a darker shadow—blood? essence?—spilled from the new wound; head thrown back, he shrieked soundlessly at the sky.

And the sky answered. Briefly, the world seemed to yawn apart—the clouds parted like tearing fabric, and Cordelia saw past them to a vast plain of darkness, starless and infinite. Out in that darkness swirled the great horrors of the voids between worlds, the emptiness where evil grew hungry and intemperate, where the Princes of Hell stalked in all their power, the cold rulers of nothingness.

Belial stretched up toward that nothingness, reaching out his hands. Cordelia jerked Cortana free—for a moment, Belial seemed to look at her, his face a mask of ferocious hatred—and then it was as if he was seized, and carried up into the outer darkness. There was a flash of whiteness, the ragged flapping of wings—and he was gone.

Slowly, James let go of Cordelia. As his arm loosened around her, color came back to the world, color and sound: Cordelia could hear birds again, the sound of wind in trees, distant voices. She could hear Lucie, whispering words of farewell.

Cordelia opened her hand, releasing Cortana. It fell to the ground, striking the earth with a sound like a tolling bell. She backed away from it—it was not her sword now, despite what had just happened. No one who had sworn fealty to the Queen of Demons should bear a blade like Cortana.

"*Daisy!* Are you all right?" James caught at her shoulders, turning her toward him. His eyes raked over her anxiously, checking for injuries. "You're not hurt?"

Cordelia glanced down. She was scratched, but that was nothing to the spot in her heart where the knowledge that she was Lilith's paladin now bit like teeth. She couldn't look at James—she glanced over and saw Lucie, who was kneeling by Jesse's body. He lay where he had fallen, motionless and unbreathing. If he had not been truly dead before, he was now. Lucie looked utterly lost.

Cordelia closed her eyes, and hot tears spilled down her cheeks, scorching her skin.

"Daisy," she heard James say; she felt his stele brush over her arm, the faint sting and then the numbness of healing runes being applied. "Daisy, my love, I'm so sorry—"

"James!" called a puzzled voice, and Cordelia opened her eyes and looked over to see Matthew waving from beside the bronze statue. He looked utterly baffled; he was kneeling beside Charles, who was sitting up with his back against the side of the fountain. Charles looked pale, his hand to his chest, but seemed very much alive.

"*James!*" Matthew called again, cupping his hands around his mouth and shouting. "What on earth is going on?"

The three of them—Lucie, James, and Cordelia—bolted back across the park toward the Fairchild brothers. James fell to his knees beside Matthew, who still had his stele in one hand. His other hand rested on Charles's shoulder.

It was quickly clear that Charles and Matthew had been frozen the moment Belial had entered the park; no time had passed for them at all. As far as Matthew was concerned, he'd looked up between one moment and the next to find James and Cordelia standing at the other end of the park with Lucie, who seemed to have appeared out of thin air.

"Charles? What on earth?" Lucie gasped; she was already white as a sheet, and the sight of Charles bleeding on the ground didn't seem to be helping. "I don't understand—"

"Neither do I," said Matthew grimly, drawing two more healing runes on Charles's bare forearm. Charles seemed only half-conscious, his eyelids drooping, his shirtfront wet with blood. "We need to get Charles to the Institute—they can summon the Silent Brothers—"

James shook his head. "Not the Institute. It won't be safe."

Matthew's forehead creased in confusion. "Why wouldn't it be safe?"

Cordelia sat down on the edge of the fountain as James explained, as quickly as he could, what had happened. It seemed a great deal to him, and yet it also seemed to have taken no time at all: already the events were a blur of motion, shock, and blood.

When he reached the part of the story that involved Lilith, he found himself slowing down. Charles was resting against his brother, breathing harshly but steadily. Lucie said, "I don't understand. Why would Lilith—Lilith, the Queen of Demons—think that Cordelia was her paladin?"

"Because I am." Cordelia was sitting on the edge of the fountain. She had placed Cortana back in its scabbard. Her posture was rigid— she looked like someone who'd been dealt an awful blow and was tensed for another. "I swore fealty to someone I thought was Wayland the Smith." James saw Matthew's expression change; he looked down, suddenly, at the ground. "But it was Lilith, disguised. I was foolish to assume Wayland the Smith would want me as a paladin. It was a trick."

"We were all tricked, Daisy," said Lucie. "We all believed it was Magnus Bane we spoke to at the Shadow Market. You were not foolish."

"I was arrogant," Cordelia said. James wanted more than anything else to get up and to put his arms around her. He held himself back. "If it had not been for James—and for you, Lucie—this might all have ended in more disaster."

"That is not true," said James intently. "You are the one who delivered the second blow to Belial—without you, I could never—"

"Don't go." The voice was a hoarse whisper. James froze; it was Charles. His eyelids fluttered, though he seemed barely conscious still. His head moved restlessly from side to side, his bare hand clawing at the ground. Matthew laid a hand on his brother's shoulder, guilt and worry etched on his face, just as Charles said, very clearly, "Alastair. Don't leave."

They all stared at each other in astonishment—all, James realized, except Cordelia. She looked chagrined, but not at all surprised.

Matthew blinked. "He's hallucinating," he said gruffly. "He needs another blood-replacement rune—"

"I'll do it," James said, and was in the process of following through when Lucie cried out and leaped to her feet, pointing toward the main entrance of the park. Riding toward them through the gates, on a brown bay horse with a white star on its nose, was Malcolm Fade, High Warlock of London.

Catching sight of them, he dismounted from his horse and strode over. James, feeling he had lost the ability to be shocked or surprised by anything, finished the blood-replacement rune and rose to his feet. "Mr. Fade," he said as Malcolm approached. "What are you doing here?"

"Just happened by," said Malcolm, crouching down to peer into Charles's face. He put a gloved hand under Charles's chin and muttered a few words in a low voice. There was a spark of dark purple flame, and Charles jolted, blinking around as if he'd just woken up.

Matthew stared. "Is he—all right now?"

"He ought to see one of your Silent Brothers," said Malcolm.

"But he's better, certainly. Whoever he is." He squinted. "Is that the Consul's son?"

"Warlocks never just 'happen by,'" James said. "Not that we don't appreciate your help—"

For some reason Malcolm looked sharply at Lucie. She stared back at him, her expression hard for James to read. At last Malcolm straightened up. "The gate between worlds has closed," he said gruffly. "Leviathan has been forced out."

James sprang to his feet. "The attack on the Institute—it's over?"

Malcolm confirmed that the Institute had been attacked, the attacker had been a single monster: the Prince of Hell, Leviathan, who had slipped through a door, a gap between dimensions. "There were a few injuries, and quite a bit of property damage—but your people were very lucky, in fact. The Portal connecting Leviathan to Earth was very small, only about the size of the Institute courtyard."

"That doesn't seem *small*," said Cordelia.

Malcolm smiled thinly. "For Leviathan, it was as if you wished to enter your house through a mousehole. He could only poke a few of his lesser tendrils through."

"Those were his *lesser tendrils?*" James said. He pushed his hair back out of his face; there were bloodstains on his hands. "It's because the sigil wasn't completed. Because Charles didn't die."

"I'm feeling much better," said Charles, though James would not have described him as *looking* much better. He was still quite pale, his lips bluish. There was only so much quick spells and blood-replacement runes could do. He squinted at Malcolm. "Are you the High Warlock?" he said. "I'm delighted to make your acquaintance at last. I'm Charles Fairchild—you might know my mother, the Consul."

"*Charles*," Matthew muttered through clenched teeth. "You've just been *stabbed*."

Charles was undeterred. "I regret, of course, that we didn't meet under more auspicious circumstances—"

"Save your strength," Malcolm said, rather curtly. "You'll never get your political career off the ground if you die of your wounds today." He turned to James. "This talk of a sigil is very interesting, but I can keep mundanes out of this garden for only so long. There is a school here, *and* a church; fairly soon there will begin to be a commotion. I suggest we return to the Institute."

"Not without Jesse," said Lucie. "He fought back, he—" She broke off, looking at Malcolm. "He ought to have the Shadowhunter funeral his mother denied him years ago." She turned to Matthew. "Math, could we borrow your ridiculous overcoat? To wrap Jesse in?"

Matthew looked both sympathetic and slightly vexed as he shucked off the coat. "Yes," he said, "but it isn't ridiculous."

"It isn't nearly your *most* ridiculous overcoat," James allowed. "But it is also far from your least."

Muttering, Matthew rose and handed the overcoat to Lucie. James and Matthew maneuvered Charles to his feet, draping his arm over Matthew's shoulder. The group made their way the short distance across the park to where Jesse's body lay, the Blackthorn sword fallen nearby.

Lucie knelt down and, with her fingertips, closed his eyes gently. She laid the sword on his chest and folded his arms over it, tucking his hands over the hilt.

"*Ave atque vale*, Jesse Blackthorn," said James, looking at the pale face he remembered from Highgate Cemetery. The ghost who had saved his life. *Hail and farewell, my brother. I wish I had known you.*

Flame sparked from Malcolm's fingers as he began to open a Portal through to the Institute. James wrapped Jesse's body in Matthew's medium-ridiculous overcoat, and Malcolm scooped him up as though he weighed no more than a child. Matthew and Charles approached, slowly; Charles was walking under his own power, although leaning heavily on Matthew. Cordelia had taken hold of Lucie's hand, and she held it tightly as—without a glance back—Malcolm went through the Portal carrying Jesse.

The rest of them followed.

26

OLDER THAN GODS

With travail of day after day, and with trouble of hour upon hour;
And bitter as blood is the spray; and the crests are as fangs that devour:
And its vapor and storm of its steam as the sighing of spirits to be;
And its noise as the noise in a dream; and its depths as the roots of the sea:
And the height of its heads as the height of the utmost stars of the air:
And the ends of the earth at the might thereof tremble, and time is made bare.
Will ye bridle the deep sea with reins, will ye chasten the high sea with rods?
Will ye take her to chain her with chains, who is older than all ye Gods?
—Algernon Charles Swinburne, "Hymn to Proserpine"

The Portal deposited them just inside the front gates of the Institute.

Lucie had tried to prepare herself, but her first glimpse of the church was still a shock. The courtyard had been rucked up like a rug. Stones lay in great uneven piles, scattering the ground from the iron gates to the front steps. Water ran in rivulets through the cracks in the remaining flagstone, smelling of brine and ocean. A massive hole in the center of the courtyard seemed punched there by a giant.

For once, Lucie didn't feel as if any of this would make a good subject for a novel. She felt drained and exhausted, and worried for Cordelia. Since finding out she was Lilith's paladin, Daisy hadn't smiled once; she seemed locked away in her own private unhappiness, the way James often did. Matthew kept glancing at Cordelia covertly, his own expression troubled.

They had battled both Belial and Lilith and survived, Lucie thought, yet it felt very little like a victory. She was finding it more difficult than she would have thought to preserve the impression that she and Malcolm barely knew each other, and had very definitely *not* previously had several intense and secret conversations about necromancy. Secrets were horrible things to keep, she reflected: she'd only barely remembered before they stepped through the Portal to warn James that their parents thought she'd spent the previous night at Curzon Street instead of haring off to Chiswick House to try to prevent Belial from again possessing Jesse.

"I would prefer not to walk into the Institute carrying the body of a Shadowhunter," said Malcolm. "I fear it might create the wrong impression."

"I'll bring you to the Sanctuary," Lucie said. "We can lay out Jesse's body there."

James kissed her forehead. "Don't take too long. I expect once Mam and Dad realize we haven't all been tucked safely up at Curzon Street, they'll be desperate to see you."

Lucie led Malcolm toward the Sanctuary, picking her way among the rubble. Fade strode behind her silently, carrying Jesse; he was gazing around speculatively, as if assessing the damage. Lucie couldn't help but wonder: Was the Institute damaged inside as well? Would they need to move? She could see a few ragged places where stones had been torn from the front edifice, but it seemed to be standing strongly.

A cloaked figure came around the corner of the building, near the door to the Sanctuary. *Ghost*, Lucie thought at first before she realized: no, this was someone real and alive. The figure turned, and she saw Grace, wrapped in a dark gray cloak, only a bit of her hair and face visible beneath the hood.

"Hush," Malcolm said, causing Lucie to bristle slightly—it wasn't as if she'd been about to call out Grace's name. She wasn't a fool. "I told her to meet us here. Come."

Lucie glanced over anxiously at the other end of the courtyard, but if James had noticed Grace at all, he gave no sign—he was greeting several Shadowhunters who had emerged from the Institute. Lucie recognized Charlotte, who had made a distressed beeline for her sons.

Grace moved out of the shadows toward Malcolm and Lucie, then recoiled as she caught sight of the bundle in Malcolm's arms. "What happened? Is he—is that Jesse?"

Lucie put a finger to her lips and ushered her companions into the Sanctuary. Inside, there were still signs of Thomas and Alastair's imprisonment—a chair turned over, a messy pile of blankets, the remnants of food. Malcolm carried Jesse to a long mahogany table and laid him down there, discarding the overcoat.

Grace gave a little cry as she caught sight of the still-wet blood on Jesse's body. His hands were still folded over the Blackthorn sword. She darted to his side. "Is he all right?"

"He's as dead as he was before," said Malcolm, somewhat impatiently. "He's certainly better for having Belial cast out of him, but that doesn't make him alive."

Grace looked at Lucie in a little surprise, but Lucie only shook her head slightly. She had suspected Malcolm might have witnessed more of the fight in Mount Street Gardens than he was letting on.

"The anchor is gone," Lucie said. "I can sense that, but I can also sense that Jesse, the essential spark of him—that's still there."

But Grace was shaking her head. Her hood had fallen back, and her blond hair tumbled down over her shoulders, loose from its pins. "Why did you bring him here?" she said. "This is the Sanctuary, the heart of the Institute. Once the Nephilim find out what happened, they'll burn his body."

"There was no way to hide it from them," said Lucie. "Too many people know. And we were never going to be able to raise him here in London. Malcolm and I talked at the Shadow Market, before today, and the only way to do it is to take him away from here, Grace."

Grace had gone rigid. "Now?"

"Tonight," said Lucie. "They will let his body remain here until morning, but tomorrow they'll move him to Idris. And that will be that."

"You didn't ask me," said Grace stiffly. "If it would be all right to take him."

"This is his only chance," said Malcolm. "If you truly wish me to attempt necromancy, I will not do it in the heart of the city. I must have space, and my instruments and books. And even then, I cannot promise."

"But you have an arrangement," said Grace, straightening. "With Lucie. An agreement. She has convinced you."

"She has offered me an equitable exchange," said Malcolm, buttoning his sweeping coat. "And in return, I will take your brother away from London, to a safe place, and do what I can for him. If you refuse that, I will do nothing."

"No one knows you are here, Grace, do they?" said Lucie. "No one knows you're part of this at all."

"The Bridgestocks think I'm at their house. But I don't see what that has—"

"You can come with us," said Lucie.

Malcolm raised an eyebrow. Even Grace looked stunned. "What?"

"I said you can come with us," said Lucie. "No one would be expecting it, or trying to prevent you from departing. We leave tonight, with Jesse; you may join us or not. Otherwise, the matter is out of your hands now."

James had intended to tell the truth, all of it, the moment he saw his father and mother. But things had not turned out quite that simply.

Like the others, he had been stunned by the destruction wrought on the Institute—the strange juxtaposition of the cloudless blue sky above, mundanes wandering by outside the gates, and the wreckage within. He had seen the distress on Lucie's face as she hurried off to the Sanctuary with Malcolm: he could not blame her. The Institute had been the only home either of them had known.

Until these past weeks. The house on Curzon Street had rapidly become home to James, though he suspected that had less to do with the house and more to do with who shared it with him.

Charles was limping heavily, so James took his other arm to help Matthew guide him across the courtyard. They were nearly to the front doors when they opened, and Thomas, Christopher, and Anna poured out, followed by Charlotte and Gideon.

There was a confused babble of voices, of hugs and relief. James exclaimed at Thomas being out of prison; Thomas explained that he'd been tested by the Mortal Sword and found innocent.

"Though," said Christopher, "Bridgestock was still complaining about it when the demon attacked. I doubt he'd get much support for tossing Tom back in prison now, though, after he distinguished himself in battle. He defeated a whole tentacle all by himself!"

"Indeed," said Thomas. He grinned at James. "A whole tentacle."

Charlotte had raced over to Matthew and Charles; she kissed Matthew fiercely on the cheek and exclaimed worriedly over Charles until Gideon came to take over from James and help Matthew bring his brother to the infirmary. They departed, Charlotte darting off to fetch Henry to Charles's bedside.

"Henry was quite impressive with his staff," said Anna. "The chains rather put my whip to shame."

Thomas had taken Cordelia aside; James heard him say something about the battle, and the name *Alastair*, and he saw Cordelia brighten. So Alastair was all right; James realized he was relieved about it, and not just for Cordelia's sake. Interesting. Ariadne, too, was fine, according to Anna and Christopher. There had been no deaths, and the most seriously injured were in the infirmary, being tended to by the Brothers.

Ariadne appeared at the top of the steps. Usually neat and put-together, she wore torn gear, a bandage around one arm. Her cheek was scratched, her hair tangled. Her eyes were alight. "Anna, is everything—?" She brightened at the sight of Cordelia and James. "Oh, lovely," she said. "Mr. and Mrs. Herondale were just saying they were going to send to Curzon Street for you."

James and Cordelia exchanged a look. "And where are my parents, exactly?" said James. "It's best I talk to them as soon as possible."

He was still planning to tell the whole truth, even as Ariadne led them all to the library. Thomas, Christopher, and Anna were describing the attack—Gabriel had nearly been badly hurt, but a group effort had freed him from Leviathan's barbed tentacles—and Cordelia was still walking along in silence.

James wanted to put his arms around her, to hug her, to whisper comfort in her ear. But she was holding herself the way she had when her father died: still and careful, as if too spontaneous a movement might shatter her. He could not comfort her without exciting curiosity among the others, and he knew Cordelia did not want their sympathy. Not right now.

"You'll be glad to know Uncle Jem and Magnus are back," Anna said, glancing at James sideways as they reached the library door. "Apparently an Institute being attacked by a Prince of Hell is surprising enough news even to reach the Spiral Labyrinth. What happened to you lot, by the way? You were meant to be snug at home, but you look as if you've been through a war."

"Would you believe it if I said parlor games gone terribly wrong?" said James.

Anna smiled; there was a quizzical turn to her mouth. "You seem different," she said, but there was no time for her to expound: they had come into the library and it was absolutely packed full of Shadowhunters.

Will was there, sitting at the head of a long table. Tessa standing beside him. Many of the assembled Nephilim, like Catherine Townsend and Piers Wentworth, wore the marks of recent battle: bandages, torn clothes, and blood. Some, like the Bridgestocks and Pouncebys, were gathered into clusters, muttering and gesticulating. Others sat at the table with Will and Tessa. Sophie was there—Cecily and Alexander were likely in the infirmary with Gabriel—as was Alastair, who looked up as they came in. Seeing Cordelia, he got to his feet.

"*James!*" Will was beaming, and for a moment James forgot everything but how glad he was to see his family. He went to embrace his father, and hugged his mother, too: for the first time, she felt light and almost frail to him. He wished he had been here for the battle, that he had been able to protect them more directly than he had.

When Tessa drew back, she eyed James with concern. "By the Angel, what's happened to you—and to Daisy?" she said, taking in their bedraggled appearances. "How did you know to come?"

"Didn't you send Malcolm to fetch us?" James said, glancing over at Cordelia; she was being embraced by Alastair.

"No," said Will, his brow furrowed.

"I must have misunderstood what he said," said James quickly. "Never mind—"

"Where's your sister?" said Will. "And the High Warlock, too, for that matter?"

"They're in the Sanctuary," said James. "And Matthew's in the infirmary with Charles and his parents."

Sophie, who had been in the middle of unbuckling her leather gauntlets, looked up. "What's happened to Charles?"

Will sat down on the table, his booted feet braced on the nearby chair. "I am getting the feeling," he said, "that there is a story here. Perhaps the other half of the story we already know. Would you say that's correct, James?"

James hesitated. "If we could speak in private—"

"Certainly not." The voice was the Inquisitor's. "If you think there is any chance of more of this business being kept from the Enclave—"

"No one's been keeping anything from the Enclave," said Will. His eyes were heavy-lidded, which meant he was quite angry. "Least of all my son."

"We have been attacked," said Bridgestock, his voice rising. He looked as if he hadn't been in the battle at all—his robes were spotless— but his voice throbbed with rage, nonetheless. "By a creature of the Pit. Sent by Hell itself to wipe us off the face of the Earth. Someone has called the sea demon forth. 'Let them curse it that curse the day, who are ready to raise up Leviathan—'"

"And who are you suggesting has called up Leviathan?" said Tessa, crossing her arms over her chest.

"I am saying we have been lazy; we have allowed corruption among ourselves," said Bridgestock. His small eyes glittered. "We have allowed among ourselves the descendants of demons."

That was the moment that James decided telling the whole truth would not be possible.

"That's enough," he said. "You want to know what happened? Who's been killing Shadowhunters? Who tried to raise Leviathan? I was going to wait for the Consul, but if you insist, I'll tell you now. As long as you *don't* insult my mother or my family again."

Bridgestock looked furious, and James wondered if he'd gone too far—Bridgestock *was* the Inquisitor, the second most powerful figure in the Clave. But he could not go directly against the will of the Enclave without bitter scandal, and the crowd was already looking at James expectantly, even the Pouncebys. Curiosity always won out, James thought, watching all those realizations flicker across Bridgestock's face, turning his angry expression to a sardonic scowl. "Very well, then," he said, with a dismissive gesture in James's direction. "I'm sure the assembly would like to hear what you have to say."

So James talked—and, rather surprisingly, with no preparation, told a cohesive story that nevertheless left out several of the most important details. He explained that he had been concerned about Thomas's arrest, knowing they had the wrong suspect. (Bridgestock coughed and shifted from foot to foot.) He went through his own discovery of the pattern of the murders on a London map, the way they had formed Leviathan's sigil. He claimed he had woken Cordelia, then Matthew and Lucie, who had been guests at their house. Together, they had raced to Mount Street Gardens and found Charles under attack. The attacker, James explained, was Jesse Blackthorn. Jesse's body, it seemed, had been magically preserved by his mother all this time, presumably through the use of the dark arts—after all, they already knew she had attempted necromancy. It was why she had been imprisoned in the Citadel.

"So she succeeded?" Sophie demanded, looking quite ill. "She raised her son from the dead?"

Not quite, James explained: Jesse's body had been preserved as some kind of memorial. Tatiana had enlisted the help of a demon to assist her in doing so, and that demon had taken over Jesse's body, and had clearly been trying to raise Leviathan, Prince of Hell, to destroy the London Nephilim. Cordelia had stabbed Jesse with Cortana, he added, driving out the demon, which must have closed the gateway allowing Leviathan entry.

"Who would want to raise Leviathan?" Christopher wondered aloud. "Surely any of the other Princes of Hell would be less . . . disgusting."

"He might be considered quite handsome by other sea demons," said Anna. "We can't know."

"Be quiet," said Bridgestock. He was red in the face. "You're telling us the killer is some—some long-dead boy? Doesn't that seem ridiculous—and convenient?"

"Only if you're more interested in finding someone to punish than finding the murderer," said James. "Even if you're not inclined to believe me, Jesse's body is being examined by the Silent Brothers. Once they're done, maybe *you'd* like to explain to the Enclave how a boy who would be twenty-four today if he'd lived has been perfectly preserved at the age of seventeen, exactly when he's known to have died?"

There is more than that, said the familiar, silent voice of Jem, who had just come into the library with Lucie. His parchment-colored robes were spotted with blood at the sleeves, his hood drawn back to show his face—his scarred cheeks, his dark hair streaked with white. James felt a wave of relief at the sight of him; he hadn't realized quite how stressful it had been to have Jem away, in a place he could not be reached. *You would have to explain how it is that Jesse Blackthorn is covered in exactly the runes that are missing from the bodies of the murdered. Filomena di Angelo's Strength rune. Elias Carstairs's Voyance rune. Lilian Highsmith's Precision rune. Every one is a match.*

A murmur ran around the room as Will smiled at Jem. It was a smile James knew well: the very specific smile Will had only for his *parabatai.* If it was odd to see someone smile at a Silent Brother like that, the oddness had long since faded for James; this was his father and his uncle Jem, as he had always known them.

When Jem crossed the room to speak quietly to Will, Lucie stayed where she was; she smiled at her parents but did not run to embrace them. She seemed to be learning restraint, James thought; he wasn't sure how he felt about it. Lucie's exuberance had always been so much a part of her.

"Lilian Highsmith knew her killer," said Bridgestock, raising his voice to be heard over the buzzing gossip in the room. "She recognized him. The Lightwood boy swore to it under the Sword. How would she have known Tatiana's brat?"

"She didn't," said Lucie. "She thought he was his father, Rupert. They looked exactly alike, and Lilian knew the Blackthorns—she would have recognized Rupert." She met James's eyes across the room: he thought of Elias, who must also have thought he was seeing a man he'd known years ago—a man he'd thought was dead.

You?

"That's why Miss Highsmith said what she did," said Thomas. "'He was dead, dead in his prime. His wife, she wept and wept. I remember her tears.' Rupert was married when he died. She meant Tatiana."

"Tragedy begets tragedy," said Tessa. "Rupert Blackthorn died, and his son died, and it drove Tatiana Blackthorn mad. She refused to allow her son the protection spells of a Shadowhunter, and so created a vessel that could be possessed. She is a tragic figure, but also dangerous."

"Hopefully she is not a danger to the Sisters in the Adamant Citadel," said Alastair smoothly. "The Inquisitor was quite merciful to send her there, and not to the Silent City. Hopefully that mercy will be rewarded."

Martin Wentworth made a rude noise. "She doesn't need mercy," he said. "She needs interrogating. Do we really think she had no knowledge of this situation?"

The Inquisitor was spluttering silently. Mrs. Bridgestock, who had been standing quietly among the Pouncebys, said, "What about Grace? If this . . . murderous demon knows she exists—if it preyed on her brother—"

"Grace was born a Cartwright," Ariadne said, startling everyone. "Her parents were devoted Shadowhunters. She would have had the protection spells, years before Tatiana even met her."

The Inquisitor swept his cloak around himself. "I will leave tonight. I must go to the Adamant Citadel and request a formal audience with Tatiana Blackthorn. She will have to be brought out of the Citadel by the other Sisters, for no man can enter the place. But Wentworth is right—it is time to interrogate her."

As if he had called an end to civility, a hubbub of voices erupted—questions and demands:

But which demon was it, possessing the boy? What if it returns?

Well, so what if it does? Without a body, it's just a disembodied demon, isn't it?

How'd it get the runes off the bodies? James, do you know?

What demon has the power to call up a Prince of Hell? How would they expect to control him?

Demons don't think that far ahead—do they?

Will, who'd been sitting with his boots on a chair, kicked it over. It hit the ground with a crash that, to James's surprise, brought an immediate silence.

"Enough," Will said firmly. "As many of you know, the Consul is currently in the infirmary with her injured son. She has sent word, however, with Brother Zachariah." He inclined his head to Jem. "She's invested me with the power to open a formal inquiry into this matter, which I will be doing. Tomorrow. For now, everyone who is not injured or the family of someone injured, please return home. There is no indication of further danger, and a great deal of work must now be undertaken. The Clave in Idris must be notified, and repair work begun. For this is our Institute, and we will let no Prince of Hell turn it to ruins."

There was a modest cheer. As Shadowhunters began to file out of the library, Will turned to look at James, and James could tell what he was thinking. *First Belial, now Leviathan? Two Princes of Hell?* It was too great a coincidence. James's father was clever; too clever, perhaps. But he also knew how to wait and let the truth come to him. James had no doubts that it would.

"Well," said Alastair, "that was a whacking great lot of rubbish James just spouted, wasn't it?"

Cordelia almost smiled. She had been relieved beyond measure to see Alastair; she could not have borne the idea of anything happening to him. Not now. He was a mess, which must be vexing him dreadfully: his hair was tangled, his clothes torn and covered in stone dust. Sona would not be at all pleased when he returned home, but Cordelia thought he looked rather endearing, not so perfectly put together and stiff as she was used to.

Alastair had stayed by her side while James was talking, for which she was grateful. She had been feeling immensely peculiar. She was proud of James, holding his own against the entire Enclave, weaving a story that hung together while leaving out anything that would incriminate his friends—or her. She could not help admiring his boldness, yet at the same time she feared what came next. They were dancing at the edge of a cliff, she felt: they could not all manage this falsehood forever.

She had caught James looking at her oddly several times since the battle had ended, as if he wanted to do or say something, but was restraining himself. She couldn't imagine what it was. She could see him now, deep in conversation with Jem, not looking toward her at all.

"*Oun dorough nemigoft*," she said to Alastair, in Persian. She didn't think anyone was listening to them—they had edged their way into a corner of the library, next to a shelf of books on numerical magic—but better to be careful. "It wasn't lies. It just wasn't the whole truth."

Alastair's dark eyes flashed with amusement. "Yes. I am familiar with how lying works, Layla."

Cordelia's stomach turned over. She wanted to say, *Don't call me Layla.* It sounded too much like *Lilith* to her ears, and didn't Lilith mean "night," just as Layla did? "I can't tell you all of it now," she said. "But I can tell you one thing that is true. I was correct when I said I was not worthy of bearing Cortana."

"Did you not kill the demon possessing Jesse Blackthorn?"

"I did," Cordelia began. "But I am not—"

Alastair was shaking his head. "You must stop this," he said. "You will make yourself unworthy by considering yourself unworthy. We become what we are afraid we will be, Layla."

Cordelia sighed. "I will come back with you to Cornwall Gardens after this, before I return home," she said. "It has been too long since I have seen *Mâmân*. And we can discuss—"

"Alastair," Matthew said.

The Carstairs siblings turned in surprise; neither of them had heard anyone approach. The room was still full of Shadowhunters, streaming in and out of the library door, and the dull mutter of voices. Matthew must have come in with some of them; he stood looking at Alastair and Cordelia, his hands in his pockets.

His golden hair was mussed, as tangled as Alastair's, and there was a great deal of blood on his clothes. Charles's blood, Cordelia knew;

it was still unnerving. "Matthew," she said. "Is everything all right?"

He looked at her once—a peculiar, intense look—before turning back to Alastair. "Look here, Carstairs," he said. "I can't say I know what's going on, or want to, but my brother is in the infirmary, and he's been asking for you. I'd like you to go see him."

Alastair frowned. "Charles and I," he said, "are—no longer on good terms."

"Stuff good terms," said Matthew. "Alastair, Cordelia assures me that you have a heart. She says you're different than you were at school. The boy I knew at school wouldn't visit my brother, just to spite me. Don't make your sister a liar; she's a better person than you are, and if she believes in you, you should try to be someone she can believe in. I know I do."

Alastair looked staggered—which, for Alastair, consisted of going very still, and blinking slowly for several seconds. "Fine," he said at last. He ruffled Cordelia's hair. *"Ta didar-e badd,"* he said, and walked away, without looking at Matthew again.

Cordelia watched him cross the room to Jem. As the two spoke, Jem glanced over toward her. She could not see his face at this distance, but she heard his voice in her head: *Would you join us? I have missed you, Cordelia. There is much for us all to say to each other.*

Cordelia felt an ache in her heart. Since Elias's death she had wanted nothing more than to talk to Jem, to ask him for his recollections of her father, his advice for her family. But he was a Silent Brother—they could read thoughts, guess emotions. If he looked in her head now, he'd learn the truth about Lilith, and she couldn't bear that.

She shook her head, very slightly. *Not now. Go on without me.*

He seemed disappointed as he laid a hand on Alastair's shoulder, and together the two of them left the room, passing Thomas in the doorway. Thomas looked after them with an odd expression—surprise? Anger? Perhaps he was still trying to make sense of Alastair's behavior the day before.

"Matthew," she said. "That was—"

"Don't be angry." He had taken his hands out of his pockets, and she realized why he'd hidden them in the first place. They were shaking violently. He reached inside his waistcoat and removed his dented flask.

She wanted to close her eyes. Her father's hands had shaken, some-times every morning. Less often at night. She understood why now. She understood more than she had ever wanted to understand—about her father, and about Matthew, too.

"I'm not angry," she said. "I was going to say it was kind."

"To Charles? Possibly," he said, and took a drink. The muscles moved in his throat as he swallowed. She remembered her mother saying of Elias, *he was so beautiful*. But drinking was a sickness that ate away at beautiful things. "I don't think he and Alastair are well-suited, though."

"No," Cordelia agreed. "Though are you liking Charles any better now?"

Matthew sucked a drop of brandy off his thumb and smiled crookedly. "Because he nearly died? No. I suppose it was a reminder, though—I don't *like* Charles, but I love him. I can't help it. Odd how that works, isn't it?"

"Alastair!"

Thomas had seen Alastair and Jem leave the library together, and slipped out after them. They made an odd pair of cousins, he thought: Alastair in his torn, dusty clothes, Jem in his neat parchment robes. No one would easily guess that they were family. They were silent as they walked, but Thomas knew that hardly meant they were not conversing.

"Alastair!" he called, again, and Alastair turned, a look of surprise crossing his face. Alastair said something to his cousin, then beckoned to Thomas as Jem moved some distance away, offering them a sem-blance of privacy.

Alastair looked at Thomas inquiringly. Thomas, who had realized almost immediately that he had no idea what to say, shifted from one foot to another. "You're all right?" he said eventually. "I didn't get to ask you, after the fight."

He hadn't. When the battle with Leviathan had ended, he'd been swept away by Anna and Christopher, by his parents, by the arrival of James and the others. None of whom would have thought Thomas would have any reason to want to remain near Alastair.

"I'm fine," Alastair said. "I'm going to see Charles in the infirmary. Apparently, he asked for me."

"Oh." Thomas felt as if he'd missed a step on a staircase. The stumble, the disorientation. He caught his breath.

"I owe this," Alastair said. His gaze was dark and steady. "Do you remember what you said in the Sanctuary? That we should pretend that nothing in the past happened, and Paris was the first time we met?"

Thomas nodded. His stomach felt as if it had been tied in knots of ice.

"We cannot pretend forever," said Alastair. "Eventually the truth must be faced. All of your friends hate me, Thomas, and with good reason."

Matthew, Thomas thought. He'd seen his friend approach Alastair and Cordelia with a determined expression, and he'd wondered what it was about. He couldn't be angry at Matthew, either. Math was looking out for his brother, which was entirely understandable.

"No apology will make up for what I've done in the past," Alastair continued. "And to make you choose between me and your friends would only make it worse. So I will make the choice. Go back to the library. They're waiting for you."

"You followed me on patrol because you were worried about me," said Thomas. "You do realize—because you were there—that might have been why Belial didn't attack me? He always went after Shadowhunters who were alone. But you were with me, even if I didn't know it."

"That's just guesswork." A vein pulsed in Alastair's throat. "Tom, you patrolled alone at night because you like things that are dangerous and unhealthy for you. I won't be one of those things."

He began to turn away. Thomas reached out to catch at him, and the feel of Alastair's shoulder under his fingers almost undid him. He had touched him, like this, in the Sanctuary: had rested his hands on Alastair's shoulders, letting Alastair bear up his weight as they kissed.

"Don't," Alastair said, not looking at him. "It isn't possible. It won't ever be."

He pulled away, hurrying to rejoin Jem. Thomas stood looking after them as they vanished down the hall. Somehow, he kept expecting Alastair to turn and look back at him, even once. But Alastair never did.

You are being a fool, Malcolm Fade told himself.

It was the same thing he'd been telling himself for the past few days; it made no more difference now. The sun was bright overhead as he crossed the Institute courtyard. A wind had picked up, scattering flurries of snow, white and glittering in the sunshine. He wondered how long it would take for the Shadowhunters to put their broken Institute back together. Less time than one might expect, he guessed. They were surprisingly resourceful, Nephilim, and stubborn in a way warlocks were not. There was little point being stubborn when you lived forever. You learned to bend rather than break.

He thought he had bent, all those years ago when he had first lost Annabel. *She has become an Iron Sister,* he had been told. *You will never see her again. It is her choice.*

He had walked the world since that moment bent and twisted into a new shape: the shape of a man who had lost the only thing that mattered in his life and had to learn to live without it. Food tasted flat; the wind and sun visited him differently; the sound of his heartbeat was always audible in his ears, a broken metronome. This was his life now—it had been for more than nine decades—and he had come to accept it.

Until Lucie and Grace had appeared in his life. In learning that Annabel was dead, he had realized how much he'd resigned himself to never seeing her again. Though it ran counter to sense, learning of her death had brought with it the hope that there was a chance of somehow—after all this time—being able to save her.

He could see her, in his mind's eye, in her plain calico dress, the ribbons of her bonnet streaming in the wind. May Day in Padstow—so long ago now—but he could remember the girls with flowers in their hands, and the blue of the water. Her dark brown hair. Annabel.

You are being a fool, he told himself again. He drew his overcoat around him as he reached the gates of the courtyard. There was someone there, leaning against the iron railings. Not a Shadowhunter—a tall man dressed in green and black, an emerald stickpin gleaming at his lapel.

"Magnus," Malcolm said, slowing his gait. "How odd to see you here."

Magnus had his arms crossed over his chest. His expression as he surveyed the courtyard was somber. "Is it?"

"I would have expected you to rush to the rescue earlier," said Malcolm. He was fond of Magnus, as fond as he could be of anyone. But the other warlock had a well-deserved reputation for throwing his energy away on Shadowhunters. "Are you regretful to have missed the battle?"

Magnus's gold-green eyes glittered like the emerald in his pin. "Mock my guilt if you like, but it is real. After the last series of attacks, I rushed to London, settled myself here, and waited for something else to happen. But it has been quiet. When I was asked to bring some of the spell books from the Cornwall Institute to the Spiral Labyrinth itself, I thought it safe to go. And now *this* has happened in my absence."

"The Labyrinth required you for some time," said Malcolm. "I know Hypatia was—displeased."

The corner of Magnus's mouth twitched upward. "It turns out that moving a collection of powerful spell books from one place to another without awakening an ancient evil is more difficult than expected."

Malcolm felt a mild stirring of interest. "An ancient evil?"

Magnus skimmed a glance over the courtyard. "Unrelated to this one, admittedly, and less destructive." He cocked his head to the side. "Speaking of which. You seem—different, Malcolm. Are you, too, affected by what you see here?"

At another time, in another world, Malcolm would also have been concerned. Now he could think only of Annabel, of the cliffs of Cornwall, of a different future. "I learned something while you were gone. Something I had given up ever knowing."

Magnus's gaze was unreadable. He did not ask what Malcolm had discovered; he was wiser than that. "How did you learn it?"

"From no one of import," Malcolm said, quickly. "A—faerie." He turned his gaze back to the broken courtyard. "Magnus," he said. "Do the Nephilim really understand what is happening to them? It has been thousands of years since Princes of Hell walked on the Earth. The Nephilim are descended from angels, but to them angels are fairy tales. A power that exists but is never seen." He sighed. "It is not wise to forget to believe."

"They are human," Magnus said. "It is not in their capability to understand that which by its nature is almost beyond understanding. They see demons as what they fight. They forget that there are unimaginable forces that can bend the laws of the universe. The gods are walking, Malcolm, and none of us are prepared."

In the end, it was decided they would all return to the house on Curzon Street—the Merry Thieves, Anna, and Cordelia—though Cordelia was to stop briefly at Cornwall Gardens first. All except Lucie.

Lucie had already decided it would be impossible. The timing was too constricted, and she wanted the few hours she could have with her parents before the night fell—though Will and Tessa had told her it was all right to go to James's house, as they'd be fending off Enclave members for hours. But telling Cordelia she couldn't come back with them because she was too tired still hurt.

I hate lying to her, she thought dismally, even as Cordelia hugged her and told her that she understood. *I absolutely hate it.*

"I wish you could be there," Daisy said, squeezing her hand. "No one knows about—about Lilith—save you and James and Matthew. I don't know how the others will react. They may hate me."

"They won't," said Lucie. "They will stand by you, every one of them, and if they don't, I will hit them with my bonnet."

"Not your *best* bonnet," said Cordelia somberly. "That would be a dreadful waste."

"Certainly not. The second best," said Lucie. She hesitated. "In the Shadow Market—when I told you I was keeping secrets to help someone . . . it was Jesse."

"I had guessed that." Cordelia's dark gaze dropped for a moment: she was looking at the locket around Lucie's throat. The locket Lucie had finally adjusted so that it hung correctly, showing the circlet of thorns etched on its front. "Lucie, if you cared about him—you must have spent quite a bit of time in his company. And hidden it from me."

"Daisy—"

"I am not angry," Cordelia said; her eyes met Lucie's. "I just wish I had known. You are mourning him, and he is a stranger to me. You could have told me, Lucie; I would not have judged you."

"And you could tell me of your own feelings," Lucie said quietly, "for I think perhaps loving someone you cannot be with is a thing you understand better than I had guessed before today." Cordelia flushed. "Next time we train," Lucie said, "we will talk about everything."

But a shadow had fallen over Cordelia's expression at the mention of training. "Yes," she said, and then James was there, and he and Cordelia were bidding goodbye to Lucie and joining the others, ready to leave for Kensington and Mayfair.

Lucie watched them silently. She wanted to go with her friends, wanted it badly, but it was her duty to save Jesse; no one else could do it. It was her power. She had used it, abused it even; if she did not turn it into some kind of good, then what was she? James had used his power more than once to save lives.

It was her turn now.

"There is nothing to worry about, *Mâmân*, see?" Cordelia said, gently laying her hand against her mother's cheek.

Sona smiled up at her. To Cordelia's relief, when she and Alastair had arrived at Cornwall Gardens, they had found Sona wrapped in a velvet dressing gown, installed on the plush drawing-room sofa before a blazing fire. Sona was not wearing her *roosari*, and her dark hair spilled over her shoulders; she looked young, if more than a little tired. "You two are so dirty," she said, indicating Alastair, who was hovering in the drawing-room doorway. "A mother always worries when her children come home looking as if they have fallen in a mud puddle."

When her children come home. But this was not Cordelia's home, not any longer. Home was Curzon Street. Home was not this house, where they had all been unhappy in one way or another.

But now was not the time to say such a thing to her mother. Not now, with everything so uncertain.

"It was a small fight, that is all," Alastair said; he had already described the battle to Sona in abbreviated terms. Not the full truth, only a part of it: Cordelia felt, with some discomfort, as if she were getting quite used to that phenomenon. "And the Institute was defended."

"You have been so very brave," said Sona. "My brave son." She patted Cordelia's hand where it now lay beside hers. "And you, my brave daughter. Like Sura or Youtab."

At another time, Cordelia would have glowed at being compared to heroines of Persian history. Not now, though, not with the bitter thought of Lilith still at the forefront of her mind. She forced a smile. "You should rest, *Mâmân*—"

"Oh, nonsense." Sona waved a dismissive hand. "You would not know, but I was also confined to bed before you were born, and Alastair, too. Speaking of which, Alastair, darling, would you give us a moment alone for women's talk?"

Alastair, looking horrified, could not absent himself soon enough; he muttered something about packing a valise, and fled.

Sona looked at her daughter with bright eyes. For a moment of terror, Cordelia wondered if her mother was going to ask her if she was pregnant. She couldn't bear the thought.

"Layla, darling," Sona said. "There is something I wished to speak to you about. I have thought a great deal about many things in the days since your father died." Cordelia was surprised; her mother spoke clearly, an undertone of regret in her voice—but the terrible grief Cordelia had expected from a mention of Elias was absent. Something sad and quiet and bittersweet seemed to be in its place. "I know that you did not want to marry James Herondale—"

"*Mâmân*, that is not—"

"I am not saying you do not love him," said Sona. "I can see from the way you look at him that you do. And perhaps marriage would have come, later, but it came when it did because scandal forced it. And that was never what I wanted for you." She drew her wrapper more closely about herself. "Our lives rarely turn out the way we expect them to, Layla. When I married your father, I knew him only as a great hero. Later, when I realized the extent of his troubles, I distanced myself from my family. I was too proud—I couldn't bear for them to know."

In the kitchen, Risa was singing; the sound seemed miles away. Cordelia whispered, *"Mâmân..."*

Sona's eyes gleamed, too bright. "Do not worry yourself over it. Only listen to me. When I was a girl, I had so many dreams. Dreams of heroism, of glamour, of travel. Layla—what I want for you above all things is that you follow the truth of your dreams. No scorn, no shame, no part of society's opinion matters more than that."

It was like a knife in the heart. Cordelia could not speak.

Sona went on. "What I am saying, and I will say the same to Alastair, too, is that I do not want you hovering over me, doting on me until the baby comes. I am a Shadowhunter too, and besides—I want to know you are pursuing your own happiness. It will make *me* happier than anything else in the world. Otherwise I will be miserable. Do you understand?"

All Cordelia could do in response was murmur assent and embrace her mother. *One day I will tell her all the truth,* she thought fiercely. *One day.*

"Layla." It was Alastair, having changed out of his torn and ichor-stained clothes. He looked less rumpled but still weary, and grim about the mouth, as if he were not looking forward to returning to the infirmary and Charles. Cordelia had tried to talk to him about it in the carriage on the way to Kensington, but he had been tight-lipped. "The carriage is waiting for us. You can always return tomorrow."

"Don't you dare," whispered Sona, releasing Cordelia with a smile. "Now—run along back to that handsome husband of yours. I am sure he misses you."

"I will." Cordelia straightened up. Her eyes met her brother's across the room. "Only I need to speak with Alastair first. There is something I must ask him to do."

"Excellent lying, James," said Matthew, raising a glass of port. "Really top-notch."

James mimed raising a glass in return. He had wanted to collapse into a chair the moment they'd walked through the front door; rather luckily, Effie had appeared and proceeded to lecture them thoroughly about not getting ichor and dust on the rugs.

"I was warned you'd be coming home filthy," she said. "But no one told me about the smell of fish. Lord, it's awful. Like a bunch of rotted oysters."

"That's enough, Effie," said James, seeing Christopher turn green.

"And where's Mrs. Herondale at?" Effie inquired. "Did the stink drive her off?"

James had explained that Cordelia was visiting her mother and would be returning shortly, which seemed to energize Effie. She packed them all off to clean up and return brushed, washed, and ichor-free to the drawing room, where a fire had been laid in the hearth.

In his bedroom, James found that someone—Effie, most likely—had placed the broken pieces of Grace's bracelet on his nightstand. Not wanting to leave them out in the open, he put the two halves in his pocket. He would have to return them to Grace, he supposed, though it was hardly what he wanted to think about right now.

By the time he changed clothes and made his way downstairs, he found Anna—who had managed to produce an entire new outfit out of seemingly thin air—lounging in a tapestry chair, wearing matching velvet trousers and a loose jacket in a deep gold color.

Cordelia arrived back at Curzon Street just as Effie came in to lay out a small feast on the table: Lancashire spice nuts, curried shrimp and lauretta sandwiches, London buns and French eclairs.

The sight of Daisy made the back of James's throat hurt. As the rest of his friends fell on the food like starving wolves, he watched Cordelia make her way to the sofa. She wore a dark emerald dress that made her hair look like rose petals against green leaves. It had been gathered up in soft curls at the back of her head, held in place by a silk bandeau. There were green slippers on her feet. He caught her eye; when she glanced at him, he saw that she was wearing the necklace he'd given her, the small gold orb gleaming just above the neckline of her gown. She did not seem to have Cortana with her; she must have laid it away upstairs.

His heart gave a slow, hard thump. When they were alone, he could tell her the necklace's secret. But not now, he told himself; it felt like the fiftieth time today. Not *yet*.

"So," Matthew said, holding up the glass in his hand so it caught the light, "are we going to discuss what *actually* happened this morning?"

"Indeed," said Thomas. He had an odd air about him, James thought, quiet and inward-seeming, as if something was bothering him. He kept touching the inside of his left forearm, as if his compass rose tattoo ached—though as far as James knew, that was unlikely. "How much of what you told the Enclave was true, James?"

James sank back in his chair. He was so tired he felt as if there were sand under his eyelids. "What I told them was true—but I left a great deal out."

"May we assume," said Anna, "that the demon possessing Jesse Blackthorn was Belial?"

James nodded. "Belial wasn't possessing me, but he was the architect behind the killings. Behind all of it."

"So the dreams you were having—you were seeing through Belial's eyes, while he was in Jesse Blackthorn's body?" asked Christopher.

"I don't believe Belial was even aware that I was seeing through his eyes. I'm not sure why I was, to be honest. Perhaps it had something to do with Jesse, rather than Belial—but I can't guess." James had picked up an empty teacup; he turned it over in his hands. "The person who knows the most about Jesse is Lucie, and we may not have all of that story until we speak to her, too. But it appears she has been acquainted with him—or his ghost—for some time."

Anna, picking the currants off a London bun, frowned. "Lucie was looking into the circumstances of his death—"

"She was?" Matthew said. "We know she saw his ghost—interacted with him—but why would she do that?"

"I think," Anna said, in a measured voice, "that she was trying to help Grace. It seems they know each other rather well."

James recalled Grace, in this drawing room. *I know Lucie, like you, can see the dead—but you can also travel in shadows. Can Lucie do the same?*

"They do?" The surprise in Cordelia's eyes was clear. She glanced away quickly, though. "Never mind, Anna. It's not important."

"I went with her to question Hypatia Vex," Anna said. "She told us that Tatiana had refused to have the protection spells placed on Jesse and had hired our old friend Emmanuel Gast to do it instead."

So that's how Lucie knew to summon Gast, James realized. There was clearly far more to what Lucie could do, and indeed, what she had already done, than any of them had guessed. He thought of her gold locket. Part of the way Tatiana had preserved her son, it seemed, yet that same son had sacrificed the magic of it to save James's life. He remembered what Grace had said to him, after: *My mother says she knows now there is no chance Jesse will ever return. She says it is as if you stole his last breath.*

He had not understood her at the time. But Lucie had known . . .

Tomorrow, he told himself. He would speak with Lucie then.

"Belial had his hooks in Emmanuel Gast," said James. "He forced the warlock to place a piece of his essence inside Jesse, so that as Jesse grew older, Belial would have an anchor in him, and a body Belial could possess on this Earth."

"But why now?" said Christopher. "Why possess Jesse now?"

"Because I refused him," said James wearily. "Because his attempt to possess me went disastrously wrong. Not only did he not possess me; he was wounded by Cortana. He has remained in fear of it."

"Belial wanted to make a warrior," said Cordelia. "He believed that if he murdered Shadowhunters, took their runes and gave them to Jesse, he could create a warrior capable of defeating Cortana—half Prince of Hell, half Shadowhunter."

Anna smiled at her. "But it sounds as if you fought and defeated this being. Belial, as it turns out, was no match for our Cordelia."

Cordelia's voice was low, and ragged around the edges. "Anna, no. That's—that's not what happened."

Anna did not look surprised. She set her teacup down, her blue eyes fixed on Cordelia. "Daisy," she said. "Tell us."

James wanted to jump in, to tell the story, to save Cordelia from having to say the words. He found his fingers digging into the arm of his chair as, steadily and without emotion, she told them the story from the moment the faerie woman had approached her at the Hell Ruelle, to her trip to the White Horse, her vision of the forge, her oath and subsequent discovery that it was not Wayland the Smith she had sworn loyalty to, but the Mother of Demons.

As she spoke, Matthew rose and went to the window. He stood there, hands in his pockets, his shoulders stiff, as Cordelia finished explaining that Lilith had sent the demons in Nelson Square. "She wanted me to understand," she said, "what it meant to have that power. To be able to wield Cortana as a paladin."

"I should never have taken you to the barrow," said Matthew. He faced the window, unmoving.

"Matthew," Cordelia said gently. "It's not your fault."

Thomas rubbed at his arm, where the compass rose tattoo showed through the white of his sleeve. "So all this time, Lilith has been taking different forms to manipulate and trick you—trick us. When you saw Magnus at the Shadow Market, that wasn't the real Magnus, was it?"

Christopher looked stunned. "But why—?"

"It was never the real Magnus," said James. "I should have guessed when he came to our home here. His magic was the wrong color."

Christopher's brow was furrowed. "But Magnus was rather helpful," he said. "He helped us solve the question of the *pithos*." He tapped his breast pocket, where the *adamas* object now rested. "Why would Lilith do that?"

James watched Matthew, who was still staring out the window. "She had to earn our trust and make us believe she was Magnus. And remember, she is Belial's enemy. They hate each other. She would not mind helping us defeat him. What she really wanted was to have me take her back to Edom, and it almost worked."

"I must tell Magnus about this," said Anna. "He can be sworn to secrecy, but he must know. Who knows what else Lilith may have done, while pretending to be him?"

There was a murmur of agreement. Thomas, his eyebrows knit together in thought, said, "So if Cordelia is Lilith's paladin, how were you able to get rid of her?"

James smiled. "Your revolver, Christopher."

"You shot Lilith?" said Christopher in disbelief.

"Doesn't seem right, shooting a demon," said Anna. "Unsportsmanlike. Though, of course, I am glad you did it."

"I don't understand," said Christopher. "There's no way Lilith could be harmed by ordinary runed weapons. And as unusual as it may be, the revolver is nothing more than a runed weapon."

"But it worked," protested Matthew.

"It's a miracle it worked. It shouldn't have worked," Christopher said. He turned back to James. "But you knew it would, didn't you?"

"I strongly suspected," James said. "You told me yourself you performed all sorts of enchantments on it, trying to make it work. I remembered you said you had done a sort of modified Nephilim protection spell. And then I thought about the protection spells."

"Yes," said Christopher, "but—oh!" His face lit up with understanding.

Thomas smiled a bit. "All right, all right, explain it, one of you. I can see you want to."

"The protection spell," Christopher said. "It's done in the names of three angels."

"Sanvi, Sansanvi, Semangelaf," said James. "They are angels of protection. In the old texts, they are angels meant to protect against Lilith specifically."

"So Christopher managed to make a Lilith-killing weapon?" said Anna. "Most amazing."

"It didn't kill her," said Cordelia. "She was weakened, I think, and fled because she was startled and injured. But she is no more dead and gone than Belial is." She looked around miserably at the group. "I will understand if you must distance yourselves from me. I am still Lilith's paladin."

"James is Belial's grandson," said Anna, "and none of us have abandoned him. That is not the spirit of the Merry Thieves."

"That's different," Cordelia said, her voice a bit desperate. "Lilith is bound to me as a Shadowhunter. She could appear at any time, as has always been true, but whenever I draw a weapon, it will *summon* her. If I wield Cortana, then so does she, through me. If you think that it would be best to throw myself on the mercy of the Clave—"

"Obviously not," said Matthew, spinning away from the window. "We will tell no one."

Anna sat back in her chair. "You don't think your mother would be merciful?"

"My mother would, Will and Tessa would," Matthew said, nodding at James. "But plenty would not. Plenty would panic, and Cordelia would be in the Silent City before we could do anything."

"Maybe I should be," said Cordelia.

"Absolutely not," said James. "It's your choice, Daisy, what you want to do. If you want us to tell anyone. But I agree with Matthew. You've done nothing wrong—you're no danger as long as you don't pick up a weapon—and the Mother of Demons has reason to fear us." He put his hand to his belt, where the revolver rested. "We've defeated worse than Lilith."

"She's not even a Prince of Hell, and we've defeated two of those today," Thomas pointed out.

Cordelia clamped her lips together tightly, as if she were struggling not to cry. Christopher looked terribly alarmed. "Oh, what ho, tears," he said helplessly. "Ghastly—not that you shouldn't cry if you wish, of course. Cry like the blazes, Cordelia."

"Christopher," said James darkly. "You are not helping."

Cordelia shook her head. "It's not Christopher. Or—I suppose it is, but it's not Christopher making me sad. It's only . . . I had not realized—you really think of me as your friend, all of you?"

"Oh, darling," said Anna affectionately. "Of course we do."

I do not think of you as a friend, James thought, but all he said was, "We will manage this together, Daisy. We will never leave you alone."

The swift winter night came, falling like a knife between one moment and the next, casting the drawing room into gold-tinged shadow. Matthew was first to leave, having borrowed a tweed overcoat from James, who walked him to the door and stood leaning against the jamb, exhausted, while Matthew pulled on his gloves.

"You're certain you don't want to borrow our carriage?" James asked, for the fifth time, as Matthew glanced up at the gray-black sky.

"No, I'll catch a hansom at Oxford Street. Might as well walk a bit. Clear my head."

"Let me know if it works." James brushed a flake of snow from Matthew's shoulder; it wasn't falling, but the wind was sending flurries skirling down the streets.

"We cannot keep all this a secret," Matthew said. He looked tired, the shadows under his eyes pronounced. "We will have to at least tell your parents."

James nodded. "I had planned to tell them tomorrow, all of it—hopefully Lucie can fill in the bits we don't know. But with Belial on the horizon, we can't keep this a secret from them. Save the part about Cordelia and Lilith, of course."

"I agree," said Matthew. "Perhaps Magnus will have some idea how the enchantment between them can be broken." He put his gloved hand over James's bare one where it rested on his shoulder. James could feel the slight tremor in Matthew's touch; Matthew had drunk a little port in the drawing room, but it wouldn't be enough. He'd be wanting to get home, not to rest but to drink until he could.

So silly of me. Who knew toys had sharp edges?

"You were not there," Matthew said. "You did not see how happy she was when she thought Wayland the Smith had chosen her to be his paladin. I—I know what it is like, to do something you thought was good, and have it turn out to be a terrible mistake."

James wanted to ask Matthew to tell him more. *What mistakes have you made, Math, that you cannot forgive yourself for? What is it that you are drowning in bottles, and glasses, and silver flasks? Now that I can see you clearly, I see you are unhappy, but why, when you are more loved and loving than anyone else I know?*

But the house was full of people, and Cordelia needed him, and there was no time or chance just now. "I know, myself," James said, "what it is like to live with a darkness inside you. One that you fear."

Matthew drew his hand back, knotting his scarf around his neck. His cheeks were already pink with cold. "I have never seen darkness in you."

"Nor have I known you to make such grave mistakes as you say," said James. "But if you did, you know that I would do all I could to help you fix them."

Matthew's smile was a flash in the dark, illuminated only by distant streetlights.

"I know you would try," he said.

27

WAKE WITH WINGS

Though one were strong as seven,
He too with death shall dwell,
Nor wake with wings in heaven,
Nor weep for pains in hell.
—Algernon Charles Swinburne, "The Garden of Proserpine"

Ariadne had been waiting outside the house on Curzon Street long enough for her fingers and toes to have gone numb. As night approached, she had watched the lamplighter come with his ladder and sparking tool, and the lights had gone on inside James and Cordelia's house too. She had been able to see them through the drawing-room window: Thomas and Christopher, James and Cordelia, Matthew and Anna.

She had not minded Anna going off to Curzon Street after the battle at the Institute. Of course she would want to see her friends and cousins. But home had been miserable and tense: Grace had locked herself in her bedroom, and Mrs. Bridgestock was crying in the parlor, as she believed Mr. Bridgestock should not have gone alone to the Adamant Citadel. Goodness knew, she said, what that Tatiana Blackthorn would do to him.

Ariadne had grown used to creeping out of the house using the servants' entrance. Anna would not mind her coming to Curzon Street, she told herself; she was friendly enough with the Merry Thieves and had fought side by side with Thomas and Christopher that morning. It was not until she'd reached the house itself that she'd lost her courage.

She could see Anna through the drawing-room window, her lean body sprawled in an armchair, her hair a soft dark cap, fine and straight as silk. Her smile was gentle, her blue eyes soft, and Ariadne realized in that moment that the Anna of her memory had never really vanished. *She is still here*, Ariadne thought, hesitating on the doorstep. *Only not for me.*

After that, she could not go in, and found herself waiting by a nearby streetlight until the door of the house opened and Matthew emerged, wearing an outsized tweed overcoat. He spoke with James in the doorway for several minutes before departing; Ariadne ducked behind a leafless tree to prevent him catching sight of her.

The sun had gone down by the time Thomas, Christopher, and Anna stepped out into the frost-sharp night. Their breath came out in clouds as they descended the stairs. Catching sight of her, Thomas and Christopher exchanged a look of surprise before approaching; Ariadne was dimly aware that they were greeting her and telling her she had impressed them during the fight that morning. She returned the compliments, though she was acutely aware of Anna, who had paused on the stairs to light a cheroot.

She wanted Anna to come down the steps. She wanted to take her hand, here on the street in front of Christopher and Thomas. But the boys were already bidding them goodbye and loping off down the lane, the sound of their chatter and footsteps swallowed up quickly by fog and snow.

"Ari." Anna joined her on the pavement, the tip of her cheroot glowing as cherry red as her ruby pendant. "Taking a walk?"

"I wanted to see you," Ariadne said. "I thought we could—"

"Go to the Whispering Room?" Anna blew a smoke ring and watched it drift on the cold air. "Not tonight, I'm afraid. Tomorrow afternoon, if you—"

"I was hoping we could go to your flat."

Anna said nothing, only watched the smoke ring come apart in pieces on the air. She was like starlight, Ariadne thought: it seemed warm and radiant and near, but was in truth uncountable miles away.

"I don't think that would be a good idea. I have an assignation tonight."

Ariadne supposed she ought to have known. Anna had been clear: nothing in her life, about her life, would change for Ariadne's sake. Still, she felt a dull hurt, as if she had been struck with an unsharpened blade. "Today," she said, "when we were in the courtyard—when we were first attacked—you pushed me behind you."

Anna's delicate eyebrows went up. *"Did I?"*

And Ariadne knew: Anna remembered. She herself had relived the moment a dozen times since it had happened. Anna had been unguarded in that instant, the fear on her face real as she thrust Ariadne out of the way and turned to face Leviathan, whip in hand.

"You know you did," Ariadne said. "You would protect me with your life, then, but you will not forgive me. I know I asked you earlier—"

Anna sighed. "I am not angry at you, nor trying to punish you. But I am happy with who I am. I do not desire a change."

"Maybe you are not angry with me," Ariadne said. Dampness had gathered on her eyelashes; she blinked it away. "But I am angry with myself. I cannot forgive myself. I had you—I had love—and I turned from it out of fear. And perhaps it was foolish of me to think I could pick it up again, that it would be waiting for me, but you—" Her voice shook. "I fear it is because of me that you have become what you are. Hard and bright as a diamond. Untouchable."

The cheroot burned, disregarded, in Anna's hand. "What an unkind characterization," she said lightly. "I cannot say I agree."

"I could have managed with you not loving me, but you do not even want me to love *you*. And that I cannot bear." Ariadne laced her cold hands together. "Do not ask me to come to the Whispering Room again."

Anna shrugged. "As you wish," she said. "I had better go—as you know, I do not like to keep a lady waiting."

Ariadne did not stay to watch Anna leave; she did not think she could endure it, so she did not see Anna walk only a short distance before sinking down onto the front steps of a neighboring house. Flicking the half-burned cheroot into the snow, Anna put her head into her hands and shook violently, dry-eyed and silent, unable to catch her breath.

* * *

Lucie had waited what felt like hours upon hours for the household to fall into silence. With Gabriel injured and in the infirmary, Cecily and Alexander had remained at the Institute. Lucie had spent much of dinner playing with Alexander, letting him walk on the table and feeding him biscuits. In times of crisis, she had found, busying oneself with the care of children meant no one troubled you with questions.

Eventually she had retired to her room. She had heard Christopher come home, and voices in the library, but she had already wedged a chair against her door and was busy packing. She wasn't at all sure what one was supposed to wear to visit a warlock's house in Cornwall and engage in necromantic rituals. Eventually she decided on a few warm wool dresses, her axe, five seraph blades, a gear jacket, and a bathing costume. One never knew, and Cornwall *was* the seaside.

She left a note propped against her vanity table, took her packed valise, and crept out of her bedroom. Making her way through the halls of the Institute, she found them dark and silent. Good—everyone was asleep. She slipped downstairs and into the Sanctuary without a sound.

The room was a blaze of light. Every taper had been lit, filling the space with wavering illumination. In its center Jesse's body had been laid on a muslin-covered bier, surrounded by a circle of white candles, each in a single long holder. Around the bier were scattered squares of parchment, each inscribed with a rune: most were of mourning, though a few represented honor and courage in combat.

The Silent Brothers had done their work well. Lucie was glad the Sanctuary had been kept sealed, save for them. She did not like the idea of strangers gawking at Jesse's body. He would be a curiosity to them, and she could not bear that.

Lucie set her valise down and approached Jesse slowly. He had been arranged with the Blackthorn sword on his chest, his hands folded atop the cross guard. A white silk blindfold was bound over his eyes. The sight made her stomach turn cold; he looked *dead*, as he never had to her before in his coffin at Chiswick House. His skin was the shade of porcelain; his lashes lay long and dark against his colorless cheeks.

A beautiful faerie prince, she thought, felled like Snow White, neither alive nor dead. . . .

Lucie took a deep breath. Before Malcolm came, she wanted to be sure. She believed—she had told herself it had to be true—that Jesse had cast out Belial entirely. Surely there was not still a piece of the Prince of Hell in him. Malcolm had not asked—perhaps it had not occurred to him—but she could not imagine he would countenance trying to bring Jesse back if doing so would offer Belial a foothold in the world.

She laid her hand on Jesse's chest. It was cold and stiff beneath her touch. *If he were to touch me, I would feel so warm to him—scalding, even.*

She closed her eyes and *reached.* As she had done once before, she sought Jesse's soul among the mist and shadow behind her eyelids. For a moment there was blankness. Her heart tripped, stuttered—*what if he was gone, gone forever*—and then there was light around her, inside her.

But there was not the sense of wrongness she had felt before, when she had told him to live. Instead of shadowy monsters, she saw a dusty parlor—she was inside it, kneeling on a window seat, looking over the garden wall at a neighboring building: Herondale Manor. In the pane of the window, she could see Jesse's face reflected, small and pale. She was inside his memories, she realized, looking around the room in wonder. Cobwebs were already forming in the corners, the wallpaper beginning to peel. . . .

She was whirled away to another scene, and another—the decrepit corridors of Blackthorn Manor; a memory of Tatiana Blackthorn, face twisted into a rare smile. She was standing in the open front door of the manor. Lucie could see the briar-covered gates in the distance. There was a small girl standing behind Tatiana, cowering away as though terrified to enter the house. Her gray eyes were wide and frightened.

Then Jesse and Grace were laughing together, climbing the overgrown trees that grew on the grounds of Blackthorn Manor. Grace had a smudge of dirt on her face, and her hem was torn, and she looked happier than Lucie had ever seen her look. But then the memory shifted abruptly. She—Jesse—was in the same cobwebbed parlor, dressed in formal gear that was a little too large, and one of the Silent Brothers was approaching, stele in hand. Tatiana hovered by the doorway, twisting her hands together. Lucie wanted to shout, to reach out to demand that they stop, that the Voyance rune would be Jesse's death sentence—but then the scene shifted again. She was in Brocelind Forest, the trees bathed in moonlight. Jesse was walking the moss-covered paths, and this was Jesse as Lucie knew him—as a ghost.

Then she was in the ballroom of the Institute, and now she could see *herself*—her blue lace dress that matched her eyes, the curls escaping from her bandeau, and she realized with a shock that through Jesse's eyes she looked different than she imagined herself. Graceful, desirable. Beautiful. Her eyes were bluer than she knew them to be, her lips fuller and redder, her lashes long and secretive. She looked like a woman who was capable, adult, who had intrigues and secrets of her own.

She felt his longing for her, as if it would crack her own chest open. *Jesse*, she thought, though she was not really thinking at all—she was reaching for him, as she had always done, reaching out to draw him back to her. *Live.*

I command you to live.

Wind tore through the Sanctuary, though the doors were closed. Lucie opened her eyes to see the tapers blow out, plunging the room into dimness. In the far, far distance, she seemed to hear a sort of howl, like a tiger whose kill has been torn away from it. The air was full of the scent of singed wicks, of parchment and candle wax. . . .

Under her hand, Jesse's chest quivered and rose with a breath.

She staggered back. Only then did she realize she was shivering uncontrollably; she felt weak, drained, as if she had lost pints of her own blood. She wrapped her arms around herself as Jesse's hands moved, fluttered—raised themselves to his face. He tore at the blindfold, gasping, his back arching off the bier.

Lucie wanted to go to him, to help him, but she couldn't move. She swayed on her feet as Jesse sat up, the Blackthorn sword clattering to the floor. He swung his legs off the bier—he was breathing hard, his eyes darting around the room. She saw him register the extinguished candles, the runes of mourning on the floor, the bier.

And then he saw her.

His lips parted, his eyes widening. *"Lucie."*

She sank to her knees. *Oh, you're alive, you're alive,* she wanted to say, but there was not enough strength in her to form the words. The world had begun to blur at the edges. Darkness was creeping in around her. She saw Jesse spring up. He was a blur of white as he came toward her. She heard him call her name, felt his hands on her shoulders.

The world tilted. She realized she was lying on the floor and Jesse was leaning over her. She heard the sound of a door opening in the distance, and now there was someone else there too. Malcolm had come in from outside, bringing the chill of night with him. He wore a white traveling coat and a furious expression. "What have you done?" he demanded, his rage cutting through the hissing in her ears.

She smiled up at both of them. "I did it," she heard herself whisper. "I brought him back. I *commanded* him."

Her eyes drifted shut. Malcolm was still talking, saying that they had to get her out of here now, had to get her to the carriage before anyone discovered what she'd done.

And then there were arms under her, and someone was lifting her off the floor. Carrying her. *Jesse,* she thought, clinging to consciousness as they crossed the Sanctuary floor. She let her head fall against his chest, a sound in her ear she had never before heard: Jesse's heartbeat, steady and strong.

I did that, she thought wonderingly. There was a creak of hinges, a blast of cold air. She heard Malcolm say something about getting her into the carriage, but she could no longer hold on. She slipped away into the darkness and silence.

As quietly and hastily as she could, Grace filled her valise, repacking it with the things she'd brought to the Bridgestocks' when she'd left Chiswick House. Her clothes, she knew, were entirely impractical for a visit to rural Cornwall. Her mother had always insisted she dress in the height of feminine fashion—yards of lace, acres of silk, nothing warm or waterproof. But it would have to do.

Having closed the valise, she hurried to her vanity table. Not hers, she reminded herself. Nothing here was hers; she was only a guest, and not a particularly wanted one. The Bridgestocks would be relieved to be rid of her. Opening a drawer, she dug around inside for the small silk bag full of coins. It was all she had—not much, but enough for a hansom cab to the Institute. Malcolm would be arriving there any moment to meet Lucie. She couldn't be late. Hurrying back across the room, she picked up her valise, went to the door—

"Grace."

It was like a kick to the stomach. The valise slipped out of her hand and struck the floor, spilling petticoats, stockings, a lace shawl. Shaking, Grace turned slowly, swallowing hard against her own fear.

"Mama," she said.

There, her face glowering from the surface of the mirror on the vanity table, was Tatiana. She wore the robes of an Iron Sister, as she had the last time Grace had seen her. Around her forehead was bound an iron circlet, and her long gray-streaked hair hung unkempt over her shoulders. She looked like the oldest of the three Fates, the one who cut the threads of human lives.

"You have been a foolish and disobedient girl, Grace," Tatiana said, without preamble or greeting. "You have helped others against our family, and you have put me in an awkward position with my patron."

Grace took a long, slow breath. "You mean Belial."

Tatiana rocked back. "Oho. The chit has been sneaking about, spying on me. Learning my secrets. Is that how it is?"

"No," Grace said, "at least—I had not intended to learn anything. I was trying to help Jesse."

"Trying to bring him back from the dead, you mean," said Tatiana, "with your silly little spells. Activated moth powder indeed." She chuckled. "That's correct, chit—I know it all. How foolish you have been. You couldn't trust that your mother knew best, could you? It is my alliances, my patron, who will return Jesse to us, not your miserable fumblings."

"What Belial tells you cannot be trusted," Grace said breathlessly. "He is a Prince of Hell. A demon."

Tatiana snorted. "It is not *demons* who have betrayed me. My patron has kept every promise to me that he ever made. His word is more reliable than yours, as far as I am concerned. If it were not for you, Jesse would not now be in the hands of a Shadowhunter. And not just a Shadowhunter, a *Herondale*. How could you have done such a thing?"

Grace wanted to scream. She wanted to run out of the room, run to the Institute, to Malcolm and Lucie. But it would do no good. Tatiana would follow. "You have to be careful, Mother," she said, as steadily as she could. "The Inquisitor is on his way to the Citadel. He is going to question you."

"Fiddlesticks," said Tatiana, with a dismissive wave. "Question me about what? I am an innocent old woman."

"About Jesse," said Grace. "About his protection spells. About whether you knew that Belial had left a piece of himself inside Jesse, so he could possess him. I know, of course, that you must not have been aware of what your 'patron' did. I know you would never have put Jesse in danger."

Tatiana's voice sharpened. "It was Jesse's fault," she said, startling Grace. "If he hadn't been so insistent on wanting runes, it would never have happened. How could Belial have guessed? He assumed I would raise my child properly—to despise the Nephilim and everything that is theirs. Though I did not know what would happen, it was my fault and my boy's fault. That is why I have worked so very hard, Grace. So very hard to bring him back *properly*. With the right loyalties. The right desires. The right commitments."

Grace shuddered. "You want Jesse back, but only obedient to you."

"You can't understand," said Tatiana. "You're only a girl—stupid and foolish. Don't you see what will happen? The Herondale girl will bring him back, and turn him against us. They'll teach him to hate us, to hate everything he came from. Don't you understand? *This* is what they were always going to do. Take Jesse away from his family. That is why you must go and get him back."

"Get him—back?" Grace stared. "You mean try to kidnap him? Steal his body from a warlock and—Mother, no. I can't do that. My power doesn't even work on Malcolm."

"But it would work on Jesse," Tatiana said.

There was an awful silence. It was like the silence that had filled the room after Jesse died. "I don't," Grace said at last, "understand what you mean, Mother."

"Let them bring him back," Tatiana drawled. "Let them do the difficult work. Then convince him his place is with you—with us. When that is done, return with him, to me. I will furnish you both with instructions. It will all be very simple. Simple enough even for you."

"I don't—" Grace shook her head. She felt physically sick. "I don't understand what you're suggesting."

Tatiana's face hardened. "Must I spell it out for you? You only have one power, Grace, one thing that makes you special. *Seduce* him," she said. "Compel him. Make him believe he loves you above everything else in the world. Make him yours, as you were never able to make James Herondale yours."

Nausea rose in the pit of Grace's stomach. Her pulse was racing and her chest was tight. "Jesse is my *brother.*"

"Nonsense," Tatiana said. "You share no blood. You are barely even my daughter. We are partners, you and I. Partners in a common cause."

"I won't," Grace whispered. Had she ever said no to her mother before so plainly? It didn't matter. There was no world in which she could do what Tatiana asked, no world in which she could make filthy and horrible the only pure love she had ever known.

Tatiana's eyes burned. "Oh, you *will* do this," she hissed. "You must. The strength is all on my side, not yours. You have no choice, Grace Blackthorn."

No choice. It was at that moment that Grace realized something she had never realized before. That her mother had cursed her with power over men, but not women—never women—not because she did not believe women had influence, but because she could not bear the thought that Grace might ever have power over *her.*

With her blood screaming in her ears, Grace took three steps forward, until she was inches from the vanity, inches from her mother's grinning face. She picked up a heavy silver hairbrush and looked into Tatiana's furious eyes.

With a cry, she hurled the brush at the mirror as hard as she could. The glass shattered, Tatiana's image splintering into sparkling shards. Sobbing, Grace ran from the room.

* * *

As James closed the door behind Thomas and the others, he exhaled a long breath. It was a cold, clear night, with no hint of snow. The moon burned like the solitary light at the top of a watchtower, and the shadows cast by lampposts and carriages were stark and black against the icy white ground.

James wondered if he would sleep tonight without fear of nightmares. He felt gritty with exhaustion, his throat and eyes dry, but there was a bright wire of excitement that ran underneath his tiredness. For the first time today, he was about to be alone with Cordelia.

He closed the front door and went back to the drawing room. The fire was burning low. Cordelia was still on the sofa; she had raised her arms to readjust the combs in her hair. He watched silently from the doorway as a few unruly red locks spilled over her hands: the fire turned their edges to blood and gold. It was beautiful, but so was the upraised curve of her arms, the turn of her wrists, the shape of her capable hands. So was everything about her.

"Daisy," he said.

She slid the last comb into place and turned to look at him. There was an incredible sadness in her eyes. For a moment, he felt as if he were seeing the girl she had been, every time her father had let her down, every time she had been lonely, disappointed—all the pain she'd borne silently, without tears.

He ought to have been there for her. He would be now, he told himself, striding across the room. He sat down beside her, reaching for her hands. They were small in his, and freezing cold. "You're cold—"

"I cannot be Lucie's *parabatai*," she said.

He looked at her in surprise. "What do you mean?"

"I am bound to Lilith," she said. "Her paladin—I cannot raise a weapon save in her name. How can I train with Lucie? I cannot touch a seraph blade, raise a sword—"

"We'll fix it," said James. "We'll get help—from Magnus, from Jem, Ragnor—"

"Perhaps." She didn't sound convinced. "But even if we can find a solution, our ceremony is barely a month away. I cannot ask the

Clave to—to delay it without explanation, and I cannot explain without awful consequences. And the result would be the same. The Silent Brothers would never approve Lucie binding herself to someone who serves a *demon.*" Her voice was full of loathing. "I could not put that burden on Lucie either. I will tell her tomorrow that there isn't any—that it can't happen."

"She won't give up hope," said James.

"But she should," said Cordelia. "Even if we could free me from Lilith, I will always have made this mistake. I will always be someone you shouldn't trust to be your sister's *parabatai.*"

"That's ridiculous." James remembered that moment in the park, when Lilith had revealed the truth. He had been furious. But not *at* Cordelia. He had been furious *for* her. She wanted to do good more than anyone else he knew, wanted to be a hero because it would be the best way to help the most people. In tricking Cordelia as she had, Lilith had turned what was beautiful about Cordelia's nature back on itself—like a faerie who made the deepest desires of a mortal a weapon with which to hurt them. "Daisy, Lucie and I share a bond with Belial, a monster worse than Lilith. If anything, this makes the two of you more alike. It makes *us* more alike."

"But that is not your fault," she said passionately. "You cannot help who your grandfather was! I *chose* this." Her cheeks were flushed now, her eyes bright. "I may not have known what I was choosing, but does that make a difference? All I wanted, all I ever wanted, was to save my father, to be a hero, to be Lucie's *parabatai.* I have lost all those things."

"No," he said. "You are a hero, Daisy. We would have lost today, without you."

Her eyes softened. "James," she said, and he wanted to shiver. He loved the way she said his name. He had always loved it. He knew that now. "You were right." She tried to smile. "I *am* cold."

He drew her closer, settling her against his chest. Her body relaxed against his, her head against his shoulder. He smoothed a palm down her back, trying not to let his mind wander to the warm curves of her body.

"There's something I always wonder," she said, her breath against his neck. "We are raised to see demons, and we do. I cannot even recall the first I ever encountered. Yet we do not see angels. We are descended from them, but they are invisible to us. Why is that?"

"I suppose," James said, "because angels require you to have faith. They want us to believe in them without seeing them. That is, I think, what faith is meant to be. We are to believe in them as we believe in all things intangible—goodness, and mercy, and love."

Cordelia said nothing; when James glanced down at her, concerned, he saw that her eyes were very bright. She raised her hand slowly and laid her palm against his cheek. "James," she said, and he let himself shiver as she drew her finger from his cheek to his lips. Her pupils darkened, expanded. She tilted her head back, and he kissed her.

She tasted like spiced honey. Sweetness and heat. He cupped the back of her head in his hand, let himself fall into the kiss. He drew her against him—she was soft, strong, curving. Perfect. He had never felt such tenderness—never even quite known what people meant when they spoke of it, for it had formed no part of his feelings for Grace. Pity and need, yes, but this—this overwhelming mix of passion, admiration, adoration, and desire—was something he had never felt before, and he realized with some wonder that it felt so new, so different, that he had not at first known to label it correctly. He had thought it was not love precisely because it was.

He loved Cordelia; no, he was *in love* with her. He had been pushing the thought back all day, knowing he could not let himself fully realize it until the danger was over—until he was alone with Daisy, until he could tell her—

She broke away, breathless. Her lips and cheeks were bright red, her hair tousled. "James—James—we *must* stop."

Stopping was the last thing he wanted to do. He wanted to kiss her so hard it lifted her off her feet. He wanted to tangle his hands in her thick, smooth hair, and tell her that the curve of her collarbone made him want to write sonnets. He wanted to taste the notch at the base of her throat. He wanted to ask her to marry him again, properly this time.

"Why?" he said instead. It was not his most eloquent moment, he knew, but it was all he could manage.

"I . . . *appreciate* what you have said about how we will face this together." Her brow furrowed; she looked enchantingly puzzled. "I know you would do anything to help your friends. But I cannot rely on you so completely, cannot behave as if this is a real marriage. It is not. We both must remember that."

"It is real," he said roughly. "What we have is—is a marriage."

She looked at him squarely. "Can you say you feel about me as you have felt about her? About Grace?"

He felt a twisting inside himself. Anger. Revulsion. He thought of the bracelet, the two broken pieces of it in his pocket. "No," he said, almost savagely. "I do not feel about you at all as I feel about Grace. How I *ever* felt about Grace."

Only when she looked as if he had slapped her did he realize what he had said. How it would sound. She stood up from the couch, looking a little stunned, reaching up automatically to fix the combs in her hair. "I," she began, "I ought to—"

There was a knock on the front door. The sound echoed through the house. James mentally cursed Effie for most likely being asleep, then cursed doors and people who knocked at them.

The knock came again, louder this time. James bolted to his feet. "That," he said, "is almost certainly my father. I had rather expected he might arrive here once everyone left the Institute."

Cordelia nodded. She still looked a little stunned. "Of course you should talk to him, then."

"Daisy." He caught hold of her shoulders. "I'm not going to talk to him. I'm going to send him away. We must talk, you and I. It is past time for it."

"But if you want to—"

"I want to talk to *you*." He kissed her forehead, then let her go. "Wait for me upstairs, in your room. There is a great deal I need to explain to you. It's desperately important. Do you believe me?"

"Well," she said. "If it's *desperate*." She tried to smile, abandoned the effort, and left the room; he heard her footsteps on the stairs. James paused to brush his clothes off—it wouldn't do to tell his father to go to blazes, politely, while totally rumpled—and headed for the vestibule. His mind was full of what he would say to Cordelia. How he would tell her. He barely knew how to explain it all to himself—what he suspected, what he knew, what he *felt*. But he needed to tell her, more than he had ever needed anything in his life.

James had reached the entryway. He flung open the front door, letting in a blast of cold air—and found himself staring into Grace's ice-gray eyes. He stood frozen in shock as she threw herself into his arms.

GRACE:
1900

In the moment when Grace stood in the forest and fastened the bracelet onto James's wrist, she saw something change in him. It was as if she had taken a lamp and turned down its flame.

From then on, James loved her. Or believed he loved her. To him, there was no difference.

28

NO WISE MAN

I am caught in Love's web so deceitful
None of my endeavors turned fruitful.
I knew not when I rode the high-blooded steed
The harder I pulled its reins the less it would heed.
Love is an ocean with such a vast space
No wise man can swim it in any place.
—Rabi'a Balkhi

For a moment, James could not move. He stood frozen with shock and horror as Grace clung to him, her slim arms tenacious, her body pressed flat to his. For years he had dreamed about holding Grace in his arms, with a sort of restless hunger, wanting it almost without knowing why.

Now he knew why. And now, with her in his arms, he felt only revulsion.

"James." Grace drew back a little, though her fingers were still laced behind his neck. "I came as soon as I got the message."

What message? He didn't ask. He had to keep her here, he realized. If he gave her a chance to run, he might never get answers.

"I had to tell you, darling," she went on, her gray eyes wide and earnest. "I am going to end it with Charles. I cannot bear it anymore, James. I will not marry him. There never was anyone for me but you."

"Thank God," he said. He saw her smile; now was his chance.

He drew back and reached around her to slam the door closed, bolting it. When he turned back to her and caught at her hand, cold and bony in his, she let him take it almost eagerly. Didn't she even wonder where Cordelia was? James thought. Whether they might be interrupted? Was no one in the world real to her except herself? Did nothing matter but her immediate needs?

"Thank God," he said again. "Thank God and the Angel that this farce is finally over."

Her smile vanished. James could not help but marvel at what he was feeling—or rather, *not* feeling. Gone was the need for her so strong it felt like an illness. Gone was the sense of shock and amazement he felt at the sight of her.

In its place was something else. A rising anger.

Her lips were moving, starting to shape questions. But James could hear footsteps—the sound of the door had probably roused Effie. The last thing he wanted was to be interrupted. Tightening his grip on Grace's wrist, he marched her down the hall into the drawing room. Once inside, he let go of her immediately, yanking his hand back with such force that her mouth opened in indignant protest. He slammed the door behind them, locked it, and placed himself in its path.

She stared at him. She was panting a little. Objectively, he knew, she was still beautiful. Her features, her fine hair, her slender figure, none of that had changed. But they revolted him now as surely as if she'd been a monster extruding warts and tentacles in all directions. "James," she said. "What's wrong?"

He reached into his pocket, his hand closing around the broken pieces of bracelet. A moment later he had flung them on the floor. They clanged as they dropped, looking rather pitiful against the carpet—two tarnished half-moons of bent metal. "'Loyalty binds me,'" he said mockingly. "At least, it did."

Grace's whole body tensed. He could see the calculation in her eyes—she had come hoping the enchantment of the bracelet would still work. That she would be able to charm him. Realizing the truth, now, she was considering her options. "How did it break?"

"It happened while I was kissing Cordelia," he said, and saw her wince a little, as if the words were distasteful. Good. She could consider her options all she liked—he had no intention of being cooperative or friendly.

She narrowed her eyes. "It wasn't that long ago that you were kissing me—in this room."

"Shut up," James said dispassionately. "I am not an idiot, though I suppose I might as well have been, for some years now. I ought to just call for the Silent Brothers. They can determine what should be done with you. But I wanted to give you the opportunity to explain yourself."

"You're curious." He could see her determining the price of his questions, her answers. It filled him with rage. He knew he ought to summon the Clave, the Brothers, but his need for the truth overrode everything else. She *would* tell him what he only half guessed at now—what he dreaded, and needed, to know.

"Not curious enough to put up with you toying with me," said James. "Did you know what the bracelet did? Have you always known?"

Her lips parted in surprise. "How do you—"

"Did it just make me think I loved you, or did it do more than that?" James said, and saw by her expression that his question had hit its target. There was no pleasure in having guessed correctly; he felt physically sick. "*What did it do to me?*"

"There is no point shouting," she said, rather primly. "I'll tell you all of it—God knows there's no point protecting anyone now." She gazed past him, at the dark window. "After Jesse died, my mother took me into Brocelind at night."

"This," he said, "had better be relevant."

"It is. There was someone there—a man in a cloak, I couldn't see his face—who gave me what my mother called a 'gift.' The ability to make men do as I said and feel what I wished them to feel. When I use the power, men give me what I want—from a glass of wine to a kiss to a marriage proposal." She shifted her gaze to him. "But oh, the irony. It didn't work on *you*. I tried everything. You resisted all of it. My mother was furious, never more so than when you came back from Cirenworth to Idris and I told her you had fallen in love with Cordelia."

"I was fourteen—"

"Old enough for puppy love," said Grace, without sentiment. "All you would talk about was Cordelia. How she talked, how she walked, how she read to you when you were ill. The color of her eyes, her hair. My mother was desperate. She went to him, the one from the forest. He gave her the bracelet. It would counteract the effect of your demonic grandfather's blood in your veins, she said. And it did. From the moment you put it on, you forgot Cordelia. You believed that you loved me."

James could hear his heartbeat, thudding in his ears. He remembered Cordelia, in the study, trying to get him to remember the summer he had scalding fever—the hurt in her eyes when he did not seem to recall it.

He had already loved her then.

"But the bracelet was not perfect," said Grace. "The spell that bound you to me weakened when we were distant. Each summer, in Idris, its power would be refreshed, and you would love me again, and forget everything else. But then, this past summer, you did not come to Idris, and the spell began to truly falter."

James remembered how unhappy he'd been that they were not going to Herondale Manor over the summer, because his parents insisted on remaining in London to help the Carstairs. Memories had tormented him then: the walk up the road to Blackthorn Manor under the leafy branches of the hawthorn trees; long conversations with Grace at the iron gates; the cool water she brought him in china cups she'd pinched from the kitchen.

But none of it had been real: he had been longing for a drug, a fever-dream. Grace had manipulated him since they were children. James felt his body respond as it did in the face of any threat, his muscles tightening with coiled rage.

"So that is why you came to London?" he spat. "To tighten my leash? Grace, why? I know your mother is mad, twisted by grief and spite. But why would she go to these elaborate lengths to make me think I loved you?"

"Don't you see?" Grace cried, and James thought it was the first time he'd ever heard her burst out with any sort of real emotion. "Because of *him*. Belial. Everything was because of him. He wanted to control you, and she wanted you in pain, so they both got what they wanted."

James felt as if he could barely catch his breath. "Belial," he echoed. "He was the one in the forest? He gave you this . . . curse?"

"He called it a gift," Grace said, in a small voice.

It only made James more furious. "How long have you known that I was Belial's grandson? Did you know even before I did?"

She shook her head. "I found out when I took the bracelet from you four months ago. It was Belial who sent a demon to threaten me, to command me to put the bracelet back on."

James remembered, suddenly, what he could not remember before —the words Grace had said to him the night Blackthorn Manor had burned. The day she'd placed the bracelet back on his wrist. *It had to be you. My mother made me her blade, to cut every barrier raised against her. But your blood, his blood, is a barrier I cannot cut. I cannot bind you without his chain.*

"'I cannot bind you without his chain,'" he said. "That's what you said to me. You couldn't control me without *his chain*—the bracelet." He began to pace back and forth in front of the door. Grace watched him— she seemed unafraid in the manner of someone to whom the worst has already happened, leaving nothing left for them to dread. "So why did you break it off with me, four months ago? How was that part of Belial's plan? He must have wanted to use you to convince me to give myself up to him. To let him possess me. When I saw him in Belphegor's realm, he was furious that the bracelet was not on my wrist."

"It wasn't part of his plan," said Grace, with an odd flash of pride. "My mother had fallen ill—she was not there to stop me. I know you will not believe me, James, but I always thought of you as a friend. My only friend. As the years went past, I hated using the bracelet on you. You were the only person other than Jesse who was ever kind to me, and I was hurting you."

"So you—you meant to set me free? You cannot expect me to believe that."

"Well, it is true," Grace said, with a flicker of temper. "It is why I went to Charles—I thought him powerful enough to withstand my mother's wrath when her health was recovered. I knew she would be furious I had taken back my power over you. But I was sick to death of it." She looked away. "I was wrong. The threat of Charles, of the Consul—it did not matter. I did not realize how powerful my mother's allies were until it was too late."

"The marriage to Charles," James said, feeling his way back through half-clouded memories. Would his mind ever be entirely clear? "You used your power on him, convinced him to drop Ariadne. Marry you."

She nodded.

"Who else have you used your power on?" James said, his voice hard. "Any of my family? My friends? It only works on men, you said."

"He—they would have forgotten—"

"*Stop.*" James ceased pacing. "Never mind. Don't tell me. If you do, I cannot answer for what I will do."

She shrank back, and he hated her, and hated himself.

"I tried and tried to take the bloody thing off," he said. "Every time I went to remove it, I would find that I was doing something else, thinking of something else. If I had been stronger . . ."

"You can't blame yourself," Grace said. James thought she probably meant it. "The bracelet was forged by a Prince of Hell. Woven into it was the power to make those who had observed the bracelet and what it could do forget what they had seen. If you tried to think about it, if your friends or family tried to think about it, they would quickly forget. No matter your behavior, they would accept that you loved me." She took a ragged breath. "But you didn't, did you? You loved Cordelia despite everything. Loved her enough to shatter the spell, break the bracelet." There was wonder in her voice. "I know I have done you an immense wrong, James. But truly, if any mortal in this world has proof of the truth of love, it is you."

James regarded her for a long moment, taking in her damp pale eyelashes, the sharp planes of her cheekbones, the mouth he had once thought he would die to kiss.

"I cannot imagine the life you must have had," he said harshly, "that would lead you to offer that to me as comfort."

"No," said Grace. "You cannot imagine my life."

"I will not pity you," said James. "The bracelet broke only last night, and even in the short time since then, I've been remembering. I can remember Cordelia reading to me—how I felt about her—and it may have been puppy love, but it was new and wonderful and you smashed it underfoot as if you were crushing a butterfly with a brick." He could hear the bitterness in his voice. "I remembered how, when you took the bracelet off me four months ago, I felt as though a fog had been lifted from my brain. I could *think* again. I've only been half-alive since I was fourteen. You have not just made me think that I loved you, you have subsumed my will over and over until I no longer know who I am. Do you even understand what it is that you've done?"

"You want me to say I will atone," Grace said, in an oddly flat voice. "It does not matter, I suppose. I will do what I am told, save one thing. I came here to beg you for help because I can no longer bear to do my mother's bidding."

"Yet you still pretended you loved me when you did, and expected me to love you," said James. "You did not *ask* for my help—you expected it to be compelled. Why should I believe anything you say?"

Grace put her hand to her head as if it pained her. "No matter what my mother did to me, I thought that she loved Jesse, and that everything she did was in service of raising him—of bringing him back. But now I see that she cares only for herself. Letting Belial use Jesse as he did, to commit murder—it is unconscionable."

James laughed shortly. "So Anna was right, you roped Lucie into this Jesse business. As if it wasn't bad enough, you dragged my sister into your schemes."

"About Lucie—"

"No," James snapped. "Enough. Not another word out of you. You came here tonight thinking I was still under the spell's power—that I would hide you from your mother because I was your duped, doting fool. You had no intention of telling me the truth—"

"I know no other way to ask for help," Grace whispered.

Bitterness made it hurt to speak. "I would throw you onto the street," said James, "but this power of yours is no better than a loaded gun in the hands of a selfish child. You cannot be allowed to continue to use it. You do know that?"

"Yes." Her voice shook. "I am throwing myself on your mercy. I have no one else in this world. I will do whatever you advise."

James felt suddenly weary. He was exhausted—by his own fury, his own regret. He could not bear to look at Grace and think of all he had lost. He certainly did not want the responsibility for her now.

But he couldn't risk abandoning her. As long as she and Tatiana

Grace Blackthorn

were both alive, Grace was at risk of being used as her mother's weapon. When Tatiana discovered Grace had broken with her, it would only seal her alliance with Belial, her rage and fury.

"We must go to the Clave," James said. Grace started to object, but he shook his head. "This power you possess is evil. No human should be able to force others to act against their own free will. If you wish to prove that you indeed have broken with your mother, you will tell the Clave what she did to you, and ask the Silent Brothers to remove this power. No good can come of it. I will protect you from your mother and her demons however I can, but I will not do it alone. I will work with the Clave to help you. We are not friends, Grace. I do not want that intimacy with you. But I will help you. You have my word."

Grace sat down on the sofa, folding her hands in her lap like a child. For a moment, James remembered the little girl who had passed him the briar cutters through the gaps in the fence around Blackthorn Manor, and felt a wash of sadness. "I don't want to look at you," he said. "I am going to summon the Silent Brothers. Do not think of going anywhere. They will hunt you down."

"You needn't worry about that," Grace said. She was staring fixedly at the broken halves of the silver bracelet, where they had fallen on the floor. "I have nowhere to go."

James felt sick to his stomach as he left the drawing room—shutting and locking the door behind him—and headed upstairs. How could he ever have thought he loved Grace? Even in the throes of enchantment, he had never felt for her what he felt for Cordelia. She had never made him happy. He had only felt agony when she was not there, and assumed that that was love. *We suffer for love because love is worth it,* his father had told him once: James had thought that meant that to love was to endure anguish. He had not realized his father had meant there should be joy to balance the pain.

The sort of joy that Daisy brought him—the quiet happiness of playing chess together, or reading, or talking in the study. Reaching the door of her bedroom, he threw it open, suddenly unable to wait to see her.

But the bedroom was empty. The bed was made, corners neatly tucked. Cortana was gone from its place on the wall. There was no fire in the grate. The air felt cold, the space very quiet. Desolate. He raced to his room; perhaps she was waiting for him there.

His room was empty too.

He hurried downstairs. A quick search of the ground floor yielded no Cordelia. A cold pebble of dread was now lodged in his stomach. Where was she? He started back up the stairs, only to hear footsteps. He spun around, his heart lifting—then falling again.

It was Effie, in a billowing gray dressing gown, covered in frills. Her hair was up in paper curlers. She sighed mightily at the sight of him. "I tell you," she said. "A body can't get a night's rest around this bloomin' place."

James decided not to comment on the impropriety of a parlormaid appearing before the master of the house in her night attire. He didn't care. "Have you seen Cordelia? Mrs. Herondale?"

"Oh, yes," Effie said. "She was coming down the steps, like, and she saw you all cuddled up with that blond popsy. She tore out the back door like a scalded cat."

"What?" James seized the newel post to steady himself. "Didn't you think of going after her?"

"Not a bit," said Effie. "I don't get paid enough to run about the snow in me nightie." She sniffed. "And you should know that decent men don't embrace women other than their wives in their vestibules. They rent a nice house in St. John's Wood and do it there."

James felt dizzy. He had been angry when he'd opened the door to see Grace, angry that she'd thrown her arms around his neck, but he'd let her hold on to him, wanting to keep her in the house. It had never occurred to him that Cordelia might have seen him embrace Grace, heard what she'd said. *I had to tell you, darling, I am going to end it with Charles. There never was anyone for me but you.*

And what had he said back? *Thank God.*

Three steps took him to the entryway. A pair of Cordelia's gloves was on the side table; he stuffed them into his pocket, not wanting her to be cold—the night was freezing—he would give her his coat when he found her, he thought. "Effie," he said. "I want you to summon the Consul. Immediately. There's a treacherous criminal in the drawing room."

"Cor." Effie looked intrigued. "The popsy? What'd she do, then? Nicked something?" Her eyes widened. "Is she dangerous?"

"Not to you. But get the Consul. Ask her to bring Brother Zachariah." James yanked on his coat. "Grace will tell them what they need to know."

"The *criminal* will tell them everything about the crimes she committed?" said Effie, looking baffled, but James didn't answer. He had already bolted out the door into the night.

After what had seemed an interminably long day, Will was glad to retire to his bedroom, kick off his shoes, and watch his wife do what she did best: read. Tessa was curled up in a window seat, her hair hanging thick and lustrous around her shoulders, her nose buried in a copy of a book called *The Jewel of Seven Stars*. It always amused him that even though her life was filled with demons and vampires, warlocks and faeries, his wife made a beeline for fantastical fiction every time they entered Foyles bookshop.

As if she could hear his thoughts, she glanced over and quirked her mouth up at him. "What are you looking at?"

"You," he said. "Did you know, you grow more beautiful every day?"

"Well, that's odd," said Tessa, resting her chin thoughtfully on the spine of her book, "because as a warlock I do not age, and so I should look the same day to day, neither improving nor worsening."

"And yet," said Will, "you continue to accrue radiance."

She smiled at him. He could tell she was as relieved as he to be home, despite the extended and alarming events of the day. Their trip to Paris had been more harrowing than either of them had let on—it had taken all their joint diplomacy to smooth over the bitter anger of the French Downworlders. There were moments when, alone with Tessa, Will had worried aloud about the possibility of war. He had worried, too, about Charles: the boy had been too angry and defensive at first to realize the scale of his mistake, and then had sunk into a bitter gloom. He had not wanted to come back to London, either, and had agreed to it only when Will had pointed out that he was no longer welcome in Paris.

"You're fretting," Tessa said, reading his eyes. When she tilted her head up and brushed his lips with hers, he cupped her face in his hands. So many years, he thought, and each kiss was new as the break of day.

Tessa let her book fall to the floor, her hands rising to grip the front of Will's shirt. He was just thinking that his night was markedly improving when their reverie was broken by a sudden shriek of horror.

Will spun around, surprising Tessa greatly, then frowned. "Jessamine," he said sternly. "Don't carry on. We're married. And don't be rude, show yourself to Tessa."

Jessamine did whatever she did that allowed her to be visible to non-Herondales. It firmed her up around the edges, making her appear more solid and less translucent. "Of course I'd find you two kissing," she snapped. "There's no time for such nonsense. I need to tell you about Lucie."

"What about Lucie?" Will inquired, perturbed by the interruption. He did not think that kissing was nonsense and had been eager to continue with it, especially after such a stressful day.

"Your daughter has got herself mixed up in bad business. I don't like to tell tales, but it is a dreadful situation involving necromancy."

"*Necromancy?*" Tessa exclaimed in disbelief. "If you're talking about Lucie being friendly with Jesse Blackthorn's ghost, we already know about it. It's hardly that surprising; she's been friends with you all her life."

"And I must point out that you *love* to tell tales, Jessamine," Will added.

"It would be all well and good if Lucie just wanted to be *friends* with ghosts, but that's not the end of it." Jessamine drifted over to Tessa's dresser. "She can *command* them. I've seen her do it. They do whatever she tells them to."

"She *what?*" Will said. "Lucie never—"

Jessamine shook her head, impatient. "Your lovely child summoned up the ghost of Emmanuel Gast, that disgraced warlock. She compelled him to answer her questions, and then at the end she—" Jessamine broke off, dramatically.

"At the end she *what?*" Tessa said, exasperated. "Really, Jessamine, if you truly have something important to tell us, we could do without the theatrical pauses."

"At the end she destroyed him," Jessamine said, and a shudder ran through her silvery form.

Tessa stared at Jessamine as though she wasn't sure how to respond.

"That doesn't sound like Lucie," Will said, but a terrible prickly feeling was coming over him. He wanted to believe Jessamine was mistaken, or even lying, but what reason would she have? He'd never known her to be the kind of ghost that played pranks or made mischief. Of course, she was no help around the place either, but that didn't mean she'd tell falsehoods about Lucie.

"On the other hand," said Tessa, "she certainly concealed the fact of her friendship with Jesse's ghost all this time. She's entering a rather secretive age, I think."

"I'll talk to her," Will said, then turned to Jessamine. "Where is she now?"

"Holed up in the Sanctuary," Jessamine said. "I couldn't follow her. I daresay it's an *oversight* that no one has removed ghosts from the list of supernatural creatures forbidden to enter."

"We can discuss that later," Will said. If Jessamine truly was concerned for Lucie, that concern didn't seem to stop her from registering her usual complaints.

Jessamine vanished with an outraged sniff.

"It's so hard to take her seriously sometimes," Tessa said, frowning. "Do you think there's any truth to what she's saying?"

"Perhaps a kernel of it, but you know as well as I do that Jessamine loves to exaggerate," Will said, reaching for a jacket. "I'll just go talk to Lucie and be back before you know it."

29

A Broken Mirror

And thus the heart will break, yet brokenly live on:
Even as a broken mirror, which the glass
In every fragment multiplies; and makes
A thousand images of one that was,
The same, and still the more, the more it breaks;
And thus the heart will do which not forsakes,
Living in shatter'd guise, and still, and cold,
And bloodless, with its sleepless sorrow aches,
Yet withers on till all without is old,
Showing no visible sign, for such things are untold.
—Lord Byron, *Childe Harold's Pilgrimage*

Cordelia ran.

She ran through Mayfair, along the wide streets, among the rich
and wealthy houses with warm golden light spilling from their windows. She hadn't bothered to glamour herself, and the few passersby
on the streets stared openly at the running girl with no coat. Not that
she cared.

She had no destination in mind. She had taken nothing with her
from the Curzon Street house save what was in her pockets: a few
coins, a handkerchief, her stele. She had bolted out the back door without a single thought for anything but getting away. The ground was icy
and she was wearing only silk slippers; she could feel her toes freezing.

It was strange to be fleeing without Cortana, but she had done what she needed to do with the blade earlier that day. She had hated to do it, but there had been no choice.

Her feet skidded on a patch of ice, and she caught at a lamppost, leaning against it to steady herself. She could still see them in her mind's eye. James, and wrapped around him, her hands locked behind his neck, Grace Blackthorn.

They had not been kissing. But in some ways, the ease of their intimacy was worse. As she watched, Grace lifted her face to James's; her arms tightened around him and her body pressed against his. They were lovely together. His hair so dark and hers so fair, both of them strong and slender, both of them achingly beautiful. They looked as if they belonged together in a way Cordelia was sure she and James never could.

Unwelcome thoughts came thick and fast: James laughing with her over a game of chess, saying, *Touch me—do what you want—anything*, the way he'd recited the words of their marriage vows to her in Mount Street Gardens. All the tiny little bits of nothing that she had gathered up and stored away, fragments of hope that formed a mirror of dreams through which she saw a life with James spread out before her.

She had been lying to herself. She saw that now.

I had to tell you, darling, Grace had said, and every word was a new spike in Cordelia's heart. *I am going to end it with Charles. I cannot bear it anymore, James. I will not marry him. There never was anyone for me but you.*

Cordelia had known she shouldn't be listening—she should back away, give them their privacy, hide herself upstairs, where she could shield herself in not knowing. But she couldn't make her legs move. Frozen in place, she'd watched helplessly. Watched the blade rising, hovering over her life, her dreams, her carefully kept illusions. The blow about to land.

James had exhaled with relief. *Thank God*, he'd said.

The blade came down, shattering her dream-mirror into pieces. Leaving them to fall away in glittering, once-beautiful shards, abandoned now to tumble through the darkness into the whirlpool of her shame and horror. Even finding out she was Lilith's paladin had not been as terrible as this. Lilith's scorn she could stand, and her friends had stood by her.

But James must despise her, she thought. She'd found herself backing away blindly down the hallway, her hand against the wall to steady herself. What a fool he must think her. Oh, he had affection for her, of that she was sure enough, but he must have guessed her feelings. No doubt he pitied her for them.

She had to get away.

She had slipped silently down the back stairs, passing the ground floor, making her way to the kitchen. It was full of warm yellow light. She could remember James taking her through the house on their wedding night, pointing out each painting, each piece of furniture, with love and pride. He should never have spoken like that, she thought. Like she had a future in this house, as its mistress. One day Grace would be in charge of all this; she and James would share a bedroom, and Cordelia's room would be turned into a nursery for their certain-to-be-beautiful babies. Perhaps they would have dark hair and gray eyes, or blond hair and golden eyes.

She had stared around almost blindly, seeing the patterned china that had been given to her and James as a wedding present by Gabriel and Cecily, the samovar that had been her mother's, the silver cup her grandmother had brought with her to Tehran from Erivan. Gifts of love and pride given in the expectation of a happy marriage. She could not bear to look at any of it anymore. She could not be in that house one more moment.

She had fled, into the garden and the darkness, and the streets beyond.

She could still hear James's voice in her ears. *I do not feel about you at all as I feel about Grace.* What had she expected? She had woven a tissue of denial out of James's kindness, his kisses, his desire for her. It had probably only ever been his desire for Grace, subsumed into the only form of expression he could allow it. She had only ever been a substitute. They'd never even given each other their second wedding runes.

She began to shiver—now that she was no longer running, the cold had begun to make itself acutely known to her. She pushed away from the lamppost, making her way through the snow and slush, her arms wrapped around herself. She could not stay out in the night, she knew. She would freeze to death. She could not go to Anna—how could she make Anna understand without making herself sound a fool and James a villain? She could not go to Cornwall Gardens and face the shame and horror of admitting that her marriage was over. She could not go to Lucie at the Institute, because that would mean Will and Tessa and again, another admission that her wedded union to their son was a sham. Not to mention the new knowledge that somehow, Lucie and Grace were acquainted. She supposed she could not blame Lucie, not really, but it was more than she could bear hearing about.

Only when she was passing by the doorman in front of the brick edifice of the Coburg Hotel did she realize that her feet were bringing her to Grosvenor Square.

But Matthew no longer lives in Grosvenor Square.

Her pace slowed. Had she been looking for Matthew without realizing it? To be fair, Grosvenor Square was smack in the middle of Mayfair. She might have wound up here by accident. But her feet had, without her noticing, brought her directly this way, and it did make sense. Who else could she go to but Matthew? Who else lived alone, away from the prying eyes of parents? More importantly, who else knew the truth?

This may be a false marriage, but you're in love with James.

She glanced once at the Consul's house and walked on, passing through Grosvenor Square and continuing until she reached Oxford Street. She looked up and down its length. Normally it was jammed with people and carriages, noisy with vendors selling from carts and the swarming activity of the busy department stores. Even at this hour it was not empty, but she had no trouble flagging down a hansom cab.

It was a short drive to the place where Matthew lived. Whitby Mansions was a wedding cake of a building, an edifice of pink stone that rose in turrets and spires like dollops of icing. Matthew had probably taken the flat without even looking at it, Cordelia thought as she stepped out of the cab.

A bored-looking mundane porter appeared when she rang the brass bell beside the black double doors. He led her into the lobby. It was dimly lit, but Cordelia had an impression of a lot of dark wood and a mahogany desk such as one might find in a hotel.

"Ring Mr. Fairchild's flat, please," she said. "I am his cousin."

The porter raised his eyebrows slightly. She was, after all, a Lone Young Lady, turning up in the evening to visit a single man in his flat. No girl of good family would do such a thing. It was clear the porter thought she was no better than she should be. Cordelia didn't care. She was freezing and desperate.

"He's upstairs in flat six, third floor. Get along with you." The porter turned his attention back to reading the newspaper.

The lift was luxurious, all gold fixtures and expensive wallpaper. She tapped her feet as it creaked slowly upward to the third floor, disgorging her into a red-carpeted hallway lined with doors, each marked with a gold numeral. Only now was Cordelia's courage starting to flag; she hurried down the corridor before she could have second thoughts and knocked sharply on the door of flat 6.

Nothing. Then footsteps, and Matthew's voice. The familiarity of it sent a pang of relief through her. "Hildy, I've told you," he was saying, as he swung the door wide, "I don't need any washing done—"

He froze, staring at Cordelia. He was in trousers and an undershirt, a towel around his neck. His arms were bare, patterns of runes twining up and down them. His hair was damp and tousled. She must have interrupted him shaving.

"Cordelia?" he said, and there was genuine shock in his voice. "Has something happened? Is James in trouble?"

"No," Cordelia whispered. "James is well, and—very happy, I think."

Something in Matthew's expression changed. His gaze flickered. He stood back, opening the door wider. "Come in."

She stepped into a small square hall, an entryway of sorts, where one's eye was drawn compulsively to the massive neoclassical vase standing in one corner. It was of the Greek sort, the kind a maiden would use to pour oil into a bath, though in this case that maiden would have to be twenty feet tall. It was painted all over with faux Greek figures engaged in either combat or passionate embrace, Cordelia could not tell.

"I see you've noticed my vase," Matthew said.

"It would be difficult not to."

Matthew wasn't really looking at her, instead tugging nervously at the ends of the towel around his neck. "Let me give you the ha'penny tour, then. This is my vase, whom you've met, and that there is a potted palm, and a hatstand. Take off your wet shoes, and we'll go through to the drawing room. Do you want tea? I can ring for tea. Or make some; I've become quite handy with a kettle. Or . . ."

Divested of her drenched shoes, Cordelia wandered into the drawing room. It was much nicer than the vase. She wanted to collapse immediately onto the soft pile of the Turkish rug but decided that was a little louche even for Matthew's flat. But there was a warm, low fire crackling in the hearth, its tile surround glimmering like shards of gold, and a sofa with a velvet cover. She sank onto it as Matthew wrapped a blanket about her shoulders and arranged the throw pillows around her as a sort of protective fortress, like a child might.

Cordelia could only nod at the suggestion of tea. She had come here to unburden herself to Matthew, to *someone*, but now that she had arrived, she found she could not speak. Matthew cast a worried glance at her and vanished through a set of pocket doors, presumably on his way to the kitchen.

Chin up. Tell him the truth, Cordelia thought, gazing around at what she could see of the flat. What was most surprising was how well-kept it was. She might have expected something more like Anna's place, with its mismatched patterns and clothes thrown about. Matthew, on the other hand, had furniture that looked like it had been ordered new when he took the flat, massive heavy oak pieces that must have been murder to get up to the third floor. In a stylish touch, he had hung his many colorful jackets on a row of hooks in the hallway. A steamer trunk bearing various stamps on its canvas surface was propped near the door. Oscar, wearing a bejeweled collar, was asleep by the fire, just beneath a framed drawing of several young men in a garden of plane trees—the Merry Thieves, Cordelia realized. She wondered who'd done the sketch.

She marveled again at the sheer freedom Matthew seemed to possess. Anna was her only other friend with the same kind of liberty, and she would always think of Anna as from an older set, more mature simply because she would always be years ahead of Cordelia. But Matthew was her own age and lived as he pleased. His family was wealthy, of course, much wealthier than hers or her other close friends here—he was the son of the Consul, after all—and surely that bought a certain level of freedom, but most of it was Matthew himself. Shadowhunters were a people bound to duty, but somehow he seemed unbound—to duty or anything else of earthly weight.

Matthew—who had found a shirt and thrown it on hastily—appeared with a silver tea tray and put it down on the side table. He poured and passed her a cup. "Have you thawed yet?" he asked, dragging a dark green velvet armchair close to the sofa. "If not, the tea should help."

She sipped at it obediently as he flung himself into the armchair. She could taste nothing, but the liquid was hot and warmed her insides. "It does," she said. "Matthew, I . . ."

"Go on," he said, having poured himself a companionable cup of tea. "Tell me about James."

Perhaps Matthew was right; perhaps tea *was* the solution to everything. Either way, something unlocked the words inside her. They came out all in a rush. "I had thought it might all work out, you see," she said. "I knew when we agreed to marry that James didn't feel for me what . . . I felt for him. But there were moments—not all the time, but moments—where I thought it was changing. That he cared for me. And the moments were becoming more frequent. More real. I thought. But it seems those were only moments that I was deluding myself. It was my delusions that were becoming more frequent." She shook her head. "I knew, I knew how he felt about Grace—"

"Has something happened with Grace?" Matthew interrupted, a sharp note in his voice.

"She is with him now, at our house," she said, and Matthew sat back in his chair, exhaling. "Matthew, don't look like that—I don't hate her," Cordelia said, and she meant it. "I don't. If she loves James as he loves her, all this must have been rather awful for her."

"She does not," said Matthew icily, "love him."

"I didn't think—but perhaps she does? She seemed panicked. She must have heard he was in danger today. I suppose they felt they had to see each other, after everything." Cordelia's hand shook, rattling the teacup in its saucer. "She told him she would break it off with

Charles. And he said, 'Thank God.' She was holding him—he was holding her—I had never thought—"

Matthew had set his tea down. "James said, 'Thank God'? When she told him she was going to end things with my brother?"

Charles, Cordelia knew, would not care in any real way about Grace's abandonment. But Matthew did not know that. She sighed. "I'm sorry, Matthew. It's not very nice to Charles—"

"Never mind Charles," said Matthew, propelling himself savagely out of the armchair. Oscar gave a concerned woof. "And as for James—"

"I don't wish you to be angry with him," Cordelia said, suddenly worried. "I would never want that. He loves you, you are his *parabatai*—"

"And I love him," said Matthew. "But I have always loved him and understood him. Now I love him but do not understand him at all. I knew he loved Grace. I thought it was because of the way he met her. She seemed to desperately need saving, and James has always wanted to save people. Even those who very clearly cannot be saved. And I, of all people, cannot fault him for that." He pressed the heels of his hands into his eyes. "But to let her into your home, to embrace her with you standing right there—how could I not be angry with him?" He dropped his hands. "Even if just on his own behalf. Grace will never make him happy."

"But that is his choice. He loves her. It is not something he can simply be talked out of. There is nothing that can—or should—be done about it."

Matthew gave a sharp, disbelieving laugh. "You are remarkably calm."

"I always knew it," said Cordelia. "He has never really been dishonest. I was the one who was not honest. I did not tell him I loved him. I do not think he would have consented to marry me if he had known how I felt."

Matthew was silent. Cordelia, too, had run out of words: she had finally said it, the dark, awful thought that lurked in her soul. She had tricked James into marrying her, pretending to an indifference she did not feel. She had lied to him, and earned this consequence.

"It is only that I do not know what to do," she said. "Divorce now, after such a short time, would ruin me, I think. But I do not—I cannot go back to that house—"

At last Matthew spoke, with a sort of jerky precision, like a windup toy coming to life. "You—you could—stay here."

"With you?" She was startled. "Sleep on the sofa? That would be very . . . bohemian. But it wouldn't do, my family would never—"

"Not with me," he said. "I am going to Paris. I was planning to leave tomorrow."

She flashed back to the steamer trunk by the door. "You're going to Paris?" she said, feeling suddenly, terribly alone. "But—why?"

"Because I couldn't bear to be here." Matthew began to pace. "I took an oath to stand by James's side. And I love him—he has always been all the things that I am not. Honest where I am not. Brave where I am a coward. When I thought his choice was you—"

"It was never me," said Cordelia, setting her teacup down.

"I thought he took you for granted," said Matthew. "Then I saw the way he ran to you, after that battle in Nelson Square. It seems a thousand years ago now, but I remember it. He ran and caught you up and he seemed—desperate—to know that you were all right. As if he would die if you weren't. And I thought—I thought I had misjudged him. So I told myself to stop."

Cordelia licked her dry lips. "Stop what?"

"Hoping, I suppose," he said. "That you would see that I loved you."

She stared at him, motionless, too shocked to speak.

"I fully expected James to come to his senses," he said. "Good Lord, when I saw you two in the Whispering Room, I thought it would barely be seconds before he was hitting himself with a brick for ever having thought he loved Grace while at the same time throwing himself at your feet and professing his adoration."

Cordelia thought of Matthew saying to her, what felt like a long time ago now, *I have wished for a long time for him to place his affections somewhere else, and yet, when I saw him with you in the Whispering Room, I was not happy.*

Yet it had never occurred to her that he intended anything by it but flirting—Matthew's flirting, which meant nothing at all.

"I suppose I merely thought it would be enough for you to know," he said. "That you might—if anything were to happen to me, you would remember I loved you desperately. And if for some reason, at the end of a year, you and James divorced, I would—well, I would have waited. But I would have hoped the time would have come when my addresses would not have been disgusting to you."

"Matthew," she said. "Look at you. *Listen* to you. Your addresses could never be disgusting."

He almost smiled. "I remember," he said. "At the ball, the first time I really met you, you told me I was beautiful. That held me for quite a long time, you know. I am very vain. I didn't love you then, I don't think, though I recall thinking how fine you looked when your eyes blazed with anger. And then at the Hell Ruelle, when you danced, and proved yourself braver than all the rest of us combined, I knew it for sure. But love is not always a lightning bolt, is it? Sometimes it is a creeping vine. It grows slowly until suddenly it is all that there is in the world."

"I don't know what to say," she murmured. "Only that I truly did not suspect..."

He gave another of those harsh laughs, clearly directed only at himself. "I suppose I should be pleased that I have been a good actor. Perhaps when inevitably I am tossed out of the Clave for some future misdeed, I will find a new success upon the stage."

Cordelia was speechless. She did not want to hurt him; she had been hurt enough and had no desire to pass it on to someone else. Especially as dear a friend as Matthew. Despite his open talk of love, Matthew held himself like a wounded animal, wary and tensed.

"I wouldn't imagine you know what to say," he said. "But... I had to tell you. You had to know how I feel. I was going to Paris because it seemed to me James finally understood what he had, being married to you—and I was glad, only I also knew I could not bear to see it. I thought in Paris I might forget. In Paris, one forgets everything."

She darted her gaze up to his. "I envy you," she said softly. "We have common cause in our anguish, I suppose, but you can flee it—you can go to Paris alone and nobody remarks upon it. What I dread as much as anything else is the gossip, the things people will say when they find out about James and Grace. What my family will say. What Will and Tessa will think—they were always so kind to me—and Lucie—"

Without warning, Matthew flung himself to his knees on the thick carpet. He was kneeling in front of her, a position that filled her with a sudden alarm.

"You cannot propose," she said. "I am already married."

At that, he actually did smile, and caught at her hand. Cordelia made no move to draw it back. For so long, she thought, she had lived with the knowledge that James did not care for her the way she did for him. And now a beautiful young man was kneeling before her, holding her hand, gazing at her with a wordless fervor. Nearly all her life she had dreamed of three things: bearing Cortana, being Lucie's *parabatai*, and being loved. She had lost the first two. She could not bear to fling this last, small thing away from her so quickly.

"I was not going to propose marriage," he said. "I was going to propose something else. That you come to Paris with me." He tightened his grip on her hand; there was high color in his cheeks, and he was speaking almost feverishly. "Hear me out. You need to forget as badly as I do. Paris is a city of wonders, my favorite in the world. I know you have been there, but you have not been there with *me*." She smiled—it was good to know Matthew's vanities had not deserted him. "We will see the Pont Alexandre lit up at night—go to Montmartre, where everything is scandalous—eat dinner at Maxim's and know it is but the start of a magical evening of cabarets and dancing and theater and art." He tipped his head back to look directly into her eyes. "I would never press my attentions on you. We will stay in separate hotel rooms. I will be your friend, that is all. Only let me see you happy in Paris. It is the greatest gift you could give me."

Cordelia closed her eyes. For a moment she was back in the motorcar, and the road was unrolling before her, the wind in her hair. She had left her agony behind for those hours. She could glimpse that liberty again in Matthew's words, in the picture he painted of a city of wonders. The thought of leaving sodden, heartbreaking London behind made her feel free. Free the way she wanted to be. Free the way Matthew was free.

But my mother, she thought. And then remembered what Sona had said to her just that afternoon: *I do not want you hovering over me, doting on me until the baby comes. . . . What I want for you above all things is that you follow the truth of your dreams. No scorn, no shame, no part of society's opinion matters more than that.*

"My father," she said, instead. "His funeral—"

"Will not be for at least a fortnight," said Matthew. It was true—the bodies of the murdered were to be kept in the Silent City until they had been purified; they had, after all, been used in a demon-summoning ritual. "If we are still in Paris, I promise you, we will travel to Idris for it."

Cordelia took a deep breath. "Paris," she whispered, testing it out. "But—I have nothing with me. I left Curzon Street in one dress and ruined shoes."

Matthew's eyes lit. "In Paris, I will outfit you in a whole new wardrobe of clothes! All the latest styles, all the best dressmakers. In Paris we can be whomever we wish."

"All right," she said, still looking straight at Matthew. "Let's go to Paris. On one condition."

Matthew's expression blossomed with shock and pleasure; he clearly had not thought this was how the conversation would go. "Anything," he said.

"No drinking," she said. She knew she was treading on delicate ground, but it was important. She thought of the broken bottle in the snow at the Shadow Market. Of Matthew stumbling, slipping during the fight in Nelson Square. She had not wanted to see it, but if there was anything she had learned from her marriage, it was that looking away from truth helped nothing. She could do this for Matthew, as no one had ever done it for her father. "A little champagne, wine, as you like, but not—like my father drank. Not to get drunk."

Something flickered in his dark green eyes. "You are serious?" he said. "I agree to this and you will come with me?"

"Never more serious," said Cordelia. "We could leave tonight. There is always an evening train."

"Then yes," he said, "yes, yes. In Paris, with you, I will not need to forget." He kissed her hand and released it, rising to his feet. "I will leave a message for James with the porter. He can deliver it in the morning. I shall tell him there is no need to worry. He can let the others know—tell them whatever he likes—Anna will be delighted, perhaps she will come and visit with us."

And she would leave messages for her mother and brother, Cordelia thought. They would still worry, but that couldn't be helped. She felt flushed with energy, an almost physical longing to be moving, traveling, free of constraint, with the wind at her back and the sound of a train whistle in her ears. "Matthew," she said. "In Paris, will you be able to forgive yourself?"

He smiled at that—a real smile; his face lit up, and Cordelia could not help but think that it was a face that would open any door in Paris to them. "In Paris," he said, "I shall be able to forgive all the world."

"All right," Cordelia said. In her mind, she was dancing down the Rue Saint-Honoré. There was music, light, joy, the promise of a future that would not be empty, and all with Matthew, her steadfast friend, by her side. "Let's find me a coat."

Fleeing out into the darkness of London was well and good, but James realized quickly it wasn't going to help him find Cordelia. He could try to guess where she'd gone, but the two most obvious places—Cornwall Gardens and the Institute—both seemed unlikely to him. If she were as upset as he guessed, the last thing she would want would be questions she could only half answer. Nor, knowing Cordelia, would she want sympathy, and certainly not anything she might interpret as pity. Cordelia would rather be set on fire than pitied.

In the end, there was nothing for it: he took shelter under the colonnades outside Burlington Arcade and set up to make a Tracking rune. It felt uncomfortable to Track Cordelia—a small voice in the back of his head said that if she wanted him to know where she was, she would have left a message. *But she's proceeding on the basis of mistaken information,* he snapped back at the voice. *She needs to know. I have to tell her, about the bracelet at least. Then she can make up her own mind about what to do, but at least I can provide her with all the facts.*

With one of her gloves in hand—delicate, kidskin, with a tracery of embroidered leaves—James activated the Tracking spell. The familiar tugging feeling led him on a zigzag route through Piccadilly, to New Bond Street, and through the shadowed lanes toward Marylebone. He had nearly fetched up on the front steps of Matthew's flat when he realized that it was his destination.

His steps slowed. Cordelia had gone to Matthew? It was good she had gone to a friend, of course—and Anna was unlikely to be home, or alone if she was—and other than Anna, Cordelia was closest to Matthew of all the Merry Thieves. But then, Matthew had been one of the first to know of James's relationship with Grace, had even comforted him when it ended four months past. (James felt sick, remembering.) Perhaps she'd thought Matthew would understand best.

He kicked the snow off his boots before entering the lobby, where the porter was chatting to a tall chap with a long, narrow face and a dog on a leash. The porter glanced over at James with a polite nod.

"Can you ring up to Matthew Fairchild's flat?" James asked, slipping Cordelia's glove into his pocket. "I need to speak with him, and—"

At that moment, the dog made a lunge for James, who realized two things very quickly: the lunge was friendly, and the dog was familiar. "Oscar?" he said, laying a hand on the retriever's head.

Oscar wagged his tail so hard his whole body vibrated.

"Well, a friend of Oscar is a friend of mine," said the narrow-faced man, and held out a hand for James to shake. "Gus Huntley. I'll be watching Oscar while Fairchild's away."

"James Herondale. Matthew's away?" James stopped petting Oscar. "What do you mean, away?"

"I was going to tell you." The porter looked aggrieved. "He left maybe twenty minutes ago, off to the Paris train. Had a pretty young lass with him too. Said she was his cousin, but they didn't look a bit alike." He winked.

"He borrowed a ladies' coat and shoes off me before he went too," said Huntley. "My sister will be furious, but Fairchild's got a convincing way about him."

"If she had red hair, then no, she's not his cousin," said James, weighing the possibility that Matthew and Anna had departed suddenly for Paris, and discarding it. Anna would never have needed to borrow a coat. "That's my wife."

A terrible and awkward silence descended. The porter looked at James in some alarm. "What'd you say your name was? Herondale?"

James nodded. It felt very odd, somehow, giving his name out to mundanes, but the porter only rifled through the desk papers and handed over a folded letter, addressed to James in Matthew's scrawled hand. "He left this for you," he said. "Probably clear the whole thing up."

"No doubt a very good explanation for everything," said Huntley, who had retreated behind Oscar.

"And the Paris train leaves from . . . ?" James said.

"Waterloo," said the porter, and James fled back into the night—followed, he suspected, by at least two pitying stares.

James elected to take a hansom cab to the station, which he realized very quickly was a mistake. Though it was past rush hour, the streets were crowded—not only were there commuters returning late from work, but the London evening was well underway and the city's revelers were hurrying to dinner, drinks, and the theater. His hansom soon came to a dead stop on Waterloo Bridge in a mass of omnibuses, carriages, and horses. The thumping and rattling of the wheels made it hard for James to read Matthew's note, but familiarity with his *parabatai's* looping, evocative script helped. By the time they inched to the end of the bridge, he had read it three times.

> *Jamie,*
>
> *I never thought to write such a letter as this to you, my dearest friend, but I hope that when it finds you, you are happy. By now you will know that Cordelia and I have gone to Paris. This was not a lightly considered decision. Though I knew what you and Cordelia have was not a real marriage, I had sworn that I would respect it, and respect also what seemed to me the clear possibility that, being Daisy's husband, you would fall in love with her.*
>
> *I understand now that you will not be happy unless you are with Miss Blackthorn. I know that you promised Daisy that you would stay away from Grace, and it seems that you cannot, which bespeaks how much you must love her. Cordelia is proud. You know that as well as I do. She would tell herself she must endure the situation, but I love her, and I cannot bear to see her suffer for the next year. I hope you will forgive me—I think*

you will forgive me. You must see that in the situation we have now, there are four unhappy people. Surely you, too, wish that were not the case. Surely you care for Daisy even if you do not love her, and want her to be happy. And surely you will forgive me for keeping the secret of my feelings for her from you—I had never meant to speak of them to anyone, before tonight.

You've always laughed at my idea that Paris is a place of magical healing, but I believe that after some time there Cordelia will smile again, and that then we three will be able to decide the best course of action, without bitterness and sorrow.

Yours,

Matthew

James wanted to throttle Matthew. He also wanted to spill out the whole story of the bracelet to him, to beg his forgiveness for everything he had not noticed for all these years, for the fog that had clung to his every emotion, his every thought, blunting them all. Matthew needed so much, and James had not been there to provide it.

"I'll get out here," he yelled to the cabbie, thrusting some money in his direction. He scrambled out of the cab into a sea of Londoners heading up the short hill to the grand arch of Waterloo Station's main entrance; outside was a crush of carriages and hansoms, unloading passengers and luggage for the overnight trains.

Inside, the massive train station was absolutely heaving with people, the hubbub from the crowds and the trains deafening. Pushing through the crowd, James narrowly missed being crushed by three small boys in Eton uniforms with an enormous trunk on wheels.

"Mind the gentleman!" said a passing porter crossly. "Need help, sir? Any luggage?"

James nearly caught the poor man by his sleeve. "I need to find the train to Southampton—the one that connects to the Le Havre ferry. The first-class cabins," he added, and saw the porter's jowly face light with interest.

"Lovely, lovely. I'll escort you to the train meself. Train leaves spot on time, it does, and finding the platform is a difficult job, sir, what with the numbers on some of them being doubled. . . ."

James followed the porter as he wove through the crowd. Bright posters overhead encouraged travelers to VISIT FRANCE, showing scenes from Brittany, Paris, and the Côte d'Azur. Then they were at the platform, where a smart-looking train with gleaming brown paintwork stretched down the track. James handed over sixpence and heard nothing of what the porter said to him in response. He was too busy staring.

The first-class carriages were down at the platform's end, near the train's head. The air was full of smoke and steam, the platform crowded with travelers, but through it all James could see them. Matthew, stepping into a carriage with a gold-painted door, then turning back to help Cordelia up after him. She wore a too-big coat, her bright-flaming hair slipping out of its combs, but she was smiling at Matthew as he assisted her into the train.

Daisy, my Daisy.

James had just started toward her across the platform when a hand came down on his shoulder. He turned, his coat whirling out about him, about to snap at whoever was delaying him. But the protest died on his lips.

It was his father. He wore a hat, a blue Inverness coat, and a frantic expression. "Thank the Angel I caught you," Will said. "You have to come with me. Now."

James's heart stopped, then started again; the shock of seeing his father there, entirely absent of any context that would make his presence seem reasonable, made words desert him. "I—I can't—I'm about to get on the train." He gestured at it wildly. "Cordelia's already in a carriage—"

"I know," Will said. He had clearly raced out of the Institute without bothering to glamour himself, though there was a Tracking rune visible on the back of his left hand. How he'd located James, no doubt. "I saw her getting in with Matthew. Where the blazes are you three going?"

"Paris," James said. "After all the terrible things that have happened—I thought Cordelia deserved to enjoy herself, if only for a few days. We never had a honeymoon, any sort of trip—"

"And you decided *now* was the proper time?" For a moment, Will looked exasperated. Under other circumstances, James knew, his father would have been more than briefly put out; he would have realized how ridiculous the story James was telling really was and interrogated him like the Inquisitor. James felt a gnawing bite of worry. His father was clearly deeply distressed.

Will passed a hand over his face, struggling to control his expression. "Jamie. I understand—believe me—one does ridiculous things when one's in love. But you can't go. This is desperate."

"What's desperate?"

"Your sister's gone," Will said.

"*What?*"

"She's gone, Jesse Blackthorn's body is gone, and Malcolm Fade is missing. According to the note she left, she and Fade intend to engage in some kind of necromancy to raise young Jesse from the dead. I don't think I need to tell you what kind of price magic like that exacts." There were sharp lines at the corners of Will's mouth; James had rarely seen his father look so worried. Will usually hid his concerns. "James, she will listen to you where she will not listen to me or your mother. I need you to come with me to find her."

Numb with shock, James stared at his father. Along the platform, the porters were walking the length of the Southampton train, making sure everything was buttoned up tight.

"You had better run to tell them you'll be staying back," Will said quietly. James knew he meant Matthew and Cordelia. "Though I must ask you to tell neither of them about Lucie. The fewer people who hear of this, the better, for her sake."

Still numb, James started down the platform. Steam was beginning to rise from the train's wheels; he could see the passengers through the windows, taking their seats, readying themselves for the journey.

He turned to glance back at his father. Will stood by himself on the platform, his broad shoulders hunched, his gaze fixed on the middle distance. James thought he had never seen Will look so alone.

"All aboard!" a porter shouted, passing James as he strode toward the front of the train. "All aboard for Southampton and Paris!"

Paris. James thought of Cordelia, on the train. Daisy would be settling into a plush velvet seat, maybe drawing off her scarf and coat, looking across the carriage at Matthew, full of excitement for the journey to come. . . .

He tried to imagine himself bursting into that carriage, spoiling the cozy scene with frantic demands. But what could he possibly say? He could not beg Cordelia—or Matthew, for that matter—to abandon their plans, to come back, only to then immediately depart London himself, with no explanation as to why he was leaving, or where he was going.

It would be impossible. And worse, it would be cruel.

The train whistle sounded. James had never imagined that the hardest thing he would ever do in his life was nothing at all. He stood motionless as the screech of releasing brakes filled his ears. There was one last second during which he thought, *I could still run, I could catch up to her, call to her through the window*—and then came the plume of smoke and the *thump-thump* of wheels on tracks, speeding up as the train rolled smoothly out of the station.

The world blurred around James, a rain-spoiled watercolor in browns and grays. He made his way back to Will through the acrid smoke of the departed train. He heard himself say something to his father, something about how Matthew and Cordelia had agreed to journey on to Paris without him, that he would join them after his family business had been concluded. It was all nonsense, he thought dully, and at another time his father would have known it. But Will was too distracted now to examine the situation closely: he was already leading James back through the station, dodging the crowds as he reassured James that he'd done the right thing. After all, they had dozens of friends in Paris, and Matthew would look after Daisy—no one else could do better—and surely Paris would lift her spirits after the loss of her father?

James nodded blankly as they passed back through the arched entrance. Will glanced around, tapping his walking stick impatiently on the pavement. His expression lightened, and he herded James forward. An unfamiliar carriage waited at the side of the curb: it was shiny, black, and drawn by two matched gray horses. Leaning against the side of the carriage, resplendently attired in a pure white wool coat with a mink collar, was Magnus Bane.

"I managed to catch him just before the train left," Will said, releasing James, who felt a bit like a cocker spaniel that had bolted in

Kensington Gardens and was now being returned to its owner.

"What's Magnus doing here?" James said.

Magnus tipped back his white trilby hat and eyed James. "Your father summoned me as soon as he read your sister's note," he said. "If you know someone who's run off with a warlock, it's best to engage another warlock to help you find them."

"Speaking of finding people, have you had any luck?" Will asked.

Magnus shook his head. "I can't track them. Malcolm's blocking any attempt. I'd do the same."

"Do you have *any* idea at all where she might have gone?" said James. "A direction? Anything?"

"She mentioned Cornwall," said Will. "We'll head to the Institute there. Get a list of local warlocks, Downworlders. Magnus can ask them some judicious questions. They'll trust him more."

"And you must let me approach Malcolm, when we find him," said Magnus.

Will's expression darkened. "Like hell," he said. "He *ran off* with my daughter. Who is sixteen years old."

"I would urge you not to think of it in those terms," said Magnus. "Malcolm didn't kidnap Lucie. According to her note, it's her goal to help Jesse. That's what they both think they're doing." He sighed. "Malcolm has something of a focus on the Blackthorns."

Will looked intrigued. "There is more to this story, and I will get it out of both of you before we reach Cornwall." He sighed. "I'll check on the horses. Then we leave. We can make it to Basingstoke by morning; we'll rest then."

He stomped away, and James could hear him murmuring to the horses. Magnus's horses, presumably, though Will generally loved all horses. All animals, really, with the exception of ducks. And cats. *Focus,* James told himself. His mind was spinning; too many shocks and reversals of the day had left him as stunned as if he had fallen from a great height.

He would get used to the new situation, he knew. And when he did, it would hurt. Only shock was cushioning the pain of losing Cordelia—and Matthew—and when that shock passed, the pain would be greater than anything he had ever felt in association with

Grace. One day he would be able to reach Cordelia again, to explain to her, but by then, would she care? Or believe him?

Magnus raised an eyebrow. "So Cordelia has suddenly decided to go to Paris with Matthew, the same day that you stopped Charles Fairchild's murder and Leviathan, an ancient Prince of Hell, attacked the Institute?"

"Yes," James said shortly. "It's been a very long day."

"You will forgive me if I say that you don't look like someone whose wife just left for a pleasant trip to Paris," said Magnus. "You look like someone who just had his heart kicked out on a train station platform."

James was silent. *We suffer for love because love is worth it.*

Magnus softened his voice. "You know Matthew's in love with her, right?"

James blinked—how had Magnus known? Perhaps Matthew had told him—an odd thought—or he had guessed; he was very observant. "I know it now. I should have known it before." His head ached dully. "There isn't much I can say to defend myself. I have been very blind. In that blindness I have hurt Cordelia and I have hurt Matthew. I have no right to be angry that they have gone."

Magnus shrugged. "Rights," he said. "We all have the right to feel pain, James, and unhappiness. I would venture to guess that Cordelia and Matthew are fleeing from their own. It is natural to believe that you can outrun your miseries. There have been times I have fled mine halfway across the world. But the truth is that sorrow is fleet and loyal. It will always follow you."

James tilted his head back. The air was full of fog and smoke; he could not see the stars. He wondered if Cordelia could see them yet—if the train had carried her far enough from London for the skies to clear. "I fear it has been following Matthew for a long time," he said. "I fear that in that time I have been . . . disconnected from the people I love the most, the people who I should have been able to save from such pain."

"You cannot save people who do not want to be saved," said Magnus. "You can only stand by their side and hope that when they wake and realize they need saving, you will be there to help them." He paused. "It's something to keep in mind as we go to help your sister."

Magnus straightened up; Will had returned, rubbing his ungloved hands together to warm them. Seeing James standing miserably on the pavement, he reached out to gently ruffle his hair. "I know it's hard, Jamie *bach*. You'd rather be in Paris. But you made the right choice." His hand fell to James's shoulder; he held on tight for a moment before letting go. "All right," he said gruffly. "We can't delay. Everyone into the carriage."

James clambered into the carriage and sank back against one of the velvet seats. Sliding his hand into his pocket, he took hold of Cordelia's glove, the kidskin soft against his palm. He held it tightly, silently, as the carriage pulled away from Waterloo and rumbled into the night.

Epilogue

The wind whipped across the rocky plain like the tail of an angry cat. Tatiana Blackthorn pulled her tattered cloak more tightly around her as she struggled up the lee of a jagged hill. Far below her, she could see the Adamant Citadel, growing ever smaller in the distance, encircled by its red-penny moat of hot slag and magma. The Iron Sisters disposed of *adamas* weapons that could not be used in the lava, so dangerous was the material outside of the right hands.

Not that they had noticed when she had smuggled a chunk of it out herself, Tatiana thought with satisfaction. They thought of her as a sort of mad Cinderella, muttering to herself in ashy corners, flinching when spoken to, given to long walks alone on the emerald-moss plains. She could not help but wonder when the alarm would be raised today. When they would realize she had left the Citadel for good, and would not be back.

The alarm would be raised, but that did not matter now. She had cast the last die, crossed the Rubicon. There would be no going back. She did not care. She had been done with all things Nephilim for a long time. She could not outrun them and their pursuit, not on this Earth, but that did not matter either. She had chosen her allies well.

At that moment, she saw him. He stood atop the hill, smiling down at her. He was beautiful as ever, beautiful as sin and freedom were beautiful. She was panting by the time she reached him—he was leaning his back against a mossy boulder, examining his translucent nails. All of Belial was translucent, as if he had been formed out of human tears. She could see through him to the long stretch of empty volcanic land beyond.

"Do you have it?" he said in his musical voice.

"A fine greeting," said Tatiana. She could see that instead of one wound staining the white of his clothes, he now had two, one below the other. They were freely bleeding. Her lips tightened. Stupid children, she thought, as dangerously foolish as their parents, unaware of the stakes in the game they played. "Did our plan come to fruition? Were you able to use the *adamas* I provided you?"

"Indeed, and your son performed his part excellently." Belial smiled, and if there was a wince behind that smile, Tatiana did not see it. "That part of our plan is behind us. We look to the future now. And the future rests on you. Do you have what you promised me?"

"Yes." Tatiana reached for the metal object tucked beneath her thick belt. She held it up—an iron key, blackened with age and heavy with promise. "The key to the Iron Tombs." She glanced behind her. It might have been her imagination, but she thought she could see small figures swarming out of the Citadel, like troubled ants. "Now take me from here, as you swore you would."

Belial swept a bow. "At your service, my dark swan," he said, and his laughter wrapped her like the sweet blaze of laudanum, lifting her up as the black-and-green world faded all around her.

Carrying her far away.

NOTES ON THE TEXT

Sink Street is not a real location in London, but rather features in the Evelyn Waugh novel A *Handful of Dust* as being next to Golden Square. The passages Cordelia reads about Wayland the Smith's barrow (a real place you can really visit!) come from the 1899 edition of *Country Life Illustrated*; the passages about Istanbul (Constantinople at the time) are from *The City of the Sultan* by Julia Pardoe, published in 1836. "*Chi! Khodah margam bedeh,*" said by Alastair, is an expression of frustration; literally it means "God give me death."

Five thousand pounds, the amount Elias asks James for, is about six hundred thousand pounds in today's currency. Wow.

ACKNOWLEDGMENTS

With so many thanks to everyone who both helped with the crafting of the prose of this story and pitched in to keep me going during the many dark days of 2020. With thanks to my intrepid assistant, Emily Houk; my research angel, Clary Goodman; my writing partners Holly Black and Kelly Link as well as Robin Wasserman, Steve Berman, Jedediah Berry, Elka Cloke, Kate Welsh, and Maureen Johnson. Thanks to Fariba Kooklan and Marguerite Maghen for help with Farsi, and Sarah Ismail for translating the Baudelaire poem that begins chapter 2. Thanks as always to my agents, Jo Volpe and Suzie Townsend, and my editor, Karen Wojtyla. With hugs to Cat and Rò for cheering me up; my always gratitude to my family, and, of course, all my love to Josh: I have run out of ways to express how important you are to me.

Turn the page to read

One Must Always Be Careful of Books,

A BONUS STORY FEATURING

MAGNUS AND JEM.

⸺◈⸺

Albert Pangborn is right, you know, Jem said mildly. *The Nephilim do lay claim to the Black Volume of the Dead.*

Magnus rolled his eyes.

Jem put up his hands. *I am not saying I support Albert's claim that its only rightful place is the Cornwall Institute. Only that, if we are going by the strict language of the Accords, what we are doing right now is illegal.*

The illegal act they were currently engaged in was escorting the aforementioned Volume to the Spiral Labyrinth for repair and possible exorcism, having removed it from the library of the Cornwall Institute. When Jem had first accepted the assignment to examine the spell books of the Institute's library, he had not expected anything like this level of excitement. It was well known that the Cornwall Institute had a large collection of spell books whose contents could most charitably be described as questionable. But he and Magnus had already been in Cornwall nearly a fortnight when Pangborn, the Institute's head, had complained to them that one of his books kept leaping from the shelf onto the floor when he wasn't looking. When he reported that he had bound the volume with heavy chains and *still* found it on the windowsill of the library the next morning "as if it were having a look at the view," Jem had decided that the matter deserved investigation.

When he discovered the misbehaving spell book was the infamous Black Volume of the Dead, he and Magnus realized serious steps would need to be taken.

Now Magnus grimaced with effort as he gripped the Black Volume with both hands, keeping it still. It had begun shaking and flapping the moment the Portal appeared. "You can't honestly tell me that you think this . . . recalcitrant . . . spell book . . ." He paused to wrestle with the thing for a moment. ". . . is better off in Pangborn's sticky hands."

They are, Jem said thoughtfully, *unusually tacky. Like a newly painted fence. And my personal opinion matters little, as I act in the name of the Silent Brothers, and must uphold the Law.*

"Still," Magnus said. "You're allowing this powerful spell book to enter the very center of warlock power. We're going through those purple curtains, by the way." He nodded his head at the far wall.

Jem examined it critically. Magnus had Portaled them into a small stone chamber, like a monastic cell, at one end of which hung heavy velvet draperies dripping with lace, something of a tonal mismatch. "I moved them from my flat when High Victorian style went out of fashion," Magnus went on. "Pity. High Victorian was a good match for the High Warlock."

You hung these curtains? Did you get permission? Dubiously, Jem began pulling back the substantial folds of fabric.

Magnus said, "We High Warlocks are allowed to establish a little private space for ourselves in the Spiral Labyrinth. To store personal effects, or engage in research."

Like a carrel in a library, Jem said, but then stopped, because through the curtains was Magnus's so-called "private space," and it was less like a study chamber and more like a Pre-Raphaelite grotto. A brook passed through the center of the room, flowing from some unknown source to some unknown destination over a bed of round river stones, glistening like dragon scales. Over the brook passed a stone bridge, made to look ancient and crumbling (or, perhaps, actually ancient and crumbling and stolen by Magnus), and overhanging this, tall willows drooped their boughs. Here and there were small stacks of cloth- and leather-bound books—a few on the lawn next to the brook, one on the bridge, a few strangely tied up in the branches of the willows.

Magnus sighed in contentment. "Enjoy it; this is the most pleasant spot in the whole Labyrinth. The rest of it is mostly cold damp stone and weird eldritch light." He gave Jem an askance look. "You seem surprised. I mean, as much as any Silent Brother ever seems like anything."

Well, no offense, Jem said, *but I expected an atmosphere that was more—*

"Decadent?" said Magnus. "I am a complex being of many layers, Brother Zachariah." He examined the Black Volume critically; it seemed to have stopped trembling now that it was inside the Spiral Labyrinth.

This was true, of course, thought Jem, but Magnus was protective of those layers. He recognized the intimacy Magnus was showing him in allowing him into this space. In some ways it was more interesting than the strangest inner sanctums of the Labyrinth would have been, though those were what Will would ask him about when they returned.

Will. For a moment his mind was far from here, back in England; a pang of worry simmered somewhere in his chest. Magnus had sat down on the grass and was beginning to look through the stack of octavos next to him.

Does Tessa have a place here? he said to Magnus.

Magnus looked up from the book, his eyebrows raised. "You'd know better than I would," he said. "My understanding is that as a warlock she is *welcome* to a place here. Whether it would be *politically* wise for the head of a Shadowhunter Institute to have private dealings with the Spiral Labyrinth . . ."

Silent Brothers deal with the Spiral Labyrinth, Jem said. *Iron Sisters, even, if they have specific queries.*

Magnus shrugged. "You don't need *me* to tell you about the Clave's inconsistencies when it comes to relations with Downworlders. I believe they consider the Silent Brothers to be a little more warlockish than other Nephilim. Long-lived, uncanny presence, fond of cloaks with hoods . . ." He straightened up and brushed grass that wasn't there from his bottle-green trousers. He hoisted the Black Volume into his arms. "Shall we go fix up this ill-behaved penny dreadful?"

Don't insult the book, Jem suggested. He did not like the idea of a book that moved on its own. It spoke of demon possession, though

Magnus claimed that it was likely only a mistakenly activated spell from within the book itself. *What is our plan?*

"We take the book to the Brass Vault," Magnus said, "where spell books in need of certain kinds of—let's call it 'repair'—are kept. Shall we?"

Outside Magnus's garden, the Spiral Labyrinth looked more like it had appeared to Jem the last time he was here. It was a labyrinth, and it did spiral in some fashion, but beyond that he understood nothing of its layout or organization. The corridors were all long, sweeping arcs, so at the end of a hallway one faced a different direction than at the start, but at what angle was impossible to discern. Magnus, of course, navigated the endless repetitious passages as though he knew the place by heart. Jem couldn't fathom how he did it; there were almost no landmarks or features to remember, just endless shelves of books and the occasional wooden reading table. He had expected more dramatic, uncanny displays of demonic magic, but he supposed there were many parts of the Labyrinth that he would never be allowed to see, and probably those were the most interesting parts.

They encountered no one else in the halls. Jem wasn't sure if this was its own magic or if the Labyrinth was so large that it was rare to cross paths with others. Magnus was silent—silence did seem appropriate to the hushed sepulchral tone of the whole place—and Jem was left alone with his thoughts.

And behind his thoughts, the thoughts of all the Silent Brothers, a constant low-pitched hum, a reassuring chorus of lifeblood spread across the whole world. Strange that most Shadowhunters would never experience it. It was their very beating heart.

But outside that heart, pressing into it like a nail against soft skin, Jem worried about his family and his friends.

Something terrible was happening in London, and he couldn't help it; part of his heart was there. Everything had seemed calm when they arrived in Cornwall—they had received no urgent messages, no intimations of disaster until it was too late, and they had discovered the danger of the uncontrolled Black Volume. Now Shadowhunters were being murdered. Alastair and Cordelia had just lost their father, and must be struggling with the grief of mourning a man they had loved but not liked. And the Blackthorn family: Tatiana had been imprisoned for partaking in necromancy, but something strange was afoot with her daughter, Grace, as well, and Jem suspected Lucie might be wrapped up in it in some way—

Jem stopped walking abruptly. Magnus was giving him a strange look.

Yes? Jem said politely.

"I suppose I shouldn't be surprised that you're so silent," Magnus said, scratching his nose. "Considering your occupation. But—"

My apologies, Jem said. *I was only thinking about—the Londoners. All of those to whom I have close connections.*

Magnus nodded. "James, of course. I know you worked hard with him on controlling those shadow powers of his. But I imagine he struggles with his connection to Belial."

They all do, Jem said. *James, Lucie, and Tessa—even Will. It is like a shadow cast across their lives. And Matthew—*

"Ah, unhappy Matthew," said Magnus. "Unrequited love troubles him, but I sense there is something more to it. Do you know?"

Jem did know. Matthew remained crushed beneath the weight of misery, paralyzed by guilt over what he had, however unintentionally, done to Charlotte—but Jem could tell no one of what he knew, not even Will. Not even Magnus.

Nothing I can tell, Jem said.

Magnus only nodded. "And, of course, what happened to Elias Carstairs. If you had to return to London . . ."

Jem felt an un-Silent-Brother-like burst of yearning. He closed down that part of his mind quickly, locking away his most human desires. *No,* Jem said. *My purpose is as a Silent Brother. I have been assigned to this task and I must see it through.*

"Such is the nature of duty?" Magnus said, starting to walk again.

It is not only duty, Jem said, following after a lingering moment. *It is . . . who I am. One is transformed by the process of joining my order. I am not the boy I was.*

"I don't mean to be glib," Magnus said. "But nobody is the boy they were. I take your meaning, however," he added. "Pangborn only agreed to let us bring the Black Volume here because you were with me. To leave would be to betray the promise you made. Your connections to your family, to friends like Will and Tessa, must be put aside in service of a larger cause. That I understand."

With a start, Jem realized that the stone walls had fallen away, and Magnus had led them out of the endless corridors and onto a platform of black glass hanging over what seemed to be a bottomless abyss. In the center of the jeweled landscape an obelisk of bright polished brass stood, towering above both of them.

It was not in the nature of Silent Brothers to gawp. Jem turned quizzically to Magnus instead.

Magnus rolled his eyes. "I see the architects have fallen into the fashion for the Golden Dawn and all that mundane occult claptrap. It's very much in vogue right now. All pure reflective surfaces and overwrought symbolism." He patted the obelisk. "I knew this fellow in Vienna—"

Is this where the other books are? Jem said. *It's so . . . empty.*

"Oh, no," Magnus said. "This is like my purple curtains. Let me see now." After a moment's thought, he recited a low guttural phrase, some demonic language Jem didn't recognize. With a grinding noise, the obelisk began to retreat into the floor, and as it did, the floor began to lower, forming spiral stairs circling the obelisk. It was surprisingly slow, Jem thought, considering it was magic.

Magnus was looking at him. "Do you need to go back to London?" he said gently. "Before we go down into the Vault. I know you're worried about everyone there. I certainly wouldn't tattle if you went to them instead of remaining here among the warlocks."

Magnus, Jem said sternly, *no.*

"But—"

No, Jem said again. *Of course I want to return to London. I am still human. There are those for whom I still feel love.*

"Is it still as important to you as it was?" Magnus said quietly.

Yes. Jem folded his arms. *The nature of taking a vow,* he said, *is that you must apply your will to fulfilling that vow. If I could no longer choose my order, choose my duty . . .* He shook his head. *What would such a vow even mean?*

Magnus was silent for a moment. Finally he said, even more quietly, "It wasn't a choice, for you."

Jem regarded his old friend steadily. *It was.*

Magnus nodded. "All right. Then we go." He sighed. "Maybe this will be over quickly and we can rush back to England regardless. So. Once we enter the vault, we must—" He stopped and squinted, as though trying to recall something obscure.

Hmm? said Jem politely, after a moment.

"Well," said Magnus, "in order to restore the Black Volume's original inert state, we either must ensure that it is rejoined with its fellows, *or*, we must ensure that it is *not* rejoined with its fellows."

Jem stopped short his approach to the stairs. *I beg your pardon.*

"It was definitely one of those two," Magnus said.

What if it is the latter? Jem said still, he thought, quite politely. *What are we to expect to happen?*

After a moment of thought, Magnus shrugged. "I don't know," he said. "I don't know either way. Whether we do it right or we do it wrong, *something* will happen, I don't yet know what, and we'll deal with it as it happens. That's kind of the way warlock magic tends to work," he added, in an apologetic tone. "It's usually on the edge of disaster even in the best of times." He got a careful grip on the Black Volume and started down the stairs.

Feeling that perhaps it was tremendously foolish to go on—that, in fact, it showed a dangerous lack of the prudence and wisdom the Silent Brothers were meant to be known for, and that perhaps it reflected poorly on him that he was going to follow Magnus anyway—Jem followed Magnus down.

After a few turns of the spiral, the stairs opened onto a huge chamber, blindingly bright. The Brass Vault, Jem reckoned, judging by the polished metallic walls. They gleamed with an almost unbearable shine, though there were no sources of light that Jem could discern. Along the walls, books were stacked by the dozen, some precariously towering.

"A chamber without shadows," Magnus called back over his shoulder. "Very difficult to hide something in."

Jem joined Magnus at the bottom of the stairs; only then did he realize Magnus was wearing an odd pair of spectacles whose glass had been darkened.

"Obsidian spectacles," Magnus said. "They help with the glare. *Whoa!*"

The Black Volume of the Dead had begun to thrash again in Magnus's hands, and an aura of heat was gathering around it rapidly. Jem rushed toward Magnus to try to help him wrangle the unwieldy tome, but Magnus shook his head. "It'll burn your hands!" he said loudly, and Jem realized only at that moment that a wind was whistling through the chamber, a loud, piercing wind, and it was hard to hear Magnus over it. Everything was too bright, and too loud, and it was too much—

With a flapping sound, the Black Volume tore out of Magnus's grasp and flew toward the center of the room. Other books had flown out of their stacks against the walls and, as Magnus and Jem watched, collided with the Black Volume. As the impact settled, Jem realized that the books had come together to form the semblance of a stick figure of a human.

Magnus looked over at Jem, his eyebrows raised. "Maybe it's just a bit of spectacle," he suggested. "Or maybe the books like to be in the Brass Vault in the form of a friendly, helpful . . . book . . . creature."

The book-monster took a step forward. It raised its arms, and pages flapped with a threateningly loud whistle.

So we were not *meant to bring the Black Volume here, I assume,* Jem said.

"Who knows, really," said Magnus. "It's just as likely that this was the correct thing to do and nobody thought to mention the book-golem. Speaking of which, it would be a terrible idea to damage any of those spell books forming the thing. Maybe we can just leave it here. Pull the stairs up after it."

It's your Labyrinth, Jem said doubtfully, *but I can't imagine that's how the Black Volume is* intended *to be stored.*

"Well, technically, warlocks aren't allowed to own the Black Volume at all," said Magnus with an annoying cheerfulness. "But at the moment, we're just borrowing it. I can't help that it's become part of a book-monster, can I?"

As if insulted, the book-golem lunged at Jem with a hissing sound, swiping at him. Jem sidestepped the strike, though the edge of one of the books brushed the back of his hand.

"I don't expect it can hurt us," Magnus offered. "It's just books."

But a sharp pain was quickly blooming where Jem had been touched by the golem, like a cold burn. He gave a sharp intake of breath, surprised.

"Well, all right, I gather it can hurt us," Magnus admitted. "Any ideas?" He twirled out of the way as the book-golem came at him now, and took up a more defensive posture. "Under normal circumstances I would just set the whole thing on fire, but I can't even imagine the consequences for me if I destroyed piles of irreplaceable spell books."

Don't you think the other warlocks would understand? Jem suggested. He had taken his staff firmly in hand, using it to fend off the book-creature as it lurched his way again. *Under the circumstances?*

"They would not," Magnus said. "Besides, the spell books themselves have so much magic, I wouldn't be surprised if a fire couldn't destroy them. Or just made them stronger."

The vows of the Silent Brothers meant that Jem was never truly able to experience exasperation of the kind he associated with his youth, but he found the semblance of that emotion creeping up on him regardless.

I have an idea, he said, ignoring that feeling. *In the original golem legend, the monster could be stopped by inscribing the word "death" upon its forehead.*

"I don't think this thing has a forehead," Magnus said, dodging its latest stagger in his direction.

It has a head, Jem said, *on which I could inscribe the rune for Death that is known to Silent Brothers.*

"What?" Magnus said, raising his voice. "There are secret runes known only to Silent Brothers?"

Of course, said Jem. *That itself is not a secret. All Shadowhunters know that.*

"Do they know you have a *secret death rune*?" Magnus said, sounding a bit strangled.

It's not a death rune, really, said Jem. *It's a complex representation of—I cannot speak of it.* He caught Magnus's eye. *You must trust me.*

"I do," Magnus said, and whatever he might have said after was lost, as the book-golem took a great leap and crashed directly into the far wall of the Vault, crumbling through it as though it were paper. Beyond Jem could see more shining brass, in a corridor extending away. Jem gave Magnus a querying look.

"Well," said Magnus, heaving a great sigh. "Now it's escaped into the Brass Arcades. And while I would like to pretend that means it is no longer our problem . . . in fact it is now doubly our problem." He gave Jem a sympathetic smile. "No hurrying back to London just yet, it seems. All right. We pursue, I will try to trap it in some kind of magical cage, and we try your death rune."

And if that doesn't work? Jem said.

"Then at least we'll have it in a magical cage," Magnus said. "All right, Brother Zachariah, shall we delve even deeper into the Spiral Labyrinth, where mortals fear to tread?"

Jem took a moment to give a thought for his friends, his family struggling back in England. For just an instant, he felt an almost unbearably powerful love seize him, so strong it was only bearable for that moment. Then he said, *I suppose we must.*

CASSANDRA CLARE is the #1 *New York Times* bestselling author of *Chain of Gold*, as well as *The Mortal Instruments*, *The Infernal Devices*, *The Dark Artifices* and *The Shadowhunter's Codex*. She is the co-author of *The Bane Chronicles* with Sarah Rees Brennan and Maureen Johnson, *Tales from the Shadowhunter Academy* with Sarah Rees Brennan, Maureen Johnson and Robin Wasserman, and *Ghosts of the Shadow Market* with Sarah Rees Brennan, Maureen Johnson, Robin Wasserman and Kelly Link. She also co-wrote *The Red Scrolls of Magic* with Wesley Chu. Her books have more than 50 million copies in print worldwide. They have been translated into over thirty-five languages and made into a feature film and a TV show. Cassandra lives in Massachusetts, USA. Visit her online at CassandraClare.com. Learn more about the world of the Shadowhunters at UKShadowhunters.com.